Moon Queen

A novel

Katharine Branning

BLUE DOME

New York

17 16 15 14 1 2 3 4

Published by Blue Dome Press
244 5th Avenue, Suite D-149
New York, NY 10001, USA

www.bluedomepress.com

Library of Congress Cataloging-in-Publication Data Available

Branning, Katharine.
Moon Queen : a novel / Katharine Branning.
pages cm
ISBN 978-1-935295-25-9 (alk. paper)
1. Seljuks--Fiction. 2. Turkey--History--To 1453--Fiction. 3. Women--Turkey--Fiction. 4. Art patronage--Turkey--Fiction. I. Title.
PS3602.R36496M66 2014
813'.6--dc23

2014005986

Printed by
İmak Ofset , Istanbul - Turkey

Table of Contents

to üstad Muhsin İlyas Subaşı,
whose every breath is a poem

Introductory note

From the middle of the 12th century to the beginning of the 14th, the Seljuks of Anatolia (present-day Turkey), created one of the most significant centers of Islamic Middle Eastern culture. The Seljuk Empire, while lasting only one hundred and fifty short years, is considered one of the most glorious periods of Turkish history.

Alaeddin Keykubad I (r. 1220-1237) was the most renowned of the Seljuk sultans. The legendary figure of Alaeddin Keykubad looms large in the consciousness of the Turkish people. Streets, squares and universities bear his name today; his buildings grace towns across the Anatolian plain, children are named after him and study his exploits in school.

This novel tells the story of Mahperi Hatun (120? - 1255?), the wife of this celebrated sultan. Mahperi Hatun used her influence, wealth, and creative intelligence to build an important series of monuments after the death of her husband. She is one of the earliest female art patrons in Turkish history.

Yet, almost nothing is known of her life. There are only a few mentions of her name in the works of the historians Ibn Bibi, Bar Hebraeus, and Simon de Saint-Quentin. There are no archives to bring her to life, no wondrous letters, memos, or remembrances by contemporaries.

This leaves us with her built works as the sole voice to tell her story. Although the real person of Mahperi may seem as distant as the moon for which she was named, the stones of her architectural legacy still shine strongly today.

Kayseri, 1255

Would that my stones last longer than my bones!

It is hard for me to believe that just a few months ago I was full of vigor. Now, all energy is drained from my soul, and my body struggles to answer the call of my mind to rise and start the day. One day soon I will not be able to rise at all. I end my days in accordance with the way I lived, and for that, I have no regrets, for everything was done as it could have been done, and now there will be only judgment.

For me, life was always different than for others. Everyone scrutinized each move I made, and I am certain their eyes will continue to be on me after I am gone. Perhaps I was different, yet what I made of this difference was of my own choice. I had choices, and I didn't have choices; and my fate always seemed framed by those choices and the people in my life. Yet I did take charge of so much of what happened to me: I had vivid dreams, I was curious, I dared, I was passionate for what I believed in – even when that created problems for me.

My eyes are emptying out of this world now so that I may have a white and pure view to confront God face to face, just as I confronted every other challenge in my life. Where are you now, Jesus and Muhammad? Jesus, take my one hand! Muhammad take the other and lead me up to paradise!

Soon, in a few months or maybe even in a few breaths, I know the angel of death will come to call for me. I will then be able to look onto this world from another place; a higher and more peaceful one. Yes, from there I will look down at the *caravansarai* I have built at Pazar. I will continue to see what is happening to my kingdom and people, and hear what they are talking about. I will be able to question each merchant as he enters its door: where are you from and how is your trade? Is my kingdom still flourishing? Come in, come in, merchant; unload your tired beast and warm your aching feet by the fire in the courtyard. Eat some soup and tell me what you have seen and heard along the roads all across my Empire. Tell me everything. Tell me that my Empire lives on, and that all was not just a dream.

And if those merchants look hard enough, they will be able to read my story written there; for I am certain those stones will indeed last longer than my bones. Tell my story, oh stones of the caravansarai I have built; you are my witness and my testament….

Yes, Maryam Mahperi, I, your caravansarai at Pazar, promise to tell your story for all eternity.

I am an open door that welcomes
I am a haven for weary merchants
I am a destination for churning footsteps
I am the name on the lips of tired travelers
I am the compass point of everyone's mind!

I am the sentinel of a beautiful valley
I am the crossroads for peoples from East and West
I am the landscape of this empire
I am the guardian of the quilted plain of Tokat
I am the happy goal of the end of the day

I am a courtyard wide
I am arcades broad for beasts of burden
I am carved flowers on a portal and an engraved lintel stone
I am a fountain of cool water for thirsty passersby
I am a safe treasury for the gold of the Seljuk Empire

I am a pot of bubbling stew to feed hungry stomachs
I am stories told around the campfire
I am the storehouse of goods from all the markets of the world
I am the scent of perfumes and spices from lands afar
I am an inspiration and a purpose

I am you, the Golden Mother
I am your messenger dove bringing goodwill and peace
I am your hope for the people of this kingdom
I am the voice of your heart's deepest dreams
I am the trace of your passage on earth

I am the testament of your willful victory
I am your eternal spirit

I am your caravansarai -

PART 1

A MOON QUEEN IS BORN

1221-1227

Come here, my love, the crown of my home –
Walking so tall, so slender, like a cypress,
With your black hair falling to your feet,
With brows like a tightened bow;
With a mouth too small for two almonds
And cheeks red like the apples of autumn –
My woman, my mainstay, my love.

Tribal chieftain, ca. tenth-century
from The Book of Dede Korkut

Come to me here,
The crown on my head, the throne of my house,
Son-in-law of my royal father,
The apple of my lady mother's eye,
You, who were given to me by my parents,
You, whom I saw when I opened my eyes,
The man I loved at first sight.

Wife of chieftain
from The Book of Dede Korkut

Prologue to Part 1

This was the time when I was still a pile of mud in a field.

I, the great caravansarai at Pazar, was not yet born to the grassy plain. My site was still unchosen, my shape still unreconciled, my spirit not yet understood. It was the beginning of a time when springtime after springtime would follow and lead into the exceptional summer when Anatolia took on its face for all eternity.

I, the great caravansarai at Pazar, was not even yet an idea, a dream or a destiny; I was without a plan or purpose. I was but a pile of simple brown mud, like so much in Anatolia at this time. But my mud had the chance to lie in an area of purple and green mountains, bright blue sky, and crisp air. No wonder such a beautiful place called out to you, my Lady, to forge me from its mud!

And you, too, my Lady, were still of the clay of innocent youth, not yet shaped into your providence. Others would try to mold-cast you into the profile they wanted, but it was you, and you alone, who molded the clay of your youth into the bricks of a determined woman capable of building not only me, but an entire powerful nation.

It was this time, the 7th era of our Hegira, or as your Christian people call it, the 13th century: an era of tumult, violence, adventure, sacrifice, joy and passion. You were not alone on the road of this adventure, for men of faith and folly, humble peasants, royal sultans, bandits and dreamers would come forth to help you create your vision from all this mud. I stand in humble recognition of your efforts.

You were such a young girl then. It was the time before his rising moon awoke everything in you and allowed all your dreams to take wing. If I exist today, it is because you realized that you could step out of the shadows and blossom under the hot Anatolian sun.

Yes, who could have imagined that you, green bashful maiden, would rise to become a mighty queen with a forceful hand, a politician able to transform all that mud of Anatolia into an empire for all times? Who could have imagined your destiny at this moment when you stood trembling behind a castle door waiting for it to open onto your future? Certainly none of us did, and especially, not I.

Chapter 1

A Dowry of Castle and Sea

The clatter of eighty thousand horse hooves echoed all the way out to sea. Even the great Alaeddin Keykubad, *Al-Sultan-al-Mu'azzam,* Glory of the Faith and the Magnificent Sultan of the Seljuk Empire, was powerless to quiet down the restless horses. He could invoke his men to do anything he commanded, but their mounts were another army altogether. Snorting, stomping in a skittish frenzy and shaking their manes and tails, the stallions were impatient for the significant moment that beast, soldier, and Sultan had all been eagerly awaiting for almost four months.

Twenty thousand men stood in front of the tall wooden doors of the fortress castle perched at the top of the mountain at Kalonoros, waiting for them to swing open in surrender. The army was prepared for the last assault on the castle, eager to cry out the invocation "*Allahu Akbar*" the moment the portal cracked open. Even the Mediterranean Sea below the cliff top was calm, as if it, too, was waiting with bated breath for the opening of the doors.

"It can't be much longer now," said the Sultan, turning to his Vizier, Mubarizeddin Ertokush, mounted on the horse next to him. "Their hunger and thirst and your adroit negotiations are finally bringing this long siege to an end!" Alaeddin Keykubad turned to look back at the door, and could not believe that his dream for conquest was soon to bear fruit far sweeter than any grown in the lush groves surrounding the city. Even though it was winter, the sun was strong on their backs and bright in their eyes, warming their excited blood even more.

It had been a long time coming, this moment. Ever since he took the throne the year before, in the holy year 1220, Alaeddin Keykubad had dreamed of nothing but this day. He wanted more than anything to rule over the entire eastern Mediterranean coast, and this goal would not be possible without taking the region around Kalonoros. This important port would provide access to the sea for his inland capital of Konya. It would solidify the Seljuk military dominion of the Mediterranean Sea, and establish them as the greatest power in all of Islam. It would open trade potential with Cyprus and the Venetians, which would enrich his kingdom beyond belief. His father, Giyaseddin Keyhüsrev I, had captured the coastal city of Antalya fifteen years ago, and now it was his turn to capture the city that would solidify the Seljuk hold over the entire

Mother Sea. He had to have this city under his wing, this Kalonoros high, for it would be the shiniest pearl in the strand he planned for his empire, and this necklace dream woke him every night in a fever of sweat. Everything, yes everything, depended on those doors opening.

The fortress city of Kalonoros was in the hands of Lord Kyr Vart of the Roupenid Dynasty of Armenian Cilicia. The Armenians held on to this region as strongly as the Mother Sea held on to its merciless rock cliffs. Aware of Kyr Vart's resolute determination to defend his city, Alaeddin Keykubad had given the order to spare no trouble or cost for storming this nearly impregnable fortress and its massive walls, set atop a sharp mountain that thrust into the sea. He planned the campaign against Kalonoros with meticulous attention, setting up his camp outside the castle walls over four months ago.

Yet the siege did not go as easily as the impatient Sultan had planned. Alaeddin soon learned that no amount of catapults from land or sea could capture this castle. He had to find a weapon more powerful than bows and arrows, and that weapon he found in the diplomatic skills of his Vizier Ertokush. This trusted elder statesman had many years ago taught him that mediation could be more efficient than warfare.

Ertokush turned to face the Sultan, all the while keeping one eye on the door.

"Yes, it won't be much longer now, my Sultan. Even though they have stored much water in their cisterns and foodstuffs in their larders, they know their meals are now counted. But, in the end, it was your insistence that they surrender without bloodshed that was the most important key to opening that door."

Alaeddin Keykubad nodded.

"You are too modest, my Vizier. Perhaps I had to change my tactic, but it was your skill that made it work. I needed only to look to the actions of my ancestors to find the inspiration for victory. My forefather, Tuğrul Bey, entered Baghdad in 1055 without striking a blow, taking the most important city of Sunni Islam without spilling one drop of blood! And then, a mere twenty years later, Alp Arslan rode victorious over the Byzantine Christians in the battle of Manzikert. It was the first time in history that a Byzantine emperor was taken prisoner by a Muslim army! I, too, do not wish to make Kyr Vart a prisoner, but would rather give him the opportunity to be free and live in peace. And you, my wise Ertokush, have made that possible with the negotiations you have led with him. You spoke well on my behalf and achieved a victory for all parties concerned."

Ertokush bowed his head. "All in your service, Father of Conquests. Yes, I tried to offer him the best possible outcome to this situation, yet, in the end, it was he who came up with the suggested terms of his surrender. He agreed to hand over Kalonoros, its castle and subjects to you. He has agreed to promise you his allegiance, and to pay an annual tribute to you. The borders of this Armenian Kingdom of Cilicia will be redrawn in your favor. In exchange, he has requested safekeeping for all his family, and demands that you offer him a parcel of land in Ilgin, near your capital of Konya, in order to live out his days in peace."

Indeed, the Vizier Ertokush, governor of the Seljuk town of Antalya, two days' ride west along the coast from Kalonoros, had worked hard for many months now on this agreement, trying to carve a dignified and honorable settlement for his old friend and neighbor, Kyr Vart, and at the same time, negotiating an advantageous treaty for his Sultan Alaeddin Keykubad. He was a proud man, this Kyr Vart, but Ertokush sensed at the same time that he preferred saving his own life to defending his city to the death. Ertokush knew this was the card he had to play. He did not have much difficulty putting forth his proposal, especially since it was obvious to Kyr Vart that he could not hold out against the siege much longer. It was pointless to resist, so when Ertokush went in for the final negotiations, the Armenian agreed to the terms. Ertokush was quite satisfied with the outcome and knew that his Sultan would be pleased to win this victory so easily, without bloodshed or violence, just as he had wished.

Yet when Ertokush returned from his negotiations and presented Kyr Vart's conditions of surrender, the Sultan balked. "My Vizier, you have made this too easy for him! He must understand that I am the most powerful man in the land, and that it is I who dictates the terms, not him! I want you to go back to him, and tell him that he must give up something precious of his so that he understands that my victory is not just an exchange of a fortress on a platter in return for rich lands on the Anatolian plains! No, I ask for more. Yes – I ask that he give me his daughter as a bride, as a true testament of his submission to the Seljuks. Go back and see what he says to that!"

The startled Ertokush knew this would be a difficult negotiation. Nothing would deter the determined Sultan on his quest for total victory, yet he was confident that he would return from Kyr Vart with the promise of his daughter's hand for the Sultan in exchange for his life. And so it was done, and now the day of reckoning was upon them all.

"I would have to say, my Sultan, no woman has ever come with a dowry as spectacular as the one Kyr Vart is offering you – the city of Kalonoros shines brighter than any bag of precious jewels!"

Alaeddin Keykubad laughed heartily, and swept his arms out in front of him. "Could any woman be as brilliant as the topaz yellow of this southern sun, or as sparkling as the white diamonds glistening on that sapphire sea below? I hardly think so!"

Yet now as they both turned to look at that closed door, somewhere inside of him the Sultan dared to dream that yes, there could be a woman just that priceless standing behind the tall wooden door of the mountaintop castle of Kalonoros.

Chapter 2

Battered and Bartered

"My sweet child Maryam, you must realize that after I open this door, nothing will be the same for any of us. You understand, too, that I have no choice but to do this, don't you?"

Her father's words echoed in her ears as they stood together behind the castle door. No, she thought, I don't understand any of this. Our lives were so happy and peaceful in this castle perched high above the bright blue sea, under a sun so hot that no one ever felt a chill in their bones or in their hearts. No, she didn't understand at all what had become of this happy life over the past four months. Its peace had been broken by the incessant thud of stones battering against the outer walls, balls of fire being tossed over their tops into the streets and courtyards below, and ugly shouting. Everyone remained penned-up inside their homes with their doors shut tight, frightened to come outside and face this world of battering and bellowing. Maryam turned to look at all the eager faces of the frightened citizens who had gathered there in front of her father, Kyr Vart, Lord of the castle, who had called them to come out of their homes so that he could publicly address them.

He spoke again to his daughter with a tired voice. "I have no choice but to open this door, Maryam, and I need you to understand what I have agreed to do so that our lives can return to normal once more." Maryam sensed, however, that their lives would never return to normal, and she saw a guarded look on her father's face that worried her.

Kyr Vart continued, carefully forming his words. "I have tried to hold out, despite all this battering. Our Armenian ancestors have lived here for 200 years, and I was not about to give all of this up without a fight! Our Heavenly Lord has given us great strength to defend our walls and we have been successful up to this day. All the Sultan's men and weapons have not made even one dent in our thick walls! But alas, our four cisterns and larders are not as strong as our walls. Maryam, our water supply is running out, and our cupboards will soon be empty. Then what will we do? Will our pride or those strong walls feed us? No, I cannot allow my subjects to suffer hunger because of my pride! I have no choice: I must surrender to him."

"But Papa! You cannot do this! We cannot give up our home to these heathens!" Maryam looked at her father indignantly.

Her proud father now looked her directly in the eyes. "I repeat, I have no choice. They are not about to go away, these stubborn Turks! But we have a friend who has helped us out of this terrible situation. Our neighbor in Antalya, the Seljuk Vizier Ertokush, has come to speak with me on behalf of the Sultan. He is a good man, wise and just, and we have worked together to craft an agreement that will respect and honor both our sides."

"So what have you agreed with him, Papa? What will happen to all of us?"

Now Kyr Vart found himself at a loss for words. How could he best explain to his beloved daughter what he had negotiated with the Sultan's emissary? How could he soften the situation he now had to present to her?

"Ertokush has been very generous to us. He has agreed that in exchange for ceding Kalonoros Castle and its port to the Seljuk Sultan, all our people will be saved. No one will be harmed, killed or taken as slaves. Everyone can stay here and continue to live as before. Our churches will not be destroyed, we can continue to pray to Jesus and the saints, and we can continue to speak our own language. Not one hair on our heads will be touched, that he has assured me, and I believe his word, for although they batter walls, those Muslims are honorable people."

He looked at the frightened and confused face of his daughter, and realized he still had to convince her that all would be for the best. "Most importantly," he emphasized, "My head will be spared, and our family will be safe. The Sultan has agreed to give me a parcel of land next to his capital at Konya in which to make my home. I will go there to live immediately once this door is opened."

"But I do not want to go there! I will not leave my home here!"

Kyr Vart took a deep breath to give him the courage to continue. "My sweet daughter Maryam, I must tell you that you will not be staying here, nor will you be coming with me to my new home. No, my dear daughter, you will be going to live with them, the Seljuk victors, in their capital city of Konya. The Sultan has requested your hand in marriage, and I have agreed to it. In this way, you will form a true alliance among our two peoples. I am very happy that the Sultan's conditions have been so generous."

Maryam just stood there, feeling as if one of those flaming war balls had landed in her heart. Happy, he said? Happy that she was to be separated from her family and her beautiful castle, to be led out like Abraham's sacrificial lamb to this wall-battering barbarian? No, this could not be happening to her!

"No Papa! You cannot mean what you have just said! How could you think that I would accept such a horrible idea? My place is here, with my people, in my home, with you, Papa, and not with them! Papa, please! No, no, no!"

"Maryam, stop and think for one moment about this! I risk invasion and the death of my people! Your life is certainly worth saving us all from that! I have no choice in this, don't you see? You will go as his bride or all of us will perish, there is no other way!"

She stared at him, frozen. This could not be happening to her! She could not speak or understand this betrayal at the hands of the person she loved the most on earth.

Kyr Vart realized that he had spoken too harshly to the young girl and now tried to put the situation in a softer way for her.

"My beloved daughter, do you think this is easy for me to do? But I know they will take good care of you. You will be well-provided for, my dove. He is a Sultan, and you will be his Queen! You must be brave and try to understand that you will be saving the lives of all your family, your friends and the subjects of our city. You, at this moment, are more powerful than I ever was, or even than this Sultan now at our door. You have the capacity to turn this dreadful situation into one of peace and honor for all involved. You must make this sacrifice for a good greater than yours and mine alone, just like Jesus Christ did for us."

"But Papa! I have never been away from you for one day of my life, and now you are sending me all away from home, to go off with this barbarian who has done nothing but batter our walls and starve us for the past four months? How could you sell me off to someone so evil? No, I will not leave all that I love to go with this horrible man, to live on his ugly lands on the plain, so far from my beautiful blue sea!"

Kyr Vart sternly pressed on, for it was important that she accept this destiny.

"Maryam, I am sorry, but you are no longer a child. You are almost fifteen years old now; you are soon to become a woman. Your childish ways must now be put behind you. If I had stayed here, if all of this had not happened, you still would have been given away in marriage in the upcoming months. The time has come for you to make your own home and family, away from your old father. And what finer future could you hope for, than to be the wife of the most powerful man in the land? You will want for nothing! You will have riches, diamonds and lands, with servants to tend to your every desire and wait on you night and day! Don't you see that this brilliant future is the most generous gift I could give you?"

"No, Papa, it is selfish! You are not thinking of me at all. How can you be so unloving to me, so uncaring? How could you trade me away like a jar of olives? Mama would never have let you do this to me!"

The mention of her mother cut the wind of his determination. Kyr Vart thought of his precious Serpuhi, now gone for three years. He missed her with the same pain every day since her death, and he continually sought in Maryam's face the shadows of her smile and her gestures. Little did Maryam know that by sending her away, he would be reliving the loss of his beloved wife all over again.

"No, Maryam, your mother would have supported me in this decision and would have encouraged you to go. She would have told you that you were lucky to be given the chance to marry the most powerful man in the world. She would have told you that by doing this, you would become a sainted person, a child of God who has in her hands the opportunity to do great good for those around her. She would have told you that you would become a true Mary of her time to her people. She would have told you that you would be blessed by all the people whose lives you are saving. She would have told you to hold your head high, to understand your responsibility; to be generous, caring, unselfish and loving in the image of our Savior, Jesus Christ, who died for our sins. She would have told you that this was a God-sent opportunity for you to show the world the courage and generosity that is in you. She would have told you that you were being given a gift that would allow you to become a great Lady, a queen of hearts and souls. She would have reminded you that you bear our sacred Mary's name and must show that you are worthy of it. Yes, that is what your mother would have told you."

Maryam bowed her head, and reflected upon her father's words. Her father was right; she was being selfish and childish. She remembered how strong her mother had been during the final days of her illness, and she needed to show the same resolve in her memory. It was up to her after this to craft her destiny, her future with this man now waiting outside the castle door. As difficult as it was, she had to accept this situation. She lifted her teary face and looked her father in the eyes.

"Yes, Papa, you are right, and I am sorry I have acted so selfishly. I will do whatever it takes to survive, to help preserve your honor, to save our people, and to make Mama proud of me. I accept to leave your side and to go to this man as his bride. I will make a life for myself with these heathens, against all odds. It is my duty to serve, and I know that this is what I must do."

Father and daughter fell into each other's arms and embraced. Yet, despite her fears, an intense curiosity now filled Maryam. She lifted her eyes over her father's shoulders and peered at the castle door. Just what sort of man was this Sultan, now outside the door, this man who was soon to become not only her destiny, but that of the entire world? Somewhere deep inside of her, despite the unknown ahead of her, she sensed this man stood as tall as the wooden doors of her mountaintop castle of Kalonoros.

Chapter 3

An Ocean of Blue and Green

Now, who was the most anxious of those standing at this castle door? The 10,000 troops and their stallions, pawing in eagerness for the door to open so that they could rush in and seize the city? Or the great Sultan, waiting with each breath for the first crack to appear, so that he could taste the victory whose tantalizing aroma had been in his nostrils for so many months? Or the castle Lord, worried for the safety and the future of his people and the veracity of the word promised? Or would it be the trembling fourteen year old girl, whose entire life had been changed with one sentence a mere moment ago?

Kyr Vart turned away from his still-stunned daughter and faced the people standing in front of him, huddled together in fear for the uncertainty of this day. He raised his arms in the air to gather their attention and began to speak to them.

"My dear citizens of Kalonoros, my beloved and faithful subjects, I have called you here today to inform you of an important decision I have made concerning your future. You have shown great bravery throughout these past torturous months and have never failed to sustain me with your resolve to hold out against our aggressor. I will never forget your bravery and fidelity. But we can no longer aspire to win this battle. I have made a difficult, but necessary, decision to ensure your safety. And safe you will be, I promise you. The siege of our castle is over. I have come to an agreement with the emissary of the Seljuk Sultan, the good vizier Ertokush of Antalya. We have worked out an agreement that will save all your lives, and I know it will be honored."

The crowd looked at him in silence, not believing that this siege would soon be over and that they could move about freely once more.

"There are, however, several conditions to this pact on our end, and I am counting on your total support to ensure your future," he continued. "The first is that you must now pledge your total allegiance to the Seljuk Sultan Alaeddin Keykubad and to the orders of his emirs and troops. He is now your master and Lord. I will hand over the key to this castle door to him, and it is he who will now wear it around his waist, not I. I ask you thus to show him the same loyalty and devotion that you have always shown me. He will return it to you. He has already promised that he will keep our Sacred Magdalene Church open and that you may all continue to pray there. You will carry on with your lives as before, only now, you will pay your tribute and taxes to him. You may maintain your homes, your businesses, your trades, your language and your faith, or you may leave to go live elsewhere in the parts of Armenian Cilicia the Seljuks have not yet reached. You may even decide to adopt their ways and their God. All those choices are yours. I have surrendered my Lordship of this city so that you may be allowed to have those choices and freedom. It has been a hard decision for me, but I believe it is the best one. Finally, I announce to you that I am giving the hand of my beloved daughter Maryam to the Seljuk Sultan Alaeddin Keykubad. In this way, I am sealing the fate of our two peoples with a peaceful marriage, not bloodshed. Pray for her happiness!"

He paused, giving them a few moments to absorb the news. The crowd listened in total silence, too stunned to immediately grasp the meaning of all of this, just as Maryam had done a short while before. Soon the crowd buzzed with whispers and comments. Then from the back of the crowd rose a cry of "*Long Live our Lord!*", and all joined in a rousing cheer, relieved that their worst fears were allayed: they would survive!

Kyr Vart raised his hands again and urged them to silence.

"My dear subjects, it is now time for me to open this door and walk out of this castle for the last time. May God's grace protect you, for now and ever more, and know that no lord served a better people with more pride than I have for these last years."

He turned to face the door and lifted the heavy metal key to its position at the end of the timbered bolt that held the door shut tightly. He gave the order for the gatekeepers to release it. The first sliver of light that appeared in the opening crack went through his heart like a sword. This is my destiny, he thought, this is our destiny: the Seljuks have won.

☪ ☪ ☪

On the other side, the soldiers heard the clunk of the heavy timber log sliding in its slot and knew the door would soon be opened. They began to cheer with all the might of their lungs, exciting the horses even more. To Alaeddin Keykubad, it was the sweetest sound he had ever heard in his life. Yes, it is true, he thought. This place, where the mountains run into the sea, yes, this place is now for me! No victory will ever be as sweet to me as this one!

The Sultan was well-prepared for this moment. In order to prove his good intentions to the citizens, pouches filled with a fortune of 10,000 *dirhams* of gold were given to each soldier to hand out to the people. Over 100 oxen and 1000 sheep stood outside the door, waiting to be distributed to the starving people. His lieutenants had given orders to the soldiers that there was to be no bloodshed or plunder and to keep their swords in their sheaths. His heart beat faster than it ever had in his entire life as he saw the first crack of light in the opening door.

The Seljuk drummers struck up a noise that reached to the heavens and almost blew down Kyr Vart and his priests as they opened the castle door to its whole width and stepped out into the sunlight. Alaeddin and Ertokush rode up to Kyr Vart, who held up a giant iron key to the Sultan.

"I place this iron key in your hands, the key to this sapphire gem of my city, and to the golden citizens it holds. I trust that you will honor our agreement and treat both of them with respect and equity." The Sultan took the key, and then planted the royal banner in the walls of this city on the sea, just as his father had done before him in Antalya and his brother in Sinop on the Black Sea years before.

At this moment, the soldiers released their pent-up energy. They madly rushed into the castle, shouting "*Allah Allah Allahu Akbar*" while tossing gold coins up into the air. The citizens eagerly rushed out to catch the golden shower like little children. Alaeddin's white charger pranced in every direction in the ensuing chaos, uncertain which direction to take. The Sultan looked over the scene of joyous turmoil with a broad smile on his face, throwing his head back in laughter at the sight of all this good fortune, far richer than the gold coins from his treasury now being pitched in the air like grains of seed.

☪ ☪ ☪

After her father opened the door and stepped outside, Maryam remained in the cool shadow of the portico and looked out at the scene swirling in front of her. She heard booming music, whooping in a strange language, cooks banging wooden spoons on kettles, a band of drums and trumpets, and everyone on both sides shouting out in joy. She saw colorful silken flags with strange black squiggles on them and big poles with horsetails hanging from them bobbing up and down among the soldiers, and out of the corner of her eye she saw a sheep getting its throat slit, and several others awaiting the same fate. The sun beat down on the silver swords and stirrups of the horses, blinding her eyes, and she found herself suddenly shoved ahead by the force of the people behind her pouring out of the castle gate. She saw her father approach the black stallion of Ertokush, and then everything became a dizzying scene of madness and confusion that made her feel faint.

Suddenly, all motion froze and the din silenced for her. She saw him. There was no mistaking it. It had to be him, the great Sultan Alaeddin Keykubad himself, the man who was to become her husband. The sun's rays shone down more strongly on him, it seemed, or was it just the reflection off the blinding white coat of his stallion that shimmered brighter than silver? He sat taller in his saddle than any other officer and even the Vizier Ertokush. His teeth were very white, glittering like the fresh snowfall on the mountain peaks behind Kalonoros. She could see that brightness about him immediately, as he kept throwing his head back in joyous laughter at the scene in front of him. Erect and confident, he danced in the saddle in perfect turning rhythm with his stallion as it pranced about in the mayhem, shaking its mane in unison with the Sultan's laughing head. He glowed like gold atop this silver horse, as if he had his own inner sun. This was indeed a victor; this was a wave of a man above all others.

Suddenly, she was no longer afraid. The sun broke out inside of her as well, a sun that burned the blood in her ears. This was not what she had been expecting at all. She envisioned an old, cruel, thick and brutish monster, but in front of her was an elegant man as tall and strong as a poplar tree. His body was thin and he held himself with assured carriage, and his hands – yes, she could see them as his gloves had been cast aside – those fingers were as thin, elegant and powerful as the rest of him. She watched the way he grasped the bridle reins of that silver stallion with authority and firmness, never losing control of the animal in all the chaos. Suddenly she wanted to reach out and touch those hands. So this was to be her destiny; this sleek and assured man would be the one who would take her beyond this castle door, beyond the gate of the city of her Kalonoros home to an intriguing future she could not yet imagine.

And now she knew, as strongly as the powerful sun that beat down on her, that she wanted to go towards this mystery, to a future that would be held in those strong and elegant hands. The attraction of this promise pulled her forward out of the gate. Dazed, she began walking through the crowd towards that prancing silver stallion reined in by those long fingers. She was shoved and jostled along the way and was almost pushed down to the ground two times by the crowd, but she continued to weave her way through the mayhem with increasing determination until she found herself right under the shadow cast by the shining stallion. She looked up at the Sultan's face. The sun was shining behind it so she could not see it clearly with her blinded eyes, but even so, she knew that his eyes were upon her as well. She saw that he abruptly snapped the reins to pull the stallion to a halt and stared down at her for a second, or perhaps it was a minute, she could not tell, and then he kicked the horse to move to the other side of her. As she too spun around to follow his movement, she saw his face clearly for the first time. He had the traits of a hawk, with a nose like a beak as sharp as the long edge of the sword blade at his side. His lips were thin and pulled into an imperious curve. Then she caught her first glimpse of his eyes, a pair of the most startling blue eyes she had ever seen, bluer even than her Kalonoros sea; eyes filled with a light that shamed the brightest azure skies under the southern sun. It was hard to hold their blinding gaze, yet at the same time she could not take her eyes away from that piercing blue stare now fixed upon her. So these are the eyes I will gaze into for the rest of my life, she thought; these are the eyes that will guide me, inspire me, love me and lead me forever. Yes, these eyes and those fingers; yes, I want them. I do not understand how this can be possible, but I want both of them, right now and forever.

☪ ☪ ☪

How can it be that in all this mayhem, one person causes my horse to lurch? Who is this girl standing below me, staring impudently at me with such intent? No one approaches a sultan like this! How is it possible that my stallion could stumble at the sight of her, shaming the dignity of my horsemanship? I never lose control of Night Shining White, never! I can take Kalonoros without a blow, and yet my horse trips before the penetrating gaze of a young girl? Impossible!

But yet there you are below me, young girl, standing tall, very tall, among all those soldiers and townspeople, you and you alone, calm and collected in all this mayhem. Perhaps it is your height that startled my horse – my, I have never seen a woman this tall – but no, it is the bearing of those determined shoulders, unafraid and defiant, that freezes my horse and now rivets my gaze. I look down at your face and cannot believe the color of your eyes, an intense green, like no emerald in my treasure chest, flashing brighter than any glint off my silver sword. Never have I seen such eyes, and I cannot break away from them to take in the rest of you. As I maneuver Night Shining White to the other side of you, I suddenly realize that it has to be you – yes, you, the daughter I have requested as marriage booty to seal an alliance. I do not yet know your name; I do not know when we shall meet, but I know that a woman this tall and with such audacity cannot be mere booty. This woman is more, much more. The mettle of this woman will be the spirit linked to my destiny. She will offer me waves more sparkling than the waters of the Mediterranean Sea below me. Of this I am certain.

And so at this moment was an ocean born, filled with waters both blue and green, deep and bountiful and wide enough to quench the thirst of an entire empire.

Chapter 4

So Joins the Steppe with the Sea

"My Alaiye! This glorious city will now bear my name for all eternity!" The Sultan bellowed out for the entire crowd to hear. "I hereby rename this city Alaiye, and forever more shall this name be associated with this day of triumph and happiness. Long life to the Seljuk Empire, and may our victories be many!"

Alaeddin Keykubad, the Lion of Sultans, the Most Revered Lord, the One renowned around the World, the Holy Wise One, the Sultan of Sultans, whipped his horse past the green-eyed girl and rode into the gates of this paradise city that now bore his name. Passing through the shade of the entry portico, he took his first glimpse of his new conquest.

Yes, he thought, turning his head from side to side to take it all in, this is much finer than I imagined. He trotted his horse past the Byzantine church and went over to the edge of the fortress wall. The cliff underneath him plunged straight down into the Mediterranean Sea. He could see the irregular coastline of rocky headlands and secluded coves running to the horizon in both directions east and west, and in front of him the blue sea stretched to the end of the world. Behind him to the north, he saw the profile of pine-clad Taurus Mountains as they swept down to the sparkling sea. He nodded his head to the west towards Antalya, thinking of how proud his father Giyaseddin Keyhüsrev would have been of him now. Yes, *Baba*, I, too, have captured a city on the sea like you did with Antalya. Both you and I will go down in history as creators of an Empire unknown in the world before us! We, from the grassy steppes, have reached the sea, and there will be no stopping us now. While he was savoring the view and the rush of his new-found power, Ertokush trotted up to his side.

"My Sultan, before anything else, we must first call the sheikhs to lead an invocation prayer in praise to God for his mercy in this victory." The first blessing and invocation prayer in the holy language of the Qur'an was soon pronounced in the castle of Kalonoros, which had only yesterday echoed with church bells and hymns.

After the prayer ceremony was finished, the Sultan's troops set to work, establishing their camp, staking out the headquarters and erecting barracks, kitchens and latrines for the men. Tents were pitched, and the generals made arrangements to occupy the living quarters in the former palace of Kyr Vart.

Before being escorted out of Kalonoros, Kyr Vart requested to have one last moment together with his daughter to bid her farewell. He entered his daughter's room and saw her sitting at the window looking out at the sea and hugging her cat Angel close to her chest. He sat down next to her and spoke very softly, reaching out to stroke the silken white fur of the cat along with her.

"My dear Maryam, I am leaving now. An escort is ready to take me and some of my most faithful servants to my new lands in Ilgin. I am depending on you to be brave for your marriage tomorrow, and to carry yourself with the high manners and dignity that distinguishes our people. I am counting on you to be happy and to make this Sultan a good wife."

Maryam was unable to tell her father that she was now more afraid than when he had first told her the news of the surrender. She was now afraid of something much bigger than the military victory of a man over her father and her city: she was afraid of the power this stranger with the blue eyes now held over her.

"Oh Papa, please do not worry about me," she said, throwing her arms around his neck and trying to sound convincing. "I will be strong, just as you must be strong to start your life all anew, alone, in a strange land without me by your side. Go now, Papa, I will be fine, everything is being prepared for the wedding ceremony tomorrow and I will show the Seljuks that we are people of virtue, and that I am more than worthy to be their Queen."

☪ ☪ ☪

Indeed, the wedding of Alaeddin Keykubad, Sultan of Sultans, and the young daughter of Lord Kyr Vart was scheduled to take place the very next day after the capture of the castle. The Sultan wanted the marriage performed as soon as possible to send a message to the world that an alliance had been made with the Armenians. She was a child of not yet fifteen summers, and he was a mature man double her age. He was the representative of the Caliph; she a devoted child of Jesus. What form was this marriage to take?

The next morning started off with the promise of a hot day, even though it was in the middle of the month of January. Women servants of the sultan came into Maryam's room and served her apples, quinces and some yogurt. A bath was prepared for her with crushed lavender leaves and warm almond oil was massaged into her skin. A Turkish woman came in and tried to apply a paste of henna and olive oil to her hands and feet, but Maryam pushed her away. She made it very clear to those women that she chose to dress herself, and needed no one to fuss over her. She chose the dress she loved the best: a turquoise tunic embroidered with her favorite flowers, the tiny white blossoms of the almond trees that grew in the hillside groves around Kalonoros. She knew that the turquoise set off her green eyes particularly well, and she wanted to make sure this man was aware of this one feature of hers that she thought set her apart from others. She placed a small round cap on her head, with two rows of gold coins which hung down over her ears. As a final touch, she fastened around her neck the intricate crucifix of gold and pearls that had been given to her by her mother on the occasion of her Holy Communion six years before, and she carried her mother's set of rosary beads in her hands. Perhaps this ceremony will be led by a Muslim preacher, she thought, but this crucifix will represent the holy Christian sacrament of marriage for me. She bent her head and started to pray, harder than she had ever prayed in her life. *May this man be ever kind to me! Jesus, please do not desert me now!*

The Sultan was in his tent preparing for the ceremony as well, assisted by his male servants. His beard was trimmed, his hair washed, and a fresh set of undergarments and a white linen tunic was laid out for him. Flat-soled boots with pointed toes made of the softest lamb's leather were placed on his feet. As he tried to attach his golden belt, he noted that his hands were trembling. Why am I so nervous about this event, he thought to himself. It is true I have had little time for women over these past few years, but now I am a mature man, and the time has come for me to think of my succession and the future of this empire. This diplomatic marriage makes sound sense. And yet – if it is just a trade agreement, why are my hands trembling so? What is the power of that green-eyed gaze? He shook his head to rid it of those thoughts just as his valet entered the room carrying one of his most prized possessions, his brocaded coronation mantle. It took two men to assist him to slip on the heavy, full-length tunic that had been woven for him last year for his coronation ceremony in Sivas. What a glorious day that had been! The silk cape was crimson red with scrolling writing embroidered in gold thread at the hem, highlighted with pearls and precious stones. No citizen of Kalonoros will ever doubt my authority when they see this cape upon my shoulders, he thought, least of all that impudent green-eyed girl!

The Sultan had erected a square white tent in the middle of the fortress courtyard to host the wedding ceremony. The green banners bearing the Sultan's insignia, which had been planted in the fortress walls, relentlessly snapped in the breeze coming off the ocean and orchestrated their own wedding march. Hundreds of witnesses from the Seljuk camp were gathered in the courtyard, jostling for positions near the tent. Many notables and priests from the church had been allowed to gather there as well, and their sober black robes contrasted sharply with the white turbans and colorful gold embroidered silk and velvet tunics worn by the Seljuk retinue. All eyes were upon Maryam as she crossed the courtyard to the tent, but she held her head high and walked with a determined step.

She entered the tent and was greeted by a retinue of soldiers and male servants, dressed in the finest of casings and gowns. Sparks of light glinted off weapons incrusted with silver and gold. In the middle of the tent stood the Sultan, resplendent in a red gown brocaded in gold, far richer than anything she had ever seen on a priest. A sword with a ruby-studded hilt jutted from his hip, and a dagger and embroidered leather gloves were tucked into the green sash that was tied around his waist over the gown. The red, gold, green and white costume and the blue of his eyes seemed to form a rainbow arch over the room. Engrossed at the sight of him and all this brocaded and colorful magnificence, she stumbled over the carpet, but quickly regained her poise.

Standing next to the Sultan was a man wearing a green robe and a high white turban. He proceeded to introduce the two witnesses for the ceremony, Ertokush and Father Vartanian. Maryam had requested that her family priest from the Magdalene Church be present at the wedding, and was relieved to find that her request had been granted. She needed to reassure herself that the Holy Sacrament of marriage would be recognized by her faith, even if this were to be a Muslim ceremony. The ladies-in-waiting of the Sultan led her to the side of the rainbow glowing in front of her. Maryam felt faint from the heat in the tent, from so many people and the lack of air, or perhaps was it because the Rainbow Sultan seemed to absorb all of the air in the tent? The ceremony began with the Sheikh offering prayers to God and reciting verses from their holy book. Maryam could understand none of it and was impatient for it to end before the perspiration now running down her back would spoil her turquoise dress. The ceremony seemed to go on forever, but finally the Sheikh approached a table in the middle of room and asked that the couple sit with him.

The Sheikh took out from his belt a brass inkpot, a pen and a large sheet of paper. The inkpot was inscribed with tiny decorations and filigree markings, which Maryam assumed was the writing of the Seljuks. The Sheik proclaimed, "In the name of God, the All-Merciful, the All-Compassionate!" and dipped the pen into the inkpot and began to write on the paper in a flowing script. He then brought out a seal and pressed it to the paper, rose and bowed to the couple. Maryam now understood that she was as of this moment a married woman with a husband.

When the ceremony ended, servants assembled an enormous feast. Wool carpets had been laid out all over the courtyard, and were covered with fresh linen cloths set with bowls, wooden spoons, carafes for sherbet and cool water, and goblets of brass. Several tent-like canopies had been erected to shade the guests from the hot afternoon sun. Dozens of lambs were roasting over open flames, and mounds of steaming bulgur, vegetables and chicken with currants were served on golden platters. In front of the royal carpet a whole array of sweet delicacies tempted the fingers of the guests: honey cakes, candied fruit, heaping bowls of nuts and trays of fruit. She also noticed that contrary to wedding feasts in her church, no wine was served, only fruit juice. The guests sat on the carpets and shared course after course, served on a large brass platter set in the middle of each group. The meal was followed by a pudding made with cream, sugar, nuts and pistachio seeds, and Maryam was surprised to see how much she enjoyed it, even though she was too nervous to eat much of anything. Servants fluttered around the guests, continually serving more food and refreshing the goblets with cool drinks. Out of the corner of her eye, Maryam watched as her husband took part in the meal. He was laughing with his officers, with that same hearty laugh she heard in the crowd the day before. He was popping nuts and fruit into his mouth with those graceful long fingers as he talked. She observed how he did not drop a morsel, not even into the palm of his hands. He seemed to be in control of everything, from the smallest of raisins to the tallest of fortresses.

At last the meal was finished, and silver bowls of perfumed water were brought by servants in silk robes so that the guests could wash their hands. The imam said a short prayer. The food was cleared away and servants approached with metal ewers and sprinkled rose water on the guests and the carpets. Musicians and reciters of poetry then appeared, and the Sultan paused between sips to listen to the musicians who sang his favorite ballads to him.

By this time, Maryam was very tired and her head hurt from listening to that foreign tongue in her ears all afternoon. She was thankful when a group of women gestured for her to rise and follow them away from the crowd in the courtyard.

She was led to an inner room that had been prepared for her, with soft cushions and lit candlesticks. She looked around her and saw a low mat covered with a bright blue quilt and turquoise cushions. On the floor in front of it was the most magnificent carpet she had ever seen in her life. Palace maids entered and helped her undress, bathe and change into a white silken robe and green slippers. They left her alone and closed the door. Despite her excitement and apprehension of what was to follow, she was unable to keep her eyes open, and fell sound asleep upon the cushions in complete exhaustion.

The Sultan watched as the servants gestured for his bride to rise. It was then that he stole a glance at her, as he had been avoiding looking at her all afternoon for fear of losing his composure if he took one look into those green eyes. As he watched her leave, he smiled to himself as he recalled what had been the most memorable event of this day for him. It was the moment when she had entered the tent and stumbled. Yes, thought the Sultan, she stumbles too, and I now I have regained my honor. It will be the last time we stumble in front of each other, for soon we will be equals. I must remember that I will enter her room this night as a man, not a sultan. This night will be a long one; he thought to himself, for I have still another important victory to win, here, in this fortress city on high.

Chapter 5
Fairy of the Full Moon

The Sultan entered his private rooms and found his bride sound asleep. He was thankful to have the opportunity to finally take a long look at her, made easier by the light of the full moon which poured into the room and shone on her profile. He took his time to fully observe her before lying down at her side.

She was dressed in a thin gown of white silk, glowing silver in the cool light of the moon. He had already seen that she was tall, so very tall, almost as tall as he was, and her emerald eyes had bewitched him the first time he glimpsed at her. But what was the rest of her like? He noted her long neck and the copper hair that spilled over it, but he realized that her beauty was not one of curls, dewy lips or almond eyes. Hers was different, one of an inner strength that already became apparent to him that very first afternoon. She was different than he in faith and language, but at the same time, he felt her determination would be a match for his. This woman would be the fresh fountain from which he would drink his fill each day.

He knelt down next to her on the mat, and touched his hand to her cheek. She opened her eyes. The Sultan suddenly felt shy, and as he looked down at her felt somewhat at a loss for words. He smiled to himself when he realized that she would not understand anything of what he said anyway, which gave him the courage to plunge ahead.

"My bride, what a beautiful day we have lived together today, the first of many more to come. To remember this day, I wish to present you with your wedding gift, this rug that you see glittering at your feet. Most women would be offered pearls and gems set in gold for their wedding, but I wanted to offer you something as original as you are. I hope this rug will forever bless this wedding ordained by God for us; and will show how our lives are now knotted together."

Maryam did not understand anything of what he was saying, but she knew exactly what he meant as he gestured to the rug. She felt his eyes directly upon her. He then stepped forward and she heard him take in a breath. She understood that she would become his from that moment on, and with her heart beating faster than it had ever beat before and propelled by that strange new fire she felt within her, she placed her arm on his to invite him to her side.

Maryam kept her head bowed, but lifted her eyes slightly to look at him, and took in all of the color, shape and size of the man that she saw, and realized once again that he had his own power upon her. She was more curious than frightened, more intrigued than intimidated. Here stood in front of her the most sacred and powerful man in the entire kingdom, the man that would ensure her happiness and create the generations of sultans to come.

He looked directly into her eyes and fell into them. He placed one hand on her arm and then on her other arm. He pulled her up from the mat and brought her closer to him, and then kissed her cheeks and forehead. He lifted her chin with his hand and stopped.

"No, this will not do. This is not how I wish to take you as my bride. For you, it must be something very different, something as unique as you, like that rug. You must be given my pearls for the first time in a setting that is as memorable as you are." He looked in her eyes and wondered how she would understand anything he would say to her. I can speak the Greek I learned from my mother, he thought, the Persian and Arabic I learned from my tutors in Tokat, the Turkish of my forefathers: but this language of hers? Confound it, no! I must rely on my eyes and my touch to do the talking tonight, and may they be as eloquent as possible!

He suddenly opened the door to the chamber, barking an order to the surprised page standing outside.

"Bring me Night Shining White immediately! Just put a bridle on him, but you don't need to saddle him. Now move!"

He turned back to Maryam and flashed a bright smile. "Come, my bride, I have something to show you. We will ride out to an area east of the city that I have come to love very much. I promise you a night of exquisite beauty."

When the horse was brought to him, he rolled up the wedding carpet and tossed it on the horse. He picked up his bride by the waist and hoisted her up on the horse, and then jumped up behind her. Kicking the bareback stallion to take off, they headed out of the castle gate and down the hill towards the sea, leaving behind the stunned guards in their wake. Their way was lit by the rays of the full moon, and they headed out to the east of the city, to a long stretch of sand that came right to the lip of the sea. In a secluded area, a few feet from the lapping waves of the sea, the Sultan stopped his horse, jumped off and spread the rug on the sand. He then reached up and pulled his bride down off the horse, and then held her out in front of him and looked directly again into those green eyes. There was no laughter now from him, no fear from her. He placed one hand on her arm, and then the other, and drew her close, and then made a sash with his long silver fingers around her waist, pulling her even closer to him.

He was totally captivated by her, and stroked her cheek with his finger while trying to find his way with words. He finally spoke softly to her. "This is the happiest full moon of my life. Your face is as radiant as that moon in the night sky, and how I hope that it will always shine this brightly throughout my life! Yes, my little emerald-eyed one, you are a moonbeam sent down to me from the heavens; a fairy from the moon. Yes! That is exactly it! That is what you are – my bright moon fairy! I will name you this to remind me of this moment forever. Maryam, royal daughter of Kalonoros, from this night forth, you will be known as *"Mahperi"*, my Moon Fairy Queen, as beautiful as the face of that silvery full moon. The double capture of Kalonoros and you as my Moon Queen will be my good luck tokens for the rest of my life and reign."

He then held her face in his two hands and spoke softly to her. "Keep looking at me, my Moon Fairy Queen, right into my eyes. Hold your green eyes to mine; do not remove them for a second. I want to remember forever the look in your eyes when you realize that we will become one, now in this moment."

Chapter 6

That It Bear My Name and Mark

Happiness does not know gravity. This was certainly true for Alaeddin and Mahperi after their marriage, for their moments together fluttered as lightly as birds' wings. They spent entire days in each other's company, unable to be separated for more than a few hours. The Sultan found himself incapable of thinking of anything else but her, unable to concentrate on the matters needed to transform Alaiye into a new Seljuk city. All he wanted to do was to run to her; to discuss with her his plans and ideas, to watch those green eyes sparkle at his words, even though they did not yet share a common language. He had trouble understanding this intoxication, for he had never experienced anything so dizzying. Whereas a few days ago, he had been a powerful sultan; now, after only one night, he was reduced to a slave eager to serve his master and nothing else.

Mahperi, too, was lost in the giant blue waves of this man. They told each other stories; they told each other secrets and dreams, each one in their own language, hoping to be understood. They shared their passion in many ways and in many places, above and under the quilt, under the sun and under the moon, inside the palace and deep in the caves of the surrounding coves of the bay. They were not timid with each other; no gaze was too deep, and all was mutual discovery and conquest of body, soul and heart.

☪ ☪ ☪

At the same time they discovered each other, the couple spent days exploring the hidden corners of the city and the surrounding region. When Mahperi would cry out, "Come, my Sultan, let me show you my favorite parts of Kalonoros!" it was the most exciting thing Alaeddin Keykubad could hear each morning. He would have his pages saddle Night Shining White and a horse for Mahperi, and, leaving the palace complex at the top of the mountain, they would slowly pace their way down the steep hill towards the sea. Alaeddin never tired of the vistas they encountered at every turn of the switchback; each one offering a different, but equally spectacular, window onto the sea below.

They would pause to look out over the city, and it was during these moments that Alaeddin began his plans to rebuild the city, this Alaiye, named after him.

Although they often had trouble understanding each other, they managed well-enough to communicate their thoughts to each other. Alaeddin marvelled at how quickly she was learning Turkish, and, despite her hesitations, mistakes and strange accent, she always seemed to express her ideas clearly. Yet everything I really need to know is written in those clear emerald eyes, he thought, for they are more eloquent than the finest sermons pronounced by the famed imams in my medreses at Konya.

☪ ☪ ☪

On a fine February morning, they set out, as usual, down the hill. Alaeddin shielded his eyes with his hand against the sun, intense even though it was still winter. "Ah, my Mahperi, if you only could know all the plans I have for this city and for my empire! We Seljuks have been in Anatolia for 150 years now. My ancestors survived the sack of Konya by the armies of the Christian Crusader King Barbarossa, the Infidel, some thirty years ago. Those dark days are over. My ancestors brought Islam to this area, and it is my role to ensure it becomes the basis of the customs of this land, the foundation of our society and the source of all inspiration and strength."

The Sultan Alaeddin Keykubad pointed to the narrow spit of land that jutted out from the rocky promontory and continued. "But I do not just wish to conquer. I want more than that. I want development and happiness for my subjects, with stability and prosperity everywhere. I will set the stage for a program of building that will be more ambitious than anyone else before me: the Persians, Lydians, Romans and Greeks will pale in front of me! And I shall start by transforming this city. Just wait and see, you will not recognize the city in which you played as a child!

Mahperi was not used to hearing such forceful self-assurance, and it fascinated her at the same time that it frightened her. She knew she would never totally understand this man or the drive that made him want to be stronger and more powerful than anyone on earth. Yet she knew she wanted to be a part of this dream to build his Kingdom for all centuries.

Alaeddin continued. "I will define wealth and power as no one before me. My ports will be full of riches, my fields will bloom, my *medreses* will hum from the voices of students reciting their lessons, and my kingdom will be adorned with buildings so strongly built and richly-decorated that all visitors will stand in awe of them. My scholars will write the finest treatises, and my universities will define the new concepts of science. I will make my Kingdom as sweet as a honeycomb, dripping honey on all my subjects. This will be my legacy, far more poetic than any epitaph on my tombstone."

The words continued to tumble out of him in a torrent. "Alaiye will be my first port of many to come. I signed an agreement with the Republic of Venice last March, the first major political decision I took as a Sultan. Masters of seas and markets, the Venetians live in a world run by money and refinement, and I want to be a part of that, for I know that the most important key to building my kingdom will start with commerce. After much negotiation and hard bargaining with them, we exchanged signed letters of agreement. In order to encourage trade, I agreed that each of us would pay reduced customs fees in our mutual ports. Instead of the normal 10% duty I charge, I agreed to charge them a mere 2%, and, to boot, I exempted them from duty on wheat, pearls, precious stones, gold and silver. I may have been too generous, but I think it was a wise tactic in order to promote the export of the wheat grown in our Anatolian fields to an increasingly hungry Europe! The more this Europe realizes how much Anatolia can bring them, the more powerful we will stand and the more prosperous will be my citizens!"

He was flush with excitement when speaking about this agreement, which Mahperi sensed was as important to him as the one he had just won with Kalonoros.

"Venice will have privileged status in all trade passing through my kingdom to points east, and, in return, they have agreed to carry Seljuk goods to Europe in their vast ships. I dream that the rugs of my weavers will adorn their *palazzi*, and their silvery blonde women will be even more alluring when they slip on my embroidered silks and the rose perfumes from my gardens. They will feast on our apricots and olives, and savor the sweet sugar of our refineries. Their lives will never be the same after they taste what we Turks can bring them!"

He turned to her and smiled. "As for your city, I will soon give the order to reinforce the walls of your father's castle that crowns the great rock above the port, so that they will be as strong as the walls of my capital at Konya. I will also create a new palace for myself and new barracks for the men, and add two additional fortresses, one seaward and one landward. Your city also needs to have its cisterns rebuilt in order to store the winter rainwater to last over the long summer months. This is one big, waterless rock, and I need plentiful water supplies for my troops – you saw what a lack of water did to your father. I will also link the fortress atop the castle rock to the harbor below by a series of walls, and I will develop the harbor to welcome those Venetian traders. All of this may take me five years to build, but I will do it!"

Mahperi heard the determination in his voice and had no doubt in her mind that he would achieve his goal to build up her city. She could not resist the urge to participate in his excitement.

"I wonder," she timidly asked, "if it would be possible to think farther than just trade. If you established a naval power for the Seljuks, you could use this port as a base to develop a part of your campaign that has never existed. Step off the steppes and venture into the seas to expand your territory and claim even more power! Why, look down there, you could build a naval arsenal and an armory for weapons at the crook of the harbor. Make your tower massive and solid, of bright red brick that can be seen for miles down the coast! Inside the arsenal, you can incorporate a system of hidden docks, so that the narrow black ships of your navy may secretly slip out of the waters and rule the sea. You can build there the ships that will extend your influence around the shores of the Mediterranean. You already rule the waters of the Black Sea, and with Alaiye, you are primed to take possession of the southern sea as well. Yes, behold my Sultan of Two Seas!"

She stopped there for she felt she had perhaps gone too far suggesting to him what he should do. Yet she had never held her tongue or her opinions, and she was not about to start doing so with her husband. She waited a moment for him to grasp her words, and timidly went on.

"You see, my father never had that idea, or the dreams that you do. He was content to stay at the top of his fortress and live in this jewel of a city under the warm sun. He had no desire to leave it, to go elsewhere and expand his life and provide more opportunities to his people. You are not like him. You have a vision; you always wonder how long it will take you to reach the next horizon, and you are never afraid to set out for it. You instill in all a sense of potential, be it your officers, your soldiers or your government officials. You instill it especially in me: I never want to stop riding to that next horizon with you. Let me help you build your dream, my sultan, my love."

The Sultan now realized that he had achieved far more than a political ploy by marrying this woman. She was intelligent, eager and resourceful, the perfect ally for his mission.

"Yes, I want you to help me be that builder, my Fairy Moon Queen! With you as my lucky charm, my kingdom will grow and my battles will all be victorious!" He leaned over and squeezed her hand.

Yes, thought Mahperi, I will help him build this empire of his. What an adventure it will be! He wants my help and support, and I am here to give it to him, just as I give him my sweet kisses and anything else he asks of me.

Chapter 7

Farewell, Almond Blossoms and Rosemary

When Alaeddin first heard the sound of the woodpeckers drumming out their territory, he knew the time had come to return north to Konya. They reminded him that his empire was calling him back to duty, as did all the other signs of winter's end along the Mediterranean: the white feathers of almond blossoms now opening on the trees, newborn goat kids starting to stand on their own four legs, homely toads coming out of hibernation, the intoxicating scent of rosemary flowers drawing the honey bees to their task, and the dawn chorus of birds chirping louder than the muezzin's cry from the minarets at prayer time. He thought of the swallows that return from Africa year after year to the same nest site. I will be like you, little birds, he mused, for I will return to Alaiye each winter, and like you, I will laboriously collect mud to build this nest above the world.

The winter had indeed passed all too quickly, but the Sultan could not put off his departure any longer. The time had come to plan for more conquests and for more expansion; not just here, but in the whole empire, the one the two lovers now dreamed to build together.

☪ ☪ ☪

"There is an entire nation to build!"

Alaeddin raised his arm and swept it around in an expansive circle over his head. He and Mahperi were on a morning ride in the hills around Alaiye and had stopped to enjoy the view over the sea.

"Mahperi, the time has come for me to return to Konya. I must organize my summer campaigns, train my troops, oversee building projects, discuss issues with my ministers, confer with my emirs, check with my treasurers...I have a kingdom to run, and to build, and we must now return to the affairs of state after this magnificent moment of respite I have enjoyed here with you and your city, now my city named Alaiye! How you have helped me to shape the future of this city – I can only imagine what you will do for the rest of my Kingdom!"

His white teeth flashed in the sun, just as they had when she first set eyes on him, and she realized that this man was too big to keep all to herself. She had understood that the first time she set eyes on him, yet it was painful to think that their days of honey were soon to be over.

He sensed her sadness and tried to excite her about this new adventure. "I cannot wait to show you off to the city as my queen, to present you to all the people at my court who never thought I would take the time for a wife! And now they will see that although I may have waited a long time to marry, when I did, it was with an exceptional woman with eyes brighter than the tail feathers of the peacock that prances through the palace gardens!"

Mahperi blushed and still could not believe that she held this man as hers. Instead of being jealous of his other passion, his kingdom, she loved him all the more for his devotion to developing his vision.

"But I must tell you Mahperi," he continued, "that life there will not be the same as it is here. Konya is a very different place than Alaiye. Although it is beautiful in its own way, it does not sit next to a deep blue sea. The flowers of its gardens are not as abundant and the air is not as sweet and fresh-smelling as it is here. But you will soon come to love it. It is now your city as well! Perhaps you may even see your very first snowfall, for it often storms well into the month of March. But what really makes Konya so different from Alaiye is that my entire court and army are there. It is not only the small retinue that follows me when I travel. No, there resides the entire foundation of my kingdom: the men in charge of government, justice, religious affairs, education, agriculture, commerce and construction! There are hundreds of officials there, my viziers and emirs above all."

He gazed into the distance, and his voice became more remote as well.

"There will be many people there taking up my time, needing my judgment, my orders, my vision," he continued. "I am occupied by them from morning until night; they demand all of my time and energy and I am often overcome by all the business they bring before me. I go to bed with worries; I wake up with worries! I tell you this, sweet Mahperi, because I will not be as available to you as I am now, for picnics, horseback rides, meals at leisure and afternoon rests under our quilt. You will see much less of me and you must understand that I have no other choice – my kingdom comes first!"

Mahperi realized that he was counting on her to be as supportive as possible. Seeking to reassure him, she replied, "Of course, my Sultan, I understand. I will help you grow your kingdom in whatever way I can. I will share those problems with you and perhaps lift some of them from your shoulders. Do not worry, I am sure I will have much to do and learn as well!"

He smiled at her optimism, but his voice became even more serious. "I also want you to know that all eyes will be upon you, Mahperi," he continued. "Some of these eyes will admire you and love you. Other eyes will be envious of your power over me and your position. Women will be jealous of your magnificent emerald eyes. Men will not take kindly to your authority and directness, and the way I rely on you for counsel. Some will say malicious things about you, many will seek to make you stumble and make you look foolish. Human nature is not always kind; people do not always follow the lessons taught by our Prophet. You have grown up in a world of pure sunshine and sparkling waves. Konya is not such a place. It is bustling, dynamic and developing, and everyone wants his part in this new dream, and they may see you as an obstacle in their way. Ambition rules and breeds greed and jealousy. I say this not to frighten you, but just to make you aware that all eyes will be upon you. But I know you will be magnificent, of this I am certain. You will bring the same light to the entire court as you have brought to my heart and life. We will all be the richer for it."

Mahperi looked up directly into his eyes. "Yes, my love, know that I will follow you everywhere, and I will be at your side to help you build your empire, starting with its capital at Konya!"

He smiled at her and went on enthusiastically once more. "You will meet so many important people who will become a part of your life: my vizier Karatay, wise and plodding, serious and honest. Our religious teachers, gentle and all-seeing, will guide you in the ways of our faith and the will of God. And then there is my superintendent Köpek: oh, he is a handful most certainly! Brilliant and hardworking, volatile and perhaps too decisive at times, but what a man of action! My emirs as well are a band of ambitious men as interested as much in their own personal gain as they are in developing the kingdom, but if I am clever and play to this ambition adroitly, I should be able to get what I want from them. My generals are all fine and loyal men. My old friend General Hüsameddin Choban is as dependable as he is courageous, and I foresee an ever more brilliant future for him in coming years. And I promise we will go to visit your father in his new home at Ilgin near Akşehir. I enjoy soaking my battle- and saddle-worn bones in the hot springs there! You will be able to spend time with him in the lovely orchards of the region. And trust me; once you have tasted an apricot from Ilgin, you are spoiled for life! And you will meet women too, women who will not just be your attendants but will become your friends. Noble women of birth and character like you. I will introduce you to the ladies of the court, wives of the viziers and officers. Oh, I know you will be very happy in Konya if you give it a chance!"

Mahperi saw how excited he became when he spoke of his capital city. His eyes sparkled, his hands waved about, his words ran together in a jumble, so quickly did he speak. She managed to smile and brighten her face, but inside, she could not shake a sense of foreboding. This certainly did not sound like such an exciting place to her. No sea? No sweet-smelling breezes? No lush flowers? Malicious remarks? Their carefree time alone was over, and she would now have to share him with an entire court, all speaking different languages, all praying to a different God, with some out to make her stumble. The thought of leaving her home at Kalonoros for this new place on a dusty plain filled her with sadness. Would it be possible to find beauty there in that dust? Could it be possible to live without seeing the blue sea from her window the first thing in the morning upon rising? She was not feeling reassured about any of this. She shuddered despite the hot sun and tried to shake these dark thoughts from her head, but still, they remained. Why do I have such apprehension that hard winds will blow on me here in this new city on the plain?

And yet....in this capital city, Mahperi knew she would be received as a Queen and live in a palace with servants and attendants and have everything she could imagine at her hand. In some odd way, the unknown was an intoxicating prospect to her; an open garden gate that beckoned. There will be so much for me to do and learn there, she thought, so much more than here. Wasn't this the strange force that pulled you outside of that castle door and drew you to his side that very first day? Yes, this Konya will be a place where I can grow; it will be the place of my destiny. Yes, she would follow him anywhere, even to this city with no sea.

"My Sultan, my heart will heed your every command," she said, reigning in her horse, impatient to continue with their ride.

"Now that is the spirit of my Moon Queen!" he laughed. "That is where I will find all the strength I need to build that Empire, right there in those emerald eyes and with that determination of yours! Now come, let us race over to that olive grove I see on the crest of the next hill – and I warn you, I do not like to lose!"

Chapter 8

Charms of Fortune

"My Moon Queen must not ride into my capital on just any horse! She must mount a horse whose beauty rivals that of my Night Shining White! I have looked long and hard for such a horse for you, my love, and I have finally found just the one. My stable master thinks that he is too spirited for you, but I told him no horse was too much for you to hold – so let's see who is right!"

The morning of their departure had arrived, and Alaeddin and his officers were assembled outside the castle door, ready to leave. He had waited until this last moment to give his bride a gift that would be as impressive as this day. His stable master led out a small Arabian horse, black as the night, with a glossy coat and intense eyes.

"My love, I can imagine you on the back of this horse, riding it to every horizon of your dreams! It is a sleek and swift mount, as spirited as you are. Few people could handle such a horse, but I know you will be able to catch his fire and move as one. You two will define flight, and I wish for you many hours of freedom together. When we enter Konya, I can't wait to see the reaction of my people when they see my silver moon of a queen glowing brightly against the flank of a horse black as the winter night!"

Mahperi walked out and scarcely dared to touch this animal, whose coat shone like iridescent blue silk. She had never owned a horse before, but on their long days together, Alaeddin had taught her to ride like a Turk. Overwhelmed by the emotion of this day, by the departure from her cherished home, by the beauty of this animal and by his gesture of love, Mahperi's eyes welled up with tears. She looked up at her Sultan and was unable to express herself, but as usual, he was able to understand everything in those shining emerald gems.

They started off down the slope of the mountain. All the men were excited to return to their homes and command posts, but Mahperi was filled with tremendous sadness. She leaned down and whispered into the ear of her new horse. "Please, please, lead me to a land of happiness. You are in charge of taking me to a place where we will both be able to live in joy. Be my lucky star in the night sky! I shall call you Eclipse, for you and I will always be perfectly aligned in the eyes of the sun!"

They continued along the road westward for several hours, with the sea bobbing in and out of view. They camped for the night at the point on the coast where they would turn northwards and leave the sea at their backs. This part of the journey headed up an arduous mountain pass that would lead from the sea to the steppe. The next day they climbed for hours up the steep road, and, after one difficult switchback turn, the sea disappeared completely from view. Now Mahperi was alone with pine trees and shrubs. They needed to camp several more times along this pass, as the horses became too tired to climb for more than a few hours at a time. She began to wonder if they were ever to arrive at that plain she was so secretly dreading.

Finally, after several days, the road leveled off and became flat. In front to them stretched a beautiful blue lake as far as the eye could see, surrounded on its western shore by a range of small mountains. Mahperi's heart leapt in her chest. "Why it is almost as beautiful as the sea!" she cried out, charmed by its still waters of a color she he had never seen before in her sea: a pale and pure milky blue that rivaled the summer sky.

"Yes, I am very fond of this spot as well," added the Sultan, trotting up to her side. "It is a place of peace and unrivaled natural beauty, that is certain." When they left the calm blue waters of the lake behind them to continue on the road east, Mahperi could not stop thinking about it, and hoped that she would be able to return there often.

"Now we are on my favorite road of all," Alaeddin said turning to Mahperi. "It climbs steadily, and then turns abruptly down to Konya. I find this open land as intriguing and expansive as your sea, Mahperi. One day, too, you will be able to read its fascinating mystery just as you do with the waves of your Mediterranean."

Mahperi looked around her and, on the contrary, saw nothing that would make her call this a favorite place. They had finally reached the plain. In front of her stretched a dusty and flat expanse of land, without one tree on it, with only the distant horizon as decoration. Her heart sank. So this was to be the place of her new home. She wanted to jump off her horse and run back across the plains to her perch above the sea. She wanted to hear the voice of her father and the bells of the church in her castle. She wanted to hear sounds she understood, for she was so tired of not being able to comprehend this language being spoken around her; tired of thinking that all the laughter seemed directed at her. She wanted to go home, not to this ugly place in the middle of a dusty field! Tears started to fall and she bowed her head so that no one would see them.

At that moment, Eclipse reared back his head, swished his tail and bolted off full gallop down the road. Mahperi held on to him tightly as he raced ahead like an arrow shot out of a bow. After a few minutes of this mad dash, he abruptly stopped, and she flew over his head and landed in the soft dirt of the road.

Alaeddin rushed up to her, and cried out," Are you alright? I warned you this horse would be a handful!" and despite his concern for Mahperi, he could not keep from smiling at the antics of the spirited horse.

Mahperi picked herself up and dusted herself off. "I'm fine, I'm fine, I don't know what got into him – he just caught me off-guard, that is all. That was a good lesson for me to learn: never take your mind off the reins!" She took the bridle and led the black comet of a horse away from the group.

"Just what was that you did to me, you, who are supposed to be my friend and lucky star?" she hissed into the horse's ear. The horse placidly looked at her as if nothing had happened, and then Mahperi understood what the horse had instinctively sensed. Eclipse had done what was needed to shake off her fear and take the leap down the new road that she was afraid to take herself. By giving her this spirited horse to manage, Alaeddin had handed her the reins of her new life. She felt embraced by his loving gesture, stronger than any she had received from her family. I must put the past behind me, she thought; I must now make this dustbowl my homeland. At that moment, she took a vow to always look forward, never back. A different kind of expression appeared on her face, and a smile suddenly broke over it like the sun peeping behind from a cloud. "You little black devil, you!" she laughed, kissing her horse's neck. "Yes, the two of us must always race ahead together. Thank you, my friend, for giving me the courage I needed to make this leap forward!"

☪ ☪ ☪

They continued on for several hours until they saw a roadside inn perched on a small slope in the distance. With each step of the horses, the wide front door of the caravansarai, or han, as the Turks called these buildings, became more and more inviting.

"We will halt here for the night," ordered the Sultan to his chief aide-de-camp. "This han is large and sturdy, and I am sure it can hold all of us. We have a long and important day tomorrow and I want to be well-rested."

The Sultan's retinue approached the han, and he pointed up to the marble inscription plaque in Arabic that hung over the main door.

"I read to you, My Lions," said the Sultan: '*Built in the reign of Keykhosrow ibn Kilich Arslan, master of the Arabs and Persians, by his servant Emir Kandemir in the year 602.*' Yes, this han was built in the time of my father, Giyaseddin Keyhüsrev, may God praise his soul and give him peace. His emir Kandemir was a man who clearly understood his obligation to the Sultan and to the empire! By building this han, he ensured that merchants could travel safely to and from Konya."

The guards standing under the portico immediately recognized the Sultan's banner, and scurried to open the doors. The Sultan trotted into the expansive courtyard of the han, which was already filled with many travelers on their way to the nearby capital city of Konya. A flurry of small boys rushed out to help with the horses, and the superintendent of the han barked out orders to others to come assist the Sultan's retinue. The horses were led away to the large covered hall to the rear of the han where the animals of the other travelers were stabled.

"Pay special attention to my Night Shining White," Alaeddin urged his aide, "And make sure no filthy camel or donkey gives him a kick back there!"

Preparations were made to lodge the Sultan's retinue in the individual rooms that lined each side of the courtyard. The staff was familiar with travelers from all corners of the world coming through these doors, but the arrival of a Sultan was a rare and exciting event.

"I will bathe now," the Sultan declared, and headed to the hammam located next to the covered hall. "Afterwards, I will say the afternoon *ikindi* prayer," pointing to the small mosque above the entry gate, reached by a small set of stairs. "I would suggest you all do likewise, and we will meet for dinner afterwards." The superintendent of the han ordered the servants to heat water for the Sultan's bath, and then gave instructions to the head cook to begin preparing a lavish *tepsi kebab* in honor of the Sultan's arrival. He did not need to tell him that it had better be the most delicious one he had ever prepared in his life.

Mahperi was bewildered by all she saw in this little universe of the Kandemir Han, a machine that seemed to run with great precision and efficiency, serving everyone's needs, with no attention left out. She was tired, hot and dirty and she looked forward to the bath that was promised her. She would rest tonight and prepare herself for her momentous entry into Konya the next day.

Later that evening, the men gathered around a huge campfire that burned in the middle of the courtyard. They sat on mats and rugs and took out their wooden eating utensils from their saddle bags. Cooks had prepared giant pots of bubbling okra soup and coarse bulgur. Flatbread was grilled on hot metal *tandir* griddles, and several lambs were roasting for the kebab. The Sultan and his retinue ate alongside the merchants, all sharing the giant tray of sizzling kebab that had been set in the middle of their circle, scooping up the juicy bits of meat with the griddle bread. The Sultan was in a merry mood, reveling in the stories the merchants told about their homelands. They informed him of the goods they were selling to Konya merchants and those they were taking back to their countries from the Seljuk lands. He asked them questions and listened to their concerns. For Alaeddin Keykubad, this news was invaluable, for it gave him insight into the state of affairs in his land and abroad.

After dinner, glasses of sweet pomegranate juice were served and men brought out stringed musical instruments and began to play songs from the repertoire of each of their countries. A Syrian rose to recite a poem about a famous folk hero. An Egyptian told a joke about a donkey that fell in love with a camel, and laughter rose to keep tempo with the tunes played by the musicians.

A stout Persian merchant then pulled out a chessboard from his sack and proceeded to set up the board with its set of green ceramic pieces.

"All right, my friends, enough of these silly jokes about donkeys and camels! I am here to challenge you to a serious game of chess. As you know, we Persians are the most skillful chess players in all the lands of the earth. Our great shahs play chess with the same ease that you Turks drink water! Come on, now, does anyone have the courage to take me on?"

Alaeddin whipped his head around at this provocation. Why, you impertinent little Persian! So you think your little board game shows you to be the cleverest of peoples on earth, far superior to the Turks? You have yet to run across a Turk like Alaeddin Keykubad! Although slow to seethe, the Sultan could not accept this brazen effrontery to his people by a guest in his lands.

"Well, well, my merchant friend from Mashad, I know your bags are full of many treasures from your lands of Khorasan," cooly responded the Sultan. "So are mine; full of gold from the coffers of my treasury. I know as well that in that bag of yours is a beautiful and rare piece of turquoise, set in a gold filigree bezel that hangs on a gold chain. I heard you speak of it earlier, telling the other merchants that it was so rare and costly that you could not find a client to buy it from you, even among the richest dealers in the bazaars of the big city of Konya."

"Oh yes! Indeed!" nodded the merchant. "It is superior Angushtari first quality, of the richest of God's blues, from the Ali-Mersai Mountains of my Khorasan province. There has never been a finer piece mined in all the mountains of Persia!" he proudly boasted.

"Well, then, this is your special night, my friend, for I think you have found a buyer for it right here. Yes, I would like to buy that stunning piece of turquoise. I am sure you would agree that it is worthy of a Sultan, wouldn't you?"

The merchant nodded his head excitedly, unable to believe his good fortune. "Oh yes, quite worthy I am sure!" he gushed.

"Actually, I am intrigued not only by your fine Persian goods, but also by your boast about the unrivaled skill of the chess players of Persia. I have often heard, too, that your people have the reputation of being unchallenged on the board. Yet, as Sultan of the Turks, I feel it is my obligation to try to defend the honor of my people – who drink water so well, as you say. Yes, my good merchant from Mashad, I think we should play a game of chess together. The winner takes home that piece of turquoise set in gold – either you, with the gem and the four hundred gold pieces I will pay you for its value, or me, with the gem in my pocket to take to my palace in Konya. That is my offer. Do you accept my challenge, my Persian champion of chess?"

The entire courtyard went silent and stared at the faces of both men. The arrogant little Persian had seen his boasting called to task, and the Sultan was risking a veritable fortune to defend the honor of his people. Had the Sultan gone mad? Would the Persian accept such a gamble?

The Persian merchant tried to maintain his composure at the thought of this match of a lifetime, but beads of sweat appeared on his upper lip. He had to think quickly here, for this slender Sultan seemed impatient. How could he pass up the opportunity to triple his fortune with one or two clever moves of a chess piece that only a Persian champion could know? Yet if he lost, he would return to Mashad with very little in his bags and the wails of his hungry children in his ears. But the glow of the gold pieces he could earn flared up in front of his eyes, blinding him to all prudence. He had confidence in his skills, for he was undefeated, even among the finest players in the bazaars of his homeland. How could this rustic Turk, even if he were a Sultan, think that he could equal a Persian, with our centuries-old heritage of education and refinement?

"Yes, my Sultan, Mirza Abdullah of Mashad will accept your challenge. I will even offer you the opening move, for, after all, you are the Sultan and I am enjoying your hospitality in this fine caravansarai! Let us begin!"

He bowed to the Sultan and sat down at the board, facing his opponent for the most important game of his life. In his eyes, the surface of the board was well-lit by the glow of those gold pieces – and that light would guide every move he made with great clarity, of that he was sure.

☪ ☪ ☪

Later that evening, Alaeddin entered the small room off the courtyard that had been reserved for Mahperi. He found her sound asleep, despite the racket made by the men sitting around the campfire. He sat down on her quilt and stopped for a second to gaze at her before planting a kiss on her cheek and shaking her shoulders to wake her.

"Mahperi! Wake up my love! I want to speak with you!" She opened her eyes and sat up, still filled with sleep.

"Tomorrow will be one of the most important days of our lives. I will enter my capital city with a new queen at my side. You will enter a city whose subjects will bow at your feet. We are starting a new life together, there in our palace home, and we are to begin a new era for my kingdom. All things will be possible for me with you by my side, for you are truly my lucky star, my lucky moon. To honor this most important day tomorrow, the day when you will become a queen in the eyes of my subjects, I want to give you a special gift. You are already the queen of my heart, and I want you to always wear this around your neck as the symbol of our love."

Alaeddin extended his closed fist to her and then turned it around and opened his palm. Even in the dim candle-lit cell, the flawless turquoise gemstone nestled there shone as brightly as the sea. She gasped at its size, as large as an apricot, and at the purity of its color. She had never seen a piece of turquoise so pure, so free of matrix and veins. It was as smooth and round as a bird's egg, and its color was a blue that reminded her of that lovely lake they had passed earlier.

Alaeddin held the gem up by the end of its golden filigree chain and dangled it in the candlelight in front of her eyes. "You see how it glows like the moon, from deep inside its core? That is how you glow in my heart. This stone brings together the colors of the spirits of the sea and the Anatolian sky to bless our love. It will never lose its color, just like our love. It will always lie next to your heart like the end of a rainbow. When I see it around your neck, I will know that I am beloved of you, and when you wear it, I hope you will feel how much I desire to swim in the turquoise waters of our ocean. You will wear it under your robes, warm against your skin, where no one but I may see it. It is our secret together. Wear this forever, my turquoise Moon Fairy Queen, and feel it against your heart as we ride into Konya tomorrow to give you courage."

He placed it around her neck and she closed her hand around it to feel its warmth, and reached up to kiss her Sultan. Mahperi thought how the blue of his eyes and the green of hers had mixed together to create a color so unique that only a gemstone of this rareness could capture it.

"How I envy this turquoise gem," he laughed, "As it will live warm next to your heart! As long as I know it is there nestled, I shall know that you are faithful to me. Let us sleep now, my love, for this has been a long day and tomorrow will be an even longer one."

Before drifting off to sleep, Alaeddin whispered in her ear.

"Remind me one day to tell you about the Persian tutor I had when I was growing up in Tokat, who taught me the epic poetry of Firdowsi, the lessons of the great politician Nizam al-Mulk, how to write script with a graceful flowing hand, and how to play the royal board game of their shahs called chess. He was very important to my education, indeed...."

And so they slept that night in a lover's embrace, Mahperi with the fingers of one hand wrapped around her turquoise gem and the other ones interlaced in the hand that had placed it there; Alaeddin with his arms around his bride, who now nestled the proof that one must never, ever, think of defying the honor of a Turk without serious consequences to pay.

Chapter 9

Whirling World on the Plain

Had you been an eagle flying above the fawn-colored plains of Anatolia, you would have noticed, with no small curiosity, a very peculiar identity to a sprawling city there located, a trait like no other city possesses anywhere else on your path of flight. Noble eagle, you would have seen that everything below you is a whirl in this flat city on the steppe, a never-ending eddy of motion and activity.

That this city should be in the midst of whirling forces of energy was accepted by all who lived there. Yes, a whirling city; a city spinning on its own endeavor and determination, with all its citizens joining to make it twirl faster than the globe on its heavenly axis. Everything whirls in this city, my eagle; can you see and hear it all?

Dust balls whirl across the plain and race with camel caravans that arrive from every point of the compass on the pinwheel of roads leading to the gates of the city, jostling with the spinning wheels of farm carts coming to market day. Streets spiral round and round the mound in the center of the city like the helix of an ancient sea nautilus.

Whirl the voices of Persian in the court, Turkish in the fields, Hebrew in the temples, Arabic in the hans, Greek in the markets and Armenian in the weaving studios. Can you hear, too, the swelling refrains of divine guidance fusing into one song in every neighborhood of this basin of mystical inspiration? The faithful raise *Bismillah* prayers in praise of God in dervish lodges, tombs and mosques; bearded priests recite verses of Scripture in front of candlelit altars, and rabbis incant their ancient wisdom from the rolls of the Holy Torah.

Listen more closely now, my eagle, to all the whirling sounds of the city. The muezzin's cry from the royal mosque on top of the hill echoes in the swirling calligraphy brushed on manuscript pages in the medrese schools below. The sermons of Saint Paul still resonate in the symphony of consonants, vowels, and syllables recited by Qur'anic students in the classrooms of the city. Clusters of flies buzz around the meat hanging in market stalls in cadence with grist wheels grinding grain to flour to sate the bread-hungry stomachs of the city. Packs of mongrels roam through the night and hurl their howl against back alley walls. The memory of thundering Crusader hooves across the plains now murmurs in the buzz of honey bees of the hillside hives outside the city. Whirring lathes turn bowls and spoons from the strongest of woods; birds flutter their wings above mosque courtyards at dusk. The gibbering of the Babel of languages negotiating sales at breakneck speed in the bazaars rumbles like thunder during a flash storm over the plain.

Now look down here, noble eagle, at all the whirling activity in the city's core. Water carriers spill their buckets as they scurry away from public fountains. Dancing strands of wool unravel from spiraling bobbins on rug looms where fingers tie row after row of wool knots faster than the eye can see, racing with those whipping off strips of skin from purple eggplants for pots of juicy stews. Chips fly into the air off the hammers and chisels of stone carvers racing to build monuments for a Sultan as fast as the wheat grows in the surrounding fields. Whirling hammers tap out intricate designs on copper trays in backstreet workshops, beating in tempoed time with the spoons of dervish apprentices stirring fat cauldrons of soup to nourish their devoted brothers in the convents of the city.

Horse tails twitch in circles to shoo away flies with the same steady rhythm as the bobbing heads of the Islamic scholars memorizing by heart the entire Qur'an. Eddies of leaves flurry down narrow neighborhood streets in autumn, and snowflakes spin in fury during blinding winter blizzards. Hoe handles in spring lift clods of dead winter earth to ready it for sowing, followed by dancing scythes chopping wheat, oats and barley in late summer fields. Children chase balls with sticks and dogs chase their tails round and round in the dusty squares of the city. Falling stars twirl and comets spin across the dark night sky above the steppe.

Whirling are the prayer beads flicked by the fingers of the faithful outside the mosque before the start of prayer, clicking like the flying warp shuttles that go back and forth, back and forth on looms of rugs woven in red and yellow. Flying shears strip the lush wool of spring lambs as fast as rain clouds scud across the sky before a sudden hail storm. Spirals of dancing chaff from wheat thrown into the air to winnow scatter as swiftly as silvery fish in countryside streams. Wafts of rosewater perfume rise from the bottles opened each morning by the beauties of the city for their daily dressing ritual, reviving the memory of the refrains of the folk singers that fired their love the night before. Streams of blood from the throats of the lambs sacrificed for the feasts of Holy days whirlpool with the ruby red juice pressed from the heavy grape clusters from the garden hill above the city. Storm-tossed straw swirls into the cracks of the crumbled stones of antique temples, now lying abandoned in the prairies of the past.

Nights and mornings revolve one after another at a pace faster than the old people can count, in this nucleus of motion and newborn babies; in this city filled with the whirl of calls to market, calls to dinner, calls to prayer, calls to secret lovers, calls for children to come home to dinner, calls to God both silent and loud, and calls for the Sultan's troops to head out to battle.

Whirling, whirling, faster, faster, now, how is it that this vortex never loses its balance from so much movement? Yes, soaring eagle, it has always been this way; never stopping, this holy hub that whirls at every moment of the day and night. And so will it whirl in the eyes of the world for all eternity, this blessed heart of divine destiny on the plain; this sceptered City of Seljuk Kings, this capital station of the steppe, this blue dome of a domain named *Konya*.

Chapter 10

New Home on the Hill

Soon after the dawn prayer the next morning, the stable hands of the Kandemir Han saddled all the horses of the Sultan's retinue and loaded the pack animals with their goods for the final leg of the journey from Kalonoros to Konya. The han manager opened the heavy gate, and one by one, the animals of the royal caravan passed under the deep portal and headed eastward to Konya.

Led by the Sultan Alaeddin Keykubad himself, the caravan climbed towards a high pass for several hours, and then continued down the other side towards Konya. They passed three more hans along the way. When they came up to the last one, Alaeddin turned to Mahperi and said,

"The good Vizier Altinapa built this han several years ago. He also built a very beautiful mosque in the center of Konya, and I will take you to see it soon. Its adjoining medrese is the most important one of the entire city, and it is there that the most famous imams come to teach, enthralling the whole city with their inspiring words. I myself often go there to ask their advice, for they often show me ways to look at a problem that are otherwise blind to me."

A short while later, the road bent in a sharp turn, and suddenly in front of them opened a panoramic view onto the valley below, stretching as wide and far as the eye could see. Mahperi had never seen a space so vast and so flat. Not even the horizon of the sea that she saw from her window at the castle atop Kalonoros could compare to the sense of distance she felt here, a sense of being as small as one of the flies now buzzing around her head. In the plains surrounding the city, all was dry stubble, grain fields and stillness. Mahperi raised her hand to shield her face from the sharp light of the hot sun. Coming from the seacoast, she had trouble imagining how such a place like this could exist, with no trees and no blue – yet at the same time, she was fascinated by its starkness and severity.

"Perhaps you find this countryside monotonous, but you will soon discover that these plains change color all throughout the year. Our seasons are as varied as the people who live within the walls of Konya: in summer, we cook and burn, and in the winter, the snow blankets everything for weeks on end."

She focused her eyes to the middle of the plain directly in front of her. At first she thought it was a mysterious mirage, but then she realized that it was Konya itself, gripping the horizon with all its force.

Alaeddin turned around to the caravan behind him and shouted out for all to hear. "We have arrived! There lies the blessed city of the Seljuk Kings, daughter of the steppes, my Konya, my city of power and peace!"

There was no turning back now, thought Mahperi. Once more, a foreboding chill ran through her at the thought of what awaited her in the city below, sensing that somewhere there laid challenges that would test her courage. But when she felt Eclipse start to prance, ready to bolt off again, she held tightly to the reins and gazed with anticipation at this prize of a city, lying in a basin, just like the stars that rest in the bowl of heaven.

Alaeddin turned and reached over to take her hand. "Hold your Eclipse steady for a moment! I always stop in this spot to savor this view over the plain and my city, the one my ancestors staked out as our capital and which I am in the midst of turning into one of the most famous cities in all Islam! My Konya is there waiting for me like the open arms of a lover, and beyond Konya and the next dawn lie the far cities of my realm! The view from here inspires me, and reminds me that you can stand up tall and straight in my town and in my lands. You can stretch your arms out wide from side to side and feel the space of God's creation around you. You see, even Eclipse feels it! Come, my love, let us ride down to our city."

As they rode down the hill, the mirage of the city came in and out of view at each turn of the road, but it kept reappearing, larger and larger each time. Soon they approached a tall, square gate which controlled the entry into the city. The pointed arch over the entry was decorated with two giant figures carved in stone, each one with hovering wings on their backs.

"Why, look! Your city is guarded by a pair of Holy Angels!" Mahperi cried out in glee.

"No, those are not angels, but are winged *houris*!" laughed the Sultan, amused by her remark. "They are the messengers who greet devout Muslims at the door of paradise. I want these houris, with their wings, crowns, and flowing braids of hair to tell all they are about to enter a city as beautiful as the Gardens of Paradise. I put them here on this Larende road entrance, which is the official entry to the city. I plan to add over eight more of these gates to the entry points to the city when I finish repairing the city walls, and all of them will glisten with gilded verses from the Qur'an to beckon people from the entire world to enter our city!"

"Well, they look like angels to me, and I will always think of them as such!" she said, urging Eclipse to ride past the army of merchants who had set up stalls to sell their wares on either side of the gate under colorful canopies. She was dizzy looking at all the sculptures, for there wasn't one surface left undecorated.

The townspeople had been told by advance messengers that the Sultan's procession would be arriving that morning, and many had already lined the street to greet the caravan as it entered the city. Multicolored cloths and carpets lined the pathway, and women jostled each other in windows to get the best view of the procession. After passing through the gate, the great conqueror of Anatolia rode through his capital waving his staff to all the citizens, but in reality, they had not come out to greet him so much as they had come in eager anticipation of catching a glimpse of their new queen. News about her flashed through the crowd like lightning, with everyone commenting on her impressive height and her remarkable bearing atop that blue-black horse. They noted the strange-colored clothes she wore, her lack of veil, and the odd way she wore her hair pulled behind her ears. All remarked on her simplicity and her lack of affected manners – why, here she was, smiling at all the people as she rode by, not at all shy! The jubilant crowds took to their new queen with enthusiasm, and the Sultan was pleased to see that she was on her way to winning their affection.

Alaeddin rode straight to the center of the town to his palace, which was located on the central hill Mahperi had seen from the distance. The entire town radiated from this small hill, as if it were the center of the earth. The mound was nothing like her Kalonoros Castle mountain – why, it seemed just a mere hillock, sticking up from the city like the fat belly of a rich merchant! In any case, it was evident that it was a magnet and that the town radiated around it, like the planets in the heavens, with the Sultan's palace and royal mosque as the sun.

A palace page came out and took the bridle of the Sultan's horse, and led the royal caravan into the castle precinct.

"My grandfather Kilich Arslan transformed an old Byzantine defense tower into the imperial residence you see today," explained the Sultan proudly, pointing to each building. "When I came here, I made considerable alterations, and added fresco work, stucco decoration and tiles. In addition to the kiosk that will be dedicated to our living quarters, there are also several buildings linked together which serve as my treasury, barracks for troops and living quarters for the other emirs and viziers," the Sultan explained. "Be it servants, cavalrymen, soldiers, family, clerks, officials or emirs, I like to keep my eyes on everyone!"

He pointed to the palace building. "Come; let me show you your new home, my lovely bride."

The palace was a square structure of brick and fine cut stone, two stories high. It was clad with tiles, and even the bricks were laid in a fancy pattern. The upper floor had windows on each side, as well as balconies.

The Sultan pointed up to the balcony. "I put a balcony on it so that I may step out and greet my people and view my city in front of me. Standing there, I can dream of lands to conquer in the horizon ahead, while at my back, I have the support of God and my mosque. I love to build, Mahperi, and I was very happy when I designed this palace. It was as if I knew that one day you would be coming to live here as my Queen. Welcome to your new home, my love; may you be happy and prosper here."

Mahperi held her breath as she entered this palace that was now to be her home. They climbed to the upper level and she was pleased to see that the view over the city from this part of the palace was indeed impressive. It was not the stunning view onto the sea from her window in Kalonoros, but it was exciting to sense all the motion of the bustling city below her. What enchanted Mahperi the most was the dark blue color that exploded from the tiles set everywhere on the walls and the floors of the palace. There were low couches against each wall, covered with bright red and yellow carpets. White stucco fragments in lacy patterns shaded the windows. Although it was lavish, it retained a handsome air of simplicity, and Mahperi could not help but admire the impeccable and refined taste of the Sultan.

That night, they climbed up to the flat roof of the palace to share their first night together as the royal couple in their capital, sleeping outside and watching the stars and moon like nomads on the plains, each one dreaming of the future in front of them.

☪ ☪ ☪

Early the next morning, Mahperi was awakened by the predawn call to prayer from the mosque located immediately to the rear of the palace, reigning supreme at the top of the little mound. It was so close to the palace that she thought for a moment that the muezzin was shouting right into her ears. The Sultan had already left for the mosque to perform his prayers.

When the Sultan returned to the palace, he grabbed Mahperi's arm and said, "Come, let me show you the most beautiful mosque in all Islam, even more beautiful than the Great Mosque of Damascus! This mosque has taken over 70 years to build and I have just finished a major renovation of it, adding a new section to the west. I installed over forty columns of marble that I had brought here from the antique sites and Byzantine temples lying in ruin in the countryside around Konya."

The Sultan pointed to the inscription over the northern door and read out to her the name of the architect from Syria that had been hired for the project. "His name was Muhammad ibn Khawlan, and what a genius he was! I tell you, Mahperi, if you pick an architect with talent and passion, your building will rise like a nightingale's song!" He then pointed to a dark blue faience roundel that was placed high above the door on the northern façade of the mosque, complete with a white inscription in thick glaze. "It reads," he proudly boasted, '*Al-Sultan al muazzam, Ala-üd-dunya v'ed-din*: the greatest Sultan, eminence of the world and faith!' I hope all of my people view it with reverence and my enemies with fear!"

The Sultan became more reserved in tone when he showed her the octagonal tomb with a tall, conical dome to the north of the mosque, which contained the graves of the past Seljuk sultans.

The royal couple then entered the mosque and Mahperi gasped at the size of the spacious interior, filled with a forest of columns of wood, and some of fine marble. She had never seen anything like this before, so different from her tiny church at Kalonoros. Despite the heavy mass of the walls, the space seemed to float in air. She saw several old men kneeling on a sea of small, colorful carpets. They rocked forward, brought their head to the ground and then stood up, staring at their hands held out in front of them as if they were holding a book, before cupping them to their ears as if to hear better. But there was no sound in the mosque. What were they listening to, she thought, but then realized they were trying to capture the sound of God's voice in their ears. She was intrigued, for it was nothing like the way one prayed in her church in Kalonoros. She looked around her and saw no altar, burning candles, icons, or pews. All was light and silence.

A brightly-colored niche on the southern wall drew her eyes towards it, for it was the focal point of the entire space. The Sultan saw her eyes light up at the sight of it.

"That is the mihrab, which indicates the direction to pray. During my restoration project last year, I added the dome above it, which I have set off with turquoise, cobalt, black and white tiles fanning out in five borders. No one will ever be confused about the direction to face in prayer when they see all of this sparkling glory!"

"This piece of furniture is so lovely!" exclaimed Mahperi, looking at the set of stairs to the right of the mihrab. "It looks like carved lace!"

"That is the minbar, where the imam faces the worshippers in front of him to address his sermon. It is made of dense ebony wood that came all the way across the sea from Africa! The minbar was especially commissioned by my ancestor, Sultan Mesud. Look, you can read his name and that of my grandfather, Kilich Arslan, engraved right here in the wood!" the Sultan said, pointing to the script with the end of his slender finger.

The Sultan took special pride in showing her the large carpets he had commissioned for the floors of the mosque, each one with a striking design and color scheme.

"Along with my renovation of the western part of the mosque, I also commissioned a series of large rugs to line the floors for the worshippers. I felt that by adding these tiles and rugs to the mosque, I was completing the work of my forefather Mesud, my grandfather Kilich Arslan and my brother Izzeddin. But it is my work that will be the most lasting in the eyes of the world!"

☪ ☪ ☪

Just as she had taken joy in showing the Sultan her city of Kalonoros, Alaeddin was only too happy to lead Mahperi to all four corners of Konya to show her its sights. Starting from the core of the city that was their palace, they would take a different direction each day. Night Shining White knew the city as well as he did the plains of the Kingdom, and he deftly steered the couple with ease down the many backstreets of the city. Wherever they went, the people in the neighborhoods were always surprised to see their great Sultan in their midst, riding simply through the streets as if he were any other visitor or merchant.

Alaeddin loved his city, and enjoyed showing Mahperi every part of it. As they rode along, he would comment on each sight.

"There are hundreds of small square mosques in every neighborhood, big enough for no more than thirty worshippers. They have bloomed like spring flowers, and were all built by pious local donors to enhance the life of their neighborhood."

Alaeddin took more pride in showing her the city walls than he did anything else.

"These walls have existed since my grandfather Kilich Arslan's time, but it was I who gave the order to rebuild them last year right before I went down to besiege your city. I asked my many emirs to participate in the construction costs. I added four gates, as well as several important towers, and I plan to build more, each one with a large tower," the Sultan beamed, with the same pride as he showed when he started to build up Kalonoros.

"I decorated the walls with sculptures and statues in glistening white marble that I found in the fields surrounding the city. These old carved stones are to be found everywhere in this Konya region, lying on the ground near old Greek temples that have fallen down, and I had them collected from the fields and brought here. We Turks must ensure that all the peoples who have lived here before us are not forgotten. We are the keepers of this heritage, and we will show all citizens of the world that we are a place of peace and tolerance. I also engraved the walls with verses from the Qur'an, sayings of the Prophet and lines from my favorite stories of the *Shahname*, the book of the Iranian kings, taught to me in Tokat by that Persian tutor I told you about when we stayed in the Kandemir Han. When the walls were completed, I inscribed the names of the emirs who helped build them in gold. Look, here, for example, is the name of the Emir Jelaleddin Kaysar!"

Mahperi marveled at all the stone and marble sculptures on the city walls: dragons with open mouths, harpies, eagles with two heads, roaring lions, sphinxes, leopards chasing leaping antelopes, falconers, fish and all types of animals, one with a nose so long that it reached all the way down to the ground. It was so strange; she could believe it only to be a myth. There was certainly nothing like this at Kalonoros!

The Sultan continued as they turned down a street near the Ertaş gate.

"Ah, eternal Konya! This has been a place of mystical inspiration ever since the creation of man: the Greek goddesses Cybele and Aphrodite reigned here, the Christian Paul came here to preach to the Jews and Greeks about the new faith of the Prophet Jesus, the bishop Sosipatros held councils here, the Monks of the Monastery of St. Chariton prayed together, not to forget the Islamic scholar Muhyiddin ibn al-Arabi, whose teachings of universal love still echo in our medreses. Important things will continue to happen here, Mahperi, I know it, I feel it, and I am going to do everything I can to make this vision of mine happen. As Konya builds, so will the rest of my kingdom. There are other important cities in my Empire: Kayseri, Sivas, Akşehir, Malatya, Tokat and Ankara, but it will be Konya that will set the tone for the rest of them. Where Konya leads, all will follow! This city was inhabited by peoples from the dawn of creation, and now it is ours to leave the Seljuk mark upon its history till Judgment Day. May God grace your new home on the hill, my Queen, with every blessing and prosperity!"

Chapter 11

Everything to Discover

Mahperi's first months in Konya were filled with such activity that her head felt as cluttered as the city walls. She had everything to learn, and although she was grateful for the history lessons her husband gave her, she wanted to know more. She was eager to discover the life behind those walls and inside those mosques and medreses. She needed to explore the city in her own way, in order to discover the parts of it that she liked the best, to see its people in their daily lives, and to understand how this Turkish world turned.

And so the Seljuk Queen would saddle up her streak of blue midnight, Eclipse, and together with several guards, would slip out of the palace in the early morning to explore the city. Mahperi visited a different neighborhood of Konya each time she ventured out, but her favorite place was the hill to the west of the city. It was a lovely area called Meram, filled with vineyards and gardens. It bloomed with hyacinths in the spring, red roses in the summer and purple grapes in the fall. It was always brushed with color, in contrast to the otherwise monotone fawn hills surrounding the city. The vineyards and cool, shaded gardens never failed to lift her spirits. The fast-flowing streams and springs of Meram irrigated not only these gardens, but flowed down to provide the city its drinking water.

☪ ☪ ☪

Although Mahperi knew these jaunts would probably not be approved by the Sultan, she needed this liberty in order to survive. As beautiful as that palace was, she felt many moments of melancholy in her first few months there. She dearly missed the green hills full of almond blossoms and especially the sea of her Kalonoros. She dreamt of the wind and the sea's horizon; for now all she had was fawn plains and the smell of dust in her nostrils. Yet it wasn't just the urban setting or the difference in geography that was unsettling to her.

As much as her new life was exhilarating, at the same time it was often confusing, and she made many mistakes. The new Queen had to learn to speak Turkish and to read and write Persian and Arabic. She had to master the manners of Islam and the customs of the court, so different from those of Kalonoros. She also had no friends or family with her other than the Sultan to show her the way, and she was often frustrated, lost and lonely. Nothing seemed to flow easily, and she felt out of place by her looks, her accent, and her viewpoint. She had lost much freedom, and felt she was constantly being supervised by all the eyes of the court, the ladies especially, who would whisper among themselves about her. Her husband had changed as well. As he had warned her, things were not the same as they were in Kalonoros, for he was often away, and when he was in Konya, he was always busy with court matters. The Sultan seemed different here; preoccupied, impatient, testy to the point of losing his temper. He definitely spent less time with her in pleasure, but at the same time, he came to her more and more to speak of his concerns and ask her advice about matters that troubled him. She missed his attention and the tenderness of their life in Alaiye. She was also confused by the frightening hold this man held over her, and with each passing day, she was more and more lost into his sultanate of love.

Sometimes the gentle coolness of those Meram gardens at the top of the hill would prompt an intense feeling of homesickness. Suddenly, tears would spill forth from her eyes; tears of longing for her people, her language and everything familiar to her; tears apprehensive of this new future in front of her, even if she desired it. She knew that she would have to forge a life for herself among all these strangers, to find her place in this new world, to fulfill the role that was expected of her as queen and to prove herself through actions and achievements. She wasn't quite sure how she was going to do this, but she vowed she would find the way, for she was now the Moon Queen of this empire.

Chapter 12

A World to Radiate from Konya

Although Mahperi loved mornings in Konya, she eagerly anticipated the cool evening as well, for it was the time she could be alone with her Sultan. After dinner was finished and the evening prayer completed, she and Alaeddin would climb to the terrace at the top of their palace and watch night close in on their city until the very last rays of the pink sky disappeared below the horizon. Shopkeepers shut their stalls, birds went to roost, children were tucked into their beds and dreams, and the city became as quiet as a village.

"The call to the evening *akşam* prayer," explained the Sultan to Mahperi, "marks the beginning of a new day in our Islamic calendar. It is a time for me to think not only about the events of this past day, but also to collect my thoughts for the new day to come, and the many challenges ahead."

If the Sultan was not too preoccupied or tired, he would share his ideas with her long into the night, telling her about his plans to develop the city. Alaeddin also loved to tell her about the history of Konya and the glorious deeds of his forefathers.

"Our illustrious ancestor Kilich Arslan I, after the defeat of his troops at the battle of Doryleum in 1097 against the Crusaders, left his capital at Iznik to come here. At Konya he felt that he could better oversee the Crusaders and the Byzantine offensive, as well as better protect the lands we had already conquered. What a wise move it was to settle in the center of the country, for it is here, on these steppes, where the destiny of this Empire will be determined! Now I must turn our Empire into the strongest and most influential power of this region, by expanding our territories in all directions – to the Caucasus, to the Crimea, to Iran and beyond!"

He paused and adjusted his thin frame on the cushions.

"But what a task this is going to be! I must first start building my capital city before I can venture out into the rest of the kingdom. Each goal in its own time! But you tell me, my dear Mahperi, how is it going to be possible for me to govern a city which has as many different peoples as pieces on a chessboard? All the peoples of the Mediterranean and Black Seas, from Central Asia to the Far East are here: Christians, Muslims, Kurds, Circassians, Persians, Georgians,

Syrians, Greeks, Egyptians, Algerians, Iraqis, Khwarezmians, left-over mercenaries from the Crusader armies, Provençals and Italians from the West, and Armenians like you! How can I bring all these varied groups together under one unified Muslim banner? Now, that is the challenge for my Kingdom!"

He looked deeply into her green eyes. "Yet, when I think of the success I am having with you, I have confidence that I am off to a good start!"

Mahperi looked at his bright face and said, "You will build a fine city here, my Sultan, there is no doubt about that! But if I may speak to you frankly, perhaps creating a capital should not just be about building mosques and repairing walls. Also, perhaps it is easy to conquer lands, but you must capture the respect of your citizens as well! Start here in Konya, and make it into a beacon to the world, my love! Build a reputation for Konya as the leading center for intellectual endeavors. Invite the finest cultural and scientific personalities to make their home here and create great works: jurists, doctors, poets, astrologers, theologians, mystics, writers, scientists and philosophers from every walk of life and thought and from every corner of the Islamic world. This city should become the capital of great minds and spirits, not just of sultans! By encouraging artists and thinkers to be the best that they can be, their light will shine on your city as well as on all generations to come. Create a city that will leave its mark for all eternity – a touchstone for the entire world; a place of pilgrimage where people will receive their fill of culture, beauty and spirituality. Make Konya the name on everyone's tongue!"

The Sultan propped himself up on his cushion, astounded both by her frankness and her foresight. She never fails to astonish me with her ideas, he thought to himself, and she is indeed worthy to be my queen.

"You are very wise, my Moon Fairy, and I will heed your advice. But Konya is only the beginning of my dream to build! He raised his hand and pointed to the horizon distant to the east.

"This mother of earths in front of me, called *Anatolia,* is a heaven of grass, like the green carpet of paradise. It is an ancient land, older than the Greek gods, older than your Jesus, older than all the emperors of Byzantium. We will add our Seljuk sweat, our blood, our bones, and our victories to this rich earth. We will plant not only our victory banners in this ground, but also fruit trees and cotton. The promise of this land awaits us!"

He turned back to her and continued. "You are right. To conquer lands is perhaps easier than conquering the hearts of a people, which is the hardest task of all. Hand in hand with my subjects, I will pull together these many threads that will create an identity for my people. I want to make the glory of God visible to my subjects: on their table and in the stability of their government. Just as spring greens under the layers of snow, my empire will flower with creation.

I will develop an entirely new style of building. My emirs will establish just governance. And if I invite poets and mystics as you suggest, they will one day write the most beautiful poetry ever sung, which will bring tears to the eyes of all who will hear it. Yes, I will create a new soul for a new society, ready to welcome all people: it will be a prairie for the Turkmens, a nave for the Christian monks, a mihrab for Muslims, a tree for the Shamans....all faiths will be welcome in my land, but they must work alongside of me for goals that are above any religion: the goal of peace, prosperity and love for fellow man."

He stopped and took a sip of cool grape juice from his silver goblet.

"Yes, you are right, I may build my Konya, I may build monuments all across my land, I may conquer new territories; but if my people are not happy, I have failed. The most important element in building my economy is money: money and trade lead to prosperity and the well-being of my citizens. Without a rich kingdom, I am doomed, so I must do everything I can to produce goods and export them through trade. First and foremost, I want the Seljuk Empire to be an agricultural powerhouse, for a country that can feed itself will always be strong! Our raisins, fruits, apricots, almond oil, pistachios, yellow plums, cotton, nuts, grapes, cereals and grain will be sold the world over! Secondly, our textile production and livestock can be further developed into important exports. Not to forget that this land is filled with mines of alum, silver, iron and tin, and the world will come knocking for these minerals, giving us their gold in return for them!"

The Sultan continued to elaborate his vision for the future.

"Yes, build I will too, but not just mosques and tombs for holy men. The true holy men are those who work in the bazaars, who learn medicine, who create laws. I will build the finest buildings to house them. Hard work is the best praise God can hear! May God accord me grace so that I may build Him a new Empire to praise His glory, with no famine, no pestilence, no natural disasters to mar it. I will be an administrator of a just land, a *ghazi* warrior to conquer new ones, and a craftsman of prosperity. Such are my goals. The doors of history will swing from the hinges of Konya!

Mahperi listened with eagerness and saw the look of rapture on the Sultan's face as he spoke. She wanted to be a part of this movement and this energy, and was eager to find a way to help him with his goals. As if reading her mind, the Sultan paused to look at her.

"You, of course, my Moon Queen, with the sensible advice you always furnish me from that sound head upon your shoulders, will be invaluable to me. You are the moonbeam that will guide me to better understand the complexity of my diverse populations. You will help me to become more tolerant, patient and encompassing in my viewpoint. You will help me to see more clearly the needs of our people. I count on you above all others for advice, Mahperi, for you are wiser and more reasoned than the majority of my viziers, and certainly more trustworthy than my emirs!"

Mahperi was genuinely moved by his words and rose to kneel next to him on his cushion.

"Thank you, my beloved Sultan; nothing gives me greater pleasure than to know that I am esteemed in your eyes for the help I give you. I want to join with you to build your kingdom of prosperity and peace. Yes, in love and in partnership, we will build together."

She blushed and looked downwards. "Yes, my Sultan, I already know that you are a builder!" and placing his hands over her stomach, she looked at him deeply in those blue eyes that never failed to capture her dreams.

"You need to know that you are not just building the future of your empire in stone, but also in flesh. My beloved Sultan, know that your first child, our first child, will be born this fall."

And just then, as the *yatsi* prayer was called and the last light of day disappeared, the Sultan swept her in his arms and cried out for all of Konya to hear:

"I will be master of my territory, architect of civil institutions, artisan of political unity, and above all, ancestor of Sultans to come!"

Chapter 13

A Carpet of Friendship Is Knotted

One morning as the days greened into springtime, the Sultan burst into Mahperi's room and clapped his hands in front of him.

"Come, rise up my lovely, for today I have a splendid treat in store for you. Hurry, let's go!"

Mahperi scurried to follow Alaeddin who let her up the palace hill towards the eastern door of the big mosque. They entered the vast sanctuary inundated by the bright morning light. As usual, the brilliant turquoise tiles of the mihrab drew everyone's eyes to it. Turquoise, a color so unique in nature, is truly captivating, thought Mahperi, and she hoped the necklace around her neck enhanced her beauty in the eyes of the Sultan as much as this mihrab did for the mosque. She understood now why the Sultan had waged such a dangerous bet for that turquoise necklace – he loved the magical power of this rare color, and was making it the symbol of fortune for his reign.

Standing in front of the mihrab was a woman who appeared to be a bit older than Mahperi, along with several young girls and two men. A long bundle was rolled up at their feet.

"Good morning, my Hanife Hanim, what happiness to see you here today!" exclaimed the Sultan with a broad smile on his face. "I have waited many months in eager anticipation of this day, and I know my patience will be rewarded a thousand-fold. Before you show me the blessings of your hands, I would like you to meet a blessing that is now in my hands. Hanife Hanim, may I present to you Mahperi Hatun, my Queen."

Mahperi felt the firm dark eyes of Hanife inspecting her with intense curiosity. After what seemed like several minutes of scrutiny, she looked Mahperi directly in the eyes and smiled.

"My Lady, I have waited for this moment for a long time, and I see that what I have heard about you is true. You stand as tall as one of the columns in this mosque, you appear as powerful as a stallion, and your face is as pure and open as the full moon. Welcome to this city of ours, and I wish you every happiness here. I hope our paths will cross often."

Since her arrival in Konya, no woman had spoken so directly and honestly to her. This woman welcomed her as an equal, not like the emir's wives who curried her favor with shallow flattery. Mahperi was immediately drawn to the aura of confidence this woman exuded.

"Hanife is the finest weaver in our land, and she is here today to unveil a significant gift that she has created for my mosque," the Sultan explained. "I commissioned from her and her studio of weavers a rug to occupy the place of honor in front of my turquoise mihrab. She has worked months on it, and would never allow me to have a glimpse at it, even though I begged her. She wanted it to be a surprise; to be viewed only upon its completion. Now that day has come. Hanife is an artist above all others, not only for the skill of her technique, but for her capacity to translate her dreams and the inspiration of the world around her into the language of knots. I am certain that she has created a masterpiece that will be as glorious as the mihrab in front of which it will lie."

The Sultan turned to Mahperi. "And today is the day that I will finally be able to gaze upon her creation! I am as excited as the time I awaited that castle gate of Kalonoros to swing open!"

He walked over to Hanife who stood proudly behind her rolled-up rug.

"Now, my Hanife, I will unroll this carpet and contemplate my long-anticipated treasure at last!" He nodded to the two men who stood on each end of the carpet to help him, and he leaned over to start to unroll the rug.

"*Stop! Don't you dare touch that rug!*" Hanife's sharp voice echoed against the walls of the mosque. She stepped over the rug and defiantly stood between it and Alaeddin Keykubad, protecting it like a mother lion with her cubs. Everyone gasped in surprise at her forceful reaction. No one ever tells a Sultan what he can or cannot do, and here was this slip of a woman barking at him as if he were a kitchen scullion. She squared her shoulders and lifted her chin in a resolute pose, and spoke out in a defiant tone while looking him directly in the eyes.

"My Sultan, you have already given me the honor of weaving several rugs for this mosque, and I am eternally grateful to you for the confidence you have shown me and my workers. This rug is the most complex one I have ever woven, and will be certainly the most important one in this mosque. In this rug I have tried to translate all the strength I receive from God, all the power you aspire to and all the hopes of your citizens. I have put my soul into this rug, and there were many times when I felt that it was stronger than I was and that I would never be able to finish it. It is my most accomplished work yet, and I hope it will please you and grace this masterpiece of a mihrab. But it is not for you to unroll it first. No, that honor must be given to our new Queen. I want her to be the one who opens it, and I want her gentle green eyes to be the first ones to gaze upon it."

She turned to Mahperi without waiting for the Sultan's reaction.

"Please accept this gift, Queen Mahperi, Lady Hatun, from my hands to your eyes. May each one of its knots represent a citizen of Konya who has been graced by your arrival among us."

The giant space of the mosque was as quiet as a tiny room. No one dared move, for they were not sure if the Sultan would consider her gesture an insolent insult to his standing. Men were put to the sword for less than this.

Suddenly, the Sultan burst out in peals of laughter, and Mahperi recognized that same exuberant look of joy on his face that she had first glimpsed when she peeked at him from inside the Kalonoros gate.

"Ah! You see, Mahperi, I told you she was an exceptional woman! She is as headstrong as you are! Well, well, my Hanife, you certainly can weave your words as well as your knots!"

Hanife nodded to Mahperi, who then bent over and started to unfold the rug, aided by the two men at the ends, and soon everyone joined in the excitement. All pushed and pushed until the large rug lay flat. Once unrolled, a resplendent gleaming jewel of many hues shone up from the floor with the same intensity of light as the mihrab. All stared at it for a long while before bursting into cheers, laughter and applause.

Mahperi had never seen anything like this. Much like her wedding rug, it was full of intricate designs woven in bright colors, but here, it was on a monumental scale. While the patterns on her wedding rug were compact and restrained, the patterns on this rug exploded off the surface and into the air. The field was of a dusky, muted red color, but it was the spectacular border that dominated the rug. The border was a deep blue color, almost the hue of Mahperi's sea during a winter storm. Running around the rug on all four sides were thick geometric motifs in a lush teal blue color, all framed by a row of tiny, six-sided stars, twinkling like the Pleiades in summer.

This rug was thus to become the prelude to all the prayers directed by the thousands of eyes of the faithful facing the mihrab of this mosque. This was no mere rug; this was praise to God's greatness in and of itself. It was indeed a masterpiece, both in beauty and divine inspiration, produced by the heart and hands of an exceptional woman.

Mahperi could not get the memory of the rug out of her mind all day, and its shining light in her dreams woke her up several times that night. The next morning she asked one of the court pages to ride with her to show her where Hanife lived. Mahperi wanted to visit the workshops where this imaginative artist worked and to discover what this world of weaving was all about.

After a short ride, they approached a series of low mud-brick buildings in the easternmost area of Konya. The page descended from his horse and knocked on a small wooden door. A young girl opened it and waved them in, not at all fazed by the fact that the Seljuk Queen had come calling.

Mahperi entered a wide room redolent with a strong feral smell, which she soon realized came from the many bundles of sheep's wool that were stored there. The young girl led Mahperi to a room in the back, where several large upright looms were set up to face the light. Sitting at the looms were the girls she had seen at the mosque the day before, and at the middle and largest loom, sat Hanife herself.

She looked up at Mahperi and did not seem surprised that she was there. She did not rise to greet her, but instead called out, "Welcome, Mahperi Hatun. Come over here and sit next to me and watch me work."

Mahperi timidly approached her and sat down on the cushion at the foot of the loom. The most powerful woman in the empire now sat on the ground next to a weaver, and yet Mahperi never felt more honored than at that moment, to have been invited to this revered spot of creation. A new rug was already starting its creative climb up the warps of the loom. Mahperi watched her work in silence, fascinated by the rapidity of her movements while knotting and the decisiveness with which she selected the colors she used. Mahperi did not dare speak for fear of disturbing her intense concentration. Finally, after a long period of time, Hanife paused her knotting and turned to her.

"So, tell me, what did you *really* think of my rug yesterday?" she asked, and Mahperi could not help bursting into a broad smile.

"Why, it was the most marvelous moment I have lived since arriving in Konya! Your generous gesture, the stunning rug with that bold beautiful blue border, the power of its design, and...." She stopped there, but Hanife picked right up to complete her thought.

"Yes, I don't think I will ever forget the look of shock on the great Alaeddin's face when I forbid him to touch it!"

They both burst into laughter for a long time at the memory of that moment, and Mahperi realized that it was the first time that she had truly laughed since leaving Kalonoros.

And so in this way, with shared knots and laughter, two earnest and determined women began to weave together a carpet of friendship.

☪ ☪ ☪

Mahperi now visited the workshops of Hanife several times a week. She was drawn by this new world of smelly wool, vegetable dyes, carding, drop-spindling, planning the design, knotting, flying shuttles and combs, bouncing bobbins of oily wool on the sides of looms, and dried herbs that turned grey wool magically into jeweled colors. It was a world ruled by fast fingers and the artist's third eye of imagination; a world where many hands turned lowly materials into art of the highest order.

Mahperi could not get enough of this world, for it seemed so much more real than the frivolous life of the court. But above all, she could not get enough of Hanife. They sat for hours together at the loom, shoulders together and heads bent over the work on the warps. They talked about anything and everything, and the more they talked, the better she felt. Her Turkish skills improved and her melancholy vanished. How could one be sad in this world of jewel colors and soft wool, women's laughter and constant activity? She felt confident asking Hanife the most probing of questions about life in Konya and about Islam; how women lived their daily lives, about food, henna, clothing, confusing expressions, veils, prayer, children, love: nothing was too small or too large to ask her. She knew that Hanife would never betray her confidence. She also knew that Hanife enjoyed asking her questions about her life, for it seemed that she, too, had few women friends that she could speak to as an equal. Hanife tried to teach her to knot and laughed at her clumsy fingers which were always dropping the knife; Mahperi brought her court news, sweets and *halvah* from the palace kitchens; they brought each other joy.

☪ ☪ ☪

One day, sitting side by side, Hanife showed Mahperi how she would beat each row of knots down tightly with a heavy, comb-like tool before starting to knot the next row. She then turned to Mahperi and asked, "What color will the next row of knots in your life be, my Lady? What do you want to do as a Queen, Mahperi Hatun, and what do you want to do as a woman, my friend?"

Mahperi turned to her, not quite sure she understood her question. "Why, well I suppose I will strive to be a good wife to my Sultan, a good mother and a good queen to my people."

"Yes, that is all very well, but I ask you again, what do *you* want to do?"

"I guess… why, I really don't know!" sputtered Mahperi, unsettled by the question. "My life here is all so new and confusing, and yet… I keep hearing a voice inside of me that is pushing me to do something of importance, something with an impact, like the teal border on that rug of yours! This same voice helped me leave my country and my family, for I knew I would have the opportunity for a destiny here on these plains. But what that destiny is still remains quite unclear to me."

"Well, whatever you do," Hanife advised, "It must involve creating something tangible with your dreams, and I am not speaking here about birthing and raising children, even if they will become future sultans. You can do more than that. As an intelligent woman, you will know how to make yourself invaluable to the needs of the Sultan in his bed and on his throne, but whatever you do, don't waste your time with those court ladies and all that backstabbing intrigue! Your life must be involved with a creative expression of some sort, because you have that gift inside of you. You see the promise of the world around you, and I can tell that you are able to translate it in a generous way – perhaps you will write poetry like a wandering dervish, perhaps you will establish a school, but one thing I can tell you: you certainly won't weave rugs, not with those clumsy fingers of yours!"

When their laughter died down, Mahperi tried to respond to her initial question. "I really don't know what I will do, but there is one thing I do know for sure. I so admire the vision of Alaeddin for his Empire that I must find a way to participate in it."

"Yes, I have no doubt that you can," said Hanife, "and I know you will find that road in the near future. But whatever you do, find it, because in the end, as women, it is the only thing which is truly ours: men deceive us, children grow up and leave us, beauty abandons us – but our creation and the gifts we give to others remain ours and ours alone. Now go, Mahperi, and find your skill and create; for you, your God and your Empire. I wait with eagerness to see what you will do, and I will be with you every step of the way down that road, and I will think of you with every knot I twist."

Chapter 14

Orders to Emirs

Had Mahperi arrived in Konya one year earlier, she would not have been able to revel in its fascinating walls. She would not have seen marble statues and the golden writing there, for the walls of the capital city were in a sorry state of disrepair. To gird the city with glory was then only a hopeful dream in the eyes of a determined new sultan.

During their rides around the city, Mahperi learned from the Sultan Alaeddin Keykubad that one of the first goals he had set when he came to power was to beautify his capital. With great pride he had told her how he had solicited the help of his emirs to pay for repairing the city walls, and in return, how he had inscribed their names in gold on the towers, gates and walls to show citizens their munificence for all eternity.

But what Mahperi did not know was that when the fortifications of the city of Konya were finished, complete with those shining marble statues and golden inscriptions, something much darker had also risen. Walls of wretched resentment now rose in the hearts of the emirs. Rather than feeling pride in their accomplishments, the emirs were angered that their wealth was being spent to fuel the Sultan's ambitions. They began to loathe the man who was depleting their pockets, and their seething bitterness now polluted the atmosphere of the court.

☪ ☪ ☪

The emirs were the most powerful men in the empire, and held influential responsibilities as military leaders, governors of distant provinces, administrators and counselors. They were the viceroys of the Sultan throughout his Empire, serving his interests, and in turn, he was very generous in offering them opportunities for success. Although the Sultan believed that most of them were faithful and loyal servants to God and the Sultanate, he was also well aware that some were too avid for power to be trusted. The Sultan knew he had to devise a way to keep these ruthless men in check. He thus decided to assign them building projects in their own fiefdoms; projects that would both occupy them and serve his empire at the same time.

It had all started one day in the late fall before the Sultan left to besiege Kalonoros, when he summoned his emirs to a meeting. He had prepared his plan of action carefully, and was now ready to put it in place.

"My emirs, I have called you here today because I want to discuss with you a very important issue for our future and I need your support for it," the Sultan began, turning his piercing and imperious blue eyes on them and riveting them in place. "As Sultan, I have set a specific political agenda for this Kingdom. In my mind, it is a two-pronged approach. First, I will implement an external policy of military action to increase our territory and defend ourselves against enemies – the Artukids, the Ayyubids, and the Armenians shall all tremble at the mention of our name!"

The men cheered and all nodded their head in agreement. The Sultan continued.

"The second part of my goal is an internal one. I wish to build up this empire, to make it solid and prosperous. When we have peace in our lands, we will also achieve peace in the world."

He looked at each and every one of them directly in the eyes before continuing his proposal.

"In both of these policies, I require your help to be builders of our empire. Everyone must participate in this effort; if not, we will not be able to create a new world for our citizens."

The emirs listened, but the Sultan could see in their eyes that they still did not understand what he was asking of them. He plunged ahead to reveal his plan.

"I tell you, my fine men, the road to world peace is through world trade. In order to increase our commercial potential, we need to be pragmatic. I need your help to repair roads, erect bridges, and build caravansarais along the roads of our Empire, so that merchants will feel safe and want to come here to trade. I also need you to take care of our cities and the needs of our citizens. I need you to repair and build the walls that surround the great cities of our empire, and then build mosques inside of them so that the people may grow in God's light. I need your help to raise medreses where our brightest young people may develop their minds to become the leaders of the future. All these efforts must be carried out with your help. I cannot do it alone; nor should I do it alone. You are my Lions. Your participation in this is as important as your courageous place on the battlefields of our enemies."

The Sultan spoke more quickly now, excitedly explaining his plan of action for the development of the Seljuk Empire.

"Architecture will serve as a very powerful weapon against our enemies. Through a brilliant program of building, we can achieve immortality for our

Empire. People will admire our buildings for centuries to come! They will not lie crumbling like those of the ancient Greeks we see in our fields, and our roads will be more important than those built by the Roman Emperor Hadrian! Through architecture, we can send to our adversaries a message that says we are a realm of economic might. At home, this building program will forge a new identity for our Empire, a Turkish one, different from that of the Byzantines with their churches, monasteries and palaces. Our buildings will communicate to our citizens a clear religious, commercial and philosophical statement about where we stand as a culture, and will make all of them proud to live in the land of the Seljuk Turks!"

Lowering his voice, he now spoke more calmly, delivering his ideas with persuasive talent.

"As a group, we can work together to build this Empire. This is our duty to God. And so I am asking that each of you donate one quarter of your wealth to the state, in order to help finance the developments we need to undertake. This money will be put towards building projects, both military and civil. I will give you the freedom to choose what you wish to build in your region, but in many cases, I will need to decide what is necessary for the kingdom. Each one of you will take on a project according to your means and capability, and in return, your names will be inscribed on these buildings, and all eternity will honor your memory as just and generous men. In your lifetimes, the citizens who will benefit from these buildings will rise each day and bless you in their prayers. You will be famous and celebrated in your regions for these acts and receive God's grace. Now, let us see where we can begin!"

A few of the emirs started to whisper among themselves, but the Sultan riveted their silence with one stern look before continuing.

"To start – you, over there, Emir Zeyneddin Basara," he said, pointing to a young emir sitting at the rear of the group, "I am commissioning you today to build a mosque in the city of Niğde, the finest city in the region under your control. Make it the most majestic mosque outside of Konya, destined to show all people east of here that we are an empire of holiness. You will name this mosque after me, and as such, the Alaeddin Mosque of Niğde will be famous for all times!"

He turned and nodded to the older man sitting next to him, "I am ordering you, Badr al-Din Yakut, Emir of Sivas, to build a mountain-like fortress for the city. We will build city walls around Sivas and Konya as well as around other cities of the Empire." The stunned emirs all squirmed on their mats at his barking frenzy of successive commands, but none dared to react.

"We will construct buildings in this Empire so strong that the ominous hoe of deceitful time will never be able to plow them down. Yes, my Lions;

mosques, hans, and medreses will storm across our steppes like a herd of wild horses!" the Sultan concluded with enthusiasm.

☪ ☪ ☪

Yet, many of the men did not share his fervor. Instead of being inspired to greatness by the Sultan's rousing words, a bitter resentment began to rise in the hearts of many of the emirs.

Chapter 15
Cloud across the Moon

Now that her heart was filled with friendship and her belly growing each day with new life, Mahperi became more settled into her role as the Queen of the Whirling City of Konya. She especially savored the time spent with the Sultan discussing his projects, offering him advice, and sharing ideas. She also began to meet other key people in the Sultan's court, and made her first visits to the Altinapa medrese to hear the celebrated Islamic scholars who taught and lectured there. She thought of Kalonoros less and less, for she now had a city to reign over, a Sultan to love and guide, and a child to prepare for. Gone were her bouts of melancholy, gone was her embarrassment about speaking Turkish. She would always have an accent, she would always hold the love of Mary and Jesus in her heart, but she was now earning her right to claim this city as her own as much as any other citizen.

One summer morning, the Sultan entered her room and picked her up in his arms.

"My shining Moon Fairy, today I want you to meet a very important person, for he is without a doubt the central man in my entourage. His name is Sadettin Köpek. He is not a minister, emir or vizier; he is more than that. For him, I created a special post adapted to his outstanding skills. He is my Superintendent of Works, and as such, he is my closest assistant for all building projects – and you know how important those are for me! He has just returned from the city of Kayseri where he has drawn up the plans to build a palace for me there, and I want you to sit with us so that you meet him and hear about it. Sadettin Köpek is quite an unusual man, with a personality and a bearing all his own. Perhaps this difference may startle you, but believe me, this man is brilliant, hard-working and totally devoted to me, and for that, I count myself lucky to have him in my service."

Mahperi listened with great excitement, not only about this new building project, but also about this man who had earned such respect in the eyes of her husband. The Sultan so often grumbled about his emirs, whom he considered as hard to handle as unbroken stallions, so she was pleased that he had such a dependable and illustrious man at his side. She found it curious that he was called "*Köpek,*" which she knew meant "dog" in Turkish, and wondered why he had such an odd name, but thought that it was surely because he was as faithful to the Sultan as a hunting hound to his master.

Mahperi jumped to her feet. "The last time you came into my room to announce you had a special person for me to meet, it was quite an event, so I can't imagine what is in store for me today!" she laughed, remembering her first meeting with Hanife and the defiant unfurling of her giant mosque rug.

She hurried to prepare herself, and soon entered the *divan*, the council chamber where the Sultan met with his advisors and emirs. Perched cross-legged on the low bench against the window overlooking the city she saw her Alaeddin, and next to him sat a decidedly homely man, a bit older than the Sultan. Her husband, with his red-blond hair and his piercing blue eyes, was a strikingly handsome man, so perhaps it was unfair to compare anyone to him. Indeed, the luminous Sultan cast quite a shadow over this man, whom Mahperi now saw was more than homely – he was decidedly ugly. Yet there was something more than his mere physical appearance that made him appear unattractive.

"Ah, my Queen, welcome to the divan!" bellowed out the Sultan, rising to greet her. "It is with great pleasure that I present to you one of the most illustrious men of my entourage, and indeed, in all the Empire: Sadettin Köpek, my Master of Works and Building. He was just beginning to give me the details about the magnificent palace he is proposing to build for me in Kayseri. Come, sit with us and learn about your new Palace in the East!"

Köpek made no effort to rise or greet her, but remained seated on the carpeted bench. He peered at Mahperi with hard eyes that sent an uneasy chill down her back. No one had ever looked at her in such a way: there was something unsavory about the way his eyes took her in, and she found her composure shaken.

Finally, Köpek leaned forward on the cushions and slowly stood up to bow to her.

"Welcome to our court, my Lady. I wondered what you would look like, ever since I heard that the Sultan took you as his bride. I hope you are finding our customs and our city to your Christian liking."

What an odd thing to say, thought Mahperi. It immediately made her feel even more ill at ease, as if he were judging her adversely because she was not a Muslim. His voice was unsettling too, for it was high-pitched, nervous and jumpy in tone. Nothing about him was pleasing to her; everything about him roused her instincts to wariness. He is a dog, alright, she mused, one that must certainly bite.

She tried to regain her composure after this unfriendly introduction.

"I am pleased to meet you, Vizier Sadettin Köpek. My husband has spoken very highly of you, and I look forward to appreciating the fine qualities you put at his service. The Sultan has discussed with me at length and with great enthusiasm all that he wishes to build in his empire, and I know he is counting on you to help him with this enormous responsibility."

Instead of acknowledging her greeting and compliment, Köpek whipped his head around to Alaeddin and sharply barked: "You mean you speak to her about your plans? You inform this Christian woman about all that we are doing in the Empire?"

Instead of becoming angry, the Sultan laughed out loud. "Now calm down, my trusted advisor, you will soon see that this woman has a head on her shoulders that both of us would envy having! And may I remind you that my mother was a Christian, too? Sultana Mahperi is intelligent, generous, can put cause and effect together, and always has an uncanny way of being able to predict unforeseen circumstances. I am learning to count immensely on her advice."

Köpek did not answer the Sultan, and slowly turned his head back to Mahperi. "Well, aren't we lucky, then, to have a Queen as intelligent as she is comely?"

Again, the chill ran down her back and she reddened in shame. What impudence he had, this man! Mahperi reached up instinctively to touch the turquoise stone underneath her gown to give her strength. Why was this man so aggressive with her, she wondered, whatever have I done to offend him? She tried to think that perhaps they had just gotten off to a bad start, or perhaps this pregnancy was playing tricks with her moods. Perhaps it was sheer jealousy. To give herself courage, she thought back to when Alaeddin introduced her to Hanife and what a friend she had now become. The Sultan spoke so highly of him that she was perhaps just inventing all of this. And yet… The Sultan and Köpek returned to their discussion about the new Palace in Kayseri.

"Come over here, Mahperi, and look at the splendid drawings Köpek has prepared for this new palace!" the Sultan said, waving her over to his side. As she neared to consult the drawings, she sensed that Köpek bristled at her approach. Köpek handed her a roll of sketches, and touched her hand in doing so. His fingers lingered on hers and almost dawdled over them as he slowly withdrew his hand. There was no doubting it now in her mind: something was not quite right about this man.

Köpek lowered his head and spoke directly to the Sultan, as if she were not standing there.

"My Sultan, I know that you use Kayseri as your headquarters to prepare for your military campaigns in the East. You use the nearby Mashad plain to train your troops in a variety of exercises which are so important to ensure success on the battle field. I also know that your Devlethane Palace in the center of town is too small and inconvenient for your needs. That is why I propose to create for you a complex nearer to the area where you train the troops. Rather than returning each night from the Mashad Plain into town to rest in the Devlethane palace, you can conveniently retire here in this new palace, which will be safer and more pleasant than staying in a tent out on the plain as you do now."

Köpek spread out onto the floor one of the large rolls that he held under his arm.

"Come closer, my Sultan, I will show you what I have in mind," motioning Alaeddin to look down at the drawings that were sketched on paper rolls. "The palace will be located west of the city, on a well-traveled ancient road already in use when the Romans were here. I have found a dramatic site in which to set your complex, with views onto the big mountain that dominates the city. Everything you love, my Sultan, is here on this site: abundant water, greenery, and beautiful scenery. I am certain it will become one of your favorite residences."

It would appear that the Director of Works had thought of everything. He continued his presentation to the eager Sultan.

"You are destined to become the greatest of Sultans in all Islam, and you can also use this spot for receptions and feasts for foreign dignitaries. Imagine the great celebrations you will host with music and feasting off vessels of precious metals!"

The Sultan laughed and nodded for him to continue.

"You can use it as well for hunting parties. I have set the pavilions very near the edge of a lake, and I have planned to construct a pier extending into the lake to use for boating excursions. There will be a marina to house the flat-bottomed boats you can use to slither among the reeds to hunt wild birds."

The Sultan peered closer to the drawings, caught up in the enthusiasm of his Superintendent of Works.

"Yes, my Sultan, you heard me well! A lake! As you know, my specialty is hydraulics, and I have devised a plan for this site, which is located next to a spring. I will dam it to create a sizeable, but shallow lake. Yes, I will create a lake just for you in the middle of the plain where there was none before; can you imagine such a thing? You will want for nothing here, my Sultan!"

Mahperi listened to this description with as much enthusiasm as the Sultan. How happy she would be to gaze upon water from her window again, even if it is just a small lake!

"Just how big will be this river next to the Palace?" she excitedly asked Köpek.

At that moment Köpek let out a shrill and uncontrolled fit of laughter, stunning her.

"Oh, my Queen, I think we need to get you a new Turkish tutor or perhaps you are not applying yourself to your studies as much as you should be! It is not a river, I said, but a lake: I am surprised you would confuse two such simple words! Or perhaps it is because of your accent that I couldn't really understand what you were saying." He laughed with his mouth wide open, showing a set of dirty, crooked teeth.

Mahperi reddened at her silly mistake. Of course she knew the difference between those two words! Confound this pregnancy which is befuddling my mind, she thought. She stammered a response, excusing her confusion, but she was now convinced that this man was truly a brute to have upbraided her for such a simple vocabulary mistake, especially in front of her husband, who did not in the least take her defense in front of the Vizier's mockery.

The Master of Works returned to his presentation, not before he smugly smiled at her, pleased that he had seemingly put her in her place. Köpek pointed with his finger to the cluster of square shapes on the drawings. "I will build three pavilions out of stone and other masonry, which can always be supplemented by tents if you wish to receive guests or important military contingencies."

Seeing the bright smile of the Sultan, the Master of Works was encouraged to continue.

"And once inside, you will be dazzled by the plans I have for decorating the palace. I have devised a scheme of stucco decoration that will shine as brightly as the white coat of your stallion! I also will incorporate a frieze of engraved silver above your throne in the largest of the *iwans* of the palace. Everyone who comes to speak with you will be blinded by its brilliance."

Mahperi listened to all of this but now felt that she wanted to speak up, not only to share her views but also to show she was not cowed by his recent remarks.

"Perhaps, may I suggest that white and silver might not be exactly suitable for this type of country structure – that is possibly too fancy and pretentious? Tile, like the ones that are used in our palace here at Konya, are perhaps more appropriate. I think they are sturdier and reflect the light better. And if I may make another suggestion, perhaps these tiles could be in the color turquoise, for I know that is what the Sultan favors," she said, blushing as she looked at the Sultan, and touching her necklace underneath her robes in a secret gesture between them.

Köpek lifted his head and looked at her without a word, but she noticed that he crumpled the drawing with his fist. She had not meant to contradict him, only to suggest an idea, as she was used to doing with her father and the Sultan, but she could see that this was obviously something he was not accustomed to.

He turned away from her without acknowledging her remark, and continued as if she were not even present in the room.

"And of course, my Sultan, I will construct a small mosque for your prayers, not to forget kitchens, hammams and housing for the servants. Everything will be provided for, and it will be a complete city unto itself. It will take several years to build, but I am certain that once it is done, you will not want to be anywhere else! So what do you say, my Sultan? Shall we proceed?"

The Sultan looked up from the drawings with a dazed, yet dreamy, look on his face.

"By all means proceed! Your ideas and plan are brilliant. And just like Alaiye, I want this place to bear my name: it will go down in for all history as the Palace of Keykubadiyye!"

As they continued to pour over the drawings with their heads bent closely together, Mahperi slipped out of the room. They were so engrossed in them that they did not notice she had left. But one thing was now certain in her mind: she and Sadettin Köpek were never going to become friends.

Chapter 16

Blood Runs Readily

"*Allahu Akbar!*"

In the fields outside of Konya, the voice of the Sultan's butcher rang out loudly each time he slit the throat of each of the thirty sheep lined up to be slaughtered that day. Another morning had dawned on Konya, and the bellies of the court kettles rumbled hungrily for the meat needed to cook the stews for the royal household and for the poor who gathered daily at the palace gates each day for alms. Red blood flowed on the ground as the butcher went from sheep to sheep, all in the service of his Sultan.

"*Allahu Akbar!*"

In a nearby field, a second voice cried out the same incantation as a knife drew across the necks of the sheep butchered for the kitchens of Emir Seyfeddin Ayaba. Only this time it was a herd of eighty sheep that were lined up to be sacrificed. The blood from his sheep, which ran so readily and red in the fields outside the city, would soon trickle all the way down to the Sultan's palace, and seep into his royal soul.

☪ ☪ ☪

"Eighty sheep! What brazenness! Who does he think he is? It is I who am the Sultan of Two Seas! No emir shall show off his wealth by butchering more sheep than I! These emirs have got to remember that I am the most powerful man in the land and they must heed my supremacy! I distribute power to my emirs, not the other way around!" bellowed the angry Sultan when his guards reported the activities of Ayaba.

The situation of the eighty sheep forced the Sultan to acknowledge a situation he could no longer ignore: the emirs were acting out of bounds, and an atmosphere of tension could now be felt in the palace. The very same emirs who had lobbied to put him on the throne after the death of his brother Izzeddin two years before now sought to become more powerful than the Sultan himself. They had begun to live in a way full of pride and pleasure in the face of the abundance of provisions and property they had amassed as senior servants. Flaunting their wealth and defying decorum, their way of life had become disrespectful to their positions as trusted and veteran advisors to the Sultan, and certainly did not set a good example as servants of God to the people of the Empire. Something needed to be done.

When the Sultan heard about the blatant impertinence of the 80 sheep, he sent an emissary to Ayaba's home to bring him to the palace to explain his actions. However, when the Sultan's emissary arrived at Ayaba's home, the door was slammed in his face. An indignant Ayaba then sent a letter to the Sultan resigning from his service, and told everyone from the palace to leave him alone.

Alaeddin Keykubad could only interpret Ayaba's insolence as a sign that his own authority was at stake, and he now became suspicious of the intentions of all the emirs. Were they all like Ayaba, he wondered? Yet, despite the insubordination of this one man, the Sultan still believed that his emirs were working hard in support of his Empire. Indeed, most of the emirs were entranced by the charisma of the Sultan and were faithful to his person and ideals. His refined looks, his bearing, his self-assurance were all qualities they admired and wanted for their own. These were the men that he owned; the ones that would go with him to the ends of the earth. But could he be so sure about the others?

☪ ☪ ☪

Behind the closed doors of his home, Emir Ayaba had already started his campaign to influence other important emirs to follow his lead. They were reluctant at first to act against the Sultan individually out of fear of reprisal, but like sly foxes, they united in a subversive movement to unseat the Sultan.

One night a group of emirs met at the house of Emir Ayaba for an evening of feasting. The conversation soon became animated among the twenty-five men who sat on the carpets and cushions of his salon. Emir Ayaba was the first one to boldly put forth the subject of the Sultan and his demands for discussion.

"I don't see why we have to see our personal fortunes dissipated to promote his glory! He and his government have no business interfering with the way we run our private lives! I have worked very hard to establish myself and I will not let him take away the fruits of my work!"

Many of the other emirs nodded their heads in agreement, yet others were more cautious.

Emir Bahaeddin Kutluğu felt the need to calm his friend down a bit and offered a comment in defense of the Sultan.

"But my friend, what the Sultan is asking is only normal! You owe it to your fellow citizens to share the fruits of your work! Your wealth is not yours entirely, but has been given to you as a blessing from God. Yes, you have worked hard, but you have also been shown mercies from God and you must return this favor to others. It is the foundation stone of our Holy Faith of Islam. We must live to serve God and others."

Ayaba whipped his head around to face him and retorted sharply: "Perhaps God has given me special favors, I grant that, but it is the Sultan Alaeddin Keykubad who is benefitting from our money, not God! He is using it to build up the kingdom in his name, to leave his mark as the most generous sultan ever to walk on the earth, yet it is with *our* money that he is building his fame! And I certainly don't see many programs for which he is putting up money, other than for building his fancy palaces! Have you heard about the new one he is building out in Kayseri?"

His words resonated among the other disgruntled emirs who cheered him on. Despite the grumbling, Bahaeddin Kutluğu continued to defend the Sultan in front of the others.

"Yes, I suppose it does look like that. But in reality, I do not think it is an entirely selfish act on his part to ask us to join him. It actually is quite generous, for he is allowing us to participate in the building of this new world as he envisions it in his wise leadership. The Sultan believes that in order to build a strong state, all members of the community must have their say and participate. So, I ask you, what is wrong with that?

"Oh, my friend, forgive me, but you are so naïve!" Ayaba poured himself another goblet of wine, spilling it in his agitation. "I have a lot of trouble believing what you say. I do not see why my personal fortune should go towards building roads and feeding, clothing and nursing poor people! It is not for me to do this! The Sultan says it is to build an empire, but I say his plan is meant merely to flatter his pride."

"No, I regret, it is your duty," Bahaeddin Kutluğu persisted in a firm tone. "Firstly, as a Muslim, it is your obligation to share your wealth with those less fortunate than you. You know this well and good, just as you know you should not be partaking of that wine you are now drinking so freely. Put down those goblets of wine and drink the Holy Word of the Qur'an instead! This duty to share and serve is not a matter for debate. Secondly, it is up to you to do this because you are a part of a state with a new type of rule; one where all citizens have the right to participate in their governance. Sultan Alaeddin Keykubad is not a tyrant – he wants to create an egalitarian society like the ancient Greeks had, only much better. We will all be the stronger for it, you included, even if you share your wealth, because you are being given the chance to become a leader and a visionary. Why would you want to pass up this golden opportunity for fame?"

"Ha! It is not an opportunity for me, but only one for that egotistical Sultan!" Ayaba spat out, slamming his fist down on the table, spilling his wine.

Bahaeddin Kutluğu would not let go of his argument. "We have a long road in front of us. God has shown us the true and holy way in which we should live our lives. The Sultan Alaeddin Keykubad has formulated a vision to implement this sacred mandate for sharing, and yet some of you choose to ignore it. Come, my friends, let us be the leaders and builders of this new empire alongside our Sultan, instead of selfish and intoxicated hotheads. And when the empire has been built and is flourishing beyond our dreams, shining far brighter than any other in the history of the world, then you, the nay-sayers, will hang your heads in shame."

The emirs continued to feast well into the night, and enjoyed the performances of musicians that Ayaba had hired for the evening. Despite the sweet music and the attempts of Bahaeddin Kutluğu to appease their anger, an air of rebellious bitterness continued to circulate among the men. After a while, Ayaba dismissed the musicians and then spoke privately to the few emirs who remained behind. By this time, many of them were lost to the ill-effects of the wine.

"I have decided what we are going to do. We all agree that this Sultan must be removed from power if we are to have any control over our wealth. And we need to make sure that the person who replaces him will not start up again with the same nonsense, but will heed us instead of opposing us. My friends, when we worked to elect Alaeddin to power a few years ago, we made a mistake and chose the wrong brother. At the time we believed his younger brother, Keyferidun, was too docile to be an effective ruler; but in reality, that is exactly what we need now: someone we can easily lead and who will give us no problems! This brother is weak and will do anything we tell him! His time has now come!"

The men all agreed and cheered at this plan. Emir Ayaba lowered his voice and continued.

"Yes, this is what we will do, my brothers! I will organize a banquet here tomorrow night. I will go to the Sultan tomorrow morning to invite him to it, saying that I wish to ask his forgiveness for having slammed the door in the face of his emissary the other day, and that I regret my rash action to resign. I will beg for him to accept my apology and ask to be reinstated in his service at the palace. Cocky as he is, he will grin from ear to ear to see me groveling at his feet, and will certainly accept my invitation! During the banquet, the rest of you will come in with heavy chains and ropes, and we will tie his legs and arms together and lock him in the cellar below. A group of you will ride over to Koyluhisar Castle and fetch Keyferidun. Once Keyferidun safely arrives here, we will descend to the cellar and kill the Sultan Alaeddin Keykubad. And the next day, we will stand next to the new Sultan and cheer our good fortune!"

The men all rose to their feet and slapped Ayaba on the back in support of his brilliant plot.

"So who is with me here? All in favor of this plan, raise your goblets high!"

And when he counted the raised goblets of twenty-three men, Emir Ayaba knew that his seditious plan would succeed. Continuing long into the night, the emirs made toast after toast in anticipation of the moment Sultan Alaeddin Keykubad would be sacrificed like a sheep in the fields of Konya.

☪ ☪ ☪

In the cool of the very same late October night, a Christian princess from a castle high above the sea sat on her wedding rug in her room in the palace on the hill in the center of the City of Sultans, preparing to add to the line of Seljuk kings. As the pains increased and her blood began to flow, she prayed for a son to be born this night; a son who would reign with the same determination as his powerful father, and a son who would love his mother with devotion.

One after another the pains went through her like a knife, just like the sheep that fell in the fields that morning. Her blood kept flowing until her first-born child, son and heir, slipped out of her womb.

☪ ☪ ☪

And so this day, which started with the flow of the blood of eighty lambs and which continued with seditious cold blood beating in the angry hearts of twenty-three wicked men, now ended at midnight with the birth of a Sultan's son, covered with the warm blood of his loving mother's womb.

All the blood of this day was fated to swirl together to form a river, flowing faster and faster until it flooded over its banks. Forever more would the soul of this newborn baby be linked to the destiny of this flood. His princely blood would join the blood of wicked emirs determined to spill his father's regal blood, and would remain a stain on all their hands that would never wash clean.

Chapter 17

Sweet, Cool Water

An heir to the throne is born!

As the news spread throughout Konya the next morning, the people of the city rejoiced one and all. Arrows were shot into the air, sheep were sacrificed and their meat distributed to the citizens of the city, bazaars were shut for a three day holiday, military bands strolled through the streets drumming the news, date candy was tossed to children from soldiers atop gaily-caparisoned horses, coins and sweet buns were handed to the poor from the steps of the mosques, and all rejoiced that the future of the sultanate was secure. The imams in every mosque in the city led prayers for the blessing of the life of this new child, named Giyaseddin Keyhüsrev, after the illustrious martyred father of Alaeddin Keykubad.

As the dawn glowed over the plain of Konya, a new mother rested on her cushions in her palace snuggling this new baby to her chest, overjoyed at all the celebration she heard in the streets below her. She would never be lonely again, for she had her very own family now. She would never feel a foreigner again, because she was mother of the next heir to the throne of the Seljuks. Most of all, she rejoiced that she had become, in one painful night, the most important woman in the land, not only in the eyes of its citizens, but in the eyes of her husband.

She snuggled the little one and whispered into his ear: "Our Heavenly Lord has graced me with divine favor. You are the first blessed fruit of my garden, my rosy-cheeked apricot!"

Her little apricot had the fair coloring of his father, with a fuzz of golden red hair already sticking up on his head. He was sturdy and pink and thrashed his little arms about in time to the commotion of the streets below. Mahperi could not wait to place him in the arms of his father, and to witness the Sultan's first glance upon his first-born child. However, the Sultan had yet to appear in her chambers, and she began to wonder where he was.

The Sultan was not feeling the same joy as Mahperi that morning. The events of the previous night had been very different for him, for he had discovered the perfidy of his emirs. He would always remember this October night not as the time his first child was born, but as the night when he discovered that his emirs wanted him dead. At the same time his son was slipping out of his mother' womb into the world, the Sultan felt his life slipping out of his powerful grip, and he would forever associate these two events together.

Perhaps his emirs wanted him dead, but God apparently did not, and had sent an angel of salvation to attend that banquet of the emirs at the home of Ayaba. After the banquet ended, a slave who had accompanied his master that evening was too excited to sleep, and so decided to visit his friend who worked for the Emir Hokkabaz Seyfeddin. The slave banged on the door to wake his friend, but instead it was the emir himself who opened the door. Hokkabaz had not attended the banquet and was unaware of the events of the evening, but when he saw the excited state of the slave, he knew that this feast had been an eventful one, and was curious to learn more about what went on. He invited him inside, and pried by a gold piece, the young man told Hokkabaz everything that had taken place, from the drinking of wine to the discussion, from the plot to the heavy chains, from the return of Keyferidun to the killing of the Sultan. Hokkabaz, a trusted and close personal assistant of the Sultan, sent the slave away and immediately saddled his horse to ride to the palace to inform the Sultan of what he had learned.

Hokkabaz Seyfeddin and the stunned Sultan now prepared their counter plan. They decided that when the Emir Ayaba Seyfeddin would show up that day to invite the Sultan to his banquet, the Sultan would thank him profusely, but decline, stating that the invitation did not come at a suitable moment due to the birth of his son. How happy he would be to attend another time, he would say; but today, I need to stay with my wife and newborn son. Because his excuse for declining was such a valid one, the Emir Ayaba would never suspect that the Sultan had gotten wind of his plan. Indeed, later that morning when Ayaba did appear, bowing and bearing congratulations for the birth of a son and an invitation to come to his home to celebrate the good fortune that evening, he perfectly understood that the Sultan needed to decline his offer.

☪ ☪ ☪

The news of this plot shook Alaeddin Keykubad to the core. He now realized there was evil in his court coming from wicked men who ignored not only his command but the laws of the Prophet as well, and that this flood would grow to tyranny were it not excised. He decided to leave Konya immediately to head south to Alaiye for the winter. In this place of beauty he would be able to calm his anger, think about this situation more clearly, and sort out his next steps. But most of all, the Sultan wanted to discuss the implications of this plot with his advisors there, who were more experienced, and yes, he had to admit, wiser than he.

When the Sultan came to visit Mahperi and his new son later that morning, she could not help but see how he nervously paced in front of her. Instead of sharing a tender moment with her, he was irritable. His hatred for his emirs and his paranoia about their action overshadowed all the joy he should have felt upon seeing his first born child in the arms of the woman he loved. He could not shake off the strange feeling that this little apricot was somehow an omen of ill.

☪ ☪ ☪

As soon as Mahperi was strong enough to travel, the royal court packed up its affairs and headed out for the pass through the Taurus Mountains to the sea. When they left Konya and passed once again in front of the Emir Kandemir han, Mahperi could hardly believe how much had happened to her in the short time since she had first stayed there. She was now a wife, a queen, and a new mother. "Wait until you see my blue paradise!" she gleefully chattered to her son. "It is as beautiful as you are!"

When they arrived in Antalya, the Sultan gave orders to remain there for a few days, as he was eager to show Mahperi this important Seljuk port on the southern coast, captured by his father some fifteen years earlier.

It was a stunning city, filled with flowering bushes, orange trees and date palms, tucked into a ring of fortifications around a horseshoe-shaped harbor. It did not have an impressive fortress like her Kalonoros, but it had a charm that she had to admit was even greater than that of her native city. Above the harbor rose a slim round tower carved with eight fluted grooves, taller than any building she had ever seen before. Made of pink-colored bricks enhanced with small pieces of blue-green tiles inlaid into its grooves, the tall tower glowed against the bright blue Mediterranean sky. Mahperi gasped when she saw it, a reaction that pleased the Sultan immensely.

"This minaret is my pride and joy, the first thing I built as a Sultan. I made it so tall that all the citizens of the region can see it for miles. I want it to become the symbol of this city, and the beacon for my Empire! I built it next to the Byzantine Church, in order to show the citizens that all our religions can coexist in this land, but that Islam is the most important of them. Just as for your church in Kalonoros, Mahperi, I will not tear down the holy places of worship that were here upon my conquest. I have inherited them, and they are now placed in my safekeeping. I want to be known as a man of tolerance."

While Mahperi settled into the palace quarters overlooking the harbor, the Sultan sought to speak in confidentiality to the three advisors who had earned his trust: the Emirs Hokkabaz, Komnenos and Ertokush. When he revealed to them the plot of the Konya emirs, they reflected upon the possible solutions to the situation.

Emir Hokkabaz tried to reassure the Sultan by saying: "If our Sultan is truly convinced that this story is true, and if their evilness comes out into the open, it will be easy for us to take care of this ugliness for you and for the good of the empire. We have our ways to make this situation go away, do not fear."

However, Mübarizeddin Ertokush, the governor of Antalya, was more reserved. He had many friends among the emirs and wanted to give them a chance to amend their thinking. The wise advisor offered a suggestion. "Calm your thoughts and do not act rashly. The emirs may come to see the error of their ways. Yet if our Sultan does decide to take disciplinary action, it should be done in Kayseri, far from the court of Konya."

The Sultan found his reasoning valid, and after further discussion with his advisors in Antalya and with the imams of his faith, he told himself he would give the emirs a year to earn his trust again. He would struggle to forgive them and offer them the opportunity to prove their loyalty before taking any reprisal against them for the plot of that fateful October night. Yet, for good measure, he doubled his security guard.

☪ ☪ ☪

The joy that Mahperi felt as they climbed the hill at Kalonoros to the palace was almost as strong as the one she had felt when her baby son was placed in her arms for the first time. She could not believe how much the city had changed, for the building projects envisioned by her husband one year ago were now starting to take form. Over the following days, she took her baby and strolled along the harbor with her guards to watch the construction of the huge red tower she had suggested and which had been ordered by the Sultan. She enjoyed eating the fresh fish and other seafood grilled on the dock by the local fishermen while the warm winter sun toasted her face. She certainly could not savor such delicacies in land-locked Konya!

But this was not a time of rest for the Sultan, who began in earnest to organize his ambitious plans for territorial expansion. He laid siege to the nearby castle of Alara, where lived a group of monks, one of whom was the brother of Mahperi's father Kyr Vart. Located west of Alaiye next to a lovely river running through the summer fields, the Alara castle sat atop a mountain, even sharper than the one at Alaiye. It was so high and so steep that only contemplative monks could find the inspiration to climb it and live there. Yet the Sultan was determined to add it to his chain of trading stations along the southern route and felt its observation post would be essential for surveying the sea. Immediately after the victory, the Sultan gave orders to rebuild the fortifications and add a castle, hammam and han near the site.

With the help of Ertokush, the Sultan also made plans to extend his territory east of Alaiye along the rough Cilician coast, with his most important conquest being the great fortress of Anamur, located on the southernmost point on the Mediterranean coast of Anatolia. The Sultan continued to fulfill his dream of taking the coast as far as he could see from his window from his castle atop the rock at Alaiye.

☪ ☪ ☪

Yet all was not just warfare for the Sultan during the winter months in the south. He enjoyed picnics with Mahperi and the baby, and rode into the surrounding countryside to discover the forests behind the Dim River. Considerable trade with Egypt was underway for the export of the timber felled here, a commerce which filled the coffers of the state's treasury to overflowing. The Sultan visited the forests to inspect the many types of trees that grew here, and to learn how all this wood and bark were making his Empire rich. Besides the huge trunks that were used for building, dwarf oaks yielded the storax gum and fragrant balsam used to make perfumes. The dried roots of the licorice plants grown there were used for medicines. The lumber was also used for firewood and for making charcoal. "The gold in my coffers certainly comes from the most curious of sources!" laughed the Sultan to his financiers.

The Sultan also loved to ride to an area east of the city to the spot where a lively spring bubbled forth. The Sultan decided that he would build for himself a small pavilion there, to enjoy at his leisure and which would offer him a convenient place to stay for the night if he were too tired to return and make the high climb up the Alaiye hill. He explained his plans for this pavilion to the court architects and Mahperi. "It is not just here, but in other places along the coast that I want to create a series of garden pavilions. At these pavilions, I will enjoy hunting the rich game of these forests by day, and at night, I will enjoy banquets, music, and poetry. I will call this one, set next to this sparkling spring, my "*Hasbahce*," my private garden, and I will take strength from the sound and taste of its sweet, cool waters."

Little did Mahperi know how much the Sultan needed a place of refuge from the terrible threat of treason that never ceased to loom in front of him. Suspicion obsessed his thoughts all day and haunted his dreams each night. Little did she realize how much he needed to build a private garden, where the terrible faces of the twenty three evil emirs would never be allowed to enter.

Chapter 18

A Christmas Child

It was so warm. It was hard to believe that it was in the middle of winter, deep into the month of December. Winters in Kalonoros were always mild and sunny, but even so, Mahperi had never remembered a Christmas season this balmy. It was more than warm; it was hot, hot as the month of June, and although the sun soothed everyone's bones and spirits, there was an odd feeling in the air due to this peculiar state of the weather. The Sultan's troops wore the light tunics of their spring troop maneuvers. Meals were taken outdoors, and Alaeddin and Mahperi enjoyed sitting in the afternoon hot sun near the edge of the fortress wall to look at the sea below. The almond trees bloomed early, their leaves curling from the heat.

In the week before Christmas, the temperatures exceeded those remembered by any of the old men who sat in the courtyards of the houses on the hillside. Yet everyone was so busy preparing for the midnight Holy Mass and the family celebrations that would be held on Christmas Eve that they had little time to think about the heat. Islam might be the official religion of Alaiye now, but its Armenian citizens never forgot the joy and significance of their holiest day of the year, soon to be upon them. The birth of Jesus still remained for all of them the symbol of their faith and their relationship with God. Young and old had stopped eating meat in preparation for the *Hisnag* season of Advent. Purple candles were lit in the church and in homes at sunset, prayers and hymns were sung, visits were paid to families and friends, and excitement reigned in the entire city. Blessed Holy Christmas, the gift of the Christ Child is soon upon us! Even the Muslims anticipated all the interesting dishes they would soon discover. Women were readying dried and fresh fruits, cheese, yogurt soup, olives, and dishes of fish, rice, chick peas and green chard, along with the favorite *peda* bread. Children dreamed of the sweets to follow the banquet, with all kinds of cookies, walnuts threaded on strings and covered with grape jelly, and everyone's favorite, the rich *anushabour* pudding. Every house stocked up on pomegranates, ready to break open on their doorsteps on Christmas morning, as was the tradition of Kalonoros. Such was the excitement of the city at this time, with everyone so eagerly anticipating the arrival of Christmas

Day that they forgot that their paradise city had been scorching for weeks under a searing sun.

When Mahperi woke before dawn a few days before Christmas, she thought that it was all the excitement of the upcoming festivities that kept her from sleeping. Her baby's first Christmas! As she let her thoughts drift to the upcoming Mass, she suddenly realized that it was far too bright outside for this time of the night, and that the sky seemed to flutter in a peculiar way. She rose and looked out her window and saw a glowing light in the distance – not the star of Bethlehem; no, something much closer to the ground to the east. It was then she smelled the smoke at the same time as did the rest of the town, shaken from their sleep by the pungent odor and the light coming from a huge forest fire now raging in the direction of the Sultan's sweet-water Hasbahce pavilion.

The forest fire spread quickly, as the vegetation of the coastline had become dry as tinder from the weeks of hot temperatures. By the next afternoon, the entire region to the east of the castle rock was on fire. Flames swept across the grass faster than galloping horses and crashed through tangled undergrowth. The rampant fires crawled along the ground, engulfing the bushes and moss, and flames jumped from treetop to treetop in their mad rush to consume everything in their path. The fires raced up the sides of the terraced hills to the east of Alaiye with a frightening speed. There was nothing that could be done to stop it, except to wait until it burned out of its own accord, for there were no signs that rain would come any time soon. The heat generated by the fire was so intense that it could be felt all the way to the top of the castle rock. In order to impede the advance of the fire to the city, the citizens of Kalonoros began to dig trenches around the base of the castle rock to break the fire should it creep closer.

The fires continued to burn for three days until the supply of dry leaves and brush ran out and the flames reached a dead-end at the sea. As if to answer the many prayers of the people, the rains finally did arrive, leaving the entire area a sopping patchwork of charred and untouched areas. The odor of the fire stuck in everyone's nostrils and clothes, despite the strong sea breezes. No one felt the desire to light the purple candles each night for the Christmas celebration, but everyone believed that the city had been spared from disaster due to the miracle of the blessed arrival of the Christ child.

On Christmas Day, the day after the fires stopped, Alaeddin and a contingent of soldiers set out to inspect the damage. Ashes and charred vegetation greeted them at every turn; tree trunks had either toppled over or stood defiantly erect yet blackened. In some patches, the trees had been totally spared by the flames. Wisps of smoke rose from the ground and blue flames lingered here and there among charred logs. It was a scene of destruction like no one had ever witnessed.

"Whatever could have caused such a catastrophe?" the Sultan asked his men, unable to comprehend how such an intense devastation could have struck with such a sudden force. One of his aides quickly spoke up.

"I come from Melas in the west, my Sultan, and these kinds of fires are common there. All it takes is several weeks of hot weather, no rain, and one flash of lightning to set off the dry leaves, and the whole world can explode like the Day of Judgment! It does not happen often, perhaps every generation or so, but everyone in my region will see a fire like this at least once in their lifetime. But do not worry; you will see that within a few weeks, green shoots will start to appear. Nature is God's most perfect and persistent creation: He will resurrect the beauty of this area in no time, and you will see that the forest will be as healthy as before!"

Alaeddin had difficulty imagining that the lush green paradise he so admired was not scarred forever. "Are you sure of this?" he asked the soldier, who nodded his head vigorously.

"Yes, my Sultan, it is like an intense fever. You shiver, you are delirious, but afterwards, you feel a tremendous sense of strength and renewal. The small buds will sprout and even new types of plants will arise where there were none before, finding fresh nutrients from the soil. The insects will soon return, with the woodpeckers right after them, and then the other small animals will burrow their homes again. Believe me! God protects his forests, for they are one of his most important gifts to us."

At that moment, the pack of hunting dogs accompanying the outing started to bark frantically. They had run ahead into the underbrush, eagerly sniffing all the new odors released by the burning matter, their paws oblivious to the hot earth and their tails wagging furiously. The Sultan's head animal keeper, Tahajan, whistled for them to come back, but they had all grouped around a giant trunk that had fallen to the ground, rooting under it with their noses and madly digging at it with their paws. There would be no calling them back, as they had found prey and were eager to rout it.

Alaeddin trotted over to the fallen massive tree trunk which had completely split in two, but which oddly had not burned.

"This is exactly where the lightning struck that started the whole fire!" exclaimed one of the soldiers. "I have seen trees like this struck before, cracked open by lightning right in two like a walnut!"

Still, the soldiers could not understand what so riled the dogs, and the trainer Tahajan went over to silence the barking dogs and to discover the reason behind their agitation.

"Come, my Sultan, come! Take a look at this!" he cried out excitedly. All the men gathered around the tree trunk and were startled by what they saw there.

Underneath the tree trunk, a magnificent wild mountain leopard laid crushed to death in a flat heap. It was a female, and she must have had the unfortunate fate of lying under the tree when it was struck by the lightning bolt. Her body had been charred by the electric current of the flash, and then had been totally crushed when the tree fell on top of her. In a matter of seconds, she had gone from being one of the most impressive beasts in the forest to a lump of petrified charcoal. Such is God's *kismet,* thought all the men to themselves.

And then the Sultan saw it, the reason of the furious agitation of the dogs. Lying underneath the female were two cubs. Trapped under the tree, there was nothing the mother could do to save herself, but she would give her last moment of life to try to spare her cubs from death. She had covered them with her body as best she could to protect them against the encroaching flames. Fierce and loving, she died with the hope that she had been able to save them, as any mother on the face of the earth would have done in the same situation.

"Are they alive?" asked the Sultan, dismounting from Night Shining White to approach the fallen tree trunk.

Several soldiers heaved the heavy log off the dead leopard to reveal the two cubs. One was silent, but the other one lay whimpering in fear and pain, which was the noise the sharp ears of the hounds had picked up. Alaeddin stared at the little cub, and realized that it was still alive and in need of help.

He picked up the cub by the scruff of the neck, and turned it over in his hand. It was a female as well. Her spotted fur was charred black, her eyes were burned and swollen shut, her tail broken, raw patches of flesh oozed blood, and her head too heavy to hold up from hunger, injury and thirst. At that moment an unknown and strong feeling of compassion came over Alaeddin, something he had not even felt upon the birth of his son. In some strange way, he identified with this cub, for he was a survivor, too. He had survived when he was a young boy against his brother; he had survived being held in prison after he tried to wrest the throne from him, and was now trying to survive in the face of a raging forest fire of emirs. This cub was linked to his destiny, and she needed his help to stay alive. He felt as if the same blood that ran in her veins also ran in his, for they shared a heritage that went back thousands of generations – the heritage of the survivor against all odds.

He held her near his face and whispered in her ear. "Well, my little one, you have endured a terrible test, and so have I, and it is God's will that our futures shall be forever linked! You have been victorious over adversity, and you will share with me your strength from this day forth. Come, my little one, do not worry; you will be safe in my hands. I may not be your mother, but I will love you with the very same intensity."

The little cub whimpered softly, and it seemed so close to death that the Sultan did not know if even all the medicines and tinctures of the court physicians could save her from her brush with the tail of the angel of death Azrail.

He continued to whisper in her ear.

"I shall name you Ruby, since the red of the flames that killed your family will always be reflected in your eyes. Ruby, because you are a precious gem of the finest beauty. Ruby, because the red hot blood to defy the odds of fate flows in your veins. Ruby, because your life is as treasured as the rarest of nature's hues."

For the next two months, the two of them spent every moment together. The Sultan dipped the edge of his sleeve into a bowl of ewe's milk and dribbled it into the cub's open mouth. He spoke to her gently, soaked her raw burns with compresses of chamomile and eucalyptus oil, washed and combed away the charred fur until it was clean, tucked her in a chest next to his bed at night, and stroked her head constantly to allay her fears. When the swollen eyes of the little cub were finally able to open again, their first sight fell upon a man who gazed into them with the same tenderness as her mother. The cub trusted him; her animal instinct informed her that she owed her life to him, and for that, she would share her loyalty with him for the rest of her days.

☪ ☪ ☪

So was born the unique friendship that linked a Sultan with a savage animal. And on Epiphany Day, in the Church of Kalonoros, high upon the castle rock, Mahperi lit a purple candle for the arrival of this other Christmas Child, a miracle gift from the holiest of mothers.

Chapter 19

Twenty-Three Trees

In April of the following year, the Sultan Alaeddin Keykubad departed for the Mashad Plain near Kayseri for his annual spring military training, in preparation for the expeditions and battles in the East. It was at this time his soldiers practiced their horsemanship skills, trained on archery finesse, engaged in wrestling matches to build up their physical prowess, and marched hard for long hours to gain endurance. In addition to the regular training, there were many opportunities for games, for the Sultan knew that a rousing match of *cirit* polo could provide valuable lessons in horsemanship. He also worked with his soldiers on their leadership skills, and instilled in them a sense of duty as warriors in his service. When summer arrived, the army would head east to do battle with the various adversaries of the Seljuk Empire, be they Ayyubids, Danishmendids, Byzantines, Armenians, Khwarezmids or Artukids. All were in the ambitious path of this dynamic Sultan, and all needed to fear the arrival of his well-trained troops.

The Sultan still worried, however, that his worst enemy was not the one that awaited him on a distant battleground, but the one that surrounded him daily, in his own court. Although the Sultan depended on the support of the faithful emirs who shared his commitment to the goals of the Empire, he knew there was still dark enmity in the hearts of many others. The names of the twenty-three men who plotted against him on that October night were engraved in his heart like a black scar.

It was difficult for the proud Sultan to swallow his anger and to accept that this hatred was aimed against him, but he knew that unless he gave these traitors the chance to prove their loyalty, he would regret forever any brutality taken against them. So for the time being, his life was one of struggle, as his rage seethed in him at the same time as he tried to keep his outward composure neutral and his heart open to forgiveness.

And so in this way passed the year he had promised to give the emirs to prove their fealty. Although the twenty-three emirs continued to bow and scrape and pay the workmen for the construction projects consigned to them, the Sultan could still feel the anger in their hearts. He charged his emissaries and spies from all corners of the empire to inform him of their activities, and the reports coming back to him from Akşehir to Niğde contained both good and bad news. The good news was that many emir-sponsored building projects were well underway, and the empire was being built up in all the ways the Sultan had dreamed. The bad news was that many emirs continued to live a lifestyle full of pride, self-absorption, alcohol and pleasure, abusing the wealth they were amassing through abusive taxes and from the sale of the crops raised from the people under their rule. The exploitation of their stations as trusted advisors to the Sultan defiantly continued.

One clear spring morning in Kayseri, the Sultan Alaeddin Keykubad decided that he could no longer put off his decision concerning this defiance. The time had come to excise, once and for all, this evil from his court, his Empire and his heart. Fear needed to change camps.

He sounded a first warning against their errant behavior in reprisal to a vile practice they had adopted. The emirs had taken the habit of bringing their weapons and armed guards into the mosque when they went to perform the ritual prayers. To carry arms in the holy precinct of a mosque was an intolerable and defiant insult to the words of peace contained in the verses of Qur'an.

The Sultan sent out a formal decree forbidding the practice of bearing arms in mosques, but it went unheeded. He found it thus necessary to publically punish several defiant emirs who continued the custom. Humiliated and enraged by these whippings, the emirs once again began to vocalize their enmity for the Sultan, swaying more and more men over to their side. Yet they failed to realize that by continuing to flagrantly defy the decree, they were giving the Sultan the pretext he needed to take the final step to redress the situation.

When men loyal to him informed the Sultan that there were continued acts of insubordination and renewed plotting against him, he knew that the time had come for him to put his own bold plot into action. He had passed many sleepless nights since that October banquet, and long were the hours he had to prepare the punishment plan he was now ready to put into effect.

The Sultan planned to host a feast for the emirs at the Devlethane palace in the center of Kayseri, the likes of which had never been seen. He would invite the emirs from all corners of the Kingdom to come, telling them that he wanted to host a special celebration in honor of Zeyneddin Bashara for the opening of the newly-completed Alaeddin Mosque in Niğde. This emir had been assigned the duty to construct this mosque several years previously, and had carried out his orders to perfection. The mosque was a masterpiece, and the first prayers had been led in it that very week. The Sultan also told the emirs that he would be rewarding them for their building efforts by attributing a higher tax percentage for their lands. The sweet bait of the palace setting on the evening of a full moon in June, a fine banquet, and the anticipation of the announcement of an increase in their annual earnings was too appealing for any of the emirs to resist.

The Sultan informed his trusted emirs Komnenos, Hokkabaz and Mubarizeddin Isa of their role in his master plan.

"Komnenos, once the emirs have all arrived, you will ensure that the garden walls of the palace are encircled with your armed soldiers. Mubarizeddin Isa, as my Head of the Royal Guard, you will make sure that my personal servants will stand guard outside the palace with their weapons. Emir Mubarizeddin Behramshah, in his role of official Organizer of Receptions and Audiences, will then enter and escort the emirs into the main banquet hall of the palace, as he does each and every time I host an event. Nothing will appear to be out of the ordinary. Once all the emirs have entered, the palace guards will firmly shut the doors and I will give instructions that no one is to enter or leave the rooms of the Devlethane."

The Sultan paused and lowered his voice before continuing to inform them of his plan.

"Servants will bring out dinner, one sumptuous dish after another. The emirs will be so taken with the food and the celebration of the good fortune of the Emir Zeyneddin Bashara and his mosque that all of their inhibitions will fall. Yet, after several hours, they will tire and want to go home to sleep. As each one steps out of the main banquet hall to head for the entrance door of the palace, my armed guards will seize them and put them up in an adjoining room. Once they have all drifted out and are locked up in that room, I will put the next step of my plan into action."

Finally, the day of retribution arrived. The night sky was silvery and luminous from the beams of the strong June moon, but the rays in the Sultan's heart shone black. After the night prayer had been called, the emirs began to arrive at the Sultan's palace for their highly-anticipated evening of entertainment and feasting. As planned, Komnenos kept watch under the garden walls of the palace together with several trusted armed guards.

The emirs entered and took their places on the plump cushions spread out on the luxurious carpets which had been laid out in the room. Adjusting themselves in a comfortable cross-legged position, they settled in for an evening of robust celebration. The food service began and plate after plate of fine foods appeared: yogurt soup, kebabs tender as a maiden's kiss, freshly-baked tandir bread, and freshly-picked June apricots soaked in sugar syrup. The *saz* players started to enchant the men with their songs and virtuosity.

Meanwhile, Emir Mubarizeddin Isa, together with his brothers and guards, made sure that all the doors of the palace were firmly sealed.

At one point late in the night, Seyfeddin Ayaba could not hold up his head any longer and told the Sultan that he needed to leave the feast and go home to bed. As Mubarizeddin Isa escorted him out, he motioned to him to enter the other room first before leaving, but Ayaba refused, not understanding why it was necessary to pass through that room to get to the front entrance.

Mubarizeddin Isa insisted, and taking him by the arm, spoke slowly into his ear. "When I was walking the other day with the Sultan in the palace gardens, he turned to me and said, 'What a shame it will be to cut these old trees down and plant new ones in their place, but this is what my gardeners are telling me that I must do. They advise me that even if I do not want to harm them, sometimes drastic action must be taken to allow for fresh growth. They tell me that it would be better to remove them and plant newer, healthier trees in their place. If I do not do this, my palace gardens risk falling into a disgraceful state, and we wouldn't want that, would we? So now I must cut down these old trees which are robbing the sun and nutrients from the other trees in the forest and hindering their growth. I must prepare my hatchet for action.' Yes, my emir Ayaba, that is exactly what the Sultan said to me."

Ayaba was too tired to understand the parable, and followed Mubarizeddin Isa into the room. Next, it was Zeyneddin Bashara's turn to come outside of the banquet hall. He, too, was locked in the same room along with Ayaba. One by one as they left the banquet, the emirs were put by the guards in the same room as the others. Towards dawn, all had been locked up, and Hokkabaz returned to the Sultan and said, "May your Sultanship be blessed. All has been carried out as you wished: we now turn the plan over to your hands."

The emirs were held in the room for a long time, too tired to understand what was happening to them. The Palace guards made them comfortable and reassured them that the Sultan wanted them to rest before they returned to their wives and homes. Finally, towards mid-morning, the doors were opened and they were released from the Sultan's Palace.

Yet when they returned to their homes, the emirs found to their great astonishment that their doors were barricaded by the Sultan's guards. They soon learned that all their property and fortunes had been inventoried on paper, and that their doors had been sealed shut. Deputies had been appointed to their estates, and had distributed all their possessions and the deeds to their houses to their slaves. With no bloodshed, the Sultan had taken his revenge: the former force of the emirs was now rendered meaningless by stripping them of their wealth.

Most of the bewildered and out-maneuvered emirs knew that there was nothing they could do to reverse this situation. However, the ever-enraged Emir

Seyfeddin Ayaba and several others refused to allow the Sultan to rob him of their possessions, and persisted in spreading poisonous venom about him.

This time, the retaliation of the Sultan was swift, decisive and merciless. He had given them the chance to amend their ways and they had refused to heed it. Orders were given to the henchman. They brought Emir Ayaba to the tower of the castle and cut off his head. At the same time his wayward soul lifted to the gardens of heaven like a bird, the heaviness on the chest of the Sultan floated into the air above the city.

The revenge of the Sultan would not stop with the removal of just one traitor, and he vowed to eradicate this hatred against him from the other miscreants once and for all. Zeyneddin Bashara was locked up without food in a fortress cell until he ate his own flesh from hunger, before meeting the same fate as Seyfeddin Ayaba. Mubarizeddin Behramshah was sent with his servant to be locked up in the Zamando fortress before he, too, was executed by the Sultan.

From this day forward, the lesson had been taught, and its moral learned. From the emirs, servants, commanders, and soldiers down to slaves, all knew that no one could escape their duty to the throne of the Seljuk Empire. The past vileness of conduct was remedied and vanity was banished. Those who gave goodness were shown the way to the stars, and their goblets were always filled with clear and good water. With the safety of his throne now secured, the Sultan was at last able to sleep at night.

The Sultan's garden had been cleared. Twenty-three rotten trees had been chopped down. Fear had at last changed camps.

Chapter 20

Rose Petals and Thorns

Time holds no relevance for lovers, who measure passing time with glances instead of seconds, kisses instead of minutes, embraces instead of hours and children instead of years. The next few years were peaceful for the royal couple, quiet in the way God intended. Happiness and delight blended into an ever-evolving turn of the seasons for Alaeddin and Mahperi, and they kept time in ways that were not measurable by the sand of the hourglass or the rays of a sundial. Life for the royal couple continued to glow in the silver light of the full moon with each month that passed. Their little son grew, and they looked forward to having more blessings in the future.

Mahperi could still not get enough of her husband, who seemed to her to become more handsome with each day that passed. His sharp nose and broad cheekbones came from his Turkmen fathers, while his fair skin and height were gifts from his Byzantine mother. Yet those eyes, blue as sapphires, were his and his alone. Only Alaeddin could have made them: that color, the light that shone from behind them, the clarity and intensity of their beam – only he could have made that happen. As Alaeddin continued to build his kingdom, Mahperi continued to build her life at his side, on the path lit by the beam of those blue eyes. Their passion endured, and each one took great strength in the love and devotion they gave each other.

She lived days of happiness. Her Turkish became fluent, and now she could even write poems in it. She could impose her will and style upon the household, her advice was heeded by the Sultan, and her son toddled across the rooms of the palace. She felt loved by her Sultan, her court, her friend Hanife and her little boy.

Time holds no relevance for Sultans, who measure passing time with soldiers instead of seconds, battlefields instead of days, victories instead of months, and territories gained instead of years. The Sultan too, was ever grateful for his wife's support in everything he did, and was still as fascinated by those green eyes as the first time they had transfixed him. He became used to her strange accent, forgiving it since every word she spoke was in a miraculous voice, low and rich and velvety, unlike the chirping way most of the court women spoke. With Mahperi by his side, he felt that everything was possible, in his divan chambers, before his ministers, under his quilt, and on the battlefield before his enemies.

The Sultan now embarked on a series of military conquests, first securing a resounding victory at the Crimean port of Sudak on the Black Sea. This important trading center had been seized by the Mongols, a scourge of invaders now pouring in from the Far East. Alaeddin sent an expedition to the area, with a fleet commanded by his trusted Emir Husameddin Choban of Kastamonu. The able military veteran was able to take the city back from the Mongols, and then stayed onsite and administered the entire region for the Sultan, building a mosque and a garrison to ensure their position. New trade possibilities with the north now opened up, and the Seljuk Empire grew richer in goods with each passing day.

The Sultan also sought to extend his territory eastward from Alaiye, along the inhospitable Mediterranean coast. He soon extended Seljuk control as far east as Silifke, which was held by the Knights Hospitallers of St. John under the Armenian suzerainty of King Hethoum. Losing this city was a humiliation to the arrogant King Hethoum. Now a vassal of the Seljuks, Hethoum was obliged to pay indemnities to Alaeddin, who also demanded that he supply the Sultan with troops and even to mint coins for his realm bearing the name of *"Al-Sultan-al-Mu'azzam"* – the greatest Sultan. The Seljuk Empire grew richer in territory with each passing day.

The Sultan continued to build as well, and the empire was now sprinkled with magnificent constructions. In the southern tier of his empire, Alaeddin fortified the walls of Alaiye and Antalya and built hunting pavilions at Gulefşen, Sedre, and Kemer. The city of Mahperi rose to even higher splendor, with the completion of the projects he had dreamed about when he first took the city. The Red Tower and an arsenal now dominated the harbor, and an impressive chicane entry gate to the Seljuk city was added half-way up the hill, leading to the new Ahmedik Citadel and Castle at the very top of the hill, built next to the old Byzantine church that Mahperi attended as a child. In the east of his Empire, the city walls of Kayseri were fortified, and enhanced with the impressive Arrow Tower, built at the entrance to the inner city. The walls of Sivas were rebuilt as well, and a magnificent Great Mosque now rose near the apricot orchards of Malatya. In his capital city of Konya, small neighborhood mosques continued to sprout on every corner, and hans multiplied on the roads leading to the capital city. On the shores of the nearby Lake Eğridir, the Emir Ertokush built for him an impressive han and medrese. The Seljuk Empire grew richer in stones with each passing day.

All seemed to be going so well for the Kingdom, in love, territory gained and in building projects, and yet Mahperi sensed a tension pulsing underneath the obvious successes of her husband. Although the terrible episode with the emirs was behind them, the memory of the incident still fouled the air. Mahperi felt a contentious atmosphere every time she was in the presence of Köpek, and she avoided him whenever possible. The jealous Köpek could not bear the thought that a woman could have as much influence on the Sultan as she, and sought to denigrate her in his eyes at every opportunity.

☪ ☪ ☪

Although Mahperi felt the cold-blooded stares of Köpek upon her whenever she was in his company, she never dared to speak of it with her husband who held him in such esteem. The only person she could confide in was Hanife.

"I cannot believe he was so rude to me when we met to talk about the plans for the Kayseri Palace! And I don't like the way he looks at me, analyzing every move I make."

"Yes, I have heard that he can be very strange," replied Hanife. "My mother knew him when she worked in the palace as a young woman...."

"She did? What was he like then?" Mahperi asked, intrigued that there was a connection between them.

"Oh, I can't remember much, but please, just ignore him!" replied Hanife sharply, abruptly turning away from Mahperi to return to her knotting at the loom. Yet Mahperi noticed that her hands were shaking and that the cutting knife fell from her grip.

☪ ☪ ☪

One day when the Sultan and his Superintendent of Works were out riding to supervise the building of a new mosque in the city, Köpek leaned over to the Sultan. "My Sultan, please accept this counsel I give you with charity. I believe you are lending your wife too much importance. Do not forget she is not one of us. A woman is nothing but an empty vessel, and it is you who are the master – she lives in your shadow and should be kept in her place! It is not for her to suggest things for you to do. Turquoise tiles indeed! I also think you need to keep a closer rein on her; for I often see her talking with merchants in the bazaar as if she were a simple servant girl on an errand, and I have seen her on many occasions coming out of the Armenian Orthodox church in the southern part of the city. You must discourage this attachment she has to her faith; it is not good for a queen to be a Christian. She must become a Muslim!"

The Sultan roared in laughter. "My Queen, an empty vessel? You and I both should have a head like hers on our shoulders, my vizier! As for becoming a Muslim, I cannot force her to do that. That will come in time or it will not, so we must be patient. I will allow her total freedom to keep her faith if she wants to. I remind you, again, that my own mother was a Christian and my father's mother was a Christian, and so there is more Christian blood flowing in my veins than there is Muslim! She can pray in the churches of Konya, she can pray in her room, she can pray inside of her soul: that is her liberty, and we must be tolerant of her as we are of all the citizens of our empire. If Islam is truly the finest of all faiths, it will win converts from all the religions of the world without any difficulty. The decision of one's relationship to God cannot be mandated like a law," he admonished Köpek. Wishing to change the subject, he pointed to the building in front of them. "Now, my Superintendent of Works, what do you think about that wall going up over there by that medrese? It seems to be off-plumb, wouldn't you say?"

☪ ☪ ☪

Mahperi however had more troubling concerns than her contentious relationship with Köpek. Despite their happiness, Alaeddin had seriously changed since the discovery of the plot against him by his emirs, and it was affecting his relationships with all those around him, including her.

His outlook on life had altered; he became moody and withdrawn, and even with her, his attitude was different. His thoughts darted about his head like swooping birds at sunset; only at nightfall, these thoughts never found a roost. He slept little, and became temperamental in character, cruel one minute and loving the next. He was unsatisfied and unsettled, and looked fiercely at the four corners of the room as if he saw the four compass points of his kingdom beyond. Something had broken inside of him and his trust of everything around him seemed shattered.

Also troubling to Mahperi was the fact that the Sultan showed little interest in his child, and Mahperi could not understand why he distanced himself from the young Giyaseddin. She herself worried about the little one, for the toddler seemed secretive and quiet, somewhat too sad for a little boy of three years old. He didn't play on his own, invent games, hold imaginary conversations with his playthings, or sing along with her rhymes. He always waited for others to take the lead or for her to toss him a ball to chase. He didn't run up and down the palace stairs or investigate forbidden closets. He laughed rarely, even when butterflies flew by him or when her pet cat patted his nose with her paw. Mahperi often saw the character of her gentle father in her boy, but could not find the dynamic traits of his Sultan father in him anywhere. All in all, he was a quiet and passive child, and she would need to work hard to groom him into the fine young man destined to become a Sultan. For it would be this boy, this shy, little Giyaseddin Keyhüsrev, named for his warrior Sultan grandfather, who would one day step onto the throne of the Seljuks and take the scepter and the shimmering crown of an equally golden empire. She realized that her son was going to need much encouragement from her and those around him in order to develop his capacities. This is my true destiny, she thought. I am here to raise a Sultan to be the equal of his father, to be able to step into his shoes to lead the kingdom to even greater heights.

☪ ☪ ☪

The Sultan ignored his son, perhaps, but he adored his leopard Ruby, and lavished every attention upon her. He had the finest jeweler of Konya craft a collar of precious rubies for her neck. He now led her by a golden chain attached to this collar wherever they went, and the sleek beast accompanied the Sultan on his trips and campaigns, in her own crafted silver cage set atop a fine stallion. Night Shining White and the spotted beast became synonymous with the Sultan, recognizable by all. The Sultan fed her by hand himself, and lavished more love on this beast than he did on his very own son, from whom he remained strangely detached.

A special bond, far stronger than any golden chain and more precious than a ruby collar linked these two, for the beast knew she owed her life to him, and the Sultan knew that this beast would never betray him, would never disappoint him, and would never fail to inspire him. Despite her claws and her jaws, she was, in his eyes, the most trusted member of his entourage. As a conqueror of adversity, she had become the symbol of his destiny, and as long as she was by his side, he would be the Greatest of all Sultans.

Chapter 21

Destiny in the East

It was now the year 1225, and the Sultan rested in his rooms one bright spring morning with Mahperi enjoying the soft air of the season. The Sultan startled Mahperi with a surprising question.

"Do you think, my love, that you will offer me more sons? I would like Giyaseddin to have a little brother, which may seem odd in view of the difficulties that I have known with my own brothers. As you know, I have sent my younger brother Keyferidun away so that he will not pose a threat to my throne. But I have never spoken to you much about my other brother Izzeddin."

The Sultan drew a deep breath before continuing. Mahperi could tell that this was a difficult subject for him to discuss.

"After my father's death, my brother Izzeddin was selected to succeed him as Sultan. I could not bear the thought that my father's sultanate would pass to him. I was jealous of him, of course, but I also believed that Izzeddin did not have my force of character, for all he seemed to care about was reading poems! So I decided to attempt to seize the throne for myself. I marched to Ankara to do battle with my brother, but after almost two years of fighting, he defeated me."

Mahperi could not imagine anyone defeating her sultan, and now began to understand some of the motivations that drove him so intently to win.

"So I had to bury my perhaps premature ambition and accept that my brother had won the throne. He locked me up in a fortress near Malatya to be confined there for the rest of my life. But fate decided otherwise, for on his march south to fight the Ayyubids, Izzeddin fell ill near Malatya, coughed up blood and suddenly died. With the help of my emirs and supporters, I was released and crowned the next Sultan. This is a sad story Mahperi, sad because brothers should not fight brothers, for it endangers the well-being of the State."

The Sultan rose and went over to the window and looked down at the city below for a long time, before turning back to face her. "Such serious rambling about the business of brothers! But I am feeling most serious these past days. Are you feeling strong this morning, my love? I hope so, for I have some very considerable news to announce to you."

Mahperi's eyes grew wide at the sternness of his tone.

"My Queen, I will be leaving Konya soon to embark on a series of military campaigns in the east. There are many issues to remediate, and they can only be taken care of on the fields of battle. I need to find out if I can expand our territory and conquer new peoples for the Seljuk Empire. My challenges are many, for on all four compass points there are enemies to my Kingdom!"

"Who are all these enemies, my Sultan?" Mahperi asked, for she was totally unaware of the external threats to her husband's empire.

"Well, to start, your Armenian people in Cilicia continue to impede our progress. They are robbing merchants along the coast roads and it has been necessary to send out troops against them. Other Christians to the north, the Latins and Byzantines, are always restive and bristle under our rule, and are easily stirred up by the neighboring Georgians who interfere in their matters."

The Sultan paused before continuing.

"But my greatest dream for this campaign involves extending my influence in upper Mesopotamia and northern Syria, and the Artukid Dynasty is the key to my plan. They wish to become a kingdom entirely independent from the Ayyubids, who control most of the area. I want to step in and settle these political intrigues to my advantage. With God's help and my superior troops, I am sure I will be able to seize all of the Artukid territory for myself!"

Mahperi saw the familiar glint in his eyes when he began to speak of victories. His hunger for them was unending!

"Alas, my lovely, my rivals are not just to the north and south, they are within as well! There are several smaller Turkmen dynasties here in Anatolian territory that need to be held in check as well. I will not tolerate such affronts to my power!"

The Sultan became even more solemn. "But above all others, I fear the most important of all our enemies will be the Mongols. The brutal warriors of Genghis Khan have already swept from China into Persia, and their swarm westward has pushed many people to flee in terror. Many of the artists, poets and craftsmen that are currently building our empire have fled to our lands seeking refuge from them. I do not know if I will ever meet his armies on the battlefield, but for the moment, I am ensuring that my cities are fortified against their attack. Our world, our holy Muslim world as we know it, has never seen such a vicious foe – the Crusaders are nothing next to these Mongols. These invaders destroy any city they encounter, massacre men, rape women, sack mosques, burn the Qur'an and take children into slavery. Never have we been subjected to such a threat."

He shuddered for a second before continuing.

"And so you see, Mahperi, the list is long of enemies I have in front of me. It is my duty to continue the vision of my ancestors, and so I must embark on this campaign in the East. I do not know how long I will be gone, but it will be several years at least. I do not know how many enemies I will vanquish, but I do know I will be victorious. I want to make my lands as large as the canopy of God over these plains. God walks by my side. I know it. I feel Him there. He is on my shoulder and I hear His words in my ear. He is the one who teaches me to see beyond the horizon, the one who tells me what riches lie there, to pray for the next sunrise to show my love for His glory."

Gone several years! How would she be able to live without him at her side? Mahperi was stunned at the thought of him being away so long, but knew it was hopeless to stand in the way of the ambition of this man, who never was satisfied with his successes. Perhaps there, on those battlefields of the East, he would find the resolution to the driving ambition that haunted his soul. She tried to put on a brave face, for she knew he was depending on her support.

"My Sultan, I wish you triumph on every battlefield and I will wait here for you to return victorious. But.....if you will allow me, may I say a few things?"

"Certainly," he replied, "I always appreciate what you have to say to me."

"Does it not seem that you are perhaps attacking too many fronts and too many enemies all at the same time? The broader your frontiers, the harder it will be for you to hold them. Instead of seeking to gain territory for territory's sake, perhaps it would be more beneficial for you to focus on just one area at a time, don't you think? Do not be in a hurry to have all victories come to you at once. But you will succeed, of that I am certain my Sultan, and your name will be remembered for ten thousand years."

Although the Sultan was taken aback by her forward remarks, he said nothing, for he knew that every piece of advice she gave him was always sound.

☪ ☪ ☪

The preparations were soon completed for the Sultan's departure for Kayseri, where he would train his troops all through the spring before heading eastwards. He not only took his soldiers and their mounts, but his own imam, muezzins, Qur'an readers and viziers, secretaries, finance officers, butchers, cooks, veterinarians, doctors and all the hundreds of support staff that were needed to maintain the army. The Sultan's official seals were placed in a waterproof case by his postal service, so that he could stamp his letters from the front to be returned by courier to Konya from any point in the empire. Ruby too, was placed in her cage on the horse immediately behind Night Shining White.

At last the day of departure arrived. As Mahperi stood on the terrace of the palace to watch the departing caravan of troops and courtiers, she focused on her toddler son wiggling impatiently in her arms so that she would not lose control of her bravery. She dared not even think that he would not return to her: she could not bear to imagine that this lion of a man could be killed on the battlefield like his father. No, he would return to her, happy and healthy and loving. Clouds of dust from the hooves and the carts of the procession carried skywards all the emotions she was feeling: excitement for the Sultan's campaign, sorrow that he was leaving her, apprehension for his successes and dread that he would meet harm. One thing was certain in her mind though: He would return truly worthy of wearing that crimson mantle he wore on their wedding day, the one with the gold writing on the hem: *Al-Sultan-al-mu'azzam*, the Greatest Sultan indeed!

Mahperi watched as the bright beacon of the coat of Night Shining White faded into the distance, and when the white horse dipped out of sight over the horizon, her tears spilled forth.

"Good luck, my Sultan!" she shouted aloud to the horizon. "May God's blessings ride with you, and may you feel my heart beating inside of yours. May my love for you give you the force of 10,000 troops!"

Chapter 22
Gone Too Long

Dear beloved husband, Sultan of Two Seas and of my heart,

May God bless the eyes that read this letter and give your heart grace and your arms the strength to confront your enemies.

You have been gone so long that each day becomes a burden more difficult to bear. I long for the day when you will return to us, victorious on the battlefield, with your hopes and aspirations for the Empire satisfied. I know you are achieving great successes on the various fronts of the East, for I receive news from the overland couriers that bring your sealed reports back to Konya. How my heart skips a beat when I see that red wax on the roll, knowing that your fingers have touched it! Your kingdom is now growing and becoming more powerful with each fortress and city you seize.

The people of Konya rejoice with enthusiasm in the news of your victories. They are proud to belong to an Empire that is growing stronger with each day. The lectures in the medreses continue to attract more disciples and our markets are overflowing with goods arriving from the roads that link us to the four corners of the globe. Poets sing the praises of your city. All is well in your court: your ministers work hard; your emirs have understood that their role is to serve. Your Konya kingdom is flourishing.

Yes, I hear that all is success on your fronts. I have also learned that the horrible villain Genghis Khan has died, and that his empire has now been split into four parts, each with its own leader. I pray that his sons and grandsons are not the violent men that he was. May God protect us from their wrath!

I have also heard that you have been victorious in your plans against the Ayyubids, and that you and Al-Ashraf defeated the Artukid forces and have now taken possession of the right bank of the middle Euphrates: Hasankeyf and the fortresses of Adiyaman, Kahta and Çemişkezek are now yours. These are outstanding victories that will inscribe your name in history for all times! You will provide stability in the towns and fields of your empire for future generations to come.

Yet none of this is as exciting to me as will be the day I hear the news that you are on your way home to Konya. It has been more than two long years now that I have been waiting for it, and each day is more difficult to bear.

I am sorry to tell you some unfortunate news. My father passed away this month. I will be forever grateful to you for having offered him a dignified life after losing Kalonoros. I pray for his soul each day and I am certain that he is now sitting peacefully in the Upper Room with all the saints. Our life certainly has been a rich one since that day he opened the castle door to admit you into the city on top of the mountain of Kalonoros. I used to feel that the sea was my home, the place that always welcomed and comforted me. But now, these plains, with their billowing waves of hot air make me feel more vibrant and nurtured than I ever dreamed possible. My father's death has taught me this lesson: my destiny is now here, on these plains with you.

Your little son grows stronger each day; he is now a fine boy of four years. He is responding well to the lessons that his tutors are starting to give him. I take him on my rides through the city and he enjoys pointing to all the animals and statues that he sees on the walls, with the same glee that I did when I first came here. He is a quiet boy, but takes instruction well. Your daughter Seljuka, born soon after your departure, is growing each day as well. She is as pretty as a dancing poppy in the fields, and has the fair coloring of your mother. I am certain that both of your children will be very happy when their father returns to them.

As will I. My Sultan, I miss you terribly. You are the dewdrop of love on my lip, and I carry your taste like a sip of the sweetest sherbet. Your skin is the heat of my soul. I manage to keep myself very busy during the day with activities at the court, the children, my studies of the Persian poetry and Arabic literature, of which I have become adept, you will be glad to see, and my visits to the workshops of Hanife. But nights are a different matter. When the candles are extinguished and I am alone in my room, my thoughts turn to you. I ache to feel you lying next to me, I long to feel the touch of your long fingers and I can think of nothing but the memory of your sweet kisses. On the nights when there is a full moon, I set my wedding carpet next to the window and lie on it, feeling those silver rays upon me and remembering how the moonlight shone upon us on the very first night when we....

"The Sultan is returning!" bellowed out a palace page as he raced through the rooms of the palace, shouting as loudly as he could for all to hear. "He has just passed through the Larende gate and is on his way up the main road! He will be here in minutes! Quick, everyone, prepare for his arrival!"

Mahperi was stunned, and dropped the pen from her hand. How could this be possible? Her husband was returning to her! Her heart pounding, she rushed to the window to see if she could catch a glimpse of his caravan. How was it that she had not been told he was coming? Surely, his couriers would have informed the palace officials of his pending arrival, in order to prepare the ceremonial feast in honor of his return! Why had she not been told? This made no sense! But who cares for feasts and ceremonies, he is here, now home! Her thoughts raced frantically through her mind, dazed by the excitement of his return. He would be in her arms tonight! So much to do! Where should she start?

Suddenly, she heard the crowd on the street raise a loud cheer, and she knew the Sultan was not far away now. No time to worry about her dress or jewels, no time to fetch the children from the nursery. She raced to the top of the terrace of the palace to view his arrival from the distance and to make sure that he saw that she was there, waving to welcome him home.

Clouds of dust rose from the hooves of his retinue which stretched as far as she could see, just as it had two years ago when he left on the campaigns to the East. She caught a glimpse of his gleaming horse before she could even see the Sultan: that Night Shining White, ever like a comet in the skies! Closer and closer they came, and finally he came into focus, waiving his scepter to the crowds that came running from all directions to greet him. Even from the distance she could tell that he had lost weight and that his body seemed even leaner and harder, but his posture atop that horse seemed more firmly resolute than ever. Her heart started to thump in her chest and tremors shook her body from this unexpected moment of happiness. He was safe! He was home!

Because she was so intently focused on looking at his face and because her eyes were blurred by her tears, she did not notice the horse riding alongside the Sultan. It was a striking red stallion, smaller and more compact than Night Shining White, and was surrounded by a group of horses bearing banners and streamers of colors she did not recognize. Perhaps these are the prisoners of war, thought Mahperi, but why would they be next to the Sultan? She now discerned a figure in black sitting atop the roan horse. When she squinted her eyes to see better, Mahperi was able to see that the figure was a veiled woman, dressed in the Arabic style, with her long, black robes fluttering behind her as she trotted next to Alaeddin. Directly to her rear rode an entire army of animals wearing the same colors: some fifty mules, a hundred Bactrian camels and over three hundred dromedaries, all carrying large chests and servant girls on their backs. Drums and horns were beating madly. Whatever is all of this, Mahperi wondered. The people were cheering frantically as they passed in front of them, adding to her confusion.

Then she saw her beloved husband's face break out into a radiant smile and he tossed his head back in laughter; the very same gesture that stole her heart the first time she caught a glimpse of him outside that gate at Kalonoros. Only this bright smile was shining on the veiled woman, not in the direction of the palace. When she saw him reach over and take her hand in his and bring it to his lips for a kiss, everything became clear to her in a blinding flash – this was no prisoner of war. Now she understood the reason for the secrecy of his return. There was now another woman at his side. He was parading a new Queen down the streets of Konya; a new queen destined to take her place in the palace on the hill and in the palace of his heart, the places that Mahperi held dear with all her life.

The half-finished letter in her hand now fluttered to the ground, its words of tenderness blowing off the pages like snowflakes in a storm, melting into nothingness.

PART 2

EMPIRE RISING

1227-1237

"My warrior, I shall wait a year for you,
If you come not in a year I shall wait two,
If you come not in two, I shall wait three then four.
If you come not in four, I shall wait five then six.
I shall pitch a tent where six roads meet,
I shall ask news of every traveler.
Whoever brings good news I shall give him horses and raiment,
I shall clothe him in caftans.
Whoever brings evil news I shall cut off his head.
I shall not let a male fly settle on me;
Give me my heart's desire, take your heart's desire,
Then go, my warrior."

- from the Book of Dede Korkut

It was now the time of the summer of the Seljuk Empire, when Anatolia took on its face for all eternity.

Buildings of grandeur dotted the cities of the Empire like stars in the constellations; up from the steppes rose medreses and mosques and bridges and hospitals. The roads of the Empire sparkled with new caravansarais. I, the great caravansarai at Pazar, was destined to join their ranks one day, there to shine as one of the greatest ever built.

It was a fine time for growth perhaps, but oh, this was a sad time for my Lady! How could a woman this pure, this generous, and this loving be dealt such a painful blow from the hand of the one person she venerated above all others; the one to whom she had given everything? Yet I am ashamed to selfishly say that I owe everything to this agony of hers. If she had not been challenged, would she ever have searched for something more solid than human devotion to keep her anchored in life?

My Lady held her head high throughout it all. Gone were the carefree, almond-blossomed days of a young girl in love with a handsome sovereign with piercing blue eyes. She now became a woman determined to survive and endure, for her children, for her kingdom, for her title, for her still-honored love, for her faith, and above all, for her dignity.

Yet, she paid heavily for this determination to survive – and I can tell you that the stones she would use in time to build my high walls were the same that were destined to come crashing down upon her head, pushed over the edge by the hands of jealousy and deceit….

Yes, in this summer of the Seljuk Empire, her ever-beloved Alaeddin Keykubad led the way, and she stood right by his side. Yet, for all I know, was it not perhaps she who led the way for him to follow?

Chapter 23

Misery from Malatya

A hand touched Mahperi's shoulder and a low voice spoke gently into her left ear. Since her spinning head was thundering as loudly as the jubilant pandemonium on the streets below, she had not noticed that someone had entered the room and was now standing behind her.

A dazed Mahperi turned around and through the wall of tears in her eyes, she could distinguish the large figure of the Vizier Jelaleddin Karatay. It was rare that she had any interaction with this senior minister, and she immediately knew that if he had been sent to speak with her, the message had to be a serious one.

"Come, Queen Mahperi Hatun, please sit down here, you need to rest," he said, motioning for her servants to adjust the cushions.

Karatay was a tall and husky man, whose imposing physique contrasted with his low and soft voice. His Turkish had a distinctive accent which gave away his Greek origins, but his eloquence was always as crystal-clear as his logic. When he spoke, his words were direct and precise, with never a stray compliment or wasted breath cluttering his message – so unlike many of the other flowery-tongued sycophant viziers that surrounded the Sultan. Alaeddin Keykubad counted on his sincerity for handling the most important matters at court, and this pious and moral man had risen to become the most respected spokesperson in the Empire.

A page brought a pitcher of water and two goblets and set the tray in front of them. Mahperi now realized that preparations had been laid out well ahead of time for her to learn of the situation in a carefully-orchestrated manner.

"My Sultana, you have just seen that your husband the Sultan has returned to Konya. We must thank God that he has returned safely to us. His victories on the fields of battle and in the court divans of his adversaries have been peerless, and he has managed to expand our territories significantly. Alaeddin Keykubad, the World-Renowned and Father of Conquests, will definitely be remembered as the most illustrious of all the Seljuk Sultans if he continues on this path of glorious triumphs!"

The Minister Karatay paused, as the most difficult part of his message was now upon him. It pained him to deliver it, for he had great respect for the lovely and intelligent Queen: she, too, was a foreigner like he was, but above that, he especially appreciated her innate goodness and personal dignity.

"As you know, Sultana, your husband has always placed the needs of the Kingdom above everything else. You have witnessed his zeal for developing the infrastructure of his cities, his plans for expanding his territory, and the alliances he seeks to cultivate: all this has been done with a purposeful determination and much discussion with his counselors and ministers, of which, I am very honored to say, I am one. We speak often about the needs of the Empire and its people, and I can assure you that every decision he takes is one that is deliberately debated and considered in all aspects. He left on this extended campaign with several goals in mind, the most important being to resolve the conflicts between the Ayyubids of Syria and the Artukids of the Upper Mesopotamian region. On this campaign, he also became more aware of the increasing threat of the Mongol invasion. It became very obvious to him while he was away on this campaign that he needed to do everything possible to ensure that our part of the world is shored up against this Ocean of Malice coming from the East with increasing speed and force."

The avuncular Karatay took a deep breath and leaned his bulky frame closer to Mahperi.

"To this end, he believed that confirming dependable relations with the Ayyubids was the key element to this defense. We need them as solid allies in the war against the Mongols. With this political goal in mind, he sent a message through Emir Semsettin Altinapa to the Sultan Malik Adil of Damascus to request the hand of his daughter in marriage. Al-Malik is one of the most important of the Ayyubid leaders. By marrying his daughter, there could be no firmer proof of his intention for an alliance between our two peoples. This offer for the hand of his daughter Gaziye was accepted by Al-Malik, and the Sultan married the Arab Princess in Malatya a few months ago, on his return trip to Konya."

Karatay paused to let this last piece of information register with the Sultana before he continued.

"With this marriage, he has cleverly managed to both repair past strains and strengthen the relationship with the Ayyubid family, all the while constituting a formidable buffer against the onslaught of the Mongols, whom he fears will soon to be upon us. You must understand, Mahperi, that this marriage was carried out for the needs of crown and scepter, and the Sultan wishes you to understand that this was a necessary and well-weighed strategy for the best interests of the Kingdom. You also know, Mahperi, that the Islamic tradition allows a man to take several wives. Although this is very different than your Christian beliefs, you must understand that the Sultan has done nothing wrong here."

Karatay bowed his head and prayed to God to provide him the strength to now deliver the part of the message that was the most painful for him, for he knew to what point it would hurt the Sultana.

"Mahperi Hatun Hanim, please listen to me. I must tell you that this type of arrangement is often made between political families. You yourself saw how your father gave you as a bride to the Sultan in order to save his own life and that of the people of Kalonoros. Political alliances through marriages are a fact of life, and you must try to understand and accept this. But…" and it was here that the renowned eloquence of the vizier stumbled for a moment. "It appears that this is more than a political alliance. Just as the Sultan had the chance to fall in love with you, it would appear that he has done the same with Gaziye Hanim. They spend much time together."

Her Sultan shares his time with someone else? This could not be possible! Her head spun so quickly now that she felt ill to her stomach.

"A necessary arrangement? Is that how he has considered his life with me? No, you are wrong, Vizier Karatay, this cannot be true! It is impossible that he could love another! It just cannot be so! We share our hearts, our kingdom, our son is the heir, and we are building this Kingdom together! There is no place for her here!" Mahperi's green eyes flashed with an intensity that frightened Karatay.

The wise Vizier was used to negotiating thorny diplomatic waters, but this situation was the most challenging he ever had to broker.

"My Sultana, please be calm. I know this is a difficult piece of news for you to hear, much less accept, but accept it you must. She is now a part of our lives here at the court. I am counting on you to be gracious to her, to honor the decision of your Sultan husband, and to try and work out with him a reasonable arrangement so that all of you can live together. May I remind you that we are all in the service of the Sultan and go but for the grace of his command, and that we must honor that command. Remember, too, that I wish to be your ally, and will work with you to ease this situation as much as I can. I know you are a strong and wise woman. I also know that the Sultan needs you in his life. Do not despair. All is not lost with him. You will continue to be a part of his life, and he will continue to love and honor you. Whatever happens, we both must remember that our role is to keep the Sultan as anchored as possible. The well-being of our people depends on us as much as it does on the Sultan and his armies. Now, my Lady, hold your head high as you always have. You are a daughter of a Lord and the wife of a Sultan. You are a queen in every sense of the word. The Sultan will come to your chambers after a while to speak with you. He needs to bathe and rest from the voyage, and I think it would be best if a bit of time, perhaps several days, passes before you see him. I beg that you find in your soul the spirit to move forward and make the best of this situation. May God's grace shine upon you."

As he turned to leave the room, it was the great vizier's turn to be devastated. No arrow has ever entered a soldier with more piercing pain than the one I just shot at this innocent woman, he thought to himself. God please absolve me, provide me her forgiveness, pardon my trespasses and give me the strength to accept this torture I have just inflicted on such a pure victim. I pray that her sorrowed face will not haunt my dreams at night. Is this what my service to the Sultan should endure? Minister Karatay was not so certain, and his shuffled steps were slow to regain the palace throne room to inform the Sultan that his message had been delivered as requested.

Chapter 24
A Cold Quilt

The next two days were lost to Mahperi. Staring out from her window at the street below, she played over and over the scene she had seen there. She would turn from the window and look at her quilt on the other side of the room, shuddering at the thought that he loved another woman, and shared with her his dreams and his life. No, such a betrayal cannot be possible! He left me months ago with love in his eyes, our child in my belly, and now he has returned as if all that love never existed?

On the morning of the third day, she heard a familiar step behind her door, and soon it opened wide. The tall silhouette of the Sultan stood above her, looking down at her with a steady gaze.

"Peace be upon you, my turquoise Moon Queen, I am pleased to see you again. You are looking very well, and have grown more lovely in the months I was away, if such a thing could be possible. I have missed you greatly."

Mahperi raised her head and smiled at him, her anger forgotten. She had not imagined those tender words, he had said them! So this is all but a dream, he has not betrayed me after all! She patted the cushion next to him, urging him to sit next to her.

"Oh my Sultan, I have missed you so and longed for his day! I am so relieved that you have returned to me safely! Vizier Karatay came to speak with me about your marriage with the Arab princess, but I know it just cannot be possible that you love her as he says you do!" She threw her arms around him and hugged him fiercely.

It was then that she was given her answer, clearer than any explanation from the Vizier. The Sultan made no move to return her embrace, and slowly unwrapped her arms from around his neck. He then looked at her directly in the eyes, and began to speak in a soft voice.

"Mahperi, I have loved you these past few years with a passion I did not know was possible for me. You have given me not only your arms, but your wisdom, your encouragement and your kindness. I could not have accomplished any of the things I have done without knowing I had that support behind me. You have given me my first children. I have just seen our daughter Seljuka for the first time, and she is as beautiful as a flower! It is you who have helped me to become the Sultan of Sultans that the world now knows."

He paused and stared at his hands.

"Yet.... life changes and many aspects of our lives evolve in different ways, often beyond our will. I never thought it possible that I could even look at another woman, much less hold one in my arms, but that has now happened. I was gone too long – perhaps that was the mistake, for two years is a long time for a man to be alone. And yes, I was lonely, and at times frightened and in the need of comfort. It does not mean that what we shared was not precious to me or will not remain so, but as difficult as it must be for you to understand, I now love another woman at the same time as I love you. Our life together from this point on will not be the one we knew before. I must be frank with you, and I know that with your dignity, you will be able to find the strength to accept it."

She just stared at him, this husband who now seemed a total stranger.

"But this cannot be so! This is impossible! How do you expect me to live under the same roof with her? Will you take her to our Kalonoros in the winter? What will become of our children? Will she give orders at the court? How will the people of Konya know who is their Queen? Do you honestly think that I can accept this situation?" Mahperi's eyes grew frantic and her words raced together in a stream of recriminations.

"My Sultana, I know this is hard for you, but you must understand that I have taken another woman into our home, and I will share my affection with her. I do not take this responsibility to care for both of you lightly. It says in our Holy Qur'an in the Surat Nisa that it is very difficult to be just and fair between women. I will strive to overcome this difficulty, just as you must strive to be just and fair to Gaziye. I promise you, Mahperi, that you will be treated with the same respect and care as before. You must understand as well that I am the Sultan, with the mandate to do what is best for this Empire. This political marriage was as strategic move, just as I took you as a bride on that day in Kalonoros. Nothing, not even you, will stand in the way of my mission to forge this Kingdom. This is the world in which we live, here in the Seljuk Empire, and as my wife, you are a part of it. I am counting on you to be strong and merciful to both Gaziye and to my decision. I am not abandoning you. I still love you deeply, and will continue to honor you and your children. But I now share my love with another as well."

As the Sultan rose to leave, Mahperi grabbed the edge of his robe and yanked it hard.

"Not only have you broken more than my heart, but you have broken a sacred trust! In my faith, marriage is one of the seven sacraments that point to what is sacred for Christians. My religion, the one of the heart, believes that love is a holy covenant that cannot be broken. The idea that you would love another is impossible for me to accept! You have betrayed both me and my faith!"

"Christian laws do not rule here in the Seljuk Empire, Mahperi. Either you recognize Gaziye as a sister and live in harmony, or you don't, and you will spend your days avoiding her and living an intolerable existence. That decision is yours. Mine has been made. I will love and honor both of you. Forgive me if I have hurt you, for that was never my intention. There is no point in continuing this conversation. I love Gaziye, we share our nights together, and she is now with child."

Chapter 25

A Confrontation of Queens

For the next several days, Mahperi kept to her rooms to hide her swollen face, her red eyes and her shame. Her mind was as numb as her heart. Everything shut down for her; she lost track of time as the days melted into nights. All she could see in front of her was the image of her husband kissing that hand. All she could hear were his words: "*I love Gaziye and she is now with child*" bombarding her ears with a racket that drowned out the knocking of servants at her door, the muezzin's cry from the royal mosque on the hill, and her own choking sobs. Her heart squeezed tightly and pushed hard upon her stomach. Everything in her body ached, as if she had been beaten with a stick.

Finally, when she had cried every drop of moisture in her body's tissues, when she had spent every emotion in prayer, when the shock of his new marriage and the resulting denial on her part wore off, she realized that she had no choice but to accept this situation. Yes, Maryam, you will rise; you will hold your head high, just as you did when you stepped out into the sunshine from that castle door at Kalonoros on that final day of siege. Yet she would never understand how her husband could love another at the same time as he loved her – for her, such a thing would be impossible.

After seven days shut up in her dark room, she decided that she needed to bathe, eat, and see her children. She was a queen with responsibilities, and she must not let this Arab woman in black robes think she was victorious over her. She rose with determination and called for her maid. While waiting for her, she walked over to her window and threw open the wooden shutters, wishing it could be the blue waves of Kalonoros that would greet her eyes. However, when she looked down, it was not her peaceful sea she saw, but Alaeddin and the Black Raven walking across the palace gardens. She noted that this woman was very tiny, barely reaching up to the chest of the Sultan. A dainty little bird, she thought, not a huge pillar like I am. Is that what my Sultan prefers? Then she heard it for the first time: her high-pitched, strident voice cackling with chatter. They were speaking in Arabic together, and Mahperi was instantly jealous of the ease of communication the two of them shared. All those months at the beginning of their marriage when she had to use her eyes to show him what she was trying to say, all those months of frustration at having her emotions locked up inside of her for lack of the tool of speech – and this woman just steps in and chirps away to share the Sultan's thoughts. The Sultan's voice was different, too, when he spoke with her; it was faster and higher-pitched, as if it were trying to match hers. Mahperi then heard him giggle – yes, this Sultan of Sultans giggled like a nervous youth in the presence of a village girl. With Mahperi, he roared like the Lion, but with the Raven he babbled with carefree insouciance. Mahperi could not take her eyes off of them, even though it was even more painful than the first time she saw them together, for those high-pitched giggles now cut through her like shards of broken glass. He was totally infatuated with her; there was no doubt about that in her mind now.

☪ ☪ ☪

Later that afternoon, a familiar knock rapped at her door. The Sultan entered without waiting for her to respond, and came over and sat on the cushions against the wall. He was nervous, she could tell, twirling his prayer beads in his fingers and avoiding her glance. At last, he spoke.

"Mahperi, I am told that you are refusing to eat or leave this room. Please, this must stop. Such behavior is not serving your children, the Kingdom, or me any good. Please, show yourself to the court, for everyone is worried about your well-being."

"And you?" she snapped. "Are you in any way worried about my well-being?"

"Please, please, Mahperi, anger will not benefit you, and such conduct is not your manner in any case. Of course I am worried about you. But I am worried that your children are deprived of their mother more than anything else, so please, come out of this room. Do not act on your anger to their detriment. In any case, this situation cannot continue. You will have to meet Gaziye at one point and speak with her. Your paths will continually cross here in my court, and I cannot have animosity between you. I have arranged a meeting between the two of you, tomorrow. You will be there, you will be gracious, and you will show her what it is to be a Queen – my noble Moon Queen. Mahperi, I told you before: I expect the two of you to be sisters. Work out this problem or all will suffer – you most of all!" Alaeddin rose and abruptly left the room.

Yes, thought Mahperi, I will suffer most of all. Oh, my revered Sultan, you told me a lifetime ago that without me by your side you would be the moon without rays, a falcon without wings, a poet without verses, bread without salt, a farmer without rain, a saddle without stirrups. You told me you would starve and wither. Do you remember any of that? I want to stand by you always, to build the world we dreamed together, to look into the horizon at the back of your blue eyes, to love you in kingdoms that your men cannot even dream of conquering. How could this love have flown from your heart and gone to another? Yet my love for you will never leave my heart.

☪ ☪ ☪

The next day, the palace servants came to fetch Mahperi and escorted her down to the main divan room of the palace where she knew the encounter with Gaziye would take place. Waiting for her in the room was the Minister Jelaleddin Karatay.

"Good morning, my fine Lady," he smiled as she entered. "I am pleased that you have come here today. I have not slept well since I brought you that difficult piece of news, and I hope you will find it in your heart to forgive me, for I would rather tear a limb off my body than bring you sadness. Just as I had to obey the orders of my Master, so must you today."

Mahperi nodded to the Vizier. "Of course, I do not hold any anger towards you. I know I can always rely on your kindness, and I will work to overcome this painful situation as best I can."

At that moment, Köpek abruptly entered the room without knocking, and Mahperi shuddered at the sight of him. Of all the pestilence upon my head these past days, the last thing I need to see is that ugly face in front of me, she thought. Surely, I will collapse if he acts in any way discomforting to me.

"Well, well, here is our Queen, looking fine indeed! I hope that you will soon rejoin our conversations with the Sultan – how I have missed your acute observations and useful suggestions," he snickered.

Mahperi had forgotten how strident his high-pitched voice was, and she couldn't help but remark that the Raven had the same grating tone.

He continued without letting her respond. "I am glad that you have agreed to meet the new Queen and to show her the ways of the court. You will see that she is a fine woman – yes, a fine Muslim woman. I encouraged the Sultan to select her as a wife, for she is much prettier than the older sister that Al-Malik first wanted to offer him! This marriage will prove to be one of the shrewdest political alliances he will ever make! The powerful Ayyubid Kingdom, capable of restoring Holy Jerusalem to its rightful Muslim citizens by banishing the Frankish Crusaders – well, that little rock fiefdom of your father's is nothing in comparison to this powerhouse of a dynasty!"

Mahperi was stunned by his insulting words to her father's memory. So he had his hand in all of this, she thought, which does not surprise me at all. I should have suspected that he would have done everything possible to put a wedge between the Sultan and me. Steady, Mahperi, steady; keep your head and nerves.

The Vizier Karatay jumped in to cut off Köpek's hurtful prattle. For the first time, Mahperi noticed that the virtuous Minister cringed as well in the presence of the Dog, and that his distaste for him was as palpable as hers.

"Peace be upon you this morning, Köpek. I did not know we were going to have the pleasure of your company with us today," he queried, suspicious of his intentions.

"Oh yes, the new Queen invited me to attend this meeting. Why, she and I have become very close, actually. We rode together all the way back from the East to Konya. She is grateful for all the counsel I have given her, and she knows that she can count on me to be her devoted servant at all times."

Oh, this is much worse than I ever could have imagined, thought Mahperi. Now my enemy here at the court is in league with the woman who has stolen my husband from me! This is worse that the plague of locusts upon the Hebrews in Egypt that I read about in the Bible!

At that moment she heard her husband's familiar footfall on the tile of the hallway and in an instant he was in the room. He entered smiling, and close behind him followed the small form of the black-clad Raven. He greeted Karatay and Köpek, and then turned to Mahperi.

"My Queen Mahperi, I would like to present you to my second wife, with whom you will have the honor of sharing this court. Queen Gaziye, or as they say in Arabic, Melike Gaziye, is very pleased to meet you, and I know you will do everything possible, just as we discussed, to make her feel a part of this court. I am also convinced that the two of you will share much and that your children will grow up together and play in harmony. I leave you now to make acquaintance with each other."

He abruptly turned around, and, motioning to the two other men to do the same, he quickly fled the room, leaving the two queens alone together.

☪ ☪ ☪

The next few seconds were awkward for Mahperi, but fortunately, a servant came in with a tray of sherbet and set it down in front of them before scurrying out of the room. An uncomfortable moment of silence followed, but Mahperi knew that by being gracious, she could show, at least for one brief moment, that she was the stronger of the two of them. She motioned for Gaziye to sit on the cushions and poured for her some of the cool juice. The two of them sat quietly for a while, and then Gaziye raised her head and blurted out, "At last, I get to meet you! I have heard so much about you from both the Sultan and Köpek, and now I will see for myself if all that they have told me is true!"

Mahperi paused, closed her eyes and took in a deep breath. I need to step back and maintain my composure, she thought to herself. I need to remember my status here as queen, the dignity of my father's memory, and the spirit of generosity that I learned from the lessons of my faith. She who loses her composure will lose the battle, and that will not be me today! I will be kind to this woman. Alaeddin is right, for I will be the one most hurt in this. I will be generous and gracious to this Raven. Yes, I will turn the other cheek in charity as I have been taught by the lessons of Jesus. Yes, I will be kind to her, let no one reproach me the contrary.

She opened her eyes and looked at her rival. "You will find life here quite agreeable, Gaziye Hatun, for Konya has a varied and pleasant climate. There are beautiful rose gardens in our city, and I will take you to see one of my favorite places here, the gardens of Meram. Its lovely nature will refresh your soul. As you discover Konya, you will see it is a vibrant city, whirling with activity. Wait until you see our busy bazaars!"

The Raven Gaziye stared at Mahperi, unsmiling, and then began to speak in the same shrill voice she remembered hearing in the courtyard.

"First of all, I would prefer that you address me as *Melike Sultana,* for that is my title, not *Hatun*. I am a Queen, not a mere lady. Although I am sure your Konya is a charming place, do not forget that I come from the greatest capital of the world, rivalled by none! Damascus is the site of the most glorious mosque ever built in Islam. When you enter into its long and wide hall, you feel as if you are in God's paradise. Alaeddin has tried to turn his mosque on the hill here into an impressive one, but I can tell you, nothing compares to the majesty of praying in the Great Mosque of Damascus! But then, what would you know about praying in a mosque, Mahperi Hatun?"

How dare she insult our imperial Konya! The dignity of our calling the very heavens attest! Mahperi was too stunned by her snide remarks to find a suitable retort, but persevered in her intent to be gracious.

"No, I suppose I don't know what it is like to pray in a mosque, but I have started to learn about your religion and am often impressed by how similar it is to mine. I especially enjoy listening to the many important scholars who preach here in our medreses. The great master Ibn al-Arabi was here and trained many disciples who are now carrying on his message of universal love. He left us to go live in your Damascus, but another master has just arrived that is filling our people, including myself, with his words of inspiration. His name is Bahaeddin Veled, and he is very well-regarded by the Sultan. I will take you to listen to him in the Altinapa Medrese where he preaches."

"Yes, perhaps, but I have other more pressing issues for the moment, starting with my rooms. The decoration here in this palace: this white stucco everywhere and these peasant rugs are just too clumsy: I will need to bring in fine woven silks and brocades from the finest workshops in Damascus!"

Her frivolous words stunned Mahperi. How could she possibly insult a rug woven by Hanife! The workshops of Hanife produced objects as refined as anything you could hope to see in the East! Perhaps the court at Damascus was more sophisticated than the one at Konya, Mahperi could allow that concession, but Gaziye was here now and had to accept what she was offered.

"I am certain we can adjust the decoration of the palace to suit your desires, *Melike Gaziye Sultana,* if that is what you would like. I will also be glad to help you learn the customs of our Seljuk court with its traditions, festivals and foods, and in no time, I am sure you will be truly at home here, especially after you have tasted your first *tandir kebab*!"

Gaziye sniffed and threw her head backwards in laughter. "So you think that you need to teach me about the ways of a court? Don't ever forget that I am a princess from the most powerful Muslim kingdom, the Ayyubids. We are all descendants of the great Saladin who seized Jerusalem back from the hands of those Frankish invaders that you Seljuks were unable to harness! I am a noble princess by birth and certainly in need of no training on how to act like royalty!"

As if those final cutting words were not enough to slay her victim, Gaziye unbound her black veil and with a flourish, she let it fall around her shoulders, allowing Mahperi to view her face for the first time. For if there was one thing she knew for sure, this *Melike Sultana Gaziye,* Ayyubid Princess of Damascus, it was that her beauty was as exquisite as the most luscious maiden in paradise. She had been told by all those around her in the court of Damascus that there was no woman, in any village or city or mountaintop in all the world, that could match her stunning and devastating allure, and certainly, this tall woman in front of her would be no competition whatsoever for the attentions of the Seljuk Sultan Alaeddin Keykubad.

Chapter 26

Colors of the Loom

For the next several months, the entire court, and for that matter, all the markets and streets of Konya buzzed with the same questions about the new queen. Everyone hoped to get a glimpse of this new wife, who remained a total secret from the city, for she remained cloistered in the palace. The people of Konya also noted that their good queen Mahperi no longer rode on her black stallion through the city and they missed her warm smile and reassuring presence on their backstreets and in their bazaars. The court tried as best they could to adjust to the new situation, endeavoring to accept the new queen and to appreciate her – but all missed the dignified simplicity of Queen Mahperi. The new queen was anything but simple – her commands to the servants were sharp, her demands for food and drink capricious, and her interest in the palace and the city around her totally lacking. Yes, the people of Konya wondered how their Sultan could have been so bewitched by this dark-haired temptress from the East.

☪ ☪ ☪

The bear had perhaps stuck his paw into another hive of honey, but he did not forsake the memory of his first wife and her sharp mind. He knew he had hurt his first wife's pride, and he became increasingly aware over the next few months how much he counted on her advice and her counsel on many matters of his court. Should the thief in the market place be put to death? Should the good service of Emir Amin al-Din Yusuf be rewarded by increased land shares in the province of Akşehir? Should a new medrese be built to house the increasingly large crowds that thronged to hear the preaching of the master theologian Bahaeddin Veled? Should he continue his campaigns eastwards against the Artukids and the Khwarazmians, or should he focus, instead, on the Black Sea region? Such questions he could debate with his viziers and ministers, yet he always found the right answers to them in the soft voice and emerald eyes of his first wife. He could not separate himself from the need to discuss things with her, and to review projects through her eyes. With her, he could voice his hesitations, show his doubts, and yes, even admit to his fears – as he could with no one else. She never judged, never criticized; she just listened and stated her opinion, which, if truth be told, was wiser than any emitted by his viziers, except perhaps for Jelaleddin Karatay. He needed his Guiding Moonbeam in his life more than ever.

☪ ☪ ☪

When he called her to the divan, Mahperi respectfully answered his command; she didn't act petulant, no matter how much it hurt her to sit next to him, knowing where he had been the night before. Not to feel warmth between them was the hardest to bear. She would look at those long fingers and ache for them to be wrapped in hers, just one more time, even if it were for a second. Keep your dignity, she told herself to steady her nerves; talk to him and accept his conversation and companionship, even if it is a crumb next to what you have known before. I will do this to serve his needs and to show him that I honor my responsibilities. I will do it as well for my son, our son, the future Sultan of his empire. For although I must now share him with another, I will make the best of this situation. Perhaps he cannot resist the charms of my rival, but I know there is one place where I hold him, and that is with my mind. I know how much he counts on me for advice, and I will continue to give it to him each time he calls me into the divan, for it is there I still stand in the silvery moonlight of his love.

☪ ☪ ☪

Mahperi, in search of solace, now spent more time with her weaver friend Hanife. She sat for hours next to her, observing her swift fingers. What fascinated her most were the choices of colors Hanife made as she grabbed pieces of yarn from the cluster of bobbins dangling on each side of the loom. That flash of orange there: why did she choose such a vibrant color to place next to the pink, a tone already so startling? Mahperi never really understood the secret meaning of all those shapes, patterns and colors; but, in the end, the master weaver always turned out a jewel of perfection. She never doubted her choices, the Queen thought, and when her rug was complete, those colors and patterns whirled together in a nebula as bright as any in the night skies.

They would sit side by side for a long time, without speaking, which was the way of their friendship. The long moments of silent communion they shared were more meaningful than hours of empty chatter. These were two women of a rare intensity of spirit; one, queen of an empire, and the other, queen of the visual world. When they did speak, it was a conversation of respect and encouragement; one where each one sought to bring joy, gentleness and love to the other. Mahperi often thought that Hanife had been sent to her by divine Providence to help her find her way in her new life. Hanife felt that Mahperi was a visitor sent by God, to help her combat the loneliness that plagued her when she was not sitting at her loom, the only way she had to communicate to the world until meeting her. God pushed His hand on their backs differently than He did on the backs of most other women, but with each other, all was mutual understanding and respect.

One morning, Hanife saw that her friend was staring off into space and not observing the knotting with the same intensity as she usually did. She knew her friend was sad, very sad, since the arrival of Gaziye, and she was unsure how to help her come out of this hole of loneliness and desolation. She stopped for a moment and ran her fingers over the bobbins of yarn hanging on the side of the loom frame.

"Look at these bobbins, Mahperi! Each color has its own personality; it is the oddest thing! I don't mean just its appearance, but also the texture of each one is different. Some yarns stand up more or less straight, and some have their own curl and spin, just like the difference between your hair and mine! Some colors fight my hand, such as orange and yellow; some, like teal and purple, glide through my fingers like water. And then there is red, dependable and steadfast and accepting of anything I choose to do with it. My challenge is to take these diverse yarn colors and respect their differences, to make sure that my hand gives each one its esteem. Each one demands a different tension on my part to knot it, and it is not easy to always sense the needs of each color. Yet, I cannot refuse to work with a color because it resists my hand, for that particular tone may be just the one that will make my rug sing. I must accept its individuality and work with it hoping that in the end I will be victorious. The tension of my hand must adapt to each one in that particular row of knots; for if I don't, my rug will be twisted and not lay flat. And a rug that buckles is a failure, for it will not catch the light evenly and its shimmer will be weakened. Feet will certainly catch on it, tripping those who tread on it to fall to the ground."

Mahperi smiled to herself, admiring how her friend had so adroitly given her a gentle lesson on working with the various strands of people and events of her life. She wanted the rug of her life to lie flat, that was certain, and if it meant sensing the various colors of her life in a way that would respect the values she wished to pursue, then she would do it. She needed to support her husband, to maintain his esteem, to raise a son to be a sultan, and to strive to use her position as Queen to improve the lives of those in her kingdom, all the while keeping the colors of her dignity and self-esteem glowing. She turned and smiled at her friend.

"Oh Hanife, you give me such courage, but I am not sure if all those colors will respond to my hands, which seem so weak right now. My heart is still so heavy; I don't know what to do to release this grief. I just cannot get over this pain. And, to add to my wound, is the woman herself, sarcastic of every remark I make! Oh, and then to make it even more excruciating for me, there is her beauty. She is so exquisite, this Raven; you cannot imagine the intensity of her black eyes and the creaminess of her skin. Even one of your rugs would pale next to her!"

"One of my rugs pale next to a woman? *Never!*" The eyes of Hanife flashed angrily, and then both women burst into laughter at the ridiculous thought of anything coming near to the sparkling magic of one of her rugs.

"Are you sure that her sarcasm is not hiding something else? Think of her for a moment, Mahperi. Are you trying to understand how she feels in this situation? Are you letting your hurt stand in the way of showing her the compassion you always show to everyone else? She is new here, and probably is very homesick for her people – you can remember what that was like. Perhaps she feels a bit insecure about her position here, and tries to brag about her Ayyubid Damascus in order to put herself in a good light. But probably more than anything, she is intimidated by you – don't forget your height, green eyes and intelligence are more than impressive – and so she stings you to protect herself. She knows, just as you do, that you are truly the first Queen in the Sultan's life. How do you think she feels when she sees the Sultan respectfully rise when you enter the room? Underneath that harshness, probably lies a woman with a good heart, but one frightened by the competition with you for the Sultan's affections, for she does know, just as you do, how much he holds you in esteem."

"Perhaps you are right," Mahperi conceded. "The Sultan still loves me, I know that, and wants to make the best of this situation. I want to forgive him, but....the fact is he calls me to the divan room for discussion, but never into his private chambers. He is totally taken with her and has no time for me."

"Give him time. Perhaps you need to get away from this court a bit, Mahperi, at least until her baby is born. For the moment, Konya and that palace on the hill might just be a little too tight for you to all find a livable peace. There are many other cities in this empire where you could find your way, and do well for the Sultan's subjects. Sivas, Kayseri, Tokat, Niğde – all these cities would offer you a bit of distance to help heal your wounds."

"But I don't want to leave him totally in her hands! The one hold I have over him is that he still comes to me for advice and counsel, and if I go away, then he will certainly do away with me! No, I think I must stay here to make myself as invaluable as possible. It is my only hope!"

"Well, you perhaps are right. Keep your dignity intact and you will always hold the most exalted position in his eyes. I know that he is the warmest color of your carpet of life, and that your wools will be forever entwined," she said, smiling at her friend.

"But, my friend, it is not just for me that I worry. I am not the only one who is suffering: my little son Giyaseddin is not faring well either with all this upheaval in his life. I know, even though I try to hide it as best I can, that he senses that his mother is sad. But it is more than just worry about an unhappy mother. He is shy and insecure and has no friends, and is detached from people, except for me. He keeps to himself and doesn't join in the games organized by the other palace children, and most of all, I never hear his laughter."

"How is he with his father?"

"He cringes when he sees the Sultan and moves closer to me, as if he fears that his father is going to say something harsh to him. In defense of little Giyaseddin, I must say that his father does not show much interest in him at all."

"And with his tutors?"

"He doesn't really have any yet, other than a few court scribes who are teaching him his letters. I suppose he should start some formal lessons, but I have been reluctant to put him in the hands of tutors until he grows out of this insecure stage. I do what I can to get him involved in games, but he doesn't appear to be good at anything – he misses the target in archery more often than not, he doesn't like to ride horses or play with balls – he just seems to want to sit quietly by himself."

Hanife laughed. "He sounds like me! Perhaps he is an artisan waiting to be born! Why don't you try to teach him a simple craft, like making bits of leather into bags or working with silver?

"You can't be serious! Do you think his father, the Sultan, would approve if his son did anything that wasn't suitable to the art of war? This is what he must learn, if he is to become a Sultan as successful as his father. I must continue to give my son all the love and affection I can and teach him to speak up for himself. I am responsible for raising a Sultan, and I will do what it takes to achieve this. Yes, Hanife, you are right, for both my life and his, I will take the varied colors of the yarns of our fate and deal with them, knot by knot, row by row, until the rug of our destinies reaches the top of the loom."

Chapter 27

The Face in Front of Us

As Mahperi and her escort of guards entered the famed Altinapa Medrese on the main road of Konya, she paused to observe the large courtyard with its dome, sunken pool and the recessed open area, known as the *iwan,* which served as the classroom. She saw students coming in and out of rooms on each side of the courtyard, teachers carrying armloads of books, and clusters of scholars in the courtyard, their heads bent together in conversation. Other students sat alone reciting their verses aloud, their heads bobbing in unison with their words. She marveled at the busy spirit of the place, and understood why so many of the people of Konya flocked here of late, including her own husband.

She had come here to meet Bahaeddin Veled, the illustrious imam who was spearheading this burst of activity in the medrese. He had been invited by the Sultan to teach in Konya, and had arrived earlier that spring with his family. Within a few months of his arrival, he had attracted a considerable group of curious students and devoted disciples. This "Sultan of the Learned," as Bahaeddin Veled was called, taught five days a week in the medrese on Islamic law, the Hadith sayings of the Prophet, and the interpretation of Qur'anic texts.

Mahperi wanted to speak with him, and he had accepted her request for a meeting. She wondered if he could provide some counsel for her in this difficult time when her soul was dark. She needed to speak about the pain in her heart that would not heal, and her own priests and prayers were not offering the answers she needed. Mahperi had heard so many good things about this man's wisdom that she wanted to get closer to his insight. If a man is holy, she thought, what difference does it make what religion he uses to answer God?

In the middle of the iwan she saw a white-haired man with a gentle face, his shoulders stooped over the low, wooden stand that held a thick manuscript on religious law. He raised his head as she approached. Her guards discretly stood along the walls of the iwan while she spoke with the imam.

"Peace be upon you, Mahperi Sultana, I am glad you are here. Come, let us be friends. Sit next to me and we will talk. What can I help you with, my good Lady?"

Despite her shyness, Mahperi felt at ease in front of the imam, and plunged ahead with her questions.

"Thank you for meeting with me, Bahaeddin Veled, for I need your insight. I confess to you that I am confused. I believe that I am a good person and have done nothing to deserve what has happened to me. Try as I might to understand, I cannot piece together the mystery of the Sultan's actions. Love is eternal, is it not? That is the reason our Lord sent us Jesus Christ. I came here to Konya, and to my marriage, with that belief, and now I find that it is not true."

Bahaeddin Veled looked into her sad face and felt an immediate tenderness for this woman who was so frank with him.

"My lovely child, you are asking a very difficult question, and I will answer it the best I can with a story. You are not the only one who has come to Konya from far away to find your happiness and your providence with the belief that love is eternal – I, too, have traveled the same road as you."

He paused and looked up to the turquoise tiles on the dome above him before continuing.

"Yes, indeed, the destiny of my life has been forged by the force of God and by two powerful men – and your husband is one of them. The force of God is, however, the most powerful of all. You are never cold when the fire of God warms your blood and heart, and I serve as a humble and devoted servant of God, dedicated to sharing the warmth of that fire with all I meet. Such is my calling, just as you were called to yours to follow the Sultan here to Konya as his wife. At the same time, my destiny was also forged by another fire: the one caused by the devastating thunderbolts lashed out from the fists of a terrible force named Temujin, a warrior from the mountains of China. He calls himself "*Khan,*" the great king, and declares that he is the ruler of the Mongol peoples of his land, and wants to be the King of all the peoples of the earth. He also calls himself "*Genghis*": the Ocean. And, like an ocean, he seeks to cover all dry land in his path. He is not warmed by the love of God, but instead is driven by a different fuel: the one of hatred. This Ocean seeks to burst the walls of all the dams in his path, to cover the beds of the rivers in front of him, and drown all in his path. He has flooded across China, through Afghanistan where I lived, and now Persia, destroying all that he encounters. Blood and death and evil are the words he lives by, not those from a holy book."

The old man paused and shuddered at the thought of all this destruction.

"One morning in Balkh, my hometown, I awoke from a vivid dream which warned that the Ocean was coming near. I gathered my family, disciples and close friends together, and we took all that we owned and fled ever westwards, settling in Nishapur in Persia. My son Jelaleddin, who now teaches here in the mosque with me, was still a little boy then. But that demon Genghis has as many soldiers in his floodwaters as there are fishes in the sea, and the waves kept coming closer. After several years, we could feel our feet getting wet again. Our caravan of family and friends continued on to the illustrious cities of Baghdad and Mecca, where I continued to learn at the feet of many Sufis and famous scholars. It was there that I heard that my city of Balkh had been entirely destroyed by the Mongol army of five hundred thousand men, led by the Ocean Genghis Khan himself. Those heathens burned fourteen thousand copies of our Holy Qur'an. They killed fifteen thousand students and professors of law, and they took two hundred thousand people out into the fields and shot them to death with arrows, including my own daughter Fatima, who had chosen to remain in Balkh. Onwards we continued, to the city of Damascus, but even there, in the great sainted city of Saladin, we did not feel safe. I heard of a magical place called Anatolia, governed by a fair-minded sultan, and decided to cast my fate there. Leaving Damascus, I headed northwards, passing through many prosperous cities, finally finding one where I could settle: Karaman, to the south of Konya. We prospered there, and my son Jelaleddin grew into a fine religious scholar, married, and saw the birth of his two sons."

He stopped and smiled at the memories of those happy days.

"Our life was full of contentment, but again, our destiny was changed by a force as powerful as that of the Ocean. But only this time, the man was not a destroyer, but a builder, in the midst of creating a spectacular kingdom in his capital of Konya. How could I refuse his invitation to teach in his illustrious capital city? Do you remember that warm day last May when I first arrived in Konya? That day, there were roses in bloom to greet my family and friends, and the people that lined the roads to greet us sounded like the archangels of Paradise! The good Sultan himself met me with great ceremony, coming down from that blazing white stallion of his to walk me to my new spiritual home in this Altinapa Medrese. Here I have had the provident blessing to grow as a religious scholar, and I will ever be grateful to your husband, the great Sultan Alaeddin Keykubad, for this opportunity."

He paused to smile at her, pleased to see that she was listening so intently to his story. "So you see, my Sultana, we share very similar fates, as both of our destinies were forged by the same two men. I was chased by the Ocean and lost everything dear to me in my homeland. Fear of the Ocean pushed your husband into crafting an alliance with the Ayyubids that caused you to lose everything dear to you in love. Yet, if I had not been shown the munificence of a generous Sultan, I would not have found safe harbor for myself and my family here, as well as my very own medrese in which to teach the word of God. If you had not been shown the love of this Sultan, you would not be the mother of the two fine children, nor would you enjoy your role as Queen of an Empire. We have received much from the hand of this man, and must remember those gifts instead of being mournful about what has been taken from us."

Mahperi bowed her head and her eyes filled with tears, for she was well aware of how much her husband had brought her.

"Above all, we must be thankful for the blessings of God upon us. You asked me if love is eternal, yet I think you know the answer without receiving a lesson from me – that answer is already in your heart. Your Jesus put it there, and God shares it with you as well. Love takes many forms, yet it is always present in our lives. Never forget that the greatest force in life is love: the way of love will always be the eternal victor. This is the most valuable lesson I can leave with you. Know that wherever we turn, the face of God's love is in front of us, and you must always turn in this direction:

"May God grant you total soundness,
O travelers on the Way of Love.
May the Beloved remove the veils from your eyes
that you may see the secrets of your time and of the true center,
and may it be for each of us that Wherever we turn,
there is the Face of God."

After listening to his prayer, Mahperi nodded her head. She felt ashamed that she had so selfishly focused on her own distress. His story made her recognize all that had been given to her, which would help her find the strength to heal. Despite her loneliness, she knew that the face of God's love was indeed shining in front of her, and she needed only to lift up her heart to receive it to find the peace she sought from her sorrow.

Chapter 28
Golden Orb

It is noon, and the midwife, with her puffy baklava face, announces that the Lady's time has come. The sun is shining so brightly that all the shutters have been drawn since mid-morning, but in your heart those shutters were pulled shut long before this day. With each day that her belly grew larger, your heart shriveled like a dried plum in a marketplace stall. Wonders did not wane; the Sultan was as infatuated with the Raven as the first day she swooped to her roost. Ever since that first disastrous day, she has won battle after battle for his attention, and now is the victor once again.

Leave this palace today she tells herself; take your Eclipse and ride as far away as you can, and when you return at dusk, perhaps this will all be over; maybe it is only a mirage like the ones you see shimmering in the distance over the summer plains. Leave this place today; you will not be able to breathe the air of anticipation and joy that now fills its halls; for you, it is a suffocating gas in your lungs. Ride out until the sun burns your skin red raw, burnt like the scorched heart beating underneath it.

☪ ☪ ☪

So indeed it came later that day that a golden beam of a child burst forth in that blazing summer sun, an angel ever bright and fair, taking nothing of his mother's dusky coloring, but everything of his blonde Byzantine grandmother. A child so perfect as to capture a Sultan's heart with the first shining ray of his tiny face. Little Izzeddin al-Kilich, born on this day, as blond as the fields of golden grain stretching to infinity, incited the dreams of a Sultan.

And you, still standing on that high west hill above the city atop your jet-black stallion, staring at the palace below in the distance. Is that the Star of Bethlehem you see rising above the sunset sky? You say you are going mad, you say you must get far away from here. Yes, you dream you are standing atop a castle rock, back to a simpler time in Kalonoros, gazing from your window onto the peaceful blue sea below, unruffled by the waves. But no, it is here on the plains you now stand, your eyes blinded by the sparkling rays of the little golden orb glinting on the horizon of his father's eyes; this little newborn babe of the Other.

Chapter 29

The Valley of God's Thumbprint

Sultan Alaeddin Keykubad, Glory of Glorious Lions, Most Revered Lord, the World Renowned, Holy Wise One, Sultan of Sultans, was now, at the age of thirty-six, at the height of his manhood, strength and power. He was consumed by the hot fire of his purpose which incited his heart to pursue more and more conquests to the East. It never stopped raging; this fire of his purpose, and it needed more and more fuel to feed its flames. Now that the last patches of snow were retreating from the steppes around Konya, he headed again to Kayseri to plan for his next campaigns. The heady aroma of the earth awakened by spring filled his nostrils and the winds from the East blew through his hair, reminding him that the campaigns of summer would soon be upon him.

Now, in the spring of 1228, the place that fueled the flames of the hot fire of his purpose was the city of Erzincan. It was a place almost behind the sun, this Erzincan lying near the headwaters of the mighty Euphrates River, lost in the middle of wide plains. Erzincan, whose Armenian merchants wove fine cloths of many colors and crafted silver as easily as carving fruit; this Erzincan of blistering summers and blizzard-filled winters; a city since time immemorial the nexus for the roads to kingdoms north and east – Erzincan, this junction city filling a vast valley formed by God's thumbprint.

Erzincan was the seat of the Mengucukid dynasty. For years, the Seljuks had respected the autonomy of this small principality, which paid tribute taxes to the Sultan in return for being left alone to run their own affairs in their lands. The ruler at Erzincan, Behram Shah, was respected by the Seljuk court and was considered a dependable ally who set a good example for others. Yet such was not the same for his son Davud Shah, who came to the throne upon his father's death. Although a cultured man like his father, the young man, as is often the way of young men who seek to shine, became ambitious and wanted to stand alone against the Seljuks. He reached out to form alliances with other leaders to help him with his goal, notably with the Ayyubid al-Ashraf, Shah Jahan of Erzurum, and the notorious Jelaleddin Menguberti, leader of the Khwarazmians from Azerbaijan.

However, many of the old emirs who had been in faithful service to Behram Shah were worried about the turn of events. It was one thing to want autonomy, but to tempt the powerful Seljuk Empire was a dangerous game to play. They informed the Sultan Alaeddin Keykubad of these coalitions being formed against him. The proud Sultan would not bear any insubordination to his rule, especially since the plot of the emirs, and he moved quickly to snip off this sapling before it could grow into a tree that would cast shade over his garden. He sent his troops to lay siege to the castle of Erzincan, and within a short while, the kingdom of the Mengucukids of Erzincan was no longer.

After his defeat at the hands of the Seljuk troops, Davud Shah was summoned to the Keykubadiyye Palace to officially surrender his sword to Alaeddin Keykubad. The Sultan organized a huge banquet to mark his importance for all the lands, and to show as well his generosity to those he defeated. With a sense of charity, perhaps roused by the memory of the dignified Behram Shah, or even by his own sense of honor coming to the fore, the Sultan Alaeddin Keykubad, Glory of Glorious Lions, offered to Davud Shah the former lands of Kyr Vart in the region of Kirşehir, as a province where he could live the rest of his days in peace and dignity, despite the loss of his Erzincan.

The generosity of the Sultan shone on his own as well, for after his glorious victory over Davud Shah in Erzincan, the Sultan turned control of the city of Erzincan over to his trusted Emir Mubarizeddin Ertokush of Antalya, now promoted to the position of *atabeg*, or governor of his own province. The Sultan needed a man of confidence to manage this strategic city, and he could think of no one more reliable than the Emir Ertokush, who had served him so faithfully in the past.

In mercy so ended the story of a firebrand who dared to stare in the face of the Sultan of Sultans. So ended as well the Dynasty of the Mengucukids, not only in Erzincan, but in the cities of Kemah and Sebinkarahisar, which had impertinently rebelled as well. Once again, the lesson was learned by all: no one defies the great Sultan Alaeddin Keykubad without a price to be paid, even out there, in the valley of God's thumbprint.

Chapter 30

A Cry from the Unfavored

He knew his numbers, he did, the little boy; why, yes, he could count past his fingers and toes and all the way up to thirty. He knew his shapes and colors and patterns, and that now for a long time now, such baby tasks for him, a big boy of six!

He knew his prayers, too; he could recite them along with his mother each morning and night, and he could retell the stories of his friend, the sweet Jesus, to her as well. He especially loved the Bible story of the great catch of fish by Simon Peter, but his favorite was the victory of David, a little boy just like him, over that big, mean Goliath! He also could recite without one mistake the *Al-Fatiha* verse at the beginning of each prayer session, when he stood behind his father in the great mosque on the hill when they went to pray along with the Sultan's men and ministers. He knew, too, the little boy, many words in many languages; he spoke in one way with his mother and with Jesus, and in another way with his father and his men, and yet another one inside the big mosque on the hill. He knew his backwards from forwards, his directions right and left; he knew what smells from the kitchen signaled that his favorite halvah was being made that day. He knew secret hiding places where his father's men could not find him when they came to fetch him for his lessons. But they always did find him in the end, and his teachers taught him how to hold a pen and write letters and numbers in the flowing script of the Big Book. He knew how to say please and thank you and not to interrupt when someone was speaking. He knew, too, the little boy of six, that he loved his mother more than anything else in the world, even more than that halvah, for she was always so patient and calm and never yelled at him. She smelled of flowers and always moved with such quiet grace. She was so different than the other Lady of his father's court, the one with whom his father spent so much time now; the one who was always loudly chattering in a voice he did not like.

Yes, he knew a lot of things, this little boy, he had learned much on his own and from other people. But the one thing he knew for sure was something that had not been taught to him; it was something he sensed with an intuition that was as grounded as his sense of touch and smell. He knew, the little boy, that his father did not like him very much. His father avoided his glance, never touched or played with him, or let him crawl upon his lap to shower him with kisses. His mother told him that Sultans were serious and did not play games with children. But the little boy knew that this was not true, because he saw how his father laughed with his younger half-brother Izzeddin and the new baby Rukneddin. With Izzeddin, the Sultan sang songs, shared date candies he bought at the market place and walked hand-in-hand up to the big mosque on the hill. He got tossed in the air during games, he got his tummy tickled, and he was taken on special trips up to the Meram gardens. He knew, the little boy of six, these were things his father would never do with him. His father did not like him, of that he was certain, as sure as he could write his name in big black letters: *Giyaseddin Keyhüsrev*.

☪ ☪ ☪

Nobody notices me; nobody cares about what I do, except my mama. She loves me so much and always hugs me. I like that, because it makes me feel warm and happy. I am forgotten at every moment of the day. Activities are planned but never include me. My brothers get to do everything and I get left behind.

I want to go places, and have fun and laugh, too! My father always yells at me, no matter what I do. Is it my fault my arrow did not hit the target? Even my sister Seljuka hisses at me like a snake. Although I am the biggest, I don't understand their games even when they explain them to me and I feel stupid around them. I don't like any of them; they are all so mean to me. I want to be a part of my papa's life, too, not just an annoying shadow behind my shining little brother. I want to be loved by him, too.

The little boy of six went into the room next to his father's quarters that was reserved for his beautiful leopard cat. If only he would love me as much as he does this cat, all would be better. Between this cat with the ruby collar and my brother with the golden curls, he has nothing left to give to me. I deserve his attention, too! Me, look at me, he thought, as he reached his tiny hand through the bars to unlock the cage door and to grab one of the two cubs that had just been born to the regal Ruby after his papa had mated her with the leopard of the defeated prince of Erzincan. Come here, little cub, come with me, I will show you who is a big boy.

The little boy grabbed the wriggling cub by the scruff of his neck and tucked him under his shirt and ran outside of the palace to the rear of the kitchens where he knew few people went, there at the secret place where he hid from those boring old teachers at lesson time. He picked up a large, sharp rock that was on the ground, and pulled the cub out of his shirt. Bad cub, you are bad, bad, like my brother, my papa loves you and not me, you are bad, bad, bad, and he held it down onto the ground and banged the rock again and again against its head. I will hurt you so you can feel what it is like when papa hurts me with his hard words and his sharp looks of anger. *Whack, whack, whack.*

It was only after the little cub stopped whimpering and the little boy saw the cracked skull and all the pink goop did he realize that what he had done was very bad. He had only wanted to hurt the cub, but now he had killed it, just like those bugs he squished with his sandal when he played outside in the palace gardens. But this was no bug; this was the baby of his papa's beloved cat. He had killed it for certain, as it lay there motionless and bleeding just like the sheep he saw slaughtered on the high holy days, their blood running in rivers down the hill. Now what do I do, thought the little boy, my papa will be very angry with me and will beat me just as I have done to this baby cub. My head will be pink goop too. Oh, I am in trouble now! I will run away! But no, I can't leave my mama; that would be too sad – no, I must hide what I have done so no one will know and I must pretend nothing has happened, even if it means lying to my mama and to Jesus. But mama says I must never lie, oh, what am I to do?

The little boy picked up the sharp, bloodied stone and threw it as far away as he could. Then he scooped up the limp form of the cub and ran over to the well in the courtyard and threw it over the edge. When he heard the splash he knew he was safe. It was gone, gone under the water, that bad cub; no one will know what happened. But for certain when Papa sees that one of his beloved cubs is gone, he will want me to take its place. He will feel sorry for me then and see that I am a lost cub, too.

☪ ☪ ☪

Back in the palace, a mother leopard paced back and forth, back and forth in her cage, anxiously awaiting the return of her cub. Yet her instinct told her this cub would never be returned to her, and she would never forget the smell of the hand that had lifted it from the cage.

Chapter 31

Blue and Banished

"Let me see now, so many choices!" mused Gaziye as she opened her jewel chest to select the earrings to wear for the day. Shall I wear the ones with the dangling pearls that set off my black hair so well, or the silver filigree ones with the emeralds that glow against my olive skin? No! Certainly not the emeralds; they will remind the Sultan of her eyes. I will wear the topaz ones, yes, all shimmering brilliance, just like me.

Yes, those emerald eyes…I have got to find a way to get the Sultan to stop looking at them. He is seeing more than their beauty; he is admiring the woman behind them, and I will not have this! I must find a way to diminish her, and get that son of hers out of sight as well. As long as that first-born son is around, he casts a shadow over my two boys, as if one could cast a shadow over my two bright little twinkling stars! Gaziye smiled at the thought of her two boys, and how much the Sultan especially adored the little Izzeddin. Yes, I want him away from this court, away from my boys, and out of the Sultan's view….Suddenly her face lit up as brightly as her jewels, for she now knew how she could achieve both goals at the same time.

Gaziye immediately dispatched her maid to deliver a message to Köpek, telling him to secretly meet her in the palace rose garden after the evening prayer. She knew the Sultan listened to everything this vizier said, and she also knew that he didn't like Mahperi either. The time has come for us to work together, she mused.

That evening, she chose a rosewater perfume to blend in with the heady aroma of the famed palace rose gardens. Soon Köpek appeared from the shadows of a hedge and approached her, looking right and left for her guards.

"Do not worry, Köpek, I am alone. Thank you for kindly coming to meet with me, honored Vizier Köpek, and I appreciate your discretion. I know this meeting is highly irregular, but I wanted to meet with you alone to ask your advice on an issue that is bothering me," she murmured, trying to charm this often-difficult man.

"I am at your service, my Lady, in any way I can."

"You see, I am concerned about the Sultan's son Giyaseddin, who seems entirely under the influence of his mother. I think he spends too much time with her; why, I have even seen them coming out of the little church in the Şekerfuruş neighborhood together! It is one thing for her to continue to practice her religion, but to raise her son in the ways of the incense lovers is another. Why, it is an insult to Islam!" she insisted, eager to plant the seed that she knew he would take up and water.

"You bring up an important point, my Lady, and I thank you for the consideration you show to the first-born child of the Sultan. He is being raised in the Islamic faith, rest assured, but I can understand that you worry about her influence over him. Giyaseddin is a timorous little boy, but the time has come to start his official education. It is the usual practice for young princes to be sent away to a distant town, where they learn to govern a small outpost. We must find such a place for the prince Giyaseddin, as well as a trusted tutor to take him in charge. I will broach this topic with the Sultan and see what he thinks."

"Thank you, Köpek, I now see that what they say about you is true! You are indeed the most intelligent of all the Sultan's counselors!" Gaziye cooed to the homely man.

That is correct, thought Köpek, bowing his head. I am intelligent, way too intelligent to be taken in by your fussy compliments, perfumed curls and batting eyes! I know both of us want exactly the same thing: to reduce the influence of the emerald eyes and keen mind of that Christian woman over our Sultan.

"I am at the service of my Sultan and his empire, and if I can be of service to you as well, I would be most grateful and honored," said Köpek as he turned and left her. Gaziye, pleased with her victory, snapped off a fragrant red rose and tucked it in her hair.

☪ ☪ ☪

Early the next day Köpek requested an audience with the Sultan to discuss the plan that he had devised during the night after his discussion with Gaziye, a plan he was sure would serve everyone well – especially himself.

As usual, the Sultan smiled and greeted Köpek heartily. He ordered his page to bring in some cold sherbet, and motioned for Köpek to sit next to him on the cushions to share a cup with him.

"What is the subject you wish to discuss with me today, Köpek, and at such a bright hour?"

"My Sultan, the subject is your son, Giyaseddin. He is a fine boy whom I am certain will make an outstanding Sultan. With a father as brave as you and a mother as intelligent as Mahperi Hanim, why, how could it be otherwise? Yet we must ensure that he is given all the tools to carry on your illustrious path!

The time has come for him to receive a formal education to prepare for that day, may it still be many, many years away, *inshallah!*"

"You are right, Köpek," said the Sultan as he looked down at his cup of sherbet. "We need to appoint tutors for the boy so that he may become equipped to handle the responsibilities of leadership."

"Actually, my Sultan, I have a suggestion to put forth to you. After your glorious victory in Erzincan, you turned control of the city over to Emir Ertokush, and no one deserved this more than he! Who can forget that glorious day when we stood outside the castle door at Kalonoros!" Köpek paused before continuing, making sure he had the Sultan's full attention. "A fine man, indeed, and one that perhaps deserves an even greater reward for his loyalty and the esteem he holds in your eyes. He has proven himself over and over again as a competent officer. But I also think he can assume an even more significant appointment: the tutor of the heir to the throne of the Seljuks!"

Köpek watched for the flicker in the Sultan's eyes before continuing his plea. When he saw it, he knew he could finalize his proposal. "Frankly speaking as well, my Sultan – and I mean this only with the greatest respect for her Ladyship – it might be best to remove Giyaseddin from his mother's care as soon as possible. He is also quite withdrawn in nature, probably because he spends too much time with a woman, and not enough with men. Ertokush will be able to deal with his delicate personality and help him bloom into a fine young warrior."

Köpek stopped and waited for the Sultan's reaction. He must not realize that this plan serves me first and foremost, for it is I, Vizier Sadettin Köpek, who wants to dominate this boy. Once away from his mother, it will be easier for me to exert my influence over him. And by sending him away, I will also hold Gaziye in my debt and crush the domination of that Armenian queen.

"Köpek, as usual, I find your idea a brilliant one! It is true that the time has come to take this boy's education into hand, and you are correct, there is no one more competent for this task than Mubarizeddin Ertokush!"

☪ ☪ ☪

Later that day, the Sultan called Mahperi into the divan. He was not anticipating this conversation with any pleasure, for he knew how attached she was to the little boy, and dreaded having to tell her that he would soon be taken away from her.

Indeed, since the arrival of Gaziye, Mahperi had turned all her attentions and energy to her son. The love of her child eased her pain, and the responsibility of raising an heir to the throne gave her encouragement to confront each day. She knew that the boy, even at this tender age, felt overshadowed by his father, and could not hope to compete with his father's brilliant image. He was a boy of humor blue, not one of gold like his half-brother Izzeddin.

When the Sultan saw her at the door, he motioned her into the divan. "Mahperi, come, please sit down, I have something important to announce to you."

Mahperi shuddered at the memory of the last time she had heard these words, and somewhere in the depths of her heart, she knew that it had to do with her son.

"Mahperi, the time has come for us to think of the well-being of our son. He will one day become sultan of this glorious empire, and we must start preparing for that time as of today. He needs to receive a formal education at the hands of skilled tutors. He must be trained not only in letters and philosophy, but also in combat skills, horsemanship, archery and battle management. Most importantly, he must learn morals and leadership, the tenets of a wise ruler. I have discussed this situation in depth with Köpek, who agrees with it. Mahperi, your son will be sent to the good care of Mubarizeddin Ertokush in Erzincan. He will live there from now on. I spent my formative years in Tokat, and it was there that I learned to read and write in four languages, to lead troops and manage the needs of citizens – and, not to forget, to play chess like a champion! Our son needs to go away to have a view onto the world that is larger than this hill and the rooms of the palace, for that will be the vision of the world he will inherit. He will learn passages of the Qur'an by heart to provide him moral fortitude. He will learn arithmetic so that he can understand the ways of the marketplace and participate in discussions with the finance ministers. He will learn the refinements of Arabic grammar, and he will master Persian to speak with his administrators. He will also study history, poetry, ethics, law, geography and the military arts. As you can see, he has much to learn. Please prepare for his departure as soon as possible. I know this is a difficult thing for a mother to hear, but you must help your son, the future Sultan, walk tall towards his destiny."

Mahperi's head spun at the news. Although she knew that someday this separation would take place, she was not ready for it just yet. He is the one thing that still unites me with the Sultan, and once he is gone, I will be placed in a cupboard like a broken piece of pottery, never to be used again. So Köpek thinks this is a good idea, does he? I should have known he would interfere to harm my life. Steady now, maintain your dignity, Maryam, do not collapse, do not cry. You are a Sultana, of head high and heart strong. You will survive this tribulation as well.

No one thought of the little boy in this situation, except his mother. A pawn he now became, this little Giyaseddin Keyhüsrev, haunted blue boy, now banished.

So it was announced to both the court and the little boy that a departure for Erzincan was imminent. When Köpek related the news to Gaziye, it was hard to determine which one gloated the most. When Mahperi announced the news to the little boy, it was hard to tell which one shed the most tears. When the Sultan summoned his boy to explain his future, the child heard only a cold voice announcing exile, not opportunity. He felt rejected by a mean father who was taking him away from his mother, the only person who ever smiled at him and made him feel loved. Yes, at this moment, he felt like the little David standing before the cruel, giant Goliath.

Chapter 32

Just Listen, I Am Here

Mahperi and her guards walked into the Altinapa Medrese and she immediately saw Bahaeddin Veled sitting cross-legged on the prayer rug. His white head was bent over a book opened on a low, carved wooden stand. He was so engrossed in his reading that she hesitated to disturb him, but the hour had come for their weekly discussion.

Mahperi now regularly met with this renowned religious scholar to learn more about Muslim traditions and thought, which she felt would help her better understand the ways of the court of the Seljuks. Yet, she sought more than this. She needed to understand how to reconcile her Christian faith with the practices of Islam. With each passing visit, Mahperi became more and more attached to the gentle old man. She found much solace in his words and in the mystic poetry he recommended for her to read. He inspired in her an interest in Islam that grew with each day.

It was not possible for Mahperi to remain insensitive to the religion of the court, for her ever-curious mind wanted to understand everything about this world of the Seljuks. She could speak to Bahaeddin Veled freely about her own search for God, the differences between Islam and Christianity, and the customs she found perplexing in the Islamic faith. No question of hers was dismissed or went unanswered by Bahaeddin, who always responded with attentive patience. Mahperi became encouraged by the lessons of the Prophet, and she was drawn to the order she found on the pages of the Qur'an, so much like the peace of the parables of Jesus in the Bible.

The departure of her son had left her bereft. She still needed to look after her daughter Seljuka, but this child with an independent nature thrived on her own like a wildflower in the fields. The daily life of the court, her rides on Eclipse and visits to Hanife's studio occupied her days, but they were not enough to fill the void left by the loss of her son Giyaseddin. She felt that the entire driving responsibility of her existence – to raise a future Sultan – had been taken away from her, and that she was now useless. First her father, then her husband, and now her son – somedays, she was overcome with unbearable sadness by the losses of her loved ones.

"Master Bahaeddin, sometimes I do not know where to turn, for I am not sure anymore of the purpose of my life. I want to be linked to something outside of myself, and I don't know what it is and where it is. I want to feel joy in my deeds, in my life, with the people I love. Yet, my loved ones have been taken from me, and joy eludes me."

The old man remained bent over the pages of his Qur'an for a long time before lifting his eyes.

"My child, that joy is all around you, but you are not seeing it. Trust me; you need to connect with all the daily miracles in both the inner and the manifest worlds in which you live. You sense the need to give; you seek, you search, you read, you pray, you desire to connect with something bigger than yourself. That is the first step. You see, the road towards happiness here on earth starts with the path to God. Yet finding that road is difficult, because there is not just one path."

"Yes, my teacher, I am sure of that!" interjected Mahperi. "There are so many sources of wisdom! Which one am I to choose to find a richer and deeper life? I know that good works are important. I know that quiet contemplation with myself, whether it be with nature or with the Holy Scriptures is important. How can I confront the world around me, find truth and understand the sacred? I ask you, how do I grow in devotion and sincerity? How do I translate the inner guidance that I receive from reading the Scriptures or the lessons from the Qur'an into my daily life?"

Bahaeddin smiled at her and answered slowly:

"I repeat, my child, the road towards spirituality is real and sometimes hard to choose, for paths to truth are not one but many. But I can help you to discover the one that I feel is the most universal: the way of love, pure love. God willing, a new time is opening for greater spirituality among men and women, in kindness, patience and mutual support, as we turn in steadfast and trustworthy devotion to the One who turns us all. We must work towards the creation of a place where we will share a sacred brotherhood. Yes, we all turn together on this earth. Do you remember the first verse I ever recited to you?

"May God grant you total soundness,
O travelers on the Way of Love.
May the Beloved remove the veils from your eyes
that you may see the secrets of your time and of the true center;
May it be for each of us that Wherever we turn,
there is the Face of God."

The old man took a deep breath after reciting his verse.

"Never forget this verse, and carry it with you forever. I am feeling old now, Mahperi Hatun, and I am not certain how much longer I have on this earth. But my son Jelaleddin is turning into a fine spiritual leader, and I expect great things from him. Put your faith in him as you have with me, and you will find your path to Love alongside of him. Support him and encourage him, just as your husband has encouraged me here in Konya these past years. His message will be the same as mine, because it is the only true message. Love is the only constant in an ever-changing world: whether you remain a Christian or whether you choose Islam, the paths are paved with the same stones of love. Live your life with love, and God will accept your soul always."

At that moment, Mahperi heard the call for the noon prayer. First she heard the muezzin from the Altinapa mosque, then a split second later another one from the mosque down the street and then another, and soon the skies over Konya reverberated with an echoing refrain to the greatness of God:

Allahu Akbar. Allahu Akbar.
Allahu Akbar. Allahu Akbar.
Ash-hadu an la ilaha ill-Allah.
Ash-hadu an la ilaha ill-Allah.
Ash-hadu anna Muhammad-ar-Rasoolullah.
Ash-hadu anna Muhammad-ar-Rasoolullah.
Hayya 'alas-Salah. Hayya 'alas-Salah.
Hayya 'alal-falah. Hayya 'alal-falah.
Allahu Akbar. Allahu Akbar.

God is Most Great. God is Most Great.
God is Most Great. God is Most Great.
I bear witness that there is none worthy of being worshipped except God.
I bear witness that there is none worthy of being worshipped except God.
I bear witness that Muhammad is the Apostle of God.
I bear witness that Muhammad is the Apostle of God.
Come to prayer. Come to prayer.
Come to deliverance. Come to deliverance.
God is Most Great. God is Most Great.

Bahaeddin turned to watch the face of Mahperi as she listened to the call, and he could see there a brightness that was not there previously. After the call was finished, he spoke to her quietly:

"When you hear the call of the muezzin, stop what you are doing. Just listen. Quiet your mind, gather your thoughts inwards. Let the vibrations of his voice resonate in your soul. Just listen. Think about what you are doing at this moment, quiet down, collect your thoughts in your arms and hold them to your chest. Think about how you could be doing better towards others and to yourself. Just listen. Think about what you are doing this day to praise God, your fellow man and life. Just listen. Think about how you can be honorable and generous. Just listen. Think about the negative thoughts and actions you have committed since the last call. Take strength from the beauty of the words and the rhythm of his song. Just listen. Let the voice lift you higher than where you are now, and truly hear what you have just listened to, in your ears, in your head and in your heart. Let the call to prayer be your first introduction to Islam and its wonders of love, Mahperi Hanim. And when you feel in your heart that you understand what could truly be behind this call, I will be there to take that heart and your hand and lead you to a field wider and greener than any you have ever known. Listen now. When you are ready, I am here."

Chapter 33

Starry Portal of Dreams

The Sultan paced back and forth in the divan in front of a group of his emirs. Since returning from the Erzincan campaign, he had become increasingly restless. The disappearance of Ruby's cub troubled him and he believed somehow the emirs were responsible for it, sending him a sign that they were plotting against him once again. To take his mind off this event, the Sultan again directed his energy to the development of his empire, and called his emirs together to discuss his plans with them.

"My emirs! There is a vast nothingness in the middle of this land! I want to fill this emptiness with people and buildings. The world's horizon will be widened by my efforts, and all eyes will turn to Anatolia as a beacon for trade and wealth!"

The emirs stole glances at each other, for they knew what this would mean for them. The last time the Sultan had given an order to build, a serious revolt had ensued, with unfortunate consequences for many of them. Perhaps this time the Sultan would be more reasonable and not overburden them like before, but the fiery machinery churning behind those blue eyes said otherwise.

"Yes, I must encourage travelers to come to my lands. I have spent much time rebuilding the cities of my kingdom, but now I must develop a program for the countryside. If travelers feel safe on our roads, they will trade here, and our lives will be enriched by the goods they will be able to sell us. From palm-shaded oases of distant deserts, from mountain mines and from workshops of the Eastern cities, from sea to sea, from Empire Byzantine to Empire Persian, all kinds of goods must pour into the baskets of our bustling bazaars: cardamom and curry, emeralds and diamonds, juicy dates, cedar wood and ivory, bronze pots and apricots, cinnamon and silk! Yes, they must all be in our hands!" he exclaimed, rubbing his palms together.

"As you know, my emirs, there are already overnight inns on the roads leading to Konya. But now, I want to dot the entire kingdom with these caravansarais, or as we call them in Turkish, *hans*. I want to build a necklace of them – hundreds of them! – a chain so extensive that everyone coming after me will say I was delirious. I believe the true strength of a ruler depends on the strength of the stones of his kingdom: roads, waterways, bridges, sanitation canals and aqueducts – not on fancy palaces and gardens! Once the state coffers are filled with the money earned from these hans, we will wisely reinvest it to serve the religious, educational and social needs of our people. Medreses, hospitals and mosques will rise from the profits earned by these hans."

The emirs now sat up and listened to him with interest, for they realized that this vision would potentially result in more gold in the pockets of their caftans.

The Sultan continued to explain his proposal. "We must consider the needs of the merchants and travelers on our roads. Let us just imagine for a moment that we are merchants – what do they need to carry out their trade? What are their fears and wants? They hunger and thirst, that is certain, and their horses and beasts may fall lame. Without strong beasts of burden, how will they drive their goods to market? They ask themselves each day as they set out: 'What lies ahead? Who awaits me on the road and in the next town? Will they be enemies or friends? What will be the unknowns of weather? Will I freeze in a snowstorm or die of heatstroke?' We must make sure that they never have to be concerned about these issues when they are on Seljuk roads!"

The Sultan walked over to Köpek and put his hand on his shoulder. "Today is a very important day: I am inviting all of you to visit the site of a han I am building on the Aksaray road. It is well underway and we hope to have it done by spring. It will be the most impressive han in the entire land. Köpek has worked with me to oversee construction of this building. He is carrying out the task with great mastery, and I am pleased. I am counting on you as well, my emirs, to support the cost of the construction of similar hans. You have already done a magnificent job building the walls of our cities, but now we can do more. These hans will be run as businesses, so there will be profits for you as well as for the state coffers."

The Sultan could see that they were already counting the gold *dirhams* in their heads, so he continued.

"But we will not practice greed in these hans. My emirs, it is our duty to show the respect and consideration for the foreign and local travelers on our lands. I propose that every traveler, whatever his nationality or religion, will be my guest for three days, and no charge to those who remain for that time. Their hungry stomachs will be filled with meals paid for from my very own purse. Medical treatment will be provided for illnesses, and their cleanliness will be assured by my hammams. Their horses will be shod, and their lame and tired animals replaced. At the end of three days, their repaired shoes will be placed in front of their door. They can then choose to leave or remain, and if they do stay, a small daily fee will be charged. We will thus show our power, influence and generosity to all the peoples of the world, who will look up to us with admiration. Such will be the Seljuk way!"

☪ ☪ ☪

The next day the caravan of emirs and court officials set off to visit the site. The Sultan invited Mahperi as well, as he always counted on her grounded advice. There is certainly no way I am going to miss this excitement, thought Mahperi as she climbed atop Eclipse, pleased to spend some time alone with Alaeddin, far from Gaziye. She remembered how impressed she had been when she first visited a han on her maiden voyage to Konya. How far ago that seemed now! But from what she heard, this han was going to be much grander, for it would bear the mark of the highest excellence and prestige: it was a royal commission, built to honor both the Sultan and his ancestors!

☪ ☪ ☪

Two days later, the royal caravan caught glimpse of a building rising above the steppes like a hulking bear. When they arrived at the main entry, the Sultan paused to give some details.

"I have faced the door towards Aksaray, so as to encourage the flow of travel to Konya. This huge portal will beckon merchants coming from the east from miles away! This door, along with the hexagonal corner towers and the smaller side towers give the han the reassuring appearance of a fortified castle. This door can be bolted shut, securing all goods and animals from harm. I can assure you, no one will ever be able to storm these walls!

Before entering the han, the Sultan asked his imam to recite a prayer for the safekeeping of all who would come through these doors and for the long life of its stones. Above the door, Mahperi saw a band of cursive writing and a frieze of the same alternating black and white stones as on the façade of the mosque on the hill in Konya. The explosion of carved decoration of blossoms, crescents, palmettes and stars on the portal stones made her dizzy, and seemed more beautiful than the stars she used to gaze at in the night sky above her palace at Kalonoros.

Her reverie was interrupted by the squawking, high-pitched voice of Köpek. "There is nothing like this in your little Kalonoros, is there, Sultana?" he snickered as he rudely pushed by her to enter ahead of her.

They walked down a long entryway which gave out onto the main courtyard. "The rooms on each side of this corridor will be used as offices for administrative operations," the Sultan explained, gesturing with his hand. "And here in the corner is the hammam."

Mahperi noted that the Sultan and his architects had thought of every detail a traveler would need. The mark of excellence was unmistakable. When they came out into the wide courtyard, the vibrant sunshine in the open space beamed off the limestone blocks like mirrors. The courtyard had a covered hall to the rear as did Kandemir han on the road to Konya. But this han had something she had never seen before: there was a mosque in the shape of huge cube in the middle of the courtyard.

Pointing to the arcade running along the right-hand side of the courtyard, the Sultan continued to highlight the features of the han. "This area will be used for storing goods and stabling animals. At the end of day, the merchants are tired, and these high and open vaults will make the unloading and loading of goods easier for the grooms." Mahperi turned her eyes to the left side of the courtyard and saw a row of nine small rooms. "Ah, and over there, we have the rooms that will be used for daily service activities: a kitchen, a refectory with carved stone benches, as well as spaces for sleeping. No need will go untended for the travelers to my lands!" boasted the Sultan.

In the courtyard, Mahperi saw a stone carver busy at work on the inscription plaques to be installed above both the entry door and the door leading to the covered section to the rear of the courtyard. She paused to admire his work, and he smiled up at her. "I am writing the Sultan's name and the date in letters so large that even the camels will be able to read it from miles down the road!" he laughed.

The Sultan turned to the masons and bellowed out, "And don't forget that I want the limestone blocks set so tightly that you won't even be able to insert a blade of grass between them!"

Mahperi contemplated the little mosque, set on four stout piers to raise it from the dust of the courtyard, and thought it resembled a long-legged camel with a heavy pack on its back. A small stone stair snaked up the side, and Mahperi climbed up it to look into the prayer room. It was decorated with a sculpted mihrab, and she estimated that the space could hold a dozen men for prayer. The stone decoration of the mosque was masterful, truly worthy of a Sultan's prayers.

The site foreman now led the Sultan's retinue through another impressive portal into the covered section of the han. "This hall will comprise the sleeping and living quarters for the winter months," he explained to Mahperi as she lifted her eyes to the high vaults. The central aisle, wider than the others, reminded her of the nave in her church at Kalonoros. In the middle was a dome, with an opening to the outside to let in air and sunshine, and which was covered by a conical cap. Mahperi admired how the stones had been laid in the pattern of a snail's shell, decorated by a handsome carved rope at the base. No element was considered too small to be denied artistry.

The Sultan turned to Mahperi and said, "So what do you think of all this, Mahperi? Tell me, my Guiding Moonbeam, am I doing a good thing here, or is this just foolishness on my part?" His blue eyes shone on her with the same sense of partnership that they shared at the beginning of their marriage, when both sought to build up her Kalonoros into his Seljuk showcase city.

"Oh, my Sultan," cried Mahperi, "this han shines brighter than all the jewels in your crown! You have truly surpassed your glory with this building!"

And with that said, the Sultan knew that his people would now live in the light of a new and secure era.

☪ ☪ ☪

Soon the doors of this han would open to all the merchants of the land. Yet on this day, a special door opened for Mahperi as well.

As she gazed up at the explosion of stars engraved on the main portal of the Sultan Han of Aksaray, Mahperi realized that she had found the solace she had been seeking since the arrival of Gaziye. It was as if a comet had streaked across those skies and flashed in front of her universe, lighting her path with a blinding light. No longer were her thoughts confused about what she was going to do with her life. The answer was written right there on that starry portal, and the path in front of her now seemed as clear as a night sky in winter.

She, too, would build.

As she looked up at the carved decoration on the portal, Mahperi realized that this was her salvation from the sadness she felt since the arrival of Gaziye. Once she had walked under that starry portal, she knew that she wanted her life to take on a reality as strong as its golden stones. When she observed the finest masons and stone carvers in the land working on this han, she knew that she, too, wanted to be surrounded by such excellence and artistry. This building is so noble, so pure, and so far from the court and its vicious intrigues – this is an endeavor as impressive as life itself! I am suffocating in Konya, thought Mahperi; I must get onto these plains, here the wind blows hard and the dust carries hopes. I want to be in charge of something grand. I want to feel the same strength that Hanife does when she weaves: so many yarns coming together, so many decisions to make that will be mine, to be shared with these workmen of excellence. I, woman and queen, am capable of making those decisions; I am capable of building something as beautiful as this han. Yes, my destiny lies somewhere here in these stones; I will pour my blood into them like mortar from this day forth.

Starry portal of my dreams, I am ready to walk through you!

Chapter 34

The Price of Pride

Kemaleddin Kamyar has returned to Kayseri!

The news of the return of the Emir to the court at Kayseri from his diplomatic mission to the far reaches of eastern Anatolia was shouted out by pages throughout the halls of the Konya palace and reached the eager ears of the Sultan. Kamyar's messenger brought news to the Sultan about the aggressive intentions of the Khawarazmian leader Jelaleddin Menguberti, leaving the Sultan no option but to depart at once to do battle with him. As his troops made ready for the journey across the plains to the East, the Sultan knew that there was one person he needed to consult before leaving. Mahperi was always his touchstone for any important political decision – and the situation with Jelaleddin Menguberti was indeed a significant one.

When Mahperi arrived in his rooms, the Sultan was pacing back and forth, spurting out his fury about the recent turn of events in Eastern Anatolia. "Many were the years when Jelaleddin Menguberti was my faithful ally and friend, and now he has deceived me! In his struggle against the Mongols, he has become reckless and irresponsible!"

The Sultan paused for a minute and shook his head in regret. "Ah, Mahperi, if you only knew what a fierce and stirring warrior he is, this courageous Jelaleddin Menguberti! At the same time I was besieging your Kalonoros, he was doing battle with the great Genghis Khan in person! He swam his horse across the Indus River to meet him face to face, and then imposed the only defeat the Khan has ever known! The forces of the Ocean had already pushed Jelaleddin Menguberti from his native homeland south of the Aral Sea westwards into Azerbaijan. At that time, he sent an envoy to me seeking financial assistance against the Mongols, and I answered his call for help with respect. I remember my exact words at that moment: 'Dear Jelaleddin, we are both of the same religion. Our world, our holy Muslim world, is under the threat of invasion from pagans, and its fate depends on our joint policy and action. We must agree to fight as a unified front.'"

The Sultan paused again, shaking his head. "Yet something happened to him, and he became too prideful. He not only refused my collaboration, but he attacked and brutally pillaged the fortress of Ahlat. Unthinkable! Ah, but the glorious city of Ahlat is too delicious a fruit to resist, there on the northwestern coast of Lake Van in the shadow of majestic Mount Ararat! Can one blame a man for being ambitious? But when that man is Jelaleddin Menguberti, my ally and friend, I am unable to pardon such an affront. It is treason!"

The Sultan shuddered at the betrayal of his former friend and ally. "But I am an honorable man, and once again, I gave him an opportunity, by sending an emissary laden with many gifts and peace offerings to salvage our political alliance. Jelaleddin Menguberti rebuffed my gifts, dismissed the ambassadors, telling them, '*Return to your court and tell your sultan that I want nothing to do with the Seljuks, those shepherds who take themselves for Kings*!' This was too much, and so I sent my legendary soldier and diplomat, Emir Kemaleddin Kamyar, to talk sense into the hot head of Jelaleddin Menguberti. Yet he too, was rebuffed, and he has just returned to the Keykubadiyye Palace in Kayseri, with the message that there is more trouble brewing with him in Eastern Anatolia. Mahperi, I must leave at once to deal with Jelaleddin Menguberti. I cannot be sure of his true intentions towards Anatolia, but now I cannot trust him anymore than the Mongols. I am convinced that he is as determined to run me out of my lands as the Ocean himself!"

The Sultan finally stopped his tirade long enough for Mahperi to speak.

"My Sultan, it would seem to me that this Jelaleddin Menguberti is afraid for his life, continuously moving westwards in search of a refuge against the growing Mongol pressure. But think about this: as long as the Khwarazmians remain in the East, a buffer exists between you and those Mongols. Remove him and you will be left standing naked against them. Let Jelaleddin Menguberti take the brunt of their aggression, and break himself against them! That will be punishment enough for his insolence! I understand that you want to avenge the incidents at Ahlat, but the bulwark he provides is too important for us. Let him shield the Seljuk Empire against the Mongols! Please, my Sultan, listen to me!" implored Mahperi.

Alaeddin turned to Mahperi with a flame in his eyes that startled her, now projecting his anger onto her. Since when has she become so unsupportive about my desire to expand my territory and conquer my enemies?

"I am sorry Mahperi! I have no other option! And I certainly do not appreciate your lack of support in my efforts to remove threats to our kingdom! Since when are you so timid?" he snarled, abruptly turning around to leave.

Mahperi was stunned. Never had he spoken harshly to her before, and she felt hurt. As he approached the door, she saw that Köpek had been eavesdropping outside in the hall, and had overheard the entire scene, adding to her humiliation.

"Excuse me, my Sultan," Köpek said, with a smirk on his face, turning to look at Mahperi from the doorway. "I have come to tell you that all the preparations have been made for your immediate departure for Kayseri to meet with Kamyar and to decide the fate of Jelaleddin Menguberti. Come, my Sultan, let us show that Khwarazmian upstart who is the strongest Lion that walks on earth!"

☪ ☪ ☪

The Sultan Alaeddin Keykubad, Glory of Glorious Lions, Most Revered Lord, the World Renowned, Holy Wise One, Sultan of Sultans, was angry indeed, and acted quickly in response. He immediately dispatched 2,000 of the finest horsemen, under the command of the Commander Chavli, to Erzincan to be ready to attack. He was not alone. The Ayyubid Sultan Al-Ashraf himself came north from Aleppo and Diyarbakir to lead a special corps of 5,000 of his elite troops. The allied forces assembled in a wide campfield at Yassicimen, a grassy meadow west of Erzincan on the route to Sivas. They were soon joined by the Sultan's Turkmen cavalry forces, under the command of Emir Kamyar. A contingent of Armenian and Latin troops was provided by the Armenian king Hethoum of Cilicia in accordance with the terms of his peace treaty with the Seljuks. The combined forces numbered 20,000. The sharp blade of the anger of the Sultan was ready to slice the air open, out there, in a meadow deep in the valley of God's thumbprint.

☪ ☪ ☪

While the Sultan was assembling his forces, Jelaleddin Menguberti was besieging Malazgirt. When he heard that the Seljuk troops had assembled for battle, he knew he needed to make haste west and deal with them. He was confident that he would be able to secure an easy victory, since he had behind him a contingent of over 100,000 men. He, the Khwarazmian Warrior of Eternity, he, who had looked the Ocean in the eye and reduced him to a tiny wave, was in no way afraid of the troops of these shepherds now playing as Kings!

He first met and defeated a Seljuk vanguard on the hot Ramadan day of July 28, 1230, and continued on to meet the main contingent at the grassy meadow of Yassicimen the next day. The Khwarazmians fought hard and were in superior number, but despite the cocky optimism of Jelaleddin Menguberti, they were crushed in the end by the Seljuk forces.

So it was there, in a meadow in that valley of God's thumbprint, on a hot August day in 1230, that one of the proudest warriors of the East was conquered by a Shepherd King. Jelaleddin Menguberti was defeated for the first time by forces other than the Mongols. After an Ayyubid soldier raided his tent in the middle of the night, he panicked and fled the battlefield. He ran all the way back to Azerbaijan, abandoning the siege of Malazgirt, evacuating the hard-won Ahlat and scattering his treasure all along the way. His remaining troops were killed or taken prisoner. A few months later near Diyarbakir, Menguberti was murdered in his tent, some say by a deranged soldier, while others say that the earth swallowed him up in an orchestrated disappearance until the day when his resurrection to power would dawn again.

After the battle, the Sultan Alaeddin Keykubad, Glory of Glorious Lions, Sultan of Sultans, went on to capture the principality of Erzurum. The Sultan Alaeddin Keykubad was truly now the Most Revered Lord, and hero of this day. Bards lauded the Sultan in their verses, the marketplaces buzzed with praise, prayers were lifted to God for his well-being, and banquets were held in honor of Alaeddin Keykubad, Glory of Glorious Lions.

☪ ☪ ☪

Mahperi sat in her room in the palace on the hill in Konya and listened to the reports brought by messengers of the events of the grassy field in the valley of God's thumbprint. She was both relieved and dismayed by the news. She was relieved, because her husband was safe and victorious. She was dismayed, because her prideful Sultan had not followed her advice as he usually did, and she somehow felt this was a bad omen. Battle follows battle; blood runs like water, personal glory and vanity are the prayers of the day. Will we ever live the blessings of peace in this land?

There is always a price to pay for pride, she thought, shaking her head. The Sultan chose not to follow my words of reason. Instead, he let the rage of his temper and arrogance lead the way. Yes, there is always a price to pay for pride, be it for cities, sultans or renegades. In the end I suppose we both were right, she thought. The Sultan was right to do away with an ambitious and volatile adversary. I was right because the removal of Jelaleddin Menguberti and his hellcat troops has now left a breach in the dam holding back the torrential flood waters of the Ocean. It is now only a matter of time before they will pour forth, she thought, shivering despite the warm weather.

Chapter 35

Polar Star above the Horizon

Mahperi was more than insightful when she counseled her husband to keep a buffer between the Mongols and the Seljuks. For now, after the death of Jelaleddin Menguberti, the Mongols stood unchecked on the doorstep of Anatolia, ready to rush through the door. A proud Sultan would now pay the price for his pride.

The Mongols were a cyclone of dust devils coming from the East, spitting blinding sand in the eyes of all in their path. These were hardy men who dropped from their mother's wombs on horseback and rode before they could waddle. The Crusader knights, in their caparisoned finery, armor and emblems of ancestry, may have believed they were the foremost warriors in the world, but the Mongol demons knew otherwise. Mongol horses were small but spirited, and their riders were clad lightly to move with lightning speed. Their weapon was the bow and arrow, and they were highly disciplined, superbly coordinated and brilliant in tactics. The world had never seen warriors such as this.

Brilliant warriors perhaps, but illiterate savages nonetheless. They were a band of 700,000 herdsmen from the grassy plains north of the Gobi Desert and to the south of the Siberian forests. They carried no dreams of creating literature, music or poetry. They were shamanists, and their Magic Men in animal furs invoked the gods of their spirit world with shaking drums, gongs, flutes, and hooting animal sounds. They climbed the World Tree alongside roosters, giant tortoises and goats, on their soul journey towards the Polar Star, the brightest of the seven stars of the constellation of their gods. They lit fires on sacred mountains and performed convulsive dances until they fell to the ground. They had no scripture, no holy word; just grunting, trances, shaking bells, falcon feathers and horsetails bobbing on sticks.

At the turn of the 13th century, before the time of Alaeddin's grandfather Kilich Arslan II, the Mongols were fragmented local bands headed by a chief they called the khan. They lived in portable felt tents. They were not builders of cathedrals, mosques or medreses; no fine buildings graced their cities. Their only concern was finding grazing areas for their animals, for they ate only meat, milk and yogurt.

This changed when a young Mongol named Temujin, which meant "the Ocean" in their language, acquired a taste for goods and finery they did not possess in their clusters of felt tents. He rose as khan over various families, due to his leadership skills and his ability to collect people of talent. In 1206, at forty-two, Temujin the Ocean took the title of Genghis Khan, the Universal Ruler, and set out to prove that he deserved it. He saw himself and his subjects at the center of the universe, the greatest of people and favored by the gods, the gods of that World Tree and shaking sticks.

Starting with northwestern China, military success after success made people believe that Genghis Khan had indeed the Mandate of Heaven. The Mongols got a taste for more than yogurt and meat and shaking sticks. Along the way they captured musicians, translators, doctors and scribes, camels and wagonloads of goods: silk, rope, cushions, blankets, robes, rugs, wall hangings, porcelain, iron kettles, armor, perfumes, jewelry, wine, honey, medicines, bronze, silver and gold. The taste was sweet on the lips of the Universal Ruler, and he hungered for more goods, as well as new lands.

Genghis Khan and his army pushed more deeply into Persia and Central Asia. His strategy was to frighten townspeople into surrendering without battle. Those frightened into surrender were spared violence. If a city chose not to surrender to the Mongols, all its fighting men were killed. The literate and learned were made prisoners. Talented and gifted artists were shipped back to China. He wasted no time in killing the city's most rich and powerful in order to seize their property. The dust devils tortured, mutilated and maimed, routed and raped women, and hacked all to pieces. Panic soon spread all the way to Bukhara and Samarkand. Citizens fled, scholars migrated, cities surrendered, and all lands were torn asunder by the dust devil warriors. Fearful word reached Europe from returning Crusaders about this Ocean Genghis Khan and his 125,000 fierce horsemen.

The heathen Mongols led a Holy War against Islam from the East, just as the Frankish Crusades were doing from the West. Only the brave Jelaleddin Menguberti was able to resist the Ocean, but he, too, found himself pushed more and more westwards. By the time the Sultan Alaeddin Keykubad stepped onto the throne of the Seljuk Empire, the Mongols were in Azerbaijan and Armenia at the doors of the Seljuk lands. Only the Khwarazmian Empire of Menguberti was left standing between them.

In 1225, the Ocean Genghis Khan abruptly decided to return East to his felt tents, pleased that he ruled all lands between the Caspian Sea and Beijing. Life was sweet, caravans toted trade, and taxes poured in from the conquered peoples. But the waves of the Ocean could not remain calm for long. Once back home, Genghis soon became bored sitting on his fine silken cushions. He longed for a hard saddle, and set out once again west to battle. Yet, behold, on route to more glory, on one hot day in 1227, the Universal Ruler, the great wave of the Ocean, it is said, fell off his horse and died.

But the waves of the Ocean did not stop there. Before his death he had chosen his third son Ogedei to succeed him as the Great Khan, and no land tempted the lustful gaze of Ogedei more than the sweet pastures of Anatolia. He dreamed that from there he would cross the Danube and conquer Europe, and after that, the world beyond. Ah, yes, he thought, I must start with Anatolia, for it is the key to Europe. Now that Jelaleddin Menguberti and his Khwarazmian Empire have been dismembered by a foolish sultan, nothing can stop me from spilling forth into the lush lands of the Seljuks. They will soon be mine – I can see that promise sparkling when I look up to the sacred Polar Star above the horizon.

Chapter 36

The Grey Satin Shroud of February

Bitter cold blew in the faces of the people of Konya, brought by the February winds across the steppes. Bitter sadness blew in the hearts of the people of Konya, brought by the news that their beloved master, Bahaeddin Veled, had died, in this grey satin shroud of February. The hearts of the Sultan and Mahperi were as desolate as the cold plains, as they had been close to the elder Master, who had become, in the three short years since he arrived in Konya, the most important spiritual leader of the capital.

The Sultan Alaeddin Keykubad, knowing how attached Mahperi was to the old man, called her into his private apartments to break the news of his passing. As he suspected, she collapsed and wept into her hands.

"I can understand your sadness, Mahperi, for all Konya is bereft. Do you remember that day three years ago when he first arrived here? He rode into town with more pomp than you did as a Queen, and even refused to bow to me, the Sultan of Sultans – he extended the tip of his staff for me to kiss instead of his hand! With one gesture, he told all of Konya who was their true leader! I soon sat in the front row with his students and listened to his lectures in the Altinapa Medrese. This was a simple man with only one ambition: to serve God with all his being."

Mahperi wiped away her tears with the corner of her sleeve. She wondered what would become of Konya now that he was gone. And now I have lost yet another person dear to me!

"He was a wise man, that Bahaeddin, and he did much to keep me grounded and fixed on the essential truths of a ruler," continued the Sultan. "I remember the time when I asked him to come with me on the roof of the palace to survey the city walls and the towers that I had just restored. Bahaeddin turned to me and said, 'Against torrents and against the horsemen of the enemy you have raised a goodly and solid defense, I will grant you. But what protection have you built against unseen arrows; the sighs and moans of the oppressed, which overleap a thousand walls and sweep whole worlds to destruction? Take care of that now! Strive to acquire the blessing of your subjects. They are a stronghold, compared to which the walls and turrets of the strongest castles are as nothing.' I will never forget those words, for they were the very same ones you said to me after our marriage. Whereas the Mongols destroy everything, I will seek to be a builder of stones and blessings. That will be Bahaeddin Veled's eternal legacy to me."

"Yes," Mahperi sighed, "He was a man of this earth and of the next one; one foot with us and one foot with God. He was like one of the disciples of Jesus, spreading the word of wisdom and love. Who will ever take his place?"

Mahperi thought back to the last conversation she had with Bahaeddin, only one week ago. She had come for their weekly lesson, but when she arrived at the medrese, she was told that he was waiting for her at his home. The wife of his son, Jelaleddin, escorted her into his room, where he was lying on his mat surrounded by devoted attendees and nurses. Mahperi realized that he was not well, and knelt beside him.

Bahaeddin smiled. "My good Lady, do not be afraid. Even though I know I will soon pass from this earth, I will be with you always. You are not alone, have I not shown you this? Remember, it is not me that you come to for comfort, it is not me that you see in my grey eyes: you are looking for the wisdom of God that shines forth from them. You will continue to see this light in the eyes of other sheikhs and other wise men who will come forth. I commend my son Jelaleddin, if I may speak as a proud father, as one such leader for you."

Mahperi lowered her eyes and spoke very softly. "Wise Bahaeddin, you cannot leave me just yet, for I still have so much to learn. I do not know where my path to God will lead, but if it should lead to Islam – if ever I am to pronounce the *shahada* – I want you by my side when I profess that declaration of the faith of God and take my first breath as a believer. I want you to be the witness to the opening of a new life; you, who opened that door for me to pass through."

"No, my dear Lady, I do not need to be there that day. When you pronounce the *shahada*, there should be no one present to hear you but God. You do not confess this to a priest but to your God. And I believe that day will come, and your heart will be so filled with companionship that the trouble-makers that surround you in the court will seem as nothing more than pesky flies. Now, let me rest, my good Lady, I am tired. Just remember to always travel on the path of love that I have shown you."

She was pained to see how difficult it was for him to breathe. She bent down and whispered in his ear. "Rest well, my Master," and turned so he would not see her tears.

Mahperi snapped back from her reminiscence when the Sultan replied to her question. "Yes, who will ever be able to succeed him? But Bahaeddin often spoke to me about his son. Let us hope that he can carry on for his father. I await great things from this Jelaleddin, and he will have my support, just as I supported his father. He is still young, only twenty-four, yet in the few days since Bahaeddin has left us for paradise, students and followers have already gathered around him, regarding him as the heir of his father. They have even now given him a title, calling him "Jelaleddin Rumi.'"

"My Sultan, let us pray that this son will honor his father's memory and make Konya a brilliant spiritual capital for the world to behold, and that his beacon of love will illuminate the path of seekers of truth from the four corners of the globe, no matter in what fashion God dwells in their hearts. Yes, that will be Bahaeddin Veled's eternal legacy to us."

Chapter 37

Muddied Doorstep

After the defeat of Jelaleddin Menguberti by Alaeddin Keykubad, the troops of Khwarazmians scattered. The forces of the Seljuk Sultan dispersed as well, returning to Erzurum, Kayseri and other cities in the Kingdom. The dispersal was not lost on the ever-alert warrior Mongols, who smelled fresh blood with every dawn. Seizing the opportunity of an unattended frontier region, the Mongol army of 30,000 under the command General Chormagan Noyan, based in northwest Persia, began to raid the Seljuk lands. Like a door left open to the stable, the robbers came in to steal the stallions. The whooping troops with their squat horses and long moustaches arrived at the very doors of Sivas and Malatya, terrifying the population, both Muslim and Christian.

The Sultan Alaeddin Keykubad had been long dreading the arrival of the Mongols, but he had not expected it so soon. Now in the year 1231, Alaeddin Keykubad smelled, for the first time, the odor of the Ocean and its pungent tang frightened him. He immediately sent his troops back to the region, under the command of the eminent General Kemaleddin Kamyar. The Sultan gave the tall order to the fearless Kamyar to meet the Mongols on the spot and to fend them off from further advances. Yet, by the time Kamyar arrived at Sivas, the Mongol raiders had returned to Persia. It seems they had come to Anatolia merely to survey the situation in the lush lands of the Seljuks. But no one was fooled: they would be back.

In order to avert a more serious invasion of the Seljuk lands by the Mongols, the Sultan decided to send a Seljuk embassy to the court of Ogedei. He wrote a letter for his ambassadors to present to the Mongols, telling them that they were to leave the Seljuk lands alone and avoid any confrontation with the Seljuk Empire, the mightiest in the world! The Sultan had every hope that the letter his ambassadors carried would be well-received by the Khan. It is certain that Ogedei would appreciate the gifts the Sultan sent – notably a carpet woven by Hanife – but the Khan needed to believe that the words in the letter glittered as brightly as any jewel he could offer him. The embassy of diplomats set off from Konya on a fine spring morning, carrying not only supplies, gifts and gold, but all the determination of a Seljuk Sultan to preserve peace for his people.

☪ ☪ ☪

Before raiding Anatolia, the Mongols first assailed the green hills of Georgia. The Queen of Georgia, Rusudan, was a headstrong woman, but did not have behind her the trained troops of the Seljuks or brave generals such as Kamyar. She only had a kingdom filled with beautiful horses and women, rose gardens, castles, domed churches and juicy vineyards, none of which would stand up to the waves of General Chormagan Noyan and his 30,000. Her only option to spare her country and her people from rampage and devastation was to accept the superiority of the Great Khan. For Rusudan, the price of salvation was an annual tribute of 50,000 gold pieces and soldiers, and she paid it willingly. So it was that Georgian troops rode alongside of the heathens of General Chormagan Noyan when they came to devastate the Anatolian countryside as far as the walls of Sivas and Malatya.

When Sultan Alaeddin Keykubad learned of this treachery by his former Georgian allies, he moved to punish them. An angry Alaeddin Keykubad retaliated by sending his army up from Erzurum across the Georgian border, trampling those rose gardens and vineyards. After the Seljuks captured a number of frontier strongholds, the haughty queen Rusudan, seeing there was no hope against the Seljuk army either, was forced to submit and sued for terms of peace. Better the Seljuks than the Mongols she reasoned, paying the tribute of 1,000 gold pieces the Sultan requested as tribute.

Yet one of the terms of surrender involved gold of a different sort. Queen Rusudan pledged her young daughter Tamara in marriage to the Sultan's son. Although this golden-haired doll was yet a child, as was the ten-year-old Giyaseddin Keyhüsrev, the marriage contract was signed on paper, with the agreement that the girl would come at a later date to the Seljuk court to become the bride of the future Sultan. Little did anyone realize that in a few years, the gold of this little girl's head would rival all the gold in the royal treasury.

Chapter 38
Flows the Black Ink into Colors

"May your pen strokes be as powerful as the slashes of my sword!" The Sultan stood in front of a small young man bent over a notebook with a pen poised in his delicate fingers. He was dressed in a stylish blue embroidered caftan, so different from the simple white cotton robes worn by the other court scribes. A white aigrette plume stuck out of his turban with jaunty panache, gold hoops dangled from his earlobes, a double strand of pearls was roped around his neck and a large topaz ring sparkled on his finger even before he began to write. Indeed, thought the Sultan as he looked down at him, this alluring and exotic newcomer is not at all like the stern scribes here at my court. This one has a rare flair, indeed.

"Al-Husain ibn Muhammad al-Munshi al-Jafari er-Rugadi Ibn Bibi, I welcome you to my court! I am honored that you and your father have accepted my invitation to come to Konya. Like many before you, you have come here fleeing the waves of the Ocean. Know that you will be safe here and that you will flourish in your chosen profession as writers."

Ibn Bibi closed his eyes and relived the events of his young life up to this moment. He had been born in the city of Nishapur in Iran, and for many years his father served as court secretary for Jelaleddin Menguberti in Azerbaijan. The father taught the son everything he could about his craft, from perfect grammar, how not to drip ink on the paper, how to listen for the important point, when to embroider, and how to write quickly, but elegantly, at the same time. It was apparent from a very early age that the boy was gifted.

"Young man, you will be pleased to know that I have appointed your father as head scribe of the secretarial handbooks. He will write letters to other rulers and state officials, conquest announcements, as well as general official correspondence. This must be done only by secretaries of great erudition, as these pieces must be showpieces of masterful style, to be copied in other diplomatic posts. I know your father will be a notable asset to my court."

The Sultan smiled down at the youth and his white aigrette plume, which contrasted with his black eyes rimmed with kohl to enhance their intense luster. "However, for you, I am thinking of another appointment. I have heard that your skill with crafting words is as refined as the great Firdowsi himself, author of the *Shah-name*, the famous Book of Kings of the Persians!"

The young man bowed his head at the Sultan's compliments and blushed slightly, pleased that he had gained his favor. "I thank you for the confidence you show me, Most Revered Lord, Al-Muazzam Sultan Alaeddin Keykubad, I am here at your illustrious court to serve you in any way I can."

"Good! Then I have a proposition for you. Ibn Bibi, as I shall call you, you are too talented to remain as a mere court scribe, documenting meetings and copying contracts and deeds! No, for you, I confer a much more significant responsibility. I charge you and that colorful plume of yours with the task of writing my history. You will become my court historian!" declared the Sultan with flourish.

Ibn Bibi opened his eyes wide and looked up at the Sultan in disbelief.

The Sultan continued with the details of this commission. "Yes, for a long time I have felt the need to ensure my legacy. Not only through enacting laws, building hans and siring sons, but by creating a document that will describe all the aspects of my reign. This is the challenge I offer you: I want you to write the journal of my reign. You will follow me wherever I go. You will sit on all of my meetings with my emirs, you will travel with me to the Palace of Keykubadiyye each spring and to Alaiye each winter and you will ride out with me on battlefields. You will be with me at all times, like my very shadow. You will write this document in Persian, for that is the language of our court. I trust you will be honest in your interpretation, but that you will depict me in the most honorable and inspiring way possible for all who will read this document in the future."

He drew a breath before continuing with more details. "I must let you know that I already have another official appointed court reporter who maintains the daybook diary of the court activities. But from you, I want something else: I want these details put into a narrative chronicle, woven into an inspiring story of my exploits and life. I want poetry and beauty from you; I want you to add elegance to the events of our daily lives in your chronicle. I will ask that you start your history with the death of my honorable father Giyaseddin Keyhüsrev and continue forth. In order to do that you will of course have to rely on others for details since you did not directly witness these events up to this day, but I am sure you will be able to do this without difficulty. So! Do you accept this task I put before you, Ibn Bibi? Will you be the written mirror of my reign?"

Ibn Bibi knew he was skillful with his pen, of that he was certain, but at the tender age of twenty-three he was still so young...but yes, I can do all of this, for I am an artist with my little quill tip! And to be in the service of this comely man with such long fingers and elegant bearing, why, this is truly a gift from God! My, those blue eyes of his would inspire anyone to greatness! The young man's chest puffed up with a pride that almost split the seams of his blue satin tunic.

"Could there be any other possible way to depict you, other than honorable and inspiring, O Muazzam Sultan, Light of our World? I will strive to the end of my days to craft with my pen a magnificent historical testimony to your greatness. May God give me the strength and gifts to translate onto paper the glories of your reign! Yes, my Sultan, I will write your story in a style that will rival the *Shahname*. I will write your name *Al-Sultan* in red ink in letters so large that it will be seen from across the room, far brighter than that purple ink used by the Byzantines! You will glow for all eternity from my pen; I promise you that, O, my Sultan!

☪ ☪ ☪

And so the ink of the talented pen of Ibn Bibi began to flow from that moment forward, never to stop until the end of his days. It was an ink that flowed with poetry and eloquence, from deep black into brilliant colors, scripted to immortalize for all eternity the reign of the Sultan with the piercing blue eyes who commissioned it.

Chapter 39

A Bone Gnawed Raw

It was almost four years now since Giyaseddin had been sent away, but the pain of his departure was still deeply felt by Mahperi. She thought of her son constantly, and prayed to the Almighty each day for his well-being and safety. She longed for news of him, no matter how small. So many questions about him continually ran through her mind. Were his lessons advancing to prepare him for his role as the next Sultan? Was he happy in his new life far from Konya? Had he learned to read and speak Persian fluently? Was he learning to play chess like his father? How tall is he now? Has he learned to become more independent and self-assured, and able to make his own decisions? Above all, Mahperi wanted to know if he missed her, and if he still thought of her with the same tenderness as the little boy who was pulled away from her with tears rolling down his plump cheeks. Mahperi feared that his memories of her had become more blurred with each day.

So starved was she for the smallest tidbit about her son that she became ecstatic when she heard that a group of court officials had just returned to Konya after an extended visit to Erzincan. Among them was Sadettin Köpek, and she knew that he would have much news of her son, for whatever she personally thought of the man, she knew that he always showed genuine interest in her son. She summoned him the very next morning to her rooms.

"Good morning, Sadettin Köpek, I am pleased to know that you have just returned safely from Erzincan. I am eager to hear of your news about the Sultan's son and heir Giyaseddin. Know that no detail will be too small for me to savor!" she said, gesturing for her maids to serve him some refreshments.

"Yes, Mahperi Hatun, I saw the Sultan's son and he is well," informed Köpek, making sure that he was not going to indulge her maternal concerns. "He is growing into a fine young man, why he is almost at the age of manhood! You will be very pleased to know that he is showing promise in his studies, and has mastered both Persian and Arabic with equal ease. He seems to favor mathematics and science, and is curious about the natural world around him."

Köpek continued to coldly describe the boy's situation as if he were informing Ibn Bibi, and not the child's mother. "He is healthy and quite robust. His hair is still a fine shade of reddish brown, and his fair complexion is becoming hardened by the intense sun and wind of the Erzincan plains. It is a place for strong men, those plains around Erzincan! He is rarely sick, eats well, and gets along very well with Ertokush and the other tutors. That is really all I can tell you, my Lady, for I did not have that much time to spend with the boy, what with all the court meetings and discussions," he finished, in as dismissive a tone as possible.

"Thank you very much, Köpek, I am glad to have this news about his progress and health. But, Köpek, I was wondering – does he ever speak of Konya? Does he ever mention his father…or me?" She swallowed her pride to ask him these questions, and she found it hard to look him in the eyes.

"Actually, my Lady, I think that he has made a happy new life with Ertokush in Erzincan, and has little thought for Konya. You know how children forget things so quickly, don't you? He is, of course, constantly reminded of the Sultan, as all of his deeds are presented to him as examples for the art of leadership. He did ask me about Ruby, and how she was, that I do remember. But other than that, I think his life in Konya is now just a vague memory for him."

Mahperi felt as if her heart had stopped beating. Could you not have found it in your heart to tell me one kind thing, you ugly Dog, about how this boy still thinks of his mother? I know that he must think of me still; it is impossible that he could forget me, for the bond that we shared was one of tenderness and love. She refused to let Köpek see her disappointment, so she immediately asked him another question.

"And his religious education, may I ask how that is progressing? As we know, this is an important issue for a future Sultan. He must show understanding of all the religious traditions in this Empire, if he is to show tolerance for all its peoples. I have always believed that Giyaseddin will be a wise leader since he benefits from the rich traditions of the religions of both his father and me."

The Dog Köpek smiled at her comment, for she had unsuspectingly given him a piece of rich meat he could rip off her bone. "Yes, you are correct, his religious education is important, and it is one that receives much attention, for you know how pious that old Ertokush is! He spends much time in learning the verses of the Qur'an by heart, discussing with scholars of the law, interpreting the lessons of the Hadith, and learning the prayers of the holy days. He is well-versed in Arabic and can read the Qur'an with ease. He did mention to me that he no longer thinks of Jesus."

Again, Mahperi's heart stopped. This was not possible, she thought. I taught him all the parables of Jesus and what they meant, and how he loved those stories so, begging me to repeat them over and over again! Didn't he tell me when he was a little boy that he, too, was going to divide fishes and loaves when he became Sultan, so that none of his people would go hungry?

"As I said, my Lady, I did not spend much time with him to know much more, but once again, rest assured that he is turning into a fine young man."

☪ ☪ ☪

Sadettin Köpek told many lies that morning, but the last comment was the biggest one, for he had indeed spent much time with the boy. He needed to assess whether the boy's timid personality was still the same as before he came under the tutelage of Ertokush. He wanted to know if the boy would listen to what he said and follow his lead, for that was the one goal that Köpek had set for himself. Yes, Köpek was formulating a plan to ensure that the boy's loyalty would be towards him and not the Sultan. This recent visit confirmed to Köpek that his plan would be an easy one to carry out. The boy was terribly lonely and missed his mother desperately. He was as withdrawn in nature as always, and still longed for the loving attention that his father would never give him. Well, my little heir apparent, do not fear, for I, Vizier Köpek, I am here to give it to you, and more, much more, just you wait and see what I am planning for you.

Chapter 40

Gardens of Blessed Moments

Blessed moment.

I live for this moment. Its memory haunts my dreams through the night. The anticipation of it wakes me before dawn. It energizes my fingers, my heart, my eyes and my whole body all the day long.

Blessed moment.

I lift my eyes to the loom. I open my mind to the color. I raise my hand and I pick up the yarn from the bobbin hanging on the side of the loom. I touch it to the loom. My fingers hold it there for one moment; yes, this blessed moment when all is possible. It is this precise moment when the color, my hand, the yarn, and the vision of the third eye inside my head all converge, ready to give birth to something that was never there before. It is the blessed moment of the weaver's dream. I, Hanife, weaver of dreams and love, command this moment towards beauty to be born. Then and only then will I start the rush of my knotting.

Blessed moment of love. Come to me. Hour after hour, row after row, from this one moment. Blessed moment of love, come to me now.

The sheep have been sheared, the wool has been washed in river water and sorted; it has been carded and combed to lie flat and clean and straight, just like my hair after a visit to the hammam. It has been spun and twisted for hours on a drop spindle by my assistants. The master dyers have soaked it in hot vats of mysterious plant syrups and magic animal serums and potent mineral mixtures to give it the colors that will now dance in front of my eyes. Even I do not know their secrets. All these hands have worked so hard, even before my blessed moment arrives.

The skeleton of my loom has been prepared and is ready, standing taller than I am. The vertical warp strings have been wrapped round and round the bottom and top bars of the loom; they are calling my fingers to flesh them out with knots. They are calling me to make the picture in my mind. Now my time has come to begin to knot. Blessed moment of skill, come to me now.

I have thought long and hard about my design. A tree of life will bloom eternally in the center of the rug. Hooks and horns I will add because they are easy to make. Curves and flowers I do not like; they are nature's greatest gift and I cannot compete with God. I will let geometric shapes tell my story, a story of happiness, sadness, love and pain.

Hear my prayer, beloved God, for this blessed moment to begin!

I weave with silence on my lips
I weave with silence in my mind
I weave with silence within my heart

I knot with a thunderstorm of colors
I knot with a starburst of emotions
I knot with a fountain of dreams

I close my ears to distractions
I close my eyes to attractions
I close my heart to temptations

I open my heart to Your love
I open my rows to Your blessings
I open my fingers to Your will

Calm me, O God, subside this storm within me
Still me, O God, keep me from harm
Soothe me, O God, bless me with Your strength

Release my pain with these knots
Deliver my fears with these colors
Cease my tumult with these patterns

Enfold me in the garden rug of Your peace, O God
I weave my rows in exalted prayer to You.
Blessed moment, now begin.

I take the first piece of wool and form the knot over the first two warps on the right side of the loom. I must already envision the entire design in my head, for I must knot horizontally to make the pattern rise vertically on the loom. No mistake is countenanced. Stay focused, stay focused; if not, you will not make a balanced design. You must become the rug, Hanife, the image of its pattern must never leave that eye in your head and those on your face; focus your eyes on the imaginary guiding red spot three-quarters up the loom until the moment the design becomes an extension of your hand; aim for that moment when your hand will take over the knotting, to draw your picture independently of your will.

Blessed moment.

The first row is done now. I cut the excess wool with my hooked knife. A few more rows and I will be pulled into it forever. There is no going back now.

Time to stop and think, as I pass two horizontal weft threads over the row of knots I have just completed, over and under the warps. Be fearless, you have done well; these threads will hold your knots firmly in place for eternity. You are confident that they must be thus preserved. Take your *kirkit* comb, so heavy in your hand, and vigorously beat down the row of knots and the wefts you have just added. *Thump thump thump*, I love that definitive sound; it is done now, the knots are packed down tight, and now onto the next row you go.

Now I pick up the scissors and cut the surplus colored threads so that all the rows of the pile are the same thickness. It becomes like the fur on the back of a cat, smooth and regular. This wool is dense; the wool is soft and pliable; they have prepared it well so that it feels like silk to my fingers. I can see the pattern emerging more clearly now. You will need to adjust that purple on the next row; oh, and yes, you will need to decrease the slope of that line, it is rising too sharply.

And now on to the next row, go, go; you are starting to warm up your fingers, soon they will fly.

knot knot knot knot knot knot knot knot knot knot thump thump thump thump thump thump

I begin again another row of knots. Each knot is a breath. Each breath is a knot. Start to breathe, Hanife start to knot, and soon you will find your pace. My lungs and my fingers are in perfect rhythm.

knot knot knot knot knot knot knot knot knot knot thump thump thump thump thump thump

How long will I sit here, how long will I weave? One year for this rug perhaps, one year of my life for one prayer to God's greatness, is that so much? How many nights will I collapse at the foot of the loom, too tired and spent to crawl over to my sleeping mat, too tired to put some wood into the stove, too tired to eat or drink? But I breathe, I knot, I am panting with exertion; with a whole day of singing knots in my ears, who needs food or fuel with that chorus of colors inside of me?

knot knot knot knot knot knot knot knot knot knot thump thump thump thump thump thump

I weave alone on most days. I am alone in this process, for only I know the way this design will play out in the end. On some days I ask my assistant to sit with me to learn and share the beauty. On other days, my beloved friend Mahperi sits with me facing this garden and we share its blooms unfolding.

knot knot knot knot knot knot knot knot knot knot thump thump thump thump thump thump

Now it is going, now it is flowing –

knot knot knot knot knot knot knot knot knot knot thump thump thump thump thump thump

This is not decoration, this is not frippery. Watch and see, my rug will move you; it will make you think of flowers and birds, or the quandaries of the symbolism of geometry. I will surprise you just when you do not expect it, right here at this spot, I will break up the symmetry just where you thought it would be; yes, and then I will shock you with a color so hot your cheeks will burn. I will rotate my design like a bird flipping in mid-air. I am not afraid to dare. I want to be insolent, I want to be gentle. I take the hard colors of blue and green and red; I take the soft colors of yellow and mauve; all are of God's great garden. This rug is my praise to Him, this is my sacred work. I try to make it as beautiful and as perfect as possible. When my work will reflect my love of Him, it will also reflect my love of those around me. Look closely, it is all there –

knot knot knot knot knot knot knot knot knot knot thump thump thump thump thump thump

Blessed moments, flowing red in wool and in the passion of my blood
Blessed moments, flowing yellow in knots like the sunshine of my hopes
Blessed moments, flowing green in rows like the bounty of blessed nature
Blessed moments, flowing blue in patterns like the domes of God's heaven
Garden of blessed moments, now come unto me

I used to be so lonely. And then you came, my beautiful friend, bringing your quiet gift of love. You taught me to read, you taught me to write. You were never ill-at-ease with my gifted fingers; you never questioned what I saw with my eye and translated here; you were never shocked when I dared to go to an unknown place with my knots

knot knot knot knot knot knot knot knot knot thump thump thump thump thump thump

You accepted my melancholy; you gave me support and friendship. I never questioned your looks, your accent, your love of Mary and Jesus, or your independence as fierce as mine. I know you express ideas from your heart, just as I do from my fingers. We do not laugh at each other's thoughts; you have the courage to say things out loud that I try to say with my knots

knot knot knot knot knot knot knot knot knot knot thump thump thump thump thump thump

You taught me to read, and I taught you about design, color, tolerance and balance, all good things for rugs, for marriage, for the world. We give each other ambitions, dreams, and thoughts warm, wise and funny to share when we are alone. I wish to create a garden here at the foot of my loom where serenity can emanate from a delicate soft signature of design and colors; we will go there together and sit quietly, my Mahperi

knot knot knot knot knot knot knot knot knot knot thump thump thump thump thump thump

I knew you were graceful by the way you held your head and sat at my side. I knew you were intelligent because you did not babble; not one word ever out of place, just like each one of my knots. I knew when you were happy, when you were sad, and when you were overwhelmed with pain

knot knot knot knot knot knot knot knot knot knot thump thump thump thump thump thump

I feel the ache you have in your heart from what the Sultan did to you, how could he imagine to find more with another woman than with what your emerald eyes and intelligence could give him. I will put your flower petals covered in dewdrops of tears here now

knot knot knot knot knot knot knot knot knot knot thump thump thump thump thump thump

Slow down, Hanife, you are too tight here, relax your tension relax your fingers what exactly was that dream I had last night about the dog and the underworld the sunrise was so rosy this morning grab some pink where is it I want to run with it don't lose sight of the guiding red spot staring at you from the crest of the loom

knot knot knot knot knot knot knot knot knot knot thump thump thump thump thump thump

And now you tell me how nasty Köpek has been to you, and how he hurts you with his words about your son. You come to me with tears in your eyes, put there by his malice. You have no idea, my beautiful friend, of the extent of his terrible terrible wickedness. I know of that evil first hand

knot knot knot knot knot knot knot knot knot knot thump thump thump thump thump thump

She must never learn, no, not what I know about Köpek she must never know what he did to my mother she must never learn how he hurt her keep him away from you Mahperi he will hurt you too with his evil

knot knot knot knot knot knot knot knot knot knot thump thump thump thump thump thump

No no she must never know pull back pull back your hands are way too tense now this row of knots is off balance steady yourself get control breathe more yellow more yellow focus focus tone on tone keep the clash of your life away from your rug

knot knot knot knot knot knot knot knot knot knot thump thump thump thump thump thump

Yes I want it all soft but the patterns keep coming out large weave weave weave until the nightmares leave knot knot knot until the pain goes away but the rugs will never be finished the pain will never be gone oh please my knots save me from my pain oh please knots now tell my story

knot knot knot knot knot knot knot knot knot knot thump thump thump thump thump thump

Chapter 41

Second City Now First

Spring came again, and the Sultan Alaeddin Keykubad made ready to head east to Kayseri. There, he would train his troops on the nearby Mashad plain, organize his battalions and prepare for his next military campaigns over the summer in the East. It was a highly-anticipated moment in the year, like the Holy Month of Ramadan.

Mahperi wondered what his life was like in the East – there, in a world dominated by soldiers, sweat and conquest. She was also interested to see what Köpek's famous palace of Keykubadiyye looked like, and she was even more curious to discover this city of Kayseri, famous in lore and legend; the city the Seljuks called *Daru'l-Feth*. Yet the East was part of the life of Alaeddin she was never privy to: the one of conquest and blood. She knew Alaeddin as majestic leader at his court in Konya; she knew Alaeddin as planner and builder during their winter months in the south, but this part of her husband's world was one she did not know.

It thus came as a great surprise to her one morning when the Sultan entered her rooms and sat down on her cushions. She could always tell when he had an idea, problem or question, because his posture, manner and voice became different – not to mention the way he nervously jiggled his prayer beads – and now he spoke in the animated tone of voice she remembered from days past.

"Mahperi, as you know we are preparing to set off for Kayseri to set up camp at the Keykubadiyye Palace. This is a great moment of my year, because from those fields of the Mashad Plain start the campaigns of my army. It seems I spend as much time in my saddle as I do in my cities! As long as I can continue to strike this balance, my kingdom will be the greatest on earth. The victories of the East start with the playing fields of Mashad, where the skills of my troops are honed to perfection, and I have many victories to achieve!" he boomed with his characteristic enthusiasm.

A familiar look came over his face, and Mahperi saw a glimmer of the complicity of their days past.

"I was wondering, however, if you would consider joining me this season in Kayseri. I ask you to come because I am building several projects there and would like you to give me your opinion on them – one is a caravansarai, almost as large as the one we visited together in Aksaray. The other project is a medrese in the middle of town, not far from the Devlethane Palace where I hold court. We could also visit the new Keykubadiyye Palace, for I am sure you would enjoy its peaceful setting. What do you say, my Turquoise Moon Queen?"

Mahperi was as surprised to hear him use her name of endearment as much as she was by his offer. She agreed at once, especially since she knew that Gaziye would never leave the comforts of the Konya court to voyage east. She would have her Sultan to herself, and dared to dream that she could once again truly be his Turquoise Moon Queen.

☪ ☪ ☪

The journey to Kayseri went smoothly, and they traveled along the same caravan route that led them to the Sultan Han near Aksaray that they had visited before, which had now been finished. After two nights of rest, they carried on to Kayseri through some of the oddest countryside Mahperi had ever seen, full of pink-hued canyons covered with tall rock formations instead of trees.

"Byzantine churches were carved out in these caves almost a thousand years ago, Mahperi," the Sultan explained. "This has been a refuge for the priests of your church from invaders and barbarians before us, when your religion was not accepted by all," the Sultan explained.

When they arrived at Kayseri, the Sultan and the court settled in at the Devlethane, his modest palace in the center of town. She visited the impressive caravansarai with the Sultan, built much in the same way as the one in Aksaray. This one had a cube mosque in the middle of the courtyard as well, decorated with a ferocious pair of entwined dragons, sculpted so realistically that they frightened Mahperi. The Sultan gave her a tour of Kayseri on horseback and Mahperi was impressed by the number of monuments of note already built in this city. They also visited the site of the medrese that the Sultan was building in the center of town.

However, it was the city of Kayseri itself that captivated Mahperi the most. There was something about its serious mien, its grey basalt walls and its determined bustle that intrigued her. She felt this city was more suited to her personality than Konya was, for it was tall, defiant, robust and resolute. Many Armenians lived here as well, and she took pleasure in hearing her own language spoken when she walked through the city's bustling bazaars. She rode around the city on Eclipse, discovering its many treasures, just as she had done in her early days in Konya. As she passed in front of the Arrow Tower in the city walls, named after the archers who crouched and shot their arrows from here in times of attack, she thought it resembled a hulking rook standing guard on the board of a chess game. When she peered into the courtyards of the dozens of medreses scattered around the city, she admired the industry of the students there, especially those in the impressive medical complex built by the Alaeddin's father Giyaseddin in honor of his sister. But it was the bazaars of Kayseri that were the most captivating aspect of the city, for they hummed even louder than those of Konya.

She saw there both the most common and the most amazing goods for sale. She saw a booth that sold the prettiest pearly white ceramics with dainty scrolls of blue flowers painted on them, which had come all the way from a country named China, far to the east of Persia. She saw people working in the rear workshops of the bazaar stalls weaving luscious velvets and silks. Kurdish women told fortunes; Arabs and Persians ground spices. She saw people in the bazaars cooking lamb heads down into broth, and hungry mongrels whined constantly in front of stalls selling slabs of pungent cured beef. Eggplants spilled out from carts and splattered to the ground, children ran everywhere, mangy cats dodged under the kilims and checkered cloths draped over the tables, and merchants peddled their wares in voices each one louder than the next. Old men sat on small stools at the side of their booths, guarding their goods, propping their chins on the handles of their canes. Copper pots sparkled in the sunlight; silver goblets and gold bracelets tempted like Satan, fat older women pushed the slender younger ones aside, fancy ladies made their way through the crowd with their servants clearing their path. Some men sauntered, some men ran, women peered and poked, news rang out about a caravan arriving with dates from Egypt, a horse kicked a dog and a dog bit a child, music played on a stringed instrument, smells of heady leather, ripe vegetables and curing sheep heads filled the air, and strolling water and sherbet sellers pushed in front of each other to get the best spot by the corner door. How Mahperi loved all the activity of the bazaars of Kayseri!

Later that evening at the Devlethane, when she commented upon them to the Sultan, he laughed and explained their importance. "As you know, Mahperi, I understand the language of pragmatism and commercial interests. In this realm, I speak twenty languages fluently! Konya is perhaps the seat of government for my kingdom, but it is in the bazaars of Kayseri that the true power of my empire rests, the power of commerce and trade, of goods bought and sold. Our money has become the strongest in the world, due to these bazaars! Konya serves religion and administration, but Kayseri will be the center of commerce and science in my kingdom. The research done in its health centers will benefit the well-being of my entire kingdom. Such is the importance of this city, considered the 'second city' of my empire – but in my mind, it is truly the Capital of Capitals!"

☪ ☪ ☪

One morning, as Mahperi gazed upon the monumental teaching hospital built by Alaeddin's father in honor of his sister Gevher Nesibe, she reflected upon her own ambitions to build, the vow she set for herself when she walked under the starry portal of the han on the Aksaray Road. Standing in front of the door of this medical complex once again inspired her thoughts, and suddenly, it all fell into place for her: Kayseri would become her city too, the key to the next part in her life. I will move here, she told herself. Yes, I will set up a household here far from Gaziye and that Konya court; yes, I will make a life for myself here, in this city of determined people. I will be closer in distance to my son Giyaseddin in Erzincan, and possibly I could even visit him from time to time. I will add a mark in my own fashion to this city of markets and medreses. Yes, here I can live. It is here I will build and live my truth. I will draw strength from the mountain that hovers over the city.

As Mahperi lifted her eyes to the big solitary mountain rising to the south of the city, she was convinced now that her life would climb as high as its snow-capped peak, here in the resolute second city of Kayseri, soon to become the first city of her life.

Chapter 42

Trade Town of Lava and Snow

That ten thousand years long ago – and no one knows for how many millions of eras before that – the great solitary Mountain on the plain had spouted its lava all over the plains, and sprinkled the valleys with ash for centuries and centuries – this was accepted, in this holy moment of time in the year of 1233 as an ongoing fact of life, understood by all who lived in the city built below the northern shadow of its massive form.

The peak of the Mountain guarded the countryside it created like a white, hovering angel, fluttering its wings of knee-deep snow at all seasons of the year. Behold, too, the demon lava that beat in the heart of this white angel, so that both snow and lava glinted at all times off the forehead of its mountaintop. The good and evil of the world were there writ large for all to fear or to admire when looking upon it. Would the giant solitary angel flutter her wings, or would the red demon breathe its fire? That was ever the question asked by all below, each day, as they scurried about their commerce and commotion, lifting their eyes many times during the day to its peak to find the answer. Try as they could to turn their backs to the Mountain, it was always there, never lifting the goggle eye of its peak from those below. For here, in this town below the Mountain, the upper world reigned over the lower world, holding its history of spouting over the lands and the fear of further spouting over the people.

And look upon it the people did, those living below in the city built in the crossroads of time, all watching for signs of further spouting, all the time struggling with their own daily battles for survival in a world of good and evil. The people lived in this city, nestled snug against the chest of the Mountain. Yet, its destiny was never the one of warm safety found in the arms of a loving mother. The very plain below was crafted from its spoutings; a countryside of valleys and rocks and soft stone and secret caves and vast forests of mineral trees.

The mammoth Mountain served as a signpost to the world, beckoning the caravans of commerce for thousands of years now; caravans that knew that all they needed to do was to drive their animals in the direction of the big Mountain, there, at the nexus of all trade routes. Below the Mountain would be held the greatest bazaar they could find, the supreme emporium, flush with products proffered by packs on the backs of beasts of burden from every compass pointing thereto. Come to me, called out the Mountain; come to me, you merchants from Iran, China, Central Asia, Russia and India; come to the marketplace at my feet. I offer you a trade colony like no other, filled with the goods of my fields, my orchards and my workshops.

Indeed, this was a trading town of commerce, commodities and cash, a town where the largest mercantile fair in the world was held each spring since the dawn of time, where droves of merchants came from all corners to hammer hard bargains and drive their deals. Baskets of bounty from the fields of all the nations of the world were sold here: wheat and wild plums, molasses and mungbeans, cheese and cumin, buffalos and barley, pomegranates and grapes, walnuts and wine, quinces and cotton. Each and every product of the mints, dye houses, slaughterhouses, cotton mills, gold shops, tanneries, linseed oil presses and looms of this city of the Mountain found their buyers here in an ever-ending pace of production and trade. Fortunes were made and lost here daily, destinies were crafted here like tin pots and wooden bowls; lives and hearts were broken here, all under the knowing nod of the big Mountain to the south.

It was a city where illustrious men were born, where peasants rose to greatness and where wise religious men of every cloth preached their prophetic words; where scientists in medical schools labored over their experiments again and again to reveal the answers they knew were there to be found; where women with bent heads knotted meadows on carpets, row after row and day after day; a place where tinkers and tailors wielded hammers and needles with equal force and determination. This was the city that churned with endeavor, its beads of sweat dropping into the kettle of commerce like the snowflakes that melted in the pools of lava at the top of the Majestic Mountain.

It was a city filled with Armenians, Greeks, Jews, and now Turks; of Christians and Nestorians and atheists and now Muslims; a city of churches and temples and now mosques. A city of medreses built of grey limestone as intensely dark as the clouds of winter, as somber and serious as its people. A city crammed with mud brick houses in narrow, crooked alleys, a population protected by stern and imposing city walls. A city of war, a city of progress, a city ever-striving to rise above the ash left by the spoutings of the great Mountain above.

Outside the city, saints and priests found refuge in the secret caves of the countryside, and long-legged pink birds and waddling ducks took harbor in the reeds of its salty marshes; waterfalls cascaded from vertiginous heights; hot springs burst upwards with mineral waters boiled by the lava of the Mountain; grey limestone was born from the bones of the seas that once covered this region; and the soft tufa stone formed from its ash was carved into homes for peasants and farmers.

This lava and spoutings were perhaps a cataclysm, but a natural one; yet that the city in the shadow of the Mountain should have known other cataclysms human was not to be denied. The plains below the Mountain were a highway for the blighted Crusaders to cross, just as Hittites, Babylonians, Assyrians, Turkmens, Persians and Romans had done before them. It would continue evermore to be a crossroads of invading men, battling empires and intense commerce. All nations of children were born in its cradle. All footsteps of humanity beat down its soil and hardened its limestone with their determination.

Come to me, calls out the Mountain, you people of the world, come to me and gather handkerchiefs full of snow, baskets of flowers in the skirts of my lower meadows, and braziers of hot embers from the fires still burning within me. Come, dip your toes in the wide marshes at my feet and watch the eagles soar at my summit. Come, taste the sweet honey of my fields, now flowing from beehives like lava once flowed from my core. Come, and see how my snowy peak rears its head like the white stallion of the Great Seljuk Sultan Alaeddin Keykubad. Come, and see if you can escape from the shadow of my protection, ever close, ever far, never sleeping, and watching all below. Come, but never think you can climb to my peak, for I will let forward an avalanche of snow, a river of lava and a blanket of ash from my frozen peak made from fire, just like glass, onto you, people of the world that come to the city at my feet!

Yes, O Mountain, we, the city at your feet, behold you; we, the peoples of this trade town of lava and snow; this crown city of Caesars named Kayseri, married to the shadow of you, the great solitary Mountain we call *Erciyes*.

Chapter 43

So Shall It Be Heard

The Sultan Alaeddin Keykubad, dressed in his formal robes, sat cross-legged on a raised platform in his Devlethane Palace in Kayseri, surrounded by the most important men of his court. He had just been informed that the embassy he had sent to the court of the Mongol Khan Ogedei had finally returned home. The ambassador brought the response to the letter the Sultan wrote to the Khan expressing his warning to leave the Seljuk lands alone to ensure a mutual peace between the two rulers.

The chamberlain clapped his hands three times and the ambassador was escorted into the divan and immediately knelt in front of the Sultan. Although exhausted from his journey, he explained in great detail how well he was received, how Ogedei savored the gifts sent by the Sultan, and that he gladly accepted the Sultan's invitation to send a delegation of Mongol ambassadors to visit the Sultan in Kayseri. Yet the ambassador knew, from what he had seen of the blunt nature of Ogedei, that the letter he brought back from him would not be full of such friendly platitudes. Fearful of the contents of the letter, he rose slowly and presented Ogedei's letter on an engraved brass dish to the Sultan.

The Sultan took the letter and asked everyone to leave the room except for a cluster of his most trusted courtiers. He handed the letter to Ibn Bibi and asked him to read it to himself first so as to be able to document its contents in his journal.

"Well?" asked the Sultan with a furrowed brow. "What kind of letter has the Great Khan written to us?"

With the letter fluttering in his shaking hand, the young man looked up at the Sultan.

"Your Highness, it is….a short letter; not particularly well-written, but what does one expect from those heathens with no literature? Yet…it must be said that its message is stated clearly and powerfully, but I am not entirely sure you will be pleased with it," the young court historian said in a trembling voice, for even though he was new to the court, he had already learned that the Sultan did not like to see his power challenged by anyone.

"Well, then read it out loud for all to hear!" bellowed the Sultan, angry that Ibn Bibi should impugn that he, the great Alaeddin Keykubad, Eminence of the World and the Faith, should have anything to fear from those goat worshippers from the Far Eastern steppes.

In the bated silence of the room, the voice of Ibn Bibi rang out as he read aloud the letter the Sultan had been waiting months to receive:

Honorable Padishah Sultan Alaeddin,

Be thee aware that our kingdom and its people hold the utmost fame in the all of the universe.

The fact that you have sent ambassadors to us shows that you are in recognition of this fact and honor it, and this is pleasing to us. I send this letter to you in recognition of your message to us.

We are satisfied. We hear this as a message of goodwill from you, and that you are willing to recognize our sovereignty.

Because of this, we wish to support your bid and offer you protection.

We invite you into the arms of our friendship and to behold our imperial orders.

And we want that you and your kingdom should live in pleasure and peace. For that, you will submit entirely unto us. The Seljuk Empire will deem the Great Khan as ruler, and will answer only to him.

The Great Supreme Being exalts us and calls us to proclaim it.

Now it has become necessary for us to make known our conditions so that you may walk on the straight and correct path.

Now, here are our conditions to you:

You will pay us the tribute in terms we set forth. Men, goods and beasts will be sent unto us. To those who heed not our mandate, we will come and seize their lands. To those who try to resist us, we will kill them. We will take from them their women and children and hold them as prisoners and slaves. We will plunder their property and their livestock, and we will destroy their territory and estates. This is not villainy from us. It is fact.

So in this year has it been written, so shall it be heard.

[thumbprint of] The Great Ogedei Khan

Chapter 44

To the Gods of the Country and to the Imperial House

Although he tried not to show it, the Sultan was quite shaken by the letter from Ogedei, for he now knew the Mongol Khan was his most fearsome enemy, and he would have to deal with him in one way or the other, either on the battlefield or in the throne room. The Mongols would soon no longer content themselves with mere raids into the Seljuk territory: they wanted his kingdom – and perhaps his head – and the destined battle loomed before him. But how soon?

Until that fateful day, the Sultan focused his considerable energy on enemies he knew he could overcome. In this Holy year of 1233, the Sultan Alaeddin Keykubad, Eminence of the World and the Faith, continued to pursue his dream to dominate all of eastern Anatolia. He took back the fortress of Ahlat from the Ayyubid Sultan al-Ashraf in September. At the same time, he rebuilt the castles and city walls of the towns in this area, starting with Ahlat, Amasya, and above all, Sivas, whose citizens had felt the hot breath of the Mongols upon their necks, just as he was feeling it now.

So it was with pleasure that he looked forward to going south to Alaiye for the winter after this eventful summer. He needed rest, and despite his glorious victories in the east, the words of Ogedei's letter continually haunted his thoughts.

Mahperi was always joyful to return to her home. Seeing many of the people who had loved her father was always a consolation to her, and the joy of celebrating the birth of Jesus was always one of the highlights of her year. Above all, the annual pilgrimage to Alaiye offered her a rare opportunity to breathe in peace without the scorn of the Black Raven upon her. For reasons obvious to all, Gaziye chose to winter in neighboring Antalya instead, which offered Mahperi time alone with the Sultan. Above all, she was home, and even though the city was now called Alaiye and not Kalonoros, the bells of the church still rang in the hearts of its citizens, especially on Christmas Eve.

The Sultan had no time for Christmas Eve candles and pomegranates, however, as he was embarked on yet again another building project. Directly between his cities of Antalya and Alaiye on the coast road stood two impressive monuments built by the Romans when they occupied this region: the amphitheaters of Side and Aspendos. Although the Sultan had no use for a stage for antique dramas, these two theaters, both over 1,000 years old, never failed to impress him, and he decided to build a small palace for himself within the walls of Aspendos. What better way to show the world that he was the Sultan of Sultans, Most Revered Lord, mightier than the Romans, than to build his own palace in the core of this monument, symbol of a fallen empire, while his empire stood glorious?

The Sultan invited Mahperi and some of his other court officials to visit the construction site of the new palace. When they arrived after a full day in the saddle, they found the site full of activity, with workers clearing away toppled stones and column capitals from the stage area, repairing walls, digging new wells, and laying out the area that was to serve as the Sultan's palace. The Sultan could not believe how far the work had progressed since he first had ordered the construction to start in the spring of the previous year. He called out to Abdullah, the main foreman on the site, to commend him on his efforts.

"Abdullah, my Lion! Why, you have worked miracles here! It looks like I can move in already! Let's forget about Alaiye and stay here this winter, what do you say?" he said, slapping him soundly on the back.

The skillful foreman was pleased that he had served the Sultan well. "If truth be told, my Sultan, it is not I who am responsible for all of this. I just barked out the orders to these donkeys of workmen here when they got too lazy, but the real reason for the success is due to a foreigner who came here looking for work one day. He could barely speak Turkish, looked a little thin to me, but there was something sharp in his eyes that told me he saw things the rest of us did not. He told me he had building experience back in his home country. I took him on, and within one day I saw that he knew more about construction than all of us combined. And to boot, he has an eye for detail and creativity that is exceptional. Come, let me introduce you to the man who gives me the reason to bully all these workers!"

Abdullah waved to a slight young man who was standing to the side of the site. He was dressed in a long brown robe, gathered with a leather sash into which he had stuck several of the tools of his trade: a small hammer, a measuring stick, plumb bob and a leather pouch to hold bits of charcoal for sketching. The young man shyly approached, a bit embarrassed by the praise of the older man.

"Come, my son, don't be timid, I won't cut your heathen head off! That I will save for those Mongols!" laughed the Sultan. "What is your name and where do you come from?" Alaeddin noted that indeed, this young man possessed a bright look in his eyes.

The Shadow of God on Earth stood above the young architect and looked at the roll of drawings in his hand. The foreigner bowed in respect and when he rose he took several seconds to observe the face of the Sultan. He noted his slim, yet strong physique, his sharp falcon beak of a nose, his intense blue eyes, his heavy dark eyebrows and the fine lines creased across his cheekbones. A face of a leader of men, the architect noted. He wanted to pick up his pen and immediately sketch this face before he could forget the traits of this distinguished man. He then laughed to himself, for he realized that one look into those blue eyes was enough to engrave that face on his memory forever.

"My Esteemed Sultan, I welcome you to this site we are trying to make worthy of your excellence. My name is Estève de Cantadou, but here everyone calls me 'Lou Cantadou', for our foreign names are so hard for Turks to pronounce. I come from the Languedoc region of southern France. I work at your service with great honor."

"Well, Lou Cantadou from Languedoc, walk me around and show me what wonders you have planned and what work has been achieved by that bully Abdullah!" the Sultan roared with delight at the prospect of discovering this new site.

As they entered the theater, Lou Cantadou pointed to the inscription over the main gate. "As you can read there in Latin, my Sultan, the inscription says, *"To the gods of the country and to the imperial house."* Perhaps the names of the Gods have changed, but this building will still stand as testament to an imperial house, that of the mighty Seljuks of Rum!"

The Sultan looked up at the inscription, whose message rang strongly in his ears. They passed through the entrance gate and the young architect began his tour of the site.

"My Sultan, the first thing we needed to do was to repair the north wing of the theater, as it was threatening to collapse, and we reinforced it with bricks to save it from further decay. It will stand for another 1000 years, I guarantee it! I have calculated by the rows of seats that over 15,000 people used to sit here when there was a performance! Can you imagine that? And now it is you who are the main actor over a theater full of citizens in your empire!"

Lou continued his animated tour to a now-captive audience.

"Rather than construct a separate palace building, I decided to reconfigure several rooms in a side wing of the theater stage on the upper floor for you. I installed your rooms into the south side of the stage, as this will offer you the finest views over the Pamphylian plain, the Köprü River and the foothills of the Taurus Mountains. I assure you, from its terrace, or as we call it at home, a *belve-*

dere, you have a view that the Roman emperors never dreamed of, to the east and south as far as the eye can see!" insisted the Frank, pointing upwards.

"To add a Seljuk touch to the building, I have painted the staircase both inside and out with red and white chevrons, much like the ones I saw used in your palace and on the gates at Alaiye. I wanted to continue that design for you here, since it was obvious it was one that pleased you, my Sultan. I will also line the staircase tower walls all the way up with glazed tiles. I have found a wonderful potter named Joseph, a Greek, who is crafting a set of luster tiles that will dazzle you! Abdullah will confirm that his work is worth every bit of the trouble it takes to deal with his cantankerous personality!" Lou said, nodding to the foreman.

Abdullah rolled his eyes upwards and nodded energetically to the Sultan.

"These tiles will be like nothing you have seen before, even in your palace at Konya. They will glimmer like stars, and I have requested that some bear the inscription *"Hafiz bilad Allah,"* the Protector of God's lands, for that is how I perceive you, Sultan Alaeddin Keykubad!"

The Sultan began to see what the resourceful foreman Abdullah was referring to. This young foreign man with the odd accent was modest and self-assured at the same time, full of ideas and capable of translating architecture into might.

"And to complete the project," Lou continued, "workers are out at the Köprü River rebuilding the old Roman bridge that stands there. I am very attentive to cost, as Abdullah will tell you, and I am sure that we will complete this project with a minimum of expense and time. I will build something that will both please you and reflect well on your standing as leader of this Empire."

As he did when he was happy, the Sultan flashed his brilliant smile, radiating throughout the theater as forcefully as any Roman thespian's voice. Placing his hand on the shoulder of the young man, he nodded to his foreman and said, "You are right, Abdullah, he may come from the country of those cursed Franks, but he has certainly proved that he has style and knows his way around the world of building! I am pleased with your work, Lou Cantadou from Languedoc, and may this be the start of many projects we will accomplish together, to both God and this imperial house!"

Chapter 45

A Sultan of Land and Seas and Lakes

As always, it was difficult for the Sultan to leave Alaiye at the end of the winter to return to Konya. The pleasures of fresh sea breezes, delicious seafood, warm sun, starry nights and clear days spent outdoors hunting, riding and picnicking in the mountains were not easy to leave behind, but the court had a fixed protocol which needed to be respected. It was now time for the Sultan to prepare his departure for Keykubadiyye for the spring training of his troops, and from there, he would set out for the East in the early summer to conquer more territories, for his ambition never relaxed.

The court caravan left Alaiye and stopped at Alara to spend the night in the han that had recently been completed there. Mahperi took great pride in reading the inscription plaque above the door as she passed under it: "*Built by the most august exalted king of kings, the master of nations, the lord of the sultans of the Arabs and the Persians, the sultan of justice, the conqueror of the regions, of the universe, the sultan of the land and sea of the Greeks, Syria, the Armenians and the Franks, Alaeddin Kaykubad, son of Keykhüsrev, son of Kilich Arslan, the Evidence of the Commander of the Faithful, on the date of the year 629.*" Yes, thought Mahperi, he truly is the "Sultan of Lands and Seas", just as he had inscribed on the Kizil Kule in Alaiye.

After a few more days of riding, the caravan finally came out of the mountains through the Emireddin Pass, one of the few paths available to cross the mountains onto the steppes. There, another delight awaited them: the view of the turquoise waters of the lake Mahperi loved since the first time she set eyes on it: *Buhayre-i Gurgurum*. The caravan would always pitch their tents here and rest, before heading out on the final leg of the trip to Konya.

Arriving at Lake Buhayre-i Gurgurum was always a bittersweet moment for Mahperi: bitter because it marked the end of the southern part of their year, and sweet because the setting of the lake was so lovely that it was possessed of an enchantment all its own. As she watched a heron wading along the edge of the lake, she felt envious that he had this lake to himself most of the time.

Mahperi often thought about this place, and how she wished she could spend more time here and enjoy its beauty. When life in the court of Konya became suffocating, or when she heard Gaziye's cackle or observed the admiring eyes of the Sultan upon her rival, all she wanted to do was jump on Eclipse and escape to the peace of these waters, which reminded her of her beloved blue Mediterranean. But alas, that was not to be, for there was no place to stay here, just remote nature at its purest. Yet, what if there were quarters to stay here, she thought, a place where I could come and stay for days on end, to ride in the hills and enjoy nature? What if I could have my own room here, with my own window to peer out at the water like I had in my castle on the hill in Kalonoros? Yes…what if?

It was then that Mahperi conceived an idea that would not let go of her until she shared it with the Sultan. After dinner, when they were sitting around the campfire watching the shooting stars, Mahperi took advantage of a moment alone with the Sultan to speak of it with him. There was a new moon that evening, so it only seemed appropriate that the Moon Queen propose a new beginning to her Sultan.

"My Alaeddin Sultan," she began, "I was wondering something. You seem to enjoy the palace that is being built for you in Aspendos, and I can understand your enthusiasm. But where we really need a palace is here, right here on this lake, so that we can rest on our route to Alaiye and back. A setting this beautiful rivals any in the world! We could use it not only for our travels, but you could also use it as a place to escape from Konya; to ride, hunt and have some peace when you need to plan for your next military campaigns."

"Mahperi!" The Sultan cut her off abruptly. "I can't believe you are saying this!" he said bursting into laughter. "At times I think you are my shadow! I was just thinking the very same thing this morning when we first hit upon the view of the lake. How my spirits lift each time I see those waters, so soft, shimmering like the colors of a peacock's tail."

Mahperi sighed with relief that her idea was well-received.

"Yes, we could build a palace here, a palace so handsome that it will rival the beauty of its surroundings, if such a thing could be possible," the Sultan continued. "I will use this palace to admire God's colors and abundance, which are some of His greatest gifts to us."

He paused and looked up at the stars in the night sky. "You are right, Mahperi, I need a place of tranquillity. I need a place to escape the horrors of my campaigns. I want to hear the birds sing and the leaves rustle instead of the groans of dying men. I want a place where the joy and beauty of this world erase the terrible cruelty of its other face."

Mahperi had never heard the Sultan reveal that he was weary of the rages of war and it surprised her.

"I want this palace to be more private than my others; a place where all my family can come together. I am already thinking that I would like to build it in two parts: one private section for my family and another part for my court. The palaces will be situated together in one large precinct, and other small buildings will be added, too. Yet this will not be a lavish palace like at Konya. I will build my palace of modest proportions, almost like a han. If I build a house much bigger than those of my subjects, I will bring down the shame of God."

Mahperi was thrilled that a new home would be built here, at this place of which she had become so fond. She was sure, as well, that the Raven would not come out here to the country, for she much preferred the comforts of the court of Konya. Mahperi also wondered if she would ever be able to bring Giyaseddin here for respite from his schooling and training at Erzincan. Her head was spinning with the possibilities of what this palace could be, and already she had one very strong idea in the back of her mind.

"If I may, my Sultan, I have one more suggestion to make. Since you were so impressed by that Provençal architect at Aspendos, perhaps we could invite him here to work on this project as well. You could not stop singing his praises to me, so you must think he has talent. What do you think?" she proposed.

"An interesting thought you have there, Mahperi, but remember that Köpek, *Amir u-shikar va mimar*, the Superintendent of Building at my court, is in charge of overseeing all of my construction projects. Actually, for this project I have my own ideas and will make many of the plans myself. Yet, the more hands, the better, and your idea is a good one! He certainly does have a creative touch, that Frank!" nodded the Sultan.

The Sultan was obviously in a good mood, so Mahperi decided to push her run of luck that evening with even one more question. "Perhaps we could invite that grumpy potter, as well?" she queried, the wheels of her mind already spinning as fast as the clay on his wheel.

"I suppose if my foreman Abdullah can put up with him, then so can I!" roared the Sultan in laughter. "Bring him along, too! I am more than pleased with what the two of them have done at Aspendos, so let's give them another chance to build yet another palace, only this time, one from the ground up, not a reworking of the ghosts of Romans past!"

☪ ☪ ☪

Ibn Bibi had much to write in his journal that evening. His pen noted how the Sultan camped by the lake of *Buhayre-i Gurgurum* and planned to build a palace more glorious than the souls of the chaste, with vaulted domes to compete with the *muquarnas* of the highest heavens.

When he was finished with the notations of the day, the court historian, himself transfixed by the beauty of the place, could not help but compose a poem in its honor:

Green lake with waters delicious as milk
Ripples over its surface looking like creases in velvet
Heavenly mountain skirts
Lands so verdant that they appear turquoise
The smell of musk in the air, earth filled with beauty
Teeming with game of all kinds

Even though Ibn Bibi made no mention of it in his court journal that night, it was so decided between a Sultan and his Moon Queen that an architect with gentle brown eyes and a cantankerous, mud-spattered potter would be invited to join the team that would build a palace next to God's most beautiful lake. There was time enough later to tell their story, thought Ibn Bibi, as well as the rest of the promising adventure of the building of this new palace for Alaeddin Keykubad, the Sultan of Land and Seas, and now of Turquoise Lakes.

Chapter 46

O, Little White Heron of Paradise

If you were a long-legged white heron wading in the lake at the base of the foothills of the Anamas Mountains, you would look up from your isolated spot along the shore and gaze all the way over to the summit of a rocky headland and admire the color of God's green paradise;

You would stalk silver fish and frogs for your banquets among the sedges in milky green waters of the lake which pour there from the melting snows atop limestone mountains and from the plentiful springs of the fertile plain;

You would feel your feathers lifted by the constant puffs of air sweeping across the lake, and be cooled by their caress; and you would pose on one leg in water so sweet and pure that the winter snowflakes cry out in envy;

You would take haven here and there and wherever you pleased among the reedbeds of the lake or on the edges of the numerous islands sprinkled among its waters, and converse in amity with your waterfowl friends, the ducks and blackbirds and pelicans and cormorants;

You would listen to the melody of the gentle breezes blowing through the trees and the reeds and believe it was God singing His call to prayer call just for you;

You would raise your graceful neck and sniff the aroma of the pine trees and cedars and junipers from the mountains to the west, spicing the crisp air breezes with their heady sharpness;

You would watch the kingfishers gorge themselves on the juicy flesh of plums, mulberries, peaches, and cherries and wonder if any would be left for the friends of the field, the rabbits and bears and the foxes;

You would be blinded by the brilliant blue hues of these waters that swirl in a whirlpool of marbled cobalt and turquoise streaks;

You would peer at your stately reflection in this silver mirror of a lake, and say to yourself that you are indeed the brightest of all the creatures of the land and skies and the waves;

Yes, you would say that the Holy Prophet himself should come to live with you here, in this place sited to perfectly catch the views of both mountains and water; this magnificent place where you wade, o little white heron, Sultan of the Waters of the lake known as *Buhayre-i Gurgurum*, but what you call *Paradise*.

Chapter 47

Till the End of My Days, I Will Lament

It was his erect and defiant posture that first caught her attention, yet everything about him stood out. Burnished by the sun, he was tall, even taller than the Sultan. He moved with the self-assurance and grace of an athlete, and was dressed in a simple brown linen tunic and short pants, in a style totally unlike the Turks. His head was uncovered despite the hot sun, and she could see a cascade of long, brown curls that reached down to his shoulders.

She was riding on Eclipse through the jumble of ruins in the fields behind the Roman theater of Aspendos when she saw him for the first time. He was standing in front of the entrance to the theater, gesticulating wildly with his arms to the Sultan, as if he were drawing in the air with his hands. She could tell that the Sultan was entirely absorbed by what he was saying, for he kept nodding eagerly at the man and flashing his brilliant smile in his direction. It was clear they both shared an equal vitality.

She watched them a while longer before the group disappeared into the theater. She was intrigued by this man, and she could not explain why, and she wanted to learn more about him. I do not know who you are, thin, graceful man, what you do, or your name, but I will find out, she vowed to herself as she rode off.

Mahperi soon learned that he was the architect working on the site at Aspendos. Yet, even after she and the Sultan left to head back to Konya, she could not let go of her curiosity about him.

☪ ☪ ☪

Soon after their return from the south, the Sultan Alaeddin Keykubad came into Mahperi's rooms in the Konya palace to inform her that the Frankish architect had arrived from Aspendos to the lake of the milky blue waters. The Sultan also told her that he would soon be riding out there to confer with Köpek to get the project for his new palace underway.

"Why don't you come along with us, Mahperi? Since you were so enthusiastic about building a palace there, I think you would enjoy being there for the beginning of the project. Plus, I could always use a dose of that common sense of yours which cuts through the knot of any problem like a sword!"

When they arrived on the site, she saw him again from atop Eclipse and felt the same sense of intrigue. It was only when Alaeddin waved at her to come over that she dared to join the group of men walking around the site with the Sultan: Köpek, several master masons she recognized from the Sultan Han site, a man with a severe limp, and the Aspendos architect. As she trotted over to them, she could see that the architect was once again motioning energetically to the Sultan.

As if he sensed her eyes upon him, the man suddenly stopped speaking and whipped his head around in her direction, his gesticulating hands freezing in mid-air. He looked directly in her eyes and held her gaze steadily until she was forced to drop her head. No one looks at me, a royal Queen, in the eyes like that! she thought to herself, her face flushed from embarrassment.

The Sultan observed the exchange of looks and broke the moment. "Mahperi, come meet Lou Cantadou from the place called Languedoc in France, who has agreed to come from Aspendos to build us a paradise palace here!"

She nodded in acknowledgement of his introduction. The Sultan turned to Lou and said, "My Queen Mahperi Hatun is very clever and full of ideas about many things, including building and the way things should fit together. I want you to consult with her on all aspects of the large palace, the one I want to build for my family, to make sure it is suitable to her taste. But I warn you: she has as many headstrong opinions as I do!" he laughed.

The architect nodded at the Sultan, and turned to Mahperi, looking at her instead of the Sultan when he gave his response.

"My Sultan, it will be my pleasure to consult with the good Queen Mahperi on any issue she would like," he said, again looking her directly in the eyes. "I serve at her orders as well."

Mahperi lowered her eyes. *Lou, your name is Lou.* I am certain that you and I will become friends, and build a palace of beauty together.

☪ ☪ ☪

I will serve at her orders with pleasure indeed. Could it be any other way? I think not. Have I ever set eyes on a more magnificent woman? Everything about her is regal: her bearing, her height and the look from the depth of those emerald pools. She is a cathedral of a woman, and I will dedicate myself to her altar. I will worship her with all my soul, for it cannot be otherwise.

That my heart began to tremble and shake;
This is why I will lament, till the end of my days.

Lou Cantadou already imagined the first verses of the *canso* poem he would compose that night to her, and for the rest of the day, thoughts of plumb bobs and bearing loads were far from his mind.

Chapter 48
A Gushing Spring of Youth and Beauty

"Right here! Yes, right here, where this spring gushes up!" cried out the Sultan, excitedly pointing in front of him to a spot on the promontory that jutted out into the lake. "This is where I want you to build my palace, right next to this spring!"

The Sultan was walking along the edge of the lake with Sadettin Köpek and Lou Cantadou. The Frank architect had arrived earlier that week from Aspendos, bringing with him the potter Joseph and several of the finest workers from his team there.

"My Sultan, before we make any decisions, may I suggest that we get a feel for the entire site? Let us walk around the grounds together, for this way we can understand how the wind flows, and where the sun hits at each time of the day. I must commit the site to memory before I can design for it, for sometimes it is the site that gives birth to the idea that will fit it, not the other way around."

Lou turned to Köpek and said, "I am sure with your building experience, you have found that to be true, am I correct?"

Köpek grumbled a vague answer and continued to stick close to the Sultan's side. He objected to the arrival of this stylish Frank for several reasons: first and foremost, because he perceived him as a threatening rival in the eyes of the Sultan, who did nothing but lavish praise upon him. As if we needed a Christian here on this site to build for a Seljuk Sultan, he grumbled to himself, and as if anyone could be more talented for this job than I am!

☾ ☾ ☾

The three of them met early the next morning; right after first light. The silence of the site at dawn was broken only by the noise of the frogs jumping at the side of the reed beds. Gnats played in spirals rising from the shore, and birds darted about frantically to catch them. Lou thought to himself that this was indeed a site of serenity, and he prayed that the palace they were to build there would reflect the tranquil peace of this spot.

Alaeddin turned to Köpek. "Vizier Köpek, as Superintendent of Building, I am putting you in charge of the organization of the construction operation.

Send out the messengers to all the lands to hire the most skilled craftsmen, stonecutters and masons possible! I want this palace to go up as soon as possible. This Frank here will draw up the plans and bring his artistic touch to the project, for he has a real flair for that, as I saw at Aspendos. I count on the both of you to work together to provide me with the finest palace I will ever know!" he said in a firm voice.

The Sultan looked out onto the still turquoise blue waters covered with the morning mist. "I already know that I want this to be a royal town of sorts, with walls, a gatehouse, baths, a dockyard to house the boats we will use for excursions to the many islands out in the lake, a fenced enclosure for animals, gardens and small pavilions scattered all around the grounds," he explained, looking to the left and right before continuing to elaborate his vision. "As concerns the residences, I want to build two palaces, one for administrative purposes and one for my family. I would like the public palace, where I will receive official visitors and such, to be perched on a hilltop with a fine view over the lake."

"I see that kiosk being built right here," said the architect Lou, pointing to the small spit of land jutting out into the lake more to the north from the gushing spring. "I can add a long central corridor, with a receiving room for the public, and then straight ahead at the end, opening on to the lake, we can construct a large deep *iwan*, a recess where you can receive visiting dignitaries. Imagine the dazzling effect it will have on your subjects when they see you sitting there on your raised platform, framed by the stunning beauty of the view behind you!" Lou waved with a sweep of his arm.

"Absolutely! You see, Köpek, I told you he had an eye for the dramatic!" the Sultan laughed, enjoying the whole discussion immensely.

Lou nodded at the Sultan and continued. "The spot next to the bubbling spring that you pointed out yesterday will make an excellent site for the family palace. The fact that you picked it instinctively tells us that it is where you will be happiest, and where you will spend many hours of enjoyment with your loved ones."

The Sultan nodded his head in agreement. "This palace must be larger than the official one, for it needs to contain many sections. I would even like you to include a large courtyard at the front, so that the children of the palace can play games and run around to their heart's content! I also want my own special room here, not a throne room exactly, but a room where I can rest and also receive my personal guests."

"That sounds very feasible, my Sultan, and we will build it for you. I will make sure that all the rooms face the lake to offer splendid views, with large openings to catch the sweet breezes. We can build a terrace to the rear of the palace, much the same as the one at Aspendos, or even the one you have in Konya. You can walk out there in the early morning and watch the mist lift off the lake, or at night to contemplate the dome of stars and the phases of the moon."

"I like those ideas very much, young Frank!" the Sultan beamed, and then turned to Köpek. "My Vizier, your challenges in this project will be many as well, due to the complexity of the construction needs. Lou Cantadou, perhaps you do not know this, but Sadettin Köpek is the finest engineer in all the land, especially as concerns hydraulics. There is nothing he does not understand about how water flows: how to bring it in fresh from the mountains and springs, and take it out once dirty after use," boasted the Sultan.

Köpek was glad to finally get some attention, and grabbed the opportunity to add his input. "Yes, my Sultan, we will have to construct aqueducts to bring in fresh water to the site from the mountains to the west," he said, pointing to the high mountains close to the shore of the lake. "I will also have to lay many cisterns to catch rain water, dig channels for water pipes, and perhaps even construct a small dam. And of course, if we are to build a fancy viewing terrace like the Frank wants, I will have many challenges to make sure that there is a sturdy supporting wall to hold it all up. But yes, it is all feasible."

"Well, all right then, let us begin! I want this palace built by the time I return from my winter visit to Alaiye, one year from now!" the Sultan ordered. "You are not to spare any expense if you feel it is necessary, but I want accurate records kept of all expenditures!"

Köpek nodded his head to the Sultan graciously, but inside he was seething. I am the one who is in charge of building for the Sultan, not this young upstart! It is I who will go down in history as the builder of the site, and I will make sure Ibn Bibi tells the world that! And you can be sure that I will make life as difficult as possible for this upstart incense sniffer and his hobbling potter friend!

Lou spoke up again, looking over to Joseph. "Before we leave, if I may, I have one last thing to propose to you, my Sultan. The inside of your palace must be as beautiful as the outside. This is a very important part of any project, for the interiors finish off the grandeur of a building. It is essential for your well-being to be able to rest your eyes on objects of splendor when you are in your rooms. For that, I propose that we decorate the walls of the palace with tiles, mosaics, stucco and frescos. Colorful silk cushions and carpets will cover the floors. We will keep the colors in harmony with the greens and blues that we see rippling in the waves of the lake. In this way, we will bring the beauty of the lake to you, even when you are sitting inside. And this is exactly where our friend Joseph will work his magic," Lou said, turning to the potter who had joined the group, quickly taking up his cue to speak.

"Sultan, I will cover the walls of your private room with large, colorful tiles – a constellation of images that will reflect the bounty of nature that God has given us – and He has surely worked his heavenly wonders here!" the potter laughed.

"Yes," Lou concluded, "we will all work to create for you, my good Sultan, a haven of harmony and refinement. You will see; this will be the most cherished of the Seljuk palaces!"

☪ ☪ ☪

That night, Köpek took great care to relate to Ibn Bibi the details of the site visit, filling in some details while leaving out others. The young scribe then picked up his quill and noted in his journal what he had been told:

> *The Sultan Keykubad ordered the architect Köpek to build a palace that would match the heavens in beauty. In accordance with the Sultan's orders, Köpek will build large and exquisitely-decorated kiosks with beautiful views and refreshing pools, and arches whose spans will compete with the domes of the heavens. He will situate the palace near a fountain, where it is said that people who drink from it became young and beautiful again.*

So was noted in his journal the beginning of the adventure of a haven of peace, built on the shores of a lake next to a spring of youth and beauty; a palace to be named for all eternity as *Kubadabad*, the Abode of Keykubad.

Chapter 49

A Bonhomme Builder

After Mahperi had arrived at the lake to visit the project site, she found she did not want to leave the stunning spot and return to Konya, and decided to stay there for the rest of the summer. She enjoyed watching the hundreds of men scurry around the site and seeing stones rise into recognizable forms. Joseph, the potter, with his lumbering limp that belied the grace of his magic hands, held a special fascination for her.

She was also fascinated by the Frankish architect, and was drawn to him in an unexplicable way, ever since that first time she set eyes on him outside the Roman theatre at Aspendos. He did not look like the people she was used to, for he was both taller and thinner in frame, with sharper features and a darker, quieter look in his eyes. She sensed he had the same artistic soul as Hanife, and perhaps they could become friends as well. One morning on a visit to the site with her guards, she found him by the side of the lake, inspecting the shoring of the terrace wall that would support the palace.

"It will hold well. Köpek has done an excellent job with the design. Are you satisfied with the way your new home is shaping up, my Lady?"

"Why yes, it seems fine!" she said, a bit flustered by his boldness to speak to her so directly. In turn, she decided to be bold. "I actually am more interested in hearing more about you than that wall there. How old are you? Why are you here, so far from your land? Why did you become an architect?"

"And you, my Lady, why are you so far from your land, your beautiful Kingdom by the sea?" he retorted without a second of hesitation.

He looked at her for a moment, holding her gaze with that bold way of his; making her feel ashamed she had been so rude. He turned his head away, and then turned it back again. He took a deep breath and slowly started to speak.

"My Good Lady, or as we say where I come from, *'Ma Gente Dame'*, I am from Occitania in southern France, a land of blazing summer heat, blue mountains, and hard winters. I was born in a small town called Roquefixade, perched high on a mountain outcrop. After I learned my trade there as an architect, I left with my mother and sisters to help build nearby Béziers, a fine burg full of markets, churches and schools, much like Konya. Occitania is a beautiful place, filled with people called the *Cathari* by the outside world. We call each other *Bonshommes* and *Bonnesfemmes*: Good Men and Good Women, for that is how we see ourselves – good and pure. We are different than other Christians because we do not accept the doctrine of the Catholic Church in Rome. We consider that those Popes in their gold robes have betrayed and tainted the original purity of the message of Jesus. We love a God of goodness, and we are men and women of justice, wisdom, and concord. Cathari women look at the world straight in the eye, just as you do, *ma gente dame*, which makes me feel at ease with you," he said, holding her gaze once again before continuing.

"Our religion is a learned one, built on writing, just like the Islam I see here in your land. Our preachers lived in modest houses, not in palaces or abbeys. They walked with us, they prayed with us and they worked with their hands alongside of us. We all knew how to read and we translated the New Testament into our Provençal language so that all could understand it. Our religion is far from all those superstitions of the Catholic Church, with their relics and statues of frozen saints, holy water and incense! We live our faith as naturally as we breathe, with no need for a liturgy to speak what is in our hearts. I have met Sufi masters here in this land, and it is very similar to the Path of Love they seek."

He stopped to see if Mahperi was following all of this. His Turkish was good, with an intriguing accent, almost musical, that she had never heard before. She nodded her head for him to continue, and many of her guards now eagerly clustered around to hear his story.

"Rome sent bishops and monks to try and convert us, but when that failed, the Pope ordered a formal crusade against us, just as he had done against the Muslims two hundred years before. Can you believe that one Christian Church would try to eliminate another? Such nonsense!" he said, kicking the wall with his boot. "Their methods were always the same. They would come into a village and round up all the Cathari. The Inquisitor would condemn some to burn at the stake, in public, in order to frighten the others to renounce their faith. But we never did renounce it. When they came to Béziers, their wrath was particularly brutal, and thousands were dragged behind horses, used for target practice or killed. They also destroyed our sacred texts. Many others died when the city was razed by fire, like my family. When I came upon the charred bodies of my mother and my sisters, I gave up all hope. With the fire licking at my toes, I knew that I had to escape all this hate. With only the singed clothes on my back, I fled through the city gates, dodging the sword blades of those vile soldiers of God that rained upon my head. I fled the burning city, my home, the unburied corpses of my family, my friends and all that was dear to me, out onto an unknown path."

Lou Cantadou lowered his head and paused for a moment, shuddering as he relived the scene in his mind. "I really had no idea where to go. I came down to the sea and boarded a ship in port that was leaving for Cyprus. On that boat I heard some merchants talking about trade with the Seljuks of Anatolia, and it was then that I decided to follow them to try my chance here in this Empire that seeks to build itself up from the ground. I knew that I could exert my profession here and live with purpose. I also knew that I did not have to be a fugitive from my beliefs. I could be respected for who I was, instead of being hated. So now I am here on this site, building in beauty at your side, looking to light and love each morning when I arise, not at fear and narrow-minded bigotry. This land has been very good to me."

As Mahperi glanced at this man who seemed so foreign, she suddenly realized that he was capable of understanding her far better than anyone she had met since leaving Kalonoros. He had been forced to leave his home, was a Christian living in a Muslim land, and was a seeker of truth in his faith. He came to his land to find an honorable place to exert his skill and his dreams. Mahperi felt a compassion for his journey, in many ways like hers.

She did not know how to respond to his tragic story and scrambled to find some words that could show him that she understood his pain. "Sometimes I long for my land, and wonder what would have been my life if I had stayed there, down south in Kalonoros. I miss our customs, the sea, my language, my foods – what do you miss the most about Occitania?"

Lou Cantadou smiled, and answered without a moment's hesitation. "In Occitania, we have a special tradition: we live to make songs about love. We try to find the right words and music to express the gracious sentiment of love. We call these songs *cansos*. Our hearts are driven by love: we dare to adore a Lady and we sing of that worship. Our Provencal language is filled with much emotion, and we use it to paint songs to convey the nobility of the heart. I think the Turkish language has much the same sentiment, and I know that very soon, great poets will come forth from these steppes, to sing in heartbreaking poignancy about the same values of love that we hold dear in Occitania."

He looked at Mahperi and remembered the lines of the *canso* he had begun to write the first time he saw her. To cover his emotion, he quickly picked up his story. "But our love, the one we sing about, is not about carnal appetite. Our *cansos* are poems that rhyme very subtly and very magically. You must love your Lady, have the courage to formulate it beautifully and then you must let it be known. Then and only then does the Lady lead her poet in the direction she wants to give to their story. A man can only propose his love in a *canso*, but the woman decides whether she will respond to that call for love. That is the honor of a Lady."

He continued to describe the tradition of the *cansos*. "Yes, we open our hearts bare to the joy of love, a love that seeks to flower in joy. The song is sometimes sung with lament if the Lady does not reciprocate the emotion, and sometimes it is sung with ecstatic joy if she does."

"I should like to hear one of those songs one day; for they sound enchanting," she replied, lifting her eyes to his.

"Oh, you shall, my Lady, you shall," he said. He held her gaze again, then turned away without another word and walked ahead along the shore of the lake.

Chapter 50

Tumble the Rocks of the Fortress

The Sultan Alaeddin Keykubad, *Shahinshah al-Azam*, the Greatest Conqueror, had other more important matters on his mind than simply building a Paradise Palace. He needed to build a paradise of an Empire. Although the Mongols were still a distant threat, he had two very real adversaries in the East: the Artukids and the Ayyubids, who continued to grip their territory with their warrior talons.

The Ayyubids, after the conquest of Ahlat by the Seljuks, had become increasingly angry at the Sultan for his expansion in the territory they considered theirs and theirs alone. The Ayyubid Sultan Al-Kamil of Egypt was especially angry that Alaeddin Keykubad had taken the hot apricot trophy of Ahlat. Seething with anger that this fruit should have been snatched so easily from his brother al-Ashraf, the Egyptian vowed to take it back and end the Seljuk Sultan's expansion efforts in the region once and for all. He decided to ride over from Egypt with his troops and take matters into his own hands. After his arrival on the Mesopotamian plain, he convened all the various Ayyubid rulers at Aleppo and amassed a joint army of over one hundred thousand men. They began marching up to Seljuk territory on the well-trod Aleppo-Kayseri caravan route. Ahlat will return to our hands! he vowed, raising his fist heavenwards.

Hearing that Al-Kamil was on his way, the Sultan Alaeddin Keykubad and Commander Kamyar prepared themselves as well for battle. The clever Commander Kamyar blocked all the Taurus mountain passages leading up from the Mediterranean with a wall of soldiers, leaving absolutely no room for even the thinnest Ayyubid soldier to slip through the defiles. In this fashion, the Seljuk forces were able to maintain their hold and keep the hot apricot prize of Ahlat nested in their basket. The vow of al-Kamil went unfulfilled.

Sultan Alaeddin Keykubad had once again shown that he was *Abu'l Feth*, Father of Conquests and Victories. Yet he still needed to defeat once and for all his other enemy in the East, the Artukids. The two powers confronted each other at Harput, in May and June of the holy year of 1234. After a siege lasting 24 days, the venerable Artukid City of the Rocky Fortress finally surrendered to the Seljuk forces on a parched August day. After this defeat, the Artukids knew that they could no longer hold out any hopes of victory against the Seljuks and withdrew from the region, carried off by the hot winds of the Mesopotamian plains.

Even the proud Ayyubid Sultan Al-Kamil, when he heard of the Seljuk victory over the Artukid forces, had to admit a temporary defeat. He turned his horse back towards Egypt and left the region to the Seljuks. As he trotted back across the Mesopotamian plains to Cairo, he reflected that perhaps those Seljuks may have been victorious at Harput, but it is I, and the Ayyubids alone, who still hold on to the glorious and prized cities of Hasankeyf and Diyarbakir.

Chapter 51

Sugared Demons

Spring bloomed once again. Vizier Sadettin Köpek accompanied the Sultan on his annual military maneuvers to the East, and took advantage of the opportunity to visit Giyaseddin Keyhüsrev at Erzincan. Using the pretext of a need to confer with Ertokush on a court-related issue, he received the Sultan's permission to head north.

Nothing Vizier Sadettin Köpek did was ever without a determined purpose, and this trip had little to do with collecting taxes from the citizens of Erzincan to fill the Seljuk coffers, or gathering information about local terrain – no, this trip was about Giyaseddin Keyhüsrev, future heir to the Seljuk throne.

Köpek had long thought about the role that the young Giyaseddin could play in his life. Köpek needed the two of them to be allies, for it would serve them both well. For this first-born son, fast becoming a man, Köpek's support would be essential for his future court life, as Köpek held many of the powerful emirs under his control – and the others lived in fear of him. For Köpek, a close association with the heir to the throne would ensure that he remained a key policy maker in the court after he inherited his father's throne. Yet, perhaps the greatest motivation for Köpek's seemingly avuncular concern for the young boy was to use him as a pawn in his avid lust for supreme power.

☪ ☪ ☪

When Köpek and his men arrived in Erzincan after a long and dusty ride, he was pleased to see that the city was flourishing under Seljuk rule. He also noted that the young Giyaseddin was no longer a child, but now an adolescent with a deeper voice and chin hair. He was tall, like his mother, but had inherited the bulky frame of his namesake grandfather, as well as his red hair. His face, however, gave away the fact that he was still introverted, for even when he smiled, his face seemed to absorb light and not radiate it. How different, thought Köpek, from the blazing blue eyes and brilliant smile of his father!

Köpek was pleased, actually, that the boy had remained timid, for he did not want him to mature into a man as headstrong as his father. No, he wanted him to remain docile so he could lead him in any direction he wanted. For it will not be Giyaseddin Keyhüsrev who will truly be in charge of the Seljuk Empire the day he becomes sultan; no, it will be me, Sadettin Köpek.

☪ ☪ ☪

Giyaseddin was thrilled to see Köpek, for he had always enjoyed a friendly relationship with him. Köpek never scolded him like his father did, or looked at him with a scowl. The young man remembered how Köpek would spent time with him when he lived in Konya, inviting him on rides to the countryside, teaching him how to string a bow tautly, sneaking him pieces of halvah from the court kitchens, and laughing with him – all of the things he wished his father would have done with him, but had not. And now he has come to visit me here! I am not forgotten out here in these far reaches of the empire! He will certainly bring me news of my mother – oh, how I miss her! I have forgotten nothing of her face, her smell of sweet flowers and what she taught me. Ertokush is a fine teacher, but he does not really show me love; no, no one does that except my mother, and now, perhaps, Köpek, too.

Köpek took the young man on long rides around the flat plains of Erzincan, using this time to talk with him and gain his confidence. He found Giyaseddin more cheerful than usual, eager and responsive to everything he said. Yes, young man, as long as you keep saying yes to me, our future together as a team will be insured.

☪ ☪ ☪

Near the end of his stay in Erzincan, Köpek moved to deepen the bond between them even further. He knew exactly what he needed to do, and how easy it was going to be. Once accomplished, this bond will be stronger than any the boy would ever know, more potent than his fawning attachment to his mother, his fear of his father, or his timidity towards life. Yes, he will be attached to me very strongly in ways both mental and physical. He will depend on me and look to me first, rather than to his mother, and certainly not to his father. Once master of this boy, I will be able to have him do whatever I tell him.

One evening after dining on an elaborate meal of roast lamb with walnut sauce, the two of them sat in Köpek's campaign tent which had been pitched in a meadow outside of town.

"My lad!" called out Köpek, slapping him on the shoulders. "Soon I will not be able to call you that much longer! You have grown into a fine young man, and I think it is time that you start living like one, and leave your boyish games behind you! It is time for you to participate in a battle campaign alongside your father. It is time for you to join in the *çirit* polo matches with your father's finest athletes, and to wrestle with his strongest champions. It is time for you to open the prayers in the mosque on Friday, and – it is time for you to take a wife!"

Giyaseddin was surprised at that last comment but said nothing. It was certain that he was becoming curious about young girls; he would look at them when he went to the bazaars and market, fascinated by their delicate shapes, dainty feet and flirting eyes, but he did not yet really understand what any of that allure meant.

"Why, yes, I suppose I am a man now!" said Giyaseddin eagerly. "When you think about it, I could become the next Sultan at any time, for each spring when my father sets out for battle, who knows, but God, if he will return?"

"Exactly, that is what I mean," continued Köpek, "and you will need your own heir as well. The sooner you set about this, the better for the future of the Seljuk Empire!"

In truth, Giyaseddin did not know if he really wanted to become Sultan. And as far as a wife, that was an issue even more baffling.

"But, Köpek, I …" Giyaseddin looked down at his hands. "I have no idea what this is all about. I mean, I have never really ever spoken to a woman other than my mother, my sister, Hanife or Gaziye – so how am I supposed to know how to act with a wife? How would I talk to her, how do I please her, and… how do I touch her?"

Köpek laughed and then patted the young man soundly on the back.

"Oh, my fine young lion, you need not fear any of that! You will see that it is all quite simple. You just look them straight in the eyes, stroke their lustrous locks, and then you will see, a magic will happen that will guide the two of you along your way!" he added with a tone of encouragement.

"If you say so… but I know that my father has already betrothed me to a Georgian princess. When will that marriage take place? Do you think she will like me? I hear that Georgian girls are the prettiest on earth!" he said, smiling eagerly.

"Indeed they are, and you are one lucky young man! Yes, you will marry the daughter of Queen Rusudan, and we will work to arrange that in due time. But for the present time, we must prepare you for that day, and tonight, we are going to start on that lesson, one you will not learn from the good Ertokush or his algebra teachers!"

Köpek clapped his hands twice, and two of his servants entered bearing a tray of refreshments: sugared pastries of all sorts, lokum and halvah, as well as a carafe and two goblets.

"I remembered how much you used to love the halvah of the palace kitchens at Konya, so I have brought you some! Here, enjoy it, and let's taste some of the fine juice from the vineyards of Meram that I have brought as well!" he said, motioning for the servant to pour the wine, making sure that Giyaseddin's goblet was filled to the rim.

Giyaseddin had never tasted wine, and was not sure if he wanted to try it. "But I cannot drink this! It is forbidden! Ertokush has always told me that alcohol is not to be touched, for it is poisonous herbage!" he said, looking at the goblet askance.

"Now, now, let's have none of that nonsense; wine is a pleasure to be enjoyed! Many of your father's emirs partake of it! Let's toast to the future Sultan of the Seljuks, Giyaseddin Keyhüsrev!" cheered Köpek, lifting his goblet high.

Giyaseddin was unsure what to do, but he certainly did not want to offend Köpek who had been so nice to him. He was more interested in gobbling the halvah than drinking the wine, but he sipped politely in response to Köpek's toast. For as long as he could remember, sweet things satisfied a longing in him that was always aching. The minute the sugar of the halvah melted on his tongue, a feeling of pleasure ran all through his body like a shiver, and he felt immediately happier and calmer. He felt *loved*. When his distant father would yell at him or rebuff him in front of the Golden Boy Izzeddin, one little pop of candied sugar in his mouth made everything bad go away.

Köpek and Giyaseddin continued drinking a while longer, until Köpek could detect the effects of the delightful grape upon him: the boy relaxed and became chattier, and opened up his thoughts even more to Köpek. He now knew he could continue with the rest of his plans for the evening. Köpek clapped his hands again, four times this time, and the flap of the tent opened widely. Only this time it was not pages with platters who entered, but rather two beautiful girls wearing long, dangling earrings and gold-embroidered tunics of red satin.

"My Lion, I have prepared a little entertainment for you this evening. These two young ladies will sing for you most delightfully. Now, if you will allow me, I must beg your forgiveness, but I am very tired from our ride today and must withdraw to rest. But do not fear, you are in good company here. These maidens will entertain you and tend to every one of your needs," he said, bowing and quickly leaving the tent before Giyaseddin could object.

Outside the tent, Köpek smiled to himself, pleased with the outcome of his evening, for he knew that by leaving Giyaseddin under the influence of the attractions of fantasy inside, he could be totally confident of the magic that would happen when they were put at the service of a young man of thirteen years. Giyaseddin was under his control now in all ways, Köpek thought contentedly. He is now dependent on me to furnish him an addictive supply of sugared delights.

Chapter 52

Sweet Cherries of Friendship

Mahperi continued to enjoy her summer days spent at Kubadabad. She often took long rides on Eclipse to the surrounding countryside and boating excursions to the surrounding islands with her servants. One hot afternoon she decided to organize an impromtu picnic for the workers on the site, who deserved a break from all their hard work. She and her servants brought out bread, cheese, spinach pastries, olives, fresh-picked cherries and jugs of fruit juices, and laid them out on tables and kilims on the worksite, much to the appreciation of the hard-working laborers.

She sent her guards to invite Lou and Joseph the potter to sit at her table. She wanted this opportunity to discuss the progress of the work on the Large Palace. She also wanted to get to know them better, both Christians and foreigners in the Seljuk lands.

As the servants passed around the cherries, Lou stole a glance at the smiling face of Mahperi. It brought to mind a verse in the *canso* he was composing. *Shining face, more radiant in beauty than gold in the sun.*

He had always observed her from a distance, for he was too much in awe to approach her. She was, quite simply, the most extraordinary woman he had ever met. So tall, so strong, so vital; even that white steed of her husband paled in comparison. She was not beautiful in the way most men saw beauty, but her bright face shone like the morning sun and her gaze was so earnest. *The all-powerful beam of her eye so riveting that my vision was troubled.* And now, she is sitting so close to me I can smell the flowers of her perfume. *Oh, ma gente dame, my senses grow weak and my heart trembles and shakes; this is why I lament, till the end of my days.*

Mahperi turned to Lou and said: "I once asked you this but you never answered me. Why did you become an architect?"

"I'm afraid the answer to that question is a very complicated and long one to provide!" he answered, startled by her boldness.

"Yes, I would enjoy hearing this story as well!" piped in Joseph, pulling his stool closer to them, pushing aside Mahperi's guards to get closer.

He now realized he could not avoid their inquisitiveness. "As you wish, my Lady, I will try to clarify it for your curious mind."

He drew a deep breath. "I build because I love God. It is that simple."

His response startled her. "But I thought you said the answer was a long one – yet you have summed it up quite simply! Yet, just what exactly does that mean, 'to build because you love God'?"

He fixed his eyes into hers and plunged ahead with his attempt to explain the essence of his life. The guards huddled closer to hear his story as well, for all were curious about this foreigner and his different manners.

"Whichever way you turn your eyes, you must always be conscious of the presence of God. That is what I want to convey in my buildings. Building is life, it is hope, it is goodness. It is God living in us. Each new building becomes the promise of a new life for me. That is why I chose to become an architect, in order to renew life that will sustain generations to come."

Lou found it a solace to speak of these inner thoughts that had possessed him since that fatal day in Béziers.

"Let me explain it more concretely. On every new site there comes the moment when I can visualize the future. I call it the moment of the Alpha: what is and what is to come. When I first set eyes on the site, I try to visualize what can rise. I walk around the site calmly, and plan for all the parts, and give free rein to my abstract ideas, visions, and dreams. You see, architecture is not a straightforward process. Architecture keeps back a part of its mystery; you must trust that all the elements will come into position one by one, and then at the end, at the moment of Omega, when all the volumes are in place, it will become reality instead of guesswork. How you worry, though, about being disappointed if you are not able to bring to life the promises you have created for yourself! But that is good, for a site without problems would be like a life without sorrow. That is why I have gotten so thin, my good Lady," he smiled at her, popping another cherry into his mouth before continuing.

"Architecture is not flat like this kilim," he explained, rubbing his hands along the rug on the table. "You must understand that volumes are in the round. A surface is sculpted and space is a volume hollowed out of a mass. If I am successful, I will make it possible for people to feel something bigger than they can physically perceive when they enter a space – they will become the space, just like we are inside of the mountain of God's love."

He was not sure if she was following him, but trusted that she was sensitive to what he was revealing to her.

"You see, volumes are full and at the same time they are empty, and the magic is that when we enter a space, we should be able to imagine both of those aspects together. We cannot see God, we can only imagine Him through the beauty of his creations, like these perfect round cherries we are eating. Full and empty, I say, just like our life: we have the daily reality that surrounds us - sticks and birds and water and these cherries – as well as the world of our dreams and our vision of perfection. For me, art and creation lies in the middle ground of these two worlds. We are often like ships, lost in the immensity of the ocean, or camels lost in search of a caravansarai to rest for the night. I seek to make us feel a little less lost in our world by showing that daily life can be infused with poetry and light – a way of love that can be visually seen and apprehended. I believe that art – and architecture – are ways to discover the reality that surrounds us, and, at the same time, they reveal our dreams. Yes, I think it lies there in the space between those two realities – or, at least that is where I want to place it. For you see, God is there in that space as well."

He dug into the basket to pick up another handful of cherries. Joseph the Potter, usually so talkative, listened in silence and nodded for him to continue.

"As an architect, my part in all of this is to organize and calculate everything, from the first dream in my head to the last stone laid, and build so that the walls will ring with life for centuries. We build for now and we build for the future. We live in extraordinary times, Mahperi, where cities are rising from the Anatolian plain, and great cathedrals are rising from the fields in my homeland of France. We can be a part of this humanity and determination. Let us be powerful in this way; what do you think, my good Queen?"

Moved by his words, it took a long time before she could answer him.

"Lou, I asked you why you became an architect because I was wondering if your answer would help me to understand my yearnings to work and to love all around me. My favorite verse from the Bible is in Psalms: '*Delight thyself in the Lord and He will give you all the desires of your heart*.' But what are the desires of my heart? Alone in my room at night and during the day in my thoughts, just like you, I draw up my dreams for a place of peace, a place that will stand for eternity, both for God and for we humans. And for me, I think that stones could offer that possibility of expressing the desires of my heart. I want to set up my own household in Kayseri and build something monumental there. I truly feel that the city at the foot of the Mountain holds much opportunity for me. Stones have souls, Lou, just like you and I do, don't you think? I know you may think that sounds strange, but they do, for they strive and struggle just like we do. And with these stones here at Kubadabad or Kayseri, I feel a little less a lost ship, as you say, than at the court of Konya. I am convinced these stones will help me fill those desires of my heart. I so admire what my husband, the Sultan, is building, and I want to be a part of that as well."

"*Ma Gente Dame*, you must certainly not hide your talents or ambitions; they were given to you by God as a gift to be used! What good is an astrolabe without the stars? Build, my lady! Build more than a palace, build your Empire! Make those stones pulse with the same warm heart that beats in you!" he said with tenderness and conviction at the same time.

☪ ☪ ☪

He speaks so gently and is so at ease with himself, thought Mahperi, and I feel that same calm when I am with him. He makes me believe that a world of beauty can rise from mud and stones. He makes me believe that a world of peace exists, far from the fear of these encroaching Mongols. He inspires me to believe that this world can be better than it is today; a beautiful world of hope and stones.

Lou Cantadou looked her directly in her emerald eyes, shining greener than the mountains behind her.

"What a gift you are," he said softly to her. "What a wondrous gift – to this court, to this Empire, and to this world. I understood that from the first day I saw you, for the intelligence of your heart sheds a light by which all around you can see their lives better. You are truly a remarkable Queen, Mahperi Hatun."

And I love you. That was the end of the phrase he wanted to pronounce, but those were words he would never be able to say.

Chapter 53

Pure, Noble and Honorable Queen

In the middle of the summer, Mahperi returned to Konya, for she realized how much she missed her weekly lessons with Jelaleddin Rumi and her visits to her friend Hanife. She was eager to tell her all about Kubadabad and the building of the palace, and as soon as she returned to the city, she went directly to Hanife's workshop. The two sat at the loom for a spell before Hanife spoke, as was the ritual of their visits together.

"I have missed you, my good friend. You have been away from the court for many months. I can only assume that your duties at Kubadabad committed you to be there at this crucial time for its development. Why don't you tell me about it? I would love to hear it described through your eyes."

Bubbling with enthusiasm, Mahperi related the stunning beauty of the lake, the clearing away of the site, the digging of trenches, the laying out of garden beds, the constant noise of hammering and yelling workmen, and the sheer energy of so many people involved in the creation of something so unique. She also told Hanife about her new friendship with Lou, and how he was bringing her much of the same joy she felt with her.

Hanife took it all in and kept knotting in silence for a long while after Mahperi had finished her story.

"Please forgive me for being away so long, but I had so much to do there!" she blurted out. "I will be returning soon, once I finish with some affairs here. With the Sultan away on his campaign in the East, I need to represent his voice on the site."

"But what about Köpek – wasn't he there to represent the Sultan's interests?" Hanife questioned.

"Yes, of course, but you know how he is. He takes over everything and I just want to make sure I have some input for the building of my own home!" she stammered.

Yes, thought Hanife to herself, I know exactly how Köpek is, and I am uneasy with you being around him alone on that site without the Sultan present. She grabbed the red yarn from the bobbin hanging to the left of the loom and mounted three rows of knots, banging them down with her *kirkit* comb, more energetically than usual. When she thought about her friend on the site in close proximity to Köpek, a chill ran down her back, despite the June heat. The muzzle of that Dog can sniff out anything, and if he reads anything into this innocent friendship she shares with Lou, he will turn it on her and destroy her in ways she cannot begin to imagine.

☪ ☪ ☪

Yet in ways I certainly can imagine, thought Hanife. No, not only imagine, but know for truth. She thought back to a time long ago, when she was a little eight-year-old girl living in the modest house with her widowed mother, who worked at the palace as a seamstress. It was from her that Hanife learned to appreciate the richness of textiles; it was her tender mother who taught her how to sew, who laughed and played with her until that one day when all went dark in their lives. Dark, like the muzzle of a black Dog.

On that long-ago day Hanife was playing in the courtyard when she heard her mother arguing with someone. Her mother never raised her voice; it was as soft as the velvets she embroidered for the wives of Giyaseddin Keyhüsrev I, the sultan sitting on the throne in those days. Frightened by this tone of voice she had never heard before, she tiptoed up the back steps of their small house and listened outside the door to her mother arguing back and forth with a shrill male voice.

"What makes you think that you can rebuff me, you haughty woman? You are nothing more than a palace servant, and I am an important man! Of course you must submit to my demands! Come with me, and I will offer you riches you never knew possible! Do you want to stay in this hovel forever? I can get you out of here, and offer you a life you never dreamed possible! I want you, now, in my life, and I will have you! No one refuses me – no one!"

"But I don't want to be with you! I am happy in my life, in this hovel as you call it! I have my work and my dignity and I will not tarnish it. I must think of my daughter, and I do not want her growing up thinking her mother is a concubine! I do not want the shame of all Konya upon my head! We both honor the memory of my deceased husband, may God protect his soul! I don't love you, you frighten me and I don't want you hovering around me anymore! Now please, stop pestering me with your advances or I will tell the Sultan about you!"

The little girl did not understand any of what this meant, but she certainly knew that her mother was in some kind of danger. She approached the door to peek in to see with whom her mother was arguing. She recognized him at once: it was Sadettin Köpek, an up-and-coming official in the court, whom she had often seen when she went to the palace with her mother. He would not stop screaming at her mother, his eyes becoming more and more enflamed with a wild look.

Then the little girl then saw him grab her mother and slam her to the ground. "*I will have you! No one says no to me!*" he screamed. The little girl's mother kicked and screamed, but he was on top of her, crushing her with his weight. He slapped her repeatedly hard across the face and screamed '*there, you see, you are mine, you are all mine now!*' He finally got up and stared down at her listless form on the floor, adjusted his robes, and wiped off his lips with the back of his sleeve. As he turned to leave, he saw the wide-eyed stare of the little girl standing at the door.

"What are you doing there? How long have you been there?" he bellowed. When he heard the little girl start to cry, he dashed out of the room, shoving her to the ground as he passed by her.

The little girl rushed over to pick up her mother's bruised head in her arms. Her eyes had a wild and empty look in them. That man has broken my mama! And break her, he did. From that day forward, her mother went dark. She never spoke again; she stared out at the world with the blank eyes of a specter, and those last words spoken in anger with the bad man were the last words the little girl ever heard her mother speak. That day would remain engraved in her memory forever.

☪ ☪ ☪

"Hanife, are you all right? You have gone all pale!" said Mahperi, putting her arm around her friend's shoulders which were shaking uncontrollably.

Hanife put her head in her hands and started to weep. "Please! Please! I beg you! Keep away from that Frank! I see only sorrow and pain for you!" she sobbed.

"But what are you talking about? What does he have to do with anything?" she asked, puzzled by her friend's reaction.

Hanife calmed down and took Mahperi's hands in her own. She pressed them to her cheek and held them there for a long moment.

"My beautiful friend, I am so happy for you that you have this opportunity to be involved in such an exciting adventure. I think that you have found the path you have been seeking for your life; the one I was always hoping you would discover. I can see on your face that you are blossoming like a rose. Yet… I feel I must say a few things to you. As you know, oh so well, people are not always kind, and often seek to harm others of whom they are jealous with their thoughts and deeds. You, as Queen, must always be pure, noble and honorable in your behavior, not only to set an example for others, but to always ensure that you are distanced from any situation that could give people reason to criticize you. Make sure you are above entanglements of any kind so as not to be a target. I fear that people may judge your friendship with this architect as more than just a tender complicity. They will spread gossip and malice and seek to destroy you. Listen to me now: keep a certain distance from that man, Mahperi, trust me! The honor of a woman in Islam is the highest of virtues, and as Queen, you must be higher than all. You are Mahperi Hatun, wife of Sultan Alaeddin Keykubad and Queen of the Seljuk Empire, the most civilized kingdom in the world! Now go and be that Queen in example to every peasant, child, shopkeeper, artisan, and woman in this land. You are a pure, noble and honorable queen, and you must never forget it!"

Chapter 54

Jealous Rainbows

Mahperi always enjoyed visiting the potter Joseph in his shed. Others called Joseph cantankerous, but with her, he was never irritable. In the rowdy commotion of the worksite, his shed was a haven, much like a church, with its massive worktable altar and his tools lined up like liturgical objects. As with Hanife, Mahperi was content to just sit and watch him work, with not a word passing between them. Joseph was a craftsman of the finest skill and the most delicate of sensitivities, and she wanted to be a part of his world of visual delight.

Wiry and agile despite his considerable limp, Joseph had forearms as large as his thighs, built up from lifting heavy lumps of clay and then massaging them for hours on end. His solid hands, full of calluses and cracks, were graceful, caressing the clay more than beating it. Joseph was always covered from head to toe with clay dust and spatters, and Mahperi wondered if it ever got entirely washed off at night.

One morning on her inspection tour of the grounds, she and several of her guards entered his shed, where she found the potter speaking with Lou. The two Christian foreigners working for the Seljuk Sultan enjoyed a close friendship based on the unspoken respect for each other's talents.

"See, my little Lou, my work is advancing nicely. The clay in the pit is moist, pliable and will fire nicely."

Mahperi turned to the architect and asked, "What are you having Joseph prepare for the site, Lou?"

Joseph whipped his head around and barked, "That man never tells me what to do, my Lady, he knows better than that! I am in charge here; I am the master who will make his plain stones sing!"

When he saw the startled look on Mahperi's face, the architect jumped in to calm down the gruff potter.

"Now, now, Joseph, she is only curious about what you are planning for her home, so why don't you tell the good Lady here – the wife of the man who is paying you a fortune of a salary, I might remind you – what you have in mind?" Lou prodded, winking at the grumbling potter.

Realizing he had offended Mahperi, the potter began to explain his plans for the palace.

"I will decorate the large and small palaces and the baths with tiles, starting from about knee-level and going up to the top of our heads. When the Sultan will sit on his raised dais of the throne room in the Great Palace, these panels will have pride of place right at his eye level, and when the members of his court sit at his feet on soft cushions, they will look up and gaze at all this glory! I will decorate each tile with a portrait of an animal or a person. I will include the Sultan and his family and court members, but also the servants and pages who are so much a part of palace life. These will be big tiles, about the size of your spread hand, and in the shape of eight-pointed stars," he said, grabbing a piece of charcoal from his bench to make a rough sketch.

"Between the tiles I will insert turquoise cross-shaped pieces decorated with interlaced tendrils and leaves to represent the bounty of the plants of the shore and forests here. These tiles will make the big star tiles stand out even more. At the bottom and top of each panel, I will place a border of simple rectangular turquoise tiles, to imitate the blue waters of the lake below, and the blue sky above us. I will bring the outside indoors; you will feel nature is surrounding you, in a place where time will stand still. On the star tiles, I promise I will draw images that will delight you. Hunting dogs will look back at their master with paws raised and noses sniffing for prey, goats will leap, birds will twitter and flit between trees, bears will lumber through the groves looking for fruit, horses will prance in mincing steps, rabbits will hop, and palm fronds will wave invitingly on the banks of the lake," described Joseph, with a rapture and tenderness that belied his usual gruffness.

The window onto his emotional side did not last long. He tossed the charcoal down and blurted out, "But all this is not easy, not like the job that Frenchman has, drawing a bunch of scribbles on paper! I take earth, water and fire and make masterpieces – do you think that happens by chance? No, it takes many years of experience and much patience!" He hobbled over to his table and grabbed the edge to steady himself. "It takes at least two weeks to make a tile," he continued, "and many weeks of work before that to prepare all the necessary materials: getting them delivered to the site, grinding the pigments, finding the correct plants, stocking the wood fuel for the ovens, and so forth. This is a complicated process that takes much forethought!"

"Yes," Mahperi nodded, "My weaver friend Hanife tells me the same thing! Months of preparation take place before she can even think of sitting at her loom!"

"Absolutely!" Softening a bit, he waved her over to his table. "Yes, Queen Mahperi, come; what if I show you how to make a tile? I certainly could use another pair of strong hands today to help me!"

Lou smiled at the image of the Sultana of the Seljuks kneading mud like a lowly worker, but that was the way she was: uncomplicated and forthright, and he admired that in her. Her lovely fingers will make this clay the most blessed that Joseph has ever fired, he thought to himself.

"The clay is as easy to make as bread dough, I tell you: just three ingredients: clay, minerals and plants. The energy and touch from your hands is the yeast of the mix!" Joseph laughed.

"To make the clay as white as possible, I have a little trick. I add pulverized quartz from river stones and a secret mix of various kinds of plant ash, which gives a nice shine to the clay. I add some pure water from the lake, and there you have it, the clay you are kneading with your lovely hands, my good Lady!"

"I can tell you, Mahperi," interjected Lou, "you do not want to be around Joseph when a batch of tiles comes out of the kiln all broken from too much lime in the clay or other impurities that often make them split. You can run all the way back to Konya and hide; such is his wrath at that moment!"

Rubbing his hands together, the potter smiled gleefully, pleased to have such an attentive pupil. "After I shape the tiles, then comes the best part. When the tile has dried hard I can then paint it. But before I draw my picture, I must first paint the background. I usually cover the tile with a colored glaze to hide the dull, natural tan color of the clay. I can add some tin to make the glaze a milky white color, or I can add some other kinds of ground metals to make a colored glaze. These metal powders are expensive, hard to get, and are wily, for I never know how they are going to turn out once fired. If there is too much manganese powder in the mix, the purple comes out almost black and the tile is useless. If I don't put enough cobalt oxide into the mix, the blue comes out pale, not dark like the sky right before sunset, that moment when the birds flutter to find their final roost for the night. I love that time of day, don't you my Lady?"

Mahperi nodded her head, fascinated by the detailed process and his sensitivity to nature.

"The hardest color to achieve is turquoise – could it ever be possible to replicate the color of the waters of this beautiful lake? No, God reminds me of that every time a batch of tiles comes out of the kiln too green, too yellow or too faded. So it's another day of work lost, but the next day I pick up again and pray to the saints above for a successful outcome. You must understand that everything affects the way the color turns out: the air, the sun, the time of day, the heat of the furnace, the impurities in the metals, the stickiness of the clay, the steadiness of my hand and even my mood. Yet, sometimes, when the grace of

God shines upon me, all these elements join together perfectly, and the explosion of beauty on the tile roars forth louder than that big leopard of the Sultan! The whole process of making tiles has a mysterious life all its own. That clay and those ingredients are alive I tell you, alive, as you or me!"

"That's what Hanife says about her wool, too!" added Mahperi. "She always is telling me that it reacts to her hand in ways she can never predict."

The potter smiled broadly. "Now you see the burden we artists must endure!"

"But when do you paint the picture, potter Joseph?" questioned Mahperi eagerly.

"That comes next. After I have covered the tile with that first glaze, I let it dry but do not fire it. Then I take pigments of different colors and paint my picture with a fine-pointed brush – leaping rabbits, pages with pomegranates, double-headed eagles, whatever my fancy tells me!"

His tone became serious. "But as an artist, I never get to do exactly what I want; for it is the hand and the brush that rule me. Sometimes the brush can fly over the surface and startle me wfith an image I had not even expected; sometimes the brush trembles so strongly in my hand that I cannot hold it. Sometimes the bristles are too hard, sometimes the color too wet. Always surprises, good and bad, that is for certain. What you must understand, Lady Mahperi, is that the pigments I use to paint the pictures all look brown when I am painting them. It is only when they are fired in the oven that the true color comes out. So it is a challenge for me to keep the design in my mind when I select my various pigments to render each part of the picture, for they all look like the same brown goop on the tile! When I have finished painting my image, I often silhouette it in black to highlight it from the background glaze color. Once the paint is dry, I then brush the tile very carefully with a clear glaze to seal it all together."

"Do you sign your name to the tiles, Joseph?" Mahperi asked.

"Bah! I do not need to sign my wares. Just look at them! My signature is there for all to see; in the subjects I depict, the special life I confer on my subjects, my sense of color – just look! My name blazes forth as loudly as if the muezzin cried it out from the minaret of the Niğde mosque!"

The potter continued his explanation. "Now for the final step: the firing. You see that row of ovens in the field over there with the beehive domes? That is where the final magic takes place. Under the dome, trays of tiles are stacked on top of each other. Underneath is a large pit where we place the branches and logs for the fire. The kiln has a voracious appetite for fuel, and my apprentice must take care to keep feeding in wood so that the temperature remains even throughout the entire firing. One spike or drop in temperature and the whole lot will be ruined! We bake the tiles for at least twelve hours at a very high heat.

After the fire goes out we let the oven and the tiles inside cool slowly for one week. They must come back to the world of the living gently after having been in the volcano of hell! We take the trays out of the ovens and that moment can be the proof of the existence of God or of the Devil, for both of them are at work in that oven! I always get my share of surprises when the tiles come out of the oven. Some of them will be broken, warped or split in two. Sometimes the colors will fire all wrong, and turn out an ugly brown or too dark. The glazes of some blister and bubble up. Designs bleed out, get smudged, and the black contours get fuzzy. But ah! For every ten tiles that are no good, one will soar out of the oven like the Holy Dove above Noah's ark! It will be perfect, in glaze and design and in color. It is at that moment, when I pick it up and hold it in my hand, that I understand what you women must feel when your child slips out from your womb and you hold it in your arms for the first time. Life has been created!"

Joseph paused and wiped off his hands on his dusty apron. "And there you have it, my Lady: the making of a tile. And so you see why I am often so cantankerous! With all the challenges of my work, is it any wonder I am able to keep a sane head on my shoulders? But that is the way of the demon of fire and the angel of beauty! Now knead harder, my Lady, your clay will never turn out well unless you put some energy into your hands! Harder, I say!" laughed the potter, pleased with his day.

Pointing to one of the tiles drying on the shelf, Lou turned to Mahperi and concluded, "Now you can understand, my Lady, why I put up with this man, for no one does work as fine as his. He is a man that can turn mere mud into miraculous splendor. I am certain these tiles will be the greatest glory of this palace for all eternity. Wouldn't you agree, my Sultana?"

☪ ☪ ☪

And certainly did Ibn Bibi agree, who noted in his journal that night:

> *"The Palace will glow with turquoise and dark blue coverings on its walls, so beautiful that the colors of the rainbow fade with jealousy."*

Chapter 55
Sullied Water

As promised, the Sultan came to Kubadabad as often as he could to inspect the progress of the work on his new palace. In between his campaigns in the East and his journeys south to Alaiye for the winter, he made sure that he came to review the building and to give additional orders and suggestions. Köpek was especially pleased one morning when he was able to walk around the site with the Sultan and explain his engineering exploits to him.

"The walls of the pavilions that you see in front of you, my Sultan, are indeed beautiful, but they are only the surface of the project. The real construction endeavors are the systems underneath the palace that make everything work efficiently: pipes for transporting fresh water, draining sewage, and irrigating the gardens. In essence, the work you cannot see is what ensures the success of the project," he explained. "It is like the stars of God's night dome: we see the constellations above us, but we know there are a million other domes of stars above them that we cannot even begin to perceive."

"Well put, Köpek!" answered the Sultan. "Yes, I do understand that the transport of water is the key to everything, especially in a project this complex. You have done an outstanding job, and I commend your efforts!"

"My Sultan, if you permit," he continued, "There is one other aspect to the project I have yet to show you. It will astound you, I am sure."

"I am intrigued, Köpek! Just what have you planned for us here?"

"I have taken inspiration from the way the Romans constructed their baths, like the ones at Ilgin you so enjoy and had reconditioned. If we think about it, the times of year you will be using this site are principally in the early spring and in the late fall. At those times of the year the sun is still bright and the days are clear, but the nights can be brisk, especially here in your palaces, where your Frankish architect has insisted on placing so many windows in every room," he interjected, hoping to cast a shadow across the glowing esteem the Sultan held of the talent of Lou. "In order to combat any chill, I have run a series of pipes underneath the floors in each room. Instead of relying only on small coal braziers for heat, here at Kubadabad, hot air heated by the bath furnaces will be forced through empty spaces under the floors. Another set of pipes will run used hot water, which had been heated for the baths, under the floors to warm the stone floors. This will toast the wool of the carpets on the floors, and make your rooms comfortable despite any outside chill!"

"Why Köpek, that is brilliant! How did you ever come up with that idea? I am astonished by your ingenuity, and my family and guests will have you to thank when they run their toes through those plush carpets warmed by your water pipes!" replied the Sultan, smiling brightly.

"Yes, I must say, I am quite pleased with the way this system has taken shape. It took me many hours of calculations, but I worked it all out in the end!" Köpek added, beaming with delight at his deserved praise.

The Sultan continued on his site visit, asking each member of the team, including Lou, the potter Joseph, and the head masons and carpenters, to explain their work. No detail was too small to escape his attention, criticism or praise.

When it came his turn, Lou Cantadou invited the Sultan to walk through the two palaces, which were almost complete.

"My Sultan, as promised, the site and buildings will be delivered by next March. As you can see, the palace walls are already in place. Left to complete are the interior finishes. Over this coming winter while you are in Alaiye, we will install the wall of tiles in the throne rooms of the two palaces. The stucco grills will be set in the windows. The gardeners are now out on the grounds planting the tulip bulbs that will greet you next spring with their dancing heads. Your preferred weaver, Hanife, is completing, as we speak, a series of large carpets that will grace your floors – now heated, thanks to Köpek's skill! – with their bright patterns. Seamstresses are stitching the cushions and pillows for the low benches that will run along the walls, and which are now being assembled by the carpenters," he explained, pointing to the walls. "All will be ready for you when you arrive next spring. I promise you, when you come up out of the Emireddin Pass and set your eyes upon the site, you will truly think you have arrived in Paradise!"

The Sultan now knew that he had made a wise choice in bringing Lou up from Aspendos to this site. The architect continued his presentation.

"The whole team of workers on the site has participated in bringing your vision to life. Guided by your initial instructions, my Sultan, we have each sought to bring our own touch of skill, artistry and love to this project. May God praise their hands!" he concluded. "There is perhaps one person, however, who has worked particularly hard on this project," said Lou, ever attentive to his friend, the lame potter, who was so often ridiculed by the other workers for his odd ways and his infirmity. "His challenges were as monumental as Köpek's, for he has to work with a matter as unpredictable as the forces of nature. With his tiles, Joseph has created for you a spectacular reflection of the beauty that surrounds you here, as well as the floating world of our dreams. You will see his wall of glory in place on the day of the inauguration, but I would like to show you an example of what he is planning," he said, nodding to the potter.

Joseph invited the Sultan to walk over to his studio, dragging his lame leg behind him as fast as he could. In preparation for the Sultan's visit, he had laid out on the table a small mock-up of nine of the star and cross tiles that would be assembled on the palace walls. The table of tiles was for the moment covered with a linen cloth.

"Welcome to my studio, my honored Sultan. I would like to give you a small hint of the future decoration of your palace," he indicated, proudly gesturing to the table with his hand. "Imagine this group thirty times this size, set in place with the lake as its backdrop. I promise you, it will be like nothing the world has ever seen. For centuries, people will stare in astonishment at this testament to the glories of the Seljuk Sultans!"

Joseph whisked away the cloth with a flourish and stood back to observe the Sultan's reaction.

"Why, this is unbelievable!" the Sultan gasped as he gazed at entire universe sparkling up at him from underneath their shiny glazes. "I cannot imagine that you have wrought such splendor from mud and water! You are truly a genius, Joseph! You are right, Lou Cantadou. By the grace of his work here, all eternity will come to this site and remember the glory of the Seljuks! You have made this project sing like the angels of heaven!" gushed the Sultan.

Köpek observed the scene with intense jealousy, unable to bear that the center of attention was no longer on him. Here was this foreign, smelly cripple getting all of the Sultan's praise for his little colored pats of mud, whereas I, who have constructed an entire hydraulic system, get but a nod and a few words of appreciation! Köpek couldn't withhold his anger, and rashly spoke up, his high voice piercing the small studio space with its sharpness.

"May I remind you, Your Highness, that this wall is standing only because of my foundation engineering, and will be enjoyable only because of the cleanliness and warmth that I have provided through my systems, built with great care and attention for you," he sniffed, looking down at the lame potter.

"Yes, yes, Köpek," interjected the Sultan, "We all know all about your systems and are most grateful for them; I have already acknowledged that! We all are well aware that you work wonders with hot water pipes and disposing dirty water from bowels and bladders – but *this* –" he said, gesturing to the tiles on the table with a sweep of his elegant fingers – "*This* is work of the highest level of artistry!"

☪ ☪ ☪

Köpek felt his ears burning as if someone had stuffed hot coals down them. The heat rose to the top of his head and lights exploded behind his eyes. *Bang-bang-bang,* burst the hot coals in his head.

"*I am good for nothing more than bowels and bladders!*" the Sultan's words echoed in his burning ears over and over again. *Bang bowels bang bladders bang hellfire.*

Pipes! That is all I am to him! I am nothing more than dirty water in his eyes, when it is my work that is the most important! *Bang bowels bang bladders bang hellfire.*

Oh, my Sultan, if you don't know what I am good for, believe me, you will soon find out. You will regret how you have just treated me. You will never look down at me again, you pitiful Alaeddin. When I am through with you, this kingdom will be mine and mine alone, to whom it truly does belong, for I am more intelligent and gifted than all of you! I will destroy you, along with that imperious Armenian queen of yours, your insipid son, your glorious kingdom, your honor, everything! I will destroy it all! *Bang bowels bang bladders bang hellfire.*

I deserve it all, much more than you do! My father begged your father the Sultan Giyaseddin to allow me to attend the palace school. And I worked hard to earn his respect, and to show him that it was not just a favor tossed out to appease my father – I was truly the smartest of all the students in the school. I grew up alongside three royal brothers who did nothing exceptional, other than having royal blood, whereas I, Sadettin Köpek, shone by my hard work and cleverness. I could solve any mathematical equation faster than all of you, I could write faster and ride faster and pull an arrow faster than the three of you; oh, yes, I could, but do you think that was ever praised by the Sultan Giyaseddin? I earned my respect and proved my worth, but was that ever recognized by him? He may have promoted me to a high rank once I graduated, but did he ever toss me a bone of kindness and praise? No, I was always the ugly dog Köpek, standing in the shadow of his royal sons. And now, you, his son, dare do the very same thing to me. *Bang bowels bang bladders bang hellfire.*

Well, now it is my turn; I will take my place as ruler of this kingdom. I, too, am every inch as important as a son of a Sultan and I will take the power that I deserve and that should be mine. I will destroy you, Alaeddin Keykubad – you, the Sultan of piercing blue eyes who now says that I am worthy of nothing more than bowels and bladders. You will see that I will destroy everything dear to you, and when you see the dirty water I will dump on you, then you will then know who is the finest man in the land, and that would be me and me alone – Sadettin Köpek!

Chapter 56

Let the Little Children Come unto Me

On one bright, late autumn morning when Mahperi's guards escorted her to Lou's shed, she found him bent over rolls of drawings spread out on the table, charcoal bit in hand.

"Good morning, Lou Cantadou! Surely you have finished with drawing all the plans for the palace by now, haven't you?"

"*Ma Gente Dame*, it never stops, and if we are to be finished on time by next March, I must ensure that not one detail is left to chance," he sighed.

"After you finish with this project, what will you do?" she asked him, walking around the table to see what he was so engrossed in drawing.

"I don't know exactly. I guess I will look for more work on another site, for building projects are not lacking in this country!"

It was then that Mahperi found the perfect opportunity to speak to him about an idea that had been formulating in her head for some time.

"Then listen to me, Lou Cantadou from Languedoc," she said. "I have a proposal for you. I would like to hire you myself as head architect for a project I want to build."

"For you! But that is impossible! I work for the Sultan!" he replied, dumbstruck.

"Perhaps now you do, but in the future, you will work for me. I will arrange the details with the Sultan, do not worry. On our last visit to Kayseri I discussed with him my idea for my own construction project, and he agreed to everything. He even promised to help with the financing, above my normal allowance. He is very supportive in all that I do, and I am most grateful to him."

"So, it seems you have thought all of this out, my Lady! May I ask exactly what you have in mind?"

"As I have told you before, I have plans to set up my own household in Kayseri. It is a city that I admire very much and its appeals for me are many. I look forward to spending more time there as soon as this project here at Kubadabad is completed."

What she did not tell him, however, was that her plan to build, already a dream since that day she walked under the starry portal of the Sultan's han, had now became an obsession.

She traced her finger over one of the drawings on the table. "Like you, my friend Lou, I have dreams in the night that keep me awake and haunt me. Mine are about what I will build out there in my husband's Empire, and the visions are starting to become clearer and clearer with each dream."

"I am listening. What are these visions of yours?"

"Promise me you will not laugh, chastise me or think I am unstable, agreed?" she pleaded.

"I am not one to chastise a queen!" he laughed, "Especially one who is going to be my future patroness!"

"Alright then. It was actually our conversation during the picnic with the workers that has provoked all of this, so I suppose I have you to thank – or blame – for this. Your words affected me very deeply," she explained.

"For that I am grateful, but just how did they do that?" he questioned.

"Because, I, too, want to build for God."

It took Lou a few minutes to grasp what she had said. "This touches me much that you are feeling this same impulse, but what and how exactly are you going to build for God?" he asked, cocking his head to the side.

Mahperi took a deep breath. "I.... I want to build a mosque."

"What! But that is unthinkable! Why, you are a Christian..."

"You promised not to chastise me, remember?

"But..."

"Listen to me, Lou Cantadou. Both you and I are devout Christians. You lost all of your family and almost died for your beliefs in a God of purity. I am a Christian who loves Mary and Jesus as strongly as I love my children – and perhaps even more so. I pray every day, I have taught my children all the verses of the Bible, and I celebrate with great joy the sacraments of Christmas and Easter. My faith is the foundation of who I am."

He nodded to her, still not fully understanding where she was leading with her remarks.

"Yet, at the same time, I spend much time discussing the faith of this land with the scholars of the medreses of Konya. Bahaeddin Veled was very influential in my life. He opened a spiritual door much wider than any I had walked through previously. And now his son, Jelaleddin Rumi, and his teacher, Buhaneddin, as well as others, continue to instruct me on the ways of the Islamic faith. They are patient with me and answer my questions. It intrigues me, this faith. It has such purity, order and reason. Again, what you told me about the *Cathari* offered me many points of contrast as well," she insisted, pausing to sit down on the stool brought to her by one of her guards.

"I have learned in this land of many religions that they all have the same spiritual source and honor the same one God, font of all creation. I have also learned in this land of Anatolia that all humans have been created equal, and that the diversity of race and culture are worthy of appreciation. Lou, I suppose what I am trying to say is that we must not be afraid to investigate other paths of spirituality than the one dictated in Rome or the one into which we were born. We grow, we change, and our faith should always be there with us at whatever point in our lives we are, supporting us and helping us evolve. I am asking myself now at this point in my life whether that support can come only from Mary and Jesus, or perhaps could the holy words of the Qu'ran guide me as well? I cannot say – but the only thing I can say is that Islam is now shining its light on me through an opened door. Perhaps one day I will walk through that door and pronounce the *shahada* and pray in the mosque on Friday instead of in the church on Sunday – or both. Who knows where my quest for God will lead, but God must be at the center of my life. Now, this quest is telling me to go deeper. It is telling me to make a gesture that shows that we are all united under God's love, whatever path we are on. It is telling me to build a mosque. I feel that such a gesture would honor all that my husband the Sultan has tried to create for this Empire. And for this, I need you, a fellow Christian and an architect devoted to 'building for God', to be by my side. It is almost as when Jesus said, '*Let the little children come unto me*'."

Lou was quiet for a while, thinking of all the implications of what she had just told him. He could not imagine the potential scandal, or even the total refusal of the idea of a Christian building a mosque. Was she thinking clearly about the impact this would have on her own faith? Would the people of Kayseri want to enter a mosque built by the hands and heart of a Christian? This was a reckless proposition for certain! Nonetheless, the potential inspirational impact of such a project fascinated him. The Seljuks preached tolerance as a part of the foundations of their governance – as his welcomed presence in their lands testified – so could this project set a brilliant example of their leadership in this direction? Would it send out a message of God's embracing love for all his children? His head spun as he tried to sort out all these thoughts. This was a totally outrageous proposition! And yet.... His head spun at the complexity and audacity of this totally unorthodox and original proposal of hers. She was right. It was daring, but she needed to go down this challenging path for many reasons. This one building could symbolize all the aspirations of this Empire, far more than all of the projects of her husband put together! What a remarkable woman she is!

He finally found the argument to answer her, based on his work.

"Mahperi, when an architect is hired to work on a religious building, he is offered an opportunity like no other, for it gives him the chance to speak from the depths of his feelings. He has the chance to achieve heights from these depths that he never thought were possible. It should not matter what your personal religion is as an architect – what matters is the building and its power to convey a spiritual message to its people. Whether you pray in a pew or on a rug, whether you answer the call of the muezzin or pealing bells, once you are inside a house of God, you must be impressed by its connection to a higher entity. It should not matter to an architect who has commissioned the building: be it rabbi, pope or imam, our task is the same: we must inspire everyone who walks into the space to lift his heart heavenwards. So, I suppose what you are saying joins much of the same spiritual challenges that are often put in front of an architect."

She smiled, happy that he understood that she was seeking to say something in praise of God, despite the path she was taking to get there. "Let me explain a few more details to you, Lou Cantadou. Sultan Alaeddin Keykubad is currently building a medrese right in the center of Kayseri, not far from an old Roman bathhouse. It will be an impressive one in a city already full of impressive medreses – it seems this city of scientists has one on every street corner!" she laughed, before becoming serious once again. "What I would like to do is make it the finest one in the city. Alaeddin's father built a remarkable hospital and medical school in Kayseri, and it has been an inspiration to me. I, too, would like to build a complex of buildings. I will place Alaeddin's medrese as its centerpiece, and build a mosque alongside it, near the old baths. The mosque I plan will be an important one, because it will be immediately visible to all coming to and leaving the city. By uniting Alaeddin's medrese with a mosque and baths, I am creating a symbolic fountain to quench the thirsts of the minds, hearts, and bodies of the people of Kayseri. It is a way for me to show my connection with the Sultan. I also want the citizens of Kayseri to know that they are loved by their Sultan's queen."

And how could they not but love you, just as I do?

Lou clasped his hands in front of him and looked down at them for a while before answering her. "As I told you before, Mahperi, you are a gift. It would be my honor to join forces with you to bring this dream to life. We will work together as a team to build a spectacular mosque for the city of Kayseri. A project this complex will take at least four years to complete. When do we start?" he said, bowing deeply to her.

"Right now!" she said, clapping her hands in glee. "Even though you are busy with this site, we must think about the next project. Perhaps you could take a trip to Kayseri to look at the site, and then you could start the preliminary drawings and the project scheme. If we have the drawings completed, we could even consider starting the actual building as soon as you are finished with Kubadabad next spring," she proposed ambitiously.

"*Ma Gente Dame*, are you *sure* the Sultan has agreed to this? Are you certain this will not create any problems for him – or you?" Lou queried, still skeptical.

"As I said, in theory, he has, yes. He refuses me nothing – he is a noble husband who supports me in everything I do. Remember, too, that his own mother was a Christian, so he has a wide tolerance for religious practice. He knows about my discussions with imams and Sufi masters, just as he knows of my devotion to Mary. He has never forbidden me to practice my faith – he is an enlightened ruler, and, if anything, he would be the first to encourage the message that my mosque will symbolize. In this way, he is as much of a patron of the project as I am. Yes, all of us will have our dreams sing in the stones of the most beautiful mosque Anatolia will ever see!"

Chapter 57

Little Song, Go Now to Tell of Me

After a hard day of work on the construction site of Kubadabad, the workers often gathered around a campfire on the lakeshore. There, they would watch the stars rise, observe the turning phases of the moon, and listen to the crickets and the frogs raise their song to the night heavens. The men shared stories, gossip, incidents of the work day, jokes and snippets of poetry, and as the evening went on, musical instruments appeared and singing and dancing followed.

One evening, the workers decided to host a special celebration in honor of a distinguished group of visitors that had come to the site. They were eager to show their accomplishments to the members of the Sultan's entourage, which included Ibn Bibi and the Vizier Karatay. Mahperi was invited as well to join the festivities, and she ordered her servants to provide refreshments for the evening. Fresh fruit was picked from the groves along the lake and melons were set to chill in the cool waters. Her cooks began preparing a kebab made with pistachios and eggplants, and the tantalizing aroma of roasting meat soon filled the site.

Lou was in a good mood from a successful day on the site, and was looking forward to celebrating with the other workers. The restraining wall under the terrace was completed and holding well, the walls of the Small Palace were in place, and Joseph had opened his kiln today to discover a particularly immaculate lot of tiles. All was coming along as the architect had hoped: on time, on schedule, and with no accidents to the men. Not that all went smoothly: there were fistfights among workers, cracked stones, late deliveries of materials, and the inevitable clashes with Köpek, who appeared to be doing everything possible to thwart his efforts. A roll of completed drawings disappeared from his shed the week before, and he could only surmise who was responsible for the theft. Yet the only true difficulty about the project he encountered was the frustration of being in such proximity to Mahperi, and being forced to hide his feelings for her.

The evening began with the honored guests arriving to take their places around the campfire. Mahperi and the other members of the court were seated next to Köpek and Lou. Everyone was regaled by the delicious feast that Mahperi's cooks had prepared for them, and men became more and more festive as the night wore on. Joseph managed to spill his juice all over a mason when he too energetically told a joke; the head stonecutter twirled a watermelon on the tip of his index finger, and a carpenter imitated the song of the bullfrog so accurately that a lake full of she-frogs answered in chorus. The levity of the evening was palpable, and soon musical instruments began to appear and the next phase of the evening's entertainment was ready to begin.

Curious, Lou leaned over and picked up the *ud* that belonged to Yusuf, one of the site masons, who was also the most talented of the amateur musicians who gathered around the fire each night.

"Do you think you are able to play it, my Frankish friend?" asked Yusuf, gesturing with his head to the *ud*.

Lou picked at the strings with his index and thumb. "Your *ud* seems similar to the stringed lutes we play in Occitania, but it is much deeper in sound. Ours give a lighter tone, more like the birds, but this instrument is still very much like ours."

"Well, why don't you show us how you Franks sing, then?" the mason continued. "I have heard that your songs are quite impressive."

"Why…yes, they are…" Lou stammered, a bit unsure of himself. "Yes, I suppose I could sing one for you. Actually, I have been composing one in my head for quite a while now, and I would finally enjoy playing it into life," he said, strumming a few chords.

All eyes were now upon him, and the crowd fell silent in anticipation. Lou looked up and realized there was no turning back now from Yusuf's request. Or from the emotions of his song, which he could no longer keep locked up inside of him.

"My friends, I will sing for you now a simple song, called a *canso*, from my land of Occitania," he announced. "It tells the story of a knight and his thoughts of battle. Our songs are much like yours, with one voice, a few strings, a few chosen lines, but the emotion is the same. I hope you will like it."

Yet Lou Cantadou from the country of troubadour poets carefully hid the fact that this knight was singing of a battle fought in his heart and not on dusty plains; a battle of love, the passion of his heart, and the duty of service to the Lady of his life.

At last, he thought to himself, at last I will be able to sing this *canso* that I have been carrying around in my head and heart for months, ever since the first time he set eyes on her at Aspendos. He knew that neither Mahperi, nor anyone else present would be able to understand the words of his song. No one spoke his language here, so he felt safe in giving full flight to his feelings and to express everything he felt in the deepest part of his heart.

The attention of every man was now focused on the architect. It seemed that even the crickets and the agitated she-frogs had hushed their song to let the verses of Lou Cantadou float over the lake. He started off slowly as if to savor this moment, the only moment he would ever have to express aloud the love he felt for her. Soon his strong and clear voice could be heard by all present that night, be it man, frog or stars:

Chanssos, va t'en dreich viatge lai on ill es
Qu'el mon non ai mais messatgequ'l tremesses
Chansoneta, vai t'en lai, non ges q'leu re il man,
Mas ben il potz mon esmai dire ses mon dan.
Digatz il c'a leis es donatz mos coratges et autreiatz !
Sieus son e sieus seri jase !
Morir puosc per ma bona fe....

Little song, go directly
To where she is
Little song, go now to tell of me
Relate my love without revealing my sorrow
Tell her my heart is given to her and devoted to her!
I am hers and always will be!
I can die for my good faith

Love! Love! You've done this to me,
Why did you have me choose a lady
For whom my heart sighs so deeply
That it cannot tell joy from sorrow,
And why do you want to destroy me for love of her?
When you make my sad heart burn
And melt in loving martyrdom, is this well done?

When her sweet eye's glance
And her shining face, white and rosy,
Fresh and sweet as a summer flower,
More radiant in beauty than gold in the sun,
By which I found myself illuminated,
Has soon overcome my five senses;
That my words dried up and my strength waned

For my heart cannot hide carrying my
Love for my Lady, nor can it cease to love her;
Rather, the love that abides in me

Is greater each day and nothing can put it out;
For when she most causes me to grow pale,
Grieve, moan and complain, then she most enslaves me
This is why I will lament, till the end of my days

In no way does my dear lady know
That I love her more than myself or anything I have
My heart lies caught in her snare,
This treasure and door-keeper of my heart
I will never dare tell her of my desire and my sweet malady
She receives me kindly and hospitably,
But I am not worthy to seek her favor

My Lady, to you, without reservation
I give my heart, thought, desire, and love
Gente Dame most excellent, I have
Such desire and longing for you
That nothing else in the world
Is so strong in my heart
This is why I will lament, till the end of my days.

When he finished, no one moved, so touched were they by his artistry. Total silence reigned over the lake. When he raised his eyes from the strings of the *ud*, he did not dare to look into hers, though he sensed they were upon him. She has heard my words, but she will never understand them. She has heard me sing, '*To you without reservation, door-keeper of my heart.*' I have spoken my feelings without compromising her honor, and no one knows what I have sung in my Provençal language, in my language of love; nothing but my yearning heart can understand it.

Go now, little words of my song, go away from my heart. Let the last vibrations of the strings of this *ud* carry you into the air with their fluttering wings, off to float over the lake into oblivion.

There, they are gone. Silence now.

Yet for you, *ma gente dame*, and for the promise of my love never to be fulfilled, I will lament until the end of my days.

Chapter 58

Golden Malice

Gaziye, wearing a dark blue velvet caftan and a necklace of amber and gold, clapped her hands for her maids to bring in yet another platter of pastries and fruit for her guests. She had taken to inviting Sadettin Köpek and Ibn Bibi to her apartments once a week, a time when the three of them shared refreshments, news, and gossip. Their ever-lively discussions revolved this week around the building of the Palace at Kubadabad.

"It is progressing very well, on schedule and without too many unresolvable problems," revealed Köpek, "Of course much of that due, if I may humbly say, to my ingenuity for the complex engineering of the site! I predict that by the time we return in late March from our winter in Alaiye, the entire complex will be finished. In fact, I am now organizing the opening ceremonies which we will plan for the month of Rabi."

"Oh, that is my favorite time of the year, when spring lambs are born and warm days start to bud," interjected the ever-poetic Ibn Bibi. "The site will be spectacular at that moment, with the surrounding hills covered with a blanket of apple and cherry trees in blossom, dancing tulips and fresh green grass!" picking up a glittering gold and enameled goblet in the air for the servant to refill with pomegranate juice.

"What exactly do you have in mind for the festivities?" asked Gaziye, always attentive when plans for parties and play were announced.

"I was thinking of organizing three days of celebrations around the time of the full moon. We will have an enthronement ceremony of the Sultan in the divan room of his new palace, followed by a lavish banquet with musicians brought in from Sivas. During the day, we will organize boating trips to the outlying islands in the lake, with picnics and song contests, and perhaps some game shooting for the men," he stated.

"Why, that sounds just exquisite, and I love the idea of bringing singers from the East – those of Sivas are unrivalled!" added Gaziye.

"The only problem I foresee is that Mahperi Hatun has also requested that we open the grounds to the surrounding villagers for a visit and a banquet at one point, but I cannot conceive of those peasants roaming around a Sultan's palace!

She is resolute in this request, however; and so far, the Sultan has not refused her," lamented Köpek.

"That woman and her ridiculous ideas! Imagine those toothless farmers tramping their dust and fleas all over our beautiful new palace! That would be a complete insult to the Sultan!" complained Gaziye, rolling her eyes upwards.

"She is insisting, and there is not much I can do, for she is quite determined in this matter," explained Köpek. "It seems long ago she made the Sultan promise to tend to his citizens as much as he does his battles and building, and he seems to go along with it."

"Oh, how I wish we could do something to tear down, once and for all, that high esteem the Sultan holds for her!" moaned Gaziye. "In his eyes, she can do no wrong. He is always seeking her advice, inviting her to the *divan* sessions; taking her along on his trips...Yet *I* am the first queen here, not her! This has got to stop! We have already managed to exile her son out to that forsaken hole in the East; couldn't we do the same thing to her? Poor woman! No one pays any attention to her; she spends her time talking with stuffy imams in town and with that odd, secretive woman who weaves the Sultan's rugs. All she can think about is riding that big black horse of hers around Konya like a soldier and building that Palace out there in the wilderness! She would do well to tend to her caftans and jewels; no wonder the Sultan pays so much attention to me!" boasted Gaziye.

"Oh, but on our recent trip to Kubadabad, I noticed someone who certainly pays much attention to her," interjected Ibn Bibi. "Have you seen how that Frankish architect is always hovering around her and looking at her when he thinks no one, especially the Queen Mahperi herself, can see him? Yes, they make quite a spectacle of themselves, walking around the site in deep discussion; he with his eager eyes upon her, both of them with their heads bent over the table in his shed, drawing plans for God knows what, and laughing. Yes, I hear them laughing together all the time; joyful laughter like children! If you ask me, this is more than a work relationship they share. Their friendship in my eyes is quite scandalous. Do you think the Sultan has gotten wind of it?" he concluded, picking up an apricot from the platter with his delicate, bejeweled fingers.

Köpek did not say anything, stunned by Ibn Bibi's perception. He hadn't noticed anything, but if this were true...The wheels of malice began to churn in his head. If the Sultan were to hear of his queen becoming too familiar with another man, what exactly would be his reaction? Gaziye's remarks also spun in his head. She is right; perhaps the time has come to deal with this woman, who exerts too much influence on her husband. Perhaps my plans for taking control of this Empire can start here and now, with this banquet. I am cleverer than any of them, and I can certainly orchestrate her downfall without any problem.

Ibn Bibi took another sip from the delicate glass goblet on the tray in front of him.

"My, I have never seen anything so lovely as these goblets! They must have come from your refined and cultured homeland of Syria, Melike Gaziye, for we have nothing this exquisite in our Seljuk lands!"

Flattered by the compliment, Gaziye laughed and nodded her head vigorously. "Oh yes, they were made by Master Tarik! You certainly have an eye for the finer things in life, Ibn Bibi! No wonder we are friends!" she teased.

"Who is this Master Tarik?" Ibn Bibi continued, ever curious where stories were concerned.

"Before my marriage, back in my land, in the town of Raqqa, I knew an extremely talented glassblower. He worked in glass like that limping Greek does with the tiles at Kubadabad. Magical work, he does. As you know, we have excelled in making glass in Syria since the beginning of time. It is our gift to the world, much like you Seljuks make carpets for all to admire. Our bazaars offer glass of all sorts, but only the rich can afford the fancy pieces, for they are very time-consuming and costly to make. This glass artist Tarik crafted several magnificent goblets for my Sultan father, covered with the most exquisite decorations in colored enamels which sparkle on the surface like jewels! On several spectacular pieces, he painted calligraphy in gold! Even for someone as wealthy as my father, they cost a fortune. My father gave me a set of Tarik's goblets as my wedding present and they are the most precious thing I own. Indeed, you certainly don't have anything as refined as this here in Seljuk lands!"

Köpek lifted his head from his reverie. *Golden glass*. Yes, that is it. I will use delicate objects of beauty to orchestrate the downfall of Mahperi. She thinks she is so strong, but she is as fragile as glass. Yes, that is it. *Golden glass*.

"Do you suppose it would be possible for me to contact this glass artist?" Köpek asked Gaziye.

"Well, yes, I know where he lives; we could send a messenger, but what for?"

"Let's just say I am going to help you in your desire to reduce the esteem the Sultan holds for Queen Mahperi, and provide grand entertainment at the inaugural banquet, all at the same time!" he snickered.

"How will you do that?" queried Ibn Bibi. "I see a good story in the making for my journal!"

"Oh yes, it will be a good story. I was just thinking....I will contact Tarik via secret messenger, pretending it is on behalf of Mahperi, and ask him to craft a set of glass plates under the pretext that they will be her gift to the Sultan to be used as the official dinnerware at the Palace of Kubadabad. I will pay for them with funds from the State Treasury, but without telling the Sultan. I will arrange for a Konya banker to ensure the loan for the gold leaf in his name, so there will be no trace of my name in any of this. Tarik will believe that it is a direct order from Queen Mahperi. These plates will cost a fortune! For you see, they will be plates like none ever seen in the Seljuk Empire, just as you said, Ibn Bibi. I will have him make them large in size, crafted from the purest crystal clear glass. I will ask Tarik to decorate the plates in painted gold, with a decoration of calligraphic expressions circling the border of each plate, saying things such as *'To the health of the user,'* or *'To his goodwill'* and other such wishes. But right in the center of every plate, I will have him inscribe something special that is sure to cause a scene, I promise you!"

The two leaned closer, spellbound, as he continued to disclose his plan.

"Leave it to me. Mahperi will be totally unaware of what is going on. But I can assure you, when the astute mind of the Sultan estimates the phenomenal cost of this endeavor, and when he reads the inscription in the center of the plate, he will become enraged like a lion! For as we all have learned, there is one thing the Sultan cannot tolerate, and that is someone trying to contest his authority. And then, all we will have to do is to sit back and watch him seethe in anger against his queen. I tell you, it will be the last time he will hold any regard for her. In one swoop, I will destroy both Mahperi and her son in his eyes....and make for great entertainment for us as well!"

☪ ☪ ☪

Yes, thought Köpek, it will be a night to remember; for I will ensure that this woman is banished from our sight forever. For once the force of Mahperi's influence is removed, it will be all that much easier for me to control the Sultan, his son and even his Arabic queen. For what I take great care to hide from the scheming little Gaziye is that I know full well that she is trying to maneuver to get her son Izzeddin appointed as heir, instead of the first-born Giyaseddin. I know it is the goal towards which she plots each night with all her wiles and charms. Yet little does she know that I have a plan of my own, which I will set in motion that night of the inauguration. I will do everything it takes to ensure that it is Mahperi's son Giyaseddin Keyhüsrev who will become the next Sultan, not her golden child. For this is the son I can control and make do whatever I want. When Giyaseddin does sit on the throne, it will be I, Vizier Sadettin Köpek, not him, who will hold all the power in my hands. My ultimate revenge over each and every one of you will then be complete!

Chapter 59

Whispers on the Wind

Köpek could not get the conversation he had with Gaziye and Ibn Bibi out of his head. He kept replaying many images in his head, images placed there by Ibn Bibi and magnified by his desire for revenge; images focused through the lens of his evil intent until they became as sharp as an arrow point.

"If you ask me, this is more than a work relationship they share...."

Over and over that sentence burned in his head, and now he sought more than images to add fuel to its fire. He thought of the times he saw the two of them together on the site. Yes, it was true; they had an easy-going friendship, but that was her way with everyone, ever since she first came here. She has no shame in her frank eyes and independent ways! She acts no differently with that Frank than she does with the mad potter, Ibn Bibi, or even with the late imam Bahaeddin Veled – and, if truth be told, even with me.

And yet....the more he thought about it, the more the images danced in his imagination. There were the times he would see the two of them with their heads bent over his worktable, peering at rolls of drawings. He had one of his men sneak into his shed and steal one just to see what was on them, but there was nothing more than some pretty drawings of intricate stone carving designs.

But there was the laughter. There was no denying that laughter seemed to accompany them everywhere, especially when they spent time with the lame potter – what a trio of infernal infidels they make! Yes, perhaps there is something more than friendship – and even if there isn't, I shall make it appear as if there is.

☪ ☪ ☪

Later that morning, when Köpek saw Mahperi's servant girl returning to the kitchens after having delivered a breakfast tray of fruit, peppers and warm eggs for her breakfast, he stopped her for a moment. Köpek had long learned to take a keen interest in the gossip that circulated among the palace staff and the workers on the site, for it often bore information more pertinent than could be gleaned from official sources, or even from Ibn Bibi. He turned to the little wisp of a girl, who had recently been brought to Konya by Mahperi from Antalya on her last winter trip, and began to press her for details on what she knew about her mistress and the architect.

"Good morning to you, my little Esma – that is your name, right? And a very pretty one indeed, just like you are! So, tell me, did you enjoy the song contest the other night? I wasn't so sure the Frank who sang a song that no one could understand deserved to win, but everyone agreed that it was the finest one."

"Oh, but I understood it!" she asserted enthusiastically. "And it was so pretty!"

"*What*? What do you mean, you understood it? How could you have?" queried Köpek, immediately intrigued.

"Oh, Vizier, come on now! It was so obvious! He was singing in the universal language of love, couldn't you hear it?" she giggled. "Besides, I understood a lot of the words and phrases in his language, oh, yes I did!" she boasted.

"How is that possible? You come from Antalya, not Occitania!"

Pleased to show off in front of such an important man, the little servant girl began to relate her story.

"Yes I am, but before coming up here to work in the palace of the Sultan, I served a rich merchant from Venice who had set up a trading business there in Antalya. He was a sly one, taking advantage of all the tax exemptions the Sultan offered to foreign traders. He made a fortune exporting carpets and foodstuffs to Venice! He had such a beautiful house, right there on the harbor, with tapestries and golden goblets everywhere! The dinner table was inlaid with ivory and mosaics, and meals were served on plates of pretty porcelains from the East. The windows opened out onto the blue misty mountains across the bay, almost as pretty as this lake here. Such a fine gentleman he was too; why, he paid me an extra coin at Christmas, Assumption Day and Easter, even though I am a Muslim!"

"Yes, my Esma, that is all well and fine, but what does this have to do with the song?" Köpek asked impatiently.

"Well…" she blushed and hesitated a second before continuing. "He received many visitors to that fine house, you know, doing his business and all. Many of them came from Cyprus and many came from Provence, all interested in selling their fine wines to my master! They love their wine, they do, those foreigners! Well, one of those merchants from Provence took a fancy to me – and me certainly to him – and we started to do a bit of trading among ourselves, if you understand what I mean; oh, yes we did! What a smooth one he was, that Frank, dark and thin and striking, much like that architect who sang the song. And well…you know…at certain moments of our trading, he would sing to me one of those rhyming ditties of theirs, always so pretty and tender, they were! He would explain to me some of the words and make me learn them so I could sing my own songs back to him, for that he liked very much! So that is how I could understand bits and parts of the architect's song. It was the very same language, the very same words, I tell you! It brought all of that back to me, his gallant way, and that song warmed me more than that campfire did, I can tell you!"

"Well then, tell me, exactly what was the song about? What was that story of the knight in battle?" prodded Köpek, still not clear on the meaning of the words of the song.

"Knight in battle indeed!" she laughed. "It was all about a knight in battle, all right, but in a battle of love for a Lady he could never have! Their songs are always about that; those Provencal men seem to favor loving women they can never have, and dedicate themselves to talking about her precious honor! Yes, the song was a painful cry from his heart for his Lady Love. Oh, it was a beautiful song I tell you, so nicely rhymed and all. But such torment he is living, that poor man!" she sighed.

"And he wrote this song, isn't that what he said? So am I to understand that this song reflects emotions he is feeling?" queried Köpek.

"Well, of course it does, my Vizier! If you had only listened to him when he was singing it, you would have heard it! He sang with all the emotion of his heart, yet never once did he look at her, and then when it was over, he bowed his head and I saw tears drop into his lap! Now, if that isn't a sign of a man in love, I don't know what is!" she concluded.

Köpek sat there stunned. "Well, my little Esma, now don't you say anything about this to anyone, do you hear? You are wrong, that cannot be the way it is, and remember, it is a sin in Islam to spread lies, you know that!" he admonished her.

"But I am not spreading lies!" she insisted. "It is as clear as the bright waters of this lake! I tell you, that architect is in love with Queen Mahperi! I may be a simple servant girl next to a learned man like you, but I am smart about some things, oh, yes I am!"

Köpek slipped a gold coin into her hand. "Oh, yes, you are indeed, my little Esma. Now, take this little coin and make sure you say nothing of our conversation to anyone, have I made myself clear?"

So it is true. Yes, little servant girl, without knowing it, you have placed in my hands a weapon sharper than any steel sword from the bazaars of Damascus.

☪ ☪ ☪

Köpek requested a special audience with the Sultan before he set out on his campaigns in the East. He knew that the Sultan was preoccupied with preparing his strategy to reconquer the cities of Urfa and Harran, as well as to attack new cities, the most important of which was Diyarbakir. Yet before the Sultan left, Köpek wanted to give him something else to think about when he was out there on those boiling battlefields. Something that would make the hot sweat of treachery drip down in rivers from underneath his turban.

After presenting the Sultan with a full report on the progress of the work at Kubadabad, the two of them discussed the remaining outstanding issues involved with the site, now nearing completion.

"You can leave with a tranquil mind, my Sultan; we will take care of everything while you are away, as you have ordered. Everything is in good hands! I will continue to be involved on a regular basis, and the Frankish architect will ensure that everything is tended to with attention, both on the site and off." Köpek interjected.

"Off the site? What do you mean by that?" the Sultan queried, suddenly curious.

"What I meant to say, my Sultan, is that the Frank is most helpful in matters other than building your palace. He is encouraging and supportive to all the workers on the site, keeping their morale up, taking a personal interest in their work, that sort of thing. We have had very few fistfights and accidents, so it would appear that he knows what he is doing! Why, I even saw him out there planting tulip bulbs with the gardeners the other day! And then of course there is your Queen Mahperi, as well..."

"My Queen?" the Sultan cut him off before he could finish. "What does she have to do with him? What are you talking about?"

"Oh, yes, my Sultan, he has become very good friends with her and they spend much time together discussing the various aspects of the site and other things as well, I am sure. They often meet in his shed or in Joseph's pottery shop for long conversations. He has done much to keep her company and entertain her. That is probably the reason she is spending so much time at Kubadabad as of late, instead of returning to Konya," he added, carefully measuring his words to incite the Sultan without being accused of disloyalty or slander.

The Sultan felt the top of his head becoming very hot under his turban. Surely Köpek is not insinuating anything about the honor of my Queen; that would be beneath him and disrespectful to both me and her! Granted, she is headstrong and fiercely independent, but she would never do anything that was not appropriate; that was just not her way. She is a bold one, that Mahperi, always has been, and that directness is just what I admire the most in her – but there are limits. I cannot have her spending time with another man in public like this, especially when I am not there! He shook his head to get rid of the image that had now crept in his mind. No, such a thing could not be possible –

she loves me and is loyal to me. She is a pure and honorable woman, my Queen of the Moon!

"I will thank you to tend to all things while I am away, Köpek," added the Sultan in a stern voice. "You read what I mean, don't you? I wouldn't want any type of scandal. You must protect her from any loose association with this man, do you understand me?"

"I serve at your pleasure, as always, my Sultan. You can rest assured that I will keep my eye on everything while you are away," he bowed, facing the Sultan as he exited the room, as the court etiquette of respect demanded.

And you, my Sultan, just you make sure that you keep your eye focused on that image I have now planted in your head.

Chapter 60

Chesspiece of Basalt and Temerity

After his victory at Harput the previous year, the Sultan Alaeddin Keykubad was even more encouraged to continue his expansion efforts in the Mesopotamian region. Basing his operations in Malatya, the city where he had married Gaziye, the Sultan sent fifty thousand soldiers to the sector, once again under the orders of Commander Kamyar. The ever-brilliant military tactician decided to undertake a two-prong approach, sending one wing to besiege Urfa, and the second wing to Harran, and soon, both cities, old as time, fell into the hands of the Seljuks. The ghosts of the prophets Abraham and Job, born in this area, now answered to the name of Alaeddin Keykubad, Sultan of Sultans, Eminence of the Faith. Raqqa, a city famed for its production of luxurious glass and ceramics, was conquered by the Turks soon afterwards.

Once the Sultan had taken Urfa and Harran, his dream for more victories became obsessive. He fixated on that one major remaining chess piece he needed to topple to the side of the board: the daunting city on the banks the Tigris river, already ancient at the time of the Bible, the city built of basalt and temerity, the seat of the famed and glorious Great Mosque built by his ancestor Melik Shah in the 11th century – the formidable bastion of Diyarbakir.

And now the time had come, in this spring of 1236, for the Sultan to set out with the most resolute of intentions for victory. He left for the East this time with General Taceddin Pervane at his side, determined to lead the supreme battle to topple the grey behemoth on the Tigris River named Diyarbakir. His purpose was firm, and he was not about to let anything stand in his way. His dreams were filled with images of victory and black walls, and, although he tried to dismiss them, his thoughts were often filled as well with images of his Queen Mahperi in indelicate and troubling situations.

Yet there are some enemies that are stronger than all men, even when they are named Sultan of Sultans, Father of Conquests and Victories. Even the great Mongol Ocean Genghis Khan himself would not have been able to overcome the thick black basalt walls of Diyarbakir, stretching around the city for almost six kilometers. Not one chink could be found by the Sultan's troops in any of its sixteen keeps and five gates. Not one soldier could scramble up its walls smooth as glass, looming twelve meters high and five meters thick. Not one step of an advancing Seljuk troop movement could go undetected from their eighty-two watchtowers. Indeed, the walls of Diyarbakir were so impregnable it was certain they could withstand an attack by God Almighty himself.

Upon his retreat from the unassailable Diyarbakir, the Sultan turned back to look at those black walls from atop his stallion Night Shining White. He vowed to God that he would never give up the dream that he would one day walk along their parapets and look down upon the city inside as his own. One does not defy the Seljuk Sultan of Sultans!

"*Shah Mat*!" he yelled at the top of his lungs, raising his clenched fist into the air. "One day I will call that out to you, oh walls of basalt and temerity; one day, you will see, Sultan Alaeddin Keykubad will call out to you '*Checkmate*' and your haughty pieces will fall one after the other to my side of the chessboard!"

Chapter 61

I Am Not What I Am

Köpek could not believe the priceless piece of information the silly little servant girl had given him. It was worth far more than the gold coin he slipped in her hand afterwards; in fact, it was worth all the gold of the kingdom, this kingdom that would soon be in his hands.

So it is true. The insinuations of Ibn Bibi were not just malicious gossip. There was something more behind this seemingly innocent friendship between Queen Mahperi and Lou Cantadou.

Yet, Köpek was certain of several things: one was that Mahperi Hatun was an honorable woman, and another was that she loved her husband. She would never do anything contrary to those guiding principles. And yet....What if he could find a way to insinuate that she was involved with this Lou in more ways than just a deep friendship? What if? If I can do that, then she will be banished from this court forever, and that will be one less obstacle in my path to achieve my goals. Mahperi Hatun, you and that little Frank who has stolen my project will be sent away forever, and it is I who will go down in history as the brilliant architect of Kubadabad.

Long into the night, Köpek thought about how he could achieve the downfall of both of them during the opening ceremonies of the Palace of Kubadabad. When the cock crowed twice as dawn broke over the brilliant blue waters of the lake, it came to him.

The turquoise necklace.

Yes, that turquoise necklace the Sultan had won from a Persian trader in a chess game in the Kandemir Han, a piece so rare it was considered the most priceless of its kind. Certainly it was priceless enough to bring down a Queen.

Köpek knew that the stone had been mounted in an engraved gold bezel attached to a filigree chain, for he had been charged by the Sultan upon their return to Konya to have the chain lengthened for the tall queen by one of the finest jewelers in Konya. He knew how much the stone meant to Alaeddin, dear to him not just for his cleverness at having tricked the Persian for it and as testament to his chess-playing skills, but for other, more personal reasons. The Sultan had once confided to Köpek that his beloved Armenian wife never took it off of her neck, and as long as it hung there, he would always feel assured of her love and the good fortune it would bring to his empire. Although Köpek never saw the stone again after the day he returned it to the Sultan from the jeweler, he believed what the Sultan said. Such a silly romantic he is! It is hard to imagine the mighty Sultan of Sultans could entertain such adoring little notions. Yet if he is as attached to this stone, as the symbol of his wife's devotion to him, as much as he says he is, then it will be the ideal tool to plant the proof of Mahperi's infidelity in his eyes. I will use her very own jewel to bring her down in disgrace!

Remembering how the maid's eyes sparkled when he slipped her the gold coin to ensure her silence over her understanding of Lou's *canso*, Köpek knew that he could count on her to be the perfect accomplice for his plan. Little Esma was definitely the type of servant who would accept a bribe, and was clever enough to carry out what was required.

☪ ☪ ☪

Köpek asked Esma to come to his quarters on the site later that evening, telling her to make sure no one saw her enter his rooms. He invited her to take some of the tantalizing refreshments he had laid out on a tray, since he was certain that she did not often have many opportunities to taste such fine *halvah* and *lokum*.

"My dear little Esma," he broached, "I want us to share a little secret together. Do you think you are able to keep a secret to yourself? Can I trust you to never tell anyone of the little game you and I are going to play?" As he said this, he placed a gold coin next to the plate of *halvah* with a resounding clink on the large metal tray.

Her eyes grew wide and she quickly responded, "Of course you can, my Vizier, as long as my pockets are kept full of your special golden *halvah*, my mouth will be empty of secrets to spill," she answered.

I was right, he thought, this is one clever and ambitious little girl.

"May I first ask you a question? As Mahperi's maid, have you ever observed a turquoise necklace that she wears?"

"Notice it! Why it is impossible not to!" she exclaimed. "You cannot imagine how beautiful it is, more beautiful than a diamond! When it glows against her skin, it makes her emerald eyes take on a hue that is as magical as the waters of this lake here. Plus it is so big!"

"Does she wear it all the time?"

"Oh yes, it is her most precious object, and she fingers it constantly like prayer beads when she is alone in her chambers, getting this far-off dreamy look in her eyes. She never takes it off, never!"

"Are you sure, never?"

"Well, except when she goes to the hammam. Then she takes it off because she is afraid the soap and heat will affect its lustrous shine," she added.

"And where is the gem kept when she is at the baths?"

"She puts it in a special box in her room, and gives me or one of her other servants the key to hold while she is bathing. She trusts us all completely with its safekeeping."

Köpek could not believe his good fortune. This is going to be easier to pull off than I imagined, he smiled to himself.

"Alright, my little Esma, here is what I want you to do to earn your golden halvah. The next time Mahperi Hatun goes to the hammam, I want you to make sure you are the maid who is entrusted with the key to the safekeeping box. While she is in the baths, you will go back into her room, open the box and break the chain of the necklace. I am sure you can snap it with your own bare hands; if not, I will provide you with a little tool that can do it for you. Then I want you to put the necklace back in the box and lock it up again, and return to the hammam. That is all I am asking you to do," he explained.

"But why would I want to break such a pretty thing? My Lady will be devastated if any harm comes to her beloved necklace! I don't want to do something like that to her; she is so nice to me! And won't I get in trouble for breaking it?"

"Now don't you worry about that at all," he stressed, plunking another gold piece on the tray. "I will have it fixed for her and she will be happy with her necklace once more. I will tell you how we are going to do that now. Are we in agreement so far, my little Esma? Yes? Good little girl, now how about another piece of this tasty pistachio lokum, my dear?"

Mahperi returned from her bath the next day refreshed and perfumed. She motioned for her servant Esma to open the chest to take out her turquoise necklace, and she saw the girl go over and open the chest with the key.

As Esma lifted up the necklace, she gasped out loud. "Oh no, my Lady, the chain is broken!"

"What! But how could that have happened?" cried out Mahperi.

"It must have caught on the hinge of the box when you shut it, Lady Mahperi. Oh this is too terrible!" said Esma, feigning dismay.

Mahperi rushed over to the chest and pulled out the necklace, devastated about what had happened to it. Her beloved necklace! As long as she wore that necklace around her neck, she could believe in the love her husband held for her. All throughout her trials with Gaziye, all she needed to do was touch this turquoise to remind herself that her husband did still love her. Now that it was broken in the bottom of the box, she became frightened that something had gone wrong with that love, and she began to sob.

Esma was taken aback by her sobbing, for although she could understand why her mistress Mahperi was so upset about the chain, it didn't seem like that serious a problem. Köpek promised that it could be fixed, but of course she could not tell that to her lady right now. She stepped over to Mahperi, ready to play the role she had rehearsed with Köpek. She knew that it was a sin to lie, so she took care with her words.

"Oh my Lady, please do not cry, it will be fine; why, we can try to fix it!"

"It is not that easy! How will I ever be able to get this repaired? The Sultan must never know that it has been broken. He will be furious that I was so careless!"

On cue, Esma sweetly smiled at her mistress.

"Oh, my good Lady, do not worry, I can help you! I know a goldsmith in the bazaar at Konya who is very skillful and especially discrete. He handles the gems of many merchant ladies who come to sell their jewels when their husband's businesses are not doing well. The jeweler buys their pieces and gives them the money that allows them to put food on the table for their children and to save their husband's face in the market place. If you let me return to Konya, I can bring him the necklace and have it repaired. The merchant will never even need to know the name of my Lady, and he certainly will never breathe a word of this necklace, for if ever his discretion were put into doubt, it would be the end to this important part of his business."

Mahperi's face brightened a bit at the thought that her necklace of love could be repaired in such a discrete fashion.

"Oh! Would you be able to do that for me? Can I trust you with this? Are you sure no one will find out? Oh, thank you, dear Esma; you cannot know how much this means to me! Thank you, thank you, Esma, how fortunate I am to have you in my service!" Wiping away her tears, she placed the necklace in the maid's outstretched hand.

Esma turned and left her tent. Fortunate, yes; but it is I who am most fortunate, thinking of the gold pieces that would soon be hers, promised to her by Köpek when she delivered the necklace to him. She rushed out and ran across the site until she reached Köpek's quarters, making sure no one saw her. Whistling the special code they had agreed upon, his door cracked open and she dropped the necklace into the palm of the hand that reached out to grab it. A few moments later, the same palm opened up to reveal the four gold pieces that had been promised to her. Which one felt the richest at that moment?

Köpek held up the necklace to the candlelight in the privacy of his rooms and gazed at its beauty. He had never seen a blue stone so luminous and flawless; it was indeed certainly worth an Empire. That poor little Persian merchant is probably now back in Mashad living in ruin after having lost his bet to the Sultan! And now Mahperi's life as well will lie in ruin because of it, once the jeweler finishes working on it as I will order him.

Here in my hand, dear Sultan, I hold the tool that will remove any consideration you have for your tall queen. This little chain will set the flaming fireball of my revenge in motion. Soon you will be humiliated in public and in the most private part of your pride.

One by one, I will crush everyone close to you. I have already started with the boy, easy to manipulate like bread dough in my hands. I will crush the high-handed architect who stole this project from me, your imperious Moon Queen, and then your little feather-brained sot of an Arab wife. And then it will be your turn to fall, you, oh Great Sultan! You will be the last one I destroy; you, who thought your greatest rival for the throne had been your brother Izzeddin – well, now you will see who is the most powerful of all! Everyone will fall, and I, alone, will remain standing!

Chapter 62

Gifts of Remembrance

The architect rose well before dawn, his emotions a mixture of apprehension and anticipation for the day to come. He quickly put on his robe, belt and slippers and crept out of the site shack, letting himself out quietly so as not to disturb the sleep of the other workers, the peaceful sleep of manual workers that knew no such thing as fear or foreboding or self-doubt; a sleep that only knew the mercy of exhaustion as reward for a hard day of work.

He followed the well-worn path down to the site of the Big Palace, passing in front of the arsenal and the Small Palace. Yes, it was always to the Big Palace he went first. The sun would soon rise and glow over the golden mist of the lake. It would define the shadows of the Big Palace and lift high enough to leave no doubt in his mind that the work of yesterday and all the days before it had really taken place, and that the forms of his dreams had truly been born.

He could hear the faint buzzing of insects and the song of the birds who reveled in this tranquil moment as much as he did. He remembered days filled with the sounds of clanging picks and scraping shovels, voices bellowing orders and shouting jokes, braying pack donkeys and the grinding of pulleys; days filled with baskets, harnesses, dust, mud, and the smell of sweat.

But now, it was done, and all was silence. These minutes were his and his alone, to savor this magnificent setting and the work that had been accomplished to this day, this day on the cusp of April when the Sultan would come to inaugurate his newly-completed Kubadabad Palace.

The architect breathed a lungful of satisfaction for a job well done. It was his moment of hope, between all the work and the praise of a Sultan to come. He took comfort from the competence of his foremen and the skill of his workers. All is going to be fine. Take courage. The Sultan will approve and admire what you have done. He will be pleased with you.

Yes, your palace has risen; it has risen and will shine as brightly as the turquoise waters at your feet. Yes, your work has come to life and your Lady will see it too, and be filled with the same awe as you that such beauty could arise alongside the muddy banks of this lake, just as love can arise from the deepest and most secret places of the heart.

The entire site of Kubadabad was living a different rhythm today. Instead of going about their business of laying stones, the workers were busy polishing them. The final touches were being completed on all the different parts of the project in preparation of the Sultan's arrival later that day for the opening festivities. Gardeners pulled their last weeds and watered their flower beds, masons swept the site clean of all dust, Joseph washed his tile wall three times with vinegar water to make it shine all the more, and the left-over building materials were hidden behind the sheds. The site was, for all intents and purposes, ready for delivery to the Sultan.

A large tent was set up in the meadow in front of the Big Palace to host the evening meal. Pages brushed and beat the dust from the carpets to be laid in the tents, and others carried armfuls of drinking goblets and embroidered napkins. Laundresses and seamstresses ensured that the costumes of the servants were spotless and tailored to perfection. Maids picked wild tulips from the fields around the lake to set out in display in every room of the palace. The lake itself preened in the sunshine, for this spring day of late March dawned bright and crisp and dry.

Palace cooks had arrived from Konya the week before and had already prepared much of the food to be served, especially the pastries and halvah. Ice was laid into the cold cellars, fruit sherbets had been mixed, and several dozen lambs were roasting in pits. The cooks were preparing *tandir kebab*, the specialty of the Konya kitchens, and a personal favorite of the Sultan. The lamb had already been roasting slowly for many long hours, and would soon fall off the bone in tender, bite-size morsels. Musicians had arrived on the site as well, some from as far away as Sivas. Mahperi was especially happy because Ertokush was bringing her son Giyaseddin Keyhüsrev from Erzincan to attend the ceremonies. It had been too long a time since she had seen her son, and she was looking forward to spending some time with him after the inauguration ceremony.

The festivities were scheduled to take place over three days. The first day would be dedicated to the Sultan's family and important invited guests from the Konya court. Even Gaziye and her throngs of handmaids had arrived on the site in eager anticipation of the evening. The Sultan would make an official visit to the site in the company of the head of each of the construction guilds. The imam would lead the afternoon prayer, with a special reading from the Qur'an. A prayer of thanksgiving to God would be followed by the slaughtering of a symbolic sheep, then the family and guests would be invited to enter the palace. In the evening, the Sultan would bid everyone to come to the large tent in the courtyard, where carpets, many made by Hanife and her weavers, lay on the ground. Lanterns would be lit, pages would pour refreshments, and servants would bring in large copper platters loaded with the *tandir kebab*. One platter would be set in front of each group of a dozen people sitting on one of Hanife's carpets, who would then delight in the roasted meat, served with onions, salt and parsley, to be scooped up with pieces of freshly cooked flatbread.

The second day would be the celebration for the workers, with an official distribution of gold coins to each one by the Sultan. It would be followed by a banquet and festivities offered by the Sultan that would go late into the night. The third day, upon the insistence of Mahperi, was dedicated to the surrounding villagers, again with a banquet and a musical performance offered by the Sultan. It promised to be a series of unforgettable events for all who had a relationship with the new Paradise Palace on Lake Kubadabad.

☪ ☪ ☪

That morning, Mahperi had one important task to do above all others. She needed to make a last visit to Joseph the potter in his shed. His kiln would continue to produce tiles for local use at the palace, but most of his work on the project was complete, now that his wall of tiles in the *divan* room had been assembled in place. It was time for him to move on and look for other work, and this is why she wanted to speak with him.

She entered his shed and found him as mud-spattered as ever, despite the fact that the workers had all been told to go to the hammam and clean up for the Sultan's inspection. He will never change, she thought, and I suppose I would never want him to!

"Joseph, I come today to thank you personally for all that you have accomplished for our palace. When I sit and gaze upon that world that you have brought to life on your tiles, I will always think of you and your talent," she told him. "You will be a part of our lives forever through that stunning room you have created for us."

The potter grumbled, embarrassed by her praise.

"I know that you still have to finish some tiles for the baths. Even though your work here is almost complete, I would like you to remain at Kubadabad and use it as your base, to continue making tiles for other projects that the Sultan – or I – may build. We can discuss the details later, but I just wanted you to know that you can carry on here and work," she explained.

The gruff potter was moved by her kindness. "Thank you, my Lady, I have been very happy in this beautiful place and will be pleased to stay here. If I can continue to be of service to you, I would be honored, for you have been the most encouraging of patrons for my work. Actually, I have a little gift for you as well for this special day, but you seem to have beaten me at my own game of preparing surprises!" he laughed.

He hobbled over to the cupboard and took out a bundle wrapped in a linen cloth, and placed it in her hands.

"My Lady, here is my gift for you, to always remember our days here together. I have crafted this tile for you and you alone. Please accept it along with all my wishes for happiness here at Kubadabad."

Mahperi unwrapped the bundle to find a tile unlike any she had seen in Joseph's repertory. It was one of his large, star-shapes tiles, depicting a couple lying in each other's arms underneath a checkered quilt. She gasped when she saw it, because the portraits of the man and woman were drawn exactly in the likenesses of Mahperi and the Sultan Alaeddin Keykubad.

"My Lady, Kubadabad will be your Palace of love; I believe it. May you live much bliss here together with your Sultan," and with that, he turned and shuffled out of the shed.

☪ ☪ ☪

"Lou Cantadou, I have a gift for you," said Sadettin Köpek, gesturing to Lou to enter his rooms of the pavilion that he had specially built for himself on the grounds of the Palace. "I have called you here this glorious morning of our project inauguration to offer you a special tool that has been crafted for you and you alone."

Lou Cantadou had been wondering all morning what the Vizier had on his mind ever since his page brought him a message saying that he was waiting for him in his rooms. So this is what he wants; to offer me a gift, as if he were capable of such a generous gesture.

Köpek continued to smile at the architect. "It comes directly from the Sultan. He wishes me to give you this token of his appreciation for all the hard work you have accomplished here at Kubadabad. This is a rather lavish gift, if I do say so myself, so it must show how pleased he is with the outcome of the project. He specifically requested that you display the gift during the official banquet after the opening ceremonies. I know how you always tuck your tools into your sash; well, tonight, you will show off to the entire court a tool like no architect has ever seen!"

He took his hands from behind his back and held out to Lou a small, silver hammer, much like the one he wore every day in his sash on the site, which he used to tap the blocks of stone to sound out their solidity to determine if there were any internal cracks before they were set in place by the masons. Lou was very impressed by the symbolism of the Sultan's gesture; for his little hammer signified that he believed the stones of the palace would be solid enough to last for eternity.

Yet when Köpek placed the silver hammer in his hands he let out a gasp. Mounted on the end of the hammer handle was a piece of turquoise larger and more beautiful than he had ever seen in his life. He drew in his breath at the splendor of the stone and shook his head in disbelief.

"But this is too extravagant! The Sultan is much too charitable! This is an extraordinary gift...I find it difficult to accept such generosity!" babbled the astonished Lou. "But....I don't understand – I would have preferred to receive it directly from the Sultan's own hands and to hear his praise personally. Why, may I ask, did he ask you to give it to me instead of giving it to me himself?" Lou asked, somewhat offended that the Sultan would have Köpek do his bidding for such an important gift. For some odd reason, the architect found it hard to believe that the Sultan, a man of great personal dignity and sensitivity, would not have had the consideration to thank him with this gift in person.

Köpek quickly answered him. "Yes, yes, that may appear odd, but the Sultan in his wisdom has his reasons. He is fully aware that you and I have had our differences on this project. He also knows that it was often difficult for us to answer to so many people and their ideas for the project: himself, the Sultana, that stubborn potter and so many others. Too many artists, too many opinions! Yet he is extremely pleased with the results and wants to offer a gift commensurate with his appreciation. The reason that he asked that I put it into your hands, is, I am embarrassed to say, his way of making me apologize to you for any harshness I may have shown you on this project. He would like us to bury our differences, and by having me give it to you, he is hoping that we will be able to put aside our past animosities. It is also his way of making sure that I know that he considers that you were the lead architect of the project, not me. I serve my Sultan and accept his wishes, so I thus present, along with this gift, my apologies, and beg you to accept them, Lou Cantadou," he implored with an oily smile. "The Sultan has even told me that he hopes we will collaborate together on future projects for him. He believes we make an exceptional team, and wants us to work together in harmony. When he sees you wearing this hammer and its gleaming turquoise in your sash tonight at the opening ceremonies, he will know that you and I have had this discussion and have agreed to put aside our hostilities for his service. That will please him very much, and will be the best gift we can offer him. There will be plenty of time, then, to hear his words of appreciation, I can assure you," said Köpek. "There will be an announcement after the dinner by Queen Mahperi, who will present the Sultan with a gift for the occasion. She has asked me to request that you stand when you are called, and at that moment, you will display the hammer in your sash, so that the Sultan and the entire crowd can see this beautiful object. Can I count on you to do that for her?" Köpek asked.

Lou Cantadou could still not shake off the feeling that the Sultan would never delegate the responsibility of giving such a significant gift to someone else, but he could not risk angering the Sultan by declining his gesture, nor the apology of Köpek. Nor could he imagine that the discrete Mahperi would ask him to intervene like that, but he was too confused by all of this to refuse.

He took the hammer from Köpek's outstretched hand and looked him in the eyes.

"I know it has not always been easy for the two of us to get along here on this site, but I think, in the end, our competition led to some creative thinking and resolution of many thorny building issues!" he admitted, despite the fact that he did not believe that he would ever be capable of putting aside past differences with the mercurial Köpek. "Thank you, Köpek. I accept your apology, and please tell our Sultan that I will wear this turquoise-studded hammer with great honor at the banquet tonight. I will make sure that he sees it and will know that I am forever indebted to him for the opportunity he gave me to work on this palace."

Köpek smiled back at him, his yellow snaggle teeth flashing in the morning sun. Yes, may you savor this gift of remembrance, for now you and that tall wife of the Sultan, for whom you lust, will both fall into the hell you deserve, all for a piece of turquoise, the charm of my future fortune!

Chapter 63

Everything Is Broken

After the official inauguration of the Palace of Kubadabad by the Sultan was over, everyone eagerly anticipated the celebrations to follow. The tents were set up as the Sultan had ordered, and one of the finest banquets ever prepared by the court kitchens awaited the guests, who were eager to tuck into the trays of succulent *tandir kebab* and other delicacies. Mahperi and her son Giyaseddin, joyfully reunited after such a long time, were seated on the carpet next to the Sultan, who presided on the central carpet of honor with Gaziye and Köpek at his sides.

Omer Ersin from Sivas, one of the most famous ud players in the land, now stepped into the center of the tent and raised his arms to get everyone's attention. The dashing musician had been instructed by Köpek to make a special announcement before the start of his concert.

"Distinguished members of the court and beloved guests! Let us wish all blessings to our honorable Sultan of Sultans, in gratitude for this sumptuous dinner he has prepared for us tonight! May God give long life to his head and to the walls of this palace!" he shouted out for all to hear.

The crowd cheered their appreciation, and the Sultan nodded his head in every direction of the tent to the guests on the carpets. Lying back on their plump cushions, everyone relaxed and settled in for the evening's entertainment. Men sat cross-legged and twirled their prayer beads; women adjusted their dainty bare feet underneath their brocaded robes, and servants stood to the side at the ready. Gaziye sat up tall so as not to miss one second of the scene she knew was about to unfold.

"Before we start our musical program, I have a little surprise to announce for our esteemed Sultan," called out the musician to the crowd. "As you all know, his Queen Mahperi Hatun has been very involved in the building of this Palace, and we must praise her dedication. She has spent many hours here on the dusty site, depriving herself of the comforts of her palace in Konya, to be here to ensure that all turned out well. And what beauty she has wrought!"

"She has especially worked very closely with the architect Lou Cantadou," he continued, making sure he said this very slowly just as Köpek had requested, so the Sultan and everyone in the room could hear him. "The two of them have earned a particular place in our esteem! And now, in honor of this occasion, the good Queen Mahperi has prepared a special gift for the Sultan, but before it is brought out, Queen Mahperi would like Lou Cantadou to come forth and stand next to me so that we can all acknowledge our appreciation to him as well," the ud player announced, beaming a bright smile at him.

Mahperi looked around her, totally confused and embarrassed by this announcement, and was all the more surprised that Lou had risen and was now walking up to the musician. What gift? I have prepared nothing! What is going on here?

Lou rose and approached the center of the tent to stand next to the musician, adjusting the hammer Köpek had given him that morning in his sash as he walked forward. At the same time, the musician clapped his hands twice. From all directions, palace pages rushed in, carrying above their heads large glass platters piled high with fresh fruit. The gilded edges of the plates glittered in the light of the torches and had all the guests gasping in admiration.

"Behold the gift of Queen Mahperi to the Sultan Alaeddin Keykubad and this blessed palace!" cried out the ud player. "Long life to all and especially to the heir Giyaseddin Keyhüsrev!" He nodded to the Moon Queen and her son. Lou awkwardly stood there, not quite sure of what was to follow.

The glass plates were set down at each carpet and the crowd murmured their astonishment at such magnificent objects. Everyone grabbed a piece of the fruit off the plates to better admire the decoration and to read the inscriptions written around the border.

Mahperi felt her head spinning. What is going on here? I had nothing to do with any of this! And why is Lou standing up there? Is this his idea of a surprise? She watched as he deeply bowed to the Sultan and then to Mahperi.

It was then, at the exact same moment, that both Mahperi and the Sultan saw the turquoise gemstone gleaming off the handle of the hammer, now prominently displayed in Lou's sash. They stared at it, then at each other, and then back to Lou, both of their mouths dropping open in disbelief.

Whatever is my turquoise gem doing there? The Sultana's head spun in confusion, dizzy from the gold on these plates and the confusion of the whole scene now unveiling in front of her.

So it is true. The Sultan seethed at the realization that Köpek's insinuations were correct. She does carry on with that man. What better proof do I need than the fact that she has now given to him the cherished symbol of our love? How dare she disgrace me publicly like this, flouting her indignity to me! I will have both of their heads, my Queen, now adulteress, and that foreign traitor!

Gaziye reached over and pulled the sleeve of the Sultan's caftan. "My Sultan! Look! Read this! Why, she has engraved the name of her son on these plates and not yours! I cannot believe she has insulted you in this way!" she smirked, pointing with her jeweled finger to the center of the plate.

The Sultan looked down at the inscription and read: *"All glory and long life to Giyaseddin Keyhüsrev, may he prosper in God's grace."*

The Sultan shook his head from side to side in disbelief. Outraged, Alaeddin stood up and raised his fists in the air towards Mahperi. "What is this?" he screamed over and over again, losing his temper in front of his guests. The normally calm Sultan, who took great pains never to show any anger to an adversary, now ranted with a fury never before seen by anyone, even his soldiers on the battlefield. "You have taken liberties that are far beyond your place, even if you are a Queen! You will pay for this! You and your son, get out of my sight, the both of you, now!" His eyes bulged in anger and he looked down at the carpet and the golden plate glittering up at him. He crashed his foot down upon it, smashing it to pieces, cutting his fine leather slippers on the shards. Then, like a madman gone berserk, he rushed from carpet to carpet, picking up each plate and dashing them one after the other to the ground, sending the fruit rolling in all directions. "And you, my son," pointing his finger at the bewildered Giyaseddin, "You will pay for your impertinence as well!"

All Mahperi could do was to stare in confused disbelief at the storm in front of her: how could her beloved turquoise now be mounted in the shaft of Lou's hammer? Where did these plates come from? It was incredible, all of this: the plates, my turquoise, my son's name in gold....

And then when she heard the cackling laughter of the Raven, and saw the smirk on the muzzle of the Dog, it suddenly all became very clear to her.

☪ ☪ ☪

Joseph as well could not comprehend the scene happening in front of him, yet he had eyes only for those spectacular golden glass plates. He had rarely seen such stunning pieces from a fellow artist of the fire, and seeing the Sultan smash them to the ground wrenched his soul. Joseph quickly grabbed the plate at his carpet and shoved it under his shirt. Limping as fast as his game leg would allow him, he fled the tent, screaming to Lou, "Run! Get out of here! Run for your life! Now! To the shed, now!"

Lou heard the smashing glass, he heard the Sultan bellowing, he heard the wails of Mahperi, he heard the screeching laughter of Gaziye, he heard the gasps of the guests, and he heard Joseph's yells. All was crashing, all was burning again. Visions of Béziers flashed before his eyes and he knew he had to get out before the flames of the fire burned him to a crisp. He saw the face of Köpek through the flames, and heard his voice crackling like the exploding wood logs of the fire at the public stake in front of the Church of Saint Mary Magdalene: *"Don't think you can run away from me, little architect. I will destroy you. I will find you one day, wherever you go!"*

Mahperi knew that she, too, had to flee the scene. With the echo of her husband's voice bellowing out, *"Get out of here, get out of my sight, you despicable woman!"* she fled the tent, running directly to the Lou's shed, the only place her feet could think to run for safety.

When she got there, she found him inside; frantically stuffing his belongings into a kilim saddlebag, and sweeping his tools with the back of his arm into his leather satchel.

"Mahperi, get out of here! You are going to get killed! Please leave! Get out!"

Mahperi saw that he had removed the silver hammer and her turquoise from his sash and laid it on the table. She went over and picked it up, incredulous to see that her precious turquoise was indeed mounted on its shaft.

"But how did you ever get this?" she gasped, still confused.

"It was given to me by Köpek this morning as a present from the Sultan, although I now realize that there is something terribly amiss in this story," he muttered, closing the flaps of his bags.

If you only knew, she thought.

When he saw her distraught face, he stopped screaming at her, and panted: "I must leave now to save your honor and your life. I cannot stay here; you understand that, don't you? I have to run from this place or we will both burn alive! Whatever is going on with that hammer and those plates, I cannot fathom, but they have put you somehow in a terrible situation. My presence will only make it worse for you. Even though you are innocent, the Sultan will never believe it!"

He turned and grabbed a thick roll hidden behind the cupboard in the shed.

"Here, Mahperi, here are the drawings for our mosque," shoving the roll into her hands. "Take them. I have completed them for you. I give them to you with the hopes that you will one day use them to build that mosque of your dreams."

He extended them to her, and she reached out to take them. Both held onto the roll, unable to move. He felt her hands touching his, even though they were at opposite ends of the paper. Everything froze in the middle of the flames while he looked in her eyes, memorizing this moment forever, a moment that he knew would be the last they would ever be together.

Don't move, my Lady, don't move. I want to memorize this moment so that every time I close my eyes, I will see it. Every time I open my eyes, I will seek this moment. This one, and so many others.

The moment you first pronounced my name

The moment you looked into my eyes over the drawing table

The moment my tear dropped into my lap after my canso

The moment of recognition of the promise of dreams

The moments of moonlight and firelight and sunlight here at Kubadabad

The memory of all of these moments of you, my rose of Love,

All the moments of our friendship, the most beautiful edifice I will ever build -

Lou snapped out of his reverie when he heard shouting voices outside the shed.

"Mahperi, I do not come from another cosmos, and I do not know any mysterious secrets. I am just a man; a simple builder, trying to work with faith and hope. I am only a servant of God holding a pencil in my hands. But you, *ma douce et gente dame*, were the lead in that pencil, the inspiration that pushed my hand forward. You will see it in this roll: I have drawn for you a magnificent mosque, one as tall, stately, serious and inspiring as you. Build this mosque, Mahperi. Build this mosque to create in the sky over Kayseri a constellation of stones that will prove the power of God. Build this mosque to give a face to the power of the Seljuks for all eternity. For however many springtimes it takes you to complete it, no matter what problems you will encounter, build it, Mahperi. Build it to show your courage and conviction."

And build it for me, treasure and door-keeper of my heart, so the world will have a testament of my love for you.

At that moment Joseph appeared at the back of the shed with a saddled horse, and in a flash Lou was on it and rode off in the direction of the southern road. Through the tears now flooding her eyes, Mahperi watched her friend disappear down the road, leaving nothing but whisps of dust in the air. As she looked down at the drawings in her hands, those tears spilled out of her eyes, smudging the ink of the inscription she saw written there:

Factum a Esteve de Cantadou ex corde anno MCCXXXVII in honorem Regina Mahperi Hatun.

Chapter 64

Sullied Scepter

"*Long life to Giyaseddin Keyhüsrev, may he prosper in God's grace!"* The Sultan stood in the Great Palace, in the very rooms he had inaugurated with such joyful anticipation that afternoon. Now the walls of the *divan* room vibrated with his angry voice, bellowing the same phrase over and over again with a force that risked shaking Joseph's wall of tiles to the floor.

"Long life to Giyaseddin Keyhüsrev, may he prosper in God's grace!"

"Whatever possessed her to dare such an effrontery to my honor, in front of all my guests, on this day that was dedicated to glorifying my reign? This is an unforgivable offense and she must be punished!" yelled the Sultan with all the force of his lungs, even though Köpek, Ibn Bibi and other court officials and important emirs were sitting right next to him on the shining new carpets of Hanife, in the shadow of the glittering glaze of Joseph's tiles.

After the Sultan's berserk rage of smashing every one of the golden plates had played itself out, his private guards had ushered him out of the tent, in front of the dazed looks of the two hundred guests assembled there. It was clear there would be no musical concert that night, no chance to savor the breezes off the lake under the sparkling glow of the full moon; no, the anticipated joy of that evening had been smashed to bits and now lay on the ground along with hundreds of glass shards.

The banquet guests dispersed, completely perplexed as to what had taken place to anger the Sultan in such a violent fashion. Pages came in serving fruit on plates, and then, suddenly, he went totally mad with rage. Gaziye took over as hostess, smiling to all and apologizing for the unfortunate incident, but what was there to be done? Apparently the gift of Mahperi has offended the Sultan, she repeated to each one as they left the tent, making sure that all would understand that it was Mahperi's fault. Gaziye knew the gossip about the outrage would soon spread throughout the entire Empire.

Köpek had whisked the startled Giyaseddin Keyhüsrev away out of the view of his enraged father.

And everyone wondered where Mahperi had gone.

Köpek went to the Big Palace and found the Sultan in a state of rage, just as he had planned it.

"Köpek!" roared the Sultan, "I thought you had this whole evening arranged and organized as per my wishes! How could you have let such a thing happen? Did you have any idea this outrageous display had been prepared?"

Lie, Köpek told himself, lie. If it suits your purposes; if it advances your plans, lie. It will not be a lie in God's eyes. No, God will forgive me and understand that this lie is not a sin, but a necessary part of my plan to claim the power that is rightfully mine.

"No, of course, my Sultan, I did not," he insisted, carefully avoiding Ibn Bibi's eyes. "I was told simply to allow for a special presentation by the Queen Mahperi for the fruit course, that is all."

"My turquoise gem! Those plates! She has shamed me beyond all boundaries! Find her and bring her to me! I will deal with her in a way befitting her effrontery," he gestured to the Palace guards.

"Please, my Sultan, calm down, a wise leader does not act rashly in anger on the battlefield or in his divan, and I should think the same policy should apply for his family. Please, I beg you, calm down before we proceed with any reprisals," urged Köpek. "I am sure she meant well and that there is a logical explanation for all of this." Köpek smiled to himself, knowing full well that his schemes were watertight.

"Calm down? Do not mock me! After what she has done to me, she deserves to be locked up in a fortress for the rest of her days! No, I will not calm down, and I am certainly not going to forgive her for the outrage of this evening! There can be no explanation for what she has done! She has dishonored my rank, she has spent a fortune on frivolities without my permission, she has tried to position her son as more important than I am, and she has flaunted in front of the whole court that she and that architect were together all along under my very own eyes! She has betrayed me!"

☪ ☪ ☪

The palace pages found Mahperi sitting by the side of the lake, her knees bent up to her chest, rocking back and forth and sobbing. They stood there and watched her, unable to move, for they felt genuinely sorry for her. She had always been so gentle and kind to each of them; always with a greeting, a smile or a caring word. It just could not be true, all of these rumors that were now spreading through the site like brushfire – it was just not possible that this honorable woman could have done anything as terrible as was being said about her. And what was this story about the architect? Why had he run away? So much confusion in everyone's minds, but their orders were firm. Find her and bring her back to the Sultan.

They led her into the divan room of the Palace. Despite the horror of the circumstances that had led her there, Mahperi gasped when she saw the beauty of Joseph's tiles, sparkling in the light of the torches. She heard all the joyful animals and birds on the tiles call out to her: "*Courage, our Queen, goodness and light will prevail! Do not be afraid, we will stand with you!*" but as soon as she heard the harsh tone of Alaeddin's voice, she knew that she now stood totally alone.

He made her stand in front of him while he dressed her down, spewing anger over what had happened. When he finished degrading her in front of the emirs, stripping her of her dignity, he finally seemed spent and was able to regain control of his senses.

"So, what do you have to say for yourself? Like a grubby thief in the bazaar, I will give you the opportunity to tell your side of the story. You have one chance to explain what possessed you to act this way!" he sputtered.

Mahperi raised her eyes to his and looked directly into them, unafraid to confront the rage she saw there. The words of Jesus before his accusers came to her ears. *My God, My God, why have you forsaken me? I thirst. It is finished. Father, into your hands I commit my spirit*. You must confront your accuser with this same grace, Mahperi.

"You have no right to be angry with me, my Sultan. There is no explanation to give you, because I have done nothing wrong," she said simply and firmly.

"*Nothing wrong*? How dare you say such a thing after you shamed me in public, blatantly promoted your son, and flaunted your liaison with that man?" Spit sprayed from his lips, so uncontrollable was his rage at her answer.

"I repeat, my Sultan, I have done nothing wrong," she continued. *My God, My God, why have you forsaken me? I thirst. It is finished. Father, into your hands I commit my spirit*. Be strong, Mahperi, be strong.

"I did not orchestrate that spectacle this evening. I never saw one of those plates before in my life. I have no idea how our beloved turquoise could have wound up on the shaft of the architect's hammer. The last time I saw it was when my maid Esma took it to a jeweler in the bazaar of Konya for repair, for the chain had broken. I swear to you on the head of the Holy Mother Mary and Jesus Christ her son, this is the truth!"

"Well, then, if that is so, bring this maid in here, and let's have her explain what happened!" the Sultan clapped to call his guards to the task.

"My Sultan, I am afraid she has disappeared," spoke up Köpek. "No one has seen her since this morning, and all her belongings are gone from her room as well. It would appear that she has left Kubadabad for good!" Köpek smiled to himself, knowing that the fortune of gold coins he had given her would allow her to build a house in Antalya as fine as the one of her former Venetian master.

Mahperi knew at that moment that there could be only one explanation for this whole event, and it could only be linked to the two people on the face of this earth who consistently showed her enmity. Now it was Mahperi's turn to seethe at the treachery that had been planned against her, but she managed to control her voice.

"My Sultan, no words I can give you will convince you of my innocence. But I am innocent. One day you will discover the names of the people who are guilty of orchestrating this vile act against you and me at the same time, I promise you. They will not be able to hide their evil from you. Rid this court of them before they turn on you next," she insisted, feeling the eyes of Köpek burning into her back. "Do with me what you wish. But I am innocent in this affair. I will not beg for your forgiveness. One does not beg pardon for a sin that one did not commit." She held her head high and never once let her eyes or her voice drop.

The faces of the twenty-three emirs that had revolted against him so many years before now flashed in front of the Sultan's eyes, and he became all the more confused and enraged. Could she be telling the truth? Is it merely a coincidence that the maid disappeared that very morning? Is that gang of emirs again fomenting against me, and is now using my queen to dishonor me? This seemed inconceivable. At that moment, when he saw her face shining in the rays of the full moon, the Sultan wanted more than anything to believe her. He thought back to the time he saw that angelic face in the turquoise moonlight on that cliff in Alaiye on their wedding night, and he could never think of a time since when those emerald eyes had not looked on him with anything but love and truth, even when he told her about Gaziye. But that was a long time ago. Today is now, and now she must be punished.

Mahperi spoke out again. "Our son is totally innocent, as well. Please, I beg of you, harbor no ill will in your heart to him."

At the mention of his son's name, the Sultan's anger flamed again, and the room broke out in murmurs. Even if I believe you, Mahperi, the Sultan thought, I cannot allow everyone to see that my honor has been challenged. He must be punished for this incident. Someone must pay for all of this, and it will be him.

The Sultan raised his hand in the air to silence the room, and then looked down at Mahperi from his dais. With the moonlight over the lake sparkling behind him through the large opening, he pronounced his verdict.

"I direct that you leave my sight at once, Mahperi. Pack your things and leave for Kayseri and stay there. I do not ever want to see you here at Kubadabad or at Konya again. I will allow you to live a normal life in Kayseri; I will continue to provide you an allowance by which you may live comfortably, but as of this moment, you are banished from my family and from the influence of my inner circle. My subjects must understand that you have been punished. No effrontery to my honor is tolerated by me, and you are no exception, despite your position as a Queen."

He drew a deep breath.

"As for our son Giyaseddin Keyhüsrev, he will go from here to Kayseri with you. He is under your care now, Mahperi Hatun, for I am removing him from the charge of Emir Ertokush. His education as heir to the throne is finished. It is finished because he is no longer in need of it. As of this moment, I hereby designate my son Izzeddin al-Din Kilich Arslan as my heir. Long life to the future Sultan and to his subjects! That is all; you and your son are dismissed, Queen Mahperi; please leave now," he ordered, although he found it impossible to look into her emerald eyes when he said it.

☪ ☪ ☪

Gaziye crept away from her hiding place behind the curtain at the door to the divan, where she had been eaves-dropping on the encounter. A gleeful smile played on her lips and a little dance animated her step. Köpek has certainly played this well, she smirked, and I must make sure to thank him generously for all his help in achieving this success! The Sultan has finally done what I have been nagging him to do for months now. Our golden son Izzeddin is designated to carry the scepter of the Seljuks, and not that dolt of a son of Mahperi! In one night, I have become, as mother of the future Sultan, the most powerful woman in the entire Seljuk Empire!

Chapter 65

Determining Dreams

The Sultan now lived days filled with troubled thoughts. As he traveled down the Long Road to Kayseri to prepare for the spring troop training, his mind was preoccupied with many of the images of the past year, all of them disturbing.

Following his failed campaign to take Diyarbakir and the events of the inauguration of Kubadabad, the Sultan felt frustration and bitterness, and it began to affect him in physical ways. His mind had trouble focusing on tasks at hand, he had no appetite, and his sleep became infected by bad dreams. Each night the images of twenty-three faces, black basalt walls, gold inscriptions on plates, Mongol sword blades dripping with blood, and his Queen's treason flared in front of his eyes. He would wake from his nightmares with a start, gasping for air, his quilt drenched in perspiration from the fire of these images that tainted his mind.

These same images tormented the Sultan with every step of his stallion on the road to Kayseri, but the most terrorizing were the ones he heard about the horrors committed by the advancing Mongols. Now gnawing at the Seljuk borders at the city of Mosul on the Tigris River, the Mongols would soon become an inevitable challenge for him, forcing him to make a decision on how to deal with them. Every hoofbeat of Night Shining White drummed into his head the conflicting imperatives now in front of him.

On the one hand, he had always been the most courageous of leaders, *Abu'l Feth*, Father of Conquests and Victories, scoring victory after victory for his empire. No one before him had achieved such territorial glory, and it was the hallmark of his reign. On the other hand, his internal policy was just as significant for him, as he always tried to improve the well-being of his people. *Clip clop clip clop* trod the hooves of his horse; back and forth back and forth went his conflicting thoughts. Should I take on these Mongols and believe in my capacity to destroy them, or should I think of the safety of my citizens and this Empire first? Will all think I am a coward if I do not chase after the Mongols, or will all think I am a hero for surrendering to them to save my people? But if I lose to these heathens, as everyone else before me has, how will I deal with the smell of the burning flesh of my citizens in my nostrils for the rest of eternity? *Clip clop clip clop*, the torment did not let up as he trod the long road to Kayseri.

When the procession reached the Sultan Han outside of Aksaray, they stopped to rest for the night. Unable to sleep, the Sultan sat at the campfire well into the night, his thoughts crackling along with the flames of the fire. He could hear the low voice of his queen Mahperi in his ears, and, although her treason still burned as hotly as the fire in front of him, her voice remained insistently clear in his ears. She, who always told me that my conquests meant nothing if I did not have the support of my people. She, who always convinced me that if my people were not content at home, there was no point in striving to garner more territories. She, who was always the wisest of any of my viziers – oh why, why did you forsake me, my Queen of the Turquoise Moonlight, whatever happened to us? But he knew her instincts always proved right, and he knew the path she would advise him to take. He could hear her voice in his mind as clearly as if she were standing next to him:

"My Sultan! Pride and greed are two of the seven deadly sins. The Holy Scriptures have taught us that they, along with a lying tongue, hands that shed innocent blood, and a heart which devises wicked plots, will keep us in darkness. I am certain that your Qur'an says the same thing. Think about what the continued race against this Mongol mud will entail. If you lose on the battlefield, your people will lose. What is more important for you, my Sultan? Is it your pride and greed of glorious titles, or is ensuring that your citizens can live in peace, without fear? You are the military leader of this empire, but you are also its guiding force, a Father to these Turks. Which one do you believe is the most important role for you to fill? You and your ambassadors can work out an honorable agreement with the Mongols: you will send the Mongols money and they will agree to leave you alone, for booty is all they want. We Seljuks want more than that: we want peace and dignity."

She is right, as always. I, Alaeddin Keykubad, who has forged a glorious empire from the dust of these plains, cannot let it return to that dust by the hands of villainous heathens, he repeated to himself over and over again. I will not have destruction come to my lands, these lands that I have worked so hard to build up, with courts and mosques and hans and markets and farms and ports of trade and city walls and medreses of learning. I, Alaeddin Keykubad, will do everything I can to preserve what has been built in the name of God, for I am Sultan Alaeddin Keykubad, *Ala-du-dunya v'ed din*, Eminence of the World and the Faith!

His next battle would be a political one. His ministers, viziers, counselors and emirs would become his warriors in this battle, for their skills of diplomacy and policy-making would be the front guard for the attack on the Mongols. The differences with his adversaries would be discussed in the throne room and resolved there, and not on the battlefield. This is what a civilized ruler should do, he reasoned to himself, and if I cannot show this level of intelligence and order to the world, who shall?

The Sultan decided to call a meeting at Kayseri of all the states in the region, both Christian and Muslim. His objective was to convince the various factions in the area to unite to put aside their differences and to join into one alliance that would have the force to negotiate with the Mongols. Yet, soon after the Sultan dispatched his couriers with the invitations to his allies and adversaries to come to the summit conference, an unexpected event occurred.

One morning, the envoys of the Mongol Khan Ogedei arrived at the gates of Kayseri. They had been invited to the Seljuk court over three years ago, when the Sultan's embassy had visited the court of Ogedei. It had taken them three long years to arrive, but now they were here, now, at this very moment that agents from all the lands were on their way to his joint conference. Was this a mere coincidence, or a true sign that peace was to be crafted?

The Mongol ambassador stood in front of the Sultan in the divan of the Devlethane Palace in Kayseri and reread the original letter the Khan had sent back with the Seljuk delegate. He read it in a booming voice, that letter which had so explicitly stated that the Mongols would always reign supreme and would destroy anyone who stood in their path. The words *'You will submit entirely unto us. The Seljuk Empire will deem the Great Khan as ruler, and will answer only to him'* echoed in the Sultan's ears. He could clearly recall his anger when he heard Ibn Bibi reading that letter three years ago upon the return of the Turkish envoys. At that time, he chose to ignore that command, but now the situation was different.

When the Mongol ambassador finished reading the letter, he then withdrew from his leather pouch a new dispatch written by the Khan. With great flourish, he read it to the Sultan and all his court gathered there, who listened with rapt attention. There was no mistaking the message of this blunt letter. The Khan's letter reiterated the intent to maintain peace with the Seljuk state, but this time, the letter contained an official summons to the Sultan for payment of tribute money, and laid out the vast amounts expected. After he read it, the Mongol Ambassador extended the letter and a prepared treaty to the Sultan, who saw Ogedei's stamp and thumbprint at the bottom right of the page, and the empty space to the left, awaiting his. The destiny of the mighty Seljuk Empire was now in his hands and his alone, awaiting him, there at the bottom of a flimsy piece of paper.

It was not surprising that the Sultan's dream that night was particularly troubled, so disturbing that he needed to call upon the court astrologers and various imams to help him interpret it. The Sultan believed that all dreams were sent to his subconscious by God's angels as a secret message, yet the dream that night had been full of perplexing imagery that he could not fathom.

The Sultan related his dream to the astrologers the next morning. "I saw in my dream that my head was made of gold, my breast of silver, my belly of brass, my thighs of lead, my shins of tin and both my feet of pewter."

The soothsayers conferred long and hard to explain this dream, and were at first afraid to speak to the Sultan about their interpretation. Finally, Imam Ilyas, the wisest of the astrologers, addressed the Sultan. He said: "My Sultan, the meaning is clear. As long as you are alive in this world, your people will be as pure and precious as gold. All will go well in the kingdom during your lifetime. After you, in your son's reign, they will have the value of silver, after your son's son, they will have only the value of brass and it will be a time when creatures with lower thoughts will reign. When the power arrives at this generation, the world will be in great disorder. There will be no sincerity, no faithfulness, and no compassion among the men of the fourth generation. By the fifth, the territories of Anatolia will be totally ravaged and ruined, and trouble-makers and unknown upstarts will seize the reins of power. It will be the decline of the Seljuk Dynasty, and this land will be ruined. That is how I interpret your dream, my Sultan – and may God preserve your soul from harm."

The Sultan was stunned by his interpretation, but he was now convinced that God had sent this vision to guide him on the path of his destiny. For the Sultan, the meaning of his dream was clear: he had to negotiate with these Mongols; and he had to do whatever it took to ensure that they would not conquer and ruin his land.

His decision was made. The dream had spoken. All must remain gold; the feet of the Empire must not turn into pewter. With the greatest courage he would ever need to display in all his reign, he would pick up his pen, which would weigh in his hand as heavily as a sword. He would sign that treaty with the great Ogedei Khan. He would pay the Mongols the tribute money they demanded in exchange for peace. He, Alaeddin Keykubad, The Holy Wise One, would save his country from invasion and depredation by the Mongols; a devastation he knew would inevitably befall it if he did not chose to wield the red ink of his pen instead of the red blood of his sword, in this, the most important battle of his life.

Chapter 66

Roiling and Riling

The imperative now before the Sultan Alaeddin Keykubad weighed as heavily in his mind as would the pen in his hand the moment he would sign the treaty with the Mongols. He needed to inform all the court officials at the Devlethane of his decision to surrender to the demands of the heathens from the East.

The Emirs buzzed with anticipation after receiving the invitation to attend a special urgent meeting with the Sultan, and wondered what the promised important announcement would entail. Was the Sultan going to try one more time to seize the black walls of Diyarbakir for the Seljuks? Was he going to increase their annual income from the state treasury? Some thought the meeting was being called to discuss the situation with the new heir, Izzeddin al-Din Kilich Arslan. Others feared that once again, he would be demanding more money to support his building projects. Some speculated that the recent arrival of the Mongol Emissary has something to do with it. Rumors abounded, but no one was quite sure why this meeting had been convened. Yet no one could ever have guessed the news the Sultan was about to proclaim.

The *divan* room of the Devlethane had been spread with carpets and cushions, and guards were stationed against the walls. It was a fine day in May, and the breezes were sweetened by the aroma of flowers in bloom. The *Çavuş* bodyguard of the Sultan, carrying his long staff and wearing a sash decorated with precious stones, walked ahead and shouted out for all to step aside, clearing the path for the Sultan to enter and take his place. The Sultan sat down on the raised platform which opened up to a view of the Majestic Mountain.

The men assembled and took their places, all humming with anticipation about the meeting to follow. The Sultan looked out at the room and saw Köpek sitting in the front row with Giyaseddin Keyhüsrev at his side. After the events at Kubadabad, Köpek had persuaded the Sultan to show clemency to the young man, and not to punish him for the inappropriate behavior his mother had displayed. It was good policy, he reminded the Sultan, to show the court that he continued to support all his sons and that there was harmony in the royal family.

All rose and stood while the imam led his prayer: *"May God in all his strength cause us to express our gratitude for His goodwill and to the health of our Sultan-ül-azam the Magnificent, and make us aware of all the privileges He has shared with us in our glorious Empire here on earth, and accept us into Paradise with his unfailing generosity, and forever to accept our support for the love He so mercifully extends to us."*

When the imam finished his prayer of thanksgiving to God, the Sultan looked over the room, pausing to scrutinize each and every one of the faces in the audience, as if fixing them to memory. How will these emirs react to my news, he wondered. Will they understand my motivations, or will I be forced to cut down more trees if they are displeased with me? He took a deep breath, and in a clear voice, clearer than he had ever spoken in his entire life, the Sultan began to address the group.

"My Lions, leaders of this great Land, my Emirs! I have called you here today to announce a significant decision I have made concerning our Empire. As you know, I have selected a new heir, my son Izzeddin al-Din Kilich Arslan. He is young, but in a few years, following rigorous education and training, he will make a fine Sultan. I am counting on you to give him your full support. The future of our Empire is upon his young shoulders. May God protect him!"

The crowd murmured their approval and quieted down in anticipation of the rest of the Sultan's announcement.

"It is not only young Izzeddin al-Din Kilich Arslan who needs your support. I, as well, am counting on it more than ever to lead us into the next era of our glorious Empire," he proclaimed, looking out over the crowd now gone totally silent.

"As you know, we have received the visit of the emissaries of the Mongol court of Ogedei Khan. His head ambassador has informed me of their intentions towards our Empire. I do not need to tell you what a formidable foe these Mongols are, and what devastation they have wrought in other lands. As I sit here today in front of you as your Sultan, I must tell you that I believe that it is pointless for us to try and resist the waves of this mighty Ocean. These waves will crash over our heads and drown us all. Instead, I have decided that we must ride on the crest of those waves and keep our heads – and our honor – above the turbulent waters. It is our only chance for survival."

He paused and looked out at the crowd that had not yet grasped the meaning of his message.

"My emirs, I have decided to sue for peace with the Mongols. I will sign the treaty that Ogedei Khan has proposed, a treaty that will position our Seljuk Empire as his vassal. He asks that we pay him annual tribute in money, livestock and troops. In return, he promises not to invade our country, burn our cities to the ground, kill our men, rape our women and sell our children into slavery. I have thought long and hard about this and I believe that it is the best solution for the well-being of our people. I will not let them plunder and destroy all that I have built, nor will I allow them to disrupt the social stability that I have established for our citizens! These Mongols are a people led by hatred, not by God's love. I believe God has entrusted me to show His love to others. I must determine the future of my people and this nation, and, above all, ensure its protection. My decision is final, and I enjoin you to support this next era of our Kingdom," he said decisively.

The Sultan took advantage of the dumbstruck silence of the audience to continue his announcement.

"I will organize a banquet here on the Devlethane grounds next week to celebrate the *Eid al-Fitr al-Mubarak* festival which marks the end of the holy month of Ramadan. At the final banquet on the third night of the festivities, I will sign the treaty with the Mongol ambassadors in an official ceremony in front of all of you. You will come dressed in your finest attire to show him the force of our court. He will take that message back to Ogedei Khan – the message that we are a powerful kingdom of illustrious men, far superior in culture and dignity than they. We will bow our heads to the Khan, but will continue to still stand legions taller than any of his warriors. We are the Seljuk Empire, the most civilized on the earth, and it is for this reason that we will not allow ourselves to be wiped out on the whim of a rabble of bloodthirsty fiends. We will endure far longer than the waves of that Ocean, through our culture and dignity; and by signing this treaty, I am signing over this heritage to our children. A great Empire will continue to flourish for all time here on these lands of Anatolia, from the cornerstones we have already laid, in governance, religion, literature and science. We are a grand country!"

☪ ☪ ☪

For the next several days, the entire court did nothing but discuss the decision of the Sultan and what it meant for the future of the Empire. No one was sure of anything – would they still wage battles in the East? What about Diyarbakir? Would they be able to hold all of the cities they had fought so hard to win, or were they going to have to turn them over to the Mongols? Would the Mongols now sit next to – or even worse – in the place of the Sultan in the divan? Would our language be the same? Would they impose their religion of idol worship and shaking sticks upon us? But the biggest question on all of their minds, ready to spill out onto their tongues, was "Will we, the emirs of this Empire, maintain our power, influence and wealth?"

Later that week, a group of the emirs met at the home of Emir Siradj al-Din Badr to discuss these many questions. Köpek listened to them all with increasing interest, fully aware that he would soon transform this evening into the most important one of his career. It is here tonight; he said to himself, that I will maneuver the agents who will clear the path of my revenge.

Emir Siradj al-Din Badr spoke up, grabbing a handful of apricots and almonds from the bowl on the large copper tray that had been placed by the servants in the middle of the group. He lifted his goblet for his page to fill to the brim, and started to speak.

"I cannot understand this decision of the Sultan's! He, who has always been so proud and so courageous, now buckling like a scared rabbit in front of these Mongols! It just does not seem possible! What is wrong with him? These Mongols are going to seize our property as booty and we will be left with nothing!" he sputtered.

His comment spurred an animated discussion among the group, and soon two distinct sides began to form. Those supportive of the Sultan saw his decision as courageous and reasoned; those critical of him saw it as treason to their beliefs. Köpek listened and waited for the exact moment to speak up.

"My good Emirs, we must trust the leadership of our Sultan, who has always done the best for us. Now, more than ever, he needs our support," proposed Köpek. "True, it is probable that we will lose our fortunes in all of this," he added, drawing out that last sentence very slowly to make sure that it registered with everyone. "But at least we will escape with our heads still on our shoulders, and for that we should be thankful."

Several voices spoke up immediately. "What do you mean, *'Always done the best for us'*? Do you not remember, Vizier Köpek, the fate of the twenty-three emirs who dared to protest the heavy burdens put upon them in order to carry out the building follies of the Sultan?" spoke out Emir Nariruddin Ali. "How can you forget how he has depleted our pockets with his extravagant ambitions? No, I say, I will not lend my support to the Sultan in this decision! I will not accept that he will allow my fortune to feed the treasury of those demons from the East! He is a coward, I tell you, a coward if he signs that paper!"

Köpek was pleased to see that they were playing right into his hands, there where he wanted them. He continued to manipulate the conversation.

"Yes, that is probably what will happen. The tribute the Sultan will pay to the Mongols will come as much from your purses as from the State coffers, just like it was when the Sultan asked you to finance his building projects. You have always been his major source of funding, and that will not stop now."

The group grumbled their discontent.

"Yes, this will be the case, I am sure, unless…" Köpek continued.

"Unless what?" perked up several voices in unison.

"My Emirs, I was thinking that if we could broker directly with the Mongols and by-pass the Sultan, we could perhaps save our fortunes and make the Sultan assume the majority of the burden. Who needs the Sultan's approval anymore, after all? Once he puts his red ink to that treaty, he has lost that privilege. Or perhaps… we could even deal with the Sultan in a more decisive way, to ensure that he will never be able to challenge our influence again," intimated Köpek, making sure that he did not say anything that would later compromise him.

He turned to Emir Nariruddin Ali and said, "Why don't you gather together all the emirs who agree with us back here tomorrow night for a private meeting. Make sure that Chashnigir Ali is with you as well. I will discuss with you an idea that I have to ensure that we retain our power and property, despite the decision of the Sultan to surrender to those peasants from the Asian steppes!"

☪ ☪ ☪

After the emirs left, Köpek spent the rest of the evening in his tent with the young Giyaseddin, providing him his sugar as always, in the form of sympathetic words and syrupy wine. Köpek knew that the young man was confused about the recent events of Kubadabad, and that he could manipulate this confusion to serve his plan.

They spoke long into the night about what happened at Kubadabad. Carefully hiding his participation in the plot, Köpek used his utmost skill and subtlety to rile and roil the young man into anger about what happened to him since that night. Köpek prodded Giyaseddin to feel rage about how his beloved mother had been so indecently and unjustly shamed by his father in front of all those people at the banquet. Why, who could have done such a spiteful thing to her? He urged him to feel resentment about being stripped of his title as heir to the throne. He made him feel like a piece of spoiled fruit tossed aside in the gutters of the bazaar. He put anger in his head, he put the idea of revenge in his head, and he forced all the memories of the little boy, unloved and banished, to come to the surface.

When Giyaseddin had been sufficiently roiled and riled, Köpek added his last comments to ensure the participation of the young man in his scheme.

"Don't worry, my lion Giyaseddin, your Köpek is here to help you as always, and I will make sure that you can claim again what is rightfully yours as the first-born son. Just listen to me and do what I say and all will be fine. Trust me, young man, for have I not always been your friend? Above all, we will make sure that your mother's honor is avenged. And that is so important, the honor of a mother, is it not?"

Chapter 67

Fires of Avenging Desire

The Holy Month of Ramadan was over. Finished were the days of fasting and the body's painful questing of food and water that was denied during the hours from dawn until sunset. Now came the time to savor the moral merits achieved through days of hard hunger. Fasting was the shield against the Fires of Desire. Fasting served as the prayer to please God and to seek His Face with all one's sincerity. Days became victories against falsehood, ignorance and indecency. Life had become purer with each passing day, and all shared a time of joy when the fast was broken each night and man met his God. It was the moment when men improved their worship and obedience of God the Most High, an obedience destined to last long after the month of Ramadan was over, *inshallah*.

The duty of this Holy Pillar of the Faith was accomplished, and it was now time to rejoice in the bounty of God's blessings. Yet, for some at the court of Kayseri, on this third day after the end of the holy month of Ramadan, time ran backwards and the Fires of Desire still burned in their hearts. The hard hunger of revenge now gnawed.

☪ ☪ ☪

As was the custom, the Sultan organized an elaborate series of festivities to celebrate the end of the Holy month of Ramadan. The court at the Devlethane was in a state of excitement in anticipation of the final banquet to be held that night, the largest of the holiday celebrations. Attending would be the Armenian, Ayyubid, and Artukid envoys who had been invited by the Sultan to sit with the Mongol emissaries, with the hopes that tasty food, festivities and goodwill would have the power to diffuse their adversity and ambitions. The Mongols had shown that they wished to negotiate with Alaeddin Keykubad, not kill him. The Sultan ardently hoped the Mongols would confirm the same respect to the other dynasties present at the dinner, and, in this way, he perhaps would be able to create a lasting peace for all the nations of the East. Believing that such an encompassing view was the hallmark of a true leader, the Sultan found another encouraging rationalization to sign this treaty, for he was looking beyond the needs of his own kingdom towards those of all the citizens of the East. The banquet tonight would not only be in honor of the end of Ramadan, the Mongols, and the foreign court dignitaries, but it would also celebrate the appointment of the Sultan's new heir. The Golden Orb Izzeddin al-Din Kilich Arslan would sit at the Sultan's side during the festivities, so that all could see that this favored child was ready to start his apprenticeship to wear the crown of the Seljuks.

A frenzy of activity filled the palace grounds. Musicians tuned their instruments, pages girded their caftans with golden belts, and the palace cooks readied to prepare the most extensive banquet the Devlethane Palace in Kayseri would ever see: Mongols and Seljuks would share the same *tandir kebab* of peace, for it was on this night that Sultan Alaeddin Keykubad would sign the treaty with the ambassadors of Ogedei Khan. It promised to be a night to remember.

☪ ☪ ☪

On that bright May afternoon, Giyaseddin Keyhüsrev sat by himself on a wooden bench outside the palace kitchens. Ever since he was a child, he always headed to the kitchens when he felt lonely, for the aroma of cooking food never failed to comfort him. The chefs would slip him a tasty morsel, and with luck, it would be his favorite halvah. But today there would be no morsel, for the cooks were too busy to notice him, so intent were they on attending to the needs of the 1000 invited guests. Giyaseddin heard Muzaffer, the supervisor of the kitchens, firing out orders in every direction. Whole sheep were being roasted, goats were grilling on an open fire, and quails and partridges were being plucked to be roasted later on in the day. Feathers flew in the air and knives whittled vegetables and fruits faster than flying arrows.

Giyaseddin particularly needed comfort today, for tonight he would see his brother take his place next to his father as the appointed heir to the throne. Giyaseddin had been at a loss since that dreadful day at Kubadabad when his mother had been shamed and he had been stripped of his rightful inheritance. He did not understand why he had been rejected, and his anger was increasing with each day. His father never did love him, of that he was sure, but it was not fair that throne had been stolen from him for no apparent reason. It was his birthright as first born son after all! Yet what hurt him more than his own rejection was the fact that his mother had been so harshly humiliated by his father. He did not really understand what had happened on that day to anger his father so, but something had gone terribly wrong. Ever since that day, his mother sat in her room with her hands in her lap and her head hung low. She no longer ate, and Giyaseddin saw a flood of silent tears drop onto those hands from morning till night. He could not bear to see his beloved mother this way. Do not be sad, mama, please stop crying, I will make it better for you, I promise you. Köpek has said he will help me to do what must be done so that you can be the first queen again, and he says I will be heir once again, too. My father had no right to do what he did to you, and I will do anything to make sure that he no longer hurts you. Those tears of yours must stop, mama; please, I will make them stop; yes, for you I will do anything.

☪ ☪ ☪

On that bright May afternoon, a group of emirs stood at the side of the playing fields on the Mashad meadow and watched the sporting games being played there. For the past three days, dust had risen in billowing clouds over these parade grounds from the hooves of charging polo ponies and the running feet of athletes. There had been jousting, wrestling matches, archery contests, reveling and men fighting each other with spear, mace and arrow. The athletes were told they would be crowned 'Giants of the Empire', and would then receive the Sultan's kiss, ribbon and gold coins. It was even rumored that the champion wrestler would receive his own palace and lands. The emirs watched the games and thought to themselves that all life at this court was but a game and a contest. They, too, were athletes, but on a different playing field, the one of political power and influence. Theirs, too, was a game of skill and force where the stronger prevail over the weaker; where the victor was the one who could outmaneuver the less skillful. We are indeed champions, they thought; we will not let this Sultan win over us again like he did when the twenty three trees fell and Zeyneddin Bashara, Seyfeddin Ayaba and Mübarizeddin Behramshah lost their heads. We will be crowned Giants of the Empire in this wrestling match; oh, yes, our Sultan; we will win the gold ring of victory tonight and hold it fast in our triumphant hands.

☪ ☪ ☪

On that bright May afternoon, the Superintendent of Building, Vizier Sadettin Köpek, stood in the fields surrounding the Devlethane Palace and watched the workmen set up for the evening's event. He was exhausted from having worked so hard over the past days, giving orders for the installation of all the tents and pavilions needed for the celebration. Roads had been paved for the processional of ambassadors and guests to arrive that night. Gardeners were working all over the grounds like ants to set up small flower gardens with pools of water and fountains to adorn them, weaving paths throughout them for the guests to take air that evening. Köpek barked orders for the pitching of tents and the setting up of serving stations for the banquet guests, making sure not to forget stables and food stores.

As he watched the workmen erect the timber poles that would hold up the Sultan's satin tent, he thought of the many things that still had to be organized to ensure a successful outcome for the evening. So much to do, so much to do. I am in charge of everything here today; yes, but soon I will be in charge of everything, everywhere. I, too, am paving my own roads for the celebration tonight. I, too, am planting the garden of my ultimate revenge, here, among the tent poles of the satin tents on the grounds of the Palace of the Devlethane.

☪ ☪ ☪

On that bright May afternoon, Mahperi looked out from her window to the courtyard below and observed all the activity taking place there. She noted the many detached pavilions that comprised the Devlethane palace, all of them linked by an encircling wall. Since that terrible day at Kubadabad, she had been housed in a kiosk away from the Sultan's private apartments. She had been banished from them all, with her own wall of shame encircling her life.

She gazed at the gardens of the Devlethane. She noted that the Sultan had given orders to tether his menagerie of wild animals to the trees in order to impress the Mongols. Brightly-colored birds from Asia screeched and made noises that frightened the horses. She saw a shaggy brown bear from the Black Sea Mountains, two ebony panthers and long-horned graceful antelopes from Africa, and, at the end of the yard, the glorious beast Ruby reigned in all her feline splendor, enthroned on a woven rug and tethered to a rock by a large gold chain linked to her dazzling collar of rubies.

Rivaling the bright birds and Ruby's collar were the vividly-colored robes of the Mongol ambassadors, who were crossing the courtyard to and from their tents, preparing for the ceremony to be held that evening. Mahperi had never seen anything like these garments; even those worn by the bishop in her little church in Kalonoros on Easter morning and the red robe worn by Alaeddin at their marriage paled in comparison.

She watched as the head ambassador crossed the courtyard. He wore a purple ceremonial robe made of several layers of shining silk with long, narrow sleeves and a slim waistband made of tightly stitched ribbons terminating in loops and silk-knotted buttons. The gown was embroidered with roundels of gold phoenixes chasing one another inside a rim of flaming pearls. The phoenixes had hooked scimitar beaks, tall crests, big round eyes and a plumage of shining silver feathers. I am like that phoenix, thought Mahperi. I am a fighter. I will rise again from the ashes and soar again, my Sultan, for you cannot dismiss me as you have done. What you did to me and our son at Kubadabad was cruel and beyond all decency and has incited in me rage I never knew possible. Yet I know full well that it was Köpek and your other wife who were behind it all, but even so, you chose to believe them and not me, your ever-faithful and loving Turquoise Queen. The Phoenix is stronger than the Raven, and I will stand tall once again in resplendent silver feathers. These tears will stop; I will reclaim my rights and that of my son. You cannot take my honor away from me, my Sultan.

☪ ☪ ☪

On that bright May afternoon, the Mongol ambassador stood in the doorway of his tent and looked out onto the fields where the banquet was being set out. He fingered the paper treaty rolled up in the pocket of his purple silk robe. The text had been carefully prepared and was now ready for signature by the Seljuk Sultan. This will be the crowning moment of my career, he thought, as his fingers rubbed over its surface, for I will achieve a resounding victory for the Khan without spilling one drop of blood! He ran his hand over the embroidered phoenix on his robe and thought of the ceremony to come. Tonight, he would put this signed treaty into his pocket and these Seljuks into the pocket of Ogedei Khan, along with the many lavish gifts that he knew the Sultan was preparing for him to take back to Karakorum. He especially eyed that leopard with the ruby collar he saw in the courtyard and wondered if he could include her as booty in the treaty agreement. How Ogedei Khan would love to have her at his side when he sat in his throne room at the Palace at Karakorum! Yet from what he had heard of the Sultan's attachment to the animal, that would be difficult, for he had been told that the Sultan would kill anyone who came near his precious beast. I suppose then I would have to kill the Sultan first, mused the Ambassador, before I could bring that magnificent cat back to Ogedei Khan. The image of Ruby at the side of Ogedei Khan danced for a moment in his eyes, and his mind ran away with the possibility of it.

The Ambassador kept playing this thought over and over in his mind as he closed the door flap of his tent to keep out the dust raised by all the activity on the palace grounds that afternoon. Yes, without this cocky and forceful Seljuk Sultan around, how much easier it would be for us to rule this Empire! And how convenient for us as well that he has now appointed a little seven year old boy as his heir! If Alaeddin Keykubad were removed from power, we could dominate this Empire through the voice of a little boy. We would never have to worry about Alaeddin Keykubad changing his mind after signing this treaty and challenging our dominion over his Empire. Yes, if he were removed from power....if I could return to Ogedei Khan with a tribute treaty signed and a kingdom ruled by a little boy, he would be even more pleased with my talents as ambassador. And if I could bring back that spectacular leopard as well, I certainly would become one of the most powerful Mongols in the land!

☪ ☪ ☪

Such were the thoughts in everyone's mind on this bright afternoon of May 31 in the holy year of 1237, the third day after the end of the holy month of Ramadan. The lessons of the immense moral rewards of fasting and the victory against falsehood, ignorance and indecency were far from their minds. All avengers anticipated the banquet to come, with the Fires of Desire flaming in their hungry hearts.

Chapter 68

A Comet Across the Night Sky

I take a deep breath. I close my eyes for a moment.

God in Your heavens above, I express my gratitude for Your goodwill, and implore that You give me strength to confront this evening. God, bless this evening and its importance for the future of my people. God, You, who send Your love so mercifully upon us, I beg You to shine it upon me tonight.

I am ready. I open my eyes.

I enter the royal precinct that has been set up for this evening's ceremonies on the Mashad plain outside of my palace. Tonight we celebrate the end of the Holy month of Ramadan, yet I feel no joy in this festivity. I approach the giant round tent that has been set up at the edge of the field. A wall of embroidered fabrics now encircles the area, and pages stand guard every five feet on both sides of the wall. The canopied pavilions for the food are set up at the sides of the enclosed area. Lining the processional path to my tent are two rows of my strongest warriors, dressed in their most colorful livery. I see the flag bearers holding aloft the Seljuk banners of green silk. My *Silahdars* stand at attention carrying my weapons and sword. I see the groups of court officials and emirs standing outside on either side of the tent, waiting for us to arrive. I follow my *Çavuş* bodyguard and walk down the path between the rows of my warriors and approach the tent. I gesture for the Mongol ambassadors to enter in front of me. The pages open the tent flap and we enter and take our places on the cushions and carpets.

It is so hot tonight. So hot for May; too hot.

The imam leads us in prayer before the start of the meal. My *Taştdar* butler holds the washbowl for me to wash my face and hands.

I lift my glass in a toast to my guests. It is my favorite pomegranate sherbet drink, tart and sweet at the same time. I taste the drink, so refreshing on this hot evening.

Servants place bowls of yogurt soup on the copper trays in front of us. I pick up my wooden spoon and gently sip the steamy broth, but it is too hot tonight for such soup. I call for the servants to bring the other foods.

Next to me I see the Mongol ambassador grab food off the platter with his bare hands and stuff an entire chicken leg into his mouth. I hear him crunching the bones like a cat when it rips open a captured mouse.

I am repulsed.

He tells me that despite the warm night he is glad for his fur pelt. The Mongol ambassador takes another chicken in his hand and shoves it in his mouth as if he has not eaten for days. Ruby eats with more grace than he does.

I smell the strong odor of his greasy pelt and I feel sick to my stomach. What heathens they are! But I must remain gracious; I am the Sultan of Sultans who will save his empire from these animals.

I feel somewhat odd; I am queasy. All this heat, all this anticipation, all this odor. The unusual warmth of this evening has me sweating underneath my turban. That sherbet drink is very tart; too tart. I call for more water; I am so thirsty on this hot evening.

I cannot rid my nostrils of the smell of that rancid pelt.

My son, Giyaseddin, hands me another goblet of sherbet. Drink, my honored Sultan Father, drink, he says. But this sherbet is too bitter, I cannot serve it to my guests – oh, what do I care, these unrefined Mongols will not be able to tell that it is not as sweet as it should be, anyway. Drink up, I nod, drink up.

I am tired from these three days of festivities; always bending, nodding, talking, listening to the translator and waiting for the grunts of the ambassador in return. So slow he is to grunt back to me. Grunts, only grunts, no poetry from this band of brutes; Ibn Bibi is right.

I have nothing in common with this man and his people. They wear beads and bird feathers and ribbons; they live in a world of ignorance. They talk to trees and worship turtles. I am so glad my people are enlightened by the Book; we have seen God's light and read it in our Holy Qur'an.

Slowly he raises his hand and slaps it on my back, spraying food when he speaks. His manners disgust me but I must keep calm. I must bury my pride deep into the ground; underneath this red carpet.

So warm – more water – stay focused, try not to think of that rancid smell. Think of the rose gardens of Konya, full of soft, pink petals and melodious birds. I am doing the right thing for my people; yes, I must withstand this base boar at my side, here, in my noble palace of the Devlethane at Kayseri.

Ibn Bibi, I hope you are noting all of this carefully. This banquet is the most important one of my reign; so do not miss one detail. Tonight I save my people's lives by handing over my soul to this ignoble pig from the Ocean, but I swallow my pride, for my people come first. She always told me that.

So smelly, so dirty; now he wipes his greasy hands from the chicken onto my carpets. Oh Hanife, I am so glad you cannot see this; this lout who is wiping his filth on the stars that blaze across your carpets.

So hot so hot, I wave to the page to come over and fan me.

My mind wanders away from this moment; that smell, anything to keep me from thinking about it.

My queen could not have forsaken me; I do not understand anything anymore. My regal and loving queen did not betray me, no, I cannot believe that, but the proof is there. Our Turquoise of Love, where is it now?

Now he is spitting out the bones from his fat cheeks.

Page! More water please, I cannot quench this thirst; it rages within me, my mouth is so dry. My cheeks feel flushed, my head is boiling, but I cannot remove my turban in front of these guests. Why does my head spin so?

I wish she were here tonight at my side. She would tell me I am doing what needs to be done, she who was always so wise and steadfast, always my polestar. I should never have doubted her, never have tossed her aside. All glowed rainbows and turquoise moonbeams wherever she passed. But all of that is long ago; it is too late to turn back what I have done.

I hear the musicians now, jingling tambourines, reedy clarinets, clinking bells, drums and strings in flight. I hear voices singing spirited melodies. I see the cupbearers with their gold belts circling around the guests like moving cypress trees. I hear the flute introduce the refrain of the black-haired singer. Her voice warbles like a nightingale. "*Take your share of well-being and pleasure, for everything, even though the goal be far away, shall end.*" You sing for me tonight, do you not, my lovely; you feel my pain sitting next to this reeking man.

The bone-spitting, drooling boar is now holding up his smelly pelt for me to kiss. God, you endowed me with powers and properties that were sent to me for a reason. I must show courage in front of these heathens so that my people may survive.

For eighteen years I have struggled to build this empire, in the face of enemies within and without. I have withstood political maneuvers, treachery, revolts, and murder to achieve my goals, but I have built the finest empire on the face of the earth. And now I must hand it over to this heathen on a copper platter. He will eat it and spit out its bones just like that chicken. I am repulsed, but I have no choice.

Am I to survive? Yes, I will, I will continue to live in Konya in my palace, or perhaps I will flee this smell and go to Kubadabad, there, where all is so sweet. They will go away, once I have bowed my allegiance to them. They will take their smelly pelts and return to that valley of snow from whence they came. I will live in beauty and light, and will remember when moonbeams shone turquoise over my empire.

So hot, more water please

I see my emirs in front of me, goblets in hand. I take another fruit sherbet, wild blackberry this time. Still too bitter; perhaps it is too early in the season, they are picked too soon, but I drink it greedily on this hot night, my son Giyaseddin fills my goblet up again with juice, he is seeking my forgiveness; he has it, I harbor no ill will to him

Red, everything is red. I look down at the red of my robe, I note the red of the ink in the pot that I will use to sign this treaty, I imagine the red of Ruby's collar, I touch the red of Hanife's wool on this carpet, I recall the painted red chevrons on my Aspendos and Alaiye palaces, I remember the red of all the blood of my enemies that I have spilled onto the steppes in order to build this empire, all is red before my eyes now it is so hot so hot. I see blue too, blue of the Alaiye waves, blue of my Moon Fairy's turquoise, blue of those tiles in my palace, blue of the skies of God's paradise, blue red all the colors now swirl in front of my eyes

I look for Ruby but I do not see her. I specifically asked that she be brought into this tent with me! Where is she, she must be here with me tonight, she is my good luck charm, she, who is ever faithful to me, never disappoints me, never fails to inspire me. As long as she is at my side, I am the Greatest of all Sultans. I call for a page to have her brought in, I need her next to me

I see my food taster *Chashnigir* Emir Nariruddin Ali approach my rug. Behind him pages carry copper platters laden with succulent dishes. I prepare only the best for my guests, but what would this boar know of any of that? I hear the roar of the boar's guffaws in my ear, they echo so far away inside of my head. What is so funny to him? I am having trouble hearing I cannot follow what is being said

The page puts a platter on the round copper tray in front of me. He lifts up the lid to the platter. I see a flock of roasted partridges there, so tiny and fine, little delicate birds set atop lentils and onions. Steam swirls, the aroma rises, my heart lifts. This food will taste good and perhaps eating something will help me feel better. It is so hot though, my appetite is not strong

Chashnigir Ali, my trusted head taster, samples one of the birds. He approves, he nods. He takes another bird and breaks off the most succulent piece of the thigh and hands it to me. My piece is stuffed with rice cooked in butter with pistachios and raisins, and I am pleased that the palace chef has remembered my favorite dish. At least I can relish this pleasure tonight

I take a few bites and savor the tender flesh of the birds. The palace chef has done a fine job, it is juicy this food will help my head stop turning

Suddenly a knife runs through my gut. I grab my stomach and double over. I heave all over Hanife's rug

What is happening to me? My head is spinning now. Sweat pours from me in rivers. Kamyar! Kamyar is at my side; his face is white. Something is very wrong. I am sweating I tell him we must get out of here and that he must take me to the Keykubadiyye. My doctor is there and he knows all about herbs and cures. I have eaten something very rotten and spoiled; he can cure this food poisoning with his goat milk and honey water steeped in pine kernels, yes, he will help me. Get me out of here I must get to the Keykubadiyye Kamyar help me

I see my guests run away in horror at the sight of my face and my vomitus; the evening is disrupted. I can no longer hear anything. Suddenly there is motion around me. Kamyar is lifting me onto Night Shining White I slump over onto his neck

I tell Emir Karatay to stay and take care of the guests do not sign that treaty whatever you do

Kamyar leads me out of the Palace walls, we start to gallop, other men are at my side keeping me from falling off the horse. I cannot maintain my balance I cannot sit straight in my saddle

The wind is rustling in the trees outside and in my ears as I race down the road to the Keykubadiyye. Hang on to your Night Shining White, hang on, you will make it I have been ill many times before, but this burning is by far the worst I have ever felt it feels like a scalding iron from the smithy's shop in the bazaar is being twisted around inside my guts my heart is beating so fast

I feel the pain spreading in sharp, stabbing pangs to my heart and then back down to my gut again

I retch

Steeds harnessed with iron hooks are now dragging me across the Mashad plain I sit up, grasping my sides to get some air

I cramp, I am rigid, the pain diminishes I cramp again I can hardly breathe I fall from my horse

Demons are chewing on my innards, stripping my flesh as if it were a leg of roast chicken yes, that bird, I took a piece of it and all suddenly turned to pain

My face is rigid I cannot make my lips move my voice will only come out in a chopping bark

Knives are drawn out of their sheaths and are ready to plunge I feel them coming

Kamyar lifts me atop Night Shining White again we continue along our way

I slump over

I stop by the side of the road to vomit again

I hear the echo of my words in my ears I can no longer speak

We arrive at the palace I see the green lake

I cannot move I cannot breathe Azrail you are standing on my chest get off Azrail, you are hurting me

My mind clears for a moment yes it is now clear to me what has happened this is no accident I motion to

Kamyar I whisper into Kamyar's ear I tell him I know who did this to me

I look down and see green bile all over the red I heave and gasp for air

I can now smell the poison there in the green slime. There in that pile of poison lies the destiny of the Seljuk Empire

I am not afraid

I am the Sultan of Sultans, the World Renowned, the Eminence of the World and the Faith

I see turquoise

I see the angel and the demon at the top of the Majestic Mountain

I see the moon

I see a comet of bright light blaze across the night sky

I see

PART 3

A SULTANA REIGNS

1237-1243

My son, my son, O my son!
You have not gone among the enemy and cut off heads,
You have not killed men and spilled blood.
Take your forty chestnut-eyed young men,
Go up to the summit of the great mountain…
While I war and while I fight
While I struggle and clash my blade,
See! Learn! And lie in wait to help us, son.

-Lady Burla, Book of Dede Korkut

It was now the time when I, the caravansarai of Mahperi Hatun at Pazar, would rise from mere mud into an idea, and then into a reality. Perhaps it was the most exciting time I will ever know, that of leaving the mud behind and rising to my grandeur with course after course of finely-laid limestone blocks.

A fine time for me perhaps, but oh, that was a sad time for my Lady! How could a woman this pure, this generous and this loving, be dealt, again, such painful blows from the hands of those around her? But, she learned to fight, to impose and to survive.

She was desolate, certainly, but not defeated. No, she was much too strong for that, my Sultana! In that mud of despair she found the courage to build a new future, just as she found in the mud of the plains of Anatolia the substance to lead projects that would astonish her court and her people. She turned this colossal moment of malignancy into the inspiration for a willfull explosion of creation, and I, and other buildings all over the plains, now took form in her mind. Instead of bearing more children she gave souls to monuments, instead of giving kisses she drew designs, instead of whispering tender words into her husband's ear she issued firm commands to the workmen on her construction sites.

Yes. She fought, she grew, and she survived, and, along with her, the face of Anatolia changed. Alone, without her husband, perhaps, but she did not abandon his dreams for the Empire, or her dream to become a woman worthy of being called a Sultana. Would I be here today if she had not found such a will to persevere? She was a determined one, my Lady was, fiber by fiber, as determined as any man in that court, and certainly as strong as her Sultan, now gone. She stood up to her accusers and she rose above them all. My rising stones are witness to that strength.

Chapter 69

Reign of Silence

The Sultan was laid out on a clean table and the imam gave the final full ablution of his body, to cleanse him for the coming journey to eternity. The warm, scented water washed away from his skin all remains of his terrible retching of the previous evening. Perfume was applied to his head and nose, at the points which touched the ground when he prostrated in prayer to God. He was purified now, ready to meet his Creator.

The Sultan's long corpse was wrapped in a shroud of three pieces of white linen cloth and placed in a wooden coffin covered with a green shroud, which was laid out in the open courtyard in front of his palace of Keykubadiyye, in the shadow of the Majestic Mountain. The coffin was set perpendicularly to the direction of the mosque of the Holy city of Mecca. After the noon prayer, the imam walked up to the coffin and stood directly in front of it, and the men of the court gathered in rows behind him. Solemn silence reigned, and even the birds and the wind hushed their song.

The imam opened his funeral prayer by reciting the verse to the greatness of God, "*It is God who is magnificent.*" Although he had stood in front of coffins and recited this Magnification prayer many times before, on this day it was hard for him to contain his emotion, for he had never before led a funeral prayer for a sultan. Every soul will taste death, he thought, even a mighty sultan, but this death is too soon and too harsh to bear.

At the moment the imam began his first recitation of the Magnification of God, the worshippers standing behind him briefly raised their hands to their ears, and each one of them recited silently to himself the *subhaneke* prayers, at the same time as the imam called it aloud:

> O *God, You are perfect, You are to be praised and glorified.*
> *Your name is blessed.*
> *Your works are holy and marvelous.*
> *May Your name be praised.*
> *There is no god but You.*

The wooden coffin, which had been covered with a lid of tinned iron, was then set on a pair of trestles on a simple wooden wagon covered with a canopy, in order to protect the Sultan from the hot June sun on his journey back to his capital city of Konya.

Slowly, the procession left the verdant grounds of the Keykubadiyye Palace and headed for the great Long Road that linked the cities of Kayseri and Konya. Countless times had the Sultan traveled the length of this road between the two chief cities of his Empire, but now, on this final journey, he was being carried homeward in a covered litter, flanked by guards and attendants with the same ceremony performed as when he set out to conquer more lands for his great empire. Night Shining White was tied to the rear of the wagon that carried the Sultan's coffin. His tail, clipped as a sign of mourning, now laid across the top of the coffin. The proud horse did not sprightly prance this day as he usually did, and all remarked that his empty saddle appeared today a burden too heavy to carry.

The procession paused at the vast han near Aksaray for another funeral ceremony, where the imam led the same Magnification prayer from the steps of the kiosk mosque in the courtyard. It was only fitting that the Sultan should be honored here at this grand caravansarai, built by his will to the glory of his Empire. No one present was able to hold back his grief at the sight of the coffin laid out on a splendid red rug at the base of the little square mosque in the middle of the courtyard. All prayed to God for the safekeeping of the soul of this, His most devoted servant, the Sultan Alaeddin Keykubad, Eminence of the World and the Faith, now hovering at the door of the garden of God's eternal paradise.

It took them four days to reach Konya. Upon their arrival on the fourth day of June, the crowds lined the streets to watch the funeral procession pass by. Jelaleddin Rumi, the son of the Sultan's beloved spiritual master Bahaeddin Veled, stood at the side of the road to wait for the Sultan to go by on his last journey. As he watched the coffin lumber down the road, he vividly remembered the day sixteen years ago when the Sultan had ridden out to greet his father Bahaeddin as they arrived in Konya for the first time. He was a fresh young Sultan then, with a cocky assurance that gave every promise for success in everything he set out to accomplish. And now, at the age of 45, his Empire was laying him to rest.

Jelaleddin Rumi's eyes misted as the green-clad coffin passed directly in front of him, and whispered a silent prayer for the Sultan.

"Honored Sultan! When I think about my life as I live it now compared to then, it is as if I, too, have conquered many horizons alongside of you. These spiritual victories I owe to you, esteemed Alaeddin Keykubad, for your encouragement to my father, your generosity for the creation of numerous medreses and your invitation to wise scholars to come to Konya made all this richness possible. O, my Sultan! I vow to you that I will continue to work to bring glory and renown to your medreses. I will strive to create a Konya for you that will be known all over the world for its holiness and purity for all eternity! You are too large to be contained in a coffin. Your subjects will always carry your grave in their hearts and not in the ground. This is your legacy to us, and we accept its charge. May God always shine his light on your grave. Verily we are from God and unto Him is our final journey!" the young man murmured, his head hung low in sadness.

The procession climbed the last leg of the journey, up to the top of the hill in the middle of the city, the hill that would forevermore bear his name. There he was buried in all simplicity, in the sepulcher of his ancestors; there, high upon the mound in the center of his capital city, in the shadow of his great mosque with its glittering turquoise mihrab and vibrant red rugs. There, he would rest alongside of his glorious grandfather Kilich Arslan I and his father Giyaseddin Keyhüsrev I, the great Sultans who handed him an empire to expand and grow. He had not disappointed them, and could now deservedly rest honorably at their sides, his green-shrouded catafalque adding to the illustrious row of Seljuk royal heroes already lying there.

☪ ☪ ☪

The Sultan's funeral procession passed through a capital city where silence now reigned. The medreses stopped their droning of Qur'anic verses, the bazaars ceased their shouting of the delights of their merchandise, the streets were deserted of voices and the shrieks of children at play, and the hammers of the tinsmiths in the back alley workshops fell silent. Only the whispers of prayers could be heard, emanating from the lips of all the citizens of the great whirling city of Konya, imploring God for the care of the soul of their Sultan who had watched over them for these past eighteen years. What was to become of them now?

Back in Kayseri, the Mongols retired to their tents after the startling events of the banquet, for even these barbarians were dismayed by what had happened. We will be back to continue these negotiations, they thought to themselves; there is no need to push right now for this joint venture with the Seljuks. Our bid has been made, our terms have been stated. Once the succession of the new Sultan has been established, we will pursue our plan again with him. It is best to remain silent now, in order to let the Empire grieve for its beloved Sultan.

The court officials and viziers scurried about their duties in a state of disbelief. They needed to plan for the next event: the crowning of a new Sultan and the reorganization of the government. The ambitious scrambled to position themselves, the humble asked how they could best serve, and the rest of the court waited in silence for instructions to follow.

The emirs huddled together in groups and hummed among themselves about the events that had taken place. Some questioned the facts; others seemed to accept the situation. No one was quite sure of their ultimate fate, but they were ready to play their role in the building of the future empire. While some mourned and worried, others remained unemotional and calmly confident.

The troops of the mighty Seljuk army hung their heads and swords in despair, and clung to the presence of Commander Kamyar as their strength for the future, because he was the last man to speak with their Sultan. The *ney* flute and the drum beat around their campfires at night in a plaintive elegy for their courageous leader; he who had never been afraid to go farther and faster, he who always stood at the front of the line and never hid in his tent during battles. They shared their personal stories of the Sultan, he, the greatest soldier of them all, a master tactician with a singular vision; a soldier whose zeal for Empire kept him warmer than any cloak on the coldest of nights. Yes, such was their glorious warrior, Alaeddin Keykubad, Most Revered Lord, Father of Conquests and Victories, may God shine light on his grave.

A leopard with a ruby collar paced back and forth incessantly in the garden of the Devlethane in Kayseri while the others went about their business. The hand that now fed her was not the one with long, slender fingers that had taken care of her for her whole life, the only pair of hands she had ever trusted. She became irritable, she became frightened; she tugged at her chain and roared and hissed at anyone who came near her. Her feline instinct told her that her master had been taken from her and that she would never see him again, just as her instinct had informed her that she would never again suckle the cub that had been taken from her side so long ago.

The servants of the court buzzed with gossip and questions, fear and anger. No one knew what to think or what would come next. Pages were edgy and dropped their serving trays, the cooks lost joy in their work and chopped their fingers in distraction, and the palace guards now stood in futility in front of empty divan rooms.

One widow of the Sultan gleefully waited in Konya, and gave orders to her servants to prepare her baggage for the journey to join her son Izzeddin in Kayseri, where he would soon be crowned the next Sultan of the Seljuks. She would make sure to take her finest robes and jewels, for now, as the most important woman in the land, she must definitely look her most alluring.

Another widow of the Sultan sat despairing at her window at the palace of the Devlethane in Kayseri, stunned by all the disastrous events that had taken place in such a short time: smashing plates and friendships, calumny and denied thrones, banishment and shame, and now a death and the definitive ending to her life as she knew it. Alone and silent, she sat in her room and wondered what was to become of her. She grieved for the man she had loved with her entire being.

Silence reigned in everyone's heart. Silence of sadness, silence of shock, or silence of shame, each one determined that for themselves. Despite the flurry of rumors, no one dared to ask that one question now whirling in all their heads, yet everyone seemed certain of the answer. No one wished to pronounce it out loud, in this reign of silence, but it hung heavy in the air.

Yes, of one thing everyone was certain. Azrail the Angel of Death had not appeared unsolicited at the banquet for the Mongols. No, the Angel of Death had been summoned by persons still unnamed; this Angel of Death who had carried in his hand a vial of a potent tincture made from the roots of the poisonous nightshade plant, ready to pour into the fruit sherbet and the stuffing of a Sultan's partridge.

Chapter 70

Pointing Fingers

Fingers point. In the market, they indicate the chosen apple; on the road, the direction to take. They poke at the chest of an aggressor during an argument and they jab into the air during heated discussions. But above all, they point, in accusation, to the guilty.

The fingers of the many hands at the Devlethane Palace sought to point to the person that had brought such evil to the court, for it was now apparent that Azrail had not appeared unsolicited to leave with the Sultan's soul. The emirs, the Mongols, the palace cook, the family, the soldiers, the guards: no one was spared the pointing finger. The people were confused and frightened now that their leader had been taken away from them, the court had to deal with an impending crisis of government, the family mourned, and the emirs were angry. All was in disarray, and fear filled the air: there were Mongol enemies at the court, a strong leader now lay dead, and a seven year-old boy was set to step up to the throne at Kayseri. The fingers felt that if they could point to someone to punish for it, all would become better. So point they did.

☪ ☪ ☪

Köpek thought long and hard about how he would play his hand to resolve this situation. As one of the most powerful viziers at the court, he knew his word would have much impact and would be listened to by all. Ever since the meeting at his quarters a few days earlier, he knew that he had already been heard. At last, the time had come for him to take the place he felt he so rightfully deserved as leader of this Empire. He had been preparing this moment for a long time, and now his finger pointed to the golden fruit dangling in front of him on the tree of revenge, ready to pluck.

The Dog knew he had to move swiftly, for a decisive voice of reason would be the one heard above the roiled waters of fear and doubt now flooding the court. He called the emirs together again to discuss the situation.

"My Emirs," Köpek spoke, addressing them in a resolute tone, "We are faced with a critical state of affairs now that our honored leader, Alaeddin Keykubad, The Holy Wise One, may his soul rest in peace, has left us. At this moment, with the ambassadors of our Mongol enemies sitting in our very midst, we must show unity and strength or else we risk losing everything. We must not panic, but move with reasoned judgment and firm resolve to show them that we are still a force to be reckoned with."

The emirs nodded in agreement and urged him to continue.

"What we have before us is a situation which, in my eyes, is not going to prove the most advantageous one for us in the end," he continued. "We need a strong ruler right now, one capable of dealing with the Mongols in a skillful and forceful way in order to show them that we are still the masters of Anatolia. Unfortunately, I do not think that such a heavy responsibility can be borne on the shoulders of a boy who has barely learned to walk. We have able administrators in our government, such as the viziers Jelaleddin Karatay and Muhezzibuddin Ali, who are capable of managing the affairs of state. Commander Kamyar has the entire faith of the Seljuk troops. But what we need is a forceful figurehead in the eyes of the world – and in front of those Mongols – to inspire the future destiny of the empire. I do not see how this responsibility can be filled by the designated heir apparent, Izzeddin al-Din Kilich Arslan. How can a young child who does not even know the alphabet navigate our empire through the troubled waters of the Mongol Ocean? Imagine what the world will say when they see that the great Seljuk Empire is now ruled by a little boy! No, my good emirs, I feel that the Sultan's choice of heir, taken in a rash moment of anger, will not ensure the survival of our Empire!" he concluded, with an emphatic tone that rang in everyone's ears.

"But Izzeddin al-Din Kilich Arslan was designated as the heir and there can be no changing the will of a Sultan!" remarked Emir Gürcüoğlu Zahiruddevle.

"Perhaps it may seem so, but I am telling you, that youngest son of Alaeddin Keykubad cannot sit on the throne at this time! It will be a disaster for all of us! No, I tell you, there is a better solution. There is another son who should sit on his empty throne, and, as his first born, this is the son who rightfully deserves that throne," he boldly stated, fearlessly putting forth his daring proposal.

"You mean Giyaseddin Keyhüsrev?" gasped the Emir Altinbeh. "But the Sultan stripped him of that right after that fateful day in Kubadabad!"

Köpek raised his hands to calm the group which had become agitated. "Forgive me if I seem to speak disrespectfully of the departed, may God shine his light on his soul, but it would appear that the Sultan had acted out of spite when he appointed Izzeddin al-Din Kilich Arslan as heir. We are not here to judge the wisdom of our departed Sultan. We are here to make sure that his empire continues to survive and to flourish, and that is what we must discuss together."

"But, this decision has been taken! There is nothing we can do to change it! That would be heresy!" exclaimed Emir Taceddin.

"Nonsense! Stand tall, my good men!" Köpek blurted out. "Of course, we can take the reins of destiny in our own hands if we so desire! We are the strongmen of this Empire now; its forceful leaders and champions of our local lands. It is our duty to best represent the interests of our citizens. It is clear that we cannot have this little cub sit on our throne. We need a roaring lion! The Sultan chose him as heir; yes, but at a time when he believed that it would be many years before the boy would be called to reign. Fate has determined otherwise. We must now accept that the only solution for us is to support his other son, his first born, already educated by the finest tutors in the land, able and mature enough to carry out the duties of this position. Why, he himself has already fathered a son and the next heir! Giyaseddin Keyhüsrev is the son we must back, my men. This is not heresy, but common sense. We have no choice, and we must move fast."

Köpek looked around the room to see how his words were being received. The group was not arguing with him, which was a positive sign. Köpek was pleased to see how he was leading the emirs to accept his viewpoint, and that his carefully-planned scheme was falling into place. After the meeting of emirs he organized before the Sultan's death to discuss the proposed treaty with the Mongols, he had taken aside several he trusted and had garnered their support, through promises of gold and power. He knew that he already had many men on his side; those ever-slighted emirs who shared the same burning desire for power. Köpek was confident that they would carry the day, but he needed to plead his cause to the rest of the group. His plan could not appear as a total mutiny, but as a well-reasoned decision by all the leaders of the Empire.

"We will present a plan to the government. We will let them know that there will be revolts in our lands if it is not followed. I will get the support of the Queen Mahperi, who is so beloved by the people of this kingdom. We will join our forces together to make this happen. We must rally around the eldest son of our departed Sultan Alaeddin Keykubad, for only he can stand as tall as the shadow his father cast over us, may God preserve his soul! And I tell you, we must take charge and move fast, or all will be lost! He must be enthroned in the next few days before those Mongols get a chance to interfere!"

☪ ☪ ☪

Like colored pieces of tile being laid for a mihrab mosaic, Köpek began to cement his plan in place for the Kingdom, one emir at a time. With methodical precision, he went from man to man to get his support, and he found that a slight tug at the purse strings was all that was needed. Instead of pointing a finger, he crooked his index and beckoned all to come to his side and listen. And listen they did, stirred into action by a desire for revenge, albeit a different one than his. The memory of the fate of the twenty-three emirs who had been punished was flamed anew by the fan of Köpek's perfidy. He sought to show them that their fortunes would be kept intact and even grow if they backed his plan. The promise of glittering gold, Köpek knew, was the most convincing argument he could ever dangle in front of their ambitious eyes. One by one, he informed them that if they backed Giyaseddin Keyhusrev instead of Izzeddin Kilicarslan, he would make sure that they received significant rewards in land, treasure and power, more revenue, more tax exemptions for their crops, more independence from central control, and, not to forget, a share of jewels and gold coins from the Sultan's private treasury.

He convinced them that the young son Izzeddin would require constant surveillance by the State ministers and legislators acting as his regents, and who would make all the decisions. The more power held in the hands of the State viziers meant less power in theirs, he argued. Ah, but a sixteen year old youth, especially one trained for years by the eminent Ertokush, would be entirely capable of making his own decisions, especially if they were prompted by the wise counsel of the emirs. He convinced them that the new sultan would not be a coward in front of the Mongols like his father was, ready to sell out the Empire to them, a political point which had irked many of them. Köpek convinced them as well to move quickly and invest Giyaseddin before Queen Gaziye and her group of supporters arrived at Kayseri and got wind that there was a mutinous plot afoot. They needed to take control of the power, invest Giyaseddin on the throne and start to rule before anyone could object.

Although he managed to win over most of the emirs to his side, Köpek was challenged by some who remained steadfastly faithful to Alaeddin's wishes for his heir designate. Kayir Khan, Army Commanders Kamyar and Kaymeri all felt that in respect to the deceased Sultan, his wishes should be upheld. All trusted the judgment of the Sultan, and if, when still young and in sound health, he chose a young boy as his heir apparent, he must have believed that Giyaseddin was not fit to carry the royal banner of the Seljuks. They believed this because the young man seemed to do nothing but drink wine in his tent and spend time with his female servants. Even when not compared to his illustrious father, he still appeared incapable of wearing the mantle of the Seljuks on his slumped shoulders. Better to have a young lad supported by a strong regency of court viziers, they reasoned, than this dissolute young man.

To implement his plan, Köpek needed to start with the most important, and, at the same time, the easiest person to sway to his side: the young Giyaseddin Keyhüsrev. Ever since he introduced the boy to the pleasures of his sugar, he knew that whatever he said would be accepted by the young man. Already, the young man had sired children from the women Köpek had brought to live in the Palace as his wives. Köpek had deftly convinced him of the role he needed to play at the banquet of the Mongols, and he had carried out his task well. Köpek desperately wanted him on the throne, for once there, he knew how easy it would be for him to take over the reins and push the insecure young man into whatever direction he wanted.

☪ ☪ ☪

Köpek entered Giyaseddin's tent at the Keykubadiyye and found him lying on the low cushions and tickling two of his servant girls. Laughing uncontrollably at their mischief, they were so absorbed in their game that they did not hear Köpek enter.

"Giyaseddin! Get up! I need to speak with you! Send these girls away, now!" he barked.

The young son threw his head back in laughter, and it was obvious that he had been drinking. He continued on with his game, as if he had not even noticed that Köpek had entered the room.

Köpek drew his knife and flashed it in front of the faces of the girls. "Get out, I say! Get out!" he bellowed, his ugly grimace frightening the girls as much as the shiny blade. They quickly ran out of the room.

"Giyaseddin, sit up and listen to me! You need to be serious for a moment!" growled Köpek. "I and a group of emirs have convinced enough of the ministers and counselors to accept you as the rightful heir. There is even more encouraging news. Despite the objections of Commander Kamyar to your taking the throne, I have secured the support of the military behind us. I have slipped a gold coin into the pocket of every soldier who shows us allegiance, and I can tell you they follow the shine of metal more faithfully than the orders of that Kamyar! We will deal with him later, but for the present time, all is set up for you to assume power" he explained.

Giyaseddin pulled himself up and adjusted his robes, and nodded to Köpek with sheepish eyes.

"So I need you to put aside your pleasures for a few days, or at least until you take the throne. I need your head clear and unmuddled. I need you to show some serious concern for what is happening! You must go to the mosque at prayer time to show to the people that you are remorseful for the death of your father. Do you hear me?"

Giyaseddin looked up at Köpek, his flush face suddenly turning pale. Slurring his words, he mumbled, "You mean this is really going to happen? I am truly going to become the next Sultan? But...I do not know if I am ready yet...I mean I still have so much to learn..."

When Köpek heard his wavering voice, he struggled to keep his calm, for he remembered that severity and reprimand never worked well with the young man. That had been the tactic of his father, and it caused the boy to flee into his shell of insecurity. Instead, he needed to focus on the approach that works best with him: sugar and honey. He needed to remember all the self doubts that burdened the son in the face of the blinding rays of his father's image. Yet, the events of the banquet had already shown Köpek that the young man listened to whatever he told him.

"My good Giyaseddin, have no fear! The golden throne of the Seljuk Sultans awaits you! All the emirs back you and believe in you, and soon you will be sitting on that dais! You will be every measure the leader your father was; and what revenge it will be for you to show that you can take this kingdom higher than he dreamed possible; he, who had no faith in your capacities; preferring to choose that Golden Boy Izzeddin!" he emphasized, hoping to bolster the young man's confidence. "You are the rightful heir to this throne, and, if you work with me, as a team we will achieve that goal. We have one more hurdle to cross, but we can do it. We have always worked well, have we not, my good lad? Have confidence in my power to make you the Sultan, and in a few short days, the throne will be yours!"

"All right, I will do as you say, for you always do know best. But what is that one thing that is still standing in my way?" Giyaseddin prodded.

Before answering this question, Köpek paused to collect his thoughts, for this part of his plan was a delicate one, but capital to the total success of his scheme.

"Your mother. She is the last and most important part of our plan to put you on the throne."

Chapter 71

Sharp Is the Sword of Poisoned Ink

For his plan to succeed, Köpek knew he needed the support of the most prominent person in the court: Queen Mahperi Hatun. Köpek needed her influence over her son, her reassuring presence in the eyes of the people, her intelligence and clarity in front of the ministers. Without her support, his whole scheme was doomed. He had to find a way to ensure that she worked with him.

Mahperi loathed him, that he knew, but he had no doubts that she wanted her son to reign on the throne of his father. He needed her influence if he was to succeed in manipulating her son as he desired. For if there was one thing Köpek knew above all else, it was the supreme devotion her son held for her. Köpek would be incapable of managing the son if the mother was not in his camp.

He also knew he would never be able to manipulate her, for she was much too intelligent for that, but he had to find a way to keep her in line by holding a lethal power over her. He had already outmaneuvered her at Kubadabad, and he could do it again. Only this time, he did not need a glorious turquoise gem to do his bidding; now he would count on the flowing colors of the pen of Ibn Bibi to turn into poison.

☪ ☪ ☪

When the palace page came into Mahperi's rooms that evening to announce that Köpek wished to speak with her, she felt her skin crawl at the thought of seeing his ugly scowl. In her terrible grief, there was no room for more strife, and with Köpek, that was always to be expected. She had not had any contact with him since the fateful day at Kubadabad, and she was certain that he was behind the calamity of those events. She was frightened for the future, for she knew what this man was capable of doing. Would she escape with her life, now that her husband was dead? She was also convinced that somewhere in all the vileness surrounding the death of the Sultan, the signature of the Dog Köpek was writ large. Of that she was sure.

Mahperi agreed to meet him the next morning in the divan chamber. As she sat waiting for him to arrive, she noticed how gloomy the room was now, emptied of the radiant presence and firm voice of her husband. When she heard Köpek's squawking voice outside the door, she bowed her head so as not to look at his repulsive face.

"My honored Sultana Mahperi Hatun, please forgive me for intruding upon your grief, for I cannot imagine how deep it must be. May God give you the strength to confront this loss of our beloved Sultan, may his soul rest in eternal light," he said, his unctuous tone rankling instead of reassuring.

She could not bring herself to look at him, but she felt Köpek's intense eyes upon her, observing the marks of grief on her drawn face. *Stand tall, Mahperi, stand tall. You are still the Queen of the Seljuks. Show no fear in front of this man.* Mahperi stood there mutely awaiting the rest of his declaration. Köpek took note of her resistance to his overture of platitudes, and plunged on.

"I have called this meeting today because we are currently faced with a critical situation, and it is in both our interests to resolve it in the best possible way. We must put our past differences behind us and join forces for the good of the Empire, for its success now lies in our hands. I have called you here to tell you what I now expect of you," he explained.

Mahperi stood stunned at his words, and she felt her body swaying to maintain her composure. All of the hurt of Kubadabad, all of the vileness of his actions, and all of the grief of the death of her husband made her head spin and destroyed her sense of composure.

"What *you* expect of me?" she snapped. "Since when do you give *me* orders? I do not yet think that you are in a position to do that, no matter how grand you think your powers are. What vanity you have!" she spurted out.

"Ah, but my dear Queen," he retorted with a sneer, "Have you not forgotten that I am the dear advisor of your son, the one to whom he looks above all others? That I am the one who leads him in all that he does? So it would appear that we must work together for we both want the same thing: to put your son on the throne."

Mahperi was not sure what the Dog was implying by his remarks, but she held her tongue this time.

"My Lady Mahperi Hunat Hatun, listen to me, and listen to me well. While you were busy building a pleasure palace with that fancy Frenchman, I was working hard to promote the prospects of our Empire and the future of your son. I have every intention of putting him on the throne of the Seljuk Empire, and I know that is what you want as well. Any mother would. Despite the upheaval of the Sultan's appointment of the Golden Boy Izzeddin as heir, I have never lost faith in your son. I have done everything in my power to position him as the next Sultan, and in a few days I will orchestrate a coup and place him there. How dare you cross me with your pride! I am the kingmaker here;

you should bow down to my feet and kiss them for having maneuvered to place your son on the throne instead of that son of your rival Gaziye! I have always worked to ensure what is best for the court, and I continue to do the same now that the Sultan has departed," he asserted.

At this last remark of his, Mahperi could not hold back her resentment. "Always worked for the best of our Empire? Surely you take me for a fool! You have always worked for your personal gain and fame, you mean to say! I am certain that you had something to do with my husband's death, just like you orchestrated my downfall at Kubadabad!" she hissed at him.

Köpek chuckled smugly at her remark. "Now, now, those are nothing but empty accusations! Yet what we certainly do not want is for anyone to accuse your son of having had anything to do with the unfortunate death of his father, now do we? No, that must be avoided at all costs. But my dear, if you knew how the nasty rumors are flying fast and furious all over this court, reaching down the Long Road to Konya as well! They are saying the good Sultan was poisoned! These rumors must not involve your son, and we certainly do not want the emirs to be blamed, either, now would we? They will be the most important allies of your son, and it would not be a wise idea to alienate them when he takes that throne, don't you agree? And, oh yes, I certainly wouldn't want any of those rumors to swirl around *your* regal head, either. Yet, the sad fact remains that someone must take the blame for your husband's death. The people will not stop until they find that person. And who do you suppose that could be? The candidates are many....why... and as I said, even your name might be one of them," he pointed out, boring his eyes at her.

Slowly, Mahperi began to see the complexity of his vile plan.

"I have told the emirs that you will support them if they elect your son to the throne. You will support them morally, politically and above all, financially, or else all will fail and both you and your son risk losing your lives, just like Alaeddin did. You are a very rich woman, Mahperi, that I know, and luckily you are, for it will cost you much to ensure that your son sits on that throne."

Mahperi stared up at him speechless, unable to react in the face of all of this information.

"Yes, Mahperi, you will pledge your support to me. I want your son on the throne, and I will get him there. So hear me well: if you are not with me on this, I will spread rumors around this court and kingdom about you; ugly rumors to the effect that you did indeed betray your husband in an immoral fashion at Kubadabad and in a deadly fashion here, and that you have done everything possible to put your son on the throne and to destroy your rival. Yes indeed, it will be so very easy to spread the rumor that you had a very heavy hand in the invitation of Azrail to the banquet. I mean, when you look at it, you seem to be the person with the strongest motivation to seek revenge and remove the Sultan from the throne. But all of this will remain just rumors, as long as you choose to go along with my plan for putting your son on the throne."

"But no one in this land would ever believe that I was capable of killing my own husband!" Mahperi spurted out, her stomach cramping with disgust.

"Oh, of that I would not be so sure. There are many reasons why you would want to kill him. Your honor lost at Kubadabad, your son's throne stolen right from under your nose…such a shame, all will say. So once again, I repeat what I am expecting of you. Unless you go along with my plan and agree to support me and the emirs, I will take action against you. I will ask Ibn Bibi to pen a story that it was you who caused the death of your husband. All the court will read it and believe that you murdered him, after which you will be banished to the ends of the earth for all time. Is that what you want? No, I don't think so. So you see that it is completely in your power to prevent those potentially damaging rumors from spreading, my dear Mahperi," he concluded.

"And so you are holding the pen of Ibn Bibi over my head like the blade of a sword?" Mahperi asked. "Why, he would never commit such a travesty to history! He is an honest man at the service of depicting the greatness of my husband's legacy!"

Köpek laughed. "That little Ibn Bibi will do anything I ask him to do, because, unlike you, he knows how to befriend the most influential person in this court. He will dip his pen in the well of poisoned ink, and will write a story to damn you for eternity. And now, my proud and defiant Queen, you will at last bow your head to me, all for the sake of your son's future. And, if it is any consolation to you, I will take care of that other little Queen and her sons as well. Do not fear – I will make sure that they never give us any problems in the future. So! Do we have an understanding, Mahperi Hatun? Either you back the conditions of my plan, or your son will be denied the throne and you will be accused and banished – or even dare I say, beheaded – for the death of your husband. Those are your options. But take heart! You actually might like working with me. We could make quite a formidible team! Yes, this is the way it will be. It is what a mother's love is all about, is it not, Sultana Mahperi Hatun?"

Chapter 72

I Stand Behind the Door of Your Death

The fact of your death progresses in me slowly, without any understanding, yet dead you are, there is nothing to be said about that finality. I am now a widow and alone. Time is unreal, useless and uncalculated for me. I continue to say your name, your name in me as if you were there, there on the cliff in the moonlight of Kalonoros. Your death plays over and over in my mind, the veil of silence and anger of our last weeks together haunts me and freezes me, our love stopped in front of a door that someone slammed in our face, and now I stand behind it, in disbelief.

I gaze out from my window here at the Devlethane. I look at the very spot where I last saw you, a week now gone, crossing the courtyard to head out to the Mashad plain for the banquet with the Mongols. I see your tall frame stride with confidence to your destiny. Over and over again I replay that image in my eyes. I cannot leave this window for fear that image will disappear. I am fixed to this spot; my heart a leaf frozen inside a block of ice.

I will not leave this city of Kayseri. Here is where I will stay now, to be near you and the memory of that image. It is the only place where I will be able to live in peace, now that you are gone. My resolve to live here has not changed. I cannot leave this place where you last walked. I cannot set foot in Kubadabad with its painful memories of our last day together, I cannot go home to Kalonoros, I cannot return to Konya where the Raven sits perched in her tree at the top of the hill. No, I must stay here and try to heal this wound. I will bring Hanife to come and live with me here. I will survive. I must stay away from Köpek; I fear for my life now that he seems to be in charge, but I know our son will not let anything happen to me, despite all of these accusations that are swirling around this court. Yet, I feel the fingers pointing at me, as if it were I who wanted you gone.

Our son. Alaeddin, why did you forsake him? Surely not to punish me. How could you have let that Raven manipulate you to that extent?

Like any woman who has held her own ideas and defied men, I have made enemies. But I did not think the enemies would use my own son against me. Now, apparently, an enemy is set to spread the vile rumor that I have poisoned you in order to usurp the throne that you had willed to our son's younger half-brother. They seek to blame me for your death; me, who was locked away in my room that night, not even invited to attend the banquet. I was nowhere near that vileness. Yes, now Köpek is threatening me with total destruction: either I go along with his plan or my son will never see the throne. But it is he who wants to take your place, my Sultan, not our son! I am no fool; I know what he is planning behind his seemingly generous gesture. He thinks that by putting Giyaseddin on the throne there he will have no obstacles in his path, for our son has always looked up to him with admiration. You were so cold to our boy; it was only normal that he turned to Köpek. And now we will pay the price for that, my Sultan. In order to put my son on the throne, he is bribing my silence and demanding my agreement to stand out of the way so that he may dominate our son and run your kingdom as he wishes.

But you know me well, my Sultan, I will have a hard time holding my tongue and my spirit.

But I have no choice here. By standing by my son, I sustain everything you stood for and tried to build for your Empire. I will support all that we dreamed together since that first moonlit night at Kalonoros, down to that fatal day at Kubadabad when others slandered my honor in your eyes. I promise you, my Sultan, that I will continue your dream, and in that way, you will always be alive at my side. A little boy of seven is not capable of understanding anything; my son who grew up with you as his model, and with one of your most honored servants as his tutor can be the only possible heir to your throne. And I will be there to continue to remind him of his duty as the son of Alaeddin Keykubad, Eminence of the World. This is the choice I must take. I will stand back from the affairs of the court at Konya; I will remain here, and I will let Köpek have his way with my son. I will endure Köpek and accept his vile ways, all with the hope that my son will make as fine a sultan as you.

I do not wish to openly hurt Gaziye or her son, but I have lost too much to watch her take everything I have worked for. This throne belongs to my son, despite what you said. She will not deprive my son of his birthright. Oh, my beloved husband, I do not know who killed you, and perhaps it will never be known. But what I do know is that your first born son must reign.

I stand now behind the door of your death, in disbelief. But I promise you I will open it wide to the life of our son, the next Sultan of your glorious empire.

Chapter 73

Give, and It Will Be Given unto You

Thus the Dog became a kingmaker. Long and arduous had been his path to this day, but at last he had arrived. Revenge was taken and a Sultan was disposed of, emirs were manipulated and a powerful mother blackmailed. Above all, a malleable young man was persuaded to fight for the throne that was rightfully his, and to be prepared for a deadly battle. Köpek also informed Giyaseddin of the crucial role his mother would play in their plan, and that he now needed to speak with her to insure her cooperation and support.

☪ ☪ ☪

Giyaseddin entered his mother's room, and found her sitting on the cushion of the low couch, looking out the window. Her face was pale and lines had appeared on her forehead. She had lost weight since the death of Alaeddin, but her bearing was intact and her noble beauty shone forth, despite the grey pall to her skin. Any doubt that he had about the path he needed to take was erased once he saw that face. He must become the Sultan for her, for then she could reclaim the honor that had been stripped after the events of Kubadabad. I love you, my dear mother; I want to hear you call me "My Sultan" and watch the sunshine come back to your face.

"Good morning, my gracious mother," he said, bowing and kissing her hand as he sat down next to her. "I hope that you have found some peace in your soul after all the events we have been through of late."

Mahperi smiled as she looked up at the young man now in front of her. He was no longer the baby boy she bounced on her knee, or the young imp who stole halvah from the palace kitchens. In a few short days, he had become a man on the brink of his destiny. She peered up at his face and searched for the trace of his father, but it was not there. He is so different than Alaeddin, she thought, in temperament, coloring, movement, and bearing. She felt a stabbing pang of grief, for she realized that she would never be able to see the bright face of her Sultan reflected there. He was so energetic, that Sultan of mine! She recalled how the locks of the Sultan's hair always seemed to be blowing in the wind, even in the still of night. Her son did not have the blazing fire in his eyes as did his father. He did not have the sharp chisel for a nose and the chin that jutted out like a stallion tearing off into the distance, no matter what his rider did with his reins or heels. Yes, her Alaeddin had been a stallion in a world of ponies! He may not be his father, she told herself, but he is still the sultan's first son, and my first child.

Fiddling with his prayer beads, Giyaseddin seemed ill-at-ease and stammered a bit as he began to speak.

"M-m-mother, my honorable mother, I wanted to talk to you about all that is going on now and to ask your counsel. Köpek will not allow the throne to pass to my brother Izzeddin. In his opinion, the small boy will not be able to reign without the help of many courtiers and advisors, who will all fight to position themselves for power. The Empire needs one strong voice making decisions and that voice should be mine, in his view. I think he is right, but I have so many doubts. Mama, I am not sure I can do this!"

When she looked at him she saw that little lost boy on his way to Erzincan, instead of a young man on the brink of becoming the most powerful Sultan in Islam. "Oh my son, have confidence! You will be a magnificent Sultan, every inch your father! Do not doubt your capacities, or the wisdom of your vizier Köpek!" she insisted.

Yet despite her convincing tone, Mahperi knew the minute she pronounced those words, that they were hollow, for her son was definitely not the equal of his father. She knew that despite his rigid education and tutoring, her son was not a serious person, too addicted to pleasure and the ephemera of life. He had already fathered two children with two different women whom Köpek had placed at his disposal. She knew that Köpek was behind all of his addictions which reduced him to a state of docile stupor, as well the evening sessions of lavish entertainment. She closed her eyes and shuddered at the thought of these things and wondered where she had failed in his upbringing. Yet, it was not her fault that he had been taken from her direct care, and she knew she had lost the battle of his moral upbringing to Köpek. She knew as well that no matter how hard he tried, he would never stand as tall as his father. No one could. Alaeddin was too looming a figure; yes, that stallion among men could outrun them all.

"My son, I know that the events of the past few days have left you confused and frightened," she addressed him, trying her best to instill courage in him with kind words. "But your destiny as first-born is to become Sultan of this great empire. Now it is your turn to stand up for your rights and assume the mantle of the Sultan of the Seljuks upon your shoulders. You are going to make a glorious sultan, and above all, you will be *my* Sultan!" she gushed, taking him into her arms and holding him tight next to her.

After a few moments, Giyaseddin broke free of their embrace and looked into his mother's face to find the courage to continue. There was one last leg in the long upward climb to reach the throne at the top of the mountain, but it was the law and there was no ignoring it, no matter how steep the incline.

The mother of a Sultan must be a Muslim.

As sympathetic as he knew his mother was towards Islam, Giyaseddin had trouble believing that she would forsake her Christian religion. She was an intense Christian, one who prayed everyday and taught him to pray as well: *Hallowed be Thy name. Praise God from whom all blessings flow.* She never stopped attending mass when she lived in Konya. He recalled as a child when he would enter her room, he would often find her on her knees praying by the side of the bed, her head bowed and her hands clasped. Verses of Scripture enhanced her speech when she spoke to him; he remembered the Bible stories she had taught him as lessons when he was a boy. There was no possibility this dutiful daughter of Christ would give up her love for Jesus and Mary, and he felt he had no right to ask her to do so. His father had never requested it, and he could not either.

And yet...his mother wanted him to be Sultan more than anything else. Köpek had told him he must make this demand of her. He had no choice, as painful as it was. This was the law of the land. The mother of a Sultan must be a Muslim.

Giyaseddin looked down at his hands and began to speak, afraid to look her in the eyes. Yet he knew his mother loved him deeply and would always listen to him.

"Mama, I need your help. I need you by my side in every way. Even if Köpek does manage to convince the entire court that I am to be the next sultan, there is still one important hurdle standing in my way. It… has to do with you," he hesitated, still looking down at his hands. "To show the people that I am truly the leader of the faith, you must become a Muslim," he quickly blurted out.

Mahperi had been expecting this conversation for some time now, and had been going over it in her head for days and nights, especially since the Sultan's death. She knew that her Christianity would be a definite handicap for her son to be appointed to the throne instead of his brother, the golden son of an Ayyubid princess from Holy Damascus. Yet the thought of turning her heart against Mary and Jesus at a time when she needed them more than ever in her grief was something she could not face.

"Köpek says I must show the court that I am a devout Muslim. He says there can be no whiff of incense clinging to me when I enter the divan room. I beg you, Mama; you must convert to Islam to show the court that you are behind me. You must learn the *bismillah*, you must fast during the Holy Month of Ramadan, you must say your prayers five times daily…and you must publicly stop entering the churches in Konya or Alaiye. We can no longer celebrate Christmas and Easter Mass together like we always have. You must put away your rosaries, your icons and your candles. Your Bible must be kept hidden, and you must never be seen reading it by any of your servants. If you do not do this, you are condemning me to lose the throne. Please, Mama, can you do this for me? I need your help more than ever, and I need you right here by my side as I rule, just as you stood beside my father!"

Little did her son know that she could already recite the *bismillah* and that she knew the Qur'an probably better than he did. Ever since Bahaeddin Veled had opened her eyes to the Word when she first came to Konya as a young bride, she had never diverted her gaze from finding the answers to the questions he had instilled in her heart.

She reached out for his hand and squeezed it in hers. "My son, I have lived a dilemma of faith between Christianity and Islam for many years now, in more ways than you can imagine," she said, thinking about the mosque she dreamed of building with Lou. "But this is a personal issue for me to deal with. I have been moving for a long time to accept Islam in my heart, but know that it is hard to let go of my past. I cannot promise you when all of this will happen, my son, yet I give you my word that I will not let my faith stand in the way of your success – such is my love for you."

Her son remained silent. She now looked directly into his eyes, and spoke to him in a decisive tone.

"You can repeat this to Köpek and all the emirs who are backing you. I will convert to Islam to show my respect for the deceased Sultan and to honor the kingdom he worked so hard to build. I will convert to show solidarity with you so that you may reign with the same glory as he did. But understand that I will not become a Muslim just to satisfy a requisite for your sultanate. I will do this for you, but above all, I will do it for myself. I will only convert if and when I feel comfortable with this step in my heart – such is my love for myself. This conversion must be a testimony and acceptance from the deepest part of my soul, or else it will be a sin to both Jesus and the Prophet – such is my love for them."

☪ ☪ ☪

After her son left the room, Mahperi walked over to the window and gazed out at the spot where she last saw her husband, the night he confidently passed below her to attend the banquet with the Mongols on the Mashad Plain. The fleeting shadows in the courtyard below were now all she had left of him.

She then realized that she did not want to live in a world of shadows and empty air, but in one of bright, shining light.

She closed her eyes and prayed.

Dear Lord, the time has come. Help me get through the long vigil of this night. Help me find the courage to do this. Jesus, you who love me; please understand. Forgive me this trespass! Give, and it will be given unto you. Good measure, pressed down, shaken together, running over, will be put into your lap. For with the measure you use, it will be measured back to you.

Chapter 74

This Is the Covenant I Will Make

Mahperi peered out of her window and looked in the direction of the Majestic Mountain. Even in the darkness of night, she knew the Mountain loomed there, for it was always there, protecting and powerful. It had kept silent vigil with her on this long and sleepless night, and she was grateful for the consolation it provided her. Soon its humped outline would slowly define itself against the grey light of dawn, the dawn of a day she knew would become one of the most significant of her life, in a life already filled with so many days of daring. Today would be the day of new crowns, for her and her son.

She fell to her knees next to her bed, closed her eyes, folded her hands and began to pray.

> "*Blessed Mary, Mother of Jesus, I call you to hear my prayer today.* I ask for your understanding, your forgiveness, and your sustenance. I need you to stand by me when I open this new door of my life, just as you have always stood by me with your sweet love.
>
> The time has come for me to make a decision that will shape the core of my life. This is not a decision I take lightly; it has been in my mind for many years now. It is not just a duty of a mother to her son, but my reasoned choice.
>
> Mary, mother of Jesus, you know what it is to love a son. You saw your son sacrificed for the convictions he held in order to walk in the path of God. A similar path of challenge is now drawn in front of my son, for he now awaits the moment when he will succeed his father and be crowned Sultan of the Seljuk Empire. He is now called upon to be a shepherd of men, as was your son. I am told this moment will soon happen, despite the fact that my son was not the chosen heir. I leave the politics to the powerful men; I am here to offer support to my son as would any mother, and take pride in this achievement.
>
> Hear my words, Gracious Mary, Mother of Jesus, Perfect Woman, and know that I will never denounce the beauty of your being. Yet, my Mary, you must understand that in order for my son to sit on that

golden throne, he must show that his mother supports every aspect of his power. I must become a Muslim.

Ever since my marriage so many years ago, I have sought to understand the religion of my husband and his empire. Alaeddin never required me to change my religion, and he always allowed me to pray in churches and keep my faith a visible one in my life. I shared my faith, *our* faith, Mary, with my son. Yet Alaeddin in his wisdom encouraged me to take instruction in the Islamic faith so that I could better participate in the world around me. He led me to discuss this faith with the wise men of Konya, especially Bahaeddin Veled, who opened many doors of thought for me.

I have lived much since marrying the Sultan sixteen years ago. I have mastered the ways of the court, I learned to speak Turkish, and I learned to write poems in Persian. I taught myself Arabic in order to read the Qur'an at the feet of Bahaeddin Veled. But I did not stop there, for I found myself reading the Qur'an by candlelight long into the night, when I was alone in my room. I wanted to understand more, and the more I read, the more intrigued I became by its message. I hid my growing interest in Islam from all around me, for I was insecure. I was afraid my father would think that I was dishonoring my people and my heritage. Yet, today I must turn from my past to the future. I am fully Turkish now, a Seljuk queen, wife of one Sultan and mother of one to come. Regardless of what I do now, I know Jesus will always be by my side, but this conversion affirms the love I have for my adopted country, the legacy of my husband, the destiny of my son, and yes, I will confess to you, this growing yearning calling to me.

Yes, Mary, I yearn in my heart to travel down this other path. I cannot hide it from you. I want to make a place in my heart for Islam, just as I do for you, for these two faiths travel down much the same path. These two faiths, one based on the teachings of your son Jesus and one based on the word of God as communicated to the Prophet Muhammad, are similar in so many ways that I confuse them in my mind. The verses of the Bible and the verses of the Qur'an often swirl together in my head; the voices of Jesus and Muhammad speak to me one in each ear, but always with the same message: *Love God with all your heart and Love thy neighbor as thyself.*

Bahaeddin showed me that our faith and the faith of Islam are built on this same message, found over and over again in the pages of the Bible and the Qur'an. He taught me to recite the opening verse of the Qur'an, the *Al-Fatihah*, and I hear in these lines a majestic praise to

God, his mercy and power to forgive our sins. "*Praise be to God, the Lord of the worlds, the Compassionate, the All-Merciful.*" I can still hear the voice of my father in my ears, when we would read the Bible together: "*You shall love the Lord your God with all your heart, and with all your soul, and with all your strength. This is the first and greatest commandment.*"

Bahaeddin Veled taught me that Islam honors the religions that came before it, namely ours. He read to me passages in the Qur'an that speak of the holiness of our prophets – Jesus, Moses, Abraham, David, Solomon, Jonah, Noah, Isaac and Jacob. You are there in many of the verses of the Qur'an, Mary, full of love, the only woman called by name in all the Holy Book.

I hear the invitation from God, Mary, and I cannot refuse His call. Mary, allow me to accept that the Prophet can lead me farther down the road than I have ever traveled, on a long road across the endless plain that is faith and love of God. Jesus connected me with God. I know the words of the Qur'an will do the same.

I am now ready to recite the *shahada*. I accept this faith with entire peace. After so many years of searching, I am certain of the knowledge it contains and I am sincere and truthful in its recitation, and accept all the duties that it entails. I love God in heaven and the *shahada* that testifies to this love. So I say unto you, from this day forth, another profession of faith will enter my heart; another path to God's love will be lit by the Qur'an. I will honor God in my worship, manners and way of life, not in word only. This is the covenant I will happily make; this is the witness I will declare. Come to me now, light and mercy of God. *Amen.*"

Mahperi turned to the window that looked out upon the courtyard of the Keykubadiyye Palace. Her long night of vigil was over. Dawn was breaking and the fleeting shadows were dissipating. Now it was her turn to cross a path towards her destiny. She was ready.

The muezzin called out for the dawn prayer. She remembered Bahaeddin's words to her: "*Just listen, and when you are ready, I will be there.*" She was ready, and he was there.

She waited for the muezzin to finish his call to the faithful. She was now to become one of them. She drew a deep breath and said out loud:

"Lâ ilâha illallâh, Muhammadur rasûlullâh
There is no god but God, and Muhammad is the messenger of God"

It was now pronounced. A covenant was made and a witness was declared.

☪ ☪ ☪

At the same time as Mahperi pronounced the *shahada* silently in her head to her God, the emirs boomed aloud the name of her son as the new Sultan for all the Seljuk Empire to hear. In a crowded room at the Keykubadiyye Palace, there, where the mighty Alaeddin Keykubad met his fate but one short week ago, Giyaseddin Keyhüsrev, his eldest son, became the most important ruler in all Islam. Despite the various opposing factions of viziers and emirs who had come running from all the four corners of the Empire to broker the next coronation, Köpek had managed to convince them all that it was this son who should wear the crown. All the emirs, both those loyal to the wishes of the departed Sultan and those opposed to his selection of heir, now stepped up to kiss the new Sultan's bejeweled hand and pledged their allegiance to him. The scepter of the Seljuks was placed in the hands of the sixteen year old youth, still dressed in his white mourning clothes. A royal decree was issued and sent to all the corners of the Empire on the fastest of horses, to inform all the citizens that a new sultan, named Giyaseddin Keyhüsrev II, now reigned.

☪ ☪ ☪

So began this reign, at the time when the roses opened their buds, yet it was the bitter aroma of the toxins of treason that filled the air. A father is dead, the son lives. The father reigned, and now the son. A mother Mary gave birth to the King of Kings, a mother Mahperi gave birth to a Sultan of Sultans. A crown of thorns and a crown of gold were set upon the heads of the powerful. The Prophet has called to the faithful. A new pledge of devotion and service has been offered by both a son and his mother, one to his Empire and the other to her God. A covenant was made, and a witness was declared. A new Sultan and a new faith are born on this long and sunny day of June, in the holy year of 1237.

Chapter 75

The Groom and His Colt

As the summer sun beat down on the steppes throughout the land, a newborn colt took his first wobbly steps on the throne of the Seljuk Empire. Yet no step was taken without his groom, Köpek, at his side. Köpek found it easy to persuade the young sultan to appoint him as his Chief Vizier, and after that, he picked up the reins. He began working hard to prepare the colt to become a stallion that would tear across the steppes of this Empire – with him, of course, firmly seated in the saddle.

☪ ☪ ☪

The first order of business for the new Sultan was to deal with the Mongol envoys of Ogedei who were still at the court at Kayseri. The very next day after his appointment as Sultan, Giyaseddin, urged by Köpek, dismissed them and sent them back to their Khan, with a firm message that the Seljuks would respond to their demands in due time.

Köpek also found it easy to convince the young man that the emirs who had not been his partisans from the start now posed a hostile threat to him. Yet it was not really the risk against the Sultan that worried Köpek as much as their potential resistance to his influential position as groom to the colt. I must move fast, thought Köpek, and eliminate anyone standing in my way. Thus the groom began to muck out the stables of any filth that he or his Sultan colt might step in. No clod would remain unshoveled, and nothing would deter him from exerting his control over the young man and influencing every decision he would make from the divan.

The Khwarazmians were the first clod to be shoveled. They had always been a difficult and fickle faction, ever since the days of Jelaleddin Menguberti and his disputes with Alaeddin Keykubad. Kirkhan, the current leader of the Khwarazmians, was present at the meeting of the emirs held after the death of Alaeddin, where he had committed the grave error of expressing his indecision about which of the sons of Alaeddin he would support. Now the intransigent Köpek stepped in to claim his revenge for Kirkhan's lack of backing. He dripped poison into the ear of the young Sultan Giyaseddin, leading him to believe that the Khwarazmians were plotting against him to help his younger brother Izzeddin reclaim the throne of the Seljuk Kingdom. Köpek convinced the young Sultan that Kirkhan needed to be arrested and put to death.

Yet the groom had not anticipated the reaction of the wild Khwarazmian warriors. Angered by the news of the imprisonment and murder of their leader, the troops sought revenge against the Seljuk Sultan. They left the region of Kayseri and retreated across the Euphrates River to the Mesopotamian plain near the ancient city of Urfa, brutally pillaging all in their path. Once in Urfa, they offered up their services to the Ayyubids. The Sultan knew it would be highly dangerous to let them enter into the service of this perpetual enemy of the Seljuk Empire. He sent two of his father's most able warriors, the venerable Commanders Kamyar and Ertokush, to deal with them. Yet all was in vain, for the Khwarazmians soundly defeated the Seljuks, taking Ertokush prisoner and seizing a mass of Seljuk booty.

Not deterred by this defeat, the groom encouraged his colt to run even faster across the meadow of his enemies. When Köpek learned that summer of the death of the Ayyubid ruler al-Ashraf of Damascus, he knew that Giyaseddin could take advantage of the situation. Now the Sultan could reduce this most powerful enemy of the Seljuks to oblivion, for in their weakened and leaderless state, nothing would be easier than to seize their territories in Mesopotamia and Northern Syria!

The groom quickly crafted a diplomatic agreement to ensure closer relations with the successor of al-Ashraf in the important Ayyubid city of Aleppo, the young prince al-Nasir Aziz, who reigned with his grandmother acting as regent. In an ironic twist of fate, the rival of al-Ashraf, his powerful brother Sultan al-Kamil of Egypt, died only a few months after al-Ashraf. Köpek rubbed the reins in glee, for he knew that this death would bring nothing but good fortune for the future.

Thus it came to be that only several months after taking power, the young colt of a Sultan commanded all his neighbors. The Greeks of Trabzon, the Armenians of Cilicia, the Ayyubids of Syria, the Artukids of the Mesopotamian plain, the Kingdom of Bulgaria, and the Byzantine Greeks of Iznik all were now under his hooves. He held the strongest army at his call. Aleppo and Damascus answered to him. His Seljuk Kingdom was at present the richest empire in the East. Giyaseddin was now able to focus on the very same goals as his father at the end of his reign: driving the Ayyubid rivals from his southeastern frontiers and building up a bulwark against the Mongols in the east.

As the groom brushed down his colt after each hard run, Köpek thought with pride that with my hands on the reins, this colt will ride to the same glory as his father Alaeddin Keykubad. It matters not that he lacks the intelligence, character or charisma of the father. He can count on me for that, for I am the groom of the colt and my feet are firmly in the stirrups.

Chapter 76

Sketches of My Heart to Yours

Despite the fact that she was now, as mother of the reigning Sultan, the most powerful woman in the land, Mahperi found little joy in the ascent of her son to the throne. She was still confused about what had really taken place at the banquet with the Mongols, and nothing made sense to her anymore. Befuddled, she spent her days in a haze, and even visits to Hanife, who had now moved to Kayseri at her request, could not lift her spirits. The parts of her life were rough and tangled, like uncut knots on one of Hanife's rugs.

One afternoon several months after the death of Alaeddin, she decided to take a walk through the city to dispel her gloomy mood. Flanked by two discrete palace guardsmen, she set off through the congested streets, and the natural surge of traffic swirled her towards the activity of the bazaars near the city gates at the center of town. She paused at the New Gate and looked up at the impressive walls that Alaeddin had ordered repaired. She placed her open palm on the wall and felt the warmth of his hands in those stones. His dream for the Empire was still alive, radiating there in those stones.

She turned her back to the New Gate and looked over to the open area directly across from it. There stood the hulking old Roman bathhouse and the construction site of the medrese that Alaeddin had commissioned shortly before his death. How sad that he had not lived to see it completed, she thought, feeling a particular kinship with the fate of this building. She stood and watched the workers at their tasks, remembering with fondness the thrill she felt during the construction days at Kubadabad. Just then, she saw a man with a measuring stick talking to a group of workers. He was pointing to the rear corner of the site, and then started to draw in the dust with his stick.

Just like Lou used to do.

She instinctively knew the man had to be the architect for the project. The glittering gold crucifix around his neck gave away his Greek origins. She felt drawn to him in the same way as she felt inexplicably drawn to the medrese, for they both reminded her of beloved people she had lost.

Sensing her eyes upon him, the architect lifted his head from the huddle of the men, turned to look at her and smiled.

It was then that Mahperi knew what she needed to do.

☪ ☪ ☪

Alone in her room that night, Mahperi pulled out the roll of drawings that Lou had put into her hands during their last moment together. She had hidden the roll since that day at Kubadabad, and had not once dared to look at it.

But now it was time. She needed to build her gift to God, her gift to her husband's greatness, her gift to her son's new throne, and her gift to a friendship lost. And it would be right there, next to her husband's uncompleted medrese that she would build it. Both of them would rise, stronger with each passing day and with each layer of stone laid.

She unrolled the drawings on the table. Sheet after sheet of detailed drawings, sketches and scribbled notes opened in front of her eyes. She recognized his handwriting and felt the blue waters of Kubadabad and the blue waters of their friendship surrounding her once more, and she suddenly felt very lonely.

She heard a thud as a thick notebook fell out from the middle of the drawings and hit the floor. She picked it up and opened its leather covers. Inside were pages crammed with notes and even more little sketches, and a folded piece of paper tucked into the crease. She lifted the paper up to her nose, and could smell the sunlight of Kubadabad upon it. She unfolded it and began to read.

My honorable Queen, ma Gente Dame,

If you are reading this letter it means that I am far from you. I have always feared that one day we would be separated before we could finish our work, so I have prepared all the details so that you may carry on if I am not by your side. Our friendship will always live in these drawings and the project they represent.

On the rolls of drawings are the plans for the great mosque that we both so ardently desire to build. I visited the site as you requested and prepared these sketches and plans for you. All is here; all our thoughts, our hopes, our ideas and the fruit of our discussions. I hope I have not failed to translate onto paper what is in your heart. It will rise, I am certain of it.

When you decide to build our mosque, give the little sketchbook to the architect you will select for the project. The notes in this book will help explain the drawings that I have made, for I am not always certain that our building techniques in Europe are understood by those here. Perhaps, too, they will better explain to him our particular ideas. Although I tried hard to write in Turkish, most of my annotations on the drawings are in Occitan. Poetry flows better in that language, and what we are building is poetry, My Lady, is it not? I am confident that you will select a fine architect. Work with him, Mahperi; give him every confidence you can, just like you did to me. With him, our mosque and our dream will rise. Participate in the journey at his side, just like you did with me at Kubadabad. I know that you will make your mosque sing an eternal praise to God. It will be a place where prayers and poems can lift like a flock of doves to the heavens. And know that wherever I am in this world, I will hear that song. It will ring out in every church bell I hear tolling, just as it will echo every note of the muezzin's song you hear. I will hear that song just as I will always hear your voice in my ears when I wake up at the start of each day, and when I last drift off to sleep at the end of it.

May God bless your heart and soul, and give you courage in all that you do, ma Gente dame.

To you without reservation, from your devoted servant,

Lou Cantadou

Chapter 77

The Mary of Our Times

It was not long afterward that Nikolas Zonaras, the head architect hired by Alaeddin Keykubad to build his medrese in Kayseri, received a message from a palace guard telling him that none other than the Sultan's mother, Mahperi Hatun, wished to meet him as soon as possible at the Devlethane Palace. He had seen her at the medreşe construction site a few days earlier, and had known exactly who she was, but had no idea why she was now so interested in him.

When he arrived at the Devlethane, he was escorted into the garden, where he found her sitting under a tree waiting for him, attended by several guards. She held her head erect with a distinct dignity that would have marked her as a queen even in the middle of a teeming bazaar. Despite her majestic mien, she had a quiet assurance that reminded him of the faces of the Virgin Mary he saw depicted on the icons on the altar of his church.

She lifted her head, graciously smiled at him and beckoned him to her side, indicating for him to sit on the carpet spread on a low bench around the trunk of a large plane tree. Although this imposing figure could have daunted many, Nikolas kept seeing the freshness of Mary in Mahperi's translucent cheeks, and any fears that lingered about his encounter with her soon dissipated.

A palace servant brought out a tray of sherbet and pastries and served them to the guest. Indeed, thought Nikolas, relaxing slightly, it would appear I have nothing to fear from this woman if she is serving me sugared cakes. But what exactly does she want from me?

He did not have to wait long to find out. Mahperi went immediately to the point. It was there, under the shade of a plane tree and drinking sweet sherbet that the architect learned of her plans to build a mosque in Kayseri. When she finished explaining her intentions, she prompted him with questions.

"Tell me about yourself, Nikolas Zonaras! How is it that you are here in Kayseri? Where did you learn your trade, architect?"

Nikolas felt no shyness in front of her, and spoke right up to answer her. "Well, I am a Greek from the area around Nicaea and I learned my trade there, building many houses, churches and fortification walls in the region. I then wandered south and was hired by your husband to build his ship arsenal and Red Tower at the harbor in Alaiye, which I understand is your hometown. There, my skills had the fortune of being noted by your Sultan's foremen, and I started to work on more and more projects for the Sultan, may he rest in peace, each time with more and more responsibility. Your husband then invited me to Kayseri to be the architect of the medrese he wanted to build here, and the rest you know."

They continued to speak, with Mahperi asking him more and more about the work he did. Although he held definite ideas about his craft, she could tell that he was not a dreamer like Lou, preferring to take a more business-like approach to his work. Physically as well, he bore no resemblance to the Occitan. Considerably older than Lou, Nikolas was short, stocky and very dark, with a forest of thick black hair running up his forearms. His eyes were small, jet black and serious like the olives that grew on the trees in the groves surrounding his home village.

"Nikolas Zonaras, I have an offer that may surprise you. I want you to become the head architect for this mosque I wish to build here. Yes, you have heard me right. Tell me then, would you accept this job I am offering you?" she said, looking him right in the eyes.

Startled by her abruptness, Nikolas put down his goblet and cocked his head towards her. "Excuse my frankness, my Lady, but this request is most unusual. Doesn't the court appoint such positions by decree? Doesn't the Superintendent of Buildings Köpek decide such things? And why me?"

"And I would ask, why *not* you?"

They shared a smile and then she elaborated.

"I say this with no intended boastfulness, but I am now the most powerful woman in this Empire, and I do not need to ask anyone's permission to act. I never have, and I never will. I make my own decisions, and the minute I saw you directing the work on the medrese site the other day, I knew I had found the man I wanted to work for me. I could feel it with my instinct, which has never proven me wrong. Yet I still needed to meet you to know what kind of a man you are and to feel your passion for your work. I do not want to hire just a proficient architect. Those can be found in every town across this Empire. I want something else: a builder who can understand my dreams," Mahperi said, the image of Lou flashing back into her mind. "That is very important for me, and from what I can now see, you are the man who can bring them to life. And do not fear that because you are a Christian Greek there will be any issues with building a mosque to the glory of God. We all work together for God's good grace, no matter what our faith."

They continued to talk about their backgrounds and the project, and drew up a list of the buildings she wanted to build at her complex. First, the medrese of Alaeddin would be completed as planned, and then they would start to work on Mahperi's mosque. At the same time, the old Roman baths on the site would be remodeled. As they discussed the site plan, she felt the same excitement she had shared with Lou when they envisioned together what they would do at Kubadabad, but this was different. Now she was a widow, the mother of the Sultan and, above all, she had pronounced the *shahada*. Now she was building a house for God, and not a pleasure palace for a sultan.

Nikolas paused to look at her, his admiration for her increasing with each moment.

"Mahperi, all the blessings and riches that have been showered upon you are not due to your efforts alone, but also for the grace and will of God. You will build something wonderful here, and I will help you. You have made an excellent choice of site for this mosque. Although it is a small area, you are making a very strong statement, for your complex will be located in the very heart of the city. It is located directly east of the citadel and holds a key position facing all those who approach or leave the city through the New Gate. No one in Kayseri will be able to avoid it!"

Mahperi smiled at him and continued.

"Architect, as concerns the medrese, it is my understanding that you have included eight rooms on both of the long sides of the open courtyard, as well as two open halls for holding classes, one of which will also house the library of fine books to be used by the students and teachers. Each one of the student rooms will house up to four students. Am I correct here?"

Nikolas nodded.

"This may sound odd to you, but it is important for me that the medrese be the focal point of the complex, not the mosque, for it is the legacy of Alaeddin Keykubad. As a center of theology, medicine and science, what happens inside its walls will lead the city into the direction of enlightenment and progress. Those thirty-two students will become the leaders of our community, and each one will teach thirty-two others and so on and so on like a ball of yarn growing bigger and bigger. When you plan the site for the mosque, I want you to make sure to set it back from the line where the medrese sits, so that the first thing the citizens of Kayseri will see when they step out of the New Gate is Alaeddin's medrese."

Nikolas was quite impressed by her intent, and above all, by her generosity. He now realized that he had an enlightened patron, the one that every architect dreams of working with once in his lifetime. What pleasure I will have in designing this project with her input, he thought to himself, and the light of those green eyes will guide me like the rays of a lantern.

"However, there is one important condition to your accepting this position as my architect on the project," the Sultana continued. Nikolas saw her reach into a bag at her feet and pull out a book and a fat roll of drawings.

Handing him the roll and book, she said, "It is all here; all that I want is already laid out on these documents. I ask that you take them and build what is writ here. I count on you to interpret these drawings as you can, but the design of this mosque has already been planned by another architect a while back. Can you accept to work off of someone else's drawings of my dream?"

Nikolas was taken aback by this request, for he was his own man, and did not answer to others. Yet to serve a lady like her, he was willing to work with another man's vision. Who drew these sketches? he wondered. Yet it did not matter to him what her motivation was or the story behind the creation of those drawings. All he knew was that he now faced the most exciting challenge of his life, and the opportunity to work for a woman who was every ounce the leader her husband was. Furthermore, she would reconcile in this building the religious traditions of this empire. She is as courageous as she is loving and generous. *She is the Mary of our times, she is the Khadija of our times,* he thought to himself.

"My Lady, it will be an honor to work by your side. I accept your offer, and I will serve your every wish. I will do my best to adapt these drawings to the site here. I am sure that the architect who drew up these plans had your entire confidence and support, and it will be my honor to have that same blessing shine onto me from your gracious consideration."

☪ ☪ ☪

And that night, Mahperi slept peacefully for the first time since the death of Alaeddin, dreaming of a future of hope and promise, not one of fear and despair.

Chapter 78

A Christmas Gift to God

A new project, springing from a friendship of shared ideals and the dreams found on the pages of a sketchbook, began to take form. A Christian architect and a patron recently converted to Islam joined to build a mosque to the glory of God.

One afternoon soon after their initial meeting, Nikolas invited Mahperi to walk around the site with him. He knew it well and had studied Lou's drawings with care, so he was now ready to share his ideas with her.

"The most problematic element for building the mosque is the restrictions placed on it by the existing site," he said, scratching his head while pointing to the perimeters of the site. "The space available for the mosque, in between Alaeddin's medrese and those existing baths, is a tight one. The prayer hall is going to be squeezed hard against the southeast corner of the baths, but yes, yes, everything is possible! The main wall must face Mecca, so that will determine the orientation of the mosque, which must thus face to the south, but we will fit it all in!" he explained, undaunted by the limitations imposed by the site.

"Once we determine the plan, the key for a successful outcome, my Lady, is in the timing. If we start by the beginning of the upcoming year, I would think that we could be finished in three years. But everything must flow according to a precise ritual, much like the steps of a folk dance!" he insisted.

"Now, let's see how this will all work out…We are in November, 1237 now," he said, stroking his chin. "I will take these drawings you have given me and work up over the next month a definitive sketch plan of the entire project to present to you, indicating the size and the various details."

Mahperi spoke up, joining in his enthusiasm. "Yes, and while you are working on those drawings, I will set up the *vakif* trustfund that will ensure the running of the complex. It is my intention that the revenue from the baths will help support the upkeep and staff of the complex."

"Good! That will be most helpful!" interjected Nikolas. "At the same time, I will submit to you a preliminary budget for the project. By March, I will hire a foreman to be my right hand man for the project. He is a key person, as he will be the direct contact with the workmen, who can often get quite unruly! Just as the Sultan needs his Vizier, I need my foreman!" laughed the Greek architect.

"By tulip time in April," he elaborated, "after the last freeze, we will start preparing the site for construction. The land will be cleared and leveled, and we will build the sheds for each building trade, where they will work and store their supplies. At this time we will start one of the most important aspects of the project. We will place the order to start quarrying the stone. Workers will start prying the slabs of stone off the faces of cliffs several months ahead of the actual start of construction so that the blocks can be delivered to the site in time. Fine stone cutting is the basis of the whole project. If the stone is good, the building will be good. I know of an excellent quarry near Afyon – it is far away, I know, but the quality of stone there is the best in the land!"

"May will be a busy month, for we will hire all the various skilled workers. Bricklayers and blacksmiths are generally Armenians and Christians, while the stonemasons, carpenters and roofers tend to be Muslims. All hands of God work for his glory! I will need to hire hundreds of other skilled and unskilled workers: wagon drivers, night watchmen, storekeepers, and porters. I estimate that there will be over a thousand workers on the site. All this will cost you many shiny coins, my Lady!"

Mahperi nodded to him. "As I said to you before, Nikolas, I have all the resources I need to complete this project. Pay attention not to waste money, but spend what is necessary to produce a masterpiece."

Nikolas smiled and bowed deeply to his generous patron before continuing. "At this time we will start to dig the foundations of the mosque, and this groundbreaking will be the official start of the project. I can just imagine the gorgeous morning in May when the surveyors will establish the placement of the *kibla* wall and mark it on the site with wooden stakes."

"Yes! That will be an exciting day!" gasped Mahperi. "It is important for me to show the citizens of Kayseri that I am building a project to mark my son's ascent to the throne."

"Yes, and that groundbreaking date will be the one we inscribe on the inscription plaque, to be carved in fine calligraphy. We will put the commissioning date of May, 1238 on it, large enough for all to read from below as they enter the mosque to pray! Your words will trace your generous gift for all eternity. We will hang the plaque over the main portal of the mosque when it is completed. But since only God knows when that date will be, it is best for you to put the date of the official start of the project. We will have a small prayer read by the imam when the first shovel of dirt is tossed!" he said, rubbing his hands together.

"During the summer we will be as busy as locusts in the field. Once the *kibla* is marked, we will begin digging the trenches for the foundation walls. This is hard work, but if all goes well, this can be done in two months, and then in August, once the holes are dug to the correct depth, about the height of a man or so, we will fill them with a thick base layer of rubble and then lay the foundation stones in place," the Greek said, noting all in his head as he spoke.

"Over the long summer, the bricks will be formed offsite, so that they can dry in the hot summer sun. They are much like the warp and weft threads on Hanife's loom: you don't see them, but they must be strong and faultless, for they are what hold everything together. In an adjacent brickyard, the men will mix washed sand and clay in precise quantities. The molded bricks will be laid out in the sun to dry, and then baked in a kiln before they will be ready to set in place," he explained.

Mahperi paused to remember the fields of tiles drying in the sun at Kubadabad, waiting in anticipation of Joseph's magic brush to bring them to life. The images on those tiles still danced in front of her eyes.

"By this time, carts of stone should start to arrive from Afyon at the site. Once these blocks arrive, they will be cut into their final shapes, dressed and carved by the master stonemason and his team. So! By the end of summer, the foundations will be finished and we will host a glorious ceremony when we precisely orient the *kibla* wall. The kibla wall is very important for Muslims, as it denotes the imaginary line which points to the holy city of Mecca, birthplace of the Prophet Muhammad. I will make sure that I adhere to the calculations of the court religious officials."

"And now the excitement begins," he said, rubbing his hands together. "In the late summer through the fall, we can start to bring up the walls. Like wheat growing in fields, the walls of the great prayer hall will rise. Layer after layer of bricks will be added, just like the master Hanife does with the rows of knots on her loom. The bricks will then be faced inside and out with the cut stone, which will be tied together with iron clamps and bars. And to make the walls even stronger, vertical rods will be inserted to bind each layer of stone to the one above it. This is just like the weft rows that Hanife puts after tying a row of knots; for you need that extra effort to hold everything together so that it is solid and will withstand all wear. The walls will keep rising higher and higher, and as we go along, we will build scaffolding to support platforms for the workers to do their jobs."

Nikolas continued to gush forth enthusiastically as he explained the project to Mahperi. "And when it becomes too cold in the winter months for mortar work – and as you know, it can get quite cold and snowy in Kayseri – we will take the work inside. The stonemasons will continue to dress the blocks of stones and can even begin the more fancy carving work of the marble capitals, bases of columns, and decorative patterns for stones of the facade. I know you will want to create patterns of great intricacy for your main doors," surmised the architect.

He paused for a moment to frame his words. “A key part of your interior design will involve the mihrab and the wall around it. As you know, the mihrab niche is like the altar in a church: it symbolizes the entrance to paradise. We will make an especially beautiful one here! How do you want your mihrab to look, my Lady? Will you put glorious blue tiles on it like Alaeddin’s mosque on the hill at Konya or like the Güllük Mosque here in Kayseri? That mihrab, along with the wooden mimbar you will commission, will be your most beautiful gift to God. At this time, too, you can also think about the carpets you wish to have made for the project. I am sure that you will have much help here from your friend Hanife.”

“Yes, I will order many rugs from her workshops, and I will have her personally make a very large and fine piece to put as a focal point right in front of the mihrab. Hanife once told me something I have never forgotten. She said that each one of her rugs is a mosque all on its own. She said that on her rugs, the worshipper creates his own space – his own private, intimate mosque – a space defined entirely and fully by his experience at that moment in his communication with God. His worship, his holy world, is right there within the borders of her prayer rug.”

Mahperi then laughed. “Yes, and my friend also tells me a large rug takes her from one to two years to complete, so I had best get her going to get her ideas down on the loom!”

“Yes, the days do fly by as fast as her fingers on the loom!” noted Nikolas, before continuing. “Christmas will come and go, the new year 1239 will be upon us, and before we know it, winter will draw to a close. By March the snow and freezing will be over, the ground thawed and we can once again start to work on the walls, using all the bricks and stones that were prepared over the winter. Those glorious walls will be more beautiful than the heads of the spring tulips in the meadows! Window grilles will be installed, and the columns will be prepared with capitals attached. This work will continue all through the summer and fall. Then once again, it will be winter, and the work will move inside, and we will install the dome over the mihrab. This is a complicated process accomplished by building up triangular supports with bricks to make the transition from the square shape to the circular base of the dome. This the trickiest part of all architecture, but I am fearless!”

His head bobbed in anticipation. “Spring will come again, and over the summer of the year of our Lord 1240, the roof of the building will be put in place. The sky above your prayer hall will disappear and soon all will be closed in. We will also lay the water pipes leading from the baths over to the ablution fountain, as well as to the mosque latrines. Wooden shutters will be carved for the windows. The panels of the minbar will be brought in and assembled, with thousands of small pieces of wood laid out on the mosque floor to be joined together in an intricate pattern of geometric lace,” he indicated.

"In the fall of 1240, the official deed for the mosque will be recorded. All will be readied for the opening to take place, which I would like to definitely plan for around Christmas time. During the fall, you will hire the staff to run the mosque, such as cleaners, doorkeepers, imams, teachers for the medrese, muezzins, clerks, gardeners, candle keepers and lighters, and not to forget, a librarian to maintain the precious collection of books for the mosque and medrese. You will need to commission a calligrapher to create special ones just for this mosque. The final interior finishes will be completed, notably the painting and whitewashing. We will hang your carved inscription plaques over the doors. The scaffolding will be removed from inside the prayer hall; the ground will be compacted, and as a last touch, the prayer rugs of your friend Hanife will be laid in place," he concluded with a flourish.

Mahperi's mind flashed back to the day she met Hanife, unrolling her rug in front of the mihrab of the Alaeddin mosque. How far the two of them had traveled since that day!

"And then, hear my dream, my Sultana. On Christmas Day of the year 1240, three years from the start of the project, on this day, where we stand right now, we will host the official dedication ceremony of your mosque. We will invite the *ulema*, the royal family, the military commanders and emirs, as well as all the local important community leaders and merchants. We will hold a special prayer service, and a lamb will be sacrificed. Worshippers will then perform their ablutions, and all will enter and inaugurate the mosque with prayer. All will praise this new and magnificent temple to God!

"What a glorious day that will be!" muttered Mahperi, feeling a bit overwhelmed by it all. "But I would like to ask you something, Nikolas. You seem much attached to this idea of opening the mosque on Christmas Day. Why is this so important to you?" she queried.

The architect smiled and lowered his head. "Yes, I would like to host it that day for many reasons. That day for me symbolizes one of the greatest gifts God gave to man to show his merciful love. In the same way, you are offering the people of Kayseri this same kind of gesture of love. Through God's mercy, as represented by this mosque, and by the miracle of Christ's birth, God has shown man that he need never to live in ignorance and fear. Opening the mosque on Christmas Day is a unification of our beliefs. You and I were both born Christians, and yet we work in great respect with the Muslims of this city. We are all children under God's love, and on this glorious day, all the citizens of this city will be able to feel that devotion and fellowship, made possible by a generous Sultana. All will praise God from whom all blessings flow!"

As he looked at his patron smiling graciously upon him, Nikolas knew he would build a mosque as beautiful and noble as she. *She is the Mary of our times, she is the Khadija of our times*, he thought to himself, ready to set to work on this most generous of gifts.

Chapter 79

Dig Silent, Dig Hard

We dig silent, we dig deep. We are the first workers of your dream, our Sultana. Hear our prayer, God; hear our song, Lady Mahperi; hear our plea, you heavy pickaxe!

We dig hard, we dig fast. We dig the foundations of this dream, deep into the rich earth at the base of the Majestic Mountain. Earth of eternity, earth of the past, earth of the present. Our shovels throw up millennia of treasures and traces mixed with the living fury of the earth. We are the ditch-diggers.

Up come primeval demon spirits, rhizomes, silex blades, fossils, arrowheads and shells from the time when the sea covered this region. Earth of Eternity. Other ancient voices cry out from the depths to the surface: Hittite coins, larvae, fibulae, stones with strange marks scratched on them, chunks of broken marble with acanthus leaves. Earth of the past. All is topped by purple stones, red clay, white decomposing bones of animals, moist peat, and worms burrowing as hard as we. Earth of the present.

We dig silent and we dig hard, for we are burrowing from the earth a dream we hold in hands covered with dried mud and calluses and red sores that ache well into the night after the pickaxes are laid to rest. We dig and dream of a mosque that will rise stone by stone, step by step, in a staircase to the space above; there, where God dwells. Dig harder, brothers, for this mosque will be built on these foundations which ask only for the good earth to bear their weight. The harder we dig, we say to ourselves with each grunt of the shovel, the higher it will rise, and the more glory it will bear to God. Day after day, hard we dig this earth that weighs heavy in our shovels, whose mud sticks to our arms and whose lime burns the skin of our hands.

We are exhausted of all energy; we are prisoners of the pickaxe and we are slaves to the slime of the mother mud. No vicious foreman needs to crack the whip over our heads; for we dig for another Master. We dig to be free from foolishness. Hear our prayer, oh God the Great. We will be released, once we finish removing the last clod of mud from the hole of darkness and ignorance. A house of light will rise from this pit of black earth; we already see the staircase rising from the depths with each shovelful of dirt we pitch into the air. We collapse at night on our mats, dropping to sleep with the vision of this staircase in our eyes. Too quickly the dawn arrives and it starts all over again.

Your pit will soon be ready, Lady Mahperi; we have dug deep enough to find the devil's cave. The spirit of this house of light will soon float free and start to breathe. It will stretch up to touch the hand of God that reaches down to take it in its grasp. The spirit of light will take possession of the hole of humanity still filled with the fears, ancestral terror and ancient gods. The building to rise from this pit we now dig will eradicate their memory, and crush them forever under the weight of its columns. From our hole will raise a defiant testament to the glory of God, whose grace will dominate ignorance forever more. Truly we say unto you, the path to the light of truth starts from down here, in the darkness of the pit we plow. Let us climb the staircase to God together. Let us dare to look God in the face. Be you Sultana or ditch-digger, we all share this prayer of hope. *Allahu akbar*.

Chapter 80

A First and a Last Supper

The enticing aroma of roasting lamb greeted Köpek as he stood in front of the door of his newly-completed caravansarai outside of Konya. Taking a deep breath, he inhaled as well the scent of satisfaction as he looked up at the portal, with its superb keystone of alternating black and white stone courses framed by carved saw-tooth designs. He was proud of this han he had built, and the decorative touches of this door would convey his pride – and his might – to the entire world. No one will be able to miss this door, he snickered to himself; why you can see it looming ahead for miles down the road from Konya! Perhaps some will find me insolent for using the same design as the north portal of Alaeddin Keykubad's mosque in Konya, but I am equal to a Sultan in everything I do, even down to the building of doors.

Yes, Köpek had worked very hard on this han. He started it at the same time he had been pushed aside from the Kubadabad project, for he needed to have his own project after that humiliation. To build a caravansarai to rival the Sultan's very own would certainly mark a point! He chose a site about a day's ride out of Konya on the road leading eastwards to Aksaray, and vowed that his han would be just as impressive as that Konya mosque or the Aksaray han built by the Sultan.

He turned from the door and began to walk around the perimeter of the han, performing a last-minute inspection of the building with the same precision as a general reviewing his troops. Only this time, he was not setting out to do battle, but hosting a lavish inaugural banquet, to be held that evening.

As he circled the outer walls, Köpek admired the hundreds of elaborately carved stones scattered among the plain limestone blocks, many taken from Roman graveyards and Byzantine churches in the area that had fallen into disrepair. He felt no remorse in using them, for they gave a special flair to the walls when the bright rays of the sun danced upon them. These people are conquered, dead and gone, he reasoned, and the only thing that matters now is the glory of my han.

He completed his inspection of the walls and stood once again in front of his magnificent portal. Looking up at the dedication plaque over the door, he read the date of 1236 and the name of Alaeddin Keykubad inscribed in flowing script, and a sea of memories came flooding back to him.

Waves of his rivalry with him and his need to outdo him came crashing onto the shore of his forehead. Yes, I began to build this han when you were still alive, Alaeddin; yes, I even took your money to do it, but now, two years later, I have completed it under the reign of your son, the son I myself have put on the throne. And so I ask you now, whose han is the finest, yours at Aksaray or mine here?

He entered the han and walked over to the door of the covered hall, on which he had used the same black and white stone courses as the front door. This section was the last part built and completed the construction project. Köpek paused to read the inscription plaque over its door which had been hung up by the workers earlier that week. There he read the date of 1237 and the name of another sultan, *his* Sultan, Giyaseddin Keyhüsrev. Yes, at last, he beamed, this han is ready to open its doors.

The aroma of the lamb wafting from the kitchens snapped him out of his reverie and reminded him that the opening ceremonies would soon be starting and that he needed to don his finest embroidered robe to receive his guests. As proud as the fancy peacock he had tethered outside the han, Köpek had done everything to ensure that this would be a memorable banquet, one even fancier than the infamous inauguration ceremony of Kubadabad. Only this time, there would be no scandal or smashing plates!

A scullion running to the kitchens with a pot of onions bumped into him, but Köpek was in too good a mood to get angry at his carelessness. He looked around to ensure that all was in place for the celebration. The tall torches set around the perimeter of the long courtyard would compete with the full moon and the bright stars shining in the sky that night. An elaborate menu had been prepared, the entertainment rehearsed, the imam was ready with his prayer, the sacrificial lamb had been tied outside the door, and all the guests had been invited. Anyone who was anyone at the court of Konya had been summoned, with over 400 guests expected to arrive at sunset after the afternoon prayer. Everyone would be there, except for one important person Köpek had made sure not to invite.

A special troop of musicians from Azerbaijan had been hired to perform a musicale of lively Turkic folksongs. They were known far and wide for their emotional interpretations of love songs. It had cost a fortune to bring them here, thought Köpek, but they will be worth every *kuruş* once my guests hear their golden songs lift up to the full silvery moon.

Yes, he smiled to himself, all was in place.

With great pomp and ceremony, Köpek stood at the portal to await the arrival of the Sultan and his other guests. The head imam stood there as well, next to a sheep with a bright red ribbon around its neck, ready to be sacrificed after the invocation prayer.

When Sultan Giyaseddin Keyhüsrev arrived with his entourage of dignitaries, Köpek greeted him with a small military band. After bowing and kissing his hand, he nodded to the imam to begin the dedication ceremony. The imam, resplendent in his white turban, led the group in a series of prayers, and as the lamb's throat was slit, he boomed out:

> *"In the name of God, the Beneficent, the Merciful; may God's blessing be upon Muhammad, seal of the Prophets, and his family, as well as the leader of his faith, Sultan Giyaseddin Keyhüsrev. It is to his honor that Saddeddin Köpek, the High Authority, the Lordly, the great Emir, the Learned, the Just, the Holy Warrior, the Officer and Servant, the Glorious and Righteous officer, dedicates this gift."*

Afterwards, the Sultan's group entered the han and was given a tour by Köpek. None failed to be amazed by its size and magnificence, murmuring to themselves about the imagined construction costs. Others gossiped about the invocation prayer, for none had missed the fact that the imam's words glorified Köpek more than the Sultan. The men then took their places on the fine carpets, sitting around sumptuously inlaid copper trays with a large brass serving dish set on each one.

The guests continued to arrive, and soon the courtyard buzzed with animated conversations. The sun set and the curtain of the night sky rose. Servants scurried in all directions to tend to the needs of the guests, and the courtyard became a dizzying blur of colorful caftans and jeweled turbans shimmering in the glow of the torch lights.

☪ ☪ ☪

Giyaseddin had begged his mother to make the journey from Kayseri to Konya to attend the ceremony with him, and she found it hard to resist his invitation. In truth, Mahperi was curious to see what the Dog had done with his building. She had no particular desire to share his joy, but she wanted to compare it with her own mosque project now underway in Kayseri.

When she arrived, Köpek greeted her at the door, certain she would not miss the reference of the black and white stone courses.

"Welcome to my han, Sultana Mahperi Hatun, how honored I am that you have made the journey to attend my event," he politely purred, greeting her with a low bow. "May I provide you with a brief tour of the han? I know how interested you are in buildings," he smirked, with obvious provocation.

As she looked around her, Mahperi had to admit that the han was very impressive, quite different than the one her husband had built at Aksaray, but just as imposing. Köpek pointed out its features as they strolled around the courtyard, nodding along the way to the many guests now pouring into the han.

"Like the Aksaray han of your late husband, may God shine light on his grave, I have included a large covered section to house travelers during the cold winter months," Köpek said, pointing out the elaborate door and her son's name on the inscription plaque. "Mine is every bit as roomy, perhaps even a bit higher, and I have put a sizeable lantern dome in the middle. I have provided raised platforms as well to make the unloading and loading of goods easier for the traveling merchants. I have thought of their comfort first!"

Mahperi said nothing, cringing at his unbearable boasting.

"Yet, as the Chief Architect of the project, I have taken the initiative to include some interesting elements, a bit different than in your husband's han. The most obvious is that I have set the entrance off the main axis of the building. I think it is much better this way, and since the courtyard of my han is so much larger than your husband's, I judged that the travelers and beasts could move about more freely if they entered directly into the heart of the courtyard. This is quite an innovative approach, I think!" he bragged.

Mahperi thought if she heard one more reference to the superiority of his han over the Sultan's han at Aksaray, she would snap back at him, but she held her tongue for the moment.

"There is also a hammam in the southeast corner of the courtyard. See its elaborately carved and inviting doorframe? Oh, and over there is the kitchen and refectory," he said, pointing to the northern side of the courtyard. "You will soon taste the fine delicacies that will pour out of there tonight! And over here on the other side of the courtyard, I have put a section of open arcades to stable the animals. Nothing has been left out. I have built a true palace for traveling merchants!" he boomed, sweeping his arms in all directions.

"And of course, I have included a mosque, but mine is set above the entrance, not a kiosk in the middle of the dusty courtyard. In this way I will keep the courtyard space free and uncluttered for circulation, and the mosque will be in a much cleaner area. See those steps over there?" he continued, pointing to the right of the entrance. "They lead up to the mosque. Perhaps you might like to go up there one day for your prayers, now that you have become a Muslim. You do know how to pray the *al-Fatihah* now, don't you?" he queried, never missing an opportunity to goad her.

She chose to ignore his prod and turned her head to avert his gaze.

"You see, my Sultana, this is what an architect of quality can produce," he went on, and Mahperi felt the sting of this remark, decidedly intended to impugn the talent of Lou Cantadou. "And if I may say so, this is the finest han in all the land! Generations of our descendents will come to stand in its courtyard and feel the greatness of the Seljuk Empire!"

"Yes, I suppose when one has all of the coffers of the State at one's disposal, it is not surprising that such beautiful things may be wrought," she said smiling at him with clenched teeth.

Köpek whipped his head around, stunned by her remark. It was not like her to be verbally aggressive and he was taken aback for a moment.

"What do you mean by that?" he snapped. "The state coffers had nothing to do with this! I have paid for this entire project out of my personal fortune. How can you dare to say such a thing to me, Mahperi Hatun, you, who are taking any gold coin you please from our state treasury to build that folly of yours in Kayseri? Remember that as State Superintendent of Works, I am the only one who can authorize building projects in the Empire. You interfered enough with that authority at Kubadabad, and I said nothing, and you had absolutely no right to start building that complex in Kayseri without my permission, but I held my tongue and did nothing to impede you. In any case, it will be a minor piece of architecture compared to this glorious han," he sputtered.

Mahperi had been expecting his jealousy over her project, but his barbs infuriated her to react. She snapped back at him, surprised at the animosity in her heart that spilled out in her words.

"May I remind you, Vizier Köpek, that I am the mother of the Sultan? The entire fortune in the coffers of this empire is mine should I want it. I am of the ruling family, not a mere appointed court servant, as you are. Yet I am using my own personal monies to build that 'minor piece of architecture' in Kayseri as you choose to call it. The Sultan Alaeddin Keykubad left me a substantial fortune, I have my father's dowry and inheritance, and my son takes care of my every financial need. So I have no need to rob the state treasury to pay for my project," she emphasized, making sure that he heard by her tone that she had completely understood that he was doing the contrary, despite his boastful denial.

Mahperi realized now the extent of the ascending trajectory of Köpek since the death of Alaeddin. She knew that he exerted a charismatic influence over her son as his trusted advisor, and that he was an all-powerful minister at the court. With that authority came all the related benefits, and his luxurious lifestyle was without any doubt in her mind funded by the embezzlement of state funds on an astonishing scale. All the court listened to him, and all lived in fear of him. He had inside knowledge to every aspect of the court and personal lives of its actors.

He had been indispensable in ensuring that her son was sitting on the throne today, as well as for shoring up the finances of his crony emirs. The building of this han proves that he is surely unassailable, she thought. Or is he?

She continued her tirade, spewing forth many emotions so long bottled up inside of her. "And may I ask, Vizier Sadettin Köpek, just where that personal fortune of yours came from? I am curious, for just where would you have been able to amass such a large amount of money on your own as a servant to the Sultan, if you had not had your greedy fists inside the Sultan's treasure chest as well?"

"How dare you speak to me like that!" he screamed at her. "Remember what I can do to you!"

"Oh, yes, Köpek, I remember," she sneered, "And you remember, too, that I can speak to you however I wish. I have kept my end of the bargain in your business to put my son on the throne. I have supported you and stayed out of the way. But I will not have you saying untoward remarks about Kubadabad or my Kayseri project. That I will not tolerate," she glowered, surprised at how hardened she had become since the events of Kubadabad and her husband's death.

He looked at her and burst out in one of his high-pitched laughs, exposing his stained and crooked teeth. "Yes, of course, you would not want me to say anything against that fancy French architect of yours, for we all certainly knew how close you were to him."

Mahperi knew there was no point retorting to his remark, for it would enflame the situation even more. Although burning with anger, she sweetly smiled at Köpek and said, "Yes, I was close to him, for he was by far the finest architect this Empire has, or will, ever see. No one can ever come near his level of talent, no matter how hard they try," she said, abruptly turning away.

She walked over to the carpets where her group of servants had set up her cushions, feeling the eyes of Köpek boring a hole into her back. She sat down and tried to regain her composure as she looked out at the lavish banquet now being set out in the middle of the courtyard. He has humiliated me one last time, she thought. As if he had not gotten his fill at Kubadabad, now he must continue it even tonight. But I will settle my score for your remarks just now, she thought. I will show you what it is to build with love and generosity, and to create buildings of skill and beauty. She paused for a moment to control her anger, but suddenly its heat turned into flowing water. Yes, suddenly it became very clear in her mind what she needed to do to prove her point. Not only will I build my complex in Kayseri, she vowed to herself, but I will build my very own han, a han more beautiful even than this one. Köpek will regret his remarks a thousand fold, the day he stands in awe outside the door of *my* han. For I am not his servant. I am the most powerful woman in this Empire, and he will live to lament the day he gave me that authority.

☪ ☪ ☪

This first supper served at the han started out with a soup of tender okra and minced meat. Knowing that *etli bamya* soup was the Sultan's favorite, Köpek ensured that Giyaseddin would eat heartily and happily. The soup would be followed by a chopped salad of cucumbers and fresh radishes served with *su boreği*, delicate puff pastries stuffed with meat. With the guests' appetites now well opened, the servants would then bring in teeming pots of *ekmek salmasi*, a stew of tiny cubes of lamb served with buttered bits of toasted bread. The main course would be the most famous dish of the Konya kitchens, *firin kebab*, lamb grilled for hours until it was tender enough to eat with a spoon, and served on platters along with fresh green onions, parsley and quarters of white onions.

Mountains of bread poured out of the ovens of the han's kitchens as fast as the bakers' paddles could shovel them out, and other cooks sat on the ground flipping thin sheets of *saç arası*, a flatbread griddled on heated metal plates. The servants ran from group to group with pitchers of buttermilk and apricot nectar, making sure their goblets were always filled. On sideboards, gold platters covered with quinces and apples sparkled in the candlelight awaiting the end of the meal, when they would be brought out to be enjoyed during the musical performance. Above all, Köpek had not forgotten how sugar ruled the Sultan, and so had provided mounds of dates with pistachios and honeyed cakes awaiting his delight.

The evening progressed, with the excitement of the guests increasing with each course served. The emirs praised the glory of Köpek; caftans, gold rings and carved stones glittered under the bright moon and stars, and the songs of the Azerbaijani singers made the nightingales weep in jealousy. It was indeed a night to remember.

☪ ☪ ☪

After a brief intermission in the performance, the musicians struck up a long, intoxicating melody on their reed instruments. Despite the differences between the Turkic dialect of their country and that of the Seljuks, all were able to understand the poetry of their songs. While performing a particularly poignant song, the musicians were disrupted by a shrill shriek coming from the other side of the courtyard. The astonished singer and musicians paused to gape at the boisterous tussle at the front door between Köpek's guards and a screaming woman frantically trying to force her way past them.

"Of course I have every right to be here! You cannot bar my entry!" the woman screeched, thrashing in the grip of Köpek's guards. "I am the late Sultan's Queen, mother of the true heir to the throne!"

It was Gaziye, that one person of the Konya court that Köpek had made sure was not invited to the ceremony, but she had obviously refused to stay away. Despite all their efforts, the guards could not overpower the feisty woman and her private bodyguards.

Köpek rushed over to the door to impede her entry and to avoid a scene in front of all his guests, yet she glared at him and squealed out loudly enough for the entire courtyard to hear as she tussled in the grip of his guards.

"How dare you push me aside and not invite me to this banquet! You have not dared to face me since you stole the throne away from my son, so I am obliged to come all the way here to confront you! You have betrayed me! We were friends and you have used me! No one defies me! I am an Abbasid princess and mother of two sons of the Sultan, not just one, and a stupid one, to boot!"

Turning to Mahperi who had come over to witness the scene, she hissed, "And you, you little witch Mahperi! Enjoy your days as the Sultana, for they are numbered! I will get my son on that throne, even if I have to bring in all the Abbasid armies of my family to do so! I will get my revenge on the both of you!" she shrieked.

Then, as all the guests looked on, she wrestled herself free from the grip of the guards. Springing as quickly as a cat, she grabbed a large serving pot of *etli bamya* soup from the hands of a dumbstruck servant, and with a surprising force for such a small woman, she hurled its contents directly at Köpek's head. The boiling stew scalded his face and ran down the front of his embroidered caftan.

Aides rushed over to wipe off the steaming soup from his face, but huge blisters had already begun to rise on his reddened skin. Köpek looked down at the hundreds of stewed okra buds now dripping down his luxurious gown, their shapes oddly imitating the leaf patterns embroidered on the precious silk cloth.

He lifted his head and glared at Gaziye, wiping away the bits of meat from his eyes. "You should *never* have done that, woman; you will pay dearly for this scandalous affront. Your days here are over; you have just lost your battle and the entire war!"

He barked out to his guards, waving them over to his side.

"Take her away! Get her out of here!"

As they struggled to subdue her and her private guards, the fuming Köpek called his most trusted advisor, Emir Ozbaş, to his side. Lowering his voice so that no one else could hear, he leaned close to Ozbaş and hissed into his ear.

"Get rid of her! Do you understand me? I never want to see her ever again, *ever*! I am counting on you to make sure that she never returns to the Konya

Palace. Have her absconded on her way back to Konya; kill her guards if you need to! Take her directly to Ankara and lock her up in the fortress there until I give you further orders. This will be the last supper she will ever share with the court. From now on, her meals will be taken alone, amid the dark walls of the castle keep," he seethed to his aide through clenched teeth, his pride stinging as sharply as the skin of his burned face. "How dare she humiliate me on the occasion of the first supper in my glorious new han! She will pay for this dearly! Now get her out of my sight!"

Chapter 81

In the Shadow of the Sun

The entire Konya court buzzed with gossip and rumors flew in all directions the morning after the inauguration ceremonies of Sadettin Köpek's han. What really happened last night? Was it true that Gaziye Hanim had thrown a pot of hot stew at the head of Köpek? Was it true she then slapped the Sultana Mahperi's face? Was it true that the walls of the han were lined with gold tiles?

But the most insistent question on peoples' minds was "*Where is Gaziye?*" for no one had seen her since she was escorted out of the han after the incident with the bamya stew. Both she and her body guards had yet to return to Konya. Perhaps she was so embarrassed that she decided to stay away for a bit until things calmed down. Perhaps she was headed south to Antalya or even to her home in the Syria; but wherever she was, she was certainly not in her rooms, and no one had any idea of her whereabouts.

☪ ☪ ☪

The Sultan Giyaseddin Keyhüsrev woke up the next morning with a very heavy head, and he knew it would take him a long stay in a hot hammam to clear his fuzzy mind before he could face anyone. He, too, tried to remember what had happened the night before at the festivities for the opening of Sadettin's han. He remembered how happy he was to see his mother arrive; he recollected being overwhelmed by the opulence of the han, which rivaled anything his father had built; he recalled the many goblets of succulent drinks that Köpek served and the delicious food; oh yes, my favorite, that delectable *etli bamya* soup! But the one thing the Sultan had trouble remembering was the ruckus caused by a screaming and kicking Gaziye Hanim and a steaming pot of *etli bamya* soup.

The door to the hammam opened and through the steam, Giyaseddin could make out the figure of Köpek approaching him. It was rare that the two of them bathed together, and when Köpek dismissed the guards from the room to go stand outside at the door, Giyaseddin realized that the Vizier had come to discuss a matter with him in private. It was well-known that the steam and running water of the hammam guaranteed privacy from eaves-dropping ears in more public spaces.

"Good morning, your Eminence. I hope you enjoyed the events of the banquet. In fact, I come to you to speak about what happened last night," he stated, not wasting anytime with pleasantries.

"Indeed, can you explain to me exactly what did happen there at the end with Gaziye? It all is a bit unclear to me!" the Sultan confessed.

After Sadettin gave him the details about the incident of the uninvited eruption, angry insults and tossed stew, he became more serious.

"Your Highness, I am not here just to talk to you about that silly woman. It is much more serious than that. You have two sons of your own now, my Sultan. Your little Izzeddin Keykavus is now a fine boy of four and your newborn Rukneddin Kilich Arslan is in good health and growing more robust with each day. And there will be many more sons to come, I am sure, especially after your marriage to the Georgian princess, which will take place soon. I am currently completing the preparations to have her arrive at the court shortly. The succession to your throne is definitely assured now."

"And just what does this have to do with Gaziye and what she did last night?" the Sultan asked, his thoughts still befuddled by the after-effects of all that he had drunk the night before.

"If I may speak frankly, my Sultan, last night's incident is a very unfortunate augur of things to come. Gaziye's continued presence at the court does not bode well for you. This woman is volatile and bitter, and she will continue to cause trouble. If she is capable of throwing a pot of stew at a vizier's head, then what could be next? A knife in your belly? I enjoin you to remove her from this court, to distance yourself from her, for your very life may be menaced. Worse yet, as long as she remains here, your throne is continually in danger, for she is still determined to put her son in what she maintains is his rightful place. She must be dismissed from this court immediately, along with her sons, for they risk your very position as Sultan! She will organize plots to dethrone you, of that I can guarantee. You do not need the emirs riled once again into divisive factions. All the emirs must solidly back you and you alone, and the only way to do that is to remove her and your rivals totally from sight," he stressed firmly.

"Just what are you proposing, Köpek?"

"I want her locked up far from here, in the fortress at Ankara. There our men will watch over her and make sure she has contact with no one. In that way your throne will be safe," he insisted.

"And my brothers? What harm have they done to require being locked up?"

"They too, must be removed from this court, for as long as they are here, they will be a reminder that you were not the designated heir to the throne.

Their presence here will continue to inflame certain emirs steadfastly loyal to the memory of your father. And if there is one lesson to be learned from your father's reign, it is that the emirs must be held in check at all times."

"But this is a bit drastic isn't it? They are my half-brothers after all," pointed out the Sultan.

Yet as soon as he pronounced those words, they froze on his lips. How could he have forgotten? Certain memories now came back to him as clearly as daylight through his muddled brain and the steamy mist of the hammam. He saw the brilliant smile of his father shining upon the face of his brother while he, the first-born son, stood cowering in the corner of the room. He heard his father's booming laughter as he followed the toddling steps of his half-brother, sweeping him up into his arms just before he tumbled to the ground. He remembered wiping away his rejected mother's tears as they rolled down her cheeks. He remembered Gaziye's hard gaze upon him as he was sent off to Erzincan, banished from the court and away from his mother. Yes, he remembered all of those things very clearly now, and even though he could not remember what happened last night, those images were forever etched into his mind. Now I have the opportunity to banish them forever, he thought; yes, my Vizier is right, I should expel Gaziye and my brothers, especially that golden boy, Izzeddin al-Din Kilicarslan, the one who stole my father's love from me.

Sadettin Köpek continued to plead his case.

"My Sultan, we have no choice. Izzeddin is now ten years old and will soon be of an age when he can pose a threat to you. The boys must be sent in exile to a separate prison from their mother, where they will not be under her influence. If not, she will continue to fill them with the fire of revenge. Believe me, one day they will turn on you and claim their rights, and if they manage to gather enough emirs and support from the Abbasid court, your days as Sultan will be numbered!"

"But how can we do this? Surely they cannot just disappear without gossip and fear swelling all through the court!"

"Do not worry about that," Köpek interjected. "We can spread the story that after the embarrassing events of last night, all three of them have decided to return to her homeland of Abbasid Syria for an extended stay. I will send Gaziye to the Ankara Fortress, and the boys to the Burgulu Castle in Isparta, with several of our most faithful guards to watch over them. They will have no contact with their mother or anyone here at the court."

"For how long?"

"That we will see later, my Sultan; do not concern yourself with that right now. The most important thing is that Gaziye and her sons be locked away far from here, far from harm to your throne. You agree with this, do you not? I have already prepared the papers for you to sign giving the orders, and as soon as we step out of this restorative bath, we can get the process in order."

Köpek smiled to himself about how once again he had so easily manipulated the Sultan to carry out his plans. He needed to make sure that the Sultan himself issued the official order in writing under his royal signature, so that no evidence of the responsibility for this act could ever be traced back to him.

"Enough business for this morning!" Köpek clapped his hands for the bath attendants to come back into the *caldarium*. "Now that we have decided upon that issue, why don't you tell me more about your favorite song from last night's concert!" he asked, winking at the Sultan through the mist.

Chapter 82

Cutting the Stairs to Heaven

We live in a world of mallets and chisels, crowbars and pickaxes, soaked wedges and pulleys, winches and windlasses. We tear cubic yards of stone out of the earth, we carve straight and curved edges, and we cut deep grooves so the stones can grip each other once they are set in place in the wall. We sort the blocks by thickness; we stockpile and number them in inventory books; we select out the special stones, we crush the bad stones into rubble, we load the good ones on flatbed wagons to haul to the great city in the shadow of the Majestic Mountain to build a mosque for a blessed Lady. The muscles of our arms are always sore, our lungs are filled with dust, our beards are white with poultice. We are soldiers armed with mallets and chisels instead of bows and arrows. We confront a daily battle of carving stone after stone, coming at us like Mongol warriors over the crest of the hill. Instead of racing across the plains in battle, we sit on the ground with the block between our outstretched legs. We are the stonecutters.

At the same time we live in a world detached from all human reality. We must become the stone first before we can cut it; we must feel its pulse meeting ours. We must work with the same precision of movement as the beating of our hearts. All must unite so we can sense what stone to select for cutting and dressing and be able to find the tender spot where the block can be split apart. Even when we look up to the raw cliff face of the quarry we can hear the voice of the one we should go after, calling out to us from a magical instinct that is not human. It is our instinct, the instinct of the stonecutter. We know that each stone has a soul, and it is our duty to find it.

The pile of stones we dress never melts away; the work never ceases. Day after day we toil with our eyes fixed on the face of the stone, breathing in the dust raised by the chisels in their continuous rhythmic flow. Strong hands, strapping forearms, balanced hand, an eye as sharp as our tools; tapping over and over again in the same movement to dress the stones of a royal Lady's mosque. Such is our burden, to turn out one cubit of stone a day, on a good day.

We fix our eyes on the block of the moment and cannot think of yesterday's or tomorrow's work or our dinner tonight at the end of the hard day. We must be fixed to this precise moment in time; our hands and hearts beating in unison. The chips fly away with each breath, the space between the chisel and the hammer widens, and then the stone springs free. Today, it is born at this moment, just as another will spring again tomorrow. Our work is repetitive and tempoed as we lovingly caress the music and the color out of these stones. We work to reach the sacred moment when we can penetrate into the world of stone, to become ourselves the stones of the building to rise. Only the stone matters, and its quality must be perfect. Each hammer blow is a dialogue with God. Our days are filled with bloody hands, crushed feet and toes, slipped chisels that cut off fingers, eyes strained to the point of blindness; days full of work producing nothing but crumbling stone. Yet our work must be perfect. No chaos can reign in the quarry; every gesture must be measured and precise and safe, just as You, o God, make this world safe from the chaos of ignorance.

We work far from the construction site to prepare the stone that will build the mosque. Our work is anonymous, without signature or recognition. The humility of a well-cut stone is all we need to touch our reward. From the depth of each well-cut stone springs forth a prayer, a song, a musical note, a poem, or a rose: that is our dream for the stones we cut.

We dream of the ideal stone. We lift the block up with winches into the bright turquoise sky and watch its turning edges sparkle like diamonds. We lay it down on the ground as gently as a baby in its cradle. We then study it, stare at it, poke at it with sticks and place our hands on it to feel its energy, for each stone has its own heartbeat. Is there a volcano inside of it like the one inside the Majestic Mountain above the city? Will it rumble like an earthquake and crumble into bits? Will it be strong enough to bear the weight of the wall, at the same time light enough to bear the flight of the architect's vision? Does it have a deep internal crack like the secret faults of so many men? If the stone meets our hopes, we send it to be dressed. If we are lucky, the work of 100 men will yield one good block of stone per day. If it does not meet our hopes, we toss it to the graveyard of unworthy stones, to be crushed into bits to be used as fill under the foundations of the mosque. There is room for all God's matter in His world.

We dream that we can give the builders the unlimited audacity to turn our blocks of stone into weightless and opaque prayers to the glory of God. We dream of You in the exceptional dimensions that our work will build, and we work to be worthy of You.

We, the stonecutters, we dream of the staircase of light that our stones will build. We dream of the first footprints of God that will tread upon that staircase of light; the one to be built from the stones we cut here today, now, in this moment, in our world of mallets and chisels.

Allahu akbar.

Chapter 83
The Dark Face of the Mountain

The foothills of the Majestic Mountain of Kayseri are filled with lush meadows that overflow with singing birds, fluttering butterflies and colorful flowers.

Yet there is another side of the mountain, the one that faces away from the bright beauty of the blessings of God's nature. There are deep and dark shadows on this side of the Mountain, a place where storm clouds gather and avalanches fall. On this side of the mountain live wolves and scorpions, which come out at night in stealth to claim their prey. Like the souls of many men, the Mountain has two faces, one of goodness and one of evil.

Yet it is not just in the foothills of the Majestic Mountain where the predators prowl, but in Palace rooms as well.

☪ ☪ ☪

Jealousy and revenge brewed a toxin which poisoned Köpek's heart with each passing year lived in the shadow of the glorious Alaeddin. Angered by the fact that Mahperi was now building a mosque in defiance to his position as Superintendent of Works, humiliated by Gaziye in front of all his guests at the inauguration of his han, and contested at court by emirs who challenged his command, he found it increasingy difficult to control his seething anger. His scorpion stinger twitched in hate, and he vowed to make all of them pay for their disobedience to him, Sadettin Köpek, the most powerful man in the land.

He decided to begin with the easiest target: women. After banishing Gaziye, he now turned his wrath to Mahperi.

And so Köpek found himself, in the middle of a moonless night, breaking into the architect's shed on the worksite of Mahperi's mosque. He had never understood why she had hired this plodding Greek to mastermind her project, and he was enraged that she had excluded him, the talented Superintendent of Works, from all aspects of the project. Holding his lantern high above his head to scrutinize the contents of the shed, Köpek soon found what he was looking for. He approached the wooden table where the drawings for the Sultana's mosque were spread out, their curling edges weighed down by bricks. He peered at them under the flickering light of his candle for a long time, admiring the detailed tracery and masterful draftsmanship he saw there. Well, it would seem he is not so plodding after all, thought Köpek to himself bitterly, for these lines attest to the talent of a true master. His jealousy rose as he realized that he would have been incapable of producing anything as fine as this.

He turned to scan the shelves along the wall, and a leather-covered notebook caught his eye. Picking it up, he slowly opened it and flipped through its leaves. They, too, were covered with skillful sketches and markings, of the same hand as the ones on the table. It took Köpek a few minutes to understand what he was looking at, but when he saw the notations scripted in an alphabet he could not read, he realized that he was holding none other than the sketchbook of Lou Cantadou.

The face of the French architect flashed in front of his eyes, filling him with an envy rarely felt before. Köpek carefully studied the notebook, his wrath increasing with each page he turned. No, he would not tolerate any shadow cast by the memory of this man, this man who earned the admiration of both a Sultan and his Queen, who could draw with the grace of an angel and who could bring the most supreme artistry to life. No, this he would no longer endure.

His rage exploded, and with a gigantic stroke of his arm, he swept all the architect's tools off the shelf, dashing them to the floor in a huge clatter. He then grabbed the rolls of drawings from the table and frantically began to rip them into pieces, throwing the bits onto the floor. Out of malicious fury, Köpek lifted up his right foot and brought it down upon the pile, grinding his heel into the drawings until all the sketches were obliterated by the mud of his heavy boots. He then threw Lou's notebook on top of them and spat upon it. As a final gesture of wrath, he smashed his lantern down on the pile, causing the dry paper and parchment to erupt into an immediate burst of flames. Köpek's high-pitched laugh bounced off the walls of the shack in glee over his settling of scores, as he fled the shack out into the night.

☪ ☪ ☪

The next day, the construction site hummed with the news of the fire in the architect's shed. As the workers sifted through the ashes, all offered prayers of thanksgiving for the fact that the fire had been caught very early on by the night watchman, before it could spread to the entire site and cause extensive damage to the rest of the buildings.

When Mahperi arrived that morning for her daily inspection tour, she was stunned by this misfortune, despite the reassurances by Nikolas that he was able to remember most of the plans by heart and that the progress of the project would not be compromised in any way.

"How could this have happened?" she asked him, visibly upset by this omen. "I just don't understand how this could have happened in the middle of the night when the site was empty. Aren't there guards posted at the entry to the grounds?"

"Yes, there are, but this is a huge site to control. It could have happened for a number of reasons, perhaps nothing more than a cat knocking over a lantern," he said, trying to reassure her as best he could.

Yet, there was no reassuring Mahperi, for her intuition immediately told her that this was no mere accident, but rather a definite act of arson. It was the only explanation possible, and she was sure that Nikolas thought the same.

The fire was still smoldering as she walked through the damaged shed, its smoke stinging her eyes. As she brought up her handkerchief to her mouth to block the strong smell of the fumes, her eyes fell upon the most precious object of the room, now lying in the smoldering ashes. She walked over and fished out the charred notebook of Lou from the debris with the end of a stick. By some miracle of divine grace, its thick leather cover had protected it, and the pages inside had only been singed on their edges. She picked it up and held it to her chest and closed her eyes, bringing back the memory of the other attempts that had been made to destroy their friendship. Both the fuming wisps of smoke and the sad memories stung the back of her eyes, causing tears to run down her cheeks.

No, this fire was not caused by something as simple as a cat. The powerful destructive force of jealousy was a clue that Mahperi could not ignore. Images of the smashing plates of Kubadabad came flashing back to her, and she knew exactly who was behind this attempt to stop her in her tracks. She had seen this all before.

Yet, she was not worried for her personal honor and safety, nor for the outcome of her project, for she knew the walls would soon rise and that the architect Nikolas no longer needed to refer to a piece of paper to envision them. Her project was but a small piece of the overall situation at hand. What really worried her more was the insidious influence that Köpek exerted over the entire Kingdom, through his manipulation of her son and by his abuses of power.

As advisor to Giyaseddin, Köpek's influence had grown considerably. His first goal had been to secure the throne for him, and after that, there was no more controlling him. It was apparent to Mahperi that Köpek was striving to be more than a Prime Minister by usurping all the power for himself. She saw now, as he was becoming more and more powerful, that he was beginning to make rash political and private moves. He had ordered ill-advised military campaigns, such as the one against the Khwarazmians that ended badly with the rash assassination of Kirkhan. He spent the court's money lavishly, notably to build his han. He chose to close his eyes to the Turkmen revolt now beginning to seethe in the Eastern provinces. Worst of all in Mahperi's eyes was how he preyed upon the weakness of her son Giyaseddin.

Clutching Lou's charred notebook to her chest, Mahperi feared that the worst was yet to come. She knew that before long, her deepest fears concerning the eventual outcome of Köpek's ambitions would become a reality from which there was no turning back. She knew this menacing situation, now smoldering like the smoke of the ashes of the fire of the site shack, would soon burst into flames of destruction. But she had no idea what to do to prevent it.

Ever since Köpek had tried to blackmail her, Mahperi had swallowed her pride and had sincerely tried to work with him, even though she knew he would be her enemy forever. She also knew full well that he wanted all the power for himself. She noted how her son was becoming increasingly depraved under his influence. Mahperi could see the effects of all the alcohol that was being poured into her son daily by Köpek to muddle his mind. She needed to get Giyaseddin to stop this lunacy, for she knew he was totally submissive to these poisons. And for that evil, Köpek was responsible, which in her eyes was his most vile sin.

Yet, Mahperi had no idea that it was not just the two of them that were targeted as victims. Soon, Köpek would strike with an even deadlier sting than the one he reserved for her son or for drawings at a construction site.

With his ambition increasing with each day, Köpek wanted to assert that he, and he alone, was in charge, and to do this, he knew he had to eliminate each and every one of his competitors. He took no heed of the lesson learned from the backlash after the murder of the Khwarazmian chief Kirkhan. Continuing to take advantage of the weakness of Giyaseddin, he now laid a plan to use his power over the young sultan to rid the court of any rival emir he felt stood in his way.

The evil sting first fell upon an easy victim, the elderly Emir Shemseddin Altinapa. Köpek had heard rumors that the white-bearded elder statesman was telling certain members of the court that there was no cure for a rabid dog. Although Altinapa was Giyaseddin's former tutor and a strong supporter of the Sultan, Köpek would not tolerate this veiled, yet outright, criticism against him. Altinapa, one of the most revered and experienced emirs at the court, had faithfully served the five Seljuk sultans as an important counselor. He had also had built from his own purse a large han outside of Konya and an impressive landmark mosque in the center of town. In the eyes of an enraged Köpek, this made Altinapa too venerable, and gave him all the more reason to eliminate him. He concocted a pretext that Altinapa was now too feeble to be of any service to the throne, and that it was he who had incited Kirkhan to ally himself with the Ayyubids. Abetted by Emir Taceddin, Köpek assassinated the aged and defenseless Altinapa in the dark of night. No one dared to protest this wicked act, for all lived in fear that the Dog would turn on them next.

And turn he did. The next sting was reserved for Emir Kaymeri, another faithful servant to the throne. Under a flimsy pretext of mutiny, Köpek had him arrested at Malatya and imprisoned in its fortress, with the hope that he would languish there until the end of his days. It was only upon paying vast sums of money from his personal fortune to Köpek that Kaymeri was able to negotiate his release.

Yet these two events did nothing to calm the anger of his rampage, and Köpek continued to cast suspicion on anyone who threatened to outshine his need for glory.

The biggest threat of all to Köpek came from the powerful Kemaleddin Kamyar. It was the illustrious Commander Kamyar who rode with the Sultan Alaeddin Keykubad on his final journey to Keykubadiyye Palace, and who was at his side when he died. Ever since that day, Köpek sensed that Kamyar looked at him with clouded eyes. Köpek could not bear the sideways suspicious glances of Kamyar upon him, and felt uneasy each time they were in a room together. He knows something for certain about the darkness of that night, Köpek thought, and I cannot risk having it come out in the light of day.

Köpek had Kamyar arrested at Konya with a fabricated charge and exiled him to the fortress of Kayala, where he gave orders to have the valiant commander strangled to death. The noble Kamyar, the commander-in-chief who confronted Jelaleddin Menguberti at the decisive battle of Yassicimen, this valiant soldier who dealt fearlessly with the Ayyubids and who had led the Sultan's troops to so many other resounding victories, paid with his life for the honored place he held as a hero of the reign of the great Sultan Alaeddin Keykubad. Emir Kamyar, the most eminent and trusted of the Sultan's servants, his ambassador to all the lands and one of his most able government officials, now lay on the floor of a castle keep at Kayala, his breath stilled by a soul tortured by jealousy.

With the murder of Kamyar came the death of all goodness and nobility in the land. It was not just the great Sultan Alaeddin Keykubad who met a tragic end, but also all those who participated in the prominence of his reign. A dark night now settled over the sun-filled days of the Empire he had built.

The last victim of Köpek's dark rampage of envy was none other than the Emir Taceddin, who had previously helped him assassinate the aged Altinapa. Regretting his participation in this abominable event, Taceddin now realized that Köpek was overstepping all bounds of reason and decency. Fearing that one day his own end could be orchestrated in this descending whorl of madness, Taceddin left the Konya court and withdrew to live in Ankara, but even there he could not flee the wrath of the vizier. With no explainable logic, Köpek now turned his rage against his former ally.

Standing in front of the *ulema* court at Konya, Köpek accused Taceddin of intriguing against the Sultan, and procured a *fatwa* decree against him from the court jurists. To further reinforce his fabricated case, he added a dose of moral scandal, claiming that Taceddin was living with a well-known prostitute from Konya. Köpek, armed with the judgment of the *ulema*, flew on horseback from Konya to Ankara in a record speed of two days, so intent was he to deliver the *fatwa*. Once in Ankara, he arrested Taceddin, brought him back to Konya to stand in front of a tribunal in the presence of the Sultan. The weak Sultan Giyaseddin Keyhüsrev, egged on by Köpek in front of his magnates, approved the guilty sentence pronounced by the *ulema* of Konya. With the verdict in hand, Köpek took Taceddin back to Ankara where he had him publicly executed in a ghastly scene that went far beyond the vileness of anything he had done before. In one of the most despicable scenes ever known to the Empire, Köpek buried his victim in the ground up to his waist and then ordered the mob to stone him. Even in this era plagued by the violence of the Mongols, the sordid murder of Taceddin was above all bounds.

Köpek was now running totally amok. Beyond the baseness of his acts, the murdering spree of viziers was depriving the state of its most skillful administrators. It would only be a matter of time until the results of this misguided policy of eliminating wise voices in a time of external threat and increasing internal instability would be keenly felt. As much as Mahperi and the other trusted advisors pleaded with Giyaseddin to halt the spread of Köpek's reign of violence, there was no stopping his murdering rampage bent on assassinating his rivals, one after the other.

The Seljuk Empire now lived in the deep and dark face of the Majestic Mountain, there, where the wolves and scorpions came out at night in stealth to claim their prey, seldom missing their marks.

Chapter 84

A Necklace of Seven Topaz Gems

The conversation and laughter of the merchants sitting around the fire in the han courtyard crackled as brightly as its flames. They gathered there, on this chilly November night in the year 1238, warming their weary bones after a long day on the road, telling stories and sharing news, singing along with the minstrel on his ud, and sipping warm broth from a pot nestled in the glowing embers. The new Sultan had been reigning for over a year, but the men still spoke of the glories of his father, the great Sultan Alaeddin Keykubad, Eminence of the Faith.

One of the Syrian traders spread his arms wide and gestured to each of the four corners of the courtyard. "He was a glorious leader, that Alaeddin Keykubad, to have built for us this spectacular han here in Tuzhisar! It has to be the finest one in all the land, even finer than the one he built in Aksaray!"

The other merchants all nodded their agreement, and were quick to praise the late Sultan for his generosity in building this han located in a small village outside of Kayseri.

At that moment the hinges of the heavy wooden doors of the han creaked loudly and all turned to see the doors swing open to allow the entry of a large contingent of palace guards. The merchants stared at the brightly-colored retinue, dressed so differently from the usual dusty travelers with their packs of animals and goods. Their lively chatter came to a halt when they saw that the guards surrounded none other than Mahperi Hatun, the mother of the reigning sultan.

The startled merchants rose to their feet, confused about what to do in front of this venerable visitor and widow of the man whose praises they had just been singing. Sensing their awkwardness, Mahperi Hatun, Sultana of the Seljuk Empire, spoke right up.

"Good evening, my fine men; please, return to your places around the fire! My, it is certainly chilly tonight! I am thankful to see so many of you benefiting from the generosity provided by my husband. With your permission, I would like to join you."

Still stunned by this highly-irregular visit by a member of the royal family, several of the merchants scurried to make a place for her. The Sultana's guards spread out a carpet for her, and, to the astonishment of the gaping merchants, she sat down alongside them. None could believe that the most powerful woman in the land was now sitting next to them around a courtyard fire!

True to her usual direct and open manner, Mahperi wasted no time in ending their curiosity. "My good men, thank you for allowing me to join you. I have come here tonight for a specific reason. I want to ask you some questions that I believe are important ones for all of us," she broached, amused to see the puzzled look on their faces.

"As merchants, you spend much of your time on the roads of this Kingdom, and they have made you rich. Hans like this one have allowed you to broker in peace and security. The late sultan Alaeddin Keykubad, may God shine light on his existence, wanted nothing more than to ensure your well-being," she explained. All the men nodded and praised his name to God most high.

"But I think there is still more to be done to build up our empire, and for this I am asking your help. I want to know what you need in order to successfully trade in our lands. There are already many hans along the Long Road leading from Kayseri through Aksaray and over to Konya. My son is also building a series of hans along the southern seacoast road between Antalya and Alaiye. But I ask you, what more do you need? Where is the most pressing call in the land for a han like this one to be built? Where do you want bridges and roads restored? Speak up! I am listening to you!"

At first the merchants were too shy to talk. Some feared this was a trick to get them to complain and betray the goodwill already shown on them. Yet all knew the honest reputation of this woman. All knew that she was devoted to her subjects, and many had heard about the mosque she was building in the big city down the road. An elderly trader from Persia took the lead and raised his voice.

"My Lady, my name is Isfandiyar and I come from far away, from Tabriz in Persia, to trade here in your lands, mostly in furs. Journeys on the roads of this empire are often arduous, but we take solace that we will not get lost or robbed. The hans your husband built have removed this fear. We feel safe here. We are a moveable world journeying through your empire, and our sandals beat down the dust of your roads. We are our own army, but instead of soldiers, we fill your lands with traders and peddlars. On the road we are a small city on the hoof, sharing the fraternity of the journey with our animals. We answer to every God; we speak to Him in every language. All we ask is to be protected from bandits and to carry out our trade. But, if I may speak so boldly, you are right; we could use more help in our task, and I would ask that your good grace shine upon my request."

The merchants listened with bated breath, and Mahperi nodded for him to continue with his comments.

"If honest truth be told, My Lady, and I believe you are a woman who seeks such truth, there is still more to do. As you said, there are many fine hans linking the great cities of Kayseri, Aksaray and Konya, but there are fewer way-stations on the other roads of the land, especially in the north. We need more hans on the northern routes leading up from Kayseri and on the southern routes leading down to Iraq!" he urged, and the other men nodded their agreement.

"Yes! I have the same trouble coming over to Erzurum and up to the Crimea with my goods!" interjected a young tin merchant from Afghanistan.

All the men started to speak up at once, and Mahperi was surprised to see the intensity of their requests. The elderly merchant from Persia raised his hand to silence the others, and turned once more to the Sultana.

"You see, my Lady, Kayseri is a magnet for all of us. We come from afar to trade here, for this city is the hub of the commerce wheel, where two major trade routes converge. One is the northern route, the one I take, which leads down from the Caucasus through Erzurum and Sivas. The other fork is the southerly route coming up to Kayseri from Mesopotamia, Syria, and Malatya. Once we arrive in Kayseri, we can continue on to anywhere in the Kingdom between Aksaray, Konya and the Mediterranean coast. But we need help in getting our goods safely over to Kayseri in the first place before we can get them to the bazaars of the capital of Konya! There are, alas, few hans along the stretch of road coming down from the north, passing through Sivas to Kayseri. The road is an arduous climb through those parts, and we all need to stop at Tokat to rest before continuing. It would be beneficial for us to have a han there, much like this one, as well as several others in the region!"

Tokat!

The name rang out clearly in Mahperi's ears and her eyes lit up. It was there, she remembered, in this town set on a green river bordered with pink roses, where Alaeddin had spent his youth, and there where he had learned to play chess like a champion.

Yes, Tokat! This town could be the perfect place for the han she vowed to build on that humiliating night at the inauguration of Köpek's han. She could use the profits earned by this han to fund other building projects and to support charities, perhaps some for women. Yes, my destiny is to build in Tokat!

Mahperi snapped out of her reverie and looked at the men who were waiting for her reaction. She nodded to the merchant and spoke in a voice that cut through the night air. "I have heard your request, my fine merchant, and I give you my word tonight as Sultana of the Seljuk Empire that you will soon have a han at Tokat! May you always trade in prosperity in these lands!"

☪ ☪ ☪

The conversation with the merchants gave much to Mahperi to think about. Now that she was a widow, she could invest her substantial inheritance from Alaeddin in construction projects that would help her people. She no longer needed to worry about keeping a discrete profile so as not to outshine her husband. Her role as Sultana, mother of the Sultan, was now to glorify the reign of the son she put on earth. Furthermore, by building this han, she could show Köpek that he was not the only builder in this Empire. He will regret those remarks he made about Lou, she vowed; he will regret disgracing me at Kubadabad and humiliating me at the inauguration of his han; he will regret that he defied me.

☪ ☪ ☪

Two days later, Mahperi spoke with Nikolas who had accompanied her to the Sultan Han and had witnessed the scene with the merchants. As they walked around the mosque construction site on their daily inspection tour, she turned to Nikolas and shared her thoughts with him.

"In building this mosque, I have undertaken a project which designates my position as mother of the reigning sultan. But I must do more. That meeting with the merchants in the Tuzhisar han has encouraged yet another dream. We will build palaces for merchants now, Nikolas, just like my husband did! Yes! We will build a han in Tokat!"

She grabbed the arm of Nikolas and shook it in excitement. "We will work together here to draw the plans for the han exactly as I see them in my head," she exclaimed, her face flushed with enthusiasm. "I envision a simple building, actually, similar to the Sultan han at Tuzhisar, with a large courtyard and a covered hall to the rear," she continued, her emerald eyes gleaming. "I would like a straight-on entrance, like at Tuzhisar, not one on the side like Sadettin Köpek put on his han outside of Konya," she asserted firmly.

The architect stood stunned as he listened to her ideas for this new project. The fierce determination of this woman never failed to impress him.

"But I want to render the decorative details a bit differently: softer, and more graceful. Instead of a pointed niche filled with stalactite carving on the main door, I want a simple rounded arch. We can employ the stone carvers working on this project to reproduce the same decorative patterns as on the portals of the mosque here, for they are as delicate as lace. But in addition, I want to add elements that will reflect the beauty of the nature found in the hills and valleys surrounding Tokat. Leaves, blossoms, grape clusters, vines and pine cones can bloom on the column capitals. All must be elegant and subdued. I remember so clearly the Sultan Alaeddin saying to me: "*Overbearing decoration must never mask the structure. You must always feel the strength of the building first; the finery should only enhance it.*" Those were his words, and this is what I would like to achieve on this portal," she stated firmly.

"There is one other thing: I want the people of the surrounding village to benefit as well from this han. For that, I want to install a public fountain in the front wall. In this way, even when its doors are tightly shut for the night, the villagers will always have a place to draw drinking water. Oh, Nikolas, this will be a beautiful han, and I know it will serve for generations!"

Nikolas turned to her and scratched his head. "Well, then, let's get this project started, my Lady! Once construction starts, it should rise very quickly, for a han is a more straight-forward building than a mosque and will take less time to build. I am sure we will inaugurate it even before the muezzin calls the first prayer for your mosque in Kayseri! I will send out surveyors to scout the terrain and existing roads. I will make for you a master plan for the entire project, and submit it to you as soon as possible," he concluded.

Mahperi smiled at him, but her thoughts were already far away, at Tokat, where the valleys of green and blue hills would soon be dotted with the golden stones of her han.

☪ ☪ ☪

That evening, Mahperi's head was full of ideas for this new project and for the future. Our Lord made the world in seven days, she thought to herself, and I will make a chain of seven hans, one in praise of each day of His creation. A ribbon of seven hans for my empire; yes, that is what I will do.

As she stepped out on her terrace and gazed up at the stars glittering above the night sky over Kayseri, Mahperi looked past the Pleiades and imagined she saw another constellation in the shape of a glittering necklace of seven topaz gems. She then imagined this necklace of golden stones floating down from the heavens and draping itself around the snowy collar of the Majestic Mountain, its sparkling jewels lighting the roads of her empire in the East. It will be the most magnificent set of jewels any queen could ever dream to own, she mused.

Filled with happiness, she shouted out in the night air to all the stars above:

I am Maryam, I am Mahperi, I am Sultana, I am builder!

Chapter 85

Colored Silk, White Silk

I, Ibn Bibi, head scribe and titled historian of the Seljuk Empire, have seen and noted much in the course of my career. As official witness to the greatest empire the East has ever known, I have tried to describe every event I have witnessed with accuracy and eloquence at the same time. If needed, I let my imagination take flight and compose poems to better describe the emotions behind an event or to color the settings of my story. I am a talented writer, this I know, a refined poet of the noble Persian tradition, and I am certain that I have represented honestly and clearly the lives of those whom I depict, especially the great Sultan Alaeddin Keykubad, who appointed me to this lofty position and to whom I owe a debt of the greatest felicity.

I know, too, that my words will go down in history for all generations to read. If I did not directly witness an event, it is still my duty to try to relate the story as accurately as I can. Yet this is not always an easy task, for when stories are related to me I am certain jealousy and ambition enter into the depiction of the event. I suspect that truth is often manipulated. Yet what can I do?

Yes, I have always tried to tell every story to the best of my ability. I am charged with leaving a testament of this era. I sign my name at the bottom of every journal entry, and I take entire responsibility for what is there written. I am the court historian, for all that entails. Does anyone ever think of the burden upon me? I am not here just dipping a pen in an inkpot to write pretty words; I am crafting destiny.

But I know that one thing is certain here in this story I must now write: she is dead. I must tell her story, for the journal of this Empire, but mostly for her.

I write the following entry to my journal with as much dignity as I can. I am obliged here to put aside the personal feelings I felt for this woman. She was so strikingly beautiful, so sparkling and exotic; and she was so kind to me, always inviting me for cakes and conversation. Such glorious jewels and caftans she wore! No peacock in the royal rose garden glittered as resplendently!

I do not know exactly what happened, or who was responsible for this event. I pray to God to accept this account as the best I can portray, though my heart is breaking from the treachery here committed to my beloved friend. God will judge his servants; my sole task is to relate the facts. Those guilty will know who they are. The shameful will carry this abominable act in their souls for the rest of their days.

I now pick up my pen to write the story of the last day of the life of Queen Gaziye Hatun, as related to me by the imam there in attendance.

> ....When the winds of springtime began to blow and the pastures filled with the fresh smells of blooming flowers, the Sultan decided to march up from his winter quarters in Antalya, where he so enjoyed the sweet orange blossom clime of the end of the year. He decided to travel to his quarters in Kayseri, to be near his mother. He first directed his march towards Konya, with, in attendance, all his companions and servants, the ladies of his harem and their private guards, his menagerie of wild beasts, as well as his tents and silken flags. He then continued on to Kayseri. As was his custom, he made time for amusements, and when the group halted at Aksaray to rest, orders were given to stay over for several days of joyful entertainment.
>
> While the Sultan was distracted by these moments of revelry, the Vizier Köpek dispatched a group of soldiers to Ankara with orders concerning the future of Gaziye Hatun. She had been separated from her two loving sons and two devoted daughters for some time now; sent there to be locked up in the fortress after the scene at the inauguration of his caravansarai. It had so been decided that the time had come to deal with her destiny. There, on that spring day in 1239, the guardsmen were commanded to fetch Gaziye Hatun from her cell and to tell her to prepare to meet her Maker, the Almighty God, in paradise.
>
> This woman, being an honorable Ayyubid princess, demonstrated her virtue and honor by requesting permission to renew her ritual ablution before the executioners arrived.
>
> In order to bid farewell to life, she performed two *rekats* of prayer by turning her head towards the sky, the altar of supplication. In this position she prayed with the words: "*My God, I am your slave and invaluable daughter, your servant who has faced cruelty and fallen into despair. They have put a dark curtain between my children and me. They have endeavored to destroy my spirit and conscience and blaze my blood. My God, I now entrust my children to you. Please protect them! You always accept pardons and have mercy upon your servants, and I am one of your most devoted of servants!*"
>
> The religious authorities of the palace present there at that moment heard her last will and kept a record of it later. She kept repeating over and over the words: "*Please punish the cruel and pardon me, as well!*

Give me your mercy, forgive my sins and accept my apologies for any transgressions I have committed." At that moment she wrapped her head cover in three folds of cloth to swathe her face completely and then turned to the south in the direction of Mecca and sat down. She exchanged words of kindness with her servants, and words of forgiveness to her executioners. She then cited the words *'Kelime-i Shahadet'* and murmured verses of the Qur'an. Meanwhile, the executioners stood prepared to send this beautiful woman, virtue of this universe, to find solace in the garden of heaven.

The proud royal queen was ready, dressed in a caftan of the finest colored silk, carried to her by caravans from China by merchants who took refuge in the caravansarais built by her husband. And there, in a black cell, a cord of the strongest white silk was wrapped taut around her neck until her final breath was spent and she dropped lifeless onto the cold stones of the fortress floor.

Chapter 86

Eternity Is Waiting

It is now the month of April 1239 and the time of exaltation has come. The mosque of our Lady has sprung up from the earth like a giant tulip. It has now revealed its skeleton, and its first walls are raising their voices in song. The columns are pushing the clouds aside to make room for their capital crowns. The sun is already enamored with its surfaces, choosing to shine its first rays of day on the feet of its walls. Above the walls, swallows soar, dreaming of new roosts under its shaded eaves. Our work is now manifested in Thee. God will never be lost in this Empire; He will find home here and in the hundreds of other mosques rising in every city of this land, in every neighborhood and in every believer's heart. God, are you pleased with our work?

We, the masons, have not even completed one-half of your mosque, yet already the whole city is possessed by a crazed fever. As soon as the deep pit for the foundations was dug, the first columns rose, like the giant menhirs on the ancient shores of Lake Baikal in Siberia, home of the Turkic forefathers of the Seljuks. People came to gawk and gasp at the imaginary forest rising in front of them. The stones we placed to define the perimeter of the mosque allowed them to imagine what would come. All the mud has been forgotten and eyes now lift upwards to anticipated domes. People cup their hands in prayer, making their own little domes of private worship, for God is already there, in those foundation stones.

The people look for Him there, invoking His name in prayer, while standing on the sides of the immense space now defined by cut blocks of stone. Wind, rains and the sun of spring beat upon those stones, but the prayers of the passersby continue. Greatness will rise in our city and in our hearts, right here, they say. Our house of God is rising! This is the cry heard all across the city, and, with each passing day, more and more people come to gape. Where will be the door? Where will be the minbar? How tall will be the dome? All are there to see the work advance and cheer us on with their wishes. We are the masons who will make their dream come true, for we are making a miracle rise in front of them, stone by stone.

This is the miracle of our work, and we pray to You, o Great God, to give us the strength to continue. Our hammers sound with songs of praise to your glory. Underneath the weight of our bricks and stones, we bury all the demons of our world: hunger, war, violence, ignorance and sickness. We will crush them under each stone we lay; we will cement them hard in place there.

We keep our nose and our trowels to our work with the bricks and the stones. Our fingers ache from kneading mortar, our hands are burned by the lime in the stones and scraped raw by their rough surfaces, but we persevere. For that is all we, the humble masons, can offer to You: our hands, our hearts, our fatigue and our faith. We are masons of God, free and honorable men who choose a salary that will be paid a thousand fold once we are in heaven. God hears our prayer, and we hear His praise.

Yes, God, you are here on this site, leaning over Kayseri to supervise our work. No one can see You, but we know You are here. We make visible the invisible, and invisible the visible. Your transparent presence weighs as heavily as the solid bricks we are now laying. You whisper to us that we are doing a fine job; it is you, God, who blesses our faith, our sweat, our blood and our pain as we place brick after brick and stone after stone to build Your temple. We are not tired at the end of the day, for You give us our daily strength. Hurry, You say to us; hurry to finish this mosque, for all eternity is waiting for the completion of this temple built to My glory, built with the skill of your hands, the loving humility of your hearts and the power of your faith in Me.

Allahu akbar.

Chapter 87
Hard Feathers

It was not long after Gaziye had fallen lifeless on the cold stones of the fortress floor at Ankara that her memory disappeared from the Seljuk court, just as Köpek had planned it. Hard, cold stones were all she deserved, he thought, and his stone-cold mind hardened more and more each time he felt the memory of that steaming soup still stinging his face. He now vowed to erase every trace of her influence on this earth. The reign of terror of Köpek was far from finished.

☪ ☪ ☪

Köpek entered the rooms of Giyaseddin early one morning and found him still sleeping soundly, even though it was well past the time of the morning call to prayer.

"Giyaseddin! Get up! I need to speak with you immediately! Come to my rooms at once!" he blurted out as if addressing a stable hand instead of the royal head of the Empire. "Now!" he said, jabbing the Sultan's rump with his slipper.

A few short minutes later the Sultan stumbled into Köpek's rooms, and collapsed on his cushions. "What is so important that you needed to disturb my peaceful sleep this morning?" he asked, rubbing the stubble on his chin. "You know I do not like to get up this early! You know I go to sleep just as others are preparing to answer the dawn call to prayer!"

Köpek was all too aware of this, yet as he looked at his colt he felt no shame in it. That is just the way I want it, he thought to himself. The more dissolute and detached from normal life he is, the more incapable he is of running this Kingdom. That is my job.

"I come with an important proposal for your approval, my Sultan," he bowed, changing his harsh tone, "and that is why I have woken you early this morning. It concerns Gaziye."

"But you have taken care of that problem already, if I am not mistaken. So what is this issue?" the Sultan grumbled.

"Yes, that is correct, but it is not enough that she has been taken care of. We now must finish off her remaining traces on earth which risk threatening your throne, and this must be done as soon as possible," he enunciated slowly for emphasis.

Giyaseddin's head, throbbing from all the wine he had drunk the night before, had trouble understanding what his vizier was referring to. Just go away, his head hammered, just let me go to the hammam and we will talk about this tomorrow; I cannot face this right now.

Köpek had intentionally chosen this vulnerable moment to put forth a very thorny proposal to the Sultan, for he knew it would be best to do it when Giyaseddin was in a muddled state of mind.

"My Sultan, you have become a fine leader who has managed to garner the support of the court. Yet I still fear for the security of your throne. We must never forget that many were the emirs who supported your brother Izzeddin as the rightful heir to the throne and felt that you stole it away from him. I have managed to placate most of them, but I always worry that the winds of this opinion will continue to blow through the court, and that is what we must stop as soon as possible."

"So just what are you saying?" Giyaseddin asked, scratching his head. "I am afraid I do not understand your point."

Köpek looked at him and realized that he truly was not very bright. He is never able to think ahead, to put the elements together, to strategize with the facts at hand, much less make audacious decisions. No wonder it is so easy for me to manipulate him, but that is just the way I like it.

"I am saying you must eliminate that worry in its entirety. And in order to do that, you must do away not only with Gaziye, but her sons as well."

Köpek, like Alaeddin Keykubad, had observed the keen intelligence of the little Izzeddin Kilich Arslan. That bright and beautiful boy was clever, quick-witted and fast on his feet, and, even at his young age, it was evident that he had inherited all the finest qualities of his father and would make an exceptional leader. Yet it was more than Izzeddin's innate gifts that worried Köpek. He could not help but recall how Alaeddin Keykubad himself had been exiled by his brother to Tokat for all of his teenage years, believing him to be out of the range of harm to his throne. And yet in Tokat, Alaeddin had grown into an outstanding young man who contested the throne, mutinied against his brother and fought until the day he was finally able to seize it. We cannot allow this Izzeddin, so much like his father in character, to replay this same destiny. History must not repeat itself. We cannot risk having him earn the support of the emirs with just one radiant smile from his comely face. No, he must be removed to a place farther than the Ulu Borlu castle.

The Sultan bolted upright from his cushions and propped himself up on his elbows. "But you told me at the time we sent them away that we would only keep them as prisoners! Now that I have a son of my own as heir, there can be no more threat from them!" Giyaseddin protested.

"Don't be so stupid! Of course there is!"

"But they are my brothers! They are just two innocent boys! How can I wish them harm and how can they possibly be a threat to me?

"Your half-brothers, I remind you. They are the sons of that woman Gaziye, who brought such pain to your mother; that woman who deprived you as well of his attentions, and most of all, who robbed you of your rightful title when she maneuvered to have her son Izzeddin named as heir to the throne! Are you forgetting all of that? Are you forgetting all that we had to do to fix that situation and to get you onto this throne? We have already come too far, and there is still a long way to go. Remember what I told you when we sent them away from the court two years ago, after the incident at the inauguration of my han? I told you that they had to be taken away, for as long as they were here, they would be a reminder that you were not the designated heir to the throne."

Giyaseddin recalled how he had seized that opportunity to banish them from his life, purging his memories of all the pain that they and their mother had caused him. He was especially resentful of that golden boy, Izzeddin al-Din Kilich Arslan, the one who had stolen his father's love from him. But to eliminate them entirely? That seemed altogether too harsh, and he was so tired of all this cruelty. He just wanted to crawl back under his quilt and deal with it tomorrow.

Köpek continued to harangue Giyaseddin with mounting insistence, and would not let up until he had his way.

"Stop being so weak! In order to reign, you need powerful meat to feed your glory, and ambition is the juiciest of cuts! You have shown great promise by getting this far, so do not feed now on a weak broth of self-doubt!" Köpek urged. "You must make this decision, or you will regret it forever! You do not want anyone to think that their right to the throne is stronger than yours! Here, sign this order and it will be taken care of!" he urged, pushing a roll of paper into his face.

Giyaseddin began to feel unwell. His head was reeling from the alcohol and the henbane potion he had ingested the night before, and together with the poison of this proposal, he now became nauseous. Each and every one of Köpek's words hit his head like a hammer, until finally he could no longer bear to hear the high-pitched voice of Köpek ringing in his ears. He had to get out of there before he became ill. He wanted to return to the safety of his rooms and sleep under the warmth of his quilt.

Just stop nagging me shut up I do not want to hear these arguments anymore, why must I always make these hard decisions? No more killing I cannot bear it anymore everything is always spinning in my head. I am going insane I cannot bear this guilt for what I have already done, it never stops haunting me please please leave me alone I do not want to deal with this, I am going to heave up all these poisons, I want to forget it all and sleep sleep sleep.

"All right, yes, all right, Köpek! Do what you want with them; I just don't want to hear about it. Just leave me alone, I need to rest. Do what you need to do, it is up to you. Here, I'll sign! I can't talk about this any more!"

As Giyaseddin stumbled out of the room, Köpek smiled to himself. I have done it again. I convinced Giyaseddin once before to carry out an immoral act for me, and this time it has been no different. He knows not to doubt my wisdom – and my wisdom is always to kill those who stand in my way.

☪ ☪ ☪

The boys had been locked in the Ulu Borlu Castle soon after the incident at the inauguration of the Konya han. They were separated from their mother and were escorted to the castle prison with six armed guards. At ages eight and nine, they were too young to understand what was actually happening to them. The daily existence of the boys in the square-shaped tower of the castle was dark, despite the sunny climate of Ulu Borlu. As the months wore on, the little boys began to realize that there was something very strange about their lives now, for they were cut off from all that was familiar to them; most of all, the company of their mother Gaziye, whom they missed dearly.

As soon he received the official approval of his plan from the Sultan, Köpek knew he could proceed without risking any accusations of complicity in the affair. Köpek set in motion a plan to extinguish his victims without leaving one bit of evidence. Traceless murders were his specialty, and he knew that doing away with two little boys would be relatively easy in comparison to the other manipulations that he had carried out in the past. Gold coins and intimidation were the two magic keys to his formula: first bribe the executioner well, and then tell him that if ever word was leaked out about the event, that he too, would meet the same fate.

Köpek selected one of his most sadistic guards for the task, a man who had worked well with him in the past; a man who asked no questions other than how much he would be paid for his trouble. Mahmut was a man fleshed in murder, with no morality or scruples, and he eagerly accepted to take on this task at Ulu Borlu.

His plan was not a complicated one. He had to get into the castle, do his work in silence, and leave undetected. He had murdered so many times before that two little boys would be nothing more than a game for him. The henchman first spent the early part of the evening in a friendly drinking bout with the castle keeper. At about midnight when the guard's head finally collapsed into his lap from exhaustion, Mahmut slipped the ring of keys off the man's sash. He climbed up the tower facing the garden and found the room where the two boys lay sleeping in their beds, curled up side by side. Yes, he thought, this is too easy, just like two little birds on a branch! Nothing more than a game!

He crept in their room and in one fell swoop, pounced on them and wrapped them up among their bedclothes. Entangling them tightly before they even had a chance to wake up, he forcefully held them down on their quilted beds by the weight of his giant body. He yanked the *yastik* cushions from under their heads and held the pillows hard to their mouths, smothering their faces until their breath failed and they gave up their naive souls to the eternal playing fields of Heaven.

The monster Mahmut then picked up the two bodies, one under each arm, and ran down the tower staircase. He tossed them on the dirt floor of the cellar like two pillows on a bed. He spread a layer of rubble to cover them, and then walked out into the moonless night air. All traces of his crime were buried there in a stairfoot grave, under a heap of stones, deep beneath the dungeon tower. For all eternity, the names of the skeletons lying there were erased from memory, except from the knowing eye of History and God.

☪ ☪ ☪

A hard-hearted command had been barked by a vicious Dog. A weak-natured Sultan had not the strength to refuse. Two innocent boys had met death from pillow feathers turned as hard as the steel blade of a knife. Cruelty and conspiracy reigned in the land of the Seljuks that night. A threshold of the indecency of fratricide had been crossed, from which there was no return. The timeless sleep of the two princes in the tower would disturb the dreams of every leader of the land from that night forth, haunting them hard with nightmares of disgrace.

Chapter 88

To Each Woman, a Throne

Every day after the noon prayer, Mahperi would stop by the construction site to observe the progress of the work. These visits were the joyful highlight of her day, for she could witness what had been accomplished the day before and then envision the work to be achieved that coming day.

Mahperi watched the hundreds of workers scurrying around the site, and was pleased she could identify most of them. The easiest to pick out was Nikolas Zonaras, the master architect, carrying his long measuring rod and constantly moving from group to group of workers, alongside his burly foreman who barked out orders like claps of roaring thunder. She saw the teams of itinerant craftsmen hired for the duration of the project, the local workmen well-versed in building with quarried stone, the master masons specially trained for vaulting, the stone carvers of the portals, as well as the whole city of workers tending to their needs: cooks, porters, young boys running errands, tenders of kebab carts and a battalion of water carriers. The construction site was a city all on its own, populated by citizens dedicated to making this complex come to life.

To Mahperi, the progress on the site was like watching flowers springing from the earth and growing into tall, colorful blooms, and she hoped that her red tulip of a dream would soon be dancing in the sun. Her mind flashed back to the vibrant spring tulips that she used to see at Kubadabad. It was pure enchantment to discover them blooming on the forest floors of the mountains to the west of the site, when she would go riding. Memories of the magic days at Kubadabad, her first project, flooded back to her. How she missed it all, that beauty, that dream.

A sharp cry from the architect snapped her out of her reverie. "Lady Mahperi Hatun, we need to discuss the baths!"

Nikolas Zonaras and his foreman approached Mahperi and escorted her to the area of the baths. The delight he saw in her eyes during her daily visits filled him with inspiration, and he found himself looking out of the corner of his eye each day for her arrival soon after the noon prayer.

"My Lady," he said, pointing to the building that sat directly to the west of the mosque and to the south of the medrese, "I told you these baths would be a problem for me, and I was right!" he said, scratching his head.

Mahperi did notice that the building sat at an odd angle in relation to the other two buildings, and asked him to explain that to her.

"My good Sultana, these ancient baths are a testament to the history of this ancient city in the shadow of the Great Mountain. They were built over the existing well and mineral hot springs by the Romans, and have been in continuous use since then. In truth, this source of hot water was the anchor of the ancient city, bubbling forth from the lava inside the Great Mountain! The current bathhouse, as you can see, is quite dilapidated, and needs to be remodeled and reconfigured for our needs. Actually, we are quite blessed to have these large baths here, for they will comprise a distinctive element of your complex. They will tie in the ancient past of the city with the ritual of cleanliness that is so important to Islam."

Mahperi nodded her head for him to go on.

"My honorable Lady, I have a special request, however, to submit for your gracious consideration. I ask your permission to start work on the baths as soon as possible, and to do this I will need to transfer some of the workers from the mosque over to this project."

"But, why is this so urgent? I thought we said the bathhouse would be the last part done. Won't this slow down the progress on the mosque?" she queried.

"Yes, it will, and that is why I am asking your permission. But....my Lady, I need to get these baths operational as soon as possible for the morale of the workers on the site," he stammered, somewhat embarrassed by his request.

"What do you mean by that?"

"There have been requests – and some complaints – from the men concerning personal cleanliness issues, and these comments are quite justified in my opinion. That the men need a place where they can wash up at the end of the day before returning to their homes, is evident. But more importantly, the Muslim workers need a place to perform the ritual ablutions before their prayers at noon and at the end of the day. These are very pious men, my Lady. They have set up a special section with prayer rugs to the west of the mosque site where they go for their prayers, but currently there is nowhere for them to make their ablutions. Without being able to first wash up, the men cannot perform their prayers, and this is very upsetting to many of them. There is a fountain on the site but it is reserved for drinking water, and the well is used for drawing the water used for mixing mortar. Until the mosque fountain is completed and the pipes from the wells underneath the baths are led over to it, they have nowhere to wash before praying. Even though Islamic religious practice allows believers to perform a symbolic cleaning without water, this is not a satisfactory solution for such devout men. Would you have approached the altar of a church to pray if you were dirty, My Lady? It is the same thing for them. For this reason, I would request that the baths be completed as soon as possible."

Mahperi was taken aback by his request.

"I am very sorry that I have not paid the attention I should have to the workers. How could I have been so insensitive?" Mahperi said, her face reddening with humiliation. "Please accept my apologies, and I will make sure this situation is rectified. Absolutely, put all the men you need on the project, and I will even pay to hire more men for the work!"

Nikolas knew that she would offer this. That is who she is, this woman. Generosity and consideration guide everything she does.

"I thank you, on their behalf, my Lady. But, before we start, I need to talk about the baths a bit with you, so that I may have a better idea on how you want to proceed. As I said, the baths need to be remodeled. We will maintain a design that will allow the same sequence of bathing that has been in place since the Roman times, for it is the most logical and appropriate. Your husband, the Sultan Alaeddin Keykubad, used this very same plan when he built his baths at the hot springs at Ilgin."

Mahperi nodded her head, remembering the baths where he would go to soak his saddle-tired bones upon the return from arduous military campaigns.

"You recall that sequence, don't you, Lady Mahperi? The bathers move from a cold room to a warm room and finally to a hot room, and then back again in reverse. The bathers first enter a changing room and remove their street clothes and hand them to attendants who place them on hooks and in cupboards. The bathers then enter the cold room and sit around a central fountain and relax in preparation for the bath. They begin to hear the sound of water and smell the steam vapors. Next, they move to the warmer room, where their skin and lungs get used to the heat to prepare for the benefits of the steam bath to come. They enter the hot room last, ready to lie on the heated marble platform in the middle of the room. There they sweat and attendants scrub their bodies with soap and a rough cloth to remove all the dirt of the city. Massages are also given to the muscles now relaxed by the long exposure to the soothing heat. That is what your husband so enjoyed at Ilgin! The hot room is warmed by a shallow space underneath it, itself heated by the hot gasses of an adjacent furnace that pass through the space and through the flues built into the walls. This is the same system that was used to such effect in the throne room at Kubadabad. A series of small chimneys on the roof will be provided as well, to open and close as needed to regulate the flow of heat in the room," he explained to her.

"It seems you have the entire plan organized, so what did you need to speak to me about, Architect?"

"The question I have for you is this: we have two options here for the plan of the project. The first is to build one section only and have the men and women use it on alternate days. The other is to create separate sections for men and women, so that all the citizens, no matter what their gender, can have access at all times to your baths. The first option will be quicker and cheaper, and will also allow us to build a more compact building which would better fit the tight site. The second option will require a bigger building, and that may entail some modification to the wall of the mosque which is hard adjacent to it. This is my dilemma, and I would thus like to solicit your opinion."

Mahperi spoke up immediately, with no hesitation.

"There is absolutely no question about this in my mind. I want a double bath with men's and women's sections built side by side. Make them spacious and comfortable. If there is a problem with adjusting the wall later on to fit appropriately with the mosque wall, we will deal with it. These baths are important for all citizens alike. Whether they are Christian or Muslim or Jew or pagan, all citizens of Kayseri must be clean!"

☪ ☪ ☪

Even though she had given the order to build a bath to accommodate both men and women at the same time, Mahperi still felt ashamed as she stood there looking at the dilapidated building. She could not stop thinking about her insensitivity to the needs of the workers on the site. Are there others I am forgetting? She had a luxurious hammam in the Devlethane palace for her use, she thought to herself, but what about the ordinary women of the city? Where do they go to bathe and are their services comfortable? Am I forgetting them, just like I forgot the needs of the men on the site?

Yes, I must not forget them … and to ask God to forgive my inconsiderate behavior, I will make these baths my special gift to the women of this city, by making them particularly luxurious. I want them to feel the same sense of beauty and holiness I do when I bathe in my hammam in the palace. I want them to have the same restorative joy to body and soul that I feel when I am clean.

She turned to Zonaras, and said:

"You asked me for a favor earlier, and now I am going to ask one of you. I want us to pay exceptional attention to the interior of the women's section of the baths by adding a brilliant element to the walls. Please dispatch a worker immediately to Kubadabad. He is to ask for a man named Joseph, who still directs the pottery workshop there. Under my orders, he is to request that Joseph select fifty of the same tiles he designed for Alaeddin's throne room of the Great Palace. He will know which ones I am talking about. He has a stockpile in his warehouse of left-over tiles he did not use in the throne room. These tiles are to be brought back here and you will install them on the walls of the lukewarm room so that the women can gaze upon them while they are warming up their bodies to enter the hot section. We will set them in the exact star and cross pattern that was used by Joseph in the Sultan's throne room. Seen through the steam and haze of the baths, the animals and figures will seem even more evocative and magical! Wait until you see the world of nature that springs to life on them!"

"But Sultana, this is a very extravagant gesture! Those tiles are the priceless bounty of a Sultan!" he gasped.

"Nothing is too extravagant for the women of Kayseri! Every woman deserves her throne, and I will give it to her! When a woman uses these baths I have built, she will sit in the same glory as did Alaeddin Keykubad in his throne room. Each woman will be offered that very same beauty and respect, for every single woman is as important to this Empire as its Sultan. Do you understand what I am saying here?"

"Yes, my Lady, I do. These baths will serve the entire community: for the workers on this site, for Muslims and Christians and Jews, for the men and especially for the women of Kayseri. I will proceed as per your orders," he stressed, with a deep bow.

Yes, thought the Greek architect, each woman deserves her throne, thinking of Mary sitting next to Jesus on the throne of God. With this gesture, the Sultana Mahperi has ennobled every woman of Kayseri. *She is the Mary of our times, the Khadija of our times.*

Chapter 89

The Last Knot, Untied

Köpek slowly opened the door to the workshop and stepped inside. He knew she would be there alone.

By this time in the late afternoon, all the weavers of her workshop would have left to go home. He had already seen the fluttering pink headscarf of her young apprentice disappear around the last corner of the street. She would be on her way to run some errands for their evening meal: some peaches; parsley for a salad. They ate simply and sparingly these women, he thought; no red, bloody meat on their table.

He knew he could now enter and set his trap.

He had been thinking about this for some time now, with more and more urgency. Since he had begun eliminating his adversaries one by one, his thirst for violence had become increasingly intense. He was lost to it, and he knew it; the rage was wakened and would no longer be put to rest. He craved the smell of fear, of death; he craved the surge of the fire lit within him when he killed people who stood in his way. These women ate sparingly, yes, but he ate with a voracious hunger.

But this surge was different; for he now craved the power he felt when he could overwhelm a helpless woman. He remembered what he had done with the mother of this woman here, so long ago now. He clearly remembered her screams as he had his way with her. Poor little idiot thought she could refuse my attentions and reject my offer! No, he had taken care of that; not only had he ravaged her body, but he had broken her mind. After he had finished with her, she turned into a wild-eyed spook that never came back from the horror of that afternoon.

And now, the daughter. The light of day was the same, the silence was the same. It is now your turn, arrogant little weaver, with your glorious rugs, the respect of a Sultan and the love of his Queen. Yes, my little weaver, you will not continue to sit there and make art which casts a shadow over mine. I will deal with you just like I dealt with your mother; I will break you, too, into a quivering mass, limp as a skein of undyed wool.

Yes, it is right you should pay. For you see, my little weaver, that beloved friend of yours, the Sultana Mahperi Hatun, is a very dark cloud over my head. As the mother of the Sultan I cannot harm her directly; but I certainly can blackmail and intimidate her; oh, yes, that I have already done, and now she keeps her mouth shut and does whatever I say. But I want more; I want to hurt her in ways sharp as the cut of any sword blade. Her son is a weak fool who does anything I tell him to as long as I ply him with women, wine and sugar, and how I know that sainted mother of his is appalled by his immoral actions. Yes, I want to hurt her even more than I did on that day at Kubadabad, and for that, I will now smash her beloved friend just like those glass plates at the banquet. That is the price you will pay for being the soul mate of the woman I want to destroy. When I am finished with you, little weaver, Mahperi will wish it were she herself who had been hurt, such will be her suffering after I break you into bits.

Köpek crept into the large room to the rear of the low building where he knew he would find this queen of knots at the throne of her loom. She had come to live here in Kayseri to be near her friend Mahperi after the death of Alaeddin, and the two were as inseparable as ever. No expense had been spared by the Sultana to set her up in this elaborate workshop; nothing was too good for her. The other rooms of the workshop were filled with piles of wool in all phases of preparation; from recently-shorn, to carded, to spun; and gathered into skeins of every color of the rainbow. There were jars of dye stuffs and plants lined up on shelves, and benches and trays held every imaginable type of work implement. Larger tools hung on the walls. It was a quiet place, almost spooky, heady from the aroma of the feral wool and filled with a light made murky from all the wool and cotton fibers floating though it. The smell and the hazy light made him feel like an animal in a cave. Yes, he was a beast set to prowl out at the sunset hunting hour. The bear will howl; the wolf will wail in the hunt for red, bloody meat.

He tiptoed over to the large room at the rear of the workshop, where he saw the weaver sitting on a bright blue cushion at the foot of her loom. The loom was massive, approximately eight feet wide, supported between two wooden side beams the size of small tree trunks. She was obviously working on a rug commissioned by her friend for that fancy mosque she was building in the middle of town. It was a colossal carpet, with an intense red field scattered with large golden roundels that looked like the footprints of a giant mythical beast. He stared at it, overwhemed by its impressive dimensions. The contrast between its primary colors and the sparseness of its design was stunning. She certainly was an artist who saw things the rest of us do not, he jealously thought. Damn her talent!

He stood there motionless and watched her for a long time as she knotted row after row with precision and speed, never hesitating for a second in her motions. Her hands flew like butterflies across the wefts, just like the chief court musician Imran did when he plucked the strings of his *kanun* during concerts for the Sultan. Only her fingers made music from colors, so much harder to do. He watched as she picked up the heavy *kirkit* comb and beat down in place the row of knots she had just completed. *Thump-thump-thump* rang out the sound in the middle of the quiet room, jarring in its intensity. *Thump-thump-thump* came down the comb with an astonishing force of movement. She was strong this woman, that he could see. *Thump-thump-thump* as if she were killing those knots like a rabbit in the field, beating its head against a rock until it was dead. He could smell the blood in his nostrils.

Her head was uncovered and he could see her two dark brown braids running down her back, clear down to the cushion where she sat. Tendrils sprung free and framed her face, like strands of wool that refused to be contained by a knot or be beaten down by that comb. *Thump-thump-thump*. There she was; all elegance, precision, and determination. No emotion showed on her face; it was if she were in another world altogether. She sat so erect, so tall, even when sitting down, intently focusing on that row of knots. No wonder she is friends with the Sultana: they are so similar, with minds you can hear whirring like the lathe in the woodworker's shop at the rear of the bazaar at Konya.

She didn't look like that the first time he had seen her, then a small child with big round eyes, standing in the doorway of her mother's room, staring at him as he stood over her broken mother. In all the years since, she had never once spoken to him and he prided himself that he had rendered her as mute as the mother. Yet he knew that this was no broken woman; no, she was one who had entranced both a Sultan and his queen as well as a whole empire with her distinctive art. But he would break her now, just as he had done with her mother. And those plates. And the Sultan. And that fire. And Gaziye. And those boys. And Altinapa. And Kaymeri. And Kamyar. And Taceddin. And so many others still to come.

Thump-thump-thump. He would have wanted to have a woman like her or that Mahperi as a queen by his side; a strong and intelligent woman who would have made him seem even more powerful than he already was. But such a woman was out of his reach. No, women like this went to dashing sultans with blazing blue eyes and long, delicate fingers. I had wanted the mother of this weaver at my side, but she rejected my offer of love, and I still see the dismissive disdain in her eyes and the twitches of disgust on her face and the scorn in her voice as she pronounced my name and looked at my ugly face; all that scorn now ricocheted over and over in his head, *thump-thump-thump* banging against the walls of his brain and now he knew he was now lost to the pull of the inevitable.

It continued banging against his temples, louder and louder, *thump-thump-thump*, all of it, every word, every look, and every sneer. You little fiends, you think you are so much more important than I am; yet it is I who have become more powerful than you all, and yet you continue to treat me like a cur, the dog Köpek, under your feet. *Thump-thump-thump*. His rage boiled in him like the steaming vats of vegetable dyes in the courtyard outside, and all the colors of the loom suddenly exploded in front of his eyes and she appeared surrounded by a blazing fire of light. He grunted out a roar of smoke and cinders and rushed forward.

It was only then that she lifted her head from her concentration at her knots and turned towards the door to look at him standing there.

Hanife had no idea how long he had been there, but the second she heard that grunt, she knew who it was. Her memory's ear flashed back twenty years ago when he had heard that very same animal growl over the limp body of her mother on the floor. She had never forgotten that animal noise; it was nothing like the proud roar of Ruby or the wail of wild horses mating on the steppes; no, this beast rumbled like a deer impaled with arrows or a bear with his paw stuck in a trap.

Calm. Keep calm, Hanife. Do not let him smell the odor of fear. It will enrage this beast all the more. Keep calm, keep knotting.

Köpek watched as she turned her head back to her loom, finished her row of knots, set her tools down and then dropped her hands to her lap. Her face was a mask, showing no smile, no frown, no furrowed brow, no fear, no expression of any kind. Just cool insolence, nothing more. He wanted to see fear there, shock and terror, but it was not there and it enraged him all the more. *Thump-thump-thump*. He gouged the dirt floor with his boot heel like a bull ready to charge.

She had never spoken to this man, but she had formulated in her mind for years what she would say to him if she could ever confront him about the events of that day with her mother. How she would take her revenge for her mother's broken body and spirit. But now that he was standing next to her, all she could think about was her mother, and the terror she must have felt on that day. She felt it now. She took in a long pull of air into her lungs to resume her courage. *Keep calm Hanife, keep calm*.

He finally spoke up. "Too proud to rise and speak to an important visitor from the court, my little weaver? Why, you should be a bit more gracious to eventual patrons who come to visit your workshop! Perhaps I am here to commission a rug for my private palace – but then I suppose you are too busy weaving rugs for that fancy mosque your friend is building in the center of town! If her money is good enough for you, then why shouldn't mine be, too? Just like your mother; she thought she was too good for me, and look what happened to her!" he snickered, leering at her face.

Tried as she did to remain calm, the slanderous remark to the memory of her beloved mother proved too much of a goad, and Hanife began shaking all over.

"How dare you speak of my mother like that! Get out of here, you vile son of a cur! Get out of my workshop before I tell everyone of the court what you did to her! Get out, before I bring your whole world crashing down upon you!" Hanife screamed at the top of her lungs.

The high-pitched laugh of Köpek echoed in the wake of her shrieks.

"*You* speak to me like that? Who do you think you are? You seem to forget you are all alone here right now! Everyone has left for the day – why, a bit like the time I paid that visit to your mother: she too, learned that screaming would get her nowhere!" he cackled, remembering it all. He clenched his hands tightly and grinned at her with cold eyes. The blood beat hot against his temples and the voices thundered in his head and rage burned down to the very soles of his feet. He knew it was coming, as he rubbed his right hand. His killing hand. Soon the cataclysm would come, the fire, the horror, the red blood, the fury; it was all falling into place as swift as a boulder tumbling down the face of that Majestic Mountain reigning over all outside the window, crashing down sure, unstoppable and devastating.

Thump-thump-thump. The image of the mother and the daughter now became one and the same in his mind, and when he remembered the look of fear in the eyes of Hanife's mother he wanted to see it in her eyes as well. Now, right now, I want to see it. He leapt across the room and pinned her by the shoulders against the rug on her loom. *Thump-thump-thump* but where was the fear in her eyes? He couldn't see it and it drove him harder to make sure it was there.

Pouncing as quickly as a cat, Köpek straddled her and pinned her arms down with his knees. He then wrapped his hands tightly around her neck and throttled it hard. "My little witch, you will do as I say, just like I told your mother! No one speaks back to me like that!" he hissed.

He then removed his right hand from her throat and slapped her hard across the face. Ah, that's better, now I see some fear in those eyes! *Thump-thump-thump* I have her now, there where I want her, in the palm of my terror.

Still choking her with one hand, and without stopping a second, he continued to punch her with his other fist. The killing hand; yes, now it is working.

He is right here right here in my face I smell his putrid crooked rotten teeth gnashing above me so strong I cannot breathe I cannot move I need air I must survive I must move I must live

He was so intently fixed on pummeling her that he did not notice that she had wrested one of her arms free from underneath his knee. His battering blows continued to rain, but she managed to grab the heavy *kirkit* comb and brought it crashing down on his head and then raked it across the side of his face, its sharp teeth gouging deep tracks from his scalp across his fleshy ears and then down clear across his cheek to his mouth. Blood immediately spurted out onto Hanife's face from the furrows gashed by the heavy tool.

He shrieked in pain, shocked at the taste of his own blood in his mouth and from the realization that she had seriously wounded him.

"You little whore!" he gasped, releasing the hand around her throat to touch his wound, a movement which allowed the bursting lungs of Hanife to gasp for air. She immediately wiggled away from under him, but he quickly regained himself and lunged at her throat once more.

"You bitch! You will pay for this!" he growled. Now, with both hands around her throat, he lifted her head and started to bang it against the heavy wooden upright beams of the loom. *Thump-thump-thump* went her head against the poles; he shook her over and over again until her skull was crushed like a rotten melon on the side of the road and her face was an unrecognizable torn mass. Blood from his wound poured across his eyes and into his mouth; her blood poured across her rug and she then knew the fear felt by her mother.

With one final grunt, Köpek looked down at the bench and grabbed the sharp knife that Hanife used to cut the yarn after she finished tying a row of knots. Holding it in both hands, he raised his arms high above his head and brought them down hard across the rug on the loom, slashing it into two pieces. With the hacked rug crashing down from the cut wefts, he turned to lunge at Hanife, completely slicing her clothes away from her body with the knife, until she was as stripped as the rug from its wefts. Then, as she lay unconscious, lacerated and dying underneath him, he had his way with her.

☪ ☪ ☪

Before she lost perception of the world around her, Hanife lifted her gaze upwards to her loom, where all the colors now swirled together and the red of the field became the blood running in her eyes and the yellow became the bursts of pain in her skull and the shreds of her rug became the slices of her torn muscles and of her disgraced heart; and as her head swelled tight from the blood oozing into every crevice of her brain, she took one last look from the red behind her eyes to the magic red spot two-thirds of the way up the loom, and felt the memory of her last untied knot still in her hands.

Chapter 90

Joined in Life, Joined in Death

The moon had not yet risen in the sky when Mahperi's servant came into her room to tell her that a young girl in a pink scarf was at the door, sobbing incoherently, and begging to speak with her. When Mahperi saw the distorted face of Hanife's apprentice Ince, she knew something terrible must have happened. She rushed out to Hanife's workshop, giving orders for a group of palace guards to come with her, for she feared the worst. Perhaps there was a fire, perhaps there had been an accident, but whatever it was, the girl was too traumatized to speak.

Even though she feared a disaster, Mahperi was not prepared for the shock of what was she found when she arrived at the workshop. There was blood everywhere. The shredded rug hanging down from the loom was stained with it, the right support beam of the loom was covered with clots of pink tissue, the cushion where Hanife always sat was soaked in it, the *kirkit* comb laid on the floor in a puddle of it, and finally, the body of Hanife was covered with bleeding lacerations. Her torn clothes were strewn around her battered body. The shock of seeing her wounds sickened Mahperi to the pit of her stomach.

What had happened here? What kind of savage beast could have done this? She screamed out her rage and dropped to her knees and picked up the limp body of her friend in her arms. She rocked it back and forth, holding it tightly to her chest. The guards and servants stood around and tried to understand as well what had happened to the poor woman, but one thing was certain: whoever had done this had displayed a violence they had never seen, even on the battlefields of war.

Mahperi set her beloved friend's head gently in her lap and stared into what remained of her face. Her skull had been cracked open at the top and a mat of hair clotted with blood covered the gaping wound. The right side of her face was completely caved in, her cheekbones were crushed flat and her eyes were swollen shut. Her face was so mangled that Mahperi could hardly discern that it was still a face, except for the broken nose that identified the middle of her head.

It was then she heard a slight moan from the limp body, and Mahperi realized Hanife was still alive.

"Hanife! You are alive! We are here! Oh God, please help her! Hanife! You will be alright! Please live, Hanife! What happened to you? Who did this to you? Speak to me!"

The mangled left eye of the battered face flickered briefly, and Mahperi heard a low gasp.

"Know that he has betrayed us all," she wheezed, and then the eye went vacant and a whooshing sound came from her lips.

"Noooooooo! Don't leave me!" Mahperi screamed at the top of her lungs and rocked the bloody body of her beloved friend in her arms, now lifeless and lost to this world.

☪ ☪ ☪

Mahperi buried her friend in the small rose garden that stood between Alaeddin's medrese and her mosque in the center of town.

After the burial, Mahperi had her guards dismantle what was left of Hanife's loom and carry it out into the courtyard of her workshop, where she had it set afire to burn every last trace of the memory of this horror. As the bloodied upright poles crackled in the bonfire, she vowed that no one would ever weave on that loom again. As she watched the loom turn to ash, she knew there would never be another weaver like Hanife, and that she would never have another friend like her.

☪ ☪ ☪

The next day, Mahperi went to visit the grave of her friend. She sank to her knees and talked to Hanife as if she were still at her side, sitting there among the pink roses of the mosque garden. The two of them had often spent time in that garden together, chatting, laughing and sharing their dreams. She remembered how her friend had told her that she was weaving her vision of the Prophet's roses in the gardens of Paradise on the rug she was making for the big mosque, the one on which she was working when she tied her final knot.

"Oh, my Hanife!" she whispered to the earth, "What is the point of striving to achieve such beauty when there will always be evil set out to destroy it? I have survived the calumny of Kubadabad, the death of Alaeddin, the threats of Köpek, the murder of so many faithful servants, and now this – I am not so sure I will ever be able to overcome the grief of losing you, my most beloved friend," she sobbed, kneading the freshly-dug clods of earth over the grave.

Mahperi still could not believe that Hanife was gone. No longer would she be able to share her life with this gentle and proud woman, who had helped her deal with every challenge of her life, shared her every joy and walked by her side in every moment of despair.

"My dearest friend, I will never forget you or cease to hold you in my prayers. Just like my Alaeddin, I will continue to hear your voice in my ears. You will sit on my left shoulder and whisper into my ear throughout the day. I will not let you die!" she uttered to the mound of dirt in front of her.

Just as she pronounced these words, a ray of sunshine burst forth from the spring sky and shone directly on her face, as if God had chosen to offer her a moment of warmth in all of this tragedy. She turned her face upwards and smiled, remembering that despite how much despair God chose to mete out, there was always beauty to be found that made life worth living.

And it was at this moment that the idea came to her, clear and bright as that ray of sun.

I will build my own tomb right here at this spot, to be near the grave of Hanife.

Since the tragic loss of Hanife, Mahperi could not stop thinking about her own death. Would the same sudden and violent fate as Alaeddin and Hanife befall her as well?

"Hanife! I will build my tomb right here in this garden. We will rest side by side for all eternity, here in the shadow of my mosque!"

The more she thought about it, the more it made sense to her. It would be the final piece in her complex, and she could think of no better place to lay buried. She would rest near the testament of her husband's builder spirit, close to her mosque and alongside the grave of her friend Hanife, all joined in death as they had been in life.

At that moment, she heard the voice of her friend Lou whispering in her ear:

"*Ma Gente Dame*! Yes! You are right, this is where you must lie, at the heart of your life's dream! But dare to do something unique and brave here, just like you are! I have an idea for you to think about – why don't you place the entry to your tomb differently: not from the street outside, but from *inside* Alaeddin's medrese? In this way, in order to visit your tomb, people will always need to pass through your husband's medrese and render homage to him at the same time as they do to you. You will show all eternity how your life was linked to his. You will be fused together in stone – what more symbolic way to demonstrate the bond the two of you shared? As your humble architect servant, this is what I would suggest, but as usual, you will be the one to make the final decision. Would you perhaps like me to sketch up a plan for the staircase we could build in the corner of the courtyard chamber that would lead up to your tomb chamber? Here, let me show you how we could do it…"

For the first time in days, Mahperi smiled, remembering the joy her friend always brought to her life. Yes, Lou, you are right; we will do something daring here.

But when a cloud covered the sunbeam, Mahperi snapped out of her dream and came back to the reality of her grieving. Looking down at the grave in front of her, she was plunged once again into the horror of her friend's murder. She mulled Hanife's last words to her over and over in her mind. Whatever she had meant by them, she could not imagine, but they would remain engraved in her mind forever.

"I will find out who did this to you Hanife, I promise you, and when I do, I will make him suffer ten-fold what you had to endure. There will be no forgiveness possible in my heart for this villain; none, just punishment of the most brutal kind. Whoever did this to you will pay for it with his life, even if I have to kill him with my very own hands!"

She picked up a handful of dirt from the grave and raised her fist into the air.

"God, in Your sense of justice and goodness, help me in this quest! Strike vengeance onto the person who has done this with all Your possible wrath! I implore You to carry out justice to the honor of my dearest friend!"

Chapter 91

To Fan the Fires

Once she had made the decision to build her mausoleum, Mahperi wanted to begin the project as soon as possible. She could not disperse the dark clouds that hovered over her head concerning her own destiny. Firmly decided, she called her son to her rooms to speak to him about the project before proceeding, out of respect for his position as Sultan.

When he entered her rooms, the Sultan Giyaseddin could see that the rims of his mother's eyes were raw from crying. Normally ramrod straight, she now seemed bent and stooped. The fact that she appeared years older in a matter of days did not surprise him, for the shock of the brutal death of Hanife would be enough to age anyone a decade overnight.

He kissed her hand and eased himself down to the *kilim* cushion next to her.

"Come, my dear mother, why don't we enjoy some pastries and sherbet together, just like we used to do when I was a little boy in Konya, in that lovely palace high up on the hill! Do you remember those afternoons together? You used to tell me so many stories; and I savor the memory of all of them," he said, trying to comfort her as best he could.

"Of course, I remember!" smiled Mahperi. "How could I forget what a sweet little boy you were, as sweet as that halvah you used to steal from the palace kitchens!" They both shared a moment of laughter together at the memory, before her face became dark once again.

"My son, I have something to discuss with you and I do not want it to upset you, but with all that has happened recently, I cannot stop thinking about my own mortality. After the sudden deaths of your father and Hanife, I have become somewhat obsessed that I, too, may meet death soon. For this reason, I would like to start planning my tomb," she announced as gently as possible.

"But Mama, you are still so young! Your death will be many years away!" he protested, grabbing her hand and kissing it again.

"Hanife was young too, and yet she met her death this week, and not from an accident or sickness. I want to be prepared, my son, for the day the Angel of Death decides it is my turn to fly away with him. I ask you to support me on this. Perhaps we do not need to start building it right away, but I want the land set aside and the architects to be aware of my intentions. After that, let us not talk of my death anymore, and hope that it is many years before I will need it!" she insisted.

The Sultan nodded, not wanting to contradict her at this difficult time. He would go along with anything she wished, for she was so kind and sweet, now so sad and suffering.

"Actually, my son, I have some very specific ideas about it. I would like to build my mausoleum in the middle of my Kayseri complex. I want it placed in a spot which may appear odd to you, but I think it is the appropriate place for it," she continued.

"Go on, Mama, I am listening," said the Sultan, leaning forward to hear her idea.

"I want to set my tomb in between the medrese of your father and the mosque I am building. Yes, that is right," she nodded, noting his startled face. "In this way it will symbolically serve as a reminder of my connection to the lives of two sultans. In Konya I was the wife of your father, and now here in Kayseri I am the mother of the following Sultan."

Still not totally comprehending her plan, he queried, "You mean you want to put it where the rose garden is now? You will cover over the rose garden with your tomb?"

"Yes, that is right, and it will become a different sort of garden. There is not much space there, but I know we can build something fine. Yet here is where my idea becomes somewhat unusual. I want the entry to the tomb chamber to be through a passageway leading up from the back room of the medrese. In this way, people will be obliged to pass through your father's building first and be reminded of his greatness. By making people enter through Alaeddin's medrese, I am showing that I was his humble servant and that I am forever connected to him," she insisted. "But I have one other reason, a very personal one. As you know, I have buried Hanife in a section of that rose garden. I would like my tomb to stand over her grave as well, and in that way, we will rest next to each other for all eternity," she said, a tear rolling down her cheek. "This is what I want, my son, do you support this project?"

"But of course, Mama, you know you will always have my support for whatever you choose!" he said, grabbing her hand. "Yet, before we start anything, I would like Köpek to come speak with us and give his opinion – and his consent. As Superintendent of Works, it is very important that he feels involved in the construction projects of this Empire, and of course, he will need to approve the budget involved."

The thought of Köpek being involved with something as intimate to her as the building of her tomb made her shudder in disgust. Approve the budget, what for? It was her personal money she would be spending, just like she had for the rest of the complex project, and there was no need for him to have a say in how she chose to spend the inheritance from her father and her husband.

"My son, I understand your respect to protocol, but really! It is of no concern to Köpek how I choose to spend my money and build my tomb!" she flushed angrily.

"Now, now, Mama! Calm down and please try to understand! In these uncertain times, he feels it is important to control every aspect of building operations, and I must respect that. It is the least I can do for him after all that he has done to get me on the throne! There must be no controversy surrounding this project, for the last thing I want is for you to have more heartache and scandal in your life!"

He immediately regretted saying this, for he knew how much the events at Kubadabad had scarred her. He clapped his two times to call for his servant, and requested that he bring Köpek in to see him at once.

Mahperi understood the delicate position of her son, yet he was the Sultan after all, and should be answerable to no one but God! Learn to stand up for yourself and make your own decisions, she wanted to say to him, but she held her tongue. She was tired, too tired and hurt to battle.

The two of them idly chatted about other issues at the court while waiting for Köpek to arrive. It did not take him long to appear, for he knew, despite all outward appearances, whom he served. When Mahperi heard his high-pitched voice outside the door, she braced herself for the eventual confrontation with him, for there was always a clash with him every time they spoke, ever since the very first time she met this devil Dog, now her blackmailer and confirmed enemy.

When the door opened and he stepped in, Mahperi kept her head lowered, for she could not bear to look at his ugly face after all the horror of this past week. After listening to Giyaseddin's explanation of the project, the Dog's squeaky voice piped out.

"I am surprised, Queen Mahperi, that you would want to be buried here in Kayseri instead of Kubadabad where you seemed to enjoy life so much!"

She gasped at the audacity of his insinuation, and raised her head to defiantly look at him in the eyes.

But when she lifted her gaze to confront him, she was startled by what she saw. The Dog's normally repulsive face was now even more unsightly, for it was bruised and puffy. His eye sockets were nearly swollen shut, and a large white linen bandage was wrapped tightly around his head.

It was then she saw it.

The bandage had not managed to completely hide the inflamed red welts that ran from his upper cheek clear across to his mouth. He had tried to cover up his wound, but there was no denying that he had been very badly maimed in some kind of attack. A bear claw? Had Ruby swiped at him? She stared at the tracks of red wheals running across the wound on his face and suddenly she understood. These were not marks left by the claw of an animal – they were uniform, red ridges spaced exactly the same width as the teeth of a *kirkit* weaving comb.

Her head swayed as she realized what this disfigurement of his face meant. Hanife's murderer was now standing right in front of her. The blood on the *kirkit* that she had found on the floor of the workshop that day had been his and not Hanife's. My friend must have fought him with all the force she had, and that *kirkit* comb had been her last chance for survival.

Her stomach lurched and she struggled to maintain her composure. All the horror of what she saw when she entered the workshop that night flooded back to her. He had perhaps escaped death from Hanife's blows, but he will not escape the wound I will now inflict upon him, she vowed to herself. She had long learned to never show emotion or lose control in any difficult situation, and in this situation, she needed all her wits about her as she entered what she knew would be the final battle in her war with Köpek.

Calm. Keep calm, Mahperi.

She bowed her head, speechless from the shock that the killer of Hanife now stood two steps in front on her. It was then her spinning head flashed back to the last words she heard her friend utter before dying in her arms.

Know that he has betrayed us all.

But this makes no sense, what she said, thought Mahperi, her head spinning even faster. Yet Hanife never made a mistake in anything she did. What possibly could this mean? And now what was she to do? How could she punish this prominent Vizier? Yet when she flashed back to the vision of the battered and bloody body of Hanife on the floor, she knew she had no option at all. She would feel no guilt about this retribution. He was to be punished with no possible mercy.

"Mama, are you all right? You have gone all pale and look as if you are about to faint!" cried Giyaseddin, rushing over to her side and putting his arms around her shoulders.

"No, no, my son, it is just that all this conversation about death has upset me a bit; do you suppose the three of us could speak of this at another time? Please leave me, for I am so very, very tired now," she softly said, trying hard to cover any emotion in her voice.

When the men rose to leave, she turned to look at the Dog for what she knew would be the very last time. *I hope you sear in hell, Sadettin Köpek. And I will be there to fan the fires under your pyre.*

Chapter 92

An Eye and a Tooth

Mahperi immediately dispatched a messenger down the Great Road to Konya as fast as his steed could run with orders for her trusted advisor, the Vizier Jelaleddin Karatay, to come at once to Kayseri to meet with her. Utterly distraught after her discovery of the identity of Hanife's murderer, she needed to discuss this situation with the only person she could truly trust. He will know what to do, thought Mahperi; this wisest man in the entire court will help me with this horrible situation. She also knew that Vizier Karatay despised Köpek as much as she did.

When the Vizier Jelaleddin Karatay arrived four days later, she summoned him to her chambers even before he had time to shake the road dust from his cloak, so eager was she to tell him the entire story of Hanife's murder. The pious vizier was repulsed at the brutal end of the talented weaver, and images of her magnificent rugs on the floors of the mosque atop the hill in Konya flashed before his eyes. Such brilliant gifts to God's glory would never be possible again.

"Good Vizier Karatay, I beg you to help me carry out justice in this matter," sobbed Mahperi. "You are the only person I can turn to for help, for Giyaseddin is totally blind to Köpek's evil and is faithful to him to a fault. Köpek must be punished. Whether he is an important vizier in the court should be of no issue here. He has broken God's law and must pay for it. An eye for an eye, and a tooth for a tooth, I say! Completely punished, I beg you!" she implored to him.

What Mahperi did not know was that outraged Karatay had been seeking his own way to punish the evil Köpek for some time now. The murders of so many viziers and especially Commander Kamyar had been unforgivable sins in his eyes. The incident with Taceddin Pervane had pushed his tolerance to the limit. Köpek had to go, and there would be no further hesitation on his part.

"My Queen, I agree with you that the intrigues of Köpek have gone on too long. The murder of our valiant Commander Kamyar was the sounding alarm that he needed to be stopped before any further madness occurred. But we did not act soon enough. This vile act against a woman has now definitively sealed his fate. I will help you; no, – I promise you – that he will be punished to the full extent of my powers; oh yes, that I pledge to you. His madness has spiraled out of control; it must end. Leave it to me to explain to Giyaseddin the situation of the murder of Hanife. I will make sure that he understands that Köpek continues to go contrary to customs and rules of our court and to our God. His acts by the sword and his arrogance are intolerable in the civilized court we strive to build. This is not what your husband, the Great Alaeddin Keykubad, may God shine light on his grave, fought for when he laid the basis of this empire. We must put a stop to all of this political and moral wickedness!"

☪ ☪ ☪

It did not take long for the wise vizier to convince the young Sultan that his kingmaker Köpek was now a detriment to the well-being of the Empire. Giyaseddin could no longer avoid facing the fact that everyone at the Palace lived in fear of Köpek, especially since the murder of Kamyar. It was apparent that Köpek's evil was now raging like a forest fire out of control, with each act becoming more and more violent. His vile murdering spree had claimed its last victim in Hanife. The rabid Dog needed to be taken down.

Karatay called in Emir Husameddin Karaca, a devoted servant to the Empire and a fearless soldier, to help him plan the end of the rampage once and for all. Giyaseddin would order Köpek to leave Kayseri and retreat to his private kiosk at Kubadabad, citing that his swollen and bruised face at the present time was too frightening to be seen in public at the palace, and that the warm climate and bright sun of the lake would be just the medicine needed to heal his nasty wound all the more quickly.

Once at Kubadabad, the plot to rid Köpek from their presence forever would be set in motion. It was agreed that the Sultan Giyaseddin Keyhüsrev would host an elaborate party at the Great Palace of Kubadabad in celebration of the upcoming military season. Knowing how much the Sultan loved festivities, Köpek would not suspect anything out of the ordinary. The guests, especially Köpek, would relax and enjoy their unbridled evening. After a while, Karaca would invite Köpek to step outside with him for some fresh air. There, on cue, trusted soldiers of Karaca would be waiting in ambush, ready to quickly draw their swords, overpower Köpek and kill him. The Sultan reluctantly gave his nod to the Vizier, and the plan was approved and put into motion.

☪ ☪ ☪

On the night of the party, all had been made ready for the banquet according to plan: an array of fine food was laid out on bronze platters, the musicians and pages stood dressed in their finest livery, goblets were polished, and perfumed incense was burned to freshen the cushions and carpets of the Great Palace.

The guests arrived and the evening commenced with jovial conversation accompanied by cheerful music. None of the guests were aware that Köpek was to meet his fate that night, and the Sultan Giyaseddin and Karaca made sure not to betray themselves with any nervousness. The guards standing outside, charged with executing the Dog, were sworn to secrecy and paid handsomely for their efforts. All was ready to proceed according to plan.

At one point as the evening wore on, Giyaseddin stole a look at Köpek out of the corner of his eye. Suddenly, a feeling of great pity swept over him, and he felt ashamed of the trickery to which he had to resort. He was seized with a moment of self-contempt at his despicable deceit. How could it all have come to this? How could this man, who had always worked so hard to be my friend and supporter, now become the object of this plot crafted by my very own hand? What part in this have I played, he asked himself, riddled with guilt. Yet, in a second, all the infamous acts of Köpek's life flashed before his eyes: the murder of Gaziye and his half-brothers, Kamyar, Altinapa and so many others, ending with the vicious attack on Hanife. Suddenly all his qualms of conscience disappeared, and he knew he had to allow justice, albeit guided by his hand, to deal Köpek the retribution he deserved. Tonight he would help his mother avenge the death of her friend. Tonight he would save the Seljuk Empire from ruin and dishonor. Tonight he would end the reign of evil. Tonight he would act like a brave Sultan in full command of the interests of his Empire.

When the designated moment arrived, Karaca rose and asked Köpek to help escort him outside. When they came out of the palace into the night lit by a bright full moon, the hired guards greeted the two of them and asked if they needed any assistance, all the while taking care to hide from view the heavy clubs they were holding behind their backs. When Köpek passed in front of them, they raised their maces to strike him on the head. But luck never left the side of the devil Dog, for just at that moment Köpek stumbled and swerved, and the maces missed their mark on his head and came crashing down on his shoulders instead.

Suddenly, the expression on Köpek's face changed into fierce anger and he fixed his fiendish eyes on Karaca. Köpek immediately realized why this banquet had been organized and what all of these men were set out to do to him. He jumped clear of his attackers and lunged forward to strangle the neck of his betrayer Karaca. *Killing hand, do not fail me now.* Ever vigilant, one of the bodyguards quickly drew his sword and brought it down hard on the shoulder of Köpek, wounding him seriously. Köpek dropped to the ground, yet he refused to weaken. Despite his serious gash, Köpek found the strength to rise and run for his life, and he knew exactly where to go. Having built the Palace, he knew its layout better than anyone, and knew that he could find a secure hiding place in the Sultan's underground food cellar. He ran down the steps to the cool caves, but he had not realized that he would not be alone once he got there, for the cellar was filled with the Sultan's stewards on duty that night for the banquet. When the astonished servants saw the bloody and wounded Köpek in front of them, they understood what was happening and why he had run there to hide.

In the end, it was not one of the bravest of the Sultan's soldiers or one of his most intelligent viziers who would rid the Empire from its worst nightmare of evil. No, it was by the hands of simple palace servants that the destiny of the Empire was saved. Having lived in fear of the Dog like so many others, the stewards banded together and took charge. Each one pulled his knife from his sash, and in a uniform raging cry, they lunged at the neck of the Dog with all their force.

Thus it was there in the dark cellar that the dark and vile Dog emptied the last of his bitter red blood on the floor. It was then, at the break of dawn, that Köpek's dying sighs joined the echoes of the muezzin's call for the morning prayer. It was there, underneath the palace where he had orchestrated the downfall of Mahperi Hatun, that Köpek fell victim to another scheme of destruction. It was then, as he drew his last breath on this earth, that the verse of the *al-Ma'ida* chapter of the Holy Qur'an rang in everyone's ears: "*The life for the life, and the eye for the eye, and the nose for the nose, and the ear for the ear, and the tooth for the tooth, and for the wounds retaliation.*"

For Mahperi and Karatay, the raging wickedness was over. An eye for emirs eradicated, a tooth for a weaver dishonored. The meal of the table spread with retaliation was at last served to Köpek at Kubadabad, on a platter that even he could not smash to the ground. The reign of the Empire's terror had ended. The rabid Dog would bite no more.

Chapter 93

Light of Silver and Snow

The violent death of Hanife plunged Mahperi into a sadness which affected everything she did. She kept to herself, and spoke to few. She even stopped making her daily visits to the construction site of her mosque. Her daughter Seljuka tried to console her, her Sultan son brought in his two little boys to cheer her with their games and antics, but nothing could bring a smile to her face. Her grief for the Sultan had been opened wide again by the loss of her dear friend Hanife, and the horror of the death of Gaziye and the disappearance of her sons added to her despair. Although Gaziye had been her rival, Mahperi felt that her fate had been undeservedly cruel.

The only person she could speak with at this difficult time was Seyyid Burhaneddin, a wise Sufi master who had been a student of Bahaeddin Veled, just as she had been so long ago in Konya. Burhaneddin, now aged, had come to the city of the Majestic Mountain to live out his days. The minute she saw the kind eyes of the white-bearded man at their first meeting in the Güllük medrese, she instinctively knew that he possessed the same insight as her beloved Bahaeddin Veled and could offer her some of the peace she desperately sought.

The aged Bahaeddin Veled was generous in his attention to Mahperi. "I feel as if you are already my student, my fine Lady, for life has already bonded us together. I have come to your fine city from Konya, where I spent several years as the tutor of the son of your teacher, Bahaeddin Veled. I am pleased to tell you that his son Jelaleddin is now growing into a master worthy of his father. When Bahaeddin passed away, a voice told me to leave my home in Balkh to travel to Konya to take over the spiritual education of his son, for I knew he still had much to learn. Did I do it as a favor to his father's honor, or did I sense a potential in this young man and his calling? I cannot say, but even though the sermons of Jelaleddin in the Altinapa Mosque were starting to draw large crowds, I knew that he was still in need of guidance on his path to becoming an outstanding religious scholar. I arrived in Konya when the young Jelaleddin was about twenty-four years old, and for nine years I instructed him into the deeper mysteries of the science of the prophets. I even put him through three rigorous solitary retreats of 40 days in order to further his spiritual education. My Lady, you cannot imagine the teacher Jelaleddin has become! I feared sometimes the medrese walls would crack open, so popular are his lectures, for as many as five hundred students gather to attend his classes!" boasted the teacher.

"But there came a time when I knew my role had been completed, and that in many ways the student has exceeded the master. I thus decided to stand out of his way, and came here to Kayseri. He will go on to greatness, this Jelaleddin, son of Bahaeddin, our beloved friend and teacher. I predict that all throughout the Kingdoms of Islam, they will sing his praises in the future!"

"And Kayseri will be all the richer because of your presence, honored master," spoke up Mahperi to comfort him. "We have many fine medreses here as you can see, and when my mosque is completed, I would be honored if you would lead the inaugural prayer. I am so pleased to see that the faith Sultan Alaeddin Keykubad placed in Bahaeddin has now passed to his son. My husband wanted the souls of the citizens of Konya to rest on spiritual foundations as solid as the walls he was building around the city! It appears that this Jelaleddin Rumi will make his dream bloom like roses."

Mahperi then began to talk to Burhaneddin about the recent turn of events in her life, and the pain that she was experiencing. The wise man listened patiently, nodding his head at her remarks.

"My honored Sultana, as pleased as I am that you have come to me to seek out spiritual counsel, I believe there is someone else better suited to help you than I am," he confessed.

"But that cannot be! You are one of the finest scholars in all the land!"

"Yes, I am, but perhaps you need more than a scholar. You have special needs that must be attended to with great care, and you require a teacher as unique as you are. As much as I helped Jelaleddin develop, I know that one day another teacher will come along to illuminate his path with bright rays of sunshine even more than I could. I say you are special, because you carry the wealth of two religions inside of you, and your insights are all the richer because of them. I want to place you in the hands of a teacher who will honor those two traditions better than I can. Someone who imagines the mysteries of divine love in ways unfettered."

"Does such a teacher exist?"

"Yes, I believe he does, and he is right here on the streets of Kayseri. I have recently met a mysterious Sufi who has come here on the path of his wandering trail. I am not sure where he comes from, but I am attracted to his inexplicable assurance and would like you to meet him as well. This Sheikh Turesan has been teaching among the people of Anatolia for some time, and he is a disciple of the famous dervish from Turkestan, Hoja Ahmet Yesevi. Come tomorrow, and I will arrange for him to be here."

Mahperi bowed to the master, signaled to her guards and left the medrese. She had no idea what this man could bring her, but she trusted the wisdom of Burhaneddin.

☪ ☪ ☪

The next day, Mahperi returned to the medrese with her guards where Burhaneddin came each day to read the Qur'an and meet with students. As she sat next to him in the main *iwan*, the medrese door burst open and she saw a thin figure of a man backlit in the doorframe. He entered and slithered along the side wall and stopped across from them, holding onto the stones of the wall with his arms splayed out like the feet of a giant lizard. He stared wild-eyed at both of them, but she felt his eyes boring particularly into her.

He wore a plain brown wool robe edged in black felt, but the rest of him defied its simplicity. Locks of bright red hair rebelled from the confines of a rabbit fur cap and sprang forth in every direction. His beard was dyed by henna into a bright orange, and chains of ivory beads hung around his neck. Underneath his thick wool coat, Mahperi glimpsed bright green sateen pants that fell to the tops of red leather boots. He carried a rod with three tiny bells attached to the end.

After several minutes observing her, he left his position on the side wall and began to cross the medrese courtyard in her direction with a determined stride. As he approached closer, she could see that his eyes were rimmed with thick strokes of black kohl, which enhanced their intense violet color. His hands were covered with enormous silver rings embedded with impressive stones, and his fingernails were painted with henna. She had never seen anyone so wildly dressed, but his piebald clothes were only a fraction of the strange intensity she saw in the violet eyes staring at her.

He stood in front of her for a long moment, those amethyst eyes never leaving her face. She had never seen eyes of this hue, and she could not take her own eyes away from them. He then clenched his fists and slowly raised the backs of his hands upwards, holding them out right in front of her face. She was not sure what he meant by this gesture. Surely he did not want her to kiss his hands, she thought, but she could not be certain, for this man seemed to come from a place of alien manners and ways. It was all so unfamiliar to her, and for a moment she lost her poise. Flushed, she turned to Burhaneddin for guidance, but she could not read anything in his face. She turned to look back at the dervish.

The wild-eyed man then spoke. "Good Lady, I show you my silver rings, for I know you like bold jewelry too. We have that in common, so we shall be friends. I know that you wear a giant turquoise close to your heart, strung on a thick chain."

Mahperi was speechless. There was no way that this man could have known about Alaeddin's turquoise. Her hand instinctively went up to touch it. After the incident at Kubadabad, she had it removed from Lou's staff and reset in a necklace, as it had been before, and had never since taken it off. How could this wild man have possibly known about her turquoise?

At this moment outside of the medrese, she heard a group of men wildly beating on drums, adding to her confusion. Their song startled her, for its notes seemed to pulse at the same pace as the blood now flowing hotly in her veins. What was going on out there, she wondered; who are these people and why are they beating those drums? She looked out the open door and didn't see anyone in the square in front of the medrese, but she distinctly continued to hear the drumming loudly in her ears. And what is going on in here, inside this medrese, she thought, baffled by all of these confounding occurrences. She looked up from the silver rings on the dervish's clenched fists and saw that the space around him was now ablaze with light, flooding him with radiance. The drumbeat continued to vibrate within her and filled her with intense heat. Her turquoise burned against her skin, and perspiration began to drip down her forehead. The drumsong beat faster and faster and whirled within her head, and she felt buoyed upwards by a feeling of elation, brought to her by the song, the heat and this man with violet eyes and silver rings.

Now she looked up to see that the dervish was still staring at her, full in the eyes. The revolutions continued inside of her, faster and faster. Come over to me and sit here by my side, the purple eyes said; tarry a while. We are all guests. We are all wanderers. Come, let us be friends with the Friend. Be one of us. The violet eyes spoke and the drumsong continued to cast its light over her dark soul and she saw his hand hold out a shiny cup to her. It was then she felt touched by a burst of radiance that no human tongue could describe, for its brilliance surpassed the whiteness of snow and the brightness of silver, and she reached up her fingers to touch its glow.

Chapter 94

Heart at the Mountaintop

And so it was that their friendship began with a mystery, even before they had formally met. It began with a call to go beyond that which she had always known, and she did not hesitate one moment to drink from that silver cup of light he handed to her. She knew that all would change in her life from that first sip.

Mahperi, accompanied by her guards, began to meet with the dervish in the medrese on a regular basis. With each meeting, Mahperi began to feel more at peace with this odd man. Mahperi spoke at first with the Sheikh about all the evil surrounding her. The murders of Alaeddin, Hanife, Köpek, and Gaziye and the disappearance of her two little boys. The encroaching Mongols. Her son addicted to vices. Where had all of this malevolence around her come from, and had she somehow been responsible for making it happen?

The Sheikh listened patiently to her before speaking. "My honorable Lady, this wickedness is not of your doing, but the time has come to withdraw from these places that are encasing you in dread. We will retreat to a beautiful and calm spot where you can reconcile the hurt you have experienced with the covenant of love that God wishes to shine upon you. You will heal there, I promise you."

"Where could such a calm spot be? There seems to be horror wherever I go," sighed Mahperi.

"This calm spot is first in your head, but above all, it is in your heart, and I will help you find it. But to get to those inner places, we must go first to a pure place, one in the middle of nature. I know of a mountain outside of Kayseri. On top of it you hear nothing but birdsong at dawn, the wind whipping through the plains by day, and the whirring of the stars at night. You can see far into the distance in all directions, and your eyes are lifted to the heavens above. It is a place of healing, and I go there often to do my own solitary retreats, where I speak to no one but God. I would like you to come with me there, for you need to withdraw to a place deep in the countryside to go deep into yourself," he explained, the wild violet eyes never leaving her face.

Mahperi was stunned by such an audacious idea. Surely she could not go there without the approval of the court!

"My Lady, I can read your thoughts," he continued with a wry smile, "and I say unto you that yes, you can go there with me. You will be with God there, not me. You will be surrounded by many other women and in your privacy; for you see, I have many women followers. One in particular expresses her love and passion for God through her poetry; another through her dancing and tambourine playing. We are all *beings* in God's eyes, not men or women. You will find your place there, among those Sufi women and me, I promise you."

"But what kind of a place is this?" Mahperi prodded, still a bit uncomfortable with the idea. "What does it look like?"

"It is a rudimentary camp, and we use tents for living quarters. There is running water. There is a hut for our meetings, nothing more than two rooms, for our needs are small. I have hopes that one day I can build a full-fledged *tekke* lodge there, for I would like to turn this place into one that can accept more and more people, so that all can feel the holiness of this windswept hill in their souls," he explained.

Still seeing a worried frown on her face, he continued. "Do not be afraid of what is inside of you, my Lady. Come, and we will spend forty days away from the evils that so torture you. Retreats are the best way to learn humility and receive spiritual enlightenment. Do you remember how your Jesus, after his baptism, went into the wilderness in order to prepare the great work for which he had come to earth? For forty days and forty nights he fasted and prayed in the wilderness with the beasts. When he returned from that period of meditation, he was changed forever, freed from the power of the Devil. That is what I want for you, to be freed from this evil that haunts you. Come, let us together start on a path that will lead your heart to freedom."

And so it was decided that Mahperi would journey to an isolated dervish encampment in a remote place atop a mountain, with a wild-looking man of intense indigo eyes that seemed to penetrate straight into her heart. She had never done anything this daring, this frightening. But she knew that it could not be anymore trying than what she had been through at the court of the Seljuks. Or could it?

Burhaneddin accompanied Mahperi and her servants on the arduous journey to the dervish camp on the mountaintop west of Kayseri, and when the door opened and the wild man stepped out, Bahaeddin turned away and left her.

The Sheikh gestured with his jeweled hand for her to enter the small hut. Several women rose when she walked in and nodded to her. "Come sit, Mahperi, and let us open our minds only to God, purify our inner thoughts and find the beauty in our hearts. Rid yourself of the domination of the lower self in order to reach your spiritual core, and become lost in love for God. Let your bruised soul heal."

A routine was soon set, and Mahperi felt like a soldier on a military campaign, so rigid was the structure. She and the other women spent their days in discussion with the Sheikh, often conversing together from morning until night. Sometimes they just sat together for a whole day in silence. He sometimes spoke in baffling parables. At night, she was ushered into a small tent where she slept alone on a reed mat. For forty days, a bowl of simple food was placed at her door each night and a jug of water for her ablutions appeared at dawn. Yet, with each passing day, Mahperi felt she was awakening from a long slumber.

☪ ☪ ☪

Most importantly, the dervish spoke to her about the philosophy of their path and how it differed from many of the things she had learned of Islam.

"Our path of living is simplicity, My Lady. We believe in a philosophy that considers all the universe and everything therein to be coming from God as the starting point. We believe that everything that exists is in fact a manifestation of God. We are not rational, as humans understand it. There is something far beyond that. Reason cannot be the only basis of life, but rather divine love, what we call *aşk*, is the way for human beings to attain truth. *Aşk* is profound love and yearning for God in the human essence."

"So someone on this path is simply one whose heart is sincere towards God?" Mahperi queried.

"Yes, simply put, that is correct, my Lady, for as I said, we believe that all is oriented to God. There is One God, the Eternal, the Only Being. There can be only one law, the one of reciprocity observed by the selfless being. There is only one human brotherhood uniting all God's children. There is only one service, to God and humanity, and this service blooms in deeds of beneficence. The only object of praise is the beauty of the seen and the unseen. That is our path, within and without, behind us and in front of us, which leads us to wisdom and the Divine. If you follow this path out of the current labyrinth of your life, you will learn to vanquish your own doubts and break free of this maze. You will be unburdened by all dogmas and ideas and prejudices against others. You will discover your faults, and learn not to judge others, for their faults are the same as yours. You will learn humility, self-denial and patience. You will learn to stop misinterpreting others through your own vision of reality. You will learn to cherish even the smallest sign of appreciation coming from others who wish you kindness. Your life is standing now in front of the door between two worlds: the material world and the world of the Divine. Open that door, and come, step over its threshold!"

☪ ☪ ☪

And so Mahperi opened the door and stepped over the threshold, leading to times of deep discovery for her. She was not afraid to ask him the most direct of questions, like a curious child.

"My Sheikh, how do you practice this religion of yours? I come from a tradition where worship is highly structured, with rituals and procedures. I now pray to Allah in a very precise processional of prayer. How do you pray? Where is your altar? Where is your mihrab?" she asked him.

"Firstly, Mahperi, we are not a religion. We are a path to the understanding of the Divine – whom we call the *Beloved*. When I am alone I pray, I ask God for help, I open my soul to trust the messages I tell to God. I wait, I listen. I also incorporate music into my life, for I feel its vibrations are a link between my ego and the Divine. Singing and chanting helps me to let go of my conscious intentions and focus on the divine. I meditate in other ways, such as practicing *zikr*, where I repeat the same phrases over and over again, such as the ninety-nine names of God. My altar? It is right here in my heart," he said, jabbing his chest with one of his ringed fingers.

Mahperi remembered the strange drumsong she had heard when she first met the Sheikh in the medrese in Kayseri, and began to understand where it had come from. She paused for a moment and then shared a thought with the dervish.

"My friend, the weaver Hanife, used to say to me that she felt that she was praising God with each knot she tied, and that she felt that God was working through her to bring beauty to the fore. My architect friend Lou also told me that he praised God with the stones of the buildings he created. I suppose that the creation of art was their individual paths of worship, and I have seen how the beauty of rugs and buildings can touch the hearts of people."

"Yes, my Lady. Art can help us become conscious of God and all his creations and can offer us keys that can open the doors now closed to us. I can see why you were so attached to these friends, for they were on the Sufi path and were your teachers without you realizing it," he said gently.

Tears welled up behind Mahperi's eyes as she remembered the kindness her friends had shown her. Yes, their kindness, bright red knots and golden stones were their expressions of the Unity.

☪ ☪ ☪

For forty days and nights, Mahperi continued to learn about the Sufi path from the Sheikh. He answered as many questions as he provoked in her. He recited passages from the Qur'an about kindness and peace, the *al-Baqarah, al-Mai-dah, al An'am, al-Araf, al-Hajj, al-Mumtahanah, al-Mu'min,* and the *an-Nisa* suras. She began to lift the veil from her life, the veil that separated herself from humans and the true reality of God.

At the beginning of one of their sessions, Mahperi asked the Sheikh about her nagging sadness. "Will traveling along this Sufi path help alleviate the pain I feel from all the horror I have recently lived?" she looked at him with pleading eyes.

"As you lift your eyes upwards," he answered without hesitating, "paradoxes will occur. That is the Sufi way. As you gain a better understanding of yourself, you will become more human, more physically grounded in the world around you. And then, a paradox will occur, for the more you become aware of yourself, the more you will understand how you are connected to everything around you. Once you love yourself, you can love those around you, and from there you will find the heart of the creator, for we are all part of God. The life inside of you will become no different than the one you live on the outside. You will understand that you are a cup of Divine love. That cup is filled with water, and you can drink that water yourself, or you can offer it to a thirsty person near you. All of these cups of love can come together so that there is a constant flow of water and no drought in the world. The cups contain but a small amount of water, but together they form an entire sea. I believe your Jesus had much the same thought when he performed the miracle of the loaves and fishes. Everyone's plate was both filled and emptied together that day, isn't that right?"

Mahperi nodded, recalling that story which was one of her most favorite in the entire Bible.

"And so, when you become aware of the boundless opportunities to give love to the community, joy will open in you. You will not be filled with the horror of the tragedies you have recently lived, because you will have found the way to purge them and only allow the love to enter and leave your soul," he concluded.

"My Sheikh Turesan, I now understand that what you have been trying to teach me on the Sufi path is no different than the perfection which Jesus taught in the Bible, "*Be ye perfect, even as God in heaven is perfect.*"

The Sheikh smiled, pleased that she was now on the Sufi way. "Exactly, Lady Mahperi. Why is it that you love Mary so much? It is because she represents the purest form a woman can be. That is what you will become if you follow the Sufi path to the Kingdom of glory. Is that not what your Jesus said as well? '*Towards the One; the perfection of love, harmony and beauty. That is where we will go together.*' Those were his very words, I believe, were they not?"

☪ ☪ ☪

Before leaving the mountaintop at the end of her forty days, Mahperi spoke to the dervish about something he had said when he invited her there. "My Sheikh, when you first spoke to me about coming here, you said you had a dream for this place. You said you hoped one day to build a full-fledged *tekke* lodge to house mystics and the students who follow you. Is that still true?"

"Yes, my Sultana, I would like to build a lodge that will provide a gathering place for Sufis, as well as lodging for itinerant seekers of knowledge. We will make it a house of liberty, where people may speak their hearts and all views will be honored. My dervish lodge will be open to women and non-Muslims alike. We will make music a central part of religious practice, just like you do in your Christian churches. We will play the *ney* flute and drums in our ceremonies, and we will converse, recite poetry and even engage in dance, for all paths can lead to the ecstasy of love. I also wish to honor the memory of my master, Hoja Ahmet Yesevi, with the greatest appreciation, because he taught us what the magnitude of humanity can mean. That is my dream, my Lady, for my lodge."

Mahperi suddenly saw an opportunity to give back to this man who had helped her so much on her path to God's love.

"You have led me to this mountaintop, esteemed Sheikh. I started on a path to truth when I came here forty days ago. I will come down from this mountaintop a different woman than the one who climbed here, and I hope that many others will be able to travel this path. I offer to build your *tekke* for you, my Sheikh. May both God and you accept this humble gift from me."

For once, the piercing stare of his wild amethyst eyes changed into a gaze of calm gentleness. Could Mahperi detect a slight smile in them?

"Yes, I will build it for you, my Sheikh, and I will paint the door a bright green so that all may see it from afar. That door will show people that they are standing between two worlds, the one of mud at the foot of the mountain and the one of the pure heart at the top of it. If they have the courage to push this green door open, they will reap the rewards of heaven. Your *tekke* will always open its door to those who seek the heart of Truth. When a pilgrim comes here, he will be a guest of Sheikh Turesan. I would like my subjects for years to gather here and remember the spirit of your teachings. Will you allow me to do this for you?

"As you see it, My Queen, so shall it be," he replied. "That people should remember, perhaps not of me, but the lessons I have tried to teach; yes, that indeed would be of importance to my service to God. I accept your gift in the name of God most high. Generosity is one of the traits of those who reside in Paradise, and there, I pray, you will surely one day enter."

"Then I shall build it," she stated firmly, "and all will come to this mountaintop, here, where beats the heart of love, harmony and beauty."

Chapter 95

Karatay Takes Control

Soon after her return from her retreat with Sheikh Turesan, Mahperi received news that the Grand Vizier Jelaleddin Karatay had arrived in Kayseri, requesting a private audience with her. She knew immediately that there had to be an issue of importance for him to have made this journey, for he seldom left his beloved capital of Konya.

As he entered her rooms and bowed deeply to her, Mahperi looked up at this man whose impressive frame was every match for his remarkable intelligence. His sphinx-like gaze under a beetling brow never allowed his true emotions to flicker. No wonder he achieves such a success as a diplomat, she thought, for that reserved gaze serves him well. He was tall and unbending in body and although his demeanor may have seemed aloof to others, those grey eyes had always looked kindly upon her. Yet, today, Mahperi could see that they were clouded.

"My esteemed Vizier, I am honored by your visit. Yet I somehow suspect that you did not come here to inquire about my health or to gaze upon our Majestic Mountain. Please, I am listening, tell me what has sped you here."

"Peace be upon your soul, my fine Lady, and I am pleased to see that your health is indeed good. Yes, I would like to speak to you about the current situation at the court in Konya. As you know, since the death of Köpek, several dedicated ministers, including myself, have stepped in to take his place, as your son relies heavily on our counsel. We are currently working on the details for his marriage with the daughter of the Georgian queen Rusudan, as planned by your late husband Alaeddin, may God shine light on his grave, as part of the treaty made with the Georgians after they had mistakenly aligned themselves with the Mongols," he reminded her before continuing.

"My Lady, as you also know, I faithfully served in various posts for eighteen years under your husband, Alaeddin Keykubad. I helped him develop his kingdom to prominence. I am now the finance minister of your son. I am also the tutor of his oldest son, Izzeddin Keykavus. My whole life has been dedicated to this Empire, and I will continue to serve it until the end of my days. Although I put the needs of the Kingdom first, my true Sultan is God, and unto Him I bestow my total devotion. Does not the Qur'an tell how Abraham said to his people:

"*Serve God and be careful of your duty to Him; this is best for you to seek the sustenance from God and serve Him and be grateful to Him*"?

His words enjoining service with a heart full of grace rang especially true to Mahperi in view of what she had learned at the mountaintop with Sheikh Turesan. The devout personality of Karatay had always impressed her, and his dedication to the teachings of the Qur'an was legendary. There was a rumor that he had once burned a list of people in his debt, and then donated the equivalent sum to build a hospital in Antalya.

She snapped out of her reverie when she heard Karatay's booming voice once more.

"It is this very dedication to the thrones of the Empire and God that has emboldened me to speak with you today, for I am alarmed by the events I now witness in this court. Since I have replaced Köpek, I have tried to restore a sense of order to the government. While your son spends most of his days here in Kayseri, I am in Konya holding forth at the divan. I have traveled far since I was taken into the Seljuk court as a young boy, and, God be blessed, my natural gifts were recognized. I converted to Islam, and the riches I have earned from the lessons of this faith far surpass any of the gold I am paid from the Sultan's purse. You know of what I speak my Lady, for I have seen how you, too, have been affected by this gift."

Karatay now paused to tactfully frame his words.

"However, my Lady, the truth of the matter is that your son depends too much on the emirs here in Kayseri, and I sense that his weakness in front of them is growing. I enjoin you to help me, my Lady; for I know what a strong influence you have on him. We both must speak with him of the importance of his responsibilities. If you do not check this situation, you are enabling him to continue, and are risking compromising all that your husband worked so hard to create. Is that what you would want for his legacy?"

"I think you know the answer to that question, my good Vizier," Mahperi affirmed, suddenly uncomfortable with this level of directness. "But are things really so dire?"

"Yes! Your son is incorrigibly indulgent to all pleasures!" Karatay blurted out, startling her with his force of tone. "It must stop! He lives a life contrary to all the precepts of Islam, with his drinking, gambling, and lack of humility! I had thought all of this would end with that manipulator Köpek gone, but he continues to live a life totally devoted to pleasure! This court has become a playing field for Satan!"

Karatay took out a silk handkerchief from his sleeve and wiped his brow.

"His fortune is vast, coming from the income of his lands and rents, as well as from the fees earned from the posts he has distributed to the many merchants and landowners. But he must stop throwing this income into the wind! It should be spent on hiring the troops necessary to deal with the growing unrest in the East with the Turkmen tribes, as well as to parry the ever-pressing threat of the Mongols. And I tell you, my Lady, those Mongols are poised to attack soon! If he doesn't heed these signs, the safety of the Empire will be jeopardized."

Karatay calmed down somewhat, but anger still simmered in his tone.

"The biggest drain on his expenses stems from the enormous sums he lavishes upon his emirs. He is wise enough to realize that money can be a great lubricator for the wheels of government, a lesson in reverse he learned from his father. He knows that Alaeddin was too severe with them, and the consequences of such a policy. Instead, he promises them more financial liberty in their distant regions to keep them in their complacent silence," he further explained.

"I had not realized that this situation had regressed to this level," Mahperi admitted, "but surely you, as Grand Vizier of the Kingdom, can put a stop to it, can't you?"

"It is not that easy, my Lady. But there is more, I am afraid," he insisted, plunging ahead with his tirade. "Not only is the largesse to the emirs out of bounds, but so are the expenses related to the royal household. Jewelers at the bazaar of Konya have amassed fortunes, just on his commands alone. He reset Gaziye's emerald and diamond necklace to offer to the Georgian fiancée. It is rumored that he spent 180,000 dirhams for a single gem! 180,000 dirhams! Does not the Qur'an say, "O *ye who believe! Do not squander one another's wealth in vanities"*? How he has strayed from the simplicity of the Prophet's life! We must help him and his court return to a purer life before it is too late!"

The pious Karatay paced the room in front of her, still trying to control his anger.

"I know this may be hard for you to hear, my Lady, but your son is on a dangerous path!" he sputtered. "He spends too much time in pleasure at a special palace that he has built for himself out on the Mashad plain. Are you aware of the existence of this palace, my Lady? I am sure you are not, and yet it is right under your nose here in Kayseri. He has named this palace after himself, the *Josaq-ı Keykhusraviyye*, and it cost the crown a fortune! He prefers to spend his time there, and rarely leaves Kayseri because of it, neglecting his duties in the divan back in the capital of Konya."

The Vizier Karatay paused to gather his composure.

"Besides the Josaq, he has built numerous other pleasure pavilions and gardens along the southern coast for his wintertime hunting excursions. Be that as it may, I must say that his public building program is as ambitious as his father's, and I am sure, Lady Mahperi, that you have had much influence in guiding him in this direction. He has built five substantial hans along the southern roads, at Eğridir, Incir, Sarafsa, Kirkgoz, and Kargi. Again, in all fairness, he gives money and loans to merchants who have fallen on hard times. He shows a tender heart in handing out alms to the needy. Why, once I saw him hand a gold coin to three poor women and four beggars standing in front of the New Gate! But I fear these efforts are not enough to expiate his sins."

"But there is one more thing. It is a minor offense compared to the others, perhaps, but it upsets me none the less. He is increasingly mean to the wild animals he keeps in his large menagerie at the Josaq Palace. He lets the animals loose in the courtyard when dignitaries visit and enjoys watching the panic of his guests. I realize they are just animals, Mahperi Hatun, but I cannot bear to see how he teases the glorious leopard Ruby, the pride of your husband's existence. Giyaseddin keeps her tethered on a chain, and he enjoys poking her with a stick until she reacts with rage, which seems to amuse him."

The thought that her husband's beloved cat was being mistreated filled Mahperi with dismay. Such a noble beast, tethered like a goat!

Karatay continued with his invective. "We must face the gravity of this situation. I beg you, my Sultana, to help me. I cannot redress it alone. But if I do not step in and take some action, we are headed for disaster!"

Mahperi hung her head in shame that the situation with her son had reached such proportions. She knew he had a shy and withdrawn character since he was a boy. That he had allowed himself to become the prey of Köpek was perhaps a circumstance of his indecisive nature. That he felt inferior compared to his powerful father was perhaps not his fault either. This heartbreaking, doe-eyed child had defeated her; but she could not help but feeling that somewhere she had failed to give him what was needed to grow into an upright person.

Karatay realized that he was speaking to a mother, not an emir at the court, and became embarrassed by his insensitivity to her feelings. Such a fine and dignified woman, he thought, she certainly does not deserve this behavior from her son!

"I am sorry to have spoken so harshly," Karatay confessed, "but we can no longer avoid the fact that the future of the Seljuk Empire hangs in this balance of your son's transgressions. Let us act before it is too late!" he begged of her.

The Sultana Mahperi Hatun looked at him directly in the eyes and spoke out with insistence.

"Do what you need to do, Karatay; take the reins of government if you must. Be firm and resolute. I will support any measure you take to redress this situation. If not, as you say, both my son the Sultan and this Kingdom will certainly meet with tragedy."

Chapter 96

Yellow Rosebud

The more Vizier Karatay worried about the degenerate habits of Giyaseddin Keyhüsrev, the more determined he became to find a way to stop the Sultan's downward spiral. The Sultan's addictions were many – to sugar, herbed potions and intoxicating wines – but Karatay realized that there was one passion that could perhaps trump the others: his love of women. If only I could find one woman who could captivate him with her charms, the Vizier thought, I could turn this obsession into the saving hope for the Empire. If I could find one woman of exceptional beauty, wit and charm, and – one could perhaps hope – of mind and piety to match, she could encourage him to become a more responsible Sultan. As he pondered the question, the Vizier Karatay suddenly realized that he already held this saving gem of a woman in the palm of his diplomatic hand.

☪ ☪ ☪

It is said that the most beautiful girls in the world come from Georgia, the country across the border to the north of the Seljuk territories. This declaration comes from the lips of both wise men and peasants. Songs and poems written about this kingdom's legendary beauties filled the repertoire of minstrels. The Seljuk soldiers who went there on military campaigns returned with their hearts broken and their eyes spoiled to other women forever. With eyes as blue as sapphires and hair the color of golden wheat, the maidens of Georgia reigned supreme on the throne of every man's imagination. And now one was destined to reign supreme on the throne of the Seljuk Empire.

Years ago, the Queen of this kingdom filled with fine-looking horses and women, rose gardens, castles and domed churches, fearing the oncoming waves of the Mongols, found herself obliged to surrender to them. Yet the proud Sultan Alaeddin Keykubad retaliated and seized a number of frontier strongholds, forcing Queen Rusudan to surrender to him as well. She promised him not only tribute money and cavalrymen, but agreed to give the hand of her young daughter Tamara in marriage to the Sultan's son, then only a small boy of eight. Turkish blood flowed in this girl's veins, as Tamara was a granddaughter of the Seljuk Sultan Tugrul II. She spoke fluent Turkish, yet had been raised a Christian.

Now it was time, Karatay believed, to call in this debt. He was counting on the fact that this Princess Tamara would live up to the reputation of the legendary Georgian beauties. If she was anything like her headstrong mother, this princess could be just the right medicine to wean the Sultan from his poisons. We must get her here as soon as possible, Karatay reasoned, and he set the diplomatic wheels in motion by sending one of his viziers to Tiflis to bring this golden fiancée from the green hills of Georgia to the fawn-colored steppes of Anatolia.

She soon set out from Georgia, this promised bride, with her retinue of carriages and tents bedecked in red ribbons. Messengers kept the court at Kayseri informed of the progress of the Georgian royal caravan along the roads of the Seljuk Empire. Inside the largest carriage sat Tamara, Princess of Georgia. She traveled to the court with her priests, her collection of gilded and painted icons, and a retinue of servants and various attendants. In addition, her cousin David, acting as her personal escort, never left her side throughout the journey. The messengers also brought word to the Sultan Giyaseddin Keyhüsrev that her delicate porcelain skin, dancing blue eyes and golden hair would surely not disappoint him.

Karatay remained in Kayseri to await the arrival of the princess and to ensure that all went according to plan. It was he who personally greeted the procession upon its arrival at the outskirts of the city. When Princess Tamara proudly stepped down from her carriage, the Vizier noted that her beauty was as striking as the legends. She was dressed in a satin bodice over a red skirt, which set off her willowy silhouette. Two long braids of golden hair ran down her back, shining brightly in the spring sun. Another braid was wrapped around the top of her head, crowning her like the white cap of snow at the top of the Majestic Mountain behind her. She wore a white lace veil that left her face uncovered but draped around her shoulders in the back.

The grand Vizier Karatay stepped forward, bowed deeply and introduced himself. He presented a dark blue velvet case to the young girl.

"The Sultan Giyaseddin Keyhüsrev sends this gift to welcome you to his court. He awaits your arrival with great anticipation and pleasure."

The dainty young girl looked arrogantly at the sturdy figure of the Vizier, examining him as if he were a horse in the marketplace. She did not curtsy or even smile at him, but quickly reached out and tore the velvet box from his hands like an impetuous child, opening it immediately. She gasped when she saw a necklace of spectacular emerald gems set in diamond circles. Giggling, she held it up in the air and twirled it around to admire how it glittered in the sun.

"Oh, these are so pretty!" she chirped, quite pleased that she had received such an exquisite gift before even setting foot in the court.

"Indeed, my princess, those jewels are known as the most spectacular gemstones in all the Seljuk land! They are the famous emeralds that belonged to the Sultan's stepmother, the late Queen Gaziye. He had them reset for you, and he wishes you to wear this necklace tomorrow at your wedding ceremony."

The Princess Tamara whipped around and threw the jewels back into the velvet case and slammed it shut with a loud snap.

"You can take this gift back to your Sultan," she said, thrusting the case into his hands, the smile entirely vanishing from her lovely face. "You can tell him I do not care how big and beautiful these emeralds are. I am a Georgian princess, and I do not wear the jewels of another queen, and a dead one at that! If he wants to offer me a present to wear at our wedding, he had best provide me with a necklace crafted for me and me alone! I will not share the jewels of another queen as a hand-me-down. I want my own!"

Karatay's mouth dropped open at the audacity of her refusal. How could such a young thing be so imperious? How was he ever going to explain this affront to the Sultan? As he watched her insolently stomp back into her carriage, he began to realize that she was perhaps not going to be the saving grace he was hoping for.

☪ ☪ ☪

When the Sultan learned from Karatay that his fiancée had refused his gift, he was at first outraged, but then burst into laughter at the thought of her impetuous defiance. So this young upstart thinks she deserves better than that Ayyubid Princess wife of my father? Well, we shall see about that, he thought to himself, but he knew, ever since he had heard those reports about her beauty, that he wanted more than anything to please this Georgian princess.

The Sultan held the velvet box in his hands and looked up at the troubled face of Karatay. "Fine, fine, if that is what she demands, then we shall satisfy her. We just need to find some spectacular jewels and craft a new necklace for her to wear by tomorrow's ceremony," he declared.

Karatay struggled to maintain his composure as he tactfully tried to respond to the impossible demands of the Sultan.

"My Sultan, there are unfortunately no such spectacular stones currently available here in Kayseri to work with!" he sputtered. "All the royal gemstones are locked in the treasury at Konya. There is no way I can risk sending a messenger out to fetch them, and even so, he would not be able to make the trip there and back in time for the wedding tomorrow. Perhaps I can see with the merchants in the bazaar here in Kayseri if they have any available gems, but to locate fine ones on such short notice, much less to craft an entire necklace, I fear will be most difficult!" he explained.

The Sultan turned and glared at him. "Find them! Even if it is just one! Don't just stand there! We cannot waste anytime! The goldsmiths must work through the night to craft a necklace for my bride if this ceremony is to take place tomorrow, for she is expecting it! Now get out and do what it takes to find them!" he bellowed rashly.

Still fuming, the Sultan abruptly turned his back to the Vizier and went over to the window. As he looked out into the palace courtyard, his eye caught sight of the magnificent leopard Ruby tethered to a tree by her silver chain. He excitedly turned back to Karatay.

"Why, there are our jewels, right there in front of us! Grab that animal and remove the collar from her neck! Have the jewelers pry off those rubies and use them to craft a necklace for my bride! Yes, rubies will be perfect to set off her blonde beauty!"

☪ ☪ ☪

When Mahperi heard from her servants that the Georgian princess had refused the emerald necklace, she could not believe her impertinence. At the same time, she wondered if such a spirited temperament could help reform her son. But when her servants rushed to tell her that the entire palace was abuzz with the news that the famed ruby collar of the noble leopard was being stripped of its gems in order to craft a necklace for the new princess, Mahperi became outraged.

Mahperi's cries of anguish howled inside of her as loudly as those of the big cat when her precious collar was removed from her neck, the collar placed there so many years ago by the long, slender fingers of her loving master.

Mahperi wasted no time and rushed into the rooms of her son, where she found him staring out of his windows at the trainers pinning down the animal.

"My son! Have you lost your mind? Whatever are you thinking! You cannot remove those rubies! That collar is so important! It is your father's heritage to that animal and to all that she represents as the symbol of the might of the Seljuk Empire! That beast was the light of his eyes, and if you destroy that collar, it is as if you are killing both of them!" she cried out.

At that last remark, Giyaseddin whipped his head around. Mahperi saw a strange look on her son's startled face which had suddenly gone pale.

"It is too late to take that into consideration, for my father is dead already," he replied faintly, still with the odd and distant look in his eyes. He turned away from his mother and looked out the window again. After a while he faced back to her and spoke in a firm but resigned tone.

"I am sorry, Mother, but I need those jewels and I will take them. I will spare nothing to please this new bride!"

Seeing tears well up in his mother's eyes, he reached out for her hand, but Mahperi snapped it back. She had never acted this way before with him, and her anger towards him was frightening.

"Alright, my honored mother, I am sorry. I will not remove all the rubies from the collar. I will take only one large one, enough to craft a pendant necklace for her, until the time I can have more jewels sent from Konya. There are so many rubies in that collar I am sure that the cat won't miss one of them!" he smiled, trying to placate his angry mother.

Only his mother did not smile back at his remark. She continued to glare at him, unappeased, for she considered even one ruby one too many to remove. It was not just the indignity of seeing the cat stripped of its symbolic jewels that bothered Mahperi. She recalled Karatay's comment about how the big cat was being poorly treated of late, ignored and left tethered to a tree all day. She did not receive the personal attention that she had so long been accustomed to, when the long, slender fingers of a great Sultan sat at her side and scratched her head and fed her pieces of the finest meat. It was almost if her son hated this animal, thought Mahperi, or was very jealous of it. Although she understood that her husband had perhaps an abnormal attachment to Ruby, she noted that her son always seemed afraid of the cat and only wished to show dominance over it. How could he even think of poking a stick at her underbelly to get her to rise up and hiss? Yet, at the same time, she knew that her son never passed up the opportunity to parade the animal around wherever he went, for he knew well that no ruler had a beast as spectacular as this one – and thus no ruler in the world could be as mighty as he.

☪ ☪ ☪

The next day, Sultan Giyaseddin Keyhüsrev married the gorgeous Georgian princess in a lavish wedding ceremony, with the full court in attendance. He promised not to interfere with her religion, and told her she could remain a Christian as long as she wanted, and renamed her Gurchi Hatun, meaning the "Lady from Georgia". For her wedding ceremony, the spoiled upstart from Georgia wore a necklace crafted with a large gem plucked from the collar of a noble beast. But neither Mahperi nor Ruby would ever forget or forgive this affront to the memory of the great Sultan Alaeddin Keykubad, Eminence of the World and the Faith.

Chapter 97

Silver and Brass

Unfortunately, the hopes held by the Vizier Karatay for the remedial powers of Princess Gurchi did not prove true. On the contrary, she spun the cyclone of his destruction even faster. Intoxicated by her beauty and charisma, the Sultan would lock himself up in his chambers with her for days on end. The Sultan would not come out to take air, go to the hammam or attend prayers at the mosque, much less tend to any affairs of state. The entire court gossiped about the long days spent in seclusion with the Georgian enchantress, and the servants heard peals of giggles and shrieks coming from his rooms long into the night. In order to spend even more time with her, the Sultan built a tiny kiosk high on the hill to the north of the city, with a view out over the entire plain of Kayseri. It was in this Hizir Ilyas Kiosk that the couple spent many a diversionary hour together away from the court.

Karatay now realized that Gurchi had no intention of encouraging Giyaseddin to become an exemplary leader, wishing only to selfishly control him for her amusement and gain. It was obvious that Giyaseddin had no intention of attending to the affairs of state. It is now much worse than before she came, rued Karatay. This is one diplomatic mission in which I have completely failed.

☪ ☪ ☪

One morning, the Sultan called the Vizier Karatay to his rooms. When he entered, he could smell the traces of Gurchi's perfume still floating in the air.

"My Vizier, I have a request for you today. You will give orders to the silversmiths at the royal treasury to strike some new coins in celebration of my marriage to Princess Gurchi. I want them minted in the finest silver. I want her image stamped next to my own on all the coins of the realm! I know exactly how I want them to look, and I have drawn the design myself!" he boasted, pulling out a piece of paper from his pocket.

Stupefied, Karatay stared at the drawing where the Sultan had sketched their two faces side by side in a circle. He is behaving like a little child, thought the Vizier. It was inconceivable to him that their faces would appear on the coins, for Islamic tradition considered such self-glorification an insult to the supremacy of God. As a devout Muslim, the Vizier Karatay was not only shocked, but appalled at the Sultan's decision to mint coins in this fashion.

"With all respect to you, your Highness, I believe that even an honored Sultan should not go against the laws of God. This drawing of your faces on a coin is highly irregular! I would discourage you from committing such a trespass," he explained, trying to remain calm.

"It is not for you to tell me what to do! God has placed me above you, Vizier Karatay! Your fate is obedience to the Sultan and do not forget that! I want the world to see the beauty of my queen, and I want it now!" he commanded, with the same illogical impertinence he had shown with the ruby necklace.

Karatay lowered his head to contain his hurt at the insult, for the Sultan had never spoken to him so rudely. He is now learning bad manners and ways from this woman, he lamented. How foolish I was to think that his problems would end with the death of Köpek!

The Sultan, sensing he had perhaps gone too far with the statesman, tried to make amends for his boorishness.

"Perhaps you are right. I will not go against the Holy Laws that God has imposed upon me. But I do want the world to see the sun shining on this Kingdom now. I want all to bask in her golden rays like I do," pausing for a moment before speaking out again in an excited tone.

"Yes! That's it! I know what I want now! I will not depict our faces, but rather symbols that represent them. This is what we will do: we will stamp a lion with a long mane and a sword in his right paw raised in victory – that will be me. Above the lion, I would like to put the face of the sun, with rays spreading out from it, which will depict the radiant beauty of my wife. You will, of course, also stamp my name and the dates on the obverse of the coins."

Karatay again remained flabbergasted at this impetuous command.

"Now go out and give the order to start minting them as soon as possible. You must have them made in Sivas, for their tradition of silver coin production is the best in the Kingdom. I cannot wait to see them floating in all the bazaars of the land! Everyone will see what a beautiful and radiant queen I have now!" he said, clapping his hands with glee.

As Karatay bowed and exited the room, his heart was heavy. The Sultan was acting like a besotted teenager, and the welfare and leadership of the Kingdom was certainly the last thing on his mind at this moment. There is only one other person with whom I can discuss the gravity of this situation, and who will understand my concerns.

Karatay sent word that he wished to speak with the Sultana Mahperi as soon as possible.

☪ ☪ ☪

Karatay entered the Sultana's rooms, and after her servants poured him a goblet of fresh cherry juice, he explained the entire situation with the coins. He could see that she, too, was appalled by this show of ostentation in defiance of God's laws.

"Lady Mahperi, the situation is grave. He is obviously not in his right mind! Perhaps it is the potions and wines which muddle his reasoning, but you must speak to him immediately about this! He will perhaps listen to you, for he always has," urged the Vizier.

"No, dear Vizier Karatay, I will not speak to him," she said, "for that would serve no good. It is to *her* that I must speak."

Lady Mahperi immediately summoned the new bride to her rooms. She had not seen much of her since their marriage, since Gurchi made absolutely no effort to visit her mother-in-law, preferring to spend all of her time alone with Giyaseddin. Mahperi had over the years become close to the other wives of Giyaseddin, who were all honorable women. Several of them found the drinking of Giyaseddin hard to bear as well, and often came to Mahperi for solace. Since the arrival of Gurchi, they had been cast aside from his attentions, reminding Mahperi of the days when Alaeddin had returned from war with Gaziye. Adelpha, Giyaseddin's Greek Christian wife from Konya, was particularly hurt by his abandonment, and Mahperi found herself reaching out to comfort the woman for whom she had much affection.

Gurchi entered the rooms of the Sultana Mahperi surrounded by several of her maids, and at once showed her impatience at being summoned there. She did not smile at Mahperi upon entering, giving her only the weakest of greetings. Although she had never been one to indulge in all the intricacies of court etiquette, Mahperi still judged this young girl's lack of even the most simple respect to the mother of her husband to be appalling manners.

"Good morning, my dear Gurchi Hanim, you are looking well," said Mahperi Hatun, opening the conversation. "We have had little opportunity since your marriage to get to know each other better, so I decided to invite you here today for some refreshments and a little talk. Please, sit down," she said, dismissing Gurchi's servants with a gesture of her hand.

"My servants are to stay next to me!" Gurchi insisted, looking Mahperi defiantly in the eyes. "I need my attendants with me at all times."

"Not in my chambers, you do not," Mahperi replied firmly, boring her eyes right at the haughty princess. "This is a private meeting between you and me, so you will kindly ask them to step outside and wait for you at the door. Do not worry, my little one, you will be safe here," she said ironically, stunned by the insolence of the Georgian princess. As she gestured for her to sit down on the cushions, Mahperi began to see how this brazen, yet oh so comely young woman was able to persuade her son into complying with her every wish.

"I have invited you here today, my Princess, as I said, to try and get to know you better. It is important, so that I can better help you and serve your needs," she calmly explained.

Gurchi impudently cut her off before she could continue. "Firstly, I am not a Princess, I am a Queen now, she replied tartly. "And I certainly don't need any help from you, for I have all I need from the Sultan, my servants, my cousin David and my priests," she retorted.

The impudence of this sassy child is above all bounds, thought Mahperi. The mention of her cousin David reminded Mahperi of yet another problem. The abnormally close relationship between the two had created much gossip among the court, for she never did anything without his consent. Mahperi suspected the two of them were also plotting together to make deals that served their pockets and power well.

"Fine, my young woman; it is as you wish. It is true; I cannot demand your affection. However, as Queen Mother, I can demand your respect. Now listen to what I have to say, and as you are listening, remember who I am," she insisted, losing patience with the girl.

"In your position as a – Queen, as you say – it would be beneficial for you to pay more attention to the image that others hold of you," broached Mahperi. "The title of Queen must be earned, and the people of this land need to look up to you as an honorable person. You must set the example for others to follow, for the eyes of all the women of this empire are upon you. Your every gesture, your every smile, and your every kindness are observed by them, not just your jewels and brocades. I am counting on you, as well, to help my son become an exemplary Sultan to his people. He needs you by his side to encourage him to become a fine leader and to guide him in all aspects of his life," Mahperi insisted.

Upon hearing this, Gurchi burst out laughing. "Oh, you need not worry about that, for Giyaseddin does everything I say! *Everything.* So let you take note now, Lady Mahperi. It is I to whom he will listen from now on, not you. It is I who will tell him what to do, not you. You have lost that power over him. Don't ever forget that I am the daughter of a Georgian Queen, and now the reigning queen of the greatest empire of the East! My mother built a consolidated empire which dominated the Caucasus, protected Christianity and supported monasteries from Egypt to Bulgaria and Cyprus! She built cathedrals and was a champion of the Messiah! She dealt with Latin Crusaders, Kipchaks, the Mongols and the Ayyubids of Damascus. Nothing frightened her! Such was my mother, from whom I descend – so nothing frightens me either! And now I will reign as the radiant sun in this court of swarthy-souled and skinned people!" she spit out, glaring at Mahperi with hard eyes.

She continued before Mahperi could recover from her tirade.

"And I have one other piece of information for you, my Lady. I am now with child, and I know that it will be a son, destined to become the favored son of the Sultan and the next heir to the throne. So you see, it is truly I who hold the power now over the Sultan, not you, Lady Mahperi Hatun, so perhaps it is best to watch what you say to me, and – what was that you said? *'To pay more attention to the image that others hold of you'*. Yes, now it is your turn to do so" she cackled, obviously pleased with herself.

It took Mahperi a few seconds to recover from her remarks. She thought she had seen the last of such nasty aggression with the deaths of Gaziye and Köpek, but here again was the same stinging malice being thrown in her face. Perhaps she did have an intoxicating hold over her son, but one thing the Georgian perhaps ignored was the unquestioning respect and veneration Muslims hold for their mothers. Her son would never forsake her for a wife. Mahperi maintained her composure and carried on the conversation as if she had heard none of those insults.

"I would also like to talk to you about your religion, Lady Gurchi. I was in much the same situation as you when I came here. My husband allowed me to maintain my Christian religion, but if and when you give an heir to the throne, you will need to become a Muslim. In preparation of that day, I would encourage you to start studying the Islamic faith and prayers. Such insight will also help you become more aware of the empire around you, and what guides its leaders and citizens. There is much wisdom and beauty to be gained from this faith. My life has been enriched beyond bounds since I have adopted it, and I would wish for you the same. I can take you to meet scholars in the medreses here in Kayseri or even with my spiritual guide, Sheikh Turesan. I am at your service to help you on this path."

The young girl squinted at Mahperi, eyes still full of malice.

"You want me to convert to Islam? Are you joking? Never! I will not be like you, a traitor to our traditions! There is no possible way I will give up Mary and Jesus and my icons!" she glared.

"Do not be so quick to say that, my young one. Wait until you discover the richness of Islam before making such a statement. You may one day be very surprised by your desire to live by its lessons," Mahperi added.

Gurchi cackled out loud at that remark.

"Live by its lessons? I hardly think so, but if there are more jewels, money and power to be gained by becoming a Muslim, then I will do it, without hesitation. Just put a scarf over my head and tell me what to do. Teach me to babble that one line of Arabic that I must pronounce to make me a Muslim, since that is all it seems to take. If doing so will allow me to put my son on the throne, then I will do it. If it will allow me to become the most powerful woman in the land, then I will do it, my Lady, in one minute, the time it takes to pronounce that one phrase. But to do it for God and his lessons; no, that I will not," she snidely retorted.

Mahperi could not believe the callousness of this girl's soul, so hard at such a young age.

"You will live to regret those words one day, my daughter, the day the light of God's love will enter your heart and set it aflame. It will illuminate you more than those sparkling rubies you wear around your lovely neck; it will shine brighter than the sparking sapphires of your eyes or the gold of your crown of blonde hair or those gleaming silver coins with your sunny face upon them. One day, the teachings of the Qur'an will grace you with a dignity that you lack now. You will leave this existence of disdain for all around you. Your haughty head will hang in shame at the memory of the life you live now; one lived in ignorance and obsession with the ornaments of your existence. You are nothing more than a brass trinket, Gurchi Hatun. You do not deserve those rubies around your neck. You do not deserve the love of a people. Yes, one day, you will regret that you took the promise of the love of God in vain. For that, my dear little Queen, is a grace you cannot buy with all the silver coins of the realm."

Chapter 98

Brushfire Battles

Despite the chaos caused by Köpek's reign of terror and the pessimism of Karatay, the Seljuk state led by Sultan Giyaseddin Keyhüsrev in the year 1241 appeared to be as powerful as that of his father, the great Alaeddin Keykubad. Yet, like the fine fissures that can invisibly start in the strongest of stones, internal tensions now threatened to split the mighty rocks of the Empire wide open.

The Mongols of the Ocean continued to nip at the heels of the outer borders of the Empire, yet it was inside the borders of the Empire that the worst threat now appeared. The seething anger of Turkmen tribes spouted forth like the volcano in the ancient Majestic Mountain, pouring a destructive flow of lava over all the lands of the Empire.

☪ ☪ ☪

The Turkmen had been moving into Anatolia over the years, having been pushed out of their homeland fertile pastures of Central Asia by the drives of the Mongols. Yet the life they encountered on the southeastern Anatolian plateaus had not proved easy. Their native traditions often clashed with those in this land inhabited by many Christians and governed by an Islamic state. The Seljuk military expended considerable effort to keep these nomads from encroaching on sedentary farmers, forcing them to live in the undesirable barren and rocky patches of land.

These Turkmen shepherds, displaced from their lush Central Asian meadowlands, became the indirect victims of the advancing Mongol wave. Yet it was not just the lack of green pastures that plagued them. The Turkmen felt scorned by the Seljuk Empire. They knew that the Persian-speaking court in the cities looked down on them – they, the ragged peasants in the hinterlands who spoke Turkish and ate their bulgur with wooden spoons. They knew that the court in Konya made all the decisions that affected their lives, notably concerning the heavy taxation placed on their crops and herds, without consideration of their harsh life in the East.

The Turkmen tribes thus looked elsewhere for help in keeping their world in order. Confused about their economic and social status in this new community, they clung desperately to their ancestral shamanistic beliefs for comfort. These beliefs, tucked along with the bulgur in their saddlebags, told them that man descended from grey wolves, and that Spirits controlled life and death. The Turkmen trusted that their fur-capped shamans would keep their community strong, for they knew their symbols and codes and respected their identity and pride. The shamans mastered the Spirits of the sky and the night and read the omens of the Spirit world. Yes, our shamans will protect us, the Turkmen deemed, and we shall trust them and not the tax collectors sent by the Seljuk court.

☪ ☪ ☪

It was only a matter of time before the scrub brush of this volatile situation would catch fire. The forced Islamization of the Turkmen provided the spark that exploded the tinder into a brushfire blaze that engulfed the entire hinterland of Anatolia.

The Turkmen tribes were informed by the Seljuk court that if they converted to Islam, they would avoid heavy taxation. Drowning under the waves of poverty, they submitted to this new faith, but the conflicting beliefs between the many Spirit gods of their traditions and the one God imposed by Islam caused them much confusion.

Feeling isolated and spiritually bewildered, the impoverished Turkmen were an ideal brewing ground for propaganda, so it was no surprise that a new brand of religious leader appeared before them at this time, promising to help them make the transition between the old and new faiths. Called *babas* or *dedes*, these preachers were in reality nothing more than nominally-Islamized shamans who often took advantage of the unsteady circumstances for their own power gains.

One of these *babas* stood out from all the others. His charismatic personality and sermons fired the Turkmen people of southeast Anatolia with contempt for the corrupt administration of Giyaseddin's court, which he believed was robbing them through excessive taxation. The preacher incited them to take up arms and break away from the Seljuk state. The message of this Baba, named Ishak, was ripe for the ears of the nomadic Turkmen tribes. He announced that a new age was coming, away from the current appalling conditions of their lives. Yet he sought more than a rebellion. He proclaimed himself the prophet for the new age that would come under his leadership. The people believed that he truly was a new holy prophet, praying to him as "*La illaheillalah Baba Ishak Resululah,*" using the honorific title of *rasul*, normally used only for the Prophet Muhammad. The disenchanted idolized their shepherd, and followed him in flocks which grew larger with each passing day.

☪ ☪ ☪

Indeed, when wind reached the *ulema* at court in Konya that the Turkmen in the East were crying out the name of *Rasul* to a shepherd preacher, they knew they had to stop this profanation. Baba Ishak's proclamation as a holy prophet equal to the Prophet Muhammad was a heresy that would not be tolerated. There was only one God and his Prophet was Muhammad, peace be upon him. There would be no extremist forms of religion, and certainly no opposition to the established Sunnite ulema. And there could certainly be no revolt which risked weakening the government in place. Obedience was expected of all the subjects of the land. Something needed to be done.

Baba Ishak continued to incite the Turkmen to revolt, and raised the standard high for all his followers to see. The Turkmen in the alluvial plain of the southeast and in the Taurus Mountains took up the call first. Insurgents from Maraş, Kahta and Adiyaman organized themselves and began the insurrection, and they twice defeated the troops sent by the Sultan to quell them, which led many of the Seljuk soldiers to wonder if the Turkmen truly had the power of the Spirits and their new prophet behind them.

Soon, the rebellion spread into the very heart of Seljuk Anatolia. Marching up from the southeast, the rebels of Baba Ishak, now calling themselves the *Babai*, attacked Sivas, and, after pillaging it, turned towards Amasya to join their leader who had set up his headquarters there. Pressing on, the mob turned ugly and the revolt reached frightening dimensions. The Sultan Giyaseddin, instead of confronting the rebellion himself at the head of his troops, sent the administrator of Amasya, Mübarizüddin Armağan Shah, to tackle the insurgents. But before the mob reached Amasya, Armağan panicked and decided to kidnap Ishak from his *tekke* dervish retreat. He locked him up in the Amasya castle and then had him secretly hung to death.

When the outraged mob received the news that their beloved Baba Ishak had been imprisoned, they picked up their sticks and stones and steps to reach Amasya as soon as possible to free him from the castle walls. Yet when they stormed the castle and did not find Baba Ishak anywhere, tensions mounted to a frenzied state. Rumors abounded that their leader had been killed by the soldiers of the Sultan. Increasingly enraged, they attacked the Seljuk army, screaming in one loud surge "*Baba Resullah!*" The frightened Seljuk troops scattered and commander Armağan was killed in the ensuing skirmishes. With renewed vigor, the Babai took a vow to continue their rebellion against the central Seljuk authority all the way to the court capital of Konya, symbol of all their oppression.

When the Sultan heard that his troops had been defeated and that Mübarizüddin Armağan Shah had been killed, he, too, panicked. Instead of facing his responsibilities as the leader of the Seljuk Empire, he fled to Kubadabad where he knew no one find him, believing that by protecting his person against the risk of being killed by a mob of enraged peasants, he would save the Empire. Yes, in Kubadabad he would be safe, and that was all that mattered.

Enlisting the aid of their families, the Turkmen mob, dressed in their red caps, black robes and sandals, pressed westwards. They advanced on foot, on donkeys, and in carts in a great wave of movement across the steppes like a giant invasion of hungry locusts. By the time they arrived near Ankara, the Sultan could no longer avoid facing the peril, even from his hideaway at Kubadabad. The situation became so serious that Giyaseddin gave orders to recall the troops he had sent to Erzurum to protect the city against the advancing Mongols, and dispatched them to confront the mobs of the Babai rebellion.

The Erzurum troops of 60,000 contained many Frank, Armenian and Georgian Christian mercenaries. They met the Turkmen rebels on the wide plain of Malya near Kırşehir. After the Seljuk forces had neutralized the first attacks, a strange incident occurred among the Muslim soldiers. The pull and power of the Baba's preaching attracted them as well, and they began to sympathize with the plight of the Turkmen rebels. All set down their bows and arrows and refused to fight. Luckily for the Seljuk armies, the Christian mercenaries had no such qualms, and, making the sign of the cross on their foreheads before entering the fray, they were able, albeit with difficulty, to take the battle and win the day.

☪ ☪ ☪

Yet, even after this final battle, unrest continued to foment, and anger against the crown still raged. The mounds of charred ashes from the brushfire battles of the Babai continued to smolder. They lay scattered over the lands of the Seljuk Empire, scarring black the earth, and the wisps of smoke rising from these heaps of disappointed hopes could be seen far into the distance. The angry revolt had done its share to crack the walls of the Seljuk state, for it had kept its most impressive troops occupied for over two years in the central part of Anatolia, instead of taking care of the eastern fringes where the Mongols now chewed away at the frontiers like wolves on an antelope carcass.

For who can comprehend the deep waters of the counsel of God in heaven and make it right here on earth? And when will befuddled mankind ever learn what is God's destined conduct? Such were the questions that burned on the minds of the leaders of the Empire after this revolt, while the Sultan sat in the Kubadabad Palace drinking his wine of pleasure.

Chapter 99

Doors Opening Wide

Little swallow, soaring high in the skies above the kingdom of the Seljuks, you have so many new things to see underneath your wings in this holy year of 1241!

Little swallow, sweep down over the many new buildings born this year, and see how joy now rises in the hearts of the people of this Seljuk land who celebrate their completion. Speed past their doors, and skim over the heads of the people rushing into each and every one of them.

Little swallow, race down from the Majestic Mountain at the sound of the call to prayer, and dart over the shoulders of the faithful now gathering to perform their prayers in the vast hall of the new mosque in the center of their town, all ready to bend down in devoted expression to the glory of the Almighty.

A door opens to a mosque, built of stones of faith.

Little swallow, dive over the pink roses blooming in the hot June sun along a green river and then soar out over the surrounding countryside of blue hills fragrant with thyme and pine. Tip your wings to salute the camels of the caravans trodding along to and fro the seven hans now built on the roads leading to the city nestled under a fortress high.

Doors open to seven hans, built of stones of commerce.

Little swallow, pump your wings hard against the buffeting winds to reach the blue dome of heaven above a mountaintop. Seek the haven nested in the remote countryside, there, in a hushed place of retreat, where dervishes twirl and contemplate and search for the unyielding answers of truth.

A door opens to a dervish lodge, built of stones of peace.

Yes, little swallow, you are busy in this year 1241, observing all these new stones of the kingdom below you, ordered as a gift by a gracious Sultana for the people of her land. You watch as the doors of a mosque, a medrese, a hammam, seven hans and a *tekke* dervish lodge swing open to the people, doors opening as wide as the generous heart that ordered them built.

Mahperi stepped out of the New Gate and looked across at her mosque, its portal gleaming white in the sunlight. Gone were the crews of masons and stone carvers, gone were the piles of stones and bricks, gone was the mud, gone were the voices of the foremen shouting out orders to the workers. Now, only beauty and quiet remained. In place of the hubbub stood magnificence, praising God on most high with every stone of its walls.

It was finished. After three long years of construction, it was done. Three years now too, since her Alaeddin was gone; so hard to believe. Yet as she stood here, she did not feel alone. Alaeddin and her other beloved ones now gone stood next to her. She could feel the warmth of their shoulders against hers. She hoped too, that a whole nation was standing behind her, ready to cross the threshold of this mosque and her hans and her medrese and her baths and her tekke, for she had built everything for them.

She lingered for a moment to admire the fine details of the lace carving of the massive main door of the mosque. You could look at this carving forever, she thought to herself, so intricate and complex it is! I know that generations of faithful to come will pause here to stand in awe of it each time they enter this mosque, just as I am doing today. May the greatness of the Seljuk Empire live on forever in this mosque!

The mosque was dedicated just after Christmas, as Nikolas had promised, in the presence of the *ulema*, her family, the emirs, court officials, military leaders, priests from the local Christian churches and the rabbi from the Hebrew temple. Representatives of the building guilds, teachers from the medreses and merchants of the local community were invited to attend as well. Per her wish, every worker who had toiled on the project was invited to a special ceremony held before the official opening. At that time, Mahperi placed a gold coin in each and every one of their palms, just as Alaeddin used to do with his soldiers after an important victory was won. Later on in the day, with the Sultan Giyaseddin Keyhüsrev himself standing in front of the majestic portal of the mosque, the imam led the blessing invocation, a lamb was sacrificed, the faithful performed their ablutions and an entire community of believers entered the prayer hall to inaugurate the mosque with their first prayers.

Mahperi raised her eyes to the sky when she heard the fluttering wings of a swallow swooping above the mosque, looking for a place to roost. She smiled up at it, thinking about how the people of Kayseri would come here to roost as well, in the safe haven of God's grace. I am like you, little swallow; how I have flown since those days at Kalonoros!

She paused to read the marble inscription plaque that Nikolas had hung over the door before the inauguration ceremony the previous week. He had carved it just as she had requested, and became moved when she there read the names of both her husband and son, her two Sultans:

> *"The great Sultana Mahperi Hatun, moderate and honorable to the world and charitable to the faith, ordered the construction of this blessed mosque in the holy year of 1238 during the reign of her son the great sultan Giyaseddin, son of Alaeddin, protector of the faith and the world, master of victories, may God continue to shine His grace upon him and give him strength."*

She pushed open the door and entered the prayer hall, her heart beating fast inside her chest. She looked around her at the completed mosque, its columns lifting upward like giant trees. Her heart opened to prayer.

Fly, my spirit, fly like that little swallow and perch on the branches of those trees; yet may my feet stay rooted to the earth like the knots that cling to the warps of the carpets beneath me. The sap of all souls will rise up in these trees, forgetting the eons of ignorance and barbarity before us. I have created a forest grove of truth and peace. Let us now rejoice in the greatness of the Almighty, in this, the mosque I have built for You, o God, our Everlasting One.

Chapter 100

A Crown of Grey Walls

When the last of the Babai brushfires had been snuffed out on the plain near Kırşehir in the year 1241, the Sultan Giyaseddin Keyhüsrev was once again able to turn his military attention eastwards to the Empire's ceaseless adversary, the Ayyubids. The internal strife of the Turkmen revolt had kept the Seljuk army fully occupied for over three years, but now the Sultan could focus on a very particular goal. He was determined to capture the one city his father was never able to take: Diyarbakır. This Ayyubid city of grey walls was the strategic key to the upper basin of the Tigris and the maddening checkmate on his father's military chessboard.

Allying himself with the other enemies of the Ayyubids, the Sultan Giyaseddin Keyhüsrev began by capturing Meyyafarikin, the capital of the Ayyubid Emirate of the region of Diyarbakır.

He then pressed on and besieged the great city of Diyarbakır itself, and was relentless in his charge. The nobles of the city, after a valiant attempt to withhold behind their ring of thick surrounding walls, were finally obliged to acknowledge their defeat at the hands of the Seljuks. They agreed to surrender on the condition that no citizens would be harmed, and that their taxes to the Seljuk state would be lessened. The Sultan acquiesced, for he was eager to cede any concession necessary to topple the chess piece city of basalt and temerity.

As Giyaseddin sat on his horse at the top of the grey walls dark as cinders and observed the city below, he felt an achievement that he had never experienced before. He wore that ring of walls like a crown upon his head. After the humiliation of the Babai revolt and the problems with Köpek, at last he had found a victory that would distinguish him in everyone's eyes. He was a Sultan every inch as worthy as his father, for he was able to accomplish something even the great and glorious Alaeddin Keykubad could never do: he had taken the city of Diyarbakır. His father, who had set the capture of this city as one of his most important goals, failed over and over again despite all his might. And so I ask you, thought the young Sultan to himself, straightening himself taller in his saddle, who is the stronger ruler of the two?

In celebration of his victory, he immediately gave orders to repair the Great Mosque, built in the time of the Great Seljuk Malik Shah. He requested that an inscription be set in its distinctive walls comprised of black basalt and white limestone courses so that all eternity would know that he, Sultan Giyaseddin Keyhüsrev, had been there as conqueror and Shahinshah-al-Azam, the Greatest Sovereign.

☪ ☪ ☪

And so it was in this holy year of 1241 that the Sultan Giyaseddin Keyhüsrev, despite his reign being severely tested by the Babai revolt, now found himself at the height of his military powers. His praises were sung all the way to Europe, where the Catholic Church in Rome received letters about him, sent from Friar Simon de Saint Quentin, a French missionary traveling in Anatolia at the time. Giyaseddin had enjoyed hosting the good friar, and learned much from his conversations with him. In return, the monk spoke well of the Sultan in his letters home, never failing to compliment his hospitality and lavishing high praise for his richness and power. After his discussions with the monk, Giyaseddin himself began to think more and more about the promise of the West. Visions of grandeur began to flutter in his mind. Now that he had taken Diyarbakır, everything seemed possible to him, even a campaign in Europe. Why shouldn't he hold this western aspiration for his Empire? Europe would one day need to recognize the power of the Turks.

Such were the ambitions dreamed for the future by Sultan Giyaseddin Keyhüsrev, now basking in a bright sky of victory and prestige. Yet, if he had listened closely, he would have heard thunderclouds, as dark as those basalt walls of Diyarbakir, rumbling over the distant horizon to the East.

Chapter 101

Downpour Unleashed

It was not long before the rumbling clouds on the distant horizon unleashed their downpour onto the Seljuk Empire.

The Mongols, Lords of the Celestial Hordes, continued their sweep through Central Asia, destroying and slaughtering all in their path. They had trampled the verdant grazing lands of Azerbaijan, displacing Khwarazmians and Turkmen alike. They had snapped up the Georgian kingdom, forcing the haughty Queen Rusudan to flee from Tiflis. The mighty Mongol commander Chormagan Noyan captured and sacked Kars and Ani, slaughtering the entire population of the two cities.

Nonetheless, in 1241, the same year that Sultan Giyaseddin Keyhüsrev took Diyarbakir, the Mongols faced an internal crisis that risked slowing down the raging wave. Ogedei, the third son and successor of the Ocean Genghis Khan, now lay dead after an all-night drinking binge. His weakness for alcohol had achieved what no enemy sword was able to do. This favorite son of Genghis had become a world figure, expanding the Mongol Empire to its farthest extent west and south: Central Asia, China, Iran, Asia and Russia all now bowed to him! Who would be named the great Khan in his place? The succession fell upon Ogedei's son, Güyük, but he, too, died shortly after taking the throne.

In another twist of fate, the Mongols also lost their most famous general, Chormagan Noyan. He, who had served both Genghis and Ogedei with distinction, abruptly fell sick and died. He was replaced by his able lieutenant Baiju, a warrior more ferocious than any before him.

Although the Mongols were busy dealing with their own internal battles for succession and the reshuffling of their military command, none of this was evident on the battlefield. Their ardent desire for more conquests now focused on the Seljuk Empire.

Mongol spies reported back to Baiju that the Seljuk Sultan was constantly absorbed in the pastimes of pleasure. They heard the still-rumbling voices of the discontented Turkmen, and noted how the Sultan in all his glory had been barely able to subdue these ragged rabble-rousers. The spies informed Baiju that the Seljuk Sultan seemed both weak and incapable, despite his recent victory at

Diyarbakır. The strong reign of Sultan Alaeddin Keykubad was long past – the time to strike Seljuk Anatolia had come.

So in late 1242, the Mongol army under the command of Baiju set out to batter down the door of Seljuk territory. Before long, they had easily overtaken Erzurum, eastern gateway to the Seljuk lands. Helped by the treachery of a local citizen seeking to assure his survival, the Mongols seized the city on the first attempt in the bitter cold month of January, 1243. They were blocked there for several months, for even the Great Mongols had to bow before the power of the heavy snow and cold of Erzurum winters. The Mongols hunkered down and planned their next strike: a complete invasion of Anatolia, to start once the deep snows melted off the wide steppes.

Spring came, and the Mongols began their march again, trampling the blooming tulips under their hooves. And the loveliest of the blooms trampled was the city of Erzincan. Pent up from an entire winter of inactivity, the Mongol soldiers unfurled their energy in a mad furor, sacking the city until there was nothing left of it. Even the devastating earthquakes which often ravaged this region paled in comparison with the unleashed force of the Mongol troops. The Mongols butchered all the men and captured 2,000 women. They stripped them naked, made them dance in front of them and then dishonored them. Their children were taken as slaves.

Horrified by this massacre, the Seljuk commander Siyafeddin Sungurlala met with the Sultan at his Kayseri pleasure palace of Josaq and pressed him to immediately deploy troops to the region. He warned the Sultan that Erzurum was just the beginning of the Mongol wrath, and that the Seljuks needed to respond before it was too late.

Almost five years had passed since the Mongol ambassadors had been sent home after the banquet with Alaeddin Keykubad. The new Sultan Giyaseddin Keyhüsrev, backed by his emirs and Köpek, had dismissed their offer at that time, asserting that the proud Seljuks would never submit to these barbarians. Even though the Sultan had adopted this strategy, he was too weak to take the necessary action to implement it. The Sultan, still giddy from his victory over the Babai and the walls of Diyarbakır, preferred instead to sit back on his cushions and wait, wine cup in hand. He dismissed Sungurlala with a wave of his hand, insisting that this was just a Mongol trick to provoke them to react, and that there was no need to be alarmed about this little foray over the Seljuk border.

Yet Sungurlala and other emirs knew better. Refusing to accept that Giyaseddin Keyhüsrev took no advisement from them about this alarming situation, Sungurlala and several officers sent out troops to confront the Mongols. Perhaps the Sultan chooses to deny this threat, but we will not! Alas, it was not long before the heads of Sungurlala and the supreme judge of Erzurum were sent back to the Palace of the Great Khan at Karakorum as victory trophies.

☪ ☪ ☪

The Sultan Giyaseddin Keyhüsrev could now no longer deny the inevitable – the door to Anatolia had been battered wide open and the dark Mongol thunderclouds would soon unleash their torrential downpour. If unchecked, this deluge would flood over his threshold at Josaq, drown Sivas and Kayseri, and then submerge the capital of Konya.

He could hear the distant rumble of thunder roaring in his ears.

It was time to put down his wine goblet and rise.

Chapter 102

A Rainbow City of War

As much as he did not want to face the brutal truth, the Sultan knew he needed to rise from the soft cushions of his palace and go sit on the hard saddle of the war trail, towards a clash that would certainly go down in history as the most decisive Seljuk battle since the infamous day at Manzikert.

Sultan Giyaseddin Keyhüsrev left Kayseri for the city of Sivas to confer with his most able generals on a strategy for the confrontation with the heathen Mongols. At the same time, he summoned Seljuk troops from every corner of the Empire to leave their posts and converge as soon as possible at Sivas. The Sultan also sent messengers to the leaders of his vassal states. The time had come for Jean Vatatzes, the Greek Emperor of Nicaea, and King Hethoum of the Armenian Kingdom of Cilicia to send the standing troops owed to the Seljuks as part of their tribute agreements.

In great urgency, the Sultan pressed his adversaries to reconcile their past and present differences to tackle the common danger facing all, Christian and Muslim alike. They, too, were exhorted to expedite troops, and, to sweeten the prospect, chests full of gold coins were sent to them by the Sultan. The Grand Komnenos of Trabzon quickly contributed 200 crack archers. The young Ayyubid prince of Aleppo promised to send 2,000 foot soldiers and 1,000 of his finest horsemen.

In addition, the Sultan opened the state coffers to hire the mercenaries who were always ready to serve the highest bidder. A motley cavalry of ragtag Turkmen, weakened by the Baba Ishak rebellion and now at loose ends, found a new outlet for their aggressive restlessness in the war against the Mongols. Stranded Crusader Franks and deserters from the Khwarazmian, Kipchak and Abbasid armies also fed into this great mass of irregulars. A hardy contingent of 3,000 Greek and Latin soldiers of fortune was assembled under the command of the dashing Georgian prince Shervashidze. From every corner of the region, all were convening at Sivas for the confrontation of the century.

In the end, over 80,000 soldiers, bright and valiant all, arrayed in a kaleidoscopic display of differently-colored tunics, tents and banners, and praying in over twenty languages to several different Gods, formed a Rainbow City of

War. Camp was set up in a valley bowl near Kösedağ, some 50 miles from Sivas, in a field big enough to hold all the tents of these multicolored warriors. The army, arriving daily from every corner of the kingdom, grew so large that it spread across ten miles. Yet, no matter what their religion, flag, color or motivation, all were there for one purpose: to defeat the Mongol troops of Baiju. King Hethoum of the Armenian Kingdom of Cilicia kept dragging his feet about sending the 1,400 lancers that he had promised, much to the ire of the Sultan. But everyone else was now converged there, waiting for their instructions to attack – or waiting to be attacked themselves. For everyone knew that somewhere out there to the east, in a grassy field much like theirs, Baiju was making the exact same preparations.

☪ ☪ ☪

Organizing the daily life of this Rainbow City of War was a miracle of logistics, and the well-oiled Seljuk Army machine staged operations of a magnitude rarely seen in all the campaigns of its illustrious past. The military engineers knew that a successful army was comprised of soldiers, equipment and organization, and thus a battalion of ordnance officers, engineers, carpenters, ditch diggers, military police, guards, cooks, water carriers, doctors, blacksmiths, veterinarians and laborers now joined their skills to forge the systems that would keep 80,000 men fed, healthy and trained day after day.

First, orders were given to dig the trenches and lay out the wooden planks for the latrines. These deep sanitation ditches were situated far away from the center of the encampment, and were covered with sand each morning to hold down the stench of the excrement of 80,000 men.

Organizing the water camp was the next crucial step, with hundreds of wooden barrels set on the banks of the stream like battalions in marching order. The barrels were filled continuously from the stream, and then transported by wagons to the various areas of the Rainbow City of War.

Next, weapons and supplies were unloaded and set under canvas tarpaulins to keep them dry. Every possible type of war materiel used in battle was grouped in orderly stacks: swords, bows and arrows, lances, maces, shields, slingshots, daggers, pikes, bayonets and axes. Stacks of arrows were crafted daily by the smithies and woodcarvers and were stockpiled in towers tall as men.

Erected, as well, were the stockyards for the animals to be slaughtered for food. Special clean and orderly pens were set up to stable the horses. Nothing was more important to a Seljuk soldier than his horse, the wings on which he rode to victory. Seljuk horses, with their small ears, strong rumps and sturdy legs, were tended to with as much attention as the Sultan himself in his palatial silk tent.

Not forgotten either were provisions for hygiene. Special bathing pits were dug in the ground and lined with clay so that the soldiers could maintain their cleanliness, so important for their health and for showing respect to God. Much to the disgust of the Turks, the Franks found no use for bathing, and could not understand the Muslim obsession with daily cleanliness.

The last task was the digging of the pits for the mass burial of the victims for the battle to come, for no matter who the victor, there would always be fallen warriors in need of a proper and timely burial according to Muslim tradition.

However, all these measures paled in front of the massive operations for running the kitchens. Food was the utmost challenge for the Rainbow City of War: the procurement, slaughtering, preservation, storage, cooking, serving, and cleanup operations involved in feeding 80,000 men a day staggered the calculations of the most able of engineers, not to mention the patience of the cooks. Forming an army of their own, two hundred master cooks, assisted by five hundred kitchen helpers, prepared the meals for the soldiers. Each cook had 40 pots under his command, and the pots themselves were set out in their own tent city. They used kettles wide enough to hold 30 sheep heads to boil into soup broth. Young scullery helpers had to climb atop high stools to stir the bubbling soups with long wooden paddles. Two meals were served per day; usually a hearty soup after the dawn prayer, and then a more substantial meal at the end of day after the training maneuvers and the men were ravenously hungry. Following the long-standing tradition of the Seljuks on campaign, everyone ate the same meal. The commanders, ditch-diggers, grooms, generals, flag-bearers, foot-soldiers and the Sultan himself would all eat together, dipping their bread into the same bowls of bulgur and chickpea soup and sucking the meat off the same bones. All were equal in the eyes of God, especially when they were about to defend the faith.

☪ ☪ ☪

Before long, advance scouts came to the Sultan's camp with the news: the Mongols had been sighted two valley ridges away, within striking distance of the Rainbow City of War. The news that the Mongols were just over the hill spread around the city faster than a speeding arrow. All lifted their noses in the air and could smell the putrid odor of the Mongols blowing in from the distance.

A summit meeting of the commanders and viziers of the Seljuk Empire was immediately convened in the Sultan's green satin tent. All awaited their instructions from the Sultan as Supreme Commander, and he was quick to give them, without discussing strategy for the battle with any of them. He raised his head and looked them defiantly in the eye.

"My decision has been made! We will attack them first, tomorrow at dawn!" he bellowed out, jabbing his saber into the ground.

While some of his emirs agreed with his tactic, many were those who felt it would be more prudent to wait for the Mongols to strike first. Emir Mubariz al-din Chavli, commander in charge of the infantry, did not hesitate to voice his opinion.

"My Sultan, your courage is admirable! Yet do you not think it best to wait for the arrival of the troops King Hethoum promised to send us? We need every sharpshooter possible in the face of this enemy, and his are the finest!" he insisted.

Other emirs nodded their heads and murmured in agreement, but the Sultan silenced them with an irritated look. He was tired of being second-guessed about every decision. He wanted to make up his own mind this time, and act as decisively as his father would have done. Perhaps he did not have the experience of his generals, but he was the Sultan, and the final call would be his.

"No! It is decided. We move tomorrow. Our men are becoming too restless to contain, and we cannot have them lose their hunger for war. Go now, and prepare your battalions. This heat, too, is our ally! Remember that the Mongols come from lands that are covered in forests and mountains where the weather is cool. God will show them the power of our Anatolian June sun, just as He did to those Frankish Crusaders! They will bake inside their furs until they drop like parched toads!"

☪ ☪ ☪

Later, as the blue haze of evening descended across the plain and the shadows of the setting sun drew long purple patches across the field, Giyaseddin Keyhüsrev and his commanders sat around the campfire outside the Sultan's tent. All were ready for the battle, although many were uneasy about the Sultan's rashness to attack. All worried that the troops of Hethoum would not arrive in time. Other unspoken apprehensions bothered them as well: the young Sultan seemed unaware of the complexity of this battle, and lacked, despite his bravado at barking orders, the fundamental confidence of a competent leader.

Commander Chavli, a weathered army commander, decided to speak to the Sultan as if he were his own son. If only the great Alaeddin Keykubad could be here for this battle! He would now be addressing all of us, in that low and resolute voice of his, to inspire us to greatness. Instead, in front of us sits his young and unseasoned son, drinking his red wine as if he were at a festival.

He coughed to catch Giyaseddin's attention. "My Sultan, we are on the eve of the greatest battle this empire has ever undertaken. You are about to embark on the same path as your illustrious forefathers. Kilich Arslan was not yet seventeen at the very first battle of the Seljuks with the Crusader infidels at Nicaea. You are young, too, all of twenty-two years old, on the eve of this battle. Your ancestor braved the mighty Franks and reduced them to shame at Nicaea. Now you, too, must show that you can do the same to this tormenter of Islam coming from the East, just as he did to those oppressors from the West. You, Lion of us all, will take the day tomorrow!" he stirringly spoke.

The Sultan did not answer him but rather took two long sips of red wine from his goblet. Chavli interpreted this as a sign to continue his speech.

"Yet with all the respect and honor I hold for you, Great Sultan, the fact still remains that you *are* young, and with that comes the blessing of lessons yet to master. One of those lessons, a very important and hard one, is how to earn the respect of your men," he continued. "You may have inherited the supreme authority of the Empire from your father, the great Sultan Alaeddin Keykubad, may God shine light on his soul, but you must also merit it. That is a crown only you can place on your head. That was one of the great gifts of your father: he understood what it took to make men rush to their deaths upon a simple nod of his head. The soldiers in the field will respect you because you will show them what it is to be a brave warrior. God alone will decide the outcome of the day tomorrow; but you will be his agent and must show your mettle. Battles are not won only by arms or men only. They are won by faith in God and His word. Let us not fail in this Holy Covenant now upon us."

☪ ☪ ☪

After the commanders and emirs had left, the Sultan sat alone in his tent and thought about all that had been said. Rather than reassure him, Chavli's speech had shaken him to the core. He refilled his goblet and lifted it to his lips. He thought of the kind eyes of his mother who was now at Tokat visiting her hans. How he needed her to take his hand and tell him all would be fine! But she was not here and he was alone, with his fears for company.

Yes, he was afraid. Emir Chavli's unsettling words now churned in his head like the wine swirling in his goblet, each doing their share to make his tormented soul spin faster and faster. Yes, it was certain he would never be the glorious commander that his father was. As much as he tried, he did not know instinctively how to earn respect like he did. He was not brave like him. He was a little boy who stole halvah from the kitchens of the palace and did horrible things that others requested him to do. Confused and frightened, he began to question whether the order he gave that day was wise, and even if he were truly meant to be a Sultan.

As the wine flowed, the furnace roar of conflicting emotions in his ears grew louder and louder. But whether the roaring was the snarl of war desire, the craving for the ring of victory, or the drumming of his fearful heart, he was not sure.

And so he kept drinking. There was always courage to be found at the bottom of a wine goblet.

Chapter 103
Zenith and Nadir

The heat had been building in intensity with each passing day for over a week. Today, the glittering golden coin would blaze hotter than any day of the year, even though it was still the beginning of summer. The earth was uneasy, the wind was silent, birds and frogs kept their songs to themselves, the tongues of dogs hung to the ground, tree leaves crumbled like dry paper, and the stalks of grass dipped their edges down to the ground. Horses pawed the earth and all the animals took to their burrows. The sun rose quickly, bringing the morning light as suddenly as a door opened wide. Within the space of twenty minutes it went from streaks of rose to beams of yellow heat. The earth became a sizzling anvil and the sun's rays pounded down on the heads of the soldiers with the force of a smithy's hammer. The intense sunlight reflected off every surface in a blizzard mirage, and the ground glittered as if covered by snow. It was a dry, hot and silent world on this morning of June 26, 1243.

As happened every morning in the Rainbow City of War, the muezzin's cry for the dawn prayer woke Muslim and unbeliever alike. Only today, trumpets and drums sounded at the same time as the muezzin's call to ensure that all were stirred, as if anyone needed to be reminded that a day of infamy awaited them.

A hearty breakfast soup was served, as it would be the last meal the men would eat for a long time, for no one knew how long this hot day would last. After breakfast, the imam led a special prayer, and 50,000 Muslim soldiers bowed down on the plain in the direction of Mecca. Their resolve to accomplish God's will fired their hearts as hotly as the sun that burned on their turbans. The Christians looked on, excused from the prayer but obliged keep silent during this important moment. Perhaps they, too, were praying to their God, but it was Allah's day today, and Allah alone would be the Commander in Chief of all these forces.

The voice of the imam sounded out as he read the *Al-Ikhlas* "Purity of Faith" Surat 112 from the Qur'an which was believed to offer protection from evil and dangers, and evil and danger certainly perched on the dawn of this day.

In the name of God, Most Gracious, Most Merciful
Proclaim, "He is the One and only God.
The Absolute God.
Never did He beget. Nor was He begotten.
None equals Him."

The imam ended his service with a special prayer for the Sultan: *"Exalted God, preserve the power of Giyaseddin Keyhüsrev, our noble Sultan, our just and mighty Khan, protect his sovereignty and domains so he may forever be contented and victorious."*

Afterwards, small chapbooks filled with talismanic charts to ensure victory were distributed to the generals. A miniature octagonal Qur'an was placed in a metal case and attached to the Sultan's banner to guarantee that it would not be captured. Swords with the 99 names of God inscribed in gold on their handles to protect their owners during combat were placed, with great ceremony, into the hands of the emirs.

In the field, soldiers made final adjustments to their bows, arrows, sabers, and catapults. Despite the different origins of the troops, all felt a bond of solidarity in the face of the enemy. Some fought for adventure, others for salary, others for the promise of booty, others for the glory of Allah, others for the gore of bone and blood; but whatever their reason, they were all there to bring home a victory against the heathen Mongols by the end of day. They would drive them out of Anatolia, and be named heroes for all eternity.

The Sultan looked out over the troops and saw many young boys not much older than sixteen, his age when he became Sultan. Now, at twenty-two, he felt a lifetime older than they. Even his generals were young, for this was not a campaign for old men. He was ready and eager, and with the lessons of Chavli's words ringing in his ears, he knew he needed to address his troops with an inspiring speech. Yes, he thought, I will earn their respect; yes, they will see that I am as brave a warrior as my father was.

He sat up tall on his horse and bellowed out for all to hear:

"My Lions! No matter how many or few we may be, or how great in number our enemies may be, we shall fling ourselves upon them at this hour. All the Muslims of the world are with us on this morning. Either we shall be victorious and fulfill our goal, or we shall become martyrs and enter Paradise. Allah will not abandon us. We are all here together, defending the entire world from the ignorance and violence of these heathens! Know that I am not the commander here, and none are commanded. We are all one under the command of Allah. We have chosen to dedicate our lives to the Allah Most High, and those who remain alive will be heroes and acquire great riches. Eternal fire and the infamy of shame will await those who desert us. Allah's grace will be to those victorious!"

Turk or foreigner, Seljuk or Frank, Muslim or Christian, soldier or Sultan: all were now ready to confront this searing day.

☪ ☪ ☪

As had been decided the day before, the Sultan planned to send out a vanguard of 20,000 troops for the first sally against the Mongols. After stunning them with this lightening first raid, the other divisions of the army would sweep in and finish off the battle. After the vanguard, it would be the turn of the main infantry and cavalry divisions to enter the fray, followed by the right wing of Commander Chavli and a substantial left wing. The Sultan and his elite troops would then attack, and finally, the rear division, under the leadership of the experienced Emir Sahip Ataci, would close in to overwhelm the enemy. Sending out the vanguard on its own was a daring move, but the Sultan believed in his tactic. No one needed reminding that the absence of Hethoum's sharp-shooting archers would be sorely felt, but the Sultan was determined to commence the battle without them. His impatience, as well as his fears for the safety of his people against these savages, drove his resolute desire to strike as soon as possible. He wanted these Mongol monsters eradicated from Seljuk soil once and for all, and now.

Once the breakfast soup and prayers were over, and as the first blush of true day appeared over the crest of the hills, the musicians began to play their marching music. The vanguard set off to the sounds of horns and kettledrums. Emir Gurcuoğlu, the Commander in Chief of all the army forces, and the Emirs Chavli, Nizaddeddin and Sahip Ataci took command of their various sections. The honor of carrying the Sultan's flag was awarded to Atabeg Arslan.

The vanguard rode for less than a half hour in a cloud of dust before they caught first sight of the enemy. The Sultan's archers, armed with javelins and winged arrows like beasts stalking their prey, sat taller in their saddles. They paused on a ridge above the great bowl of field where the Mongols waited. The Sultan took his position at the top of the ridge to survey the troops. He nodded his head in the direction of his Commander in Chief.

Commander Gurcuoğlu gave the signal.

Suddenly, a young warrior wearing a tall, red turban lifted his sword above his head. The scraping sound of thousands of steel blades cut through the air as the men behind him unsheathed their swords from their scabbards. Leading the attack were the fearless Turkmen front cavaliers, charged with frightening the Mongols. They kicked their stallions and tore down the ridge, all of one voice shouting a cry of "*Allahu akbar*!" loud enough to be heard clear to the Holy

Ka'ba in Mecca. These wild-eyed front chargers raced down with the sound of thunder and lightning on their hooves, raising a cloud of yellow dust unto the heavens. The intrepid Turkmen whipped their curved blades back and forth in the air at the same time as they hurled their furious cry at the surprised Mongols below.

The Commander now gave his signal to the archers. The guard of 20,000 men, led by the Georgian Prince Shervashidze, was ready. They, too, charged down the hill with their bows vibrating arrows that rained forth with a din that sounded like a pack of barking dogs. The vanguard was given the task to surround the Mongols and cut them off from their rear troops. With all possible retreats blocked, the Mongols would be plunged into a big pot of boiling Seljuk stew.

Although they had been expecting an assault, the Mongols appeared taken by surprise by the advancing torrent of Seljuks, and seemed to flee in fear. The Seljuks could not know, however, that the retreat by the Mongol horsemen was nothing more than a tactic of feigned panic planned to dupe and disorganize them. Baiju quickly gave the orders for his troops to turn around and counterattack. The Mongols deployed their squadrons in a flanking maneuver, surrounding and cutting off the Seljuks from the rest of their troops. The Mongol trick completely fooled the Seljuk troops.

Baiju was an experienced warrior, and knew that he would be able to throw his opponent into confusion with this ploy of a feigned flight followed by a sudden return. He had used this classic ambush many times before, and once again, his enemy fell neatly into his trap. The Mongols pierced the front of the vanguard and ran straight through it, their shields upon their backs. Now it was their downpour of arrows that whizzed through the air with the sound of howling dogs. The Mongols pierced a wide hole that enabled their lance men and armored horses to cut through and finish the assault. The tables had completely turned. The Seljuk troops were completely encircled, with no possible way to break through and retreat. Every exit had been sealed. The brave Seljuk archers who tried to ride through the wall of Mongol fire and arrows were mowed down. Those who doubled back to reload their quivers were cut down before they could even turn their backs. The Georgian prince Shervashidze fell to the ground dead, leaving his men on the field without a commander. Other emirs fell too, and heavy casualties were sustained by the right wing. Aslan Doğmuş managed to grab the sultan's flag before it hit the ground when Atabeg Arslan was pierced through his heart by an arrow.

The Sultan remained at the top of the ridge, observing the fighting from different viewpoints, and giving out new orders as best he could in the confusion. He saw that his plan had gone terribly wrong. He conferred anxiously with his emirs, yet it soon became apparent that no new tactic would save the day for the Seljuks.

Arrows were distributed to the rear guard, but the stockpile was soon depleted. The Seljuk horsemen of the rear guard sped down the hill, but once again, the position of the Mongol troops offered them no room to advance, cutting them off from the bottom of the slope. The Mongols had chosen not only to aim their arrows at the soldiers, but at their horses as well, for they knew that a Turk without his steed was like a body without lungs. Beast after beast tumbled, and soldiers fell by hundreds as blood-spattered horses were gutted by the blades of the Mongols. The mighty wings of the Turks fell rolling on the ground while flinging their hooves in the air. The bodies of the horses soon formed a levee, barring the progress of any further soldiers down the hill. One after the other the soldiers slumped and fell. Dust ceased to rise in the air now that the ground was completely soaked by blood and viscera.

The men were running in all directions in a wild march of motion, yelling shrilly. The field howled with a mad scramble of scurrying men and horses in a heaving tangle. Waves of men continued to enter the beating heart of the furnace, unaware in their eager rush to confront the enemy that their chances for survival were grim. They were swallowed by the red flames of the war furnace, fanned by the Mongol dragons in an invincible throng. The blunt head of the Seljuk column tried to force its way through the dense mass by sheer force, but they were unable to breach the wall and faced the final and fatal encounter.

The remaining troops panicked at the sight of the carnage in front of them and realized that the Mongols had also begun to attack their rear. The Seljuk divisions now lost cohesion and broke up, with soldiers fleeing one ambush and often running into another. Soldiers scrambled back up to the ridge, abandoning the battle. Parched and afraid, they refused to return to the pot of boiling hell below.

Everyone was now in flight; shouting incoherently and riding about in disorder. From the mouths of the fleeing men came a din of wild questions, but no one had answers. The mercenaries, jealous of the Sultan's favoritism to his native troops, did not ride to their rescue. The Armenians were the first to take flight, and many Franks abandoned the battle. No one could tell who was in charge, or hear any order above the baying wind of barking arrows. Some claimed that the Sultan was firmly resisting with what was left of his army; others said that the Sultan had been captured, for no one could see his standard anywhere. Some believed that the barbarian Mongols had taken flight. Everyone had something different to report, claiming victory for each side and then denying it.

It was an earthquake of yowls, sweat, a swift rush of horse hooves and fear, clouds of dust and arrows, and hordes of fur-clad Mongols riding in every direction, all with speed, resolution and strength. It was a terrible sight, beyond any lamenting or mourning, with all the valleys and plains filled with the bodies of Seljuk warriors killed or trampled under their horses' hooves. The rest of the Seljuk imperial army was in flight, defeated and chased by the inhuman and cruel barbarians.

Prayers and supplications to God the Almighty would not help them now. Allah had forsaken them, well before the hot and high noon. The sun had not yet reached the zenith of this blistering day of hell, yet destiny had already been determined. The Seljuk Empire had collapsed to the nadir of its existence.

☪ ☪ ☪

From his vantage point at the top of the ridge, the Sultan was unable to grasp the situation any better than the men who were in the middle of the battle. Who were more wild-eyed, the men or the horses? As he looked down at the scene, the sight of all the dead and wounded soldiers affected him deeply and he began to lose what little courage he had left. Split livers, crushed heads, and severed limbs – he had seen it all before, but this time, he had no stomach for it. The air reeked of charred flesh and burning scrub. Heads covered the field like a melon patch in August, chopped stray arms lay scattered across the field like tree twigs after a violent storm, and the corpses had begun to rot in the hot sun as soon as they fell. Giyaseddin was repulsed by this assault on all his senses. He suddenly leaned over the side of his horse and vomited up the gallons of red wine he had enjoyed the night before. When it hit the ground and joined the flow of the blood of his martyrs, he was besieged with shame.

His head began to spin and he dismounted to sit on the ground. Overcome by horror, he was unable to move and accept his fate and that of his army. His officers tried to rouse him to reestablish discipline and reorganize his forces, but it was too late now. All he could do was bury his head in his hands.

What has become of me?
My head is throbbing, I cannot think clearly
I remember hearing the drum waking us this morning
I remember my servant placing the green turban on my head and strapping my sword to my sash
I remember the perfectly clear sky and the sun burning like a furnace during the morning prayers
I remember seeing each bold blade of grass
After that, all is a blurred shadow
I now see sweating faces, running madly, falling
I see heaps of bloated corpses, eyes staring into the air

I hear the shrieks of blistered beast and men alike
I cannot push out of my mind the sight of this disastrous battlefield
My fear overshadows everything
I have gone to a place of blood and hell
My soul is as swollen as the ground
I think of how my father never flinched at the sound of war
I recall how he was always the first to charge and his white horse was the fastest of all
I remember how he would shoot and shoot again before the others had even tightened their arc
But I am not my father
I cannot stand tall like him, I am mistaken
I failed to train my troops well enough
Why did that Armenian contingent of Hethoum never arrive?
I should have paid more attention to the advice of my senior generals
Why did I not wait for the Mongols to attack us first?
Allah is punishing me for hiring all these mercenaries to do His work
I should not have underestimated Baiju and his warriors of torment, each one equal to ten of my men
I think of my halvah I love so much and the roses in my palace garden
Soft and sweet and fresh dewdrops of my life
I think of my mother and her sweet smile
I think of the warm colors of the carpets on the floor of my tent
I am so very hot and thirsty
My servant gives me snow-covered water to drink
My head cools off
I now know what I must do
I must get out of here
All is lost, all are dead, and I have failed
I will run away from this battlefield just like I ran away from that leopard cub
I made his bleeding and groans go away by throwing him down the well
But I cannot hide from the moans of my men, fallen, wounded and dying
I am without a doubt the most selfish Sultan ever to have reigned
I have killed the Seljuk Empire just like I killed that cub
Ah, what more can I do?
Where can I go? I am so scared
What can I do?

I will think about that later or perhaps tomorrow
But now I must run away from here, from this smell, this noise, this smoke, this heat
I must get out of here as fast as I can
Yes right now
Now

PART 4

KINGDOM IN HOSTAGE

1243-1245

PART 4 POEM

My son, my son, O my son!
Son whom I carried for nine months in my narrow belly,
Whom I brought to the world's face when the tenth moon came,
Whom I swaddled in wrappings of fine linen,
Whom I suckled abundantly with my white milk!
Had you been a prisoner in a white-towered fortress, my son;
Had you been a captive in the hands of the infidel of foul religion,
Gold and silver I would have given to his might, and saved you, my son.
You have come to a dreadful place, to which I cannot come.
The world is sweet and life is dear;
I cannot give up my life, this you must know.

Mother of Wild Dumrul, Book of Dede Korkut

In one day, with one event, My Lady again saw her life spin into an entirely different destiny. A smashed plate, a banquet, a battle – all everyday occurrences, but these events changed her fate in the turbulent times following the arrival of the Mongols to our lands, a time when the blood of a nation was spilled and its flesh ripped from its bones.

Indeed, these were difficult days for the Seljuk Empire, and for her most of all. How ironic that I, the caravansarai she built, should begin my days in such trying times, and that I should know such success! My doors opened for business and my fame grew with each day. My doors beckoned travelers down the road from all corners of the world, and, despite the upheaval of our times, I lived days of great prosperity.

Tradesmen distant heard about my solid walls, my spacious courtyard, my well-organized stalls, and my fine array of services. All inscribed my compass points on their itineraries and came to stay here, in the blue-green valleys near Tokat. My walls were packed to brimming each night with merchants on their way to trade with all the cities of this great Empire. The sounds of a hundred tongues, the jingling of gold and silver coins, the braying of animals, the crackling of campfires, and the melodies of laughter and lively music filled my courtyard each night.

Trade to the region developed. Tokat grew as a hub of mercantile activity. I led the drive to prosperity for this part of the Seljuk Empire. More and more merchants came to our lands, even in these tumultuous times, all because they knew they could find security on the roads near Tokat. Here they discovered seven safe shelters to be exact, for the other hans built by my Lady in the region met the same success as I did.

Yet while my doors opened onto the world, hers closed and would not reopen anytime soon. While my courtyard was filled with happiness and bustling achievement, her heart was filled with darkness. It was not fair that I, the glorious caravansarai built by her generous hands, should know such prosperity, while her life became one of emptiness and obscurity.

Yet I will not despair. I take solace in the fact that citizens drink from the fountain outside my door. I take pride in the fact that my courtyard is filled each night. How happy she would be to see this success I have become! A battle was lost by her son, but a victory was won by her stones. I take hope that she will again, one day, walk through my doors and bring her own light of brilliance to shine upon my walls; I, a sturdy mass of triumph built by the hands of this strong woman.

My stones now rise as witness to that strength, and as long as they stand, the world will remember the force that it took for this woman to survive in the face of such adversity!

Chapter 104

Abandoned by God

When a shaken Ibn Bibi picked up his golden quill that night, for once, he was at a loss to describe the day he had witnessed. With a trembling hand, he tried his best to pen the scene with honor and respect. He knew that the true story would be found somewhere in between the lines of his poetry and his prose; a story he knew could be written only by the winds of history and by those who were on the battlefield on this hot day of infamy.

With a deep sigh, he dipped his pen in the inkwell and began to compose his journal entry:

> *And so on this day of June 26, 1243, when it was morning over the earth and heavens and the sun flooded the world with its light, when the golden crown enveloped the mountain peaks and a pale vest of brocade covered all the plain, the Seljuks brought their cavalry and their infantry, and they marched with the Sultan to confront the Mongols. The armies met and the fighting between them was very hard. Yet God this fatal day did not help the Muslims to stand victorious, for they were surrounded on all sides by the Mongols who destroyed, killed and captured them. So many died with the name of God still on their tongues, with their last words spoken in a low voice, "Victory is from God to the believers."*
>
> *By noon of this hot and deadly day, even before the sun had reached the summit of its brilliance, the last of the Seljuk troops had either been killed or had fled in panic. The sun was at its zenith and the Seljuk soul was at its nadir.*
>
> *By sunset of this hot and deadly day, when sheets of orange light illuminated the western sky over the blood red field, a decisive victory had been won by the Mongols, and the Sultanate of Rum and the Empire of Trabzon became their humiliated vassals.*
>
> *By nightfall of this hot and deadly day, Sultan Giyaseddin Keyhüsrev II had been humiliated as no Seljuk sultan before him. His army was destroyed and scattered and ceased to exist. His powers were demolished.*
>
> *By the time the fingernail moon rose in the night sky of this hot and deadly day, the tents of the Sultan sat abandoned and his treasures lay*

scattered on the floor. The animals of his menagerie panicked at the smell of all the blood spilled from the carnage and tugged at the chains that tethered them to the poles of the Sultan's tent. The wails of the frightened animals and wounded warrior soldiers howled like wolfwinds over the steppe, all through the long night that followed this day of dread.

God had abandoned them all before the high-noon, there on the plain of Kösedağ, on this day, the hottest and deadliest ever lived by the Seljuk Empire.

Chapter 105

Tears of the Dark Moon

After the battle, the Seljuk soldiers valiantly maintained their positions until midnight. When they heard that their Sultan had fled, they were stunned. What were they to do now, if their very own Sultan had not chosen to stay on the field to lead them? If the Sultan had given up hope, what was left for them to do? They decided there was no point in remaining to guard the field. All through the night they gathered whatever they could from their tents and stores and scattered in every direction from the shamed scene of infamy. The face of the new moon turned darkened eyes on a battlefield littered with thousands of corpses and hundreds of soldiers deserting their posts.

How was it possible that only 30,000 Mongol warriors could annihilate 80,000 Seljuk troops? An inexperienced Sultan, a rash decision, promised but undelivered troops, inadequate training, poor discipline, uninspired leadership and disjointed objectives were perhaps all to blame. But was that all? Was there not something else? As they trod down the path of retreat, many were the men who believed this would never have happened if Commander Kamyar had led the charge, and wondered if the real reason behind this defeat was God's revenge for the injustice done to this valiant warrior.

☪ ☪ ☪

Coming in from the battlefield earlier that day, Commander Mubariz al-din Chavli, covered from head to toe in dust, sweat and blood, found the Sultan crumpled in a heap of dismay outside his tent, murmuring incoherently and crying into his handkerchief.

The dazed Sultan looked up at Chavli with wild-eyes which begged him to answer the question, "Now what are we to do?"

The Emir looked down with disgust at the disheveled Sultan, thinking of the contrast with the bravery of his father, the glorious Alaeddin Keykubad. We would not have met this disaster if he had been on the field today, the commander thought to himself. The dreadfulness of the day emboldened him to adopt an impertinent tone with the Sultan.

"When it was time for precaution and ideas, you chose not to heed the advice of your generals, so what is left for me to give you now?" retorted the

Emir with scorn. "Now that all is lost, you expect me to turn this day back in time for you? No, it is too late for that, my Sultan; now you must deal with the consequences of your choices."

The Sultan whipped his head up and stared at him with wild eyes. "No! It is not I who will deal with this catastrophe! I am leaving, and I appoint you to take control of this war! When I figure out what needs to be done, we will take action. But until then, I will not stay here one second longer," he blurted out, just as a faint call for the evening prayer was heard over the battlefield for the few remaining faithful still alive to hear its murmur.

Yes, the Sultan said to himself, I have got to get out of here, now, and I know where I must go.

Giyaseddin mounted his horse and fled in the direction of Tokat, where he had previously sent his treasury and royal tents for safekeeping. Several guards and attendants came with him, but their group was small. In the panicked hurry to flee, the Sultan was obliged to leave behind most of his possessions as well as his menagerie of wild animals. Yet there was one treasure that was not forgotten in the rush. The trusted handler Tahajan would rather perish himself than have the grand leopard, Ruby, symbol of the might of the Seljuk Empire, left behind to fall into the hands of the Mongols. He shuddered as he remembered how they circled around her the night of the banquet with Alaeddin at the Keykubadiyye Palace. He would fight to his last breath before he would let one of those heathens near her.

The Sultan sped down the road towards Tokat on the swiftest of his stallions, his thoughts racing as fast as its hooves. After picking up his stored fortune at Tokat, he would flee to a safer place. He knew that once the Mongols learned that he had left the camp, they would come after him. But could there be a safe spot for him now? Wherever it was, it had to be as far west from these Mongols as possible. Sivas and Kayseri were too near and too dangerous. He would not be able to return to Konya, for the heathens would probably head there next. Oh, Konya, rose of the world! To seize the capital would be their most important victory, but that must never happen. Ankara perhaps? Yes, Ankara will be a perfect spot to reorganize and plan for the future. But from there, where? Antalya? Maybe...no, to Constantinople! His grandfather fled there after he lost his sultanate the first time, and Giyaseddin had always maintained good relations with the Latin Emperor Baldwin. He will not refuse me exile. Yes, that is where he would go. To Constantinople! With a little luck, he could arrange to move his wives and children to a safe place down south or to Constantinople as well.

But for the moment, he needed to reach Tokat, as fast as his steed could carry him, for if the Mongols got there before he did and seized his fortune, he would have no hope of escape. He knew that by leaving the battle scene before the Mongols had noticed that he had gone would provide him precious hours to get down the road ahead of them. The Mongols would never believe that the Sultan would abandon his battlefield, and with luck, it would be many hours, and perhaps even days, before they realized he was not there.

He whipped his stallion to speed faster, for he had to get to Tokat, not just to pick up his gold and jewels, but also to safeguard the most precious thing in his life: his mother. He knew she was staying there at the moment, busy overseeing details in her newly-completed series of caravansarais. But what was he going to do with her? He could not risk leaving her there or have her return home to Kayseri. She had to flee, too, but not with him; that would be too risky. She had to disappear before the Mongols captured and tortured her, as was their habit with royal family members. Nothing must happen to her, the sole remaining ray of hope in his life!

Yes, she needed to flee to save her life. She would also know how to help him; she always did. She would get him out of this predicament with her sound ideas. But he could not think about that now, he just needed to focus on getting to Tokat as quickly as possible. Every minute was valuable.

Ride faster my stallion, so late, through night and wind, ride faster!

☪ ☪ ☪

When the Mongols approached the Seljuk camp the next morning and saw no movement from the thousands of tents in front of them, they thought the Seljuks were goading them into a trap. Smiling to themselves, they retreated, for experienced Mongol warriors would not fall for such an obvious trick. We will wait patiently for the red-headed Sultan fox to come out of his hole.

Yet after three days with still no movement from their prey, they realized that they were not lying in wait there, but that the camp had been deserted. How was it possible that the Sultan had abandoned the fight and his troops and fled? Vile coward! Now, with great excitement, they went in to ransack and plunder the Seljuk camp like a plague of locusts in a field of wheat. Running and shrieking through the camp, they took everything they were able to lift with their bare hands. The Mongols knew that their Khan loved fine objects, and spent hours after his dinner contemplating the piles of goods that he had amassed from all the corners of the world. The soldiers knew that he would be very pleased with this Seljuk bounty, and that he would bestow special favor upon them. "One for the Khan, one for me!" they screamed, as they stuffed pearls, ivory boxes, brocaded textiles, jeweled belts, bows and arrows, furred hats, and all types of garments into their saddle bags to take back home. They rustled mules, three hundred camels, and three thousand sheep from the camp as well.

The satin imperial tents, symbols of the Seljuk military might and sovereignty, were taken by these men of ignoble stripe, with no education or respect. It was easy for the plunderers to find the Sultan's tent, for it was adorned within and without with luxurious treasures. Many wild animals were still tethered at its door, including lions, hunting falcons, parrots and a black panther. All types of goods from the Sultan's tent were tossed into their saddle bags and carts, along with weapons, silver coins stamped with suns and lions, brass goblets and plates. The Sultan's animals were also loaded onto wagons to take back to their Khan for his palace at Karakorum. Oh, how he will admire this sleek black panther!

The booty that fell to the Mongols from the Seljuk military encampment was beyond counting, and was even beyond the army's ability to haul it way, but they were determined not to leave one speck of value behind them. They were victors, at last, of the Seljuk Empire, and they deserved every bit of reward.

☪ ☪ ☪

By nightfall of the third day after the battle, all was motionless in the Seljuk camp. The moans of the wounded soldiers had stopped, for they had by now left on their final journey to join God in paradise. The screaming of the marauding Mongols and the thundering hooves of their horses had quieted once they had finished pillaging the camp and left. The brightly-colored tents of the Seljuks had been stripped of all their goods and honor. All was quiet, except for the noise of tent flaps fluttering in the night wind, their unfurled cords snapping angrily against the tent poles, drumming a dirge of defeat.

The east wind picked up the dusty remains of the Seljuk Empire and scattered them up to the night sky of eternity. Never again would the Empire, now collapsed, be able to regain its strength or maintain control of the Anatolian plateau.

Those who listened closely on that dark night could hear soft sobbing far into the distance, but it did not come from the ghosts of the fallen brave. It attended the teardrops falling from the new moon now gone dark from shame and sadness, a heartbroken moon that knew it would never again be able to lift its eyes to watch the comet of Alaeddin Keykubad's dreams streak across the heavens above.

Chapter 106

At the Bottom of the Well

Earlier that June, Mahperi had left Kayseri and travelled to Pazar, the village near Tokat where she had built the largest of her seven hans. She needed to attend to some administrative details, and she was curious to see how it was running. Afterwards, she returned to her more comfortable quarters in Tokat. She was exhausted but pleased with all she had seen, for the han was indeed well-managed and successful. And such a beautiful han it was! The stone carving surrounding its main door was as awe-inspiring as that of her mosque in Kayseri.

While Mahperi relaxed in her rooms at Tokat that tranquil summer evening, she had no idea that her son was racing across the plain as hard as his horse could carry him to Tokat. She had not seen him since he had left earlier that spring to prepare the battle with the Mongols. Courrier pigeons were sent daily with updates from his camp, but none had arrived for two days. A seed of worry began to sprout in her mind, but she dismissed it, for she was too happy to be troubled tonight.

In any case, she decided she would stay in Tokat a while longer. She was in no rush to return to Kayseri, for the days of late June were gentle and all was peaceful in this city on the slow green river.

☪ ☪ ☪

Towards dawn, Giyaseddin Keyhüsrev and his guards arrived at Tokat and thundered down the main road towards the royal quarters at the base of the castle fortress. Even before he lept down from his horse, he barked commands to prepare fresh horses loaded with food, water and supplies. He ordered his guards to pack his treasury into large saddlebags and strap them onto the fastest horses in the city, with all to be ready within two hours. He then sent his page to bring his mother at once to his chambers.

As soon as her servant woke her to tell her that her son was here, Mahperi knew that something had gone terribly wrong. What was he doing here, in Tokat, instead of on the field?

Mahperi rushed to his room and found her son frantically stuffing his pockets with jewels and gold coins, and shouting orders to his pages. He was filthy and covered in sweat. His movements were frenzied, his eyes wild, and his voice shrill as he screamed out to all around him. She had never seen him like this, and it frightened her.

She ran to him and took him in her arms. "My son, my son, O my son! What has happened? What are you doing here instead of at the camp at Sivas?"

She then watched as her son collapsed on the cushions, buried his head in his hands, and began to cry. In between sobs and gasps for air, he related the horror of the fatal day to her, sparing no details about the heat, the blood, and the shame. The words could not spill out of him fast enough.

Shocked by the news of the defeat, Mahperi immediately realized that this was not just any battle lost; it was a defeat like none the Seljuk Empire had ever known.

"But why are you here? What are you going to do now?" she questioned eagerly.

Taking control of himself, the Sultan lifted his tear-stained face to look into his mother's frightened eyes. "I have come here to pick up my treasury. I will go somewhere else as soon as possible, perhaps down south or to Constantinople, but I cannot remain anywhere near here, for they will capture me for sure!"

His words stunned Mahperi. Had she heard him correctly?

"But that is impossible! You are the Sultan and your responsibility is to your Empire! You cannot just run away as if you do not care about it!"

"I have emirs, I have viziers; I have able men in the court who will sort this out. But for the present time, I must ensure my safekeeping so that this Empire can continue! They must not capture me. For I ask you, without a sultan, what will happen? The Mongols will step in and name their Khan as our leader, and that will be the end of our Empire. If I manage to escape, there will, perhaps, be a chance for survival for all of us!"

"But what about your family? Don't you care about them? Your wife Adelpha and your sister Seljuka are here with me. But the others? How can you leave them in danger?" she continued, still incredulous.

"I have thought about all of that. My beloved wife Gurchi and my sons are in Konya, and I will make sure they are out of harm's way. But the most important concern I have is for *your* safety. Mama, you cannot remain here in Tokat. The Mongols will no doubt arrive here soon and will put people to the sword! You must leave here immediately!"

"But I am the Sultana! I cannot just abandon my responsibilities to my people! No, I must return to Kayseri. What if these Mongols come to destroy my mosque? I must be there to stop them!"

"No one can stop them, don't you see? They will kill you! You have heard what those Mongols do to the royals they capture! You must flee, for there is no hope. Take Adelpha and my sister Seljuka with you. You absolutely cannot return to Kayseri, for it is far too dangerous. It will take several days for the Mongols to figure out that I have left the battlefield at Kösedağ, and then they will be furious. They will most certainly head directly to Kayseri and plunder everything in their path. At best, we have a three-day lead on them. You must leave now, this very minute – there is no time to lose! I have figured out what you must do. You will go to Aleppo, and take refuge with our Ayyubid allies. You will travel with several trusted guards in a small group, as discretely as possible. We will disguise you in simple clothes like a common peasant so not as to arouse suspicion. If stopped, you must never admit that you are the Sultana!"

"But my son! You cannot just leave! You are the Sultan! Your responsibility is here, to guide and inspire your people, just like your father Alaeddin would have done! You have perhaps lost a battle, but the Empire will go on! Such is the way of war! Your father did not win all his battles, either, yet he went on to greatness, just as you will," she insisted, trying to hearten him.

Upon hearing his father's name, Giyaseddin began to tremble and a freakish look appeared in his eyes. He replied to her with an equally strange voice.

"No, mother, this Mongol catastrophe is God's retribution for all the killing I have done and for all the sins I have committed. I knew my judgment day of punishment would come, and God struck his wrath upon me today. I have brought calamity upon this Empire," he mumbled, sweat and tears pouring down his cheeks. "I cannot bear the guilt anymore. I must run away from it all!"

"What nonsense are you babbling about, my son? You do not deserve to be punished! You are a fine sultan! Your people look to you for their direction!"

"Of course you could never understand what I have done; you, so pure and good. I have things to tell you that are going to cause you much pain, my dear mother, but I must tell them to you, for perhaps it will take away some of the pain that is killing me as surely as any Mongol sword. I cannot keep this inside of me any longer! All the wine and potions I drink to erase it all from my mind serve no good. Gaziye, then my brothers, that I sent away to their fate – this torture has become unbearable."

"But it was Köpek who sent those boys away to the Burglu castle, not you!"

"No, Mama, *I* did it. Köpek forced me to sign the papers that sent them away, but in the end, it was I who did it, and that is what is so terrible. I could have stood up to Köpek and said no, but I never could refuse anything he asked of me, for I trusted his judgment. Köpek then arranged to have them killed without anyone knowing about it. Yes, Mama, those boys are dead now, not hidden like everyone thinks; dead as if I had strangled them by my own hands!"

"But this is impossible! What you have done is a dreadful sin in God's eyes! You have killed your brothers like Cain killed Abel! How could you become such a pawn of Köpek's evil?"

"Mama, please do not condemn me! You are my only hope for salvation in this hell in which I live! If it were only the sin of my brothers upon me, I could perhaps bear it, but I have sinned even greater sins – unspeakable and unpronounceable sins. I am haunted every waking moment of my life for what I did to my father. For you see, Mama, it was *I* who killed my father. Yes! There, I have finally said it! I killed my father!"

Mahperi shook her head violently to clear her ears, her heart racing and her stomach twisting in pain. No, this cannot be possible. He said that he killed his father?

"My son, repeat what you just said; I am not understanding anything here!"

"You heard me correctly. I confess to you now as I have confessed to God every day since that fatal night. I killed my father Alaeddin, with my very own hands, that night at the banquet with the Mongols."

"But this makes no sense! He fell ill, had a seizure and died. The intense heat, the emotion of the evening on his heart or something he ate; there can be no other explanation, unless..." She paused for a moment, suddenly realizing that the rumors hinting that Alaeddin's death had been orchestrated by his enemies were perhaps true.

"The Sultan was poisoned Mama, he was poisoned! Yes, it was Köpek and a group of emirs who planned to get rid of him to put me on the throne and take the power. It was their doing!"

"But then why do you say that *you* killed him? Köpek and his gang did it, not you!"

"No, it was me, I know it! My hand is dripping with blood as much as his! Köpek wanted to ensure that the Sultan would not sign the treaty with the Mongols, which he and the emirs considered a cowardly act. He gave me the task of serving papa glass after glass of a sherbet drink laced with a special potion, which he said would make him too sleepy to sign the treaty. He also gave me some berries to slip into the stuffing of the bird that was to be served to him. He knew Papa would never be suspicious of any food served to him by my hand. I had no idea that the drinks and the berries were poisonous and would kill him. I thought I was just helping Köpek save the Empire from those Mongols!"

"You willingly gave your father drinks laced with venom and put harmful potions in his food? You did not suspect for one second what Köpek was having you do? Köpek told you to hurt your own father, and you did not find anything wrong with that? Have you not been raised as a good Christian and a good Muslim to know the laws of God's universe? He used you, my son, he used you like he did every one of his pawns on his ravenous path to seize the throne way from Alaeddin!"

Hanife's last words now drummed in her brain: *"Know that he has betrayed us all."* She knew what had been done, and she was trying to tell me.

"No! He loved me! He always wanted what was best for me! Köpek told me he had a plan for me. He said if my father were dethroned we could reign together, as I deserved, not that golden child Izzeddin so favored by my father! He said that by helping him that night I was saving the Empire from the Mongols. He said I would be a hero! You see, the emirs were so angry at Alaeddin for wanting to sign the peace treaty with the Mongols, which they considered absolute treason. Köpek conspired with several of them to put me on the throne, and then he convinced the chief food taster to hand me the fowl after he tasted it, so that I could slip the berries hidden in my sleeve into the stuffing. But I never once thought that Papa was going to die from those berries. I thought they would just incapacitate him so that he would not sign that treaty and then give us time to seize the power! But we did not escape with our action – Papa was too smart for that. Kamyar confronted Köpek and told him that the Sultan had whispered in his ear right before he died the name of his betrayer. Papa knew it was Köpek – how he did, I will never know, but he did. Since Köpek could not take the risk of having Kamyar reveal this information publicly, he had the great commander killed as well. All this he did so that I could reign as Sultan! He loved me Mama, yes, he did!"

"But so did your father! How could you have wished to harm your very own father? You had to have known that those poisons would hurt him!"

"Mama, do you honestly think that Papa loved me? You know he did not. If he cared for me, then why did he hurt me so much, Mama? I was shipped off to Erzincan and my throne taken away from me. I was not allowed to be with you. He only had time for Gaziye and those two golden boys, not clumsy me. That evening of the banquet is still so confused in my mind. I drank much wine that night to give me courage, but it only made things worse. There was such tension in the air with those Mongols staring at me as if they were going to eat me alive. I have no memory of those berries; what color they were or how many of them I put in the stuffing of that bird, but I must have done it because Papa is dead. It was so hot, there was such a foul odor, and it was like a dream, except for the face of Köpek glaring at me to remind me of what I needed to do. I cannot clearly remember anything that happened that evening. But what I do remember clearly is the terror I felt when I was taken away from you and sent away to Erzincan; I remember your tears after you were humiliated at Kubadabad; I remember him yelling at you to get out of his sight. I know now what I did was wrong, very wrong. I am ashamed of myself with every breath I take."

Mahperi felt her head spinning as if she were the one who had been handed the laced sherbet. She imagined the pain the Sultan felt that evening, and she doubled over with the same piercing sting in her gut. *My son killed his very own father*. This day is truly the end of the world.

"This cannot be possible! Even if you were hurt by your father, how could you have done this to me? How could you have left me alone without my husband?"

"But he hurt you so much Mama! I wanted to punish him for all the pain he caused you when he brought Gaziye into our lives. I thought it would make you happy. And all went according to Köpek's plan – I became the Sultan, and wasn't that what you wanted more than anything? I did it so that you would be proud of me!"

"No, my son, I never stopped loving your father, despite all the pain he caused me! Now you have lost everything – this battle, all that your father worked to build, this Empire, your honor, your very soul!"

"Mama, I thought when we gave the orders to kill Köpek I would be able to erase all this shame. I thought his death would purge the sin of the others. But no, I will carry this crime with me forever, I know it. I beg you, Mama, please help me like you always have! You have never punished me, even on that day when I hurt Ruby's cub and threw her down the well – "

"*What*? It was *you* who stole her cub and then killed it?"

Giyaseddin hung his head down on his chest and was silent. Mahperi now realized her son was weak, very weak. No wonder it was so easy for Köpek to manipulate him. She felt that the harm done to the cub was perhaps the worst of all the crimes, for he had attacked pure innocence. Sickened and angered to the core, she felt no maternal pity for him, much less love.

"No, I will no longer help you make things right for you! You have now lost that right. How can I forgive you these monstrous trespasses to God's law and to me? You have lost this kingdom, your honor and my love. Take your jewels and your Georgian wife and get out of my sight forever. You are even more despicable than Köpek!"

Mahperi now watched as her son Giyaseddin sobbed into his hands.

"Giyaseddin, you have come to a dreadful place, to which I cannot come. That is your hell to live. Get out of my sight now, for I can no longer bear to look at you, a killer worse than those heathen Mongols who whipped you on the battlefield. That defeat is indeed God's retribution for your evil. Like Cain, you will be condemned to forever wander the earth in punishment. I banish you from your place in my heart as well. May God have pity on your soul, but the enormity of your sins is probably beyond even His most merciful comprehension. You may flee this place but you will never be able to run away from your sin and shame. You will be chastised until the Day of Judgment and then beyond for all eternity. You, my Cub, now lie dead at the bottom of the well of my heart."

Chapter 107
Flame of Hope

Shaken by the confession of her son Giyaseddin of the multiple murders he had committed, Mahperi collapsed on the floor and sat there stunned, unable to comprehend what she had just heard. She felt a sharp pain between her legs, just like the ones of childbirth, and looking down at her lap, she expected to see the spilled blood of those ghastly murders pouring out from her. It was not possible that I could have given life to such a monster, she thought, incredulous. Her stomach twisted as well, thinking of what her husband must have felt the night he ingested poison from the hand of his own son. Did he have any idea that night what his son had done? Probably not, for such a thing would have been inconceivable even for someone as astute as Alaeddin.

That her son had been responsible for killing all these victims was beyond any understanding. That Köpek had ordered them did not surprise her, for she always knew that he was a wicked monster, but that her son did not have the moral character to withstand Köpek's orders was still unthinkable. Yet, she should have heeded the hints of his troubled soul. His quiet, withdrawn nature and his destructive use of alcohol, women and gambling were signs for her to see all along, but she was blinded by a mother's love that seeks to see only the best in her child. It was not surprising to her in hindsight how Köpek had separated her from her son so that he could exert his evil force on the boy. Yes, it was her fault that all of this had happened.

She then cried the most intense tears of her life.

☪ ☪ ☪

Mahperi was so absorbed in her grief that she did not hear the strong rapping at her door. Finally, it was pushed open and a group of her servants entered and surrounded her, helping her up from the floor onto the cushions of the window seat. Emir Nureddin, the governor of the region of Tokat, approached and spoke to her in a firm voice.

"Honorable Sultana, I am here to help you. The Sultan has now left Tokat and has entrusted me to get you out of Seljuk territory to the safety of the southern regions. You understand that he could not take you with him, for it risked endangering you even more. Please, we must move fast, so I beg you to come with me now."

She looked up at him and still could not believe what was happening. Where in the world can I go and what is to become of me? Do I even care about surviving? I have given birth to a son that grew up to kill his own father, and I am expected to think that my life is worth saving? Let the Mongols take me, for my life is over.

Emir Nureddin, seeing her distraught face, felt pity for the woman, yet was obliged to be forceful.

"We have no way of knowing where the Mongols will go once they leave the battlefield, but it is certain they will head westwards to Kayseri, perhaps in as soon as four days. You must do as your son says and flee south."

"No! I will not flee like a coward, like my son. I will find another way to survive – or not. I cannot abandon my city of Kayseri and my mosque to the hands of those heathens! What if they destroy it? I must go there to try to stop them!" she screeched. Her life may now lay destroyed and in shambles, but she would not let them destroy her gift to God, the only pure and good thing left to her. She would rather burn along with it than leave it unattended.

"I am afraid there is no stopping them, my Lady; that is what you must understand," pleaded Emir Nureddin. "Even the hardiest of defenders will not be able to hold out against them for more than a few months. The walls of Kayseri, thanks to your husband's repairs, are solid. But even they will crack, and then all will be lost. We know how these heathens will operate after this. The first thing they will do is to kill the Seljuk soldiers. Our brave lions will be cut to the ground with no mercy! After executing the soldiers, the Mongols will separate out the people of the city who can read and write, such as doctors, imams, teachers, and engineers, and put them to their service. Then they will seek out skilled craftsmen, such as glassblowers, carpenters, dyers and tailors. They particularly prize these people, for they can often speak several languages and are expert in the many fields in which these uncultured brutes have no knowledge. These people will be shipped off east to work in the court of the Great Khan, without any concern for their families left behind. And for those poor souls who have no skills, they will be carried off to become nothing more than beasts of burden, made to tote loads, dig fortifications, and to participate in all aspects of the Mongol war effort. We have heard that the Mongols throw them into rivers to build human pontoons so that the hooves of their horses can ford the waters! For those who do not qualify even for these tasks, such as the elderly, the crippled or the simpleminded, they will be slaughtered and left behind. There is no mercy at their hands, My Lady. This is what is going to happen to your city of Kayseri, and that is why you cannot even think of going back there."

"But I cannot abandon my poor people! My city! My mosque! All is going to be destroyed!" she wailed.

"Perhaps or perhaps not, we have no way of knowing such things. It is all in God's hands now. But I must tell you, my Lady, that there is one group who suffers the most in their ravaging advance: the rich and the nobles. They seek to kill all aristocrats as quickly as they can, for they cannot take the risk of having any future betrayal. I have heard that they particularly go after the mothers of the leaders of the regions they have conquered. If they don't kill these poor women outright, they send them to live in ignominious servitude somewhere in outer regions of their territory. I have heard the most horrid stories of torture, but I will spare you those. I ask you My Lady, do you want this to happen to you? Is this how you want to disappear from history?"

Mahperi now began to understand why Alaeddin hated these Mongols so.

Emir Nureddin continued his plea. "My Lady, I repeat, you must flee here as soon as possible to save your life. As Sultana of this Empire, that is your duty. You will head south away from the regions of the fighting and seek refuge with the Ayyubids in Aleppo. They will take you in without any issue or question, for they, too, hate and fear the Mongols as much as we do. You must understand that this is more than a question of your individual safety. Our entire civilization is under siege, not just the Seljuk lands. Our magnificent Muslim civilization, now spreading its broad reach to Mesopotamian and Persian lands, is the richest in the world, and the most highly sophisticated in every branch of learning. Our medreses are filled with students learning all the sciences. Soldiers listen to orders in Turkish, judges proclaim their verdicts in Arabic, and the poets sing their verses of love in Persian! All this cultural mosaic quotes the Qur'an in unison, *Allahu Akbar*! Our scholars light the beacon of learning for the entire world. In other countries, like India, China and Europe, only the priests and court officials can read; but in our lands, there is not one village that does not have a group of men and women who can read the Holy Qur'an. The sacred words of the Qur'an have forged for us a destiny, and we cannot allow this glorious civilization to fall under the hooves of a mob of heathens! They are an empire of arrows only, and they must not prevail!"

Even though he, too, was on the verge of collapse, the Emir continued his ardent plea.

"Do you not see, my honorable Sultana, that by leaving, you can keep the flame of this Seljuk civilization lit, and that you have the potential to return and bring it to life again? It is certain that these Mongols will leave nothing standing in your city of Kayseri. The ancient bazaar will be razed into dust. Your mosque will become a roosting area for swallows, and the winds will moan through its pillars. Fifty medreses will stand empty of students. The greatest joy of these heathens is to conquer and kill their enemies and take away their possessions, and to watch the faces of their victims distort in pain and streak with tears. They do not build, they destroy. They do not live in love and hope for the greatest human potential; no, they live in hate and darkness. If you stay here, you risk becoming erased from the face of the earth. Flee, and you will save your life and all that your husband stood for; all that this glorious civilization stands for. And this Empire will survive, I am convinced of it."

☪ ☪ ☪

Suddenly, it was clear to Mahperi what she needed to do.

I will stay calm. I will not panic. I will save my life. I will go south with my daughter Seljuka and Giyaseddin's wife Adelpha. When the time is right, I will return to help lead this empire in any way I can. I will be back to carry on the dream of Alaeddin to build the greatest empire in the land. I will raise my son's three boys to lead this sultanate into the distant future. I will guarantee that an able descendant of the Great Alaeddin Keykubad, Father of Conquests and Victories, will forever sit on the Seljuk throne. I will not make the same mistake with my grandsons that I did with my own son. I will not leave them in the unloving hands of others. I, along with Vizier Karatay, if God protects his survival as well, will give them the correct tools to lead this empire to even greater heights. My son has proven to be an incapable leader, but I will make sure that his sons do not repeat his failures. Perhaps Alaeddin in his infinite wisdom was right. The golden boy Izzeddin should have reigned, for it is certain that Giyaseddin is unfit for this role. My son has lost everything his ancestors have worked for, starting with throwing a poor baby cub down a well and ending in cowardice on the battlefield.

This is my destiny. I am Mahperi Sultana. I am now more than ever a builder!

She looked up at Emir Nureddin and nodded.

"It is settled, I will leave immediately."

Chapter 108
Charred Glory

The Mongols celebrated their victory at Kösedağ with a drunken revelry that lasted for a week, but soon it came time to return to their warring, deeper and deeper into Seljuk territory. They knew they could conquer its cities with the same ease as they swatted flies. Before arriving in the Seljuk lands, the armies of Genghis Khan the Ocean had crushed Bukhara and Samarkand, Merv and Nishapur, Qazvin and Tabriz. No city withstood their onslaught, no citadel remained intact, no noble or peasant went untouched. Prayers of supplication in twenty languages to every god went unanswered. Nothing could stop the flow of the Ocean's waves, and its surge would now pound the Seljuk Empire. After Erzurum, the Mongols would smash the towns on their path towards their ultimate reward: Kayseri, the prize city at the foot of the Majestic Mountain.

☪ ☪ ☪

After the battle of Kösedağ, Baiju, the commander of the Mongol forces, gave orders to press forth to Sivas. With great hopes, the city nobles met the Mongols at the gates with presents and promises of obedience. Baiju let out a hearty round of laughter at their presumption. When will the enemies learn that there is no negotiating with the Mongols? His troops entered and plundered the city for three days, but, in an exceptional act of mercy, chose not to destroy it or kill the inhabitants.

On they marched to Tokat, but there, the citizens were not so fortunate. Once rumors reached Baiju's ears that the Sultan and his mother had been there and taken flight in separate directions, he became very angry. He took revenge by ordering a terrible sack and put the people of the gentle city upon the slow green river to the sword.

☪ ☪ ☪

Enraged that the Sultan had slipped through his fingers, Baiju vowed to push on until he found him. As he surveyed the burning Tokat below him from the castle on top of the peak which dominated the city, he wondered if the Sultan's mother had fled back to Kayseri, the city he knew was her beloved home. He barked out orders for his troops to start their journey towards Kayseri, and vowed to tear down every stone of every wall to find her. The capital city of Konya was perhaps the political heart of the Empire, but it was the city under the shadow of the Majestic Mountain that wore the crown of commerce and power. For centuries the riches of the entire Muslim world poured into this city, embellished by the Seljuk Sultans with palaces, medreses, mosques, gardens and fountains. The city was also an important center for Armenian Christians, who worked in its bazaars and workshops. The stones of their churches rubbed against those of the synagogues of the Jews. All this glory stands waiting for my plundering, thought Baiju, and I will be there soon to ravage it all.

When the Mongols neared the city, a soldier was sent to the city gates with a message that was perfectly explicit: the Mongols would offer justice to those who surrendered, but swore destruction to those who resisted. Yet Baiju did not know that the citizens of the city under the Majestic Mountain were as resolute as their peak. They chose to defy Baiju, for they believed themselves invincible, especially to ignorance. They managed to successfully resist the Mongol blockade until the day a guard betrayed them. By slipping out of the city in the middle of the night through the underground sewer pipes, he told the Mongols where the weak spots in the walls could be found. Once those spots were battered open the next day by the Mongols, the city of Kayseri paid a severe price for their resistance: total pillage, devastation and murder of most of the citizens.

The great Baiju himself and his army tore through the city that day, leaving flames, smoke and destruction in his wake. In each direction they turned, the Mongols torched every building in sight. Homes, market places, stables, churches and synagogues met a flaming demise, along with anything that symbolized the richness of the Seljuk Empire. Mosques and medreses burned to the ground. Fireballs were thrown into the Devlethane Palace in town. The royal kiosks of Alaeddin's beloved Keykubadiyye Palace and the Josaq Palace of Giyaseddin were put to the torch.

It was not just stones that burned, but flesh as well. Mothers surrounded by children ran in every direction, all seeming to be looking for someone lost. Many people found hiding places, and cringed there in terror of being discovered. Their homes were plundered and their stock driven off from the fields. Many loaded up their belongings on carts, but like demons, the Mongols rushed into the courtyards of the houses before they had a chance to flee. To the smoke-houses, the dairies, the pantries, the kitchens and cellars, like famished wolves they came; breaking locks and whatever was in their way. Thousands of pounds of dried beef *pastirma* meat in the curing houses were gone in a twinkling; flour, bulgur, oil, butter, eggs, pickles in vinegar, dried peppers on strings, and jugs of grape molasses were sucked up in a giant sweep of eager hoarding hands. Thousands of chickens, sheep and fowl were rounded up in the yards and hunted as if they were rebels themselves. The people of Kayseri were utterly powerless in the face of the drowning wave, and over 10,000 would not live to see the next dawn.

Like a brutal hail storm across the plain, the Mongols crushed all, torched all, and then in a flash, it was over. Suddenly, their hunger for pillage and killing was sated. Or perhaps it was just that their saddlebags were filled to the limit with plundered treasures and their horses could carry no more. For whatever reason, Baiju decided to turn around and go home. We have had enough for the time being, he reasoned. The capital city of Konya can wait a while longer. But be there no mistaking: I will be back.

☪ ☪ ☪

As night drew its sable curtains around the foot of the Majestic Mountain, the heavens above in every point were lit up by the flames of burning buildings, blinding the stars from view. The Majestic Mountain gazed down at the smoldering city below, now a besmirched swirl of black smoke. My people, fear not the heat of this pouring Mongol lava! O, Kayseri, my roaring lion of a city, you will survive this ardent challenge. Your walls will defiantly rise again, new babies will be born, the sound of gold coins will tinkle again in your bazaars, and your roads will be crowded with caravans once more. Your glory is not charred, only your walls. Life will go on, for your heart still beats, protected by both my angel wings and the grace of God's undying and invincible love for you.

Chapter 109

Paths of Peace

A decisive battle lost, a Sultan in flight, cities in flames, the enemy on the horizon, dark days of death: all now appeared vanquished in the Seljuk Empire. Yet, God provided salvation. Although the Sultan had fled the field and his responsibilities, experienced men of government kept their wits about them and stepped to the fore to lead the land out of this abyss of despair.

Vizier Muhadab al-Din was one such wise leader. Long a prominent administrator at the court, Muhadab was the head judge of Amasya and father of Pervane, an up-and-coming officer at the Konya court. As soon as he heard news of the defeat, Muhadab launched a daring diplomatic plan which he considered the only way to save the Empire. Acting on his own, he set off in search of Baiju. As a vizier and a man of law, all the fibers of his soul told him that this was what he needed to do. In the stead of a Sultan gone frantic, he would keep his head so that others could keep theirs.

His plan was simple but audacious: he would seek out the Mongols and offer them whatever it took to appease their hunger. He did not know if they would slice off his head the minute he appeared in front of them, sew him up in a sack and toss him under pounding hooves, but Muhadab had to show them that the Seljuks were still courageous, despite what their Sultan had done. Alaeddin Keykubad had been right after all: if that treaty had been signed the night of the banquet, none of this would have happened.

He set out to the Mongol encampment near Erzurum. Once there, he was ushered in front of a curious Baiju, to whom he explained his proposal, and, much to his surprise, it was listened to with attention. Baiju decided to bring the Seljuk vizier back with him to meet Chormagan at his camp on the Mughan steppes on the southeastern shores of the Caspian Sea. When they got there, however, they learned that the chieftain had suffered a paralyzing stroke and that his shrewd wife was now acting in his place. Would the Mongol women be as ominous as their men?

The negotiations were lengthy, but Vizier Muhadab was a steadfast and patient diplomat. Kneeling at the foot of the wooden dais where Chormagan and his wife sat on silk pillows, he looked directly in their eyes and drawing a deep breath, began his supplication.

"Chormagan, please hear my humble entreaty. You have been fighting the Seljuks for a long while now, and you know that we are a formidable enemy. We are not stronger than your glorious warriors, that is certain, for you have shown us that you are the Victors of the Universe," he uttered, hoping to flatter them before putting forth his proposal. "But there is one thing that makes us a redoubtable challenge for you. Our Empire is spread over an extensive territory, and in the end, controlling such a vast empire will prove difficult. My petition is one of pure logic. Why not allow us to maintain our government and run the Empire for you? In return, we will pay you an annual tribute and recognize your control. In this way, the Seljuk Empire will continue to prosper and fill your chests with riches. We will submit unto you, but let us run the government for you, for it will prove more beneficial for you," the Vizier exhorted in his most convincing tone.

Chormagan listened and nodded his head. Although he could not move his right side and his speech was slurred, he had not lost the powers of his mind, for the light in his eyes told Vizier Muhadab that he was clearly able to assess the situation. Chormagan leaned over to his wife and conferred with her for a long while. It was she who then turned to Vizier Muhadab and spoke in a clear, yet hard, voice.

"Chief Chormagan has heard your proposal, and finds that it makes sense. The complete conquest of Anatolia can wait for the moment. But now I say unto you – and hear this well – just as the Mongols told Sultan Alaeddin Keykubad several years ago, you must serve us with total obedience. If you work with us in this direction, pillage, fire, destruction, rape and killings in your lands will cease. You will become our vassals and pay us tribute. Against that, we will leave you alone to live as you see fit. If, after you hear and understand this decree, you are unwilling to attend to it and bring an army against us – beware, for you know what we can do. We will now write up the terms of the treaty for you to sign. There will be an annual payment of gold, soldiers, animals and foodstuffs, for our army is great and requires countless resources to keep it afloat. I can tell you that your tribute will be heavy. We exact payment of 360,000 gold and silver dirhams, 10,000 sheep, 1,000 cattle and 1,000 camels every year. You will also send to us many of your fine carpets, as well as 500 pieces of silk brocaded in gold. Once you sign this treaty here today, you may return to your capital of Konya. The treaty will still need to be validated by the Great Khan, but the terms of payment will enter into effect immediately."

On the road back to Konya, Muhadab could only flatter himself on how adroitly he had crafted the peace proposal with the Mongols. He had succeeded in forestalling further Mongol devastation in Anatolia, and, above all, had saved the throne for Giyaseddin Keyhüsrev, no small success for a diplomat! I am not sure if the Sultan will approve of this plan, but since he is nowhere to be found, it is I, Vizier Muhadab al-Din, who has shown my mettle and saved the Seljuk Empire.

☪ ☪ ☪

While Vizier Muhadab was courageously risking his neck by approaching the Mongols with his daring plan, Sultan Giyaseddin Keyhüsrev was racing down the road in the other direction of the Empire as fast as he could. After tearing out of Tokat with his treasury and a group of his guards, he first went to Ankara, and then headed west in the direction of the Menderes River. Just as he did every time he was scared, he ran to hide in the one place where he always felt safe – Kubadabad. This time, however, he knew that he could not tarry long on the shores of the bright blue waters, for the Mongols would find him even there. He thought perhaps he could flee down the pass through the Taurus Mountains to Antalya and then to Alaiye, and hole up in his mother's native town, for the fortress there was a formidable one. Yet, upon reflection, he knew there was only one place where he could truly be safe – Christian Constantinople was his only chance for survival.

At the Kubadabad Palace that August, at the same time the Vizier Muhadab was confronting the Mongols, Sultan Giyaseddin Keyhüsrev began working on a diplomatic plan of his own. He began crafting a means to strengthen his relations with the Latins in Constantinople, and his European dream twinkled again in his mind. It was time to turn eyes westward, thought the Sultan. The future of my Empire depends on forging new political alliances in this struggle against the Mongols, which now threatens each and every one of us on the globe. I am still the Sultan of this Empire, he thought, and I can still craft my own path of peace!

He wrote a hasty letter to Baldwin II, the Latin Emperor of Constantinople, concerning the possibility of arranging a political marriage with a French princess. What was one more wife in his harem? This French marriage could prove to be one of the wisest moves of his political career.

A few weeks later, a liveried envoy was dispatched from Constantinople to France to the court of the mighty Queen Blanche de Castille. In his saddlebag he carried an official petition to the queen mother for the hand of a young princess on behalf of the Seljuk Sultan, along with a letter of credence with a golden bull furnished by Baldwin, who approved of the plan. The Sultan's dream of the conquest of Europe had begun.

☪ ☪ ☪

A while later, when messengers brought Giyaseddin the news that Baiju had retreated to Azerbaijan and that the Vizier Muhadab had gone east to negotiate a peace treaty with the Mongols, he decided that it was safe to return to Konya, where the people received him with joy. They had heard of the dreadful fate of their sister city of Kayseri, and they were elated that their lives had been spared.

After Vizier Muhadab left the camp of the Mongols to return to Konya, Chormagan began to reconsider what he had done. Since he was not the supreme ruler of the Mongols, he knew better than to overstep his role and the dangers that would await him if he failed to respect protocol with the Great Khan. Furthermore, he realized that Vizier Muhadab had not been officially sent by Giyaseddin Keyhüsrev. What if the Sultan did not honor the rogue ambassador's agreement once he returned to Konya with it? Chormagan thus felt it necessary for all parties to clarify the agreement made by Vizier Muhadab. He dispatched a messenger to the Seljuk court at Konya requesting that a Seljuk embassy be sent as soon as possible to the court of Batu, the chief of the Mongols of the western territories. The definitive agreement would be formalized and signed by both parties there. The Sultan Giyaseddin Keyhüsrev had no choice but to respond affirmatively to the request, and appointed the Vizier Shemseddin Isfahani, chief deputy of Vizier Muhadab and a clever statesman, to finish the negotiations.

Soon a great caravan of soldiers and ambassadors set off to the court of the Mongols at Kaygatu, in the steppe lands between the Don and the Volga Rivers. Shemseddin Isfahani personally led the group laden with presents for Batu Khan, grandson of the Ocean Genghis Khan, and sovereign of the western part of the Mongol empire and founder of the Khanate Empire of the Golden Horde.

Shemseddin Isfahani managed to secure all of Chormagan's conditions, and the treaty was signed by both parties. It certified that Giyaseddin Keyhüsrev was Batu's lieutenant in Anatolia and, as such, the official representative of the Mongols in Konya. Batu Khan also ordered that the Sultan's five-year-old son Rukneddin travel to the Kaygatu court to officially render homage to him.

It now seemed to all that the worst possible misfortune had been avoided. The Mongols would stop breathing their fire down the necks of the Seljuks, and life could carry on as before. The people of the Seljuk Empire heaved a sigh of relief. We will continue to be governed by our own, we will build up our cities, we will be able to praise God in our mosques and we will have food on our tables. We are safe, thanks to the wily wizards of negotiation and their creative paths of peace.

Chapter 110

Thirty Pieces of Silver

As the hot July sun beat on his head, Lord Hethoum of Armenian Cilicia thought about how the events of his life had heated up over the past few months. It seemed like only yesterday that he was standing at this very spot on his castle terrace on a warm May morning, showing the emissary of Baiju the extent of his dominion.

The Mongol envoy had arrived several months earlier, sent by his superiors to ensure that Hethoum did not supply his promised archers to Sultan Giyaseddin Keyhüsrev for the battle with the Mongols. The Mongols proved as ruthless off the battlefield as they were on it. Playing behind the scenes, they sought to conquer the Seljuk Empire by forging secret ties with the Christians who lived under its rule, in particular the Armenians. Following repeated invasions by the Byzantines and the Turks of their homeland, many Armenians chose to move south to the region of Cilicia. There, in a triangle of territory wedged between the Taurus and Amanus Mountains and the Mediterranean Sea, they set up a flourishing kingdom full of independent fiefs, each with its own lord and castle. The fiefdom of Mahperi's father at Kalonoros had been located at the western boundary, and many other Armenian lords held forth from a bouquet of stronghold castles scattered across the region.

While waiting for the dreadful day of battle, Hethoum had time to contemplate his future with the Mongols. He knew that many Khans had married Christian women, and had sympathies with Christians. He knew, too, that the Mongols mistrusted Muslims whom they knew would always stand with their brothers of the *umma,* the great Muslim community of believers, in Syria, Iraq and Persia, and with the Egyptians to the West, all sworn enemies of the Mongols. He knew the Mongols counted upon Christians to serve as a tool in their quest to crush the Muslim *umma* into fractured bits of forgotten history.

Hethoum realized that he was now at a crossroads with two opposing political choices in front of him. The left fork of the road led to joining the common front of Latins, Armenians and Seljuk Turks to war against the Mongols. If he took the right fork, he would surrender to the heathen Mongols and pay them for his salvation.

When messengers finally brought word of the resounding defeat of the Seljuks at Kösedağ, the emissary of Baiju just turned to him and smiled. When the messengers also revealed that the Sultan was in flight to parts unknown, that his mother had disappeared, and that Kayseri had been sacked, Hethoum knew which one of the two was the more deadly enemy. It would be better to be a vassal to the Mongols than to the Seljuks, and he needed to ensure that his fiefdom would not meet the same fate as did the Seljuks. Little did he realize, on this hot July day of 1243, that the decisive moment to act would be in front of him that very day.

☪ ☪ ☪

Fleeing the Seljuk territories now occupied by the Mongols, Mahperi and her small retinue made their way south across the endless blistering steppe towards Aleppo in Syria. Mahperi was on the verge of collapse from the intense summer heat and the strain of the past few weeks, but she pressed on. Giyaseddin's wife Adelpha and his sister Seljuka tended to the Sultana, even though they were in truth more afraid than she was. Mahperi knew they needed to push with determination until they reached Armenian territory near the Taurus Mountains, at which point they would be out of harm's way. She reassured her family and servants that they would have nothing to fear then, for she would be among her people. From there, the final descent to Aleppo would be easier. She knew once she arrived at Aleppo, the famed city of Saladin, she would be safe from the Mongols and could plan for her future and that of the Seljuk Empire. *Hold strong! Let us get to Aleppo as fast as we can!*

Early one morning on the road, her small entourage caught sight of a group of horsemen approaching them in a cloud of dust. Fearing they were a raiding pack of Mongols sent out to find her, Mahperi tried her best to maintain her calm. There is no point to run or resist, she thought, if I am to meet my fate here on this dusty road to Aleppo, then so shall it be.

When the pack got closer and she could detect their clothes and colors, her heart leapt for joy, for she saw that they were not Mongols, but Armenians. I am among my people! She lifted her eyes heavenwards in a prayer of thanksgiving. We have at last arrived in Armenian territory and these allies of the Seljuk Empire will protect us!

The group halted in front of them, and one horseman moved to the front to address her.

"Welcome Honored Queen Mother of the Seljuk Empire! I am Hethoum, Lord of the Castle and fiefdom of Baberon!" he bellowed out. "My scouts informed me that you were on the road through our territory, so I have come to greet you and welcome you to my kingdom. You must be very tired from this baking heat! Please, come and rest at my castle. I would be honored to have the mother, sister, and wife of the Seljuk Sultan as my guests. Come; accept the hospitality I offer you."

"Lord Hethoum, we appreciate your offer of hospitality. It is most kind of you to receive us, but as much as I would like to accept your invitation, I must decline. We must reach Aleppo as quickly as possible. Just knowing that we are in friendly territory is all the rest we need!"

"I will not hear of it! In any case, you need fresh horses. You need to restock your supplies. Once you rest for a few days from the hardships of the road, you will be stronger and can make better progress. I will then send some of my men along to escort you, for they know this territory well and will guide you to the best roads. There are often bandits on this stretch, and your party will attract much attention. We cannot leave anything to chance for the Sultana of the Seljuk Empire!"

"But, really, I must not delay..."

"Please! You have been through much of late, and it is the least I can do!"

Yes, thought the weary Mahperi, if you only knew how much I have been through of late. Suddenly, she became overwhelmed by the stress of the defeat, the confession of her son, fright for her life, fear for the destruction of her mosque, and the uncertainty of the future of the Empire. It was hot, she was bone tired and thirsty and grime filled her lungs. And now this kind man was offering her a cool haven of repose, and how reassuring it was to hear her mother tongue spoken to her!

She nodded to her guards to follow the lead of his men. Nothing could happen to her in the hands of a fellow lord of her father's and an ally vassal state of the Seljuks. She could feel protected here for a few days. She was so tired she could no longer think clearly.

That night, after a long bath and a hearty meal, she slept soundly for the first time in a long while.

☪ ☪ ☪

The next morning, Hethoum's father, Baron Constantine of Baberon, burst into his son's rooms.

"Is it true what I have heard? Is the Queen Mother of the Seljuks truly under our roof?" he cried out with great excitement.

"Yes, Father, she is here. My scouts informed me that she was on the road near here, and I rode out to invite her to rest here for awhile."

"My son! Do you realize what an unbelievable fortune this is for us? You wanted to negotiate with the Mongols for peace; well, here is your golden opportunity! Holding the mother and family members of the Seljuk Sultan in our hands is the answer to all our problems! If the Mongols know we have her and are willing to deliver her over to them, our future protection from them will be assured!"

"But Father! I cannot kidnap this woman and hold her here against her will!" indignantly retorted Hethoum. "That would be dishonorable and uncharitable! I offered her our Christian help, not our treachery! She is a royal noble like us – she *is* one of us, if you remember!"

"My son, don't be foolish! Think about what the Mongols will do to you if they hear that you are harboring her without telling them! How do you plan to hide her presence here from that sneaky Mongol envoy who is still here? Believe me, what the Mongols will do to us will be ten times worse than anything you could do to her. I am telling you: it is her life or yours!"

☪ ☪ ☪

Hethoum thought long about what his father said, and even though he knew that what he was asking him to do was wrong, he had to agree that the opportunity to save his empire was now in his hands.

Hethoum told the wide-eyed Mongol emissary about his prominent guest and began to discuss the situation with him. Baberon, sensing that his son was hesitating to put forth the daring plan, cut him off and took over the negotiations with the Mongol agent.

"Listen to me! We have a rare opportunity right in front of us, which is of interest to all: Armenians of Cilicia, Mongols and Seljuks alike! It will be easy for us to detain the Seljuk Sultana here for a while under the pretext of a well-needed rest. She will suspect nothing. We will hold her as war booty for as long as it takes for your armies to completely overtake the Seljuks, which shouldn't be long. I suppose you Mongols would like us to hand her over to you so that you can kill her and show the Turks what happens to those who seek to defy the mighty Mongols. But I would advise a different tactic, more advantageous for all of us," he insisted, boring his eyes at the foul-smelling Mongol envoy.

"Here is my plan. Instead of killing her, we will hold her here for you in a secret place, and *you* will hold her as a powerful political ransom. You can play her as a wager to keep those Seljuks in line, for you can threaten that one false move and she will be strangled – or worse, for I have heard what you people are capable of doing! As long as she is in captivity, you have control over the Seljuks stronger than any battalion! Those Turks venerate their mothers, and will do anything to protect them, especially this one, for she is beloved not only by her son, but by all her people. As long as she is in captivity, they will follow your every command like donkeys on a rope. Know as well that I have no remorse about holding her locked up forever to rot in a dungeon here or elsewhere, for I will do anything to protect my family, my people and this kingdom. She may be an Armenian like us, but war is stronger than blood. And as long as we hold her, you have every assurance of our loyalty. In return, the Mongols must leave our Kingdom alone. One false step from you and I will kill her, and you will lose this bargaining power over the Seljuks. Now, have I made myself clear and do we have an agreement?"

The Mongol ambassador, mouth agape, could not believe his good fortune. What an easy victory! He immediately sent a messenger to Baiju to tell him that the royal queen had been kidnapped and was now held for them by the Armenians. In return, no harm was to come to the House of Hethoum of the Armenian Kingdom of Cilicia.

☪ ☪ ☪

The next morning, Hethoum's servant came to Mahperi's rooms to tell her that all was ready for her departure. His guards were there to escort her to her next destination, with fresh horses and supplies. Yet when Mahperi stepped out into the sunlight of the castle courtyard, she did not see her men, horses or goods. Instead, she saw only the guards of Hethoum lined up in front of her.

"Where are my men?" she asked, puzzled. "I thought we were ready to leave. Has there been a delay?"

Hethoum and his father Constantine of Baberon stepped forward from behind the row of guards. Hethoum dug his toe into the dirt before lifting up his head.

"There has been a change of plans, my Lady. You will not be continuing on to Aleppo, but will be staying with us for a little while longer," he said, dropping his eyes as he spoke.

"But what has happened? Are the Mongols on my trail? Or have the Seljuks rallied against the Mongols?" she exclaimed, with joy lighting her face and voice.

"No...no one is coming to rescue you. We are detaining you here in Armenian Cilicia and sending you to an undisclosed location not far from here for safekeeping until further notice."

"But I don't understand! You promised to help me get to Aleppo as soon as possible! Why are you telling me now that you will not allow me to continue on? Why would you want to do that?" Mahperi sputtered, but as soon as she said it, she realized that something had gone very wrong. She nervously looked at the row of guards and it suddenly became clear to her.

"Are you...am I to believe that I am being held captive here by you?"

The continued downcast gaze of Hethoum gave her the answer. "I would prefer not to call you a prisoner, but, yes, I am holding you here from this moment forth. I have notified the Mongols that you are in my hands. You will be kept here in Armenian territory as their hostage until they decide your future. It is for your own good, my Lady, for if those Mongols had caught you trying to escape, they would have sliced you alive!"

"But that is a risk I will take! I had practically made it into Ayyubid territory! You cannot hold me as a hostage! How could you have lied to me! You are a vassal of the Seljuk Empire, and as such are under the orders of my son the Sultan!"

At this point, Baron Constantine of Baberon stepped forward, angrily raising a finger to her face.

"Your son, the Sultan, has fled like a coward, leaving your Empire completely abandoned of leadership! In view of this, we have no further accounts to render to the Seljuks. We make the rules now, and we have decided to hold you as our hostage, which will save both of us. You will be kept locked up for as many days, months or years it takes for your glorious Seljuk Empire to collapse at the hands of the Mongols, and it will collapse for sure. May I remind you that you betrayed your own people and our faith by becoming a Muslim. I will not betray mine by allowing my people to be killed by these heathen Mongols. I am sorry, Lady Mahperi Hatun, daughter of Kyr Vart, now Muslim queen, but you made your choices and now I make mine. You are a prisoner of war, and a very priceless one at that, if I may add."

"But you can't do this! You are a vassal state of the Seljuks! You cannot cross them, for you have obligations to serve them!"

Hethoum now stepped in and spoke more calmly to Mahperi.

"Not any longer, my Lady. For you see, I have been contemplating an alliance with the Mongols for some time now. We live in difficult times, and we all must try to survive. Your presence here is the strongest advantage I can have to ensure the safety of my people, for now the Mongols will listen to me. Either I turn you over to them to do as they wish – and you surely know what that will entail – or I keep you here in safety until the day your people ransom you for a very hefty sum. Perhaps the Mongols will prefer to tell your son that you are their captive and will be killed if they make one rebellious step to their rule. Either way, I will earn the eternal recognition and protection of the Mongols. I am very sorry, but this is the fork of the road I must take. I have no choice but to hold you here."

"You would betray a fellow Christian Armenian, one of your own? Why, like Judas, you will take a bribe of thirty pieces of silver?" she said, looking at him with contempt in her eyes.

"I will do anything to save my life, and if you are the key to that, then yes, the price of your neck is the one I will pay. I repeat, I do not want to kill you, my Lady, or ship you off to the Mongols. That would be too cruel. I would rather keep you as a hostage to be ransomed to your family and country. Consider yourself lucky, Lady Mahperi, for if the Mongols had found you on that road to Aleppo, you would have been tortured and humiliated in the most ignoble fashion. At least with us, you have found refuge and will be treated with dignity."

Mahperi was stunned by his words. Treated with dignity? Being locked up by her own people turned traitors is considered dignity? Mahperi thought of Gaziye, and wondered if she, too, would end her days locked up in a prison cell. She had to be strong, and cling to the hope that she would see freedom again. She would show courage in the face of this trial, but she had no faith that her son would ever come to rescue her. She had forsaken him, and her brutal last words to him came back to haunt her. She told him that she never wanted to see him again, so why should he care to ransom her now? Yet, she must not let these traitor Armenians believe she was afraid or weak. *You will survive this, Mahperi; you will survive as you always have.*

Mahperi's thoughts flashed back to her father and his decision to save his people of Kalonoros when he surrendered her to the Sultan Alaeddin Keykubad so many years ago. I am a pawn once more, sold to the highest bidder in this game of survival. Only this time there is not a handsome sultan and a promise of a happy future waiting for me on the other side of the gate; this time, my destiny is in the hands of a cunning Armenian traitor and Mongol brutes. Yet, I will persevere. I must never forget that I am Mahperi, Sultana and builder of the Seljuk Empire, more priceless than thirty pieces of silver.

I will survive.

Chapter 111

A Kingdom of Six Green Leaves

Kozan Castle, September, 1244

"*This is the day the Lord hath made, let us rejoice and be glad in it.*" I recite that verse to myself every morning, as I was taught to do as a child. I may be a Muslim now, but this verse still comes to my mind the first thing when I open my eyes each dawn. But there are mornings now when it sounds hollow, and it must sound hollow to you, o, my Lord.

'*The Lord giveth and the Lord taketh away*" was also taught to me as a child, and my life here is a living lesson of this Scripture verse. Much has been given to me – and much has been taken away.

Little is given to me here, but I am thankful for what small favors have been allowed me: this small notebook in which I write, and the little plant that sits on my window ledge. I write in this journal every day and I water the plant each day. These two simple gestures of normal life keep me steady in a world gone horribly wrong. Of the two, the little plant is the most precious to me. I watch its leaves reach for the sun and dream that one day I, too, will reach for my freedom.

I cannot complain about my life since coming here. It has been over a year that I have been held captive in this castle. Days are simple and calm. I am not mistreated; if anything, I am tended to with respect and kindness. The guards and servants are all polite to me. At least with them I can speak my own tongue – how ironic that after struggling for so many years to learn Turkish, it would appear that I will end my days speaking with jailers in my native Armenian tongue. Such an irony, too, that I should be back where I started, here in Cilician Armenia, not far from where I grew up.

I was brought here to Kozan, a castle located east of Kalonoros. The castle does not lie on the coast, but at the crest of a mountain ridge. It sits on an isolated rock which commands a view over the line of valleys below, with the only access to it through a narrow passage controlled from its well-built walls and towers. Even my Alaeddin would not have been able to take this rugged castle, for there is no possibility of assault – or escape.

Ah, my Kalonoros! You, sparking white diamond in the crown of the blue sea! I think often of my days there, so long ago. I am not the same young girl who rode down the hill from that castle on a black horse at the side of a handsome Sultan on a blazing white stallion. I rode with him beyond the boundaries of my life and what he showed me changed me forever. I sit here, now, at this window, gazing into the unknown, and every shimmering glint of sunshine I see in the valleys below beckons me to the light of freedom that awaits me, be it on this earth or in God's paradise. I live for that light. I will be strong. Even in captivity, I am still Mahperi, Sultana of the Seljuk Empire.

Our cell is simple: a sleeping mat, a small table, and some low cushions. A crucifix hangs on the wall, as if to remind me of my sin of embracing Islam, nagging me by its presence to repent. No muezzin calls are heard here: this is Armenian land, Christian and holy. Clothing is scarce; we have only the few things we brought with us. My jewels and other worldly items were taken from me, but I do not mind. Ever since that day when my turquoise necklace was broken, everything else in my life fell apart, too.

My daughter Seljuka is with me. I strive to provide her solace and to teach her not to fear life. She is growing into a young woman, soon fourteen. If any blessing could be found from this imprisonment, it is that it now gives us a long, neglected chance to spend time together. We have never been close, for I favored the child that needed the most help, and that was always her brother. A mother tries to love her children unconditionally and equally, but there has always been a distance between us. Here, we sleep side by side on the same mat, and this prison tower will help bring us together. Sweet Adelpha, the wife of my son, tends to me with much attention, and she is like a second daughter.

Here with us too are a few of my devoted maids. They provide me the only contact I have with human life other than my jailers. There is no possibility here for discourse with astute minds like I had in the Seljuk court. To keep my mind sharp, I replay the conversations of my past, still echoing in my head: with my father, Bahaeddin Veled and his son Jelaleddin, the Vizier Karatay, Sheikh Turesan, my beloved Alaeddin, Hanife, and Lou. So many friends taken from me, and now I am the one taken.

I receive no news of the outside world, none. I am cut off from everything. What is the fate of the Seljuk Empire since that defeat at Kösedağ? Is my son still alive? Where is he? Does he even know that I am still alive, and where I am? I wonder who is there at the Konya court: Karatay? I wonder what is happening in the government; for that matter, does the Empire even still exist? I ask myself if the Mongols are flooding in and killing our people, sacking our cities and destroying our monuments. I pray for the well-being of my Kayseri, my Konya and my mosque and hans. Are any of my buildings still standing? I am driving myself insane with all these questions. Anything is possible in this world now gone mad. So many questions and no answers; here, in this remote tower on an inaccessible rock. All this worry has weakened me, and I am now becoming very thin. I am plagued by a deep and dull pain incubating inside of me and a fatigue that covers me like a blanket.

And so here I sit, in this stone stronghold perched above mountain valleys stretching as far as one can see, the Queen Mother of the great Seljuk Empire, now stripped of everything: power, friends, support, family, fortune, and purpose. Only my faith remains, but indeed, it is the most powerful of Empires. My mighty kingdom is now comprised of six green leaves on a small basil plant.

Although they treat me with respect, I live in fear that my jailers will one day hand me over to the Mongols. I know this would not be in their best interest, but still, I am frightened. I doubt Hethoum would touch one hair on the head of his precious treasure, but he is fickle and blows like a feather in the faintest wind. Should he decide to hand me over to the Mongols, he would do it in a second. Every time I hear footsteps pounding up the staircase, loud voices or commotion, my heart beats like a drum. Are they coming to fetch me? The vile acts of those Mongols are legendary, and I am terrorized. I have heard their stories of torture and they feed my nightmares. Will they lop my head off with a sword and then parade it about on a pike? Will they rip my bleeding heart from my body and feed it to their dogs? Will they pull out my entrails with a rope from the back of a horse? Will they put me in a kettle of boiling water and turn me into a stew? I have heard they do all this and more.

To keep my head clear and calm from these thoughts, I write in this journal every day. I also play little games with myself; for example, I count the things I see in the world around me. I count the number of swallows, flies, falling leaves, the level of snow on the mountain crest, the number of church bells or barking dogs that I hear – anything to keep my mind awake. Today, there were seven swooping falcons, two more than yesterday! I write about simple things in my journal, everyday emotions and thoughts: the amount of sun and heat, what I ate, how I feel and my health, snippets of Scripture, lessons from the Qur'an, poems, a happy memory here and there; anything I can think of is jotted down – the point is to stay focused until the day I will be released. And I know I will be released, and this forms the basis of my hope. But the question is: released to whom? Will I be handed over to the Mongols to meet a certain death, or back to the Seljuks to carry on – if there is anything left to carry on – or to someone else, the Latins or the Franks for all I know; for that wily Hethoum would sell me immediately to whoever pays him the highest for my head. Or perhaps I will stay locked up here forever – no, I cannot think that.

More than a prisoner of these walls, however, I am prisoner of my memories. Throughout the day, I fill my head with reminiscences of places, of people dear to me, of my most beautiful days. I count my blessings, every one, like beads on a rosary. I remember my father with his love of books, the sweet smile of the gentle priest of Kalonoros who fed me communion bread, the full moon of my wedding night, Joseph's brush as he brought nature alive on a tile for the throne room of the Great Palace with one thick black stroke; the shining coat of Eclipse and the smell of his pink ears, the friends of my heart, Hanife and Bahaeddin; the firm voice of my husband and the touch of his hands, the blue view over the lake at Kubadabad, the violet eyes of a wild dervish, the bazaar and walls of Konya, bustling Kayseri and the giant angel wings of the Majestic Mountain beating over my mosque, the song of Lou at the campfire, the illumination I felt the moment I pronounced the *shahada,* a turquoise on a chain dangling from the slender fingers of a Sultan and glistening in the candlelight, the inauguration days of my mosque, my hans, my tekke – all of those things, I play over and over and over in my eyes and my ears and my heart.

They help me push back all the dark images ever present: a black raven riding into Konya, the smashing of golden plates, the death of my husband, the murder of Hanife, the treachery of the Dog, innocent boys snuffed out at their play; and the unspeakable betrayal of a son, my son. Life is one of blood, not rosewater; but to survive, I must banish these dreadful moments from my mind.

In these quiet and empty days, my thoughts turn to Lou. It was he who gave me the chance to look into myself and realize that I could give my soul to building and art. By his unfailing belief in me, I became the Queen reigning in a kingdom of care and beauty, a kingdom more powerful than the one over which I officially reigned. In the darkest of moonless nights, I dream that he is telling me that we will build again and that I will climb to even more heights. Where are you now, beloved friend? You gave me days of rich hours, of order and elegance. I try to recall them to give me hope, but now, I have only the goodness of six green leaves; now, the only thing I can build is a tiny splint to shore up the stalk of a limp basil plant.

Some days a priest from the village below comes to take my confession, but I have nothing to tell him. I am a Muslim now and confess directly to God, not to a little black priest. I have lived no life of sin, and I am not ashamed of anything I have done. It is I who must show forgiveness now; it is I who must pardon, not you, my priest. I must forgive my father for giving me away in order to survive. I must forgive my husband for becoming bewitched by the charms of another woman more seductive than I could ever be. I must forgive Gaziye, too, for her beauty and the jealousy that drove her to destroy my image in my husband's eyes. I must forgive Köpek for his evil ways and for murdering so many people, and above all, for destroying those most dear to me – my husband, my son, Lou and Hanife. Yet, I will not beg forgiveness for the ambition that drove me to build and shine and, as a result, to incur enemies. Above all, I must try to forgive my son for his horrible sins. I spoke so harshly to him on that last day in Tokat, when my anger and shock overtook my senses. Those words now burn my heart. I now understand that those horrible sins were in reality those of others. I owe him the compassion that only a mother can give.

In any case, I know that this little bearded, black-robed priest could never understand the rich road of faith I have traveled in my life. He could not understand that I find inspiration in Mary and Jesus and Muhammad at the same time. Perhaps I do not understand it either, but such has been my journey.

To you, O mother Mary, Woman among all Women, lily of my solitude, rose of my dawn, star of my nights; to you, Mary, I ask, why have you abandoned me? I never failed in my fervor for you. I have awakened so many nights with your face in front of mine in my dreams, your blue veil fluttering in front of my eyes like the waves of the sea below my window of Kalonoros.

To you, sweet Jesus of mine, I hear your words on the cross: *Father, forgive them, for they know not what they do*. Yes, I must forgive them, too. May I find the strength and resistance to live long enough to climb the stairs to the glorious throne in Heaven!

And lastly to you, God, I pray the greatest of all prayers, the *Fatihah*, for in it I find the wisdom and grace for my salvation:

In the Name of God, the Compassionate, the All-Merciful.
Praise be to God, the Lord of the worlds.
The Compassionate, the All-Merciful.
Master of the Day of Judgment.
You alone do we worship, and to You alone do we pray for help.
Guide us to the straight path.
The way of those to whom You have favored with Thy Grace,
not those who deserve anger nor those who go astray.

Yes, my days are like a shadow that declineth, but my faith will cast bright sunshine on me. A day is like a thousand years to the Lord, and a thousand years is like a day. The Almighty is not slow in keeping his promise, as some understand slowness. Instead, He is patient, not wanting anyone to perish, but everyone to come to repentance. For the sun rises with scorching heat and withers the plant; its blossom falls and its beauty is destroyed.

I hold on tight to my kingdom of six green leaves.

Chapter 112

Hard Rains

The whirling city of Konya came to life again. The Sultan returned and the people were reassured. The citizens of the capital rejoiced that their holy city had been spared from the unspeakable horrors lived by Kayseri. *Allahu Akbar!* All continued to look over their shoulders in fear that the Mongols would arrive at their door; but for the moment, the people of Konya resumed their daily activities and the city took on its normal rhythm. Bazaars buzzed, the medrese of Jelaleddin filled to capacity once more, muezzins cried to the faithful, buildings rose, fields bore their rich bounty, camel caravans trod into the city from all directions, and the court carried on dispensing orders and edicts for the future projects of the Empire now under Mongol authority.

Yet, for Sultan Giyaseddin Keyhüsrev, his life could never return to normal until he found his mother. For immeasurable months, he had no news of her. Was she still alive, and, if so, where was she? It was as if she had fallen off the end of the earth. His Ayyubid envoys informed him that she had never arrived at Aleppo. The agonized Sultan dispatched spies throughout the land to bring him information about her, with a fortune in gold promised to the one who could tell him where she was. Sitting in his palace in Konya in desperation, he refused to give up hope that she was still alive, even though almost two years had passed since their last day together in Tokat. He had to find her and atone for the horror of that day; he had to make her understand how much he needed her forgiveness.

When at last the spies of Sultan Giyaseddin Keyhüsrev came to tell him that his mother had been kidnapped on the road to Aleppo by her very own people and was held hostage by them as agents for the Mongols, he was outraged beyond reason. Upon learning that Lord Hethoum was behind the kidnapping, the Sultan's anger exploded, for he was the very same turncoat who had failed to send his promised lancers to the battle of Kösedağ. The Sultan knew that the Mongols had been trying for a long while to win the Armenians over to their side. Hethoum had perhaps fallen prey to their persuasive bait, yet no one shall dare touch the honorable head of the mother of the Sultan of the Seljuk Empire, not even the Great Khan himself.

The Sultan grabbed the carafe of wine off the copper tray in front of him and heaved it furiously against the wall, shattering the glass into shards that sprayed across the floor. This is what I will do to you, Hethoum, when I get my hands upon you, the Sultan raged to himself, as he paced back and forth across the room. I will mount a campaign and go down south to Cilicia and rescue her. I will punish all those who have sought to harm my family, for it is not just my mother he holds, but my wife and sister, too. I will exact my revenge on you, Hethoum, for failing to send me those archers at Kösedağ. I will punish you for breaking your allegiance to the Seljuks and going over to the Mongol side.

I don't know where you have hidden her, but once I am in Cilicia, I will tear down every stone in every castle in the land to find her. My spies are effective, and I will ply everyone with bribes for information, and someone, somewhere, will tell me what I need to know. After that, Lord Hethoum of Cilician Armenia, I will personally crush every bone in your body for what you have done to my mother.

The Sultan immediately barked out orders to ready a campaign to head south to Cilicia. It would be an extensive campaign with multiple missions. The Sultan needed once again to quell the still-rebellious Turkmen factions in the Taurus Mountains. He would punish Hethoum and the Armenians. Lastly and above all, he would find his beloved mother and release her from captivity. It would be the most important campaign of his life.

Although a campaign of many missions, the strongest of the Sultan's motivations to descend into Cilicia was personal, not military. Giyaseddin Keyhüsrev, ever since that horrible last scene with his mother in Tokat, had been filled with crippling remorse. It had become impossible for him to carry that oppressive burden of guilt within him any longer – he had to tell her the truth that day. However, he had not counted on the fact that she would not forgive him. He thought she would understand. Yes, they were sins of an ignoble scale, but in those difficult times he had to take the actions that would best serve him and the Empire. Or so he had been led to believe were necessary, and that is where his agony increased. Had he really needed to kill all those people? Now, with hindsight, he could see how cleverly he had been manipulated by Köpek, and that what he did was wrong, very wrong. He had begged for God's mercy every day since that last meeting with her, and now he needed to ask it from her and receive her absolution. If not, he knew his life was lost. He was now twenty-four years old, with a long life still in front of him, but he could not imagine living it without knowing that his mother forgave him and still loved him.

Above all, he needed his mother's stabilizing support, for without it, he was becoming more dissolute than ever. Alcohol flowed like water wherever he went, in a vain attempt to forget his sins, his many defeats, and the loss of his mother's love. Alone in his room each night, despite the numbing effects of the wine, the pain of her last words echoed in his ears: "*Get out of my sight, for I can no longer bear to look at you, killer of your father and your brothers. I banish you from your place in my heart. May God have pity on your soul, my son, but the enormity of your sins is beyond even His merciful comprehension. You, my Cub, now lie dead at the bottom of the well of my heart.*"

I must end this pain, he thought to himself. The Sultan looked down at the bottom of his empty wine goblet. I am like you, little dregs I see here, he laughed, for my life is nothing but the sediment of the all the blood I have scattered. I lie in the pit of nothingness. I must find my mother and beg her forgiveness for what I have done. She has got to understand that I was helpless in the hands of Köpek, and that I did not know what I was doing. I must bring her back into my life. Yes, then together, we will start a new era for the Seljuks! I will stop my dissolute ways, I will listen to the lessons of the imams, I will put away my red wine, my women and my gambling pieces; I will dedicate myself to building this Empire. But I must have her by my side. Without her guidance and support I am lost. God, please send me succor for my days ahead!

He sobbed into his sleeve for a long while, and then called his servant to bring him another flask of wine.

☪ ☪ ☪

As the campaign was in territory unfamiliar to him, Giyaseddin knew he would have a greater chance for success if he aligned himself with a proven partner in the region. He had such a man in Constantine of Lampron, one of the many lords of the Cilician area. Long a faithful personal friend of the Sultan Giyaseddin Keyhüsrev, Constantine of Lampron had lent him substantial support in the Turkmen revolts. Constantine had been enraged when Hethoum had left Giyaseddin in the breach at Kösedağ, and now considered Hethoum's defection to the Mongol side an ignoble treachery. More than that, holding the Sultan's mother prisoner was, in his eyes, a dishonorable act done without faith or any sense of justice. What kind of a Christian soul could hold a woman against her will and exploit her for personal gain? The Armenian enthusiastically agreed to help the Sultan take his revenge on the traitor Hethoum.

Before setting out with his main army from Konya to the Taurus region to join Constantine's troops, the Sultan dispatched a smaller faction of troops as an advance expedition ahead of the main Seljuk army. This battalion of troops was led by the illustrious peace broker Vizier Shemseddin Isfahani. All would convene in Cilicia for a united front against the Turkmen rebels and the traitor Hethoum.

☪ ☪ ☪

The Sultan set out at last on his campaign, taking Ruby along with him as usual. She rode on the hindquarters of her dedicated horse, behind her trainer Tahajan. There would be little time, however, for the Sultan to enjoy hunting expeditions with her at the many pleasure pavilions that he had built along the southern coast, for now they were on a hunting expedition for game of a different type.

For over seven months, Giyaseddin and his troops burned and destroyed many parts of the western area of the Taurus Mountains in his attempt to quell the Turkmen revolts once and for all. Even though he fell ill with malaria in the Cilician swamplands during the campaign and suffered from frightful fever and chills that made it hard for him to keep to his saddle, he pushed on with equal fever on his quest to find his mother.

He told himself that after he finished with the Turkmen, it would be the turn to deal with Hethoum. The forces of Giyaseddin coming from the west, the vanguard troops led by Shemseddin Isfahani and the forces of Constantine of Lampron would surround the Baberon castle and squeeze Hethoum in their vise. The troops would besiege his castle and force him to negotiate his surrender. Giyaseddin did not know if his mother was held there, but, if not, he would torture Hethoum mercilessly until he gave up the name of her hiding place. *Hold on tight, dear mother; I am coming to rescue you soon.*

The strategy was laid out, the troops were convening, and the negotiators were primed. All was in place for victory.

☪ ☪ ☪

And then the rains came.

Lashing out from the heavens with a force rarely seen, the heavy rains of October fell for days on end. The hard rain pounded down the earth and filled every underground hole until it hit rock bottom. Trees died from suffocation; the ground turned to sludge. The army's horses sank up to their hocks in the mud. The drenched uniforms of the men turned moldy, arrows warped into softness, drinking water became sullied, and the dirty disease of typhoid spread. Both the Sultan and his men groaned from abdominal cramps and burned under high fever. The days were as dark as the nights, and the sound of the beating sheets of rain drowned out the drums of the military bands on the field.

Then came the floods, causing the rivers to swell and overflow their banks at every bend and meander. All prayed for deliverance before they would be swept along in the foul flow. The silted waters settled in hollows and became oceans. Some soldiers were saved by climbing on floating logs and rafters. Horses sank and suffocated. Winds began to blow, sweeping the provisions out to sea in waves. There was no food left to feed the soldiers, for soaked grain and flour laid rotting in piles. Bloated sheep floated down the river belly-up in brackish waters, waters which rushed faster than men could walk, and then faster than horses could run.

The resolve of the Seljuk troops became stuck in the mud along with the hooves of their horses. The rains continued to fall hard and harder, and nature, the most forceful of enemies, brought her own flood of defeat to the Turkish army and their Sultan.

Chapter 113

A World Torn Apart

I swish my tail in a violent snap. These mosquitoes are unbearable. They bite even through my thick fur; I feel little pins pricking my flesh everywhere. Yet they are nothing compared to the annoying black flies, drumming, drumming in my ears and crawling along the rims of my eyelids. My tail cannot beat them away fast enough. They bite hard, too, sharper and deeper than the mosquitoes, and their incessant buzzing makes my head whirl in anger.

It is hot in this place, very hot and damp, and this moist heat adds to the annoyance of these insect pests. Rain, the rain, it just will not stop. All is annoyance to me anymore. I am tired of all this traveling and confusion in my life since that horrid day on the battlefield. I carry still the odor of the rotting carrion of that day in my nostrils, disgusting even for me, a beast of the hunt.

It is the hour of the hunt now; that time when the sun goes down and the animals come out of their holes, thinking all is safe. I am ready for them. If only I could hunt down these buzzing insects like I did the deer and fox in the hills with my Sultan!

I know how to hunt. My mother died before she was able to pass on her skills to me, but the instinct of eons taught me all I need to bring down game in the wild. I can kill my prey quickly and efficiently. I know how to creep silently and close to an animal, then rush quickly to hit it and sink my claws to hook it and hold it down while I bite the neck to sever the backbone and crush the breathing tube. One swift and strong bite is all I need. Then I drag the carcass over to feed on it. My Sultan would always let me rip open the abdominal cavity, roll out the stomach and intestines and let me have them for myself. So soft, so warm, so sweet! Sometimes I would chew the ribs as well. He kept me in a cage but he also kept me savage, so I would never forget those two parts of life. Proud, strong and dangerous warriors above all, that is what he told me we both must be, the Sultan and his Ruby, together on the hunting fields of life. *Swish-snap. Swish-snap.*

Yet nothing has been the same since the death of my master Alaeddin. He, who so lovingly tended to me and raised me in the place of my dead mother. He, whose long fingers would gently nuzzle my head, stroking right there between my ears with soft caresses. He, who let me ride on the croup of a horse directly behind his bright white stallion on parade and festival days. He, who let me sit next to him in his divan in front of all the viziers and grandees of the world. He, who tied me in the garden under a sweet-smelling eucalyptus tree. He, who placed me in an airy cage on a brightly-painted wagon when we went off to war. He, who let me into his tent at night to sleep with him when he was on the fields of battle. He, whose hand fed me every day with tender morsels of the finest lamb, making sure to keep the heart and liver warm and fresh only for me. The Sultan trained me to respond to his commands; and I knew by his voice and hand when it was time to return to my cage or to have my keeper Tahajan lead me off to my picket under the tree in the garden. She is a savage animal, they all told him; you are foolish to trust her as if she were a pet dog! But no, he did not listen to them, and the good Sultan and I shared a union of trust that defied any understanding by those outside. He saved my life; I set a model of beauty and courage for his. We lived in our own Garden of Eden; a peaceable kingdom of mutual respect. *Swish-snap. Swish-snap.*

All that changed when he disappeared one night and never came back. I remember the big banquet with the hundreds of people and how noisy it was, but I was there present at his side as usual. I had been uneasy for several days before that night, tired of the hairy man who circled around me, constantly staring at me and poking me when I was tied to my picket in the garden. He was after something, he was, that smelly one; and I was not going to let him get anywhere near me. I snarled at him whenever he approached, yet that seemed to feed his interest all the more. Did he not understand that it is I who hunt prey, not the other way around? All was confusion that night, and I remember flaring my nostrils at a strange sharp odor coming from the birds placed in front of my master. Birds should not smell like that; they don't smell like that when I catch them to eat. I would not have touched that food, but that is the natural intelligence of beasts: we instinctively know when something is not right to eat. Right after my Sultan took a bite of that food I could smell terrible fear oozing out of his body and then he was gone.

He rode off into that night on his big white stallion and I never saw him again. He never came back to feed me and to scratch the top of my head with his long, slender fingers. Since then, I am cared for by the trainer Tahajan. He is kind and tends me with great attention, but he does not have the same hands as my Sultan. He does not have the same intense blue eyes that would lock into my yellow ones when he rubbed my head. I long for my master; I am adrift without him. His spark of intense energy is gone from my life. Even my coat, so lovingly brushed by him, now shines less, but whether it is dull from the lack of his daily brushings or from my grief or from these flies tearing it away in patches, I cannot know. *Swish-snap. Swish-snap.*

I am not let out of my cage enough and no one exercises me like before. I need relief from this boredom; I need challenges in order to practice my hunting skills. Alaeddin would spend hours with me tracking in the hills behind Alaiye; there, I would bring down prey for him with great pride. But now I am kept tethered up to a stick or bounced along in a cage or kept locked up alone in a room like this one. At least Tahajan unchains me so that I can move about freely, a small solace. I need to hunt. Now all I hunt are mosquitoes and black flies. *Swish-snap. Swish-snap.*

Since he went away I am bustled about like a sack of melons, from battlefield to battlefield. I am brought out like a shiny toy on the evenings when my new master holds his drinking parties. The son is not his father. There is nothing at all that unites the two of them in physique, intelligence, compassion or kindness. I sometimes wonder from whence Giyaseddin came; he is so clumsy next to his father's innate grace. Perhaps he resents that I remain the symbol of the greatness of his father that he will never come close to touching.

These black pests are like him in many ways. I have never liked him and I have never trusted him, and I know he is afraid of me. But it is his hand that is the worst of all. It is not the hand that feeds me; no, Tahajan does that. It is a hand of harm and hurt. I know this was the hand that reached into my cage and stole my cub from me so many years ago. I know this and I have never forgotten its shape or smell. I am out of routine and out of focus and I want my old life back and I want my stolen cub back. I want to pick her up by the soft fur of her neck and carry her to my lair where I can feed her and train her and wash her and nurture her. And just like he did with my cub, I know he took my master from me as well – of this I am sure, with all the natural intelligence of beasts. *Swish-snap. Swish-snap.*

Yes, that hand! How I hate it! And how I hate being paraded in front of his cronies on his drunken binge nights; how I hate being poked at by the dancing girls he brings in to entertain the men and himself. I hate witnessing their acts long into the night. I miss my master Alaeddin; I long for our life of dignity. *Swish-snap.*

Since that hot day on the plain, my life has been one of confusion and fleeing. We have done nothing but run, and I am sickened by his smell of cowardice. All the other animals of his menagerie were left behind on the Kösedağ battlefield: the poor monkeys, the parrots, the gazelles; all abandoned in the encampment after he fled the field in disgrace. All were left behind to their fate except me. Why I was spared and taken along with him to Tokat and beyond I will never know, but perhaps it was because he knew his mother Queen Mahperi would never forgive him if he did not spare me that defeat. Where is she now? She was every ounce as strong as the Sultan. *Swish-snap.*

Yes, since that day of defeat, I have been bounced along from city to city, field to field, and campaign to campaign; wandering lost with no real project or ambition. Life is no longer the adventure lived beside my dashing master in whose blue eyes I saw the dawn rising each morning; no, now it is the smell of fear and alcohol and rich perfumes that fills my nostrils instead of the smell of my master's pure feral life-force.

I am so tired of all this now. *Swish-snap.*

These flies just will not let up
They are biting my eyelids red raw
I hiss and swat my paw in the air to beat them away, but it is futile
They are like the hoards of Mongols on the field at Kösedağ
Coming again and again with no let up
I hear their buzzing in my ears
I feel them crawling on my eyes
I cannot bear this annoyance any more I am going mad
I hear footsteps outside and the door flings open
I smell the alcohol even before I turn around
Giyaseddin staggers into the room, drunk again
I hear his incoherent babbling, his noises, his ranting
He is alone
He laughs
His hand of harm reaches out and pulls my ear
I feel a black fly bite my ear
His hand pulls my ear again
Flies crawl in my eyes
All of you please leave me alone now
One fly bites my flank so hard it sends me skyrocketing into the air
I whip my head around to bite it, but he is there, reaching for my ear again
Time to hunt this prey
I am on his neck now, with all of it inside my jaws
I bite down hard
I hear a crunch of bones and feel the muscle in my mouth, soft like a piece of fresh liver
I smell the blood
I release and go back to get a bigger grasp on the side of his face
I bite down hard, very hard
I shake his head back and forth in my mouth
I hear the snapping of his windpipe
I hear more crunching

The taste of blood fills my mouth
The black flies are buzzing frantically now
I hold on for a long time despite his struggling
I hear his gurgling
I will avenge you, o my master
I will take care of this stain upon your memory
Your Ruby will save your honor
I hold on and bite down now even harder
I choke on the blood now pouring into my guzzle
I hear his cries of "Help! Help!"
I shake his neck in my jaws back and forth to shut him up
I rip the side of his neck and face away from his body and hold it in my fangs
You tore my world apart, Giyaseddin, now I will tear your life apart
I hold half of his face and neck dripping in my jaws
I hear running footsteps and see Tahajan at the door
I see the shock on his face
I see him freeze in horror at the sight of the blood spurting in air from the gash
He looks around the room
I see him dash to the window and fling the shutters wide open
I look into his eyes and I see no fear there, no anger there, but something else
I snap my head and fling the ragged chunk of Giyaseddin's neck across the room
I hear the smack of the blob as it hits the wall
It explodes into bits of pink and grey
I see the red blood streaming down the whitewashed wall
I turn my red eyes aflame with anger back to look at Tahajan
I hear him scream: "Run, Ruby, run for your life!"
I see him pointing to the window and I understand what he is telling me
I swish my tail in a violent snap
I take one leap and bound out of the window to the freedom outside
I leave the trace of my bloody paw print on the window ledge as I leap
It is the signature of my deed
I will run back to the hills of fire from whence I came
I have avenged my cub and I have avenged your honor, my Sultan,
My adored master Alaeddin Keykubad
We are now both free
I now go to find your spirit and hunt with you once more
We will run together in our hills again
We will run free forever, across this proud Empire of ours –

PART 5

A SULTANA FOR ALL TIME

1245-1255

Like a shepherd's tent my house
has been pulled down and taken from me.

Like a weaver I have rolled up my life,
and he has cut me off from the loom;
day and night you made an end of me.

I will walk humbly all my years
because of this anguish of my soul.

Lord, by such things men live;
and my spirit finds life in them too.

-Isaiah: 38:12-16

Gazel

Nideyim zâyi edip tûl-i emelle nefesi

With longing fond and vain, why should I make my soul to mourn?
One trace of love of earth holds not my heart – all is forsworn.

There ready stands the caravan, to Death's dim realms addrest,
E'en now the tinkling of its bells down on my ears is borne.

Come then, O bird, my soul, be still, disquiet leave far off;
See, how this cage, the body, is with years and suffering worn.

But yet, to weary, wasted, sin-stained Shâhî, what of fear?
Since thou'rt the God of Love, the helping Friend of those forlorn!

-Prince Shehzâde Bayazit
son of the Ottoman Sultan Suleyman
the Magnificent (1561)

Chapter 114

And I Am Escaped Alone To Tell Thee

Kozan Castle, April 20, 1250

They came this morning to tell me that my son was dead.

My son, the Sultan of the Seljuks, is dead. The last time I saw him was on that dreadful day in Tokat; and now, I will never have another chance to speak with him.

They told me that he was taken to Konya and buried in the mausoleum of the Sultans in the courtyard of Alaeddin's mosque at the top of the hill, alongside his father, his grandfather and his illustrious forbearers. I pray he rests in peace now, freed from the demons that pursued him his whole life – fear, insecurity, and the poisons of debauchery. He now lies in the same earth of eternity as his father and is seen equal in God's eyes, but in the eyes of this Empire, there will never be a doubt as to who was the greatest of all sultans.

Yet is he truly equal in God's eyes with other men? Were the doors to Paradise banned to him for the unspeakable sins he committed against his father and his brothers? Only God can decide whether he has earned his mercy and a place at His side. And can I say that I have the right to be called his mother? Perhaps not, for I have forsaken him, the ultimate sin of a mother. My last words to him were ones of banishment from my heart. Now I must ask myself if I can live the rest of my life knowing he left this earth without my forgiveness.

They told me that he died trying to save me. They said he came south to punish Hethoum and the Armenians for what they had done to me. They told me that he was searching in every castle, high and low for me, and that he had vowed in his wrath to tear each and every one down until he found me. They told me that he had died of illness, suddenly, but I think they are hiding something from me. My jailers have kept the news of his death from me for over four years – so cruel! Would it have been harder for me to know that he was dead for all these years, or to hear it now so much later after the fact? In many ways I feel it was I who killed him long ago when I plunged a knife into his heart with my words on that last day in Tokat. Despite my harshness to my son, he never abandoned his love for me, and died trying to find his way back into my heart. Perhaps he understood mercy better than I ever could, O my Lord!

And now they are telling me that I am to return home. After all this time here, they tell me in the same breath that my son is dead and that I am free. Never have I lived such a morning.

They explained to me everything that has taken place in the Seljuk lands over these past years. They told me that the Mongols ravaged my Kayseri while I was fleeing south after the battle of Kösedağ. Hethoum told me all about the agreement crafted by Vizier Muhadab to allow the Seljuks to run the affairs of state for the Mongols, and I must admit he played that one well, for he saved the Empire from destruction at the hands of those heathens. He says I am to be sent home to Kayseri with the promise that I will work with the Mongols to make sure the Seljuk court at Konya adheres respectfully to their commands. I learned that after my son's death, Hethoum began to fear that holding me prisoner was no longer proof enough to show the Mongols his antagonism towards the Seljuks, so he sent his brother Sempad on a mission all the way to the Mongol court in Karakorum to secure their protection in writing. Sempad bowed and scraped in front of Mongke Khan and gave them every assurance that the Armenians would continue to serve as their agents on the Mediterranean coast in the fight against their shared enemy, the Muslims.

Hethoum's brother also talked to the Great Khan about me, and told him that they were ready to hold me in this castle until the end of my days as proof of the their commitment to them. Yet who can ever understand those Mongols? The wily Khan surprised him and told him to send me home. Scripted right there, among the terms of the agreement letter given to Sempad was a clause concerning my release and the role I was to play once back in the Seljuk court. That Mongke certainly is a clever one, for he saw that I could be more useful out of prison than inside of it. It took Sempad four years to travel there and back with this agreement; for four long years I was kept in the dark about my fate and about the death of my son. All in all, it has been seven years that I have been languishing in this castle prison, denied information about the court, my family, my Kayseri, my mosque, my hans. Seven long years that I have been sitting here, waiting, day after day, for news; growing old, growing tired, and growing lonely. And now I learn all in the same morning that my son is dead and I am to go home.

Hethoum tells me that besides using my influence to ensure that the government runs smoothly, the Khan also believes that I can best serve their interests if I act along with the viziers as the regent to my three little grandsons. I have thought so much of them during my captivity here; missing them and wondering even if they were still alive. I am told that Giyaseddin's eldest son Izzeddin Keykavus has been put on the throne, despite the fact that Gurchi's son Alaeddin had been chosen as heir. Yet Izzeddin Keykavus is only fifteen years old, so he cannot possibly be anything but a pawn in everyone's hands, Mongols and emirs alike. Yes, the Mongols are right; I need to be there for my grandsons; especially to make sure this boy sultan, Izzeddin, is not manipulated by the emirs and viziers as was my son, their father. I will return and try to help salvage the empire that my husband Alaeddin worked so hard to build. Those boys are all I have left of him.

I have learned many things this morning, and it is all too much to take in at once, after almost seven years of sitting here in silence. I am so tired. But what will I find when I go home? Who will still be there in Kayseri? Not knowing is a torture all its own. What will my city look like now that it has been devastated by those heathen Mongols? Are its citizens starving? How will I go on if I find that my mosque is nothing more than a pile of rubble? What about my hans? Are they still standing? How will I rebuild my life after these past seven years and all that has happened? But I will, and now, instead of raising stone walls, I will raise young boys into strong leaders. I will make their grandfather proud of them. I will fight until the end of my days to ensure that the Seljuk Empire perseveres, despite the occupation by the Mongols.

They tell me that I am to be ready to leave tomorrow for the journey back to Kayseri. What do I have to ready for the journey? The clothes on my back, my basil plant and this journal are all I have. Yet I certainly have my pride and my determination to survive; yes, that I will make sure is packed in my saddlebags. Although I may be released from this prison, I will never be set free from the pain imprisoning my heart – pain from the anguish of my last words to my son. He has now gone to his last judgment alone, without a mother's love. That pain will imprison me forever with walls thicker than those of this castle. *And I only am escaped alone to tell thee, O my Lord!*

Chapter 115

Blue Dome of Hope

No matter how hard the August sun beats down on the snow at the top of the Majestic Mountain, it never melts. Every day, year after year, eon after eon, the Majestic Mountain wears its proud white crown. As I lift my eyes upward and look at the shimmering peak, I think of all the hardships life has chosen to beat down upon me. Yet, I will be like that obstinate snow and resist melting into nothingness.

It is now the summer of 1254. I have been back in Kayseri for four years now, Sultana of the Seljuk Empire once more, after seven long years as a hostage of Hethoum in Cilician Armenia. I returned to find a Kayseri devastated, but still as resolute as that crown of snow on the mountain above it. My prayers were answered, for I found my mosque unscathed, may God be praised, soaring above the city like a great phoenix! It escaped the fate of so many other medreses and mosques that were burned to ashes during the Mongol invasion. Who can say why they did not touch it? I cannot help but believe that it was a miracle of God that we were both saved by His grace. The invincible stones of God are stronger than any Mongol horde and will never crumble into ignorance.

I now foster my grandsons in whatever ways I can, for they are now the only hope left for this empire. It is not an easy task, for I must deal with ambitious and devious emirs. I returned to a difficult situation here at the court, for my two eldest grandsons are at bitter odds. Izzeddin, the oldest son of Giyaseddin, became the sultan after his father's sudden death. Izzeddin was only 11 when he was put on the throne instead of the designated heir, the young Alaeddin Keykubad II, by the manipulations of the cunning Vizier Shemseddin Isfahani. But I am not fooled, for I can see that, just like Köpek, Isfahani is using Izzeddin as a pawn in his game for power. I try to distance myself from his plots and ploys that pit brother against brother, and try to stay focused on providing my grandsons moral guidance so that they will live in peace with each other as brothers should. I have watched them grow into fine young men – Izzeddin is now 18, Rukneddin 16 and little Alaeddin is 13 – but they need guidance in so many ways. I cannot fail them like I failed their father.

My life since my return is very different than the one I led before the battle of Kösedağ. I may still be considered the Sultana, but my power and influence are not the same. I am now nothing more than a puppet in the hands of the Mongols, and I must be discrete. My days of building and dreaming are over, except for the completion of my tomb that I had dreamed about so many years before. It is not just my influence that has waned, but also my fortitude. Those years locked up in a fortress have left their mark on my spirit, and the unspeakable sins of my son have scored deep wounds into the fibers of my heart. In many ways I am broken and old, and often dark with despair. I feel so alone. When I am not at the court with my grandsons, I retreat for weeks at a time to the mountaintop dervish lodge of Sheikh Turesan, in order to try and purge this bitterness from my soul. When I am in the city I endeavor to carry out charitable works for the people of Kayseri who suffered so much when the city was plundered by those heathen Mongols.

Ibn Bibi is still here, faithfully noting all that happens in his journals, and has become quite devoted to me. I think he realizes I am his only link to the glorious past we both knew. I read in his journals about all that has happened in the Kingdom when I was down south in prison for all those years. I read that soon after Izzeddin came to the throne, the Vizier Shemseddin Isfahani led his own diplomatic mission to the court of Batu, the chief of the Mongols of the Golden Horde, in order to seek permission to allow my middle grandson Rukneddin to jointly rule with his brother. Setting brother against brother and dividing the centralized power was Isfahani's tactic to garner political influence. I know that Vizier Karatay, who served as Izzeddin's chief advisor, was furious that Shemseddin had acted alone and sought to divide the power, but he had no choice but to acquiesce once the Mongols gave their agreement to the plan. From this day forth Shemseddin became his bitter enemy.

The rivalry continued until the day Vizier Karatay plotted against Isfahani and had him executed soon after my return to the court. Karatay is now the power to be reckoned with here in the Sultanate of Rum, and I cannot say I am displeased. Since the death of Shemseddin, I have seen how he has worked hard to establish a working joint rule between my three grandsons, which he believes is the only way to end their eternal bickering and keep the Empire unified. Although the power is in his hands, Karatay does not abuse it like other viziers. He is a wise and devoted servant, and, in many ways, his dedication to the Empire is as strong as was that of my husband Alaeddin. He adroitly manages to pay homage to the Mongols and get along with them; but at the same time endeavors to maintain and strengthen the links with the rest of the Muslim world. Despite his efforts, the infighting between my grandsons endures to this day, much to my despair.

Karatay has built an impressive medrese in Konya, at the bottom of the hill in the shadow of Alaeddin's mosque. Its broad blue dome rivals the Milky Way. I traveled all the way from Kayseri to Konya for the opening ceremonies soon after my release, and it was a day of joyful celebration for the citizens of the city. At the inauguration I stood next to Jelaleddin and his strange dervish teacher Shams-i Tabrizi, who has the same wild and piercing gaze as did my Sheikh Turesan. The three of us stood shoulder-to-shoulder as we gazed up at the twinkling white stars on the sapphire night sky of its dome, and all agreed that we had never seen anything so stunningly handsome. I hold that gorgeous blue dome in my heart as the symbol of hope for the survival of this Empire, for if such a beautiful thing as this could be built, then goodness and purity will truly prevail over evil in this world. Alaeddin's dream is still alive; I can see it there in that blue dome.

We have endeavored to carry on our normal life even with the Mongol fire breathing down our backs. Baiju will be back, we are all certain of it, and the citizens of Konya especially fear his arrival. Each year, the Mongols increase their demands for tribute money, which is becoming a burden difficult for the Seljuk state to bear. Then this year came a startling request from them: they demanded that Izzeddin be sent to the court of the Great Mongol Khan Mongke in Karakorum as a sign of homage. Fearing instability at home should he be absent from Konya, the emirs decided to send the young Alaeddin Keykubad II in his place instead.

I will not hide from you the fact that Gurchi's son Alaeddin is my favorite grandson, not just because of his sunny disposition, but also because of his fragile health. He has trouble breathing and is easily overcome with dust and fatigue. I know how to keep him calm so that his lungs will not seize up, but the young boy is still frail in nature. But no one can cheer you like he does with his bright face and enthusiasm! I worried that this delicate child would suffer on such an arduous journey, so I asked if I could come along to act as his nurse. I would never forgive myself if anything happened to that sweet child. My request was accepted, and with great pomp we set off from Kayseri to the capital city of the Mongols at Karakorum. I was secretly very excited to see it, for I had heard many tales about its glories. Could it be more beautiful than Konya or Kayseri? I knew the journey would take several years, but I was ready to accept this challenge, for I needed a fresh, motivating target to stir up my energy and ambition. We were accompanied by a fine vizier named Sahip Ata, as well as other statesmen, and we enjoyed our trip thoroughly, for the joy-filled Alaeddin amused us with his stories, songs and laughter.

Yet, when I set out that day, somewhere inside of me I felt a premonition that something would go badly on this voyage. Word reached us while we were on the road that Alaeddin's two older brothers continued to fight among themselves, despite the best intentions of Karatay to keep peace. Izzeddin wanted complete Seljuk independence, while Rukneddin and his advisors stood for unconditional acquiescence to the Mongols. The two brothers became quite hostile to each other and waged a fierce competition for the throne, taking advantage that their little brother was far away.

My hopes for the success of the journey met with an abrupt end. Ironically, it was not the fragile Alaeddin who fell ill, but I did. The fatigue that began to plague me when I was in prison now overwhelmed me, and by the time we reached the Caucasus, I became too weak to travel. We stopped there for a while for me to regain my strength, but it soon became apparent that I would not be able to travel all the way to Karakorum. My bones ached so badly that I could not go on, and rather than hold up the entire mission, it was decided that I should return to Kayseri to rest more comfortably. It was with great sadness that I watched the embassy group head off into the distance; for the nagging omen that I would never see my grandson again would not let go of me.

Yet I had no choice but to return to Kayseri to rest. As I traveled home over the dusty roads, I closed my eyes and thought of that blue dome in Konya, and prayed for the long life of the young Alaeddin, namesake of my husband, the Glorious Alaeddin Keykubad, Eminence of the World and the Faith – and for a renewed triumph of the Seljuk Empire.

Chapter 116

Eclipse of the Moon

Mahperi entered the eastern door of her mosque. It was cool inside, so quiet; the light muted. There was a scattering of men in the sanctuary, some sitting, some kneeling; in the corner next to the window an old man read from a Qur'an spread open on a low bookstand.

Every time she entered the mosque, it was a miracle. Even before she began to pray, she would become the prayer itself in this space, such was its inspiration to her faith. The *shahada* echoed in her ears; it nourished her and the living prayer she had become. She was inside of this mosque just as she was immersed in the Divine. Here, there was no matter; all was eternal peace. There were no frontiers here, and no one was a foreigner to the Almighty. There were no poor here, for everyone became rich in heart in its walls. There were no downtrodden here, for this was a seat of justice and truth. There was no fear here, for it offered everyone a haven of compassion. There was no anger here, for all found an offer of peace. There was no pain here, for everyone healed their bodies and souls in the arms of this mother of mosques.

She closed her eyes, bent her head and prayed. After a moment she opened her eyes and lifted her face towards the sun pouring down in front of the mihrab. This moment is what eternity must feel like, she thought. I am both the present and the future as I stand here in this mosque that I have built.

God, You are now whispering this miracle of eternity in my ear. I hear you.

☪ ☪ ☪

Mahperi leaned against a pillar and felt its coolness run down her spine, soothing the burning pain in her bones. She felt the strength of the stones pass to her body, and her thoughts turned towards the man residing inside those stones.

Lou, can you hear me?

You were right to dare me to build this mosque, even before I was ready. You knew one day the *shahada* would be on my lips. You were right to teach me to build for the beauty of God. I hear your voice in my ears saying, *we must inspire everyone who walks into the space to lift his heart heavenwards*. I remember the prayers led by the priest in my little church in Kalonoros. I see glittering icons, I smell the incense; the prayers swirl in front of me at the same time that I hear the *bismillahs* and the cries of the muezzins. The sanctuary of this mosque is a grandiose fortress of God, and yet its stone carvings are as sweet and delicate as Mary's blue veil. All parts of stone, lead, and ebony join here in a single voice raised to the glory of God. I thank you for this gift, Lou, for offering me this moment of eternity where all the voices of my soul can come together to sing the perfect song of God's love. Now I can step away and let others stand here and feel this moment of eternity. *Allahu Akbar*, God is great, and I am His humble servant.

Yes, now we shall step aside and stand in the shadow cast by this mosque. We will be forgotten, melted into mystery, anonymous. No one will remember you or me, Lou, in the centuries to follow. But our mosque will survive, as will the faith it represents by its stones. It will offer moments of faith, hope and charity to all who enter. Yes, forgotten we will be, but that is not important; for even in the shadow of darkness of oblivion, we know we will always live in eternal light, here in this mosque we have built.

☪ ☪ ☪

Mahperi rose, crossed the sanctuary and walked out of the western door and entered the medrese of Alaeddin that stood next to the mosque.

Alaeddin, can you hear me?

How I wish you could see this building with me, my Sultan! It is the only building in Kayseri, and I think in all the land, that is joined in this way: mosque and medrese linked and ordained together, where people can pass freely as they please; a place which joins religion and science, faith and learning. This place serves well your spirit of wisdom and tolerance.

How we built, my Sultan of Sultans! Mosques and medreses and government and prosperity; we built it all side by side. People either worshipped you, ready to follow you to the ends of the earth, to die in battle for you and to answer your every order, or they detested you, jealous of your intelligence and drive and did everything they could to destroy you. The same holds true for me. People were envious of us and they became bitter. But we built, and we built well, and that is what matters.

I have fulfilled your dream, Alaeddin. Your comet will soar over the mountains and across the steppes of this Empire, above the gardens of blooming roses and the parades of saints and dervishes; over the choruses of bells and the recitations of *bismillahs* below. The glow of the turquoise moon will reflect off your comet tail for all springtimes to come. These stones we have laid, in this land, in this Seljuk Empire, in this Kingdom of the motherland of Anatolia, will sing out their golden song forever and ever.

☪ ☪ ☪

Mahperi returned to her mosque, entering by the western door, underneath its portal of filigree carving. She walked over to the minbar of her mosque and knelt next to it. She never tired of admiring the thousands of pieces of wood joined together in a galaxy of pattern. If only all the peoples of this earth could be like these wood bits, she thought; joined together in a stairway to peace and harmony. How I wish these steps could lead me as well to a place of mercy and love, past revenge and anger.

Giyaseddin, can you hear me?

I never saw you again, my son, after that fateful day in Tokat, and every day since then I have been tormented by the same question. How can I forgive a murderer, when that murderer is my own son, and his victim was his father? How can I forgive these most monstrous behaviors, disrespectful to all humanity's laws? I have begged God to provide me a sense of peace, but it has not come. Did Jesus not teach us to pray "*Our Father in heaven, forgive us our debts, as we also have forgiven our debtors. If you forgive men when they sin against you, your heavenly Father will also forgive you.*"? Yes, he said those things, but I could not hear their truth in my heart. I looked to the Qur'an as well for peace. Does not the Holy Book teach us that believers are to be forgiving, compassionate and tolerant people? I have read in the Qur'an these words: "*Hold to forgiveness, command what is right, and turn away from the ignorant. But if someone pardons and puts things right, his reward is with God. Would you not love God to forgive you? God is Ever-Forgiving, Most Merciful.*" Yes, I have heard all these same lessons, but I was still angered by the disturbing sins you committed.

I have never been the same since that last day in Tokat. Every day since that day, I have tried to figure out what would have caused you to commit such unspeakable sins. My question all these years has been whether my love should be so unconditional as to forgive them. Just what is expected of a mother's love? I have searched for this absolute love in my heart and it was not there. Yet if I step back and try to understand your reason for doing such unimaginable things, then perhaps I can find it in my heart to forgive you. I believe you were on that road to find me to give me those answers; to explain all of this to me and to ask my pardon.

Yes, I must forgive you, my son. Although I may regret having borne a son that killed his father and his brothers, I can no longer wish you ill. Was not the last person Jesus forgave before he died the repentant criminal hanging next to him? *Forgive them, Father, for they know not what they do.* For years I refused to think of you with anything but anger. Anger for having taken my husband away from me, and anger for your trespasses against God's will. You caused me unfathomable harm – but you are still my son. This pain of hating you for your deeds has caused a great hard lump to grow in my chest, and it is now killing me. But I must resolve these questions, for I cannot stand in front of God any longer with anger in my heart. I have no future on this earth or in eternity without forgiveness.

I am ready to forgive you, my son.

I now stand in the light of my mosque and yes, I say unto you, my son, yes, you are forgiven. I forgive you and I love you. If I view my life through the lens of eternity, what happens on earth is much less important than what happens after you die. And I know that I am to die soon. Faced with the choice to love or to hate, I will chose love. This is what the Sheikh Turesan taught me, and this is the ultimate trial of my faith. This will be my hard-won peace, harder than any battle fought by your father. I wish to be guided by redemption and forgiveness and love, for love has the power to make the blind see and the rains come. I now look at you with compassion and love.

I forgive you, my son.

☪ ☪ ☪

Mahperi rose and walked towards the space between the medrese and the mosque where her mausoleum was being built. She paused to admire the delicate lace carving of its walls, yet today it did not dispel her sadness.

Hanife, can you hear me?

We lived such horror in our lives, but our friendship was the purest thing I ever knew. You lie here now, and I will be here soon with you, my friend, I know it. All my beloved helpers have left me: you, Bahaeddin Veled, Burhaneddin, Sheikh Turesan; all the pure people in my life are now gone.

I have lived many things, both good and bad. I have seen a son murder his father and his brothers, perhaps because I did not give him the love he needed. I have seen jealous women betray other women, and fathers spurn their sons. I have seen loyal soldiers plot to kill their leader in the name of greed, and men crazed with power slaughter and slander those who innocently stood in their path. I have seen men of different religions slay each other and heathens spurred by greed demolish all in their path with no other end than a sadistic joy of destruction. I have seen men of honor forget the moral foundations of their religions, making them no better than the heathen Mongols who ravaged us. I have lost many times, I have accepted it all and I have gone on.

But I have also lived through much beauty. You gave me much of that, my friend. All has not been evil. Love, artistic aspirations, an illuminated path, poetry, the *shahada,* Eclipse, the waters of a blue paradise lake, my independence: I have known them all. I have seen the plains become sprinkled with dazzling monuments that sing the praises of God and the leaders who built them. I have seen dervishes and Sufis bring the lessons of love to our people. I have witnessed the growth of prosperity in the land, bread in the mouths of children, justice and law courts implemented for the benefit of citizens. I have seen colors woven, nature painted, and beauty brought to life in the world that surrounds us. I have seen an Empire rise from barren plains.

Someday all the horror will be lessened, and beauty will win the final victory. Someday the struggle for survival will be easier; someday we will learn to make life easier on ourselves. I will not lose faith in the goodness of my fellow man and his capacity to rise above the mud and float like an angel.

Ah, that mud… Yes, I have shown what can rise from mud. In the face of all this senseless brutality, warring and hatred, I have placed stones in fields of mud to create buildings that raise their fists to the sky and shout, "*God! I am at the service of your glory*!" With each layer of stone I laid, I cried out, "*We can rise above the mud!*" I pray I have left a legacy of beauty and hope to the people of this land.

I can do no more now – my body is so heavy, so tired; someone else must now walk down my path. I can no longer ignore this betrayal by my body, this throbbing ache that is becoming greedier and greedier for my energy. There is no relief from it, despite all the crushed herbs the doctors give me. Hanife, I wish to rest alongside of you, for I am tired, so tired. Not just tired from the pains of a life of treason, vengeance and retribution, but tired from this wave of throbbing pain in my side, my left side, the very same side as my heart. Can the pain I feel in my heart and in my side be one and the same? My body is becoming weaker with each day that passes. I believe that I will not be here to see another spring. I, who was always so strong and who could ride Eclipse from morning till night; now I am so feeble. I, the proud woman with her head held high, who intruded in a court reserved for men and who dared to build; now I can barely hold up my weary chin.

Just as a spider weaves its web from within itself and just like you wove your spirit onto that loom, Hanife, I put my soul into layers of stones, one above the other. I believed that with stones I could tell the story of ideas, beliefs and even my fantasies. My faith has taught me that the unreal is more powerful than the real, because nothing is as perfect as you can imagine it. I pray that these stones will last forever, but I know that it is really the fragile things of thoughts and dreams that will go on for all eternity. That is my legacy. Stones and dreams.

Yes, I dream that the comet of Alaeddin will soar above these plains forever, and that a magnificent empire, even greater than one he ever could have imagined, will come to rise.

But I am tired now, so tired… let me rest here now, for a moment; here in my mosque, under the angel wings of the Majestic Mountain.

Epilogue

Yes, you are tired; so tired, my Lady. Close your eyes and rest now, for this, your final sleep, here on this earth. I, the caravansarai you have built at Pazar, am here to continue your breath.

I was built in the time when comets blazed turquoise across the sky. I have risen above that mud, Lady Mahperi; you made me grow from nothingness into a building that will stand for all time. I am your faith in humanity; I am your voice crying out over the steppes for all to hear. I shout out your message of love and hope that all can work together to make life easier and more beautiful for ourselves. The path of your lesson for peace leads to my door and away from my door. People will tread on that path, Lady Mahperi, of that you can rest assured. Great women will follow your lead, and great men will come, too – they will have blue eyes as bright as the skies over our steppes and that will gaze far into the horizon; blue eyes as bright as those of your Sultan Alaeddin. They will be the ghazis of this Empire you both have created. They will come to lead in the path of righteousness, and the people will follow. You and your Sultan have shown us that it is possible to move forward to greatness.

I am your caravansarai of hope.

You created the miracle of art, where some stones and some carving, together with that most essential ingredient, love, can produce something stronger than time and age, more powerful than death. You are now eternal, my Lady, in my stones.

I am your caravansarai of beauty.

Cool water flows in the stone basin of the fountain on my facade, which has become a gathering place for those in the neighborhood. Your fountain of kindness will never run dry. All those who enter my courtyard look up and read the inscription plaque above the door to my great hall:

> "She has ordered the construction of this han, may God bless it, under the reign of the great Sultan and glorious Khan, Shadow of God in this world, Giyaseddin Keyhüsrev, son of the fortunate Keykubad, the prince of the believers, the good queen *Safat al-dunya wal-din,* mother of the Sultan of Sultans, Mahperi Hatun, in the year 636."

I know each and every one of them says a prayer in your memory as they pass under it to unload their goods after a long day on the road. They are tired and they are thankful for this haven of safety you have provided them.

I am your caravansarai of comfort.

More so than on that inscription plaque, I feel your spirit alive in the campfire that blazes each night in my courtyard. I remember how you dreamed to build me one night sitting with merchants around a similar fire in your husband's han, and, for me, this is where your memory will always glow the strongest. Merchants from every corner of the world come together around that fire at night; to rest, to talk, to tell stories, and play music on instruments of every kind. I never tire of hearing their tales; for each one is different; each one spreads a bit of poetry from the lands of the men that gather here.

I am your caravansarai of amity.

I heard a troubadour recite this poem last night written by a mystic poet from Konya and I thought it was quite beautiful, as if he were reciting it just for you:

Come, come, whoever you are.
Wanderer, worshipper, lover of leaving.
It doesn't matter.
Ours is not a caravan of despair.
Come, even if you have broken your vow
a hundred times.
Come, yet again, come, come.

Come, yes, come, yet again, for are we not all wanderers on some distant road? Yes, all nomads are welcome to my door. And they come, my Lady, to this place of welcome that you have built, and they will continue to arrive for all the years to come. I am one of the seven hans of the moon queen Mahperi, and I will always be open to ramblers on the road of life.

I am your caravansarai of solace.

I heard a story last night, told by a merchant from the West, for the world is now so small it seems that travelers from all corners of the globe gather around my campfire. He came from a country far away in Europe to trade in Constantinople with the Byzantines. This merchant lives in a large city in that realm of France, a city he called Paris. He described its streets filled with tradesmen of every sort, its shops bursting with elegant goods and its markets full of fine foods. He also told us about an astonishing building that is rising on the small island in the middle of the river that cuts the city in two like an apple. It is the biggest temple those Christians have ever built, bigger even than Hagia Sophia in Constantinople. They call it "Our Lady of Paris." He says its towers will scrape the skies and their bells will be heard all throughout the land when they peal to call the faithful to prayer. He told us that stone carvers are making thousands of statues of all kinds of monsters and fantastic birds to decorate the outside of the temple. Yet, I cannot imagine those stones could be any more beautiful than those on my portal here! But the most extraordinary part of his story was that one day while passing by the site this merchant met a Frenchman working there who spoke Turkish very well. When asked why, this architect told him he had once worked in our land and had built a magnificent palace for our sultan on the shores of a paradise lake. The merchant did not believe his tall tale of turquoise and tiles, and asked if any of the others around the campfire had heard of this palace. All shook their heads no, but I knew that palace as well as if it were my very own brother, my Lady. I knew that man could have been none other than your friend Lou Cantadou. After so many years, it would seem that he is finally realizing his dream to build for God. How I wish you could have heard this news! If only he could now see too, what you have built, my Lady; for God, for trade, for your country, for your fellow man! The two of you shared a bond that defied your differences, defined your dreams and fed each other's inspirations. I am sure he thinks of you with each stone he lays on that building, dedicated to their Lady of God, Mary. He will never forget you, just as all of us will hold forever the memory of our own Lady of Goodness.

I am your caravansarai of remembrance.

Yet it was another story that I heard again last night, late into the night, when most of the men had fallen silent and were listening to the echoes of the stars, that haunts me the most. A sugar merchant from the coastal city of Antalya told us a legend the natives of the Taurus Mountains relate to this day. They claim that if you look up to the mountain ridge on the nights of the full moon, you can see flashes of red glinting among the underbrush. These moving sparks, they believe, come from the reflection of the moonbeams glinting off the ruby gems on Ruby's collar, for they are certain that the great leopard is still alive and running wild in the backwoods of the Taurus Mountains, looking for her master Alaeddin to follow on the hunt. I believe this story too, and I know that as long as her spirit runs free alongside that of the great Seljuk Sultan Alaeddin Keykubad, the legacy of his Empire will remain alive.

I am your caravansarai of eternity.

THE END

Afterword

For readers interested in the fates of the historical characters in the novel, perhaps a few further facts are needed.

Although never clearly stated by Ibn Bibi in his chronicle, it is certain that **Alaeddin Keykubad** died by poisoning. Ibn Bibi relates only that during the banquet with the Mongols he ate a piece of fowl, fell ill and then died shortly after. Keykubad's assassin(s) have never been discovered and named. However, a historian known as the Anonymous Historian of Konya, writing after 1363, includes a brief line accusing Giyaseddin. As in every police investigation, fingers point first to the person with the strongest motive. As such, many modern historians have ascribed this murder to Mahperi, whom they believe killed her husband in order to put her disinherited son Giyaseddin on the throne. This accusation perpetuates to this day. I would argue, however, that the emirs had the strongest desire for vengeance against the Sultan. Continually overburdened with demands for tribute money for building projects, they had already plotted once to assassinate him. This novel thus chooses to lay the burden of guilt with them, with Köpek as master instigator and manipulator of both them and the weak Giyaseddin.

The exact circumstances of the death of **Giyaseddin Keyhüsrev** are unclear as well. Never discussed by Ibn Bibi, we are left only with the vague description by Sempad the Constable, the brother of Hethoum. This historian reports that the Sultan died at Alanya, suddenly, crying out "Help, Help!", consistent with the violent death by animal bite depicted in this novel. Other modern historians have attributed his death to poisoning by his emirs, hardship on the campaign trail, collapse after a drinking bash, typhoid, choking, drowning and animal bite.

We do not know the exact year that **Mahperi** was released from captivity or died. The historian Bar Hebraeus, writing in the early 1250's, relates that she was still held in captivity by Hethoum, and the last reference to her in Ibn Bibi briefly mentions that the *"grandmother of Alaeddin Keykubad II"* accompanied him to the Mongol court in 1254. This novel has chosen to reconcile these two historians by situating her release after the return of Hethoum's brother from his mission to Karakorum in 1250, and her death assumed in 1255. The inscription over her tomb is undated, but notably refers to her two faiths, calling her the "*Mary of her era, and the Khadija of her time.*" Khadija (in Turkish, Hatice) is the honored first wife of the Prophet Muhammad. There are three women buried in Mahperi's Kayseri mausoleum: the Sultana herself, her granddaughter Seljuki Hatun (+1284) and one unmarked grave. In this story, it is Mahperi's weaver friend Hanife who lies in this grave. The exact construction date of her tomb is also not known, and could have been built before or after her death.

All the **grandsons** of Mahperi Hatun met with tragic ends: Izzeddin Keykavus, given to drink like his father, died in exile in the Crimea in 1280, Rukneddin Kilich Arslan was strangled at a banquet at Akşehir in 1266, and the young Alaeddin Keykubad II, as predicted by Mahperi in the novel, met a mysterious death by unknown hands on the road to the court at Karakorum around 1257.

Hethoum continued his courtship of the Mongols after his brother Sempad came home from his diplomatic mission to Karakorum in 1250. Sempad returned with a protection treaty in hand as well as a journal which today constitutes a primary source document of significant importance for details about life at the Mongol court. Hethoum himself went to the court of Mongke in Mongolia in 1254, where he was received with great ceremony and was given assurance of total protection by the Mongols. This Armenian-Mongol alliance was a stroke of political genius on the part of Hethoum, for it ensured that the Kingdom of Cilicia remained protected for almost 75 years. Hethoum abdicated later in life and died in a monastery in 1271.

The daughters of **Gaziye** arranged to have her remains brought from Ankara after the death of Giyaseddin Keyhüsrev and had them reburied in the tomb they began building for her in 1247 on the outskirts of Kayseri. Oddly, the tomb's inscription gives the date of construction and the donors, but makes no mention of the fact that Gaziye was the wife of Alaeddin Keykubad.

Mahperi's prophetic words concerning Giyaseddin Keyhüsrev's Georgian wife **Gurchi** proved true. She did let the light of God's love enter her heart and set it aflame. She became a devout Muslim after her husband's death. Strongly moved by the teachings of Mevlana, she became one of his most dedicated and influential patrons, and did much to promote his Sufi philosophy among women. It was she who commissioned the first tomb over his grave at Konya in 1274, which has today become one of the most revered shrines in all Islam.

The Grand Vizier **Karatay** died in Kayseri in 1254, at approximately the same time as Mahperi. He was brought back to Konya and buried in a room located inside his medrese in Konya. He was the virtual ruler of the empire from the assassination in 1249 of Shemseddin Isfahani until his own death in 1254. Along with the death of the pious and honorable Karatay died all hope of regaining the prestige of the unified Seljuk State. In addition to being a skilled and devoted statesman, Karatay was a significant building patron in his own right. His Konya Medrese, built in 1251, is famous for its spectacular blue-tiled dome, and his caravansarai on the Kayseri-Malatya road is one of the most impressive of all the Seljuk hans. He also built a mosque in Konya and a hospital in Antalya, both no longer standing.

The Mongol warrior **Baiju** returned to ravage Anatolia in 1256, but by miracle Konya was spared through adroit negotiations and the payment of a large tribute. The **Mongols** continued their wave of destruction, most notably by the dreadful sack of Baghdad by Hulegu in 1258, which ended the 500 year old Abbasid Caliphate. After the sack of Baghdad, the Mongols advanced towards Syria and Egypt, but met defeat at the hands of the Egyptian Mamluks in the famous Battle of Ain Jalut in 1260, the first time ever the Mongols lost a battle.

After their victory over the Mongols at Ain Jalut, it was the turn of the **Mamluks** to set their eyes on Anatolia. In 1277, the Mamluk Commander Baybars mounted a major invasion of Anatolia, defeating the Mongols at Elbistan and occupying Kayseri. It was his mission to wrest complete control of Seljuk Anatolia from the Mongols. At the news of his troops' defeat at Elbistan, the Mongol Abaqa hastened to Anatolia in July, 1277 and sternly punished the Seljuk Turks, with sources citing the massacre of tens of thousands of people. This would however be the last Mongol terror sown on Anatolian soil, for their power now waned significantly.

Jelaleddin Rumi, son of Bahaeddin Veled, now popularly known as Mevlana ("our Master") or Rumi, continued teaching in Konya. After meeting a mystic named Shams-i Tabrizi in 1244, his life was transformed. The inspiration of this spiritual tutor was so powerful that it turned the sober teacher into an ecstatic poet. His principal work, the *Mesnevi*, is a vast poem of 25,000 verses divided into six books, and is considered one of the masterpieces of world literature. After the murder of Shams in 1246, Jelaleddin began his open instruction of Sufism which later included the spiritual dance ceremony called the *sema*. The Order of The Whirling Dervishes, known as the Mevlevi, founded by Rumi's son, has been famous for seven hundred years. His tomb in Konya draws 2 million visitors each year, and Rumi is now considered one of the most popular poets in the world.

In the aftermath of the Mongol invasion, the **Kubadabad Palace** was considered "lost," and remained known only through its description by Ibn Bibi, until the day in 1949 when it was rediscovered by Professor Zeki Oral. It has been subsequently excavated in the 1960s by Katharina Otto-Dorn and more recently (2001 to present) by a team of archaeologists from Ankara University under the able direction of Prof. Rüçhan Arik.

The last wild **leopard** (*Panthera pardus ssp.Tulliana*) in Turkey was believed to have been hunted down in 1974, but recent sightings in the Kackar Mountains give hope that the race is not extinct.

Years of decline under Mongol hegemony continued, with unending dynastic and administrative squabbles. Anatolia found itself in both the hands of the weakening Mongols who struggled to hold it, and the local emirs *(beys)* who had appeared over the last several years, breaking away to form their own local regional mini-states, called "beyliks," of varying size. In this period, known as the **Beylik Period**, a new era of welfare began in the country which had known Mongol destruction for so long. One of these beyliks, the Osmanoğulları ("sons of Osman"), established in the northwest Anatolia, emerged to become an unforeseen force in the world: the **Ottomans**. The last Seljuk sultan died in 1307, but already the glint of Osman's dream was seen over the horizon.

The architectural legacy of Mahperi Hatun inspired later women of influence to set up similar foundations, becoming a tradition among Ottoman sultanas. Royal women patrons have graced Istanbul with some of its most glorious mosques.

The political legacy of the Seljuk Empire of **Alaeddin Keykubad** has not been lost either, but has continued on in the destinies of the other warriors who have followed his lead. Their names are Fatih Mehmet the Conqueror, Kanuni Sultan Suleyman the Magnificent, and Mustafa Pasha Kemal Ataturk. The spirit of Alaeddin Keykubad will undoubtedly continue to inspire many more leaders to come for the Republic of Turkey.

Ars longa, vita breva

Many of the stories created by the author in this novel have been inspired by the beauty of Seljuk works of art and architecture that can be viewed today in museums and on site in Turkey. These works of art bring alive a period of history long gone, yet ever vibrant in our imaginations.

Architecture:

- The mosques, caravansarais and medreses that were built by Alaeddin Keykubad, his emirs, Mahperi and Giyaseddin Keyhüsrev may be viewed all across the plains of Anatolia. The major Seljuk monuments are located in the cities of Afyon, Alanya, Akşehir, Aksaray, Amasya, Ankara, Kayseri, Kırşehir, Konya, Malatya, Niğde, Sivas and Tokat.
- The remains of the Kubadabad palace on the western shore of Lake Beyşehir are currently under excavation and are not accessible, but the outstanding publications by Prof. Rüçhan Arik bring them to vivid life.
- For specific information on the caravansarais mentioned in this story (Aksaray Sultan, Altinapa, Kandemir, Karatay Han and the Pazar Han), visit: www.turkishhan.org.
- Aspendos is considered the best-preserved Roman theater in the world. The Palace rooms of Alaeddin may be visited.
- The blue dome of the Karatay Medrese in Konya continues to awe visitors who stand beneath it. Now a state museum, the Karatay Medrese houses a collection of outstanding pieces which offer a panorama of the Seljuk decorative arts, notably the tiles from the Kubadabad Palace.
- The Pazar Han of Mahperi was completely renovated in 2007 and is now open to visitors. Her other hans, except for the one in Ezinepazar, are in a ruined state.

Works of art (textiles and fabrics, ceramics, stone, wood and glass):

The following real works of art figure in the story in imaginative fashion:

- The red silk cape embroidered in gold thread that Alaeddin Keykubad wore at his wedding is now held in the Musée Historique des tissus et des arts décoratifs of Lyons, France (inv. no. 23475). The tunic, one of the rarest silk fabrics known, shows two adossed lions in large roundels and an embroidered *kufic* inscription with Alaeddin's name and a blessing to God. It found its way to an abbey in Auvergne, France, where it was retailored into a priest's chasuble. It is probable that the priests who wore it at the altar did not know that its hem was praising Allah most high.

- The original carved wood minbars of the Alaeddin Mosque of Konya and the Mahperi Hunat Hatun Mosque of Kayseri are in still in place.
- The tiles that adorned Alaeddin's palace at the foot of the hill below his mosque may be seen in the Konya Karatay Museum; those from his palace at Aspendos may be seen in the Antalya Archaeological Museum. Several pieces of sculpture from the walls of Konya are held in the Konya Ince Museum, notably the giant winged angels of the Larende Gate that Mahperi saw when she first arrived at Konya.
- A Seljuk-era stone carving of a leopard similar to Ruby chasing an antelope is now on display in the Ince Minareli Museum of Konya.
- An Ottoman-era ceramic plate from Iznik (c. 1575), depicting a leopard wearing a collar and chain and tethered to a tree, much as Ruby would have been, was formerly held in the Lagonikos Collection of Alexandria (cf. Carswell, John. *Blue and White: Chinese Porcelain Around the World*. London: British Museum Press, 2000, p. 148). A similar 10th century Seljuk plate from Iran is now held in the Brooklyn Museum of Art (no. 73.165).
- A rare 12th century chess set from Nishapur, similar to the one used by the unlucky Persian trader from Mashad, may be seen in the collections of the Metropolitan Museum of Art (inv. N. 1971.192a-ff).
- The tiles created for the Kubadabad Palace can be viewed in reconstructed panels in the Karatay Museum of Konya. These unsigned works, all of the same hand, are attributed to the fictive character of Joseph in the novel. They comprise a fairyland of animals, people and mythical beasts that enchant us to this day. The Cinili Museum in Istanbul also contains several of the tiles.
- The reconstructed panel of "Joseph's" tiles for the women's section of the Kayseri Hatun baths can be seen at the Güpgüpcüoğlu House Museum of Ethnology in Kayseri, Turkey.
- The great Konya rugs woven for Alaeddin's mosque on the hill are the showpieces of the collections of the Museum of Turkish and Islamic Art (TIEM) in Istanbul. Their reds and blues still glow as brightly as the day they were woven. The teal rug with the wide border that Hanife allowed Mahperi to unroll (inv. 681) and the yellow and red "Roses of Allah" rug that Hanife was

weaving for Mahperi's mosque at the time of her murder (inv. 689) are two of the most impressive carpets ever woven.

- A luster glass platter inscribed with Giyaseddin's name in gold, now displayed in the Konya Karatay Museum, was the inspiration for the story of plates ordered by Köpek for Kubadabad. This museum piece is the one in the story that Joseph the Potter tucked under his caftan at the inauguration of the Kubadabad Palace and saved from destruction.
- The name of Alaeddin's horse, Night Shining White, renders homage to the favorite charger of the Chinese Tang emperor Xuanzong. The fiery-tempered "dragon steed" is depicted by the artist Han Gan in one of the most exquisite horse portraits ever created, now in the Metropolitan Museum of New York (Dillon 1977/78).

Poetry:

- The *canso* of Lou Cantadou, composed by this author, was inspired by the poems of the troubadour poets Peirol d'Auvernha, Gacé Brulé, Arnaud Daniel, Bernard de Ventadour, Jaufre Rudel, Gaucelm Faitdit and Guillaume de Machaut.
- The poems of the Epic of Dede Korkut, the pre-Islamic folk hero, were taken from the translation of Geoffrey Lewis (Penguin Press, 1974).
- Citations and references from the Bible are from the King James Version; verses of the Qur'an are taken from the translation of N.J. Dawood (Penguin Classics, 2003).
- The poem cited in the prologue of Section 5 is taken from the History of Ottoman Poetry by Elias John Wilkinson Gibb (Cambridge, 1909), translated into modern Turkish by Ali Cavuşoğlu of Erciyes University.
- The poem in the epilog is by Jelaleddin Rumi, translation by Coleman Barks.

Dramatis Personae

*(*fictitious)*

Royal Family

Alaeddin Keykubad, Sultan of the Seljuks (r. 1220-37)

Gaziye – Abbasid wife of Alaeddin Keykubad

Giyaseddin Keyhüsrev II– son of Alaeddin and Mahperi, sultan (r. 1237-46)

Gurchi – Georgian-born wife of Giyaseddin Keyhüsrev

Izzeddin Kilich Arslan – Son of Alaeddin and Gaziye; appointed heir

Kyr Vart – Lord of Kalonoros and father of Mahperi

Maryam/Mahperi – Wife of Alaeddin Keykubad (?1206 – 1255?)

Seljuka – Daughter of Mahperi and Alaeddin

Court Figures (emirs, viziers, generals)

Ertokush – Governor of Antalya and later tutor to Giyaseddin in Erzincan

Ibn Bibi – Historian of the Seljuks for the period of 1191-1282

Kamyar – Most eminent of Alaeddin's generals; victor at Yassicimen

Karatay – Grand vizier to 3 sultans

Sadettin Köpek – Minister of Works and vizier to Alaeddin and Giyaseddin

Religious figures

Bahaeddin Veled – Religious scholar invited to Konya by Alaeddin; teacher to Mahperi

Jelaleddin Rumi – Son and successor of Bahaeddin Veled; later known as Mevlana

Seyyid Burhaneddin – Teacher of Jelaleddin; religious teacher to Mahperi

Sheikh Turesan – Dervish; spiritual guide to Mahperi

Adversaries and Allies

Al-Ashraf– Ayyubid general; ally of the Seljuks; rival of his brother al-Kamil

Al-Kamil – Ayyubid sultan, nephew of Saladin, commander during the 5th and 6th Crusades

Baba Ishak – Turkoman religious fanatic

Baiju Noyan – Mongol general at the battle of Kösedağ, successor to Ogedei

Chormagan – Mongol general under Genghis and Ogedei
Constantine of Lampron – Armenian lord and renegade; ally of Giyaseddin
Genghis Khan – Mongol Khan, known as "the Ocean"
Hethoum – King of Armenian Cilicia, son of Constantine of Baberon
Jelaleddin Menguberti – Leader of the Khwarazmians
Ogedei – Powerful Mongol general

Artists

*__Hanife__ – Carpet weaver, friend of Mahperi
*__Joseph__ – Potter at Kubadabad
*__Lou Cantadou__ – Architect at Aspendos and Kubadabad
*__Nikolas Zonaras__ – Architect of the Kayseri Hatun Complex and the Pazar Han

Animals

*__Eclipse__ – Stallion of Mahperi
*__Night Shining White__ – Stallion of Alaeddin
*__Ruby__ – Leopard of Alaeddin

Author's note

Dear Reader,

In 1993 I visited Tokat, in northeastern Turkey, where I first set eyes on the large caravansarai at Pazar, a small rural village about 20 miles from the city.

As I stood outside the han, I was entranced by the delicate refinement of its elaborately-carved portal, so different than the massive portals I had seen on other Anatolian caravansarais. As I looked up at the flowers and pine cones depicted on the column capitals on each side of the door, my initial reaction was to say to myself that this han had to have been built by a woman. There was a refined grace to it that distinguished it from any other han I had seen.

Then a strange, but very real, thing happened: the stones of that elegant han began to speak to me. The han was a ruin, but as I slowly walked through the courtyard, overgrown with weeds and filled with fallen stones and waddling geese, a voice began to whisper to me. A woman's voice. *"Tell my story"* it called to me, *"Tell the story behind the walls of my han."*

I did not know the story of this majestic han at that time, but I vowed to find out more about it, and soon I learned that indeed, it had been commissioned by a woman, and that this woman was none other than the wife of Alaeddin Keykubad, the great Seljuk Sultan. So began the desire to tell her story through this han, as much as I could, with absolutely no historical evidence about this woman to go on. For indeed, if all the known information about Mahperi were assembled, it would constitute no more than three sentences: her inscription plaques, and several isolated mentions of her name in the works of the historians Ibn Bibi, Bar Hebraeus and Simon de Saint-Quentin. Her personality and motivation for building these monuments remained even more obscure than the meager details of her life.

When I traveled to Kayseri to view her mosque complex, I was struck by the inscription on her tomb which called her the *"Mary of her times, and the Khadija of her times."* The intriguing dual faith tradition of this woman pushed my conviction even further to tell her story.

I have tried to recreate her life as I imagine it, as much as a woman living in the urban, Western world of the 21st century could ever imagine the thoughts, motivations, and ambitions of a woman in the Middle East of the 13th century.

Her story is told by my recreation of the life of Alaeddin Keykubad and the major historical characters in his world. The facts and chronology are rigidly true and are based on much research on historical sources, accounts and architectural evidence.

The story is brought to life by my creation of the characters of the architects Lou and Nikolas, the potter Joseph, and the weaver Hanife, who all surely existed in one fashion, as attested by the artistic legacy of the Seljuk era. The Sultans Alaeddin Keykubad and Giyaseddin Keyhüsrev most certainly kept a leopard similar to Ruby.

However, a few historical deviations are to be noted:

- There is sparse evidence that Alaeddin may have taken a third wife after Mahperi and Gaziye. The Carsi Mosque in Uluborlu, built in 1232, carries an inscription plaque which says that it was built by the daughter of the ruler of Erzurum, Mughith al-Din Tughrilshah (+1225), who was Alaeddin's uncle, and that she was married to Alaeddin. Alaeddin most certainly married her after his victory of Erzurum in 1230 over her brother, Rukh al-Din Jahanshah, who had allied himself with Jelaleddin Menguberti at the Battle of Yassicimen. The couple would have thus been direct first cousins. It is known that one of her other brothers converted to Christianity to marry Queen Rusudan of Georgia, and was the father of Gurchi. Ibn Bibi never mentions this third wife in his account, but she is referred to by Bar Hebraeus, who relates that Alaeddin "banished" her due to her continued support of her defeated brother Rukh al-din Jahanshah. As this story chooses to focus on Gaziye and Mahperi, this third wife does not enter into consideration in this novel, and I ask the readers' understanding for this voluntary omission.
- Mahperi was probably not in Tokat at the moment of the battle of Kösedag, but most certainly in Kayseri. However, for the needs of the final confrontation with her son, it was necessary for them to meet before they scattered in different directions, for her to be able to take with her the knowledge of the crime that I, as well as a historian writing in the era, attribute to him.

After I decided to write this book, I returned to visit the Pazar han in 2005. To my great surprise, the large courtyard was no longer filled with crumbling stones and overgrown weeds, but with churning bulldozers and forklift trucks. Fallen stones from the arcades were being tossed in heaps, and workers scurried about in all directions. A complete renovation of the han had been ordered by the Turkish government.

I stopped to talk with the construction manager and the foreman for the project, and was surprised to learn that neither of them had any idea what this building was or the story behind the woman who commissioned it. When I pointed out the original mason marks on the stones, I saw a look of intense pride in eyes of the day laborers working on the site, connecting them to the workers almost eight centuries before them.

In the same fashion, the renovation of this han will allow modern visitors to understand how and why this han was built, effectively passing on its heritage to future generations. When families come to eat the famous Tokat kebab now served in its courtyard, perhaps they will feel the legacy of Alaeddin Keykubad flowing in their veins. Perhaps the people of Pazar, as they pass by the water fountain outside, will feel pride that their village was picked by a famous queen to be the site of one of the most outstanding caravansarais ever built. Perhaps every citizen of the Republic of Turkey will feel the honor of being part of the cultural heritage of the Seljuk era.

I was then more than ever committed to telling Mahperi's story, and I hope, my dear reader, that through my story you have been able to revisit forty of the most important years of Turkish history. I ask all those who disagree with my imagination to accept this very personal vision of this woman's life, and I hope that my interpretation does not rankle, but rather honor, the historians, past and present, who have labored to reconstruct this era and the exploits of its major actors. The memory of that day I stood in front of the han in 1993 and its whispering stones formed the dream for this novel. There is a lot going on in this long story, but its ultimate message seeks to illustrate the commonality of the monotheistic spiritual experience, the strength of women, the power of art to ennoble our existence, and that love and forgiveness always prevail over revenge and hatred. I hope you will take this message with you long after the covers of the book are closed.

Katharine Branning
Tokat, 2013

photo courtesy of Selman Eştürkler

KATHARINE "KADRIYE" BRANNING, MLS, is Vice-President of the French Institute Alliance Française in New York City where she serves as the Director of FIAF's Library. For her work promoting the French language and culture through the creation of numerous libraries in both France and the United States, she was awarded the Ordre national du Mérite from the President of France in 2006, one of the nation's highest honors. Ms. Branning is a graduate of the Ecole du Louvre in Paris, where she majored in Islamic arts, with a specialty in Islamic glass. As an independent researcher, she has conducted annual field work relative to architecture and decorative arts in Turkey since 1978, which has served as the basis for her website, *www.turkishhan.org*, dedicated to promoting knowledge of Seljuk hans. She is the curator of *The Song of Stones*, the first exhibit dedicated to Seljuk art in the United States, inaugurated in New York in 2011. She is the English editor of the *Heritage of the Great Seljuks*, under the auspices of the Turkish President Abdullah Gül, published in 2013.

She is the author of a collection of essays on Turkey, "*Yes, I Would Love another Glass of Tea.*" She teaches and lectures internationally on cross-cultural issues and her articles appear in numerous newspapers and magazines. For the first time in its history, the city of Rize, Turkey, bestowed honorary citizenship on her in 2012.